No One But You

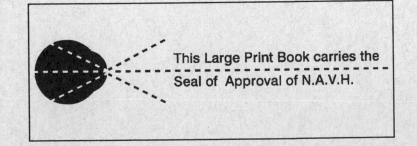

This Large Print Book carries the
Seal of Approval of N.A.V.H.

No One But You

Brenda Novak

THORNDIKE PRESS
A part of Gale, a Cengage Company

GALE
A Cengage Company

Farmington Hills, Mich • San Francisco • New York • Waterville, Maine
Meriden, Conn • Mason, Ohio • Chicago

GALE
A Cengage Company

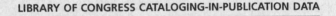

LIBRARY OF CONGRESS CATALOGING-IN-PUBLICATION DATA

Names: Novak, Brenda, author.
Title: No one but you / by Brenda Novak.
Description: Large print edition. | Waterville, Maine : Thorndike Press, 2017. |
  Series: Silver Springs | Series: Thorndike Press large print romance
Identifiers: LCCN 2017018209| ISBN 9781410499905 (hardcover) | ISBN 1410499901
  (hardcover)
Subjects: LCSH: Large type books. | GSAFD: Love stories.
Classification: LCC PS3614.O926 N6 2017 | DDC 813/.54—dc23
LC record available at https://lccn.loc.gov/2017018209

Published in 2017 by arrangement with Harlequin Books S.A.

Printed in Mexico
3 4 5 6 7 8 21 20 19 18 17

Dear Reader,

I am so excited to introduce you to my brand-new series! Silver Springs is a fictional town of five thousand people modeled a little after the real town of Ojai, California, population 7,500. Like Ojai, it boasts some lovely Spanish colonial revival architecture and is nestled in a picturesque valley about ninety minutes northwest of Los Angeles. In order to keep the town unique, chain stores aren't allowed. Instead, local business development is encouraged, and the whole area has an artsy, almost spiritualistic vibe. At the edge of Silver Springs, you'll find a boys ranch called New Horizons, where a caring woman named Aiyana Turner takes in troubled boys and turns them into admirable men.

The idea for this book struck me after watching a true-crime show where the son of an older couple came home one night to the farmhouse where he lived with his parents to find them murdered — and wound up getting blamed for their deaths. Several years later, the police were able to prove he hadn't killed them, but I could only imagine how having something like that happen would change someone's life. And since I was planning to write about men who'd once attended the same boarding school — some due to difficult backgrounds where they were orphaned or abandoned — I thought this idea would be really intriguing to explore, especially because the police would likely be even more suspicious of an adopted son with a reputation for causing trouble. Once the idea was born, my hero, Dawson Reed, stepped out of my imagination and onto the page, and, as you will soon see, he is not the kind of person most people think he is. I love to write stories like this one, where the characters overcome incredible odds and wind up proving — to themselves and everyone else — that they are far more than anyone expected. Here's hoping you enjoy your visit to Silver Springs.

I love to hear from my readers. Feel free to interact with me on Facebook at Facebook.com/BrendaNovakAuthor, or sign up for my monthly newsletter at brendanovak.com/newsletter-sign-up. I'd love to be able to stay in touch with you.

Happy reading!

Brenda Novak

To Brenda Novak's Online Book
Group, because they constantly remind
me of the value and power of story.

1

The century-old farmhouse looked haunted . . .

Sadie Harris wasn't particularly superstitious, but knowing two people had been murdered in an upstairs bedroom of this isolated white clapboard home didn't make her eager to work here. She parked outside the gate and sat in her car, engine off, angling her head to see through the passenger window.

Dawson Reed, who'd placed the newspaper ad she'd responded to, was out of jail, all right. A pickup truck that didn't appear to be in much better shape than the rattletrap Chevy El Camino her mother's brother left her when he died three months ago sat in the drive. Not only that, the 2×4s that'd blocked the doors and windows of the house for the past twelve months had been pried away, some of the weeds had been trimmed in front and the mailbox had been straight-

9

ened and reinforced. But Dawson hadn't been home long enough to get around to everything that needed tending to. What with the vandalism that'd occurred in his absence and the deferred maintenance that went along with having a house sit empty for so long, he had his work cut out for him.

She wondered what he had to be thinking, now that he'd returned to Silver Springs. After a year spent fighting for his freedom, he'd narrowly escaped a verdict that would've landed him on death row. But he couldn't be *too* excited to rejoin this small community. Regardless of what the jury said, he was guilty in the minds of all those who lived around here.

Sadie frowned as her eyes traced the graffiti that was still on the house. Someone had spray-painted the word *murderer* on the wood siding above the porch, in letters large enough to be read from the highway a quarter mile away. That Dawson hadn't scrubbed it off first thing said something about him, didn't it? But what? Was he too beleaguered after his long ordeal to care what folks thought? Too busy with items he felt should be handled first? Or was leaving it there his way of flipping off the many concerned citizens of Silver Springs?

He could be taunting his detractors because he'd wound up inheriting the property despite what they thought . . .

The alarm she'd set on her phone sounded, startling her so much she whacked her hand on the steering wheel. "Ow!" she complained as she grabbed her cell and turned off the noise. If she planned to be on time for this interview, she had only three minutes to walk the length of the dirt drive leading to the front door. And yet she wasn't completely convinced she should keep the appointment, couldn't even say what kind of job it would be. Although Dawson had advertised for a housekeeper/caregiver, he lived alone. Why couldn't he take care of himself?

Not many healthy adults had a housekeeper in Silver Springs. That sort of freaked her out right there, before she even got to the fact that it was dangerous to meet a man out here, alone, who might've hacked his adoptive parents to death with a hatchet.

She shuddered at the bloody image that crept into her mind. The gruesome details of the Reed killings had been reported in the papers and on the evening news with great regularity. *Any* murder in these parts would be shocking. LA was only ninety minutes to the south. Such a crime wouldn't be so unheard of there. But this was a peaceful artist and farming community with mission-style adobe buildings and beautiful murals. The worst thing that'd ever happened, before the Reed murders — at least in recent memory — was when the Mueller girl ran away and was kidnapped. Even that was twenty years ago, and she went to Hollywood, so she was kidnapped *there.*

Pressing the button that would bring up her display, Sadie checked the time on her phone — the clock in the car was broken, along with everything else that didn't directly contribute to the drivability of the vehicle. Two minutes. Dared she go? Or should she take off while she still could?

Sly, her domineering, soon-to-be ex-husband, would warn her to keep her distance from Dawson. He'd already put in his two cents. They'd argued about it for over an hour last night. "You don't want to work for that bastard. What kind of guy kills two old people in their sleep — the couple who took him in when no one else would? Fed him? Clothed him? Treated him as their biological child? They were so proud of him! And you wouldn't believe what he did to those people. Talk about the ultimate betrayal."

When Sadie had pointed out that no one knew for sure whether Dawson had killed his adoptive parents, that there hadn't been enough evidence for a conviction, he'd alluded to having some insider knowledge to suggest Dawson was as guilty as the infamous O.J. had been. "Trust me. You don't know everything," he'd said.

He knew everything, though — always had. She was tired of that, tired of him. He'd been playing games with her since before the murders ever occurred, drawing out the divorce proceedings, hiding any extra income he earned working security at various functions so it wouldn't be included in his child support calculation, threatening to fight her for custody of their five-year-old son if she didn't accept the pittance he offered. Since she'd been the one to move out, he was living alone in a three-bedroom, while she and Jayden were squeezed into a tiny one-bedroom guesthouse. But having the better living situation wasn't enough for him. He was trying to keep her destitute so she'd have to come back if she wanted to be able to feed and clothe their child — and eat herself.

She let her gaze range over the farm and the fields that stretched on either side. The place didn't look inviting. Several windows had been broken, an outbuilding had been burned and a pile of cast-off furniture and other rubbish from God knew where had been dumped in the yard. Even more notable, the closest neighbor had to be a mile away . . .

He's a nut job. That was what Sly had said just before he hung up. As a Silver Springs police officer, he spoke with more than a little arrogance and authority. But in recent years, he'd related *so* many stories that made the hair on the back of her neck stand up — stories about breaking up a high school drinking party but not reporting the kids so long as they gave up all their beer, or picking up a prostitute but not arresting her if she "baked the force some cookies." Although Sadie had a feeling there was a lot more involved than cookies — she'd once heard Sly make a crude joke about it — he denied any wrongdoing when she questioned him. Said he was only kidding. But if he thought he could get away with using his badge to gain some advantage in a situation, even if it was just to scare people or make someone scramble out of the way, he'd do it. And, especially toward the end of their marriage, he'd started throwing his weight around with her, too. Although he'd never seriously hurt her, he'd come close.

As far as she was concerned, he was a "nut job" himself. So why would she let him make her decision for her? She couldn't trust him. At least, as far as trust went, Dawson was still a question mark.

With only a minute left, she got out of the car. Dawson was offering full-time employment doing . . . something she hoped she was capable of, and he was promising to pay much more than she was making waiting tables at Lolita's Country Kitchen. If she wanted to escape her ex-husband for good, this was her chance. It wasn't as if she could get anything else, not with Sly using his influence to sabotage her in every way possible. No one dared get on his bad side — he'd make life too difficult — so whenever she applied for a job, she was told she didn't qualify, or a better candidate had been selected. The only reason she had her job at Lolita's was because she'd been working there since before she left him.

Dawson didn't have any reason to harm her. That was what she had to remember. If he killed Mr. and Mrs. Reed, he did it because he wanted their farm — not that that was any small thing.

As she drew closer to the house, she could see storm damage to the roof, peeling paint and bird droppings on the railing of the porch. These physical details added to her overall apprehension, but she didn't get truly chilled until a curtain moved in the window. The idea that Dawson was looking out at her, watching her approach, almost made her turn back. She stopped, but before she could do anything, the front door opened and her prospective employer strode out.

"You must be Sadie Harris."

Silver Springs had only about 5,000 residents. The town wasn't large by any stretch of the imagination, and yet they'd never met. Not only was he two years older — she knew his age because of the many newspaper reports and the trial that'd revealed so much about his life — they'd gone to different high schools. She'd attended the public high school; he'd attended New Horizons, a boarding school exclusive to boys. *Troubled* boys.

So . . . how troubled was he? Troubled enough to murder the couple who'd taken him in? Troubled enough to lure a woman out to his farm with the false promise of employment?

She hoped not.

"Yes. I —" she cleared her throat as she shoved that last thought away "— I'm Sadie."

"And I'm Dawson."

As if he needed to identify himself. Close

16

to six feet, he'd been out of jail long enough to have seen several days of sun. His sandy-colored hair, cut in a military style typical of county jail inmates, blended well with the golden color of his skin while contrasting sharply with his eyes, which were blue but not a deep blue — more ice-like. She'd known he was handsome before she came. Everyone had made a big deal about how his "angel" face didn't jive with his "devilish" actions. She'd seen so many pictures she would've recognized him even if he hadn't been standing on his own porch. "I know."

"You followed the trial."

"To a degree, yes. It was the talk of the town, pretty hard to miss."

He nodded as if her response was nothing less than what he'd expected. "Right. That's unfortunate, of course. But . . . thanks for coming."

"No problem." She wiped her sweaty palms on the flowing black skirt that constituted half of her best outfit. Sly had thrown away most of her clothes — everything she hadn't been able to carry in that first load — when he came home to find her moving out. She'd grabbed Jayden's things first, so that didn't leave her with a lot of wardrobe choices. No doubt she looked a little silly hobbling down the rutted lane in a black blouse, a flowing skirt and high heels, but she didn't feel as if she could show up for an interview in jeans.

"Would you rather talk out here on the porch?" he asked. "I've made coffee. I can bring out a cup and some chairs."

He could tell she wasn't set on staying. This was an attempt to entice her. But she *couldn't* leave, not unless she wanted to walk right back into Sly's arms. She needed the job, needed the money.

"Um . . ." She almost said it wasn't necessary that he go to the trouble. She'd been programmed from birth to say those types of things, to be polite. And although it never got very cold — their weather was much like that of Santa Barbara twenty minutes away — it was a little chilly this morning. Thick dark clouds blotted out the sun, showing signs of rain. But she was frightened enough that the idea of staying outside did raise her comfort level. She had to be cautious. Had to be around for her son, after all. She didn't like the way his father treated him. That was part of the reason she'd finally gathered the strength and determination to leave Sly, despite what she knew he'd put her through. He wasn't proud of Jayden like he should be; most of

18

the time he acted embarrassed of their sweet, gentle boy.

She drew a deep breath. "The weather's not *too* bad. Sitting outside would be a great idea. If you don't mind," she added lamely.

"I don't mind. I'll be right back."

As soon as he disappeared, she twisted around to see her car, trying to gauge the distance in case she had to kick off her shoes and make a run for it. The El Camino wasn't all that far. Since she'd parked it outside the gate, where there'd be no danger of getting blocked in, she could make a quick getaway, if necessary.

Somewhat relieved to have Dawson occupied elsewhere for the moment, she hurried to the porch as best she could without turning an ankle and gazed at the dry rot and warped boards that needed to be replaced while telling herself to calm down.

When he returned with a small table and then a tray supporting two cups of coffee, as well as cream and sugar, she wished she had said no to the coffee. She'd been so preoccupied it hadn't occurred to her he might've spiked it.

"Have a seat." Next, he brought out chairs and placed hers — rather strategically, she thought — near the stairs and away from him. "It's great to meet you. I appreciate you coming out here in spite of . . . in spite of everything."

She didn't deserve any gratitude. She wouldn't have come if she'd had a better choice. "Sure. It's okay."

"Would you like cream? Sugar?"

She went through the process of adding cream and one packet of sugar to her coffee even though she couldn't drink it.

"So . . . you live in Silver Springs?" he asked when she finished.

She met his eyes, tried to determine if they were lifeless. She'd heard that serial killers had emotionless, flat eyes, like those of a shark. But she wasn't sure a man who killed his parents for the sake of financial gain counted as a serial killer. Probably not. And there didn't seem to be anything unappealing about Dawson's eyes. The reverse was actually true. They were such an odd, arresting color and fringed with the longest, thickest gold-tipped lashes. "I do," she said.

"How long have you been in the area?"

"Since I was ten. My folks moved here, wanted to get out of the rat race of LA."

"Your parents are in town, then?"

The wind came up, but other than trying to hold her hair back with one hand while gripping her coffee, she resisted the temptation to react to the cold. After making him

20

bring everything outside, she didn't want him to suggest they go in. "No, not anymore." She set her cup on the stand with the cream and sugar. "My mother had a rare kidney disease. That was part of the reason for the move, although I didn't know it at the time. We lost her when I was fourteen. My father finished raising me, but he died of a heart attack — while jogging — the year after I was married."

"I'm sorry you lost your parents so early."

"I guess we all have our problems." She felt silly after she'd made that statement. No question his problems had been worse. At least she hadn't been accused of killing *her* parents.

He took a drink of his coffee. "Any siblings?"

"No. I was an only child."

When his free hand came up, she flinched before realizing that he was merely swatting a bug, and her cheeks began to burn with embarrassment when he scooted his chair even farther away. Obviously, he'd noticed that she wasn't quite comfortable with him. She hoped he hadn't also noticed that she had yet to take a sip of her coffee.

"So you're married."

She picked up her cup and cradled it with both hands, trying to leach the warmth from it. "Not anymore. Well, the divorce isn't quite final, but that's a technicality. We've been separated for over a year." Conjuring what she hoped was a pleasant smile, she marveled that she was able to condense the hell Sly had put her through — was still putting her through — into such a mild statement. "Trying to work out the details, you know."

He watched her closely, seemed intent on figuring out what she was thinking and feeling. Did killers do that? "Those things can take time."

"Are you speaking from experience? Or . . ." She didn't remember reading anything about him having a wife.

"No."

"No children, either?"

"Not for me. You?"

"One. A boy named Jayden. He's five." She couldn't help smiling, vaguely, when she thought of her son.

"Does he live with you or —"

She felt her smile wilt. "Yeah, he's with me. His father has visitation every other weekend, but . . . Sly's a police officer, so he works long hours." Or he was at the gym. "I have Jayden most of the time." Which was why it didn't make a lot of sense that Sly would ever sue her for custody. He didn't really want custody. He was using Jayden, along with anything else he could, as a weapon against her.

Dawson pursed his lips. "So *that's* the connection."

She peered at him. "What're you talking about?"

"I thought maybe you were Officer Harris's sister or something. But no — you're *married* to him."

She stiffened at the mention of her ex-husband's name. "*Was* married. Why? You know him?"

"Not personally." Leaning forward, he poured a bit of cream in his coffee, added one sugar as he'd seen her do and slid the cup over to her. "You saw me drink out of this, so other than a few germs you wouldn't otherwise encounter, you should be able to trust it."

Surprised he'd be so direct, she floundered for something to say in return. "That's not it. I'm just . . . jittery enough without the caffeine."

He said nothing, but she could tell he wasn't fooled by the lie.

"So . . . how have you heard of my ex-husband?" she asked, quickly changing the subject. "He didn't have anything to do with . . . with the investigation . . ."

"No. I was arrested by a homicide detective. Officer Harris wasn't involved in the case. But he dropped by last night."

Her surprise overtook her anxiety, even made her forget about the cold air that seemed to be passing through her blouse like a mesh screen. "He came *here*? Why?"

Rain began to plink on the roof. "To let me know he'll be keeping an eye on me," he replied.

"For . . ."

"Anything I might do he doesn't approve of, I suppose. Sounded like he was looking forward to the challenge of keeping me in line."

Sadie figured she shouldn't be surprised that Sly would try to bully Dawson. He was the big, tough cop — thought he could bully anyone. Of course he'd pile on when it came to the town pariah. "Was he in uniform?"

A wry smile tugged at Dawson's lips. "His appearance wouldn't have had the same impact without it."

Her nails curved into her palms as the anger and bitterness she'd had to live with for so long once again rose inside her, burning her throat like bile. "Please tell me he didn't mention *me* . . ."

"Not by name. Said there was a woman coming to interview with me in the morn-

24

ing. And that she wasn't the person I was looking for."

She felt her jaw drop. "He *threatened* you?"

"If you consider 'You've had enough trouble, it wouldn't be smart to ask for any more' a threat."

This was the first time anyone had been brave enough to admit that Sly had attempted to ruin her chances of gaining employment.

Too upset to sit any longer, Sadie came to her feet. "That . . . that . . ." She wasn't sure if she meant to say "That isn't fair" or "That really pisses me off," because both sentences ran through her mind at once. But when she got angry, she often broke into tears, especially when it came to her ex-husband. He made her feel so helpless, so easily overpowered — and he was relentless in his determination to get her back or make her pay, supremely confident he'd win in the end.

Would she *never* be free of him?

Falling silent for fear her voice would crack, she turned so that Dawson Reed couldn't see her face and stared out at the rain.

Thankfully, he didn't press her to finish her statement. He sat behind her in silence, giving her time to compose herself.

"I'm sorry," she said when she could speak without evidence of tears in her voice. "I know you've been through . . . quite an ordeal. I . . . I'll get out of your way."

She'd already started down the stairs when he spoke. "Mrs. Harris . . ."

"Please, call me anything but that." She wished she could use her maiden name, but she knew how Sly would perceive such a move, how embarrassed he'd be. She'd do it one day. She'd made a promise to herself. But, at the moment, there were too many other, more important battles to fight — and win.

"Sadie."

The rain was falling harder now, soaking her blouse and skirt, but she didn't care that she was getting wet. She closed her eyes and turned her face up to the sky, letting it wash away her makeup and run her mascara. What did things like that matter, anyway?

"Don't leave . . ." Dawson had followed her. From his voice, he was right behind her, but he didn't touch her. She wished, if he *was* a deranged killer intent on committing another murder, he'd hurry up and get it over with, because she no longer had the energy to keep soldiering on. Sly made her feel *that* cornered, *that* hopeless.

But then she thought of Jayden being stranded with only Sly to guide him through life and came back to the truth: she couldn't give up. If this wasn't going to work, she'd have to figure out some other way to build a new life.

She left him in the yard, was almost to her car when he caught up and grabbed her by the arm. Thanks to the wind and rain, she hadn't heard him following her. She nearly screamed, but he let go as soon as she turned, lifting his hands as if he'd only been trying to get her attention and had no plans to harm her. "Stay a little longer," he said. "Please. We haven't talked about the job."

Because she was unable to hold her tears in check, they rolled down her cheeks, mingling with the rain. "You can't hire me now," she said. "You have no idea what he'll do. He'll make your life so miserable you'll wish you were still in jail."

He wiped the rain from his own face. "That's a chance I'm willing to take."

"Why?"

"I need you."

Sadie shielded her eyes with one hand. "To make your meals? To clean your house? You can do that yourself — and save a lot of money."

"That's not it. I won't be able to get my sister out of the institution where they put her if I don't have someone to look after her while I'm on the farm. She's mentally handicapped, could try to cook and burn down the house. Or go outside and wander off. There's a pond out back. Wouldn't be safe if she got around it."

Sadie had forgotten about Angela Reed! She hadn't been mentioned in the media since Lonnie's and Larry's bodies were discovered. Now that he'd brought her up, however, Sadie remembered reading, early on, that the Reeds' daughter had to be institutionalized when they were killed and Dawson was imprisoned. She also remembered reading that Angela had been home during the murders but had been left unharmed, which wasn't a point in Dawson's favor. The police claimed her well-being served as proof that he was behind the killings, since only those who had to be removed in order for him to inherit had been harmed. "You want to bring her here?" she asked, gesturing at the weed-infested farm.

"I'm *going* to bring her here," he clarified as if nothing could stop him. "This is her home. This is where she'd prefer to be. And she's waited long enough. We both have."

Sadie adjusted the strap on her purse. "So

what would I be doing, exactly? I've never cared for someone who . . . who can't manage the basics. You might have to advertise for a nurse or —"

"Angela isn't on any meds. She manages, at a very basic level. She's similar to . . . to a five-year-old. Like your son. She just needs some guidance, some reassurance and oversight."

"And you can't do it?"

"What if she got confused and wouldn't come out of the bathroom? Or needed help in the shower? I couldn't go in — but you could."

"You're saying I'd be like a . . . a female companion. A babysitter."

"Exactly. You'd make sure she bathes every morning. Puts on clean underwear and clothes. Has a healthy breakfast and is able to watch her favorite shows. You'd read to her, play games with her, take her out for walks. And you'd fix her lunch and dinner, since I won't be finished until sundown or later. You'd also do laundry and help keep the house clean so I won't have that to face when I come in at night — pretty much everything you do for your son. But you could bring him along, watch them both at the same time, if you like. That would save on child care, if that's something you're paying for now. And Angela would love having a little boy around — she's always loved kids. She's gentle, sweet. You wouldn't have to worry about her ever hurting him."

Sadie loved the idea of spending more time with her son. Saving on child care, which was such a big part of her monthly budget, sounded appealing, too, not to mention how much she'd miss Jayden if she was working more hours.

But she wasn't worried about *Angela* hurting her son . . .

Besides, Sly would never put up with her bringing Jayden to this place. He'd claim she was endangering their son, would use such "reckless behavior" against her if he ever did sue for custody. "I have a good situation for him already." She paid Petra Smart, a mother who had three children of her own and lived down the street from her, to watch him, so she did feel as if he was in good hands. But the money. There was never enough money.

"That's up to you, of course."

She rubbed her arms against the cold. "So . . . while I help with your sister, you're going to be doing . . . what? Putting this place back together?"

"Yes. I have to get it up and working, make it productive again. I'll be honest.

That's the only way I'll be able to care for us both — and pay you — beyond summer."

With a sigh, Sadie wrung her hands. She'd be taking a big risk. Spending so much time alone with someone like Dawson. Letting go of the job she had now on the off chance that working as his sister's caregiver might pan out. She'd never done anything like that before, had no idea whether she and Angela would get along.

But she *had* to make a change, couldn't go on the way she was. She was falling further and further behind, and that hurt anyone who trusted her enough to give her credit. "You're not going to perform a background check before giving me the job?"

"I'm a pretty good judge of character."

"You are?"

"I knew your ex-husband was an asshole in about five seconds."

She couldn't help but laugh.

"I'm sure I'll find nothing amiss," he added. "Am I right?"

"Yes, but . . . you really shouldn't take my word for it."

"Beggars can't be choosers, Sadie. How many people from Silver Springs are there who'd be willing to work for me?"

He had a point. The whole town was

embittered. The Reeds had been well loved. Those who knew them wanted someone to pay for their deaths. And most were convinced it should be him. "Have you received any other calls on the ad?" she asked.

"I've had several. They all hang up as soon as they realize I'm the one who's looking for help." He shoved his hands into the pockets of a pair of faded jeans, which fit him so well she couldn't help noticing. "So what do you say? Will you give it a shot? I promise you'll get paid, at least for the next six months. Although I don't have a lot, it's enough to carry us through August."

What then? She had a kid to take care of. If he couldn't pay her, she'd have no choice except to go back to Sly. But she'd only have to go back to him sooner if she didn't take this chance. "When would you like me to start?"

His lean, spare features softened with relief. "Is tomorrow too soon?"

She was so wet and cold now that she was beginning to shiver. "I'm a waitress over at Lolita's Country Kitchen. I had no idea I'd get this job, still have to give two weeks' notice."

"Okay, but . . . can you come here when you don't have to be there? I was hoping you'd be able to help me get the house ready so that I can prove I have a safe and clean environment for Angela. They'll check before they let me take her."

This was happening much quicker than Sadie had expected. "Sure. Okay. I get off at noon tomorrow. I'll come over right after."

"Thank you."

With a nod and a wave, she trudged the rest of the way to her car. She had a new job. She'd be earning $3,000 a month — almost twice what she was earning now, which would allow her to make ends meet, stand on her own.

The prospect of maintaining her freedom brought such relief, such exhilaration. Finally, she had something to be happy about. She'd struck a deal with Dawson in spite of Sly. That single act of defiance felt good, as if she was taking another leap forward in regaining control of her life.

At the same time, she knew her ex wouldn't be pleased. She had no idea how badly Sly might react. *And,* even more to the point, she'd be working in almost total isolation for a man who'd just been acquitted of a brutal double homicide.

She prayed she wasn't letting desperation goad her into making a terrible mistake.

2

"You're back early. Lolita's must not have been very busy this morning."

Sadie turned from locking her front door to find Maude Clevenger, her spry but elderly landlady, standing beneath the patio cover of her own backyard. Maude lived with Vern, her husband, also retired, in the elegantly restored Craftsman that fronted the small "guest" house Sadie rented, but Maude spent a lot of time trimming plants, building rock statues or adding the occasional gnome, ceramic frog or other ornament to her yard. She loved to show Jayden her latest find or treasure. "I haven't been to Lolita's," she said. "I wasn't scheduled today."

"I'm sorry to hear that. I know you could use the hours."

Maude was aware of her financial troubles because Sadie had been forced to ask if she could pay her rent in two separate payments the past few months. "It's okay. I had a job interview somewhere else," she said. "I only came home because I needed to change. I promised Jayden I'd take him to the park."

"Where *is* Jayden?" She glanced around as if she was surprised she didn't see him.

"With Petra Smart down the street. I'm on my way to get him."

"I thought maybe his father took him . . ."

Maude was curious about her relationship with Sly, often asked leading questions, which Sadie did her best to answer without giving too much away. "No."

"Is Sly at work, then?"

"I really can't say. When I spoke with him last night, he didn't mention his schedule." And why would she ask? It wasn't as if he'd help her out even if he wasn't working. Sly never did his part when it came to parenting, but she had to be careful not to complain too loudly. She couldn't let word get back to her ex-husband that she was trashtalking him. He was such a proud and private person — hard enough to deal with when he *didn't* have a legitimate reason to be angry with her.

The jewels on Maude's rings glinted as a shard of sunlight pierced through the clouds. "So? How'd the interview go?"

Sadie held her car keys at the ready.

Although anxious to leave, she paused to finish the conversation. Maude got bored now and then and wanted to gossip. But she was essentially a good person. That she'd allowed Sadie to move in without a security deposit had been instrumental in Sadie being able to get out of the house she'd shared with Sly. Sadie would always be grateful to her. "Good. I got the job."

"How wonderful!" She clapped her hands. "But I'm surprised you didn't mention that you had an opportunity . . ."

Why would she mention it? She hadn't been sure she'd keep the appointment. And she knew everyone would try to dissuade her, if they could, just as Sly had done. She wouldn't have told him if he hadn't been so adamant that she couldn't afford to live separately from him and should come back. He'd actually invited her to live as a "roommate" for a while, until they could "figure things out." But she could guess how long that would last . . . "I didn't tell anyone, in case . . . in case it didn't go well," she explained.

"Apparently, you were worried for nothing! You got the job!"

"Yes." She could meet her expenses without having to cave in to Sly's demands. That brought her spirits up, gave her more hope than she'd felt in a long while.

The bangles on Maude's arms clanged when she lifted her colorful muumuu to keep it from dragging as she walked closer. The rain had stopped, but the ground was still wet. "So where will you be working?"

Explaining this part wasn't going to be as exciting as the rest. But nothing had been perfect in Sadie's world for a long time. She figured she might as well hold her head high and accept whatever disapproval she'd encounter as a result of her decision to work for Dawson Reed. Word would get out eventually. It wasn't as if she could keep what she did every day a secret. This community was too small for that.

"At the Reed farm."

Maude's mouth opened and closed twice before she managed a proper response. "You mean . . . where Lonnie and Larry were *murdered*?"

"That's right. Their son's planning to get the farm running again. He's home now."

"The adopted son who might've *killed* them?"

Sadie felt her smile grow strained. "Dawson was acquitted, in case you haven't heard."

"I've heard. It was all over the news. But . . . you've never worked on a farm, have you? What will you be doing?"

"I'll be taking care of his sister."

"Angela."

"You know her?"

"Not personally. The Reeds belonged to my sister's church. Chelsea saw them every Sunday, worked with Lonnie on various charity projects. She told me Angela was there the night of the murders."

According to what had been reported on the news, Angela had been sleeping soundly and hadn't been able to provide any details on what happened. First she'd said it was her brother. Then she'd said it wasn't. "He's bringing her home from the assisted living place where they put her when . . . when he was arrested."

"Why?"

The ridge of Sadie's car key bit into her palm, prompting her to ease her grip. "Because it's her home."

"But won't that be traumatic for her — to return to the place where her parents were killed?"

"He claims that's where she wants to be."

Maude began to toy with the large chunk of amber she wore as a pendant around her neck, something she did whenever she became agitated. "You understand that even though he was acquitted, he still might be . . . I mean, will you be safe?"

"I hope so." Afraid Maude would mention Jayden and her duty as a mother, Sadie shifted from one foot to the other. She had a responsibility to Jayden to be wise and responsible. That was true. But she also had a responsibility to provide, especially since Sly wasn't much help. If one responsibility warred with the other — what was she supposed to do? She wasn't going back to her ex. "Dawson seems plenty nice."

"Most killers don't announce their intentions right off the bat, Sadie."

Some of the elation she'd been feeling dissipated, as she'd known it would once she had to tell people what she'd be doing. "I understand that, but a woman's got to do what a woman's got to do."

"You're feeling a little . . . desperate. But these are drastic measures, honey."

Too drastic. That was the implication. Was she being foolish? "This is the only option I have left, Maude."

Her landlady continued to caress her amber pendant. "Does Sly know you've taken a job from Dawson Reed?"

"Not yet." Sadie didn't care to go into the fact that she'd told him she was applying, and that he'd tried to ruin her chances.

"I can't imagine he'll be pleased . . ."

He wouldn't — because this would ensure her autonomy, at least for a little while. She'd be able to finalize the divorce regardless of what he was willing to pay for child support. In order to continue to drag out the proceedings, he'd have to sue her for custody of Jayden. He'd been threatening to do so, but that would cost him in attorney fees, and he didn't really want custody or he'd be more religious about exercising his visitation rights. "No."

"He drives by almost every night," Maude said.

Sadie didn't need the reminder. She'd seen him herself. "I know."

"He's still in love with you, very concerned for your safety."

What he felt had more to do with possession and control than love. He wasn't concerned for her safety so much as worried she might start seeing someone else. He checked up on her constantly — at work, at home, at Jayden's school — all under the guise of being a loving husband and father, and a dutiful police officer. But it was a farce. As far as she was concerned, he was *stalking* her.

"Yes. Well, I'm sure I'll be fine," Sadie said. "I'll keep an eye out for anything that might be . . . worrisome."

"Isn't what's already happened worrisome?" Maude asked, but Sadie couldn't listen. If Sly was her only other alternative, she was willing to take a risk, even a big one like this.

"I'd better go. Jayden's waiting for me." She'd promised him a celebration, one that included ice cream and an hour or two at the park. She'd been looking forward to spending some time with him when she didn't feel as if she might be crushed beneath the pressure she'd been under. She'd be putting in more hours now that she had a second job, knew she wouldn't get to see him as much in the coming two weeks, so there was that, too.

But Maude's reaction had stripped the shine from her excitement. Her landlady didn't approve of her decision. Sadie doubted anyone else would, either. And now that she'd shared her plans, word would begin to spread.

Sly would be banging on her door before nightfall.

Sly contacted her even sooner than expected. Sadie's heart skipped a beat the moment she heard her cell phone ding and glanced down to see a text from him while she was at the park with Jayden.

So? Did you go this morning?

She stared at those words, wishing he could simply disappear from the planet. Perhaps that wasn't a generous thought, but she'd been feeling smothered for so long she'd begun to fantasize about a world where he didn't exist.

"Mommy! Watch!"

Sadie shaded her eyes so she could see her son go down the slide. Fortunately, the sun was out and the sand wasn't too soggy from the rain earlier. She'd been playing with Jayden for two hours. They needed to get going so she could take care of some banking, shopping and other errands. But Jayden was having so much fun she'd decided to give him a few more minutes. "Wow! Look at you!" she said. "You're getting to be such a big boy."

"I'm going again!" he announced but got distracted by a shovel and pail a little girl, maybe six, was using near the swings.

As soon as Sadie felt confident his new friend was willing to share and that the mother didn't mind, she returned her attention to Sly's text. If she didn't respond, he'd only call her or come over later.

Yes, I went, she wrote.

Are you fucking kidding me?

She blanched at the profanity. She could hear him screaming that at her . . .

Please tell me you didn't take the job, he wrote. I need the work, she wrote back.

That's a yes? You took a job from a killer????

Her phone rang. It was Sly, of course, anxious to shout at her. Texting ugly things wasn't nearly as satisfying; he craved a full verbal assault.

She pressed the Decline button, but after the ringing stopped, her phone pinged again. Answer, damn it!

When she didn't respond to that, either, he kept calling.

Finally, with a sigh, she picked up. She figured she might as well get this over with while Jayden was distracted. Why subject her sensitive child to another argument between Mommy and Daddy if she could possibly avoid it? "Sly, what I do with my life is up to me," she said in lieu of a greeting.

"That's bullshit. Don't let Dawson Reed fool you. He's dangerous. I won't have my wife anywhere near him, especially out there on the farm alone. Do you know how many places he could hide your body?"

Ducking her head so that her voice wouldn't carry, she murmured, "I'm not your wife anymore."

"Yes, you are. The divorce isn't final."

"That's a technicality."

"So? You're the mother of my child. That means I should have some say."

"No, it doesn't! I'm taking proper care of Jayden. If you're concerned that he'll be at Petra's too much, you can watch him yourself when you're not at work. That would be a great way to make sure he remains safe." She wasn't convinced spending so much time with Sly would be good for Jayden, however. She'd hate to subject him to more of his father's disapproval. Sly was so disappointed that their son wasn't the rough-and-tumble boy he'd expected that he couldn't help making snide comments: *What do you mean, you don't want to watch basketball with me? All boys — real boys — love sports . . . Why do you let him put on your lipstick? Are you trying to turn him into a fag?* On and on it went. One time when Sly *had* taken Jayden for a few hours, she'd arrived to pick him up only to find him in timeout — for telling his father he preferred dance lessons to Little League.

"You'd *like* to turn me into your baby-sitter, wouldn't you?" he said.

Not really. But she had to make the offer. No judge was going to deny Sly visitation rights. He was a police officer! And it wasn't as if she could claim he was *physically* abusive. "I'm saying it's an option."

"So you can go off and make money you'll use to keep our family apart? Screw that! Why would I help you when I haven't done anything to deserve what you're doing to me?"

"You've never done *anything* to cause the divorce?" she echoed, shocked that he could even make such a statement. "What about the day you nearly ran me over with your squad car?"

"For the millionth time, I *didn't* nearly run you down. I didn't see you standing there."

That was what he said, but she was fairly certain he *had* seen her . . .

"Besides, I've apologized for scaring you."

"So that makes it better?"

"What else can I do? I didn't know you were there, yet I apologized anyway. That's nice, isn't it? I'll make everything else up to you, too. I've told you I would, but you won't give me the chance!"

"Because I'm done, Sly. I can't do it anymore."

"This time will be different. I promise. You'll be happy. I'll make you happy. You don't need to work for some murderer!"

He *couldn't* make her happy. Any chance of that had been extinguished long ago. "We don't *know* he's a murderer."

"Who else killed those people? The mysterious hitchhiker he claims he met earlier in the night? The one he claimed was tweaking and acting irrationally?"

"Maybe. Was his story ever really checked out?"

"His story was ridiculous! What are the chances that some stranger — a drug addict — he had an altercation with is going to be able to find the Reed farmhouse and kill the Reeds before Dawson can even get home?"

His story did sound rather far-fetched . . . "I don't know. But his attorney claims the homicide detective settled on Dawson right away, that he never even looked at anyone else."

"Dawson told you this?"

Jayden was laughing with the little girl who was sharing her bucket. He didn't seem to notice that Sadie was on the phone, let alone having an argument, which brought some relief despite her frustration. "No, I saw it on the news, like everyone else," she

46

told Sly. "But maybe he was right. Maybe they focused the investigation too soon."

"No, they didn't! I'm part of the police force, Sadie. Are you saying we don't do our jobs?"

"You weren't involved in the investigation, Sly." He hoped to reach detective; his superiors just hadn't promoted him yet. She'd heard him fume when another officer was promoted ahead of him. "So that comment had nothing to do with you."

"You're talking about my friends and work associates."

"I'm telling you the truth — that we don't know!"

"Does that even matter?" he cried. "Do we *have* to know? Why take the chance?"

For the sake of freedom! She'd do almost anything to escape him. She'd gotten involved with Sly when she was still in high school. It didn't seem fair that a decision made when she was so young and naïve could have such long-reaching consequences. "It'll be okay. Dawson seems nice."

"Are you a *total* idiot? Ted Bundy seemed nice!"

Sadie stiffened. He treated her like she was stupid whenever she didn't agree with him. "There's no point in fighting about it. I've accepted the job. I'm going to work there. You have no say." She considered bringing up the fact that he'd tried to sabotage her by visiting the Reed farm ahead of her and all but threatening Dawson, but she knew that would only cause the argument to explode into something uglier, even more emotional. His attempt to intimidate Dawson hadn't been successful. She'd leave it there to protect Dawson from any backlash he'd receive for telling her.

"You'd rather work for a murderer than come back to me," he said.

"I'd rather accept a job that will enable me to remain independent."

"God, you're such a selfish bitch!"

There wasn't any way she could be more selfish than he was. That much she knew for sure. "I don't have to listen to this, Sly."

"Someone needs to knock some sense into you."

Squeezing her eyes closed, she drew a deep breath. "Who? *You?*"

"Someday, you'll get what's coming to you."

She recognized that tone, associated it with the afternoon he'd nearly run her over. He had the capacity for violence. She could sense it — and it frightened her as much or more as going to work for a man suspected of murdering his parents, maybe even more because it was directed at her. "I've got to go," she said.

"Don't hang up on me! We're not finished yet."

"I don't have to put up with your abuse anymore." She saw her son coming toward her, so she hit the button that would end the call. But she knew what she'd just told her ex-husband was a lie. She *did* have to put up with his abuse. There wasn't any way to avoid it. She'd been fighting that battle for years.

All the power was on his side.

Dawson Reed was so tired by the time he finished working in the fields that he skipped dinner. Hungry though he was, the thought of trying to prepare a meal was too overwhelming when he could hardly climb the stairs to reach his bed. Bottom line, he needed rest more than food. His body was no longer accustomed to long days of physical labor, not after sitting in a jail cell for more than twelve months. Trying to salvage what he could of the artichoke plants he'd been helping his folks grow before they were murdered, and preparing a large section of land for new plants — which he had to get in the ground before spring, since artichokes needed a period of vernalization — was more than any one man should attempt on his own. But if he was going to bring Angela home, he couldn't hire farmhands. He'd be spending what disposable income he had, what his defense lawyers hadn't already taken of his parents' estate and what was left of the money he'd borrowed against the farm on Sadie Harris, the caregiver he'd hired this morning for his sister.

He hoped he'd done the right thing. After Officer Harris had left, he'd almost decided to get the farm up and running — and turning a profit — before bringing Angela home. He'd figured, by then, maybe people would've had time to cool off, wouldn't be so angry and determined to persecute him. But Angela wasn't happy where she was, so he couldn't wait. He was too stubborn to let the arrogant ass who'd threatened him tell him what to do, anyway.

Once he reached the top of the stairs, he paused, as he always did, to stare at the closed door looming at the end of the hallway. The two people he'd loved most in the world had been murdered behind that door. When he thought of his parents, of what he'd encountered the night they were killed, he felt so much anger and grief he didn't know what to do. He tried to funnel it into his work, in the promises he told himself about the future and how he'd eventually find justice. But sometimes, the loss still hit him like a tidal wave, made him want to fight someone, anyone. Or he had to contend with a debilitating sadness that stole over him like wisps of fog, chilling him to the bone.

He reached for the knob, made sure the door was still locked, then dropped his hand. Aiyana Turner, the administrator of New Horizons, the boys ranch here in town where he'd gone to high school, had done her best to board up the place — as soon as the police gave her permission to come onto the property. She'd offered to clean up the blood for him, too. She was the only one, it seemed, who still had a kind word for him, who believed he was innocent. But he'd told her to leave the scene exactly as it was. He felt there might be some clue, some piece of evidence the police had missed that he could use to find the man who killed them — and he wouldn't rest until he did. After everything he'd lost, everything he'd been through, he'd find justice eventually.

His cell phone rang. Someone from the Stanley DeWitt Assisted Living Center in Los Angeles, where they'd taken his sister, was trying to reach him. He'd spoken to a member of their staff almost every day since he got home.

He needed to remove his dirty clothes and shower before he could lie down, so he finished the short journey to his room and sank into the wooden chair by the desk he'd been using to apply for the loan on the farm, handle the paperwork for assuming guardianship of Angela and create the spreadsheets that charted out the farm acreage, growth time, projected earnings and cash flow. "Hello?"

"Mr. Reed?"

He'd been legally adopted by Lonnie and Larry when he was fifteen, had used their last name ever since. He certainly didn't want to claim the name he'd been born with. The Reeds were the only ones who'd ever given a damn about him. "Yes."

"It's Megan. From Stanley DeWitt."

She'd called before. He recognized the name. "What's going on, Megan?"

"I'm sorry to bother you again, but . . . I thought maybe if you spoke to your sister, she'd cooperate with me."

Fighting the exhaustion that hung on his arms and legs like wrist and ankle weights, he covered a yawn. "What's she doing?"

"She's been up since six this morning, but she won't put on her pajamas and go to bed.

She insists you're coming to get her to-night."

"Tonight."

"Yes. She's waiting by the door, her purse on her arm, her coat buttoned to the top, even though it's too warm for that in here."

Dawson sighed as he pictured his sister stubbornly resisting the young Megan's pleas. The image that came to mind broke his heart. Not being able to help Angela had been as bad as everything else. "Let me talk to her."

"Yes, sir. One sec."

"It's your brother," he heard as she trans-ferred the phone.

Angela came on the line almost immedi-ately, her voice eager. "Dawson? Where are you?"

"I'm at home, honey. I can't come tonight. I told you I have to get the house cleaned up before they'll let me bring you here."

"Then clean it! Why aren't you cleaning it?"

"I *am* cleaning it. I'm doing a lot of other things, too — things that take time. I need you to be patient. I'll come for you as soon as I can. I promise."

"Okay. I'll wait here." She handed the phone to Megan, but that had been too easy, so easy that Dawson knew Angela *still* didn't understand. He had Megan put her right back on the line.

"It won't be tonight," he reiterated. "I'm not coming *now*. It might be as long as a week. These things take time."

"How long is a week?"

"Seven days."

"Seven days!" She groaned as if he'd said seven years. "That's forever!"

"That's how it has to be. Moving you requires some paperwork, too, and it's the paperwork that takes the longest. They won't let me pick you up until everything's done."

"But it's been *so* long." She started to cry. "I don't like it here, Dawson. Come get me *now*."

"I'll come as soon as I can, honey. I just . . . I need you to listen to Megan and get ready for bed. If you cooperate, the time will go faster for everyone. Then, before you know it, you'll be home."

She sniffed. "Will I get to see Mom and Dad? Or are they still dead?"

Dawson scrubbed a hand over his face. She had no concept of death, of forever. She only knew that she missed the people who'd always been there for her. He missed them, too. "They're still dead. They'll always be dead. But I'll take you to see their graves

54

and try to help you understand when you get home."

"They'll come back," she said, supremely confident. "I know they will."

"They *can't,* Angela."

"Yes, they can!"

"We'll talk about it later. For now, listen to Megan, please? Put on your pajamas and get into bed. Megan doesn't need you to make her night difficult."

"You'll be here in the morning?"

"What did I tell you?" he asked.

"I don't know," she replied, and cried even louder.

"It'll be a week. I'll be there in seven days. Have Megan count them on your fingers." He wasn't positive he could get there in *exactly* seven days, which was why he'd been careful not to name a date so far. But after what they'd been through the past year, dangling a "soon" out there wasn't comforting to her anymore. Angela needed a concrete figure, something Megan could circle on the calendar and she could look forward to in a more definite way.

He hated the thought that he might have to disappoint her at the end of the week — due to circumstances beyond his control — but it was better than disappointing her every night, like he was doing now.

"A week," she repeated with another sniff. "Seven days."

"Megan? When is a week?" he heard her ask.

There was some shuffling as he heard Megan start to count, "One, two, three . . ."

"Seven takes too long," Angela said, discouraged again, when Megan was finished.

"It won't be that long. Have Megan get the calendar and show you how far Christmas is, and you'll see that a week is soon. Very soon."

After Megan went through the months with her, and the many, many days until Christmas, Angela finally relented. "Okay. I'll go to bed. Tomorrow will be one day, right?"

"Yes." He covered another yawn as Megan thanked him and disconnected. After that, he tried to get up so he could remove his boots, take off his clothes and shower — but wound up falling asleep with his head facedown on the desk.

3

Sadie passed a restless night. She hadn't heard from Sly since their conversation at the park, but she knew he wouldn't go about minding his own business. He'd blindside her with something, sometime, which was why she kept looking out the window, watching for his squad car. If he was working, he'd think nothing of stopping by in the middle of the night and dragging her out of bed to continue their argument — regardless of what she had to do the next day. Even if he wasn't working, he could drop by very late. He'd done it before.

Fortunately, she didn't hear from him. But even when she wasn't getting up to check her windows and make sure her doors were locked, she was lying on the mattress she shared with Jayden, wondering what it was going to be like juggling two jobs for a couple of weeks. She'd be putting in long hours; it wouldn't be easy.

She kept telling herself she'd muddle through, but the closer it came to morning, the more nervous she grew. Her shift at Lolita's would go fast. She'd been there for three years, ever since Jayden had been potty-trained (what Sly required in order to watch him), so it had become almost second nature. She just hoped what she had to do in the afternoon wouldn't be too difficult or upsetting. Dawson had said she'd clean the house. But no way would she let him assign her the Reeds' bedroom. She hoped someone had already taken care of the blood that had been spilled there . . .

She hurried to focus on something else before she lost the nerve to go there at all. Did Dawson even have cleaning supplies? Or would she need to bring some with her?

She called him after she got up in the morning to check, before taking Jayden to Petra's.

"Hello?" His voice, deep and filled with a bit of gravel, was easily recognizable from the few minutes she'd spent with him during the interview.

"It's Sadie Harris."

There was a long pause. Then he said, "Please don't tell me you're already calling to quit."

She gripped her phone that much tighter.

Should she? That was what Maude and Sly wanted her to do. If her parents were alive, she'd be willing to bet they, too, would weigh in on the side of keeping her distance. But, in spite of caution, she heard herself say, "No. I'm calling to see if you'd like me to pick up anything before I come."

"You mean like groceries?"

"If you need them."

"That'd be great. I've been meaning to get back to the store, but . . . there hasn't been time."

She couldn't imagine shopping would be fun for him, anyway. The second he walked through the doors of the local supermarket, everyone would stop and stare. It was even possible the checker would refuse to ring him up. That was how hostile Silver Springs felt toward him. "What should I get?"

"I have oatmeal and eggs. That's about it."

"So . . . maybe some bread, lunch meat and fruit? Stuff like that?"

"Sure. And whatever else you like to eat. I don't want you going hungry while you're out here. Something for dinner would be nice."

What was *he* surviving on? Oatmeal and eggs, even in the evenings? "Okay. I'll swing by the store. What about cleaning supplies?"

"You'd better get that sort of thing, too."

"What do you need me to clean?"

"The whole house."

"The *whole* house?" she echoed.

She knew he'd heard her uncertainty, and understood the reason for it, when he quickly amended that comment. "Everything that's not closed off. I mean . . . the space I'm using. The living room, the dining area, the kitchen, two bathrooms, my bedroom and Angela's. I'll deal with the master when . . . when I can."

She took his response to mean it hadn't been cleaned. That she'd be working in a house where two people had been murdered and the blood hadn't even been washed from the walls and carpet made her feel slightly ill. But she wasn't sure she should let that change her mind. She'd known about the murders before she went out to meet with him.

Still, she didn't want to see that room, let alone touch anything. Maybe he felt the same. Maybe that was why he'd closed it off. "What supplies do you have now?"

"Not much. To be honest, I haven't had a chance to think about that sort of thing. All of my work so far has been outside."

"So furniture polish, disinfectant, dishwashing soap, toilet bowl cleaner, oven cleaner, a powdered cleanser and some rags? Do you have a toilet bowl brush?"

"No. Grab one of those, too. Most everything was stolen or trashed while I was . . . *away,* so I threw all the broken bits and pieces in the pile of garbage out front. I didn't have time to sort and salvage. I needed some space to be able to live so I could get out on the land."

"What are you going to do about that pile?"

"Get rid of it. I've hired someone to haul it away this weekend."

"I see." If he was as innocent as he claimed, the day he saw what others had done to his house must've been very difficult. She couldn't imagine showing up to find her home in such poor shape, the blood of her parents still in their bedroom upstairs. How was he *living* there let alone working?

And if he wasn't innocent?

Sadie wouldn't consider that. She'd decided to trust the jury's verdict, hadn't she? "What about a vacuum?" she asked as she switched the phone to her other ear.

"Don't have one. Someone . . . Never mind. I threw that out along with everything else. How much do you think a new one'll cost?"

More than she could front, and she didn't

get the impression he had money to burn, either. "I'll bring one. We can limp by using mine for a while."

"That's very nice of you. Do you have a credit card or something to put the purchases on until I can reimburse you? If not, feel free to swing by and pick up some cash to take with you."

"I've got a little room on my card." She should be able to get a few things — at least enough that she'd be able to work today.

"Okay. Thanks."

Jayden came out of their bedroom in his SpiderMan pajamas, rubbing his eyes. "Mommy? Why are you awake when it's dark?"

Sadie covered the speaker on her phone. "Because it's almost morning, handsome. We need to get you dressed and over to Petra's. Can you go potty for me first?"

With a tired nod, he went into the bathroom, and she spoke into the phone again. "I'll be there as soon as I get off at the diner."

"I'll be in the north field. Come find me, and I'll let you in."

"Okay."

"Mommy?" Jayden called with some emergency. "The toilet won't flush!"

"I'm coming, babe." Sadie was afraid he'd

filled it with toilet paper again. She had no idea how or why he'd developed such a fascination for stopping up the toilet, but she wished she had remembered and gone into the bathroom with him to protect the plumbing. "I've gotta go," she told Dawson.

"You can bring your son here, you know," Dawson said. "He'll be safe."

"That's okay. We'll see if I survive the day first." She laughed as if she was making a joke, but when he didn't respond, she cursed herself for being so insensitive. She'd been trying to feel safer by making light of the danger. Instead, she'd rubbed salt into what had to be a very painful wound.

"I'm sorry," she said. "That wasn't funny."

He made no comment on the subject. "I'll see you when you get here."

"It'll be at least one."

"Understood."

She started to hang up, but he spoke again. "Sadie?"

"Yes?"

"You don't have anything to worry about over here."

Could she believe him? He sounded sincere. But she'd once been in love with a man she could no longer stand. That showed how easy it was to be fooled, didn't it? "Good to know. Thank you for trying to reassure me."

After another pause, he said, "You're not going to ask me if I killed them?"

Them being his parents, of course. What else could he be referring to? "Would you tell me if you did?"

"No, I guess I wouldn't," he admitted. "So much for words."

He disconnected, but, as unsettling as their conversation had been, she didn't have time to mull over her gaffe or his reaction to it.

"Mommy, the toilet's going to spill!" Jayden called.

Setting her phone on the counter, she rushed into the bathroom. "Stop flushing it!"

The diner was crowded, but Sadie was relieved to be busy. The crush kept her from thinking too much. For some reason, the comment she'd made at the end of her conversation with Dawson kept running through her mind — along with the pregnant silence that'd fallen afterward — and she couldn't quit kicking herself. Just in case he was innocent, she needed to be more sensitive. She'd rather err on the side of assuming the best, of being kind, than piling on with everyone else, wouldn't she? Dawson faced enough haters. The only person who stood in his corner, and had throughout the entire ordeal, was Aiyana Turner, the woman in charge of New Horizons. Aiyana insisted the man she knew could never do what had been done to the Reeds.

Usually, Aiyana's opinion carried some weight in Silver Springs. She did a lot of good in the community, was well respected, but she was always an advocate for her "boys," had adopted eight of the students who'd attended New Horizons herself. Some of them probably supported Dawson, too. They'd gone to school together, after all. Everyone just discounted what the Turners had to say because of their close affiliation with Dawson and the fact that if he *was* responsible for those murders, it would reflect poorly on Aiyana and the school, for bringing him to town.

Now that Sadie would be working for Dawson, however, she prayed the founder of New Horizons knew what she was talking about. The man Sadie had met didn't seem unhinged or greedy. He'd seemed perfectly normal.

But what did *she* know? She'd barely met him. Maybe she was letting his gorgeous face and jaw-dropping body get in the way of her good judgment.

Sadie was just putting in an order for a Spanish omelet when two of Sly's closest friends from the police force came in. They stood at the door and gazed around the restaurant until they saw her. Then they skipped the hostess station and headed directly to her section at the breakfast bar.

"Hi, Pete. Hi, George." She handed them both menus. "How are you today?"

Young, maybe twenty-eight, and stocky, with close-cropped dark hair, Pete looked at his older and much heavier companion. "We'd be a damn sight better if we hadn't just heard what we heard," he replied.

Sadie dodged another server to be able to grab the coffeepot so she could fill their cups. She knew they liked coffee, had served them many times over the past three years. "What'd you hear?"

"Sly told us you're going to be working for the man who murdered Lonnie and Larry Reed. That true?"

Sadie nearly dropped the coffee. She'd known word would spread, but she hadn't expected to be confronted by *these* guys. Although she'd been to a few barbecues with them over the years, she didn't feel as if they were close enough — at least to *her* — to say anything. "I'll be working for their son, Dawson."

Pete's thick eyebrows came together. "Like I said, the man who murdered Lonnie and Larry."

"Dawson has already been tried in a court of law, Pete. He was found *not* guilty. So . . . I'm not sure who killed the Reeds. From everything I've seen and heard, no one is certain."

He added a touch of cream to his coffee. "When you work in law enforcement, you get a feel for these things, Sadie. You can tell when someone's lying. Dawson Reed is guilty as sin. Don't let him or anyone else convince you otherwise."

She put the coffeepot back on its warmer so that the other servers would be able to get to it. "Even cops get things wrong now and then. If that wasn't true, we wouldn't have so many innocent people in prison."

The expression on his face suggested he didn't appreciate her daring to argue with him when he was such an authority on the matter. She'd seen that look before, many times, on Sly's face.

No wonder they were friends . . .

Leaning back, he rested his hand on the butt of his gun as he appraised her. "If you think there are a lot of innocent people in prison, you're more delusional than I thought."

"*Delusional,* Pete?" Sadie said, shocked that he'd go that far.

He shrugged. "Just sayin'. You've got this one wrong, sweetheart. And you'll pay a hefty price, if you're not careful."

"You don't know I'm wrong." By the way Pete was treating her, Sly had been flapping his gums again, running her down even though she tried so hard not to disparage *him.* He was, after all, the father of her child. "But, now that's out of the way, what can I get you both this morning?" she asked, pulling the order pad from her apron pocket.

"I'll take some biscuits and gravy," George said.

Obviously tempted to pursue the argument, Pete hesitated. But then he closed his menu and handed it back to her. "I'll have the pigs in a blanket."

"Great. Your food'll be out in a few minutes." She'd already turned away when George tried to stop her.

"Sadie . . ."

The order window was right behind her, so she stuck their ticket on the rounder for the cooks. "Yes?"

"Look, you and Pete got off on the wrong foot. We're not trying to be jerks. We understand things have been a little . . . rough financially since you and Sly split up. Divorce is never easy. But is going to work for *Dawson Reed* the best solution? I mean, think about it. If we're right and you're wrong . . . something terrible could happen."

"I appreciate your concern," she said. But she didn't really believe it was concern. They were supporting Sly while attempting to isolate Dawson, to make sure he was reviled for his "crime," even though a twelve-person jury had heard all the evidence and determined he shouldn't be punished for what happened to the Reeds. "But I'm hoping my faith in our court system hasn't been misplaced."

"You're not going to listen," he said, incredulous.

She remembered the terror that'd shot through her when Dawson grabbed her arm as she was leaving the farm yesterday — and how quickly he'd backed off when she turned. That made him seem safe, but there was nothing to say he wouldn't harm her later. She just hated how certain everyone else seemed to be when they didn't know whether he was guilty any more than she did. "I'm sure everything will be fine."

Pete made a clicking sound with his mouth. "Sure hope so. Either way, you've been sufficiently warned."

"Meaning . . ."

His eyes widened at the challenge. "If you get into trouble now, you're going to have to call someone else."

Although Sadie had empty plates to collect farther down the bar, she put that off. *"What?"*

"You heard me," he replied.

Her jaw fell open. "You're on the police force! Don't tell me you're saying that if I call for help from the Reed farm, no one will come . . ."

"Of course someone will come," George said.

Pete nudged him. "But we can't promise whoever it is will come real quick," he added with a laugh.

Sadie glared at him. "You're a self-righteous bastard, Pete Montgomery. Now I know why you get along so well with Sly."

He sobered instantly. "Whoa! Sounds to me like you deserve whatever you might get!"

"And it sounds to *me* as if you've appointed yourself judge, jury and executioner — not only for Dawson Reed but for me, as well."

"You're the one putting yourself in a bad situation." He shoved his coffee out of the way as he leaned forward. "The question is why? Do you and Dawson have something going on? Is he warming your bed at night now that he's out of lockup?"

She shook her head. "You're disgusting."

"What?" He gestured as if he'd said nothing wrong. "You wouldn't be the first to want to spread your legs for him. You should've seen the women on that jury, preening and making eyes at him whenever he walked into the courtroom. If not for them, he'd be in prison right now, awaiting an execution date. So next time you think he's innocent because that damn jury handed down a 'not guilty' verdict, you might consider there were seven women on it."

"Women can weigh evidence as well as men," she snapped.

He nearly spilled George's coffee when he shoved his water glass into it. "Don't give me that feminist bullshit!"

"Pete, that's enough," George mumbled, looking around. "You're going too far."

People were starting to stare, but he didn't seem to care about that. "She's the one who won't listen!" he responded.

"Thanks for your concern, but tell Sly I'll make my own decisions," she said.

Glenn Swank, down the bar, was growing

impatient with her lack of attention. "Hey, Sadie! Are you going to bring my check sometime today or what?" he called out. "I gotta go to work!"

Sadie nodded to reassure him. "I'm coming."

"Remember, you're taking a big chance," Pete growled as she hurried away. "Are you sure he's worth it?"

Sadie was still livid when she reached the grocery store. Every time she thought about that visit at the diner from Pete and George, she wanted to go ballistic. How dare they say what they did! They had no right. They were just taking up for Sly. He'd sent his buddies over because she wouldn't listen to him.

"Pricks," she muttered.

"What'd you say, dear?"

Sadie turned to see the organist from her church standing behind her in the aisle and felt her face grow hot for cursing. "Nothing," she muttered.

"I'm sorry. I thought you were talking to me."

Fortunately, Mrs. Handley was partially deaf. "No. I was just . . . mumbling to myself."

"Nowadays you never know what people

are doing." She shook her head in apparent exasperation. "What with those little devices — blue teeth or whatever they're called — they have in their ears."

"Bluetooth. People talk on Bluetooth."

"That's it."

Sadie smiled, trying to relax. "How have you been?"

"Good, and you?"

"Busy."

"Will I see you at church on Sunday?"

If Dawson didn't murder her first. The idea that he might be dangerous had always been daunting. But now she knew the police would be slow to react if she called for help. Pete, George and Sly had all warned her not to take the job, so they felt justified in letting her go it alone. They meant to teach her a lesson, even though it could be a costly lesson indeed.

She'd almost told them she'd been forced to take the job because Sly was being so stingy with his child. It cost a lot more to take care of Jayden than the $250/month Sly was currently paying. That didn't even cover his child care! But she knew that would only cause more problems. Sly would call her up and accuse her of trying to make him look bad in front of his friends, and they'd be headed toward yet another ter-

73

rible argument.

"Yes. I'll be there," she told Mrs. Handley.

"I'm glad. I'll see you then. Have a nice day, dear."

"You, too." Sadie wheeled her cart around to the next aisle and then the next, whizzing through the store, grabbing everything on her list. She needed to get started cleaning Dawson's house so that she could accomplish something before it was time to go home.

Once she'd bought his food and supplies, she stuck the receipt in her purse and loaded the items in her car. Dawson owed her $189.03. She hoped he was good for it. She also hoped he'd like what she bought as far as groceries. She'd picked up a roast and some vegetables to put in her slow cooker, which she needed to pick up, since she hadn't thought of using it when she put her vacuum in the back of the car earlier. After being out on the farm all day, she figured he could use a solid meat-and-potatoes kind of meal.

Sadie had the slow cooker in her car with the vacuum and a few other things she thought might be useful and was walking around to get behind the wheel when Maude called out to her from where she'd been standing yesterday. "Are you heading

74

to the Reed farm?"

"Yeah, I'm off," she said, turning to wave. She couldn't help thinking Maude might be the last person she'd ever see alive. She almost implored her to look after Jayden if anything happened, but she knew, if she were to be murdered, Sly's mother would step in and raise him. It wasn't as if Marliss expected her beloved son to do much.

"Good luck," Maude said. "I hope everything goes okay."

Wading through so much disapproval was zapping Sadie's strength. She felt like she needed a nap — she probably did, since she hadn't been able to sleep last night — and yet she had a whole afternoon of menial labor ahead of her. "So do I," she said and got in the car.

4

Dawson wasn't entirely sure Sadie would show up. At one-forty, he still hadn't heard from her. He kept pausing to gaze toward the highway, hoping to see her distinctive green-and-brown car. But there was no sign of her.

Had her ex-husband gotten hold of her? Convinced her not to work for a "murderer"?

The memory of how Officer Harris had tried to bully him at his own door made Dawson long to break his jaw. The dude deserved it. If Dawson had his guess, Harris wouldn't be much of an opponent. He hid behind his badge and his gun, would have no clue how to handle himself in a fight where those things weren't allowed and his position as an officer didn't count for shit. But if Dawson wanted to bring his sister home and rebuild his life, he had to be careful. He couldn't get in trouble, especially with a Silver Springs cop. The entire force was so sure that he'd gotten away with murder, the blowback would be severe, and he couldn't afford to become a victim of police harassment right now. Law enforcement had done enough to destroy him.

At a quarter till two, he pulled out his cell phone again. He had his ringer turned on, in case she tried to reach him. He'd already checked his call history. But maybe something weird had happened and her call had inexplicably transferred straight to voice mail . . .

Nothing. No missed calls. No texts. He was dialing her number, figured he might as well face it if she had bad news, when he heard the sound of an engine and looked up to see her El Camino turn into the drive.

"Hallelujah," he muttered and hung up before the call could go through.

She was out of the car and grabbing the handles of four bags of groceries by the time he could reach her.

"Hey," he said.

She glanced over one shoulder. "Hi. Sorry I'm late. The diner was busier than usual, so they made me stay an extra half hour. Shopping took a bit longer than anticipated, too."

"I'm not upset." He was just glad she'd

come. He tried to take the groceries from her, but she wouldn't relinquish them.

"I've got these. Why don't you grab the vacuum out of the back? And the slow cooker next to it," she added as she headed to the house.

"Got it." Her vacuum didn't look like much. Neither did the slow cooker, or her car, for that matter. Even *she* looked a little beleaguered. He'd noticed the dark circles that underscored her hazel eyes when she interviewed with him, but they were more pronounced today, when she wasn't wearing makeup and had her fine blond hair pulled into a ponytail. Now that she was in jeans and a Lolita's Country Kitchen T-shirt, and not the blousy top and skirt she'd had on before, he could also tell she was thinner than he'd first thought.

Although he knew there were probably a lot of guys who'd find that waiflike look attractive, he wasn't one of them. He liked his women with plenty of curves. But he hadn't hired her for her looks. He only needed her to be reliable.

She was making room on the counter to stack the dirty dishes he'd left in the sink when he set the vacuum in the living room and put the slow cooker on the table.

"Sorry you're starting at such a deficit,"

78

he said, seeing the mess he'd created the past several days through fresh eyes. He'd thrown out everything that'd been broken — all the beer cans, cigarette butts and other trash teenagers and various vandals had left behind, as well. But he hadn't been taking the time to clean up after himself. "Daylight hours are precious to me. I haven't been able to waste them on housework."

With the sink clear of dishes, she began running hot water. "I understand."

He propped his hands on his hips as he gazed around. "So . . . you're going to start in this part of the house?"

"As far as I'm concerned, the kitchen is always the best place to start. It's the heart of the home, as they say. I'll get this clean and organized so that we can make meals and . . . get around in here. It'll take some time, though. I might have to tackle the other parts of the house tomorrow."

"That's fine." Hungry, he began rummaging through the groceries to see what there might be to eat. "How much do I owe you for this stuff?"

She wiped her hands before getting the receipt out of her purse.

Once he saw the total, he pulled $200 out of his wallet. She tried to give him change, but he waved her off. From what he'd seen, she didn't have much, either. "Consider it a very small bonus. Have you had lunch?"

She watched as he opened a loaf of bread. "I heated up some leftovers when I changed out of my uniform. Why? You haven't eaten?"

"Not lunch."

He was surprised when she took the package of ham he'd just picked up and started to shoo him out of the kitchen. "I'll make you something and bring it out."

She didn't seem to expect a lot of hand-holding. He liked that about her. "Are you sure you don't have any questions or . . . need some direction?"

"I've cleaned plenty of kitchens," she said with a wry smile.

"Right. Thanks." Dawson breathed a sigh of relief as he left the house. He hadn't had a lot to go on when he hired her, but he was beginning to think he'd found the right person.

After Sadie made Dawson a sandwich, she cut up carrots and celery and added them to his plate along with a small puddle of ranch dressing. Then she carried it all out along with a thermos of coffee. The farm was nearly a hundred acres, big enough that it took her several minutes to find him, but she eventually spotted a lone man weeding and trimming artichoke plants in the far quadrant and figured that had to be him.

He removed the ball cap he was wearing and wiped away the sweat on his forehead as she approached. Maybe he was a murderer, but no one could say he wasn't a hard worker, she thought. A glance at the field revealed that he'd done a lot to clean it up — a Herculean task for only one man. "Thanks," he said simply.

"Happy to help. Will this be enough, or —"

"Plenty. I can't overeat. Too much food will bog me down."

"I'm getting the impression you need to eat more than you have been. How else will you keep up your strength?"

He was so intent on the sandwich, he didn't look up. "Anger and determination make for pretty good fuel."

"Even that can't carry you forever."

He met her gaze. "No."

"So it's a good thing I'm here."

He said nothing, just took another bite of his sandwich.

"Do you intend to run this farm by yourself?" she asked.

"This year," he replied when he'd swallowed. "Until I start making a profit, I don't have much choice."

"Once I get the house cleaned, I can help."

"Outside?" This time he spoke as he chewed. "You'd be willing to do that?"

"Until your sister arrives, and I need to keep an eye on her, why not?"

"With all the hoops I have to jump through, there might be a few days where that's a possibility," he admitted.

"I don't have your strength, but I'll do what I can." She lifted the thermos. "This is coffee, by the way. I figured you'd have water —"

"Yeah. I've got a jug over there." He jerked his chin to indicate the edge of the field. "But —" he took the thermos "— where'd you get this? I don't remember seeing one at the house. I looked."

Sort of proud that she'd anticipated his need, she smiled. It was a small thing, of course, but she liked feeling successful at her job, especially because it was only the first day — typically the toughest. "I brought it from home. I didn't know what you had and what you might need, so I put a few things in the car, in case."

"What else did you bring?"

"Some spices and utensils. And a knife. I'm picky about my knives. They have to be really sharp." He made her so nervous she'd spoken without thinking. Only after those words were out of her mouth did she realize she was talking about an item that could be used as a murder weapon to a man accused of killing his parents.

He paused with a carrot stick halfway to his mouth, as if he could guess her thoughts, but he let it go. "I see. That was thoughtful of you."

She tried not to notice the way his T-shirt clung to his muscular torso. He looked good enough to be featured on one of those man-candy calendars, she thought. Sly had a nice body, too. He spent a lot of time in the gym to make sure of it. But he didn't have the face that Dawson did. His skin was too pockmarked, his features too angular and harsh. The pull of attraction was something she hadn't felt for anyone in a long time. Feeling it now proved a little disconcerting, considering what Dawson had supposedly done.

Embarrassed by her own reaction to him, she gestured to the field surrounding them, hoping to direct his attention elsewhere before he could recognize the romantic interest. "You're getting a lot done."

"You'd think it would go faster."

"How long have you been at it?"

Yanking on the bill of his cap, he settled it back on his head. "Since the day I got home, nearly two weeks ago."

That explained the sun-kissed color of his skin. "Then I'm especially impressed. You've made a lot of progress for such a short time."

He squinted at the ground he'd covered. "Doesn't feel like it. Not with so much yet to do."

"You had breakfast, I hope."

Her comment drew his attention back to her. "I had a bowl of oatmeal."

"When?"

"Six or so."

She frowned at him. "That's too far to go between meals, especially when you're working this hard."

"I meant to go back in and grab something else, but I was too busy — and too nervous."

This was nothing she'd expected him to say. "Nervous about what?"

He gave her a sheepish grin. His teeth weren't perfect. There was one on the right side that crowded the tooth next to it, but the fact that he hadn't had braces — that his smile was natural — worked for him. "I was afraid you wouldn't show up. I promised Angela I'd have her home in a week. That wouldn't be possible if I had to keep looking for someone to help me get the house ready and care for her."

Sadie bent to tie her shoe. "What's the rush? She's in good hands, isn't she?"

He was scowling when she looked up at him. "Of course she's in good hands, or she'd be out of there already — even if I had to bust her out."

Sadie cleared her throat. Perhaps she'd been too cavalier with that statement, but she hadn't meant to insult his ability to take care of those he loved. "Right. I wasn't implying that you would ever allow her to be mistreated." She tightened her ponytail. "Well, I'd better get going. I'll see you later."

As she trudged back to the house, she breathed a sigh of relief to be out of her new employer's presence. He made her uncomfortable for so many reasons. He had a huge chip on his shoulder, was too driven, too intense. And he was so damn handsome that she could stare at him for hours. All of which made her self-conscious. She constantly screwed up and said the wrong thing, something that shouldn't be said to a man who'd been through what he'd been through.

"Just do your work and ignore everything else. You need the money," she muttered to herself.

Once she reached the kitchen, she plugged in her slow cooker and added the roast and vegetables along with some water and a gravy packet. Then she set to work in earnest, pulling everything out of the cupboards and drawers, washing them and reorganizing them. She also cleaned the fridge and oven and scoured the sink, counters and table so she could feel more comfortable cooking in this space.

While she worked, she kept expecting to hear Dawson come in — to return his lunch plate if not to take a short break. But after two hours, she guessed he wouldn't quit until sundown. He was nothing if not determined. That was one thing that seemed sure. So she used her phone to put on some music and tried not to think about being in a house that had a crime scene upstairs. Although the unnerving images she'd seen on TV crept in now and then — whenever she heard a strange sound that was probably just a settling noise — she stubbornly ignored it. She had plenty to keep her busy where she was, she didn't have to go upstairs. She figured tomorrow would be soon enough to face that daunting prospect.

Although dinner was ready at six, she still hadn't seen any sign of Dawson. Rather than put the food in the fridge for him to warm up later, she decided to take another plate out to him. He had to be starving. She'd seen how hungry he'd been at lunch when he'd wolfed down that sandwich, and that was hours and hours ago.

She found him in the same field. Once he spotted her coming toward him, he stuck his shovel in the freshly turned earth and leaned on it as if he could hardly stand up any longer.

"You're going to give yourself a heart attack working so hard," she said. "You realize that."

"Yeah, well, I don't think there are many people who would mourn my passing, do you?"

He spoke flippantly, as if even *he* didn't much care whether he lived or died, and she realized just how lucky she'd been to be loved and wanted as a child, despite what'd happened to her parents later. At least they'd been able to give her a solid base — before she screwed up her life by marrying Sly. She wondered what the situation was with Dawson's birth parents, if he'd ever had any contact with them, or if he'd been an orphan from the beginning. "Do you have any extended family in the area?"

He wiped the sweat from his forehead. "I don't have any family at all, except Angela."

Sadie couldn't imagine a man who cared so much about his sister would murder their parents even if it did mean he'd inherit. That brought her some comfort — but it also made her question her own thoughts and feelings, made her wonder if she was building a case for his innocence because she preferred to believe he was innocent. "What about friends? I mean . . . you went to school here . . ."

"I stay in touch with a few guys. But the kids at New Horizons are sent there from other places. Most leave when they graduate. Other than the Turner boys, none of my friends stuck around here. I actually left for a while, too. Went to Santa Barbara, where I attended college and then worked, until my parents needed me to come home."

"When was it that you returned?"

"Three years ago."

The fact that the community didn't know him all that well couldn't have helped when he was accused of killing his parents. It was always easier to think the worst of a stranger — or someone with a bad reputation.

His attention shifted to the food. "Roast? Wow. Smells delicious."

She tried to hand him the plate, but he waved her off. "Go ahead and take it inside, okay? It's getting too dark to keep working out here. I'd like to wash my hands and eat sitting down for a change."

"Okay." She was glad to hear he was quitting for the night. Although he hid the extreme exhaustion she'd noted before behind a smile as if he was fine, she could see the fatigue in his eyes.

"I've got to put away my tools. It might be a few minutes."

"I'll keep your dinner warm."

She picked up his empty lunch plate on her way to the house, put his food back in the slow cooker and set a place for him at the table.

The slap of the back door alerted her when he arrived. She heard him go into the bathroom off the rear porch, recognized the slide of the pocket door as he closed it. When he came out, his hands were slightly damp as he gestured at the single place setting. "You're not going to eat with me?"

"I ate while I was waiting for you to come in. I'm just going to mop the floor. Then I'll go."

"It's after six-thirty. I'm sure you'd like to see your son. Go ahead and leave. You can mop tomorrow."

Now that she could see him in full light and not the dim twilight, he looked even more fatigued than before. She wondered if

89

he was going to be okay after she left. "I checked on Jayden not too long ago. He's watching a movie with the babysitter's kids. I'd really like to get the floor done so I can go home knowing I have one room finished, if it's all the same to you."

"It's all the same to me." He gazed around as he took his seat. "You've made good progress already."

"Only in here. Cleaning out the cupboards and drawers takes time, especially because I had to wash a lot of the stuff that was going back in them. Maybe when you're done eating, I can show you what I accomplished," she said, dishing up his food once again.

"I'm sure it's fine," he said as she carried it over.

He didn't have the energy to get up for something so trivial, she realized. He seemed grateful for the food, though.

Before she could fill the bucket she planned to use, her phone rang. She'd kept her ringer on in case Petra needed her. But when she checked her screen and saw it was Sly, she winced.

"Is that about your son?" Dawson asked.

She hesitated. Her new boss had been so intent on his dinner she hadn't expected him to be paying any attention to her, whether her phone was ringing or not.

90

"Because, like I said, you can go," he added.

"No. It's not my son."

"You don't seem pleased to hear from whoever it is."

"I'm not. It's my ex."

His chewing slowed. "Does he know I offered you the job — and that you accepted it?"

"Yes."

"What'd he have to say about that?"

"He was sure to . . . make his displeasure clear." And to send his cop buddies over to the diner to make the ramifications even clearer. She considered telling Dawson about that incident, thought maybe he should know that Sly had a lot of friends on the force, so he'd understand their bias if he ran into it. But she couldn't be entirely sure he was as innocent as she wanted to believe, felt that it wouldn't be wise to point out that she was losing support as far as the force went. Besides, she hesitated to wreck his day, especially when he'd been nice enough to hire her in spite of Sly's threats. The police had had plenty of bias against him before she came to work here. Hopefully, he understood to stay clear of them all.

"Is that what this call is about?" he asked.

91

"More displeasure?"

"No doubt." She nibbled at her bottom lip while trying to puzzle out how best to handle Sly. She didn't want her lack of response to cause another fight, and yet . . . she didn't feel as if he had the right to continue harassing her about her new job. Besides, she didn't care to talk to him, especially in front of Dawson.

After silencing the ringer, she went about mopping the floor.

She was relieved when Sly didn't call back like he so often did, thought she'd been granted a reprieve — until she heard a knock at the front door about fifteen minutes later.

"Oh no," she said, a spurt of adrenaline causing her stomach to cramp.

"That's him, isn't it?" Dawson had finished eating, was just having a glass of the inexpensive brand of wine she'd bought at the store.

"I don't know for sure, but . . . maybe. I mean, who else could it be?"

"I have no clue. I'm not expecting anyone."

"I'll get it," she said, but he put up a hand.

"No, let me." With a sigh, he pushed back his chair, seemed to summon what energy he had left and got up.

Sadie waited in the kitchen, hoping she was wrong about the identity of the visitor while listening to see.

"Officer Harris. What a surprise."

She heard the sarcasm in Dawson's greeting, knew Sly wouldn't be able to miss it, either. Dawson didn't know what he was getting himself into. If he wasn't careful, Sly and the rest of the force would make his life a living hell, and she didn't want to be responsible for that.

"Everything okay around here?" Sly asked.

"Have you received a distress call or something that would indicate otherwise?" Dawson responded.

The risks inherent in provoking such an egomaniac made Sadie catch and hold her breath . . .

"Not a call, exactly. But I have to admit, my cop's intuition is sending out a warning."

"Well, there's no trouble here. You can go on your way," Dawson said.

"Not so fast," Sly responded.

Sadie tiptoed to the entrance of the living room and peered around the corner to see her ex-husband holding the door so that Dawson couldn't close it. "I guess you decided not to take my advice, huh?"

"Advice?" Dawson echoed, using the same

facetious tone as before.

"You know what I'm talking about. Was there some confusion?"

"No, not really. Why?"

Sly's expression hardened. "Maybe you don't know this yet, but it's not smart to get on my bad side."

"Your ex needed a job, and I had one. Seemed like the perfect fit. I'm not sure why you'd have anything to do with it, to be honest."

"I have *everything* to do with it," he said. "Everything to do with *her.* And I'm telling you, she doesn't belong here."

"Actually, she does now. Technically, you're the one who has no business coming onto the property."

Sadie gripped the edge of the opening so hard she thought she might leave impressions in the wood. "Don't let him explode. Don't let him explode," she chanted silently to herself. She didn't want this to come to blows, especially because she wasn't convinced Dawson could overpower Sly, not when he was so tired. Even if he could, she was afraid Sly would make up some lie about being attacked and call for backup, which would land Dawson in jail again.

"Funny," Sly said. "A murderer with a sense of humor. I like that."

"Great. Glad to hear it. Now, I'm tired and eager for bed. Not interested in any domestic bullshit. So . . . why don't I go on about my business — and let you go on about yours?"

"I'm afraid that won't be possible," Sly said. "Not until I see Sadie. I tried calling her, but she didn't pick up. When that happens, I tend to worry."

Dawson didn't even glance her way. "Her hands were wet. She's mopping the floor. I'm sure she'll call you when she gets done."

"I want to talk to her *now*. So I suggest you make it easy on both of us and get her."

Before Dawson could refuse and thereby provoke Sly even more, Sadie walked into the room. "Sly, what are you doing here?" she asked.

His gaze shifted to her, but his expression didn't grow any friendlier. "It's after seven."

"What does that mean?"

"It means it's getting late, and I'm wondering why you're not home with our son."

She slid in front of Dawson to block Sly's view of him. "I haven't finished work. I'll be leaving soon."

"When?"

"Fifteen minutes."

"Fine. I'll wait out here and escort you home."

She wanted to tell him to leave, that she didn't need an escort, but she feared that would only tempt Dawson into trying to enforce her wishes, which wouldn't be good for him, or her. "Fine," she said and shut the door.

"Please, try to stay out of it, if you can," she whispered to Dawson when she turned to find that he hadn't moved since she slipped in front of him.

"Because . . ."

"It could be dangerous not to."

He seemed much more alert than before. No doubt Sly's attitude and the anger it evoked had given him a shot of adrenaline. "*How* dangerous? Has he ever hurt you?"

She thought of all the temper tantrums and other rages she'd witnessed over the years. Sly putting his fist through a wall. Sly throwing something and breaking it. Sly peeling out of the drive and nearly crashing his car or screaming and ranting at her until he had her backed into a corner with her arms up over her head, convinced *this* would be the time he would strike. "Not yet."

"But . . ."

"He will definitely hurt *you,* in any way he can, and I don't want to be responsible for that. Now you've had a glimpse of . . .

of what he's like, you might want to change your mind about having me work here."

He set his jaw. "You mean cop to his demands."

"I know it sounds unappealing. Believe me, I hate it as much as you do. But that's the only way to appease him."

"That's what you do?"

"That's all I can do." Suddenly feeling her own fatigue, she shoved the loose strand of hair that kept falling into her face out of her eyes again. "Anyway, I'll go now so that he'll leave, too, and you can get some sleep. But if you decide you have enough problems, that you'd rather not have me back tomorrow, just let me know." She should've known this would never work, that Sly would never allow it to work. "I'll understand," she assured him and went to get her purse.

5

The anger that welled up as his new "caregiver" left, followed closely by her ex-husband, made Dawson long to hit something. He hated to see Sadie give in to Officer Harris, to let him control and manipulate her. Just watching it happen, being a party to it, brought back the horrible feelings of helplessness he'd experienced over the past year — and with it a familiar rage. So much shit had happened to him, and he'd been powerless to stop it. When his parents were killed, he'd been swept into a vortex of pain, loss, confusion, accusation, distrust and resistance to the truth that had nearly destroyed *everything* in his life — not only his parents but all they'd left behind, including their life's work, their home and their poor daughter.

He'd often lain awake at night on that cement jailhouse bed, feeling as if he'd fallen through the proverbial "rabbit hole." That was how twisted his life had become, how distorted from what was fair, right and true. And the crazy thing was, no matter how hard he fought back, or how much he proclaimed his innocence, there was no escape. He remained at the mercy of strangers, completely subject to the rationale, judgments and will of people who had no idea who he really was or what'd happened that terrible night. They stripped him of his freedom and convicted him in the press, pointing to the anger and confusion he'd experienced as an unwanted child as the reason he'd risen up to destroy the only people who ever truly loved him.

If not for the slimmest of margins, he'd be sitting on death row *right now.* Only, he wasn't. He was here. Home. Sure, he was starting over with very little. But at least he had the chance to reclaim his sister, save the farm and find the man who *did* murder his folks. He might even be able to bring that man to justice.

If he didn't screw up.

In an effort to calm down, he walked to the table and poured himself another glass of wine. As he stood there drinking it, he couldn't help feeling a measure of relief at the transformation that'd taken place around him. The kitchen had regained its former dignity, because of Sadie. Sure, that was a small step forward, but it made him feel as if *something* had finally been put right, which gave him a shred of normalcy to cling to. Then there was Sadie's practicality in bringing groceries and supplies, her flexibility in being willing to front the money for them, so that the shopping wouldn't turn out to be a big hassle on his part, and her diligence in seeing that he got fed. She'd worked hard today. He liked her, believed he'd found a good employee.

But what she said was true: he had enough problems. He'd hired her yesterday despite Officer Harris's threats — maybe, at least partially, because of them. It felt good to fight back. But did he *really* want to get involved in a battle that had nothing to do with him when he had more than he could handle already?

No. He'd have to put off getting Angela out of Stanley DeWitt. He didn't like that she'd be disappointed, but he could continue to advertise for a caregiver — in Santa Barbara this time — hoping to find someone who was willing to commute. Santa Barbara wasn't that far. Surely, if he gave himself more time, he could find an alternative to hiring a woman connected to an abusive ex-husband who also happened to be an egotistical cop.

But if he chose that option, if he let Sadie go, what would happen to *her*?

He recalled the tears he'd seen streaming down her cheeks yesterday, the way she'd turned her face up to the sky as if she wished the rain would just wash her away. She seemed pretty desperate herself. Whether he knew her well or not, he hated the idea of abandoning her to be victimized, hated the thought that she had to be experiencing those same feelings of helplessness that'd cut him to the quick. If she wanted to get away from the guy she'd married, she should have that right. If she wanted to work for a man suspected of killing his parents, she should have that right, too. She was an adult. So why did Sly Harris get to dictate what she did — what either of them did?

You can't hire me now. You have no idea what he'll do. He'll make your life so miserable you'll wish you were still in jail.

He believed her, especially after Sly's latest visit. Her ex would not back off simply because they'd gone ahead despite his disapproval. They'd have a real fight on their hands, a fight that Dawson was ill equipped to take on in his current situation. But ducking that would only make him feel like he'd felt while he was in jail — completely at the dictates of others. And he'd never been one to back down from a fight. Perhaps he'd screw up his only chance to get his life back, but at least he'd go down swinging for what he believed in.

"You can go to hell, Officer Harris," he muttered and sent Sadie a text.

Sadie refused to speak to Sly. Her phone rang while she was driving, but she ignored his call, wouldn't even get her phone out of her purse. If he wanted to follow her home, let him. She couldn't stop him from using the same highway. But that didn't mean she had to have a conversation while she was driving.

When she pulled up to Petra's, he got out, too, and tried to intercept her. "We need to talk," he told her. "You can't keep working for that bastard."

"I'm not breaking any laws," she said.

Petra must've heard their voices, or she'd been watching for Sadie, because she came out.

"There you are," she said before her gaze shifted to Sly.

If anyone understood the truth of what her relationship with Sly was like, it was Petra. Although Sadie had been careful not to say too much, Petra knew she wished she could be rid of him, and that he refused to leave her alone.

Using the distraction Jayden's babysitter posed, Sadie circumvented Sly and continued to the door. "Sorry I'm later than originally planned."

"You warned me it'd be seven or eight. Jayden's fine, anyway. How'd it go?" Petra swung the door open to admit her but said nothing to Sly, and Sly said nothing to Petra. He hung back on the walkway, as if he was waiting for Sadie to get Jayden and come out again.

"I liked it," Sadie admitted as she went in.

Petra hesitated as if she wasn't sure whether to close the door, since Sly was outside. She settled for leaving it cracked open to suggest they'd only be a moment. "What'd you do?"

"Mommy!" Jayden came running as soon as he saw her.

She pulled him into her arms and hugged him tight as she answered. "I cleaned the kitchen while Dawson Reed worked on the farm."

Petra lowered her voice. "So . . . why's Sly with you? Nothing happened — nothing went wrong, did it?"

Sadie did her best to maintain a pleasant

demeanor. "No. He was . . . worried when I stayed so late. That's all."

"I see. And now he's . . . making sure you get home safely?"

"Apparently."

Petra's eyebrows knitted as if she understood that meant much more than Sadie was saying. "Divorce is so hard. Here's hoping I never have to go through that."

"You have no idea," Sadie agreed.

Petra squeezed her arm for encouragement. "What time do you need me tomorrow?"

"Same time, if that's okay. I have to be at Lolita's by seven."

"No problem. The kids have school, of course, so I get up early."

"Thanks. I can't tell you how much I appreciate your flexibility."

"We love Jayden. You know that." She picked up a toy that'd been left on the floor. "So it'll be another long day? You'll be going out to the farm after the restaurant?"

Sadie let her son wiggle down. He was getting too big for her to carry for long, anyway. "Um . . . not sure, to be honest."

She cocked her head. "Dawson doesn't need you tomorrow?"

If he knew what was good for him, he'd find someone else to help him. But she couldn't say where he stood on that decision. They'd left it sort of open-ended. "He told me he'll let me know."

"Okay. Text me when you find out. I'd like to take the kids on a nature walk, but if Jayden won't be here, I'll wait until he is so he doesn't miss out."

The gratitude Sadie felt for Petra brought a lump to her throat. "Thank you. Thank you *so* much."

"Of course!"

Jayden brought the bag Sadie sent with him whenever he came, but before Sadie could go, Petra caught her wrist. "I know Sly's out there waiting for you, but . . . I've been dying of curiosity. What's Dawson like?"

She thought for a moment. "He's . . . determined." Yes, she felt safe saying that, especially when she thought of the way he'd stuck it out in those fields.

"Somehow that isn't what I was expecting you to say," Petra said with a laugh.

Of course not. Everyone wanted to know if he was the killer he'd been portrayed as being. They were hoping for some small tidbit that might reveal more than what they'd seen on TV. *The way he stares at me is so creepy . . . He sits around sharpening a knife all afternoon . . . He laughs about what happened* . . . Something juicy and gossip-worthy like that. The good citizens of Silver Springs would be surprised to know all he did was work and work *hard.* "I think he's innocent."

Petra's lips formed a surprised O. Sadie was surprised herself, especially by how committed she was to that belief, so soon. She had nothing more to judge by than anyone else. Not really. She'd worked with Dawson only one day, hadn't even seen him much. But there was something about him that spoke of the kind of integrity a murderer would not possess. Maybe it was his devotion to his sister. Maybe it was the courage it must've taken to come back to this place. He could've sold the ranch and moved to friendlier climes, disappeared into the melting pot that was LA or some other urban center where he wouldn't have to face the same recrimination.

Or maybe she believed he was innocent because he'd had the guts, even after all he'd been through, to hire her in spite of Sly. He'd stood up to her ex at the door, too, probably would've done more if she hadn't intervened.

She admired him, and not only for his looks.

That was something she'd never expected . . .

"What makes you think so?" Petra asked, still eager for details.

"He's a strong man," she replied.

Petra grinned and began to fan herself. "No kidding. I've seen him on TV. What a hottie!"

"He has a nice body, but I mean he's strong in his head and his heart. He doesn't need to kill old people to get what he wants, doesn't seem like he'd ever attack someone weaker."

"Are you sure?"

She realized she was sounding like Aiyana, who'd proclaimed his innocence all along. "No. That's just my opinion."

"Well, it sounds like he's managed to impress you."

Sadie nodded. "And he wasn't even trying."

"I admit I sort of hope he's guilty — or I would if you weren't working out there. I'd hate to think of anyone going through what he's been through as an innocent man." Petra gave her a quick hug. "Good luck with Sly. Would you like me to walk you to your car?"

"No. I'll manage on my own and deal with him at home."

"Okay. See you tomorrow."

Sadie slung Jayden's bag over her shoulder and led him outside to find that Sly had gotten back into his patrol car. Jayden saw the car, too, had to know it was his father, and yet he didn't run over to greet him.

Sly rolled down the passenger window. "Want to come ride with me, bud?" he yelled.

Jayden looked up at her for some cue as to what he should do. Sadie could tell he was reluctant to leave her, since they'd been apart all day.

"It won't be for long," she whispered to him. "We only live a few houses down."

"Okay." He spoke so softly that Sly couldn't have heard him, but he let go of her hand and walked over.

"Is it really necessary to offer to drive him home when I live half a block away?" she muttered so that only Sly could hear as she unbuckled Jayden's safety seat.

"It's going to be more than half a block," he announced, full-voiced. "We're going for ice cream!"

Fun. Ice cream should make up for the fact that you haven't stepped up as a parent since the day he was born, she thought but said nothing.

Sly's hand covered hers as he took the car seat. "Care to join us?"

Sadie resisted the urge to recoil.

"Come, Mommy!" Jayden cried, but Sadie didn't have it in her. She couldn't sit around making small talk with Sly when she was so upset with him. He'd just shown up at her work, might've cost her her job, and now he wanted to take her and Jayden out for ice cream as if he hadn't done anything wrong. That was the kind of stuff he did all the time — crossed certain boundaries and then pretended he hadn't.

"I'm sorry, honey." She slid her hand out from under Sly's. "Mommy's too exhausted. I worked really hard today."

Fortunately, Jayden didn't complain. The prospect of a treat had won him over.

"I'll wait for you at home," she added.

"Don't sit around and stew," Sly said to her retreating back. "You have no reason to be mad! I was only trying to look out for you."

She pivoted and nearly gave him a piece of her mind right there on Petra's front lawn. The desire to let loose was so strong she almost couldn't rein herself in. But she knew from experience that causing a scene would only make the problem worse, and she had Jayden — and Petra and Petra's family — to think about. "I'll see you when you get back," she said in a firm voice, to let him know she wasn't willing to discuss it, and waved to Jayden as they drove off.

It wasn't until she got home and was taking her phone out of her purse to charge it that she finally saw Dawson's text.

Be here at one tomorrow, if possible. And this time, could you bring a six-pack of beer? That wine you bought was terrible.

She couldn't help laughing at the wine statement. She'd never tried that brand before. It had been in the right price range, but it *had* been terrible.

You are a glutton for punishment, she wrote back.

When she didn't get a response, she guessed he was already asleep.

By the time Sadie bathed Jayden, she was too exhausted to read to him. Promising she'd make it up to him tomorrow, she slid him over so she could climb into bed, kissed his forehead and turned out the light. But long after he went to sleep she couldn't drop off herself, couldn't get her mind to shut down. One question after another bombarded her. Why had Dawson Reed agreed to keep her on? Why would he risk his own well-being? He'd been through so much, and yet *he* was the one willing to take her side over Sly's — when so many others had decided to protect their own interests.

She understood he was in a hurry to get a caregiver so his sister could come home, and that there wouldn't be a lot of people in Silver Springs who'd trust him enough to take the job, but there were other places he could draw from. His sister had been in that institution for over a year. Why not take one or two more weeks to expand the search so that he wouldn't have to deal with Sly?

Was it because he was a nice guy, as she thought? Or something else?

When Sly brought Jayden home, she'd told him she believed Dawson could never have hurt his parents, and he, in turn, had tried to convince her that Dawson was merely "grooming her," setting her up to trust him and believe in him so that he'd be able to manipulate her. Sly said narcissists and psychopaths were experts at creating positive experiences designed to make their victims feel connected to them. Before he left, he even tried to persuade her to visit the police station in the next day or two so that he and the homicide detective who'd investigated the case could go over the details with her.

She wasn't sure that would convince her

of anything, though. If the facts of the investigation clearly indicated Dawson was guilty, why hadn't he been convicted? There had to be *some* question, didn't there?

Finally giving up on sleep, she slipped out of bed and went to the living room, where she'd left her laptop. She'd paid a fair amount of attention to the Reed murders, had listened to and read the various media reports as they came out. Like most everyone else in Silver Springs, she couldn't believe something so terrible could happen in their little town.

But after going to work for Dawson, she had the desire to look at what'd transpired from a more objective vantage point — and not while she had several police officers at her elbow, trying to sway her opinion. She also hoped to see if she could determine whether the media, in their quest for shocking headlines, had helped create a bias that shouldn't have existed, as Dawson's defense lawyers claimed.

Putting her computer in her lap, she propped a couch pillow behind her back and logged onto the internet.

A search for "Dawson Reed" called up several links. She clicked one after the other and read, with fresh eyes, what she'd given only a cursory glance before.

Silver Springs Man Denies Killing Couple Who Adopted Him featured several quotes attributed to Dawson. "I would never hurt my parents. I loved them," he said, and, "I didn't need to kill anyone in order to inherit the farm. Time would've taken care of that whether I wanted it to or not."

That made sense to her. Murder *did* seem like a drastic approach for a son who was set to inherit anyway. But the police claimed he wasn't willing to wait. They said that after Dawson achieved a master's in environmental science and management at UC Santa Barbara — quite an accomplishment, considering he'd spent his high school years at a boys ranch — he started working for a lighting conservation company, also in Santa Barbara, until he got into a disagreement with the owner and was fired after only eight months. Discouraged, since he couldn't make a go of life even with a degree, he returned to Silver Springs to work for his parents.

Although that sounded plausible to Sadie, Dawson painted his personal history in a different light. From what she could piece together, he said that he argued with the owner of the lighting company because the guy was bilking the local utility out of thousands of dollars on various state-mandated rebate programs. And it wasn't because he couldn't get a job that he came back to Silver Springs. He'd barely started to apply when he realized that his parents could no longer manage the farm on their own. So he gave up the life he was going to pursue to come help them.

Devil . . . or saint?

With a frown, Sadie opened a Word document and began to write down the various points so that she could keep them straight. On the night in question, the police said Dawson went to The Blue Suede Shoe, a local bar that offered live entertainment on the weekends, where he watched a Lakers game on the big screen and played pool with Aiyana's oldest two sons, Elijah and Gavin Turner. He left at eleven-thirty and stopped by the gas station to fill up before going home. The police admitted they couldn't figure out if he planned the murders in advance, or if he decided to kill his parents on the spur of the moment, but while everyone was sleeping, he took the hatchet from the woodpile in back, attacked his parents in their bed and then called 9-1-1 to report that there'd been a break-in and he needed an ambulance.

Both Lonnie and Larry were dead by the time police arrived to find Dawson cradling his mother in his arms. "Although that might sound like a touching act, there were no tears in his eyes," Detective John Garbo, whom Sadie had once met at a picnic, said. "His emotion felt fake to me."

Had Dawson been insincere? Or was it the police who had it wrong? Everyone reacted differently to grief. Maybe he'd been in shock after seeing such a horrifying thing.

Dawson agreed with everything they claimed about the night of the murders up until he left the gas station. At that point, he said he was approached by a tall, wiry man with brown eyes, dark hair and a scraggly beard, who asked for a lift to Santa Barbara. Dawson told him he wasn't going that far. The guy indicated a friend lived much closer and climbed in, but as Dawson drove, his passenger began to act more and more irrationally and wouldn't name a place, other than Santa Barbara. Dawson said the hitchhiker kept showing him the map of where he wanted to go on his phone, saying he had to get to a friend's place, so Dawson told him to call that friend and ask him to come, but the hitchhiker wouldn't. They were at the edge of town when Dawson finally insisted he get out. The man refused and an argument ensued, followed by a scuffle, during which Dawson managed to pull the guy out of his truck so that he could take off.

Because of the difficulty of dragging a grown man from the passenger seat through the driver's-side door, the police found that part of Dawson's story highly suspect, but Dawson looked plenty strong to Sadie. She thought the police actually made a better point when they argued that it was too much of a coincidence that some hitchhiker would be able to find Dawson's house. Dawson had an answer for that, too, though. He said he had various documents in his truck — a couple of work orders, even a bid for solar on the house — and one must've fallen out during the scuffle. His guess was that after he drove off, the hitchhiker simply used the address on that lost work order to find his house.

Sadie supposed that *could've* happened. Dawson drove a work truck, likely kept various things he thought he was going to need on the dash or seat, and loose papers could easily blow out or get dragged out amid a tussle.

Either way, he never changed his story. She felt that was important, even if the police didn't give him much credit for that. As for the rest of Dawson's explanation of the night's events, he said he wasn't far from home when that disagreement occurred. Once he got the guy out, to avoid leading him right to the farm — and because he didn't realize something with his address had already fallen out — he went back to town, where he drove around listening to music while waiting for the stranger to get wherever he was going. He even stopped at Gavin's house, but Gavin wasn't back from the bar.

When Dawson drove home, he didn't see the hitchhiker along the way, and he quit worrying — until he walked into the house and noticed the back door standing open. Once he saw that and his mother's purse dumped out on the kitchen floor, he rushed upstairs to find Angela asleep in her bed, his parents bleeding in theirs. Although he felt as if his father was already dead, his mother was making a gurgling sound. He was cradling her in his arms, trying to comfort and encourage her, when she died.

"Heartbreaking either way," Sadie mumbled, rubbing her eyes. She wanted to continue her research. There was so much left to read. But it was one o'clock and she'd had a long day, with another one to follow.

After saving her document, she set her computer on the coffee table and slipped back into her room but still didn't rest well.

Frightening images of opening that locked door at the top of the stairs at the farmhouse and finding two mangled bodies filled her dreams — along with the sound of Sly laughing at her.

Just before her alarm went off, she startled awake on her own. She'd been having a different nightmare by then, one in which Dawson was standing over her while she slept — lifting a hatchet.

6

Work at the diner proved uneventful, and much slower than the day before, so Sadie was able to leave early, swing by the store for the beer Dawson had requested and the hardware store to pick up a few items and arrive at the farm on time. She got the key to the house from Dawson, who was working in the same field as yesterday, and let herself in. Then she mixed up a quick bowl of chocolate chip cookie dough. Dawson had told her he didn't need lunch. He'd packed himself a sandwich using some of the leftover roast she'd made for last night's dinner — he seemed to really like the roast — but she figured he'd be ready for a snack in a couple of hours. Since he was keeping her on instead of hiring someone else, she wanted him to be glad, and everyone loved her cookies. Sly still asked her to bake them for certain events. Anyway, a small treat was about all she could think of to thank Dawson — partially because that was the best she could afford.

After she cleared away the dishes he'd put on the counter since she left last night, and cleaned up her mess with the mixing bowl and beaters, she decided to vacuum and dust the downstairs and wash the windows. The place needed a good de-webbing, too. She'd purchased a brush with a long handle at the hardware store so she could reach the corners.

Throughout the house, but especially in the living room, several pictures had been taken down. The wallpaper wasn't quite as sun-bleached where they'd once hung. She guessed they'd been destroyed by vandals, were among the bits and pieces Dawson had swept up and dumped out, and felt sad that people would do such a thing. Destroying the house and its furnishings wasn't right even if Dawson *was* a murderer. Trespassing was a crime. So was the destruction of private property. What made them so confident they knew what happened here, anyway? What if he was innocent? And what if the items destroyed were treasured family heirlooms? Those items had belonged to Angela, too, who was absolutely innocent.

At least Dawson still had most of his parents' furniture. The word *murderer* had been engraved in the coffee table as well as spray-painted on the front of the house. But she was going to take care of both those things. She'd purchased paint at the hardware store when she bought the de-webber, felt it was especially important she get the letters off the front of the house before she left today. Not only would having them gone make her more comfortable coming to work, she couldn't imagine the sight of them would impress anyone who visited to make sure the house was ready for Angela.

The first batch of cookies came out as she finished sanding the top of the coffee table. She'd ruined the finish, of course, but the sight of bare wood beat what'd been there before. Who wanted to be constantly reminded of someone else's judgment — someone who probably didn't know one way or the other?

She'd bought some stain at the hardware store, too, so she could cover the damage. Even if it didn't work perfectly, she was glad she'd obliterated that word. She couldn't believe Dawson would mind.

She stopped working on the table long enough to put some cookies on a plate, pour a glass of cold milk and take them outside.

She could tell Dawson was surprised when she called out to him. Chances were he hadn't expected to see her again until he came in for dinner. But she figured her timing was good. He was breathing hard when she reached him — sweating, too. As far as she was concerned, he was running himself ragged.

"What's this?" he asked as she drew close.

"I baked some cookies." She offered him the plate but kept the milk so he'd have a free hand with which to eat. "Here's hoping you're not opposed to having a little treat now and then."

"I'd *never* turn away homemade cookies. I haven't had anything like this since . . ."

When his words fell off, she guessed he'd been about to say, "Since before my mother died," which gave her the impression he really missed Lonnie. That was another reason she didn't think he'd killed her or his father. Although he seemed cautious when it came to revealing emotion, he seemed to be sincere in his love for them, seemed to miss them.

"Sly insisted I enter this recipe at the county fair," she said as he took his first bite.

He swallowed. "And?"

She regretted mentioning the county fair. That she cared about something so inconsequential made her sound like a hick, especially considering the fact that he had a better education than she did. But she was nervous. He was so good-looking that he made her self-conscious. Those eyes of his . . .

No wonder the women on the jury had been blamed for his exoneration.

She cleared her throat. "I won."

He took another bite, then nodded. "I'm not surprised."

Maybe he *didn't* think it was a stupid comment. Tough to tell. She ventured a smile. "I'm glad you like them."

"How are things at the house?"

"Good. I'm working on the downstairs. I should get most of it done today. But . . ."

When she paused, he glanced up from the plate. "What?"

"I noticed that you have a new washer and dryer."

"Someone filled the other ones with dirt and who knows what else. I wasn't going to mess with trying to clean them out."

"That wasn't right. I'm sorry."

"They were old, needed to be replaced, anyway."

"Still."

He reached for the milk and took a long swig. "We all have our problems, remember?"

"That was a pretty dumb thing for me to say."

His eyebrows slid up.

"I was nervous when I made that comment. I feel terrible about what you've been through."

He studied her as if weighing her sincerity. "Thanks," he said at length.

She accepted the glass of milk so he could finish the cookies. "Anyway, I was wondering if I could do some of my own laundry while I'm here. I have a small stackable set at my house, but there's something wrong with the washer. It's not getting our clothes clean."

"Of course. Do as much laundry as you'd like."

"I appreciate that." She'd brought her and Jayden's dirty clothes with her, in case. Now she could get the bag out of her car. "Where will I find your hamper? I'll wash your stuff while I do mine."

"There's a pile of clothes in the corner of my bedroom. I've been meaning to buy a hamper. Haven't gotten around to it yet."

"I can get one when I'm in town sometime, if you'd like."

"Sure. That'd be great." Finished with the cookies, he downed the rest of the milk and handed the dishes back to her. "Those were delicious."

Perhaps it was a simple thing, but she was happy she'd managed to please him. "I'm glad."

She was on her way to the house when he called out to her.

"How'd it go with your ex last night?"

She shaded her face as she turned back. "Better than expected. He knew he had no business coming over here, that I was angry with him for doing that, so he was trying to be charming."

"Charming means he has hope."

"Excuse me?"

"He's still trying to win you back."

"Yes."

"Is that a possibility?"

"Not if I can help it. That's why I'm here."

He scratched up under his hat. "He didn't give you any grief about working for me?"

From the moment she'd let him know about the appointment. But she couldn't repeat most of what Sly had said. "A little. He asked me to go down to the police station with him so I could talk to the detective on your case."

A muscle moved in Dawson's jaw. "And? Did you agree?"

"No."

"Because . . ."

"I already know what they're going to say."

Sadie wasn't in the house. Dawson could smell dinner simmering in that old Crock-Pot she'd brought over, but she didn't answer when he called her name. He found a receipt she'd left on the counter. Apparently, he owed her another $78.08 for supplies from the hardware store, so he left a $100 bill beside it. There was no note to indicate she'd left, though, nothing else.

He checked the front window to see if her El Camino was still in the drive. It was. And when he went to the laundry room off the back porch, he saw a stack of little boys' clothes folded on top of the dryer he'd missed when he came in.

So where was she?

"Sadie?" He moved back toward the front of the house.

No answer.

While in the kitchen again, he removed the lid on the slow cooker to see what she'd made for dinner and found some giant meatballs bathed in tomato sauce. A bowl of plain pasta sat on the counter with tin foil over the top. Garlic bread that looked and smelled as if it'd just been pulled from the oven waited nearby.

He'd been served plenty of spaghetti in

jail, but he could tell this meal wasn't going to be anything like that tasteless mess.

He cut off a chunk of meatball so he could taste it. "Damn, that's good," he muttered.

Thinking she might've decided to clean his room or Angela's, he went upstairs. She'd made great strides on the first floor. He liked the lemon smell of the furniture polish and the astringent scent of the disinfectant. But, from what he could see, the only thing she'd done upstairs was his laundry. His clothes, folded as neatly as her son's, waited on the bed.

On the way back down, he paused in front of his parents' bedroom. He doubted she'd go in there — hoped she wouldn't — and was relieved when he tried the handle. Locked, as usual. She wasn't in any of the bathrooms, either. She wasn't anywhere in the house.

Had she gone outside, looking for him?

"Sadie?" He let the screen door slam as he went out back. "Sadie, where are you?"

"Here!"

At last, he got a response. He followed her voice around to the front, where he found her on the roof, painting over the graffiti on the house.

"How'd you get up there?" He squinted to see her clearly in the fading light.

She gestured to the far side of the porch. "I climbed."

Using the railing and then the overhang. Whoever had defaced the house had probably gotten up the same way. He'd used that makeshift ladder to sneak out of the house when he was in high school, so he supposed he shouldn't be too surprised. "You need to come down before you fall and break your leg or worse. The moss on those shingles can make them a lot slicker than you might expect."

"I'm being careful."

"I can cover that up myself. I just didn't have the right paint."

"This isn't a *perfect* match, but I took a chip from the lintel of the back door when I left last night, so it's not bad. Better than leaving it as it was."

"I'll finish up," he insisted.

"Don't make me stop in the middle. I'm almost done. Why don't you go eat? Dinner's in the kitchen. No need to let it get cold."

Still a little nervous that she might come sliding off the porch and land on her back or head, he frowned as he watched. "I saw it, but I'm staying right here so I can help you down."

"Don't worry, I've got it."

"Trust me. Climbing up is a lot easier than coming down." He'd almost broken his own neck on occasion — and that was *before* he'd arrived at whatever party he was heading out to, so he hadn't been drinking. Some nights when he returned it was a miracle he'd been able to climb back up at all.

His parents had been through so much with him. He felt bad about his behavior now. But he'd had to test them, had to prove they were going to stick with him and love him no matter what. At least that was his mother's interpretation. He wasn't sure what had driven him to act out. Anger, he supposed. Youth, carelessness, selfishness. And yet they'd held fast. They'd stuck with Angela, even though she wasn't perfect, and they'd stuck with him. Whoever killed them probably saw them as two insignificant old people, people who couldn't adequately defend themselves or their belongings. But Dawson knew they were better than most people could ever hope to be. They'd made him whole, helped him find a little peace in the world, some direction —

"I guess having your help *would* make it easier to get the paint down without spilling it," she conceded, interrupting his thoughts. "Hang on a minute."

As he watched the crudely made letters disappear beneath her brush, an odd sense of relief grew inside him. Her simple act soothed some of the pain and anger that drove him like a cattle prod. But he would never forget what had started his rapid descent into hell. He'd find the person responsible for the brutal attack on his mom and dad and hold them accountable — even if it took the rest of his life to accomplish.

"How does it look?" Sadie asked when she was done. "Did I get it covered?"

He lifted his arms, in case she fell. "Whatever you do, don't step back to see for yourself!"

She cast him a disgruntled look. "I'm not stupid. That's why I asked *you.*"

"Tough to tell in this light. It's too dark. I can always throw on another coat tomorrow morning. Come on. I'm starving."

After handing down the paint and brush, she managed the descent quite nicely, for the most part. She was stronger and more agile than he'd given her credit for. Her problem was height. She was so short she had no choice but to swing freely until he guided her feet to the railing. That made him wonder what she would've done had he not been there, but he didn't ask.

Although she probably would've been

okay from there, she was close enough that he could grab her, so he set her on the ground, just to be safe. "Don't go on the roof anymore," he told her sternly.

She blinked at him with her wide hazel eyes. "I just wanted to get that . . . that ugly word off the front of the house. You could see it from the highway!"

"*I'll* take care of that sort of thing in future." He couldn't let her get hurt. Everyone was *so* certain she wouldn't be safe out here with him — especially her ex-husband.

"Then why didn't you?" She picked up the paint and brush he'd set out of the way.

That she would come back at him, challenge him, took him by surprise. "I told you, I didn't have the right paint."

"It's plain white, nothing exotic. You could've picked it up as easily as I did."

He took the supplies from her. "And I planned to."

"You just didn't get around to it."

"Not yet."

"I'm not sure I can buy that."

He said nothing, hoping she'd let the subject drop, but she didn't.

"You've been back for two weeks."

Again, he made no comment.

"You didn't want to give anyone the pleasure of knowing it bothered you," she

131

said. "That's the real answer, isn't it? You were leaving it there to prove a point."

"Oh yeah?" He spoke as he walked ahead of her, without turning back. "And what point would that be?"

He heard her slap her hands together as she dusted them off. "That you don't care what people think of you. That you don't need them to accept you, approve of you — or even like you."

"You're my employee, not my shrink," he grumbled. "Don't try to psychoanalyze me."

"I'm not. I've just been wondering why you wouldn't paint over that immediately. Having it up there had to be painful and embarrassing — a horrible thing to see every time you pulled into your own driveway. Then, after working with you for two days, I decided on the reason *I* think you left it. So . . . will you do me the favor of telling me if I'm right?"

"No," he said. "Let's eat."

Dawson paced in the dining area while Sadie was at the stove, dishing up the food. He was restless. Something about what happened outside had agitated him, but she wasn't sure what. He had to be relieved that she'd painted over that red-lettered indictment. Now *he* didn't have to. Although she didn't know him well, she was convinced she was right about his reasoning, even if he wouldn't come out and admit it. He was a proud man who didn't like to be pushed around — the kind who would sacrifice almost anything for an ideal. The way he'd reacted to Sly, that he'd refused to cave in, told her as much.

She put his plate on the table before eyeing him speculatively. "What's wrong?"

He shoved his hands into the pockets of his jeans as he pivoted and came back toward her. "I'm not sure this is going to work out, Sadie."

"This." She could tell by his voice that he wasn't talking about dinner. "You mean the job."

He stretched his neck. "Yeah."

"Why?" She would've been worried that he was about to fire her. She'd been worried last night. But this . . . this didn't feel like someone who really wanted to get rid of her. He liked her, liked what she cooked and the improvements she'd made to the house. She could tell. She also knew he'd be loath to search for someone else; he didn't want to be bothered with that. He wanted to work and put his life right. So . . . what was the problem?

"It's complicated," he said as he came

over to the table and sat down.

She studied him, trying to read his body language. She saw regret, reluctance, maybe even a little indecision. "You mean because of Sly, my ex."

He shrugged his broad shoulders. "Yeah. I guess."

She brought her own plate over to the table and sat across from him. "Except that you've gotten beyond Sly's opposition to my working here twice so far."

He turned his fork over and over in his hand. "He could always come around again."

"True. I warned you of that. And you texted me to be here at one."

"Maybe I should've thought about it a little more carefully."

"Because . . ."

He said nothing, just started shoveling spaghetti into his mouth.

"You're upset that I covered up an ugly word some asshole painted on your house. Why?"

"You could've fallen off the roof."

"But I didn't. And now that it's handled, I won't go back up there. So . . . can we focus on the real problem?"

"This isn't the best place for you, that's all."

He was wrestling with himself over *something.* "You told me I'd be safe."

"You are safe. From *me.* Problem is . . . I can't control anyone else."

"Who do you need to control?"

He didn't answer.

Pushing her plate away without touching her food, she waited as he polished off a meatball. "If I'm not around, how will you get your sister back?" she asked at length.

"I'll have to hire someone else."

"Then this *is* because I painted the front of the house."

"No, it's not. That's ridiculous!"

"You're uncomfortable because I did you a favor, and it wasn't even that big of a deal. You're so used to being judged and reviled, you no longer know what to do with human kindness."

He swallowed, his gaze finally riveting on her face. "I know what to do with kindness. It's not me I'm worried about. It's you."

"Me."

"Yes!"

"Why?"

"How do you think all the people you care about — your friends and neighbors, your ex and his family — will react if they believe you're taking my side? Befriending a man who —" he made quotations marks with his fingers "— killed his parents? They'll start treating you like they do me. You'll be an outcast. It can happen quickly, and once it does, you might not be able to turn it around — not in such a small town."

She folded her arms. "So I'd be better off finding work elsewhere."

"Yes."

"Are you sure it isn't a little more than that?"

He dropped his bread into his pasta. "More in what way? If you're talking about Sly, we've covered that."

"I'm not talking about Sly. I'm thinking that maybe you'd just feel more comfortable with someone who keeps their distance from others, like you do. I can't believe what you've been through has made you very trusting. Something like that is bound to leave scars, make you leery of those around you. But I was just doing you a good turn, trying to go the extra mile. I mean, you've done me a nice turn, too. It's not like you have to be my friend or anything."

He put down his fork. "Telling you to find other work has nothing to do with *me*. It has to do with keeping you from experiencing anything like what I've been through. How do you think I'll feel if someone vandalizes *your* house the way they did mine? A woman who has a five-year-old child to protect? If they see you coming here every day, making my meals and fixing up the place, they'll assume you're on my side, which means you're not on *their* side, and they'll make you a target, too. I should've thought of that."

Sadie remembered Sly's cop friends paying her a visit at Lolita's to warn her that they'd be slow to respond if she got herself into trouble working for Dawson. They'd made it clear she was fraternizing with the enemy, that they considered her actions disloyal. Dawson was right. Sly wasn't the only thing they had to worry about — although the problem her ex presented was difficult enough. Compared to how nasty he could get, right now he was being relatively nice. But she knew his patience wouldn't last forever. What would he do if she refused to listen and quit working for Dawson? What if she not only stuck it out here at the farm but became a friend of Dawson's — a defender?

The possibilities were frightening. She wouldn't put anything past Sly.

But she already believed Dawson was innocent. That meant she *couldn't* abandon him. "I guess we're both taking a risk, aren't we?" she said.

He drank some of his beer. "That means you're staying."

"Yeah."

He sighed before forking another bite of meatball into his mouth. "Well, at least you can cook."

She grinned at him — and laughed when he tried to scowl instead of grinning back.

7

As Sadie cleared the dishes, she was happy in a way she hadn't been happy in a long time. She couldn't point to one specific reason. She just felt . . . free. She also felt productive and capable of taking care of herself, which made her view the future in a more positive light. Then there was Dawson Reed, of course. She'd been so worried that he was as bad as everyone was saying, that she was making a mistake by answering his ad. But she didn't believe that anymore. She liked him, thought he was a decent man. Although she could be wrong — there were people who'd been fooled by killers before — she couldn't imagine him harming the Reeds. He hadn't said or done one inappropriate thing. On the contrary! What kind of killer tried to bring his mentally handicapped sister home so he could take care of her — because she'd be happier with him? What could Dawson possibly get out of assuming that responsibility? Nothing! He was paying for a caregiver for Angela when he could be spending those dollars on a farm-hand who would make his own workday easier.

Sadie certainly didn't get the impression he'd lured her into his employ for some nefarious purpose. He was less likely to engage her than she was him. She heard from him only when he came in for dinner.

She was tired when she walked out to her car to go home, but after she backed out of the drive, where she could see the house from a better perspective, she paused to look. She'd done a good job covering the writing that'd been painted on the front. She was so glad to have gotten that off.

Eager to see Jayden, she put on some music through her phone — the radio, like the clock, didn't work in her car — and finished backing out of the gate. That was when she spotted a squad car parked down the street, just out of sight from the house.

Sadie slowed as she went by. Sure enough, Sly sat behind the wheel.

Damn him! How long had he been there, waiting for her?

Determined not to acknowledge him, she pressed the accelerator. "Go home and leave me alone," she mumbled. But one glance in the rearview mirror indicated he'd pulled onto the highway behind her. She really didn't want her ex-husband waiting for her every night, didn't want to deal with him nearly that often . . .

Her cell phone rang, interrupting the music, and his name appeared on her screen. Her car was so old it didn't have Bluetooth capacity, but she had a Bluetooth device in the ashtray. She would've used it, if only the battery wasn't dead.

She pulled over so that he wouldn't follow her all the way to Petra's again. She didn't want him taking Jayden out for more ice cream. She missed her son, wanted to spend some quality time with him before bed — and she didn't want Sly involved in any way. He made her anxious, on edge. His moods could be so mercurial; she never knew if he'd be pleasant or go off on some rant in which he held her accountable for "ruining his life."

He parked behind her and came walking up.

"What are you doing?" she asked, lowering her window via the hand-crank as he approached.

"Nothing. I was just out for a drive."

She made a face. "So finding you outside Dawson's house was purely a coincidence."

His lips twisted into a wry grin. "Maybe not entirely. I was making sure you were safe. What do you think? You should thank me."

"Except that it's not necessary for you to waste your time. And it's more than I have a right to expect, since we're no longer together."

"Our separation is merely a temporary setback, Sadie. I'm going to prove that to you, prove that I can make you happy."

They'd tried for ten years and nothing had changed. She was no longer in love with him, hadn't been in love with him for at least half that time. "I'm flattered by your tenacity. But I think it's important to know when to let go. We both need to move on."

"And leave you in the hands of someone like Dawson Reed? What kind of man would I be?"

"The kind who respects boundaries. I'm fine! Dawson didn't kill his parents, Sly. He hasn't killed anyone. He's not capable of that type of thing."

Sly had his mouth open, ready to say more. He was used to dominating every conversation. But at this he clamped his lips shut. By his expression, she'd triggered one of his infamous mood swings.

"I mean . . . no one knows for sure what

happened," she added, trying to backpedal.

"He was the only one who could've killed them, Sadie — the only one anywhere nearby that night. There was no foreign DNA found in the house. If a random hitch-hiker broke in and murdered Lonnie and Larry, there would've been *something.*"

She'd read about that. She hadn't yet added the discrepancy to the list she was making, but she had a rebuttal. There was a shoe print outside in the mud — from a smaller foot than Dawson's — which the police had conveniently explained as coming from some random visitor to the farm and not the killer. She almost said so but bit her tongue. She didn't care to debate the case, especially with Sly. He had to win every argument, by getting mad and scream-ing if he didn't have a solid basis for what-ever he was saying.

"Not necessarily," she said. "There have been plenty of crimes where no DNA was found. So why can't we give him the benefit of the doubt? He hasn't made one wrong move. He works all day. That's it."

"And you . . ."

"I work, too."

"Just the two of you, out there alone together, when he probably hasn't had a woman for a year or longer."

She felt the hair on the back of her neck stand up. "I don't appreciate what you're implying."

"*I* know what men are like. *I* know what he's thinking when he looks at you."

The image Sly's words created made Sadie feel oddly overheated. She told herself that had nothing to do with Dawson. "That's not true. He hasn't acted remotely interested in . . . in me."

"Yet. I can promise you he's after more than cooking and cleaning."

"Stop it! You don't need to watch the house. I'm sure you have better things to do."

He hooked his thumbs in his utility belt. He was every bit as fit as Dawson, made sure he spent plenty of time jogging and lifting weights. He'd stepped on a scale every day of their married life. He wasn't too handsome in the face, had much plainer features, but no one could call him a slouch. He could easily find another woman.

The part of Sadie that longed to be free sometimes wished he would, but she couldn't put her heart behind that wish, not when he was so miserable to live with.

"You don't think he'd love to feel you beneath him? To feel you close around him and —"

"No!" she broke in. "I mean . . . he's not thinking like that. Why are you doing this? Why are you trying to twist everything?"

"Because you need to see the truth. You're too naïve for your own good."

"I'm not naïve! I know when a man is coming on to me. I like Dawson. We're . . . friends. That's all."

The way his eyes narrowed made her uneasy. "Friends? You've worked there two days and you're already *friends*?"

It sort of felt that way, but she shouldn't have said so, shouldn't have let Sly get the upper hand. "Not friends, exactly. Employer and employee. Why can't anything be that innocent to you?"

"Because I'm not a fool!"

She drew a deep breath. "There's no reason to worry. He's nice. That's all."

"Nicer than me . . ."

"I didn't say that. I'm merely trying to make you understand I'm not in any danger."

"And I'm merely trying to make *you* understand that you have no idea whether you're safe or not."

"I can only judge by how he makes me feel, Sly. And my intuition tells me I'm okay."

"Your intuition."

"Yes!"

"You're sure it's not something a little farther south than that? Maybe he's not the one who's looking to get laid. Maybe it's you. Does it make you wet thinking of screwing a guy who could be that dangerous?"

"Stop it!" she cried again.

"I won't stop until you listen to me. I've seen how much the women like him. Detective Garbo told me he got a ton of mail from dumb chicks sending him naked photographs and shit while he was in jail."

Sadie was beginning to sweat despite the cool, evening weather. She felt one bead and then another roll down her side. "I wasn't one of them. So this has nothing to do with me. I have to go, Sly."

"Now you're going to run away? Why don't we finally talk about this, talk about the elephant in the room? You haven't given *me* sex in forever! No matter how much I beg or grovel, you're not interested."

She *had* given him sex much more recently than she'd ever wanted. He'd pushed it upon her not long after she moved out. He'd done the same thing a few times since, and she'd gone along with it, suffered through it, because she hadn't wanted to wake Jayden and have him come out of the room to see what was going on. Sly conveniently forgot about those instances, pretended it wasn't nearly so one-sided, but she never would. The thought of sleeping with him again made her skin crawl. She tried to interrupt with a "Because we're separated!" but he talked right over her.

"Even *you* have to be dying for a man by now."

"That's enough!"

"You think Dawson can satisfy you when I can't?"

"I'm working for him! That's all! I clean the house and cook."

"You wouldn't even need to be out there if you'd come back to me. We weren't rich, but we were getting by until you decided to move out and screw up our lives."

Our lives? *She'd* been much happier since she left him, despite the problems he'd caused since. "How do you figure?"

"Name one thing that wasn't better back then!" he challenged.

Only one? She could give him a whole list. "*You* were the only one who could spend any money. I couldn't so much as buy a new blouse, even after I started working at the diner."

"That's not true."

"That's *absolutely* true."

"You weren't contributing nearly as much as I was, that's all. But I've been thinking about stuff like that. I realize I'm not an easy person to live with. I'm a perfectionist, exacting. But I'll be more generous. I promise."

"No."

"Give me a chance!" he screamed, smacking his hand against the car.

The sound reverberated like a bullet. This was how an "incident" with Sly started — and it could get far more frightening as it escalated. "I need some time on my own," she said. "I wish you'd respect that."

"But you're not on your own. You're trying to get back at me by working for a murderer!"

"I'm *not* trying to get back at you!" she yelled, suddenly unable to hold back. "All I want is for you to leave me the hell alone. Don't you get that? *I can't stand the sight of you!*"

The color drained from his face. She knew as soon as the words were out that she'd made a terrible mistake. Sly didn't allow anyone to talk to him that way, least of all her. There'd be a terrible reprisal.

"I have to pick up Jayden," she said, speaking in a calm voice. Most of the time, she managed to tiptoe around him, but she'd been too tired tonight, and he'd pushed her too far. "Petra's expecting me. I've left him too long as it is."

"If you think I'll *ever* let you divorce me, you have another think coming," he said through gritted teeth.

She threw up her hands. "Then shoot me now. Because I can't take any more!"

"Careful what you wish for," he snarled and stalked back to his car.

A moment later, he tore past her, tires spewing gravel. She dropped her head against the steering wheel, trying to calm down, but she was still shaking when she picked up her cell to call Dawson.

"I . . . I need to tell you to be on the lookout," she said as soon as he answered.

"Sadie?"

"Yeah. It's me. I just . . ." She struggled to catch her breath. "I have to warn you. Sly was waiting for me when I pulled out of your drive. He's been watching the house. He could come back. Now or . . . or later tonight. There's no telling when."

"You saw him?"

"He was waiting for me when I got off work. I just spoke to him."

"I can tell by the sound of your voice that it didn't go well."

Squeezing her eyes closed, she leaned

149

back, but the tears she'd been fighting began to flow anyway. "No. I made a mistake."

"What kind of mistake?"

"I told him I'd never come back to him, and —" she covered her phone so that she could sniff without him hearing her "— I'm afraid he'll blame you. Like I said, he could show up there now or . . . or late at night and do . . . I don't know what. Try to make things difficult for you. I'm sorry."

There was a long pause. "I'll be okay," he said at length. "But . . . you live alone, right?"

"Yeah. In a one-bedroom with Jayden."

"Will you be safe? Do you have someone you could stay with? Or should you come back here?"

"I can't come back there. He already accused me of . . . of . . ." Fresh tears welled up. She stopped talking in order to gain control over her voice. "Never mind. I'd better go. I have to get Jayden. I merely wanted to . . . to warn you that I said the wrong thing."

"You told him you won't come back to him. Isn't that what you've been telling him since you moved out?"

"Yes, but I was too absolute this time. Putting him off, that's the only way to . . . to keep him calm."

"Maybe it's time he got the message."

"No. It's dangerous to challenge him. There'll be hell to pay because of it. Anyway, will you call me if you . . . if you need help?"

"Call *you*?" he echoed.

She couldn't hold back the sob that rose up before she could cover the phone. "I don't think the police will come if you call them," she said through her tears. "I don't think they'll come for either one of us."

There was a long silence. Then he said, "You should get your son and come back here."

"I can't. Sly will view that as me running to you, and . . . and that'll just make things worse for both of us," she said and hung up.

8

Sadie fed Jayden, played with him and read to him. Then she put him to bed and continued her study of Dawson's case in the living room. But she couldn't comprehend what she read. She was too preoccupied — too anxious. She hadn't heard from Sly since their encounter on the highway, and she knew he wouldn't let that go. She'd dared to take a stand against him. He was probably planning his revenge right now, thinking up some way to hurt her.

Or he could be out at the farm, causing trouble for Dawson . . .

She almost called her boss again, but it was growing late and she hoped he was getting some sleep. He couldn't keep working the hours he'd been working otherwise, and she knew how important it was that he get the farm producing again.

After reading the same article twice, and *still* feeling as if she'd missed most of the information she was hoping to retain, she set her computer aside and got up to pace around the room. She was *so* tired of worrying about Sly. She almost couldn't remember a time when he didn't overshadow everything else. Why wouldn't he let her go? What good was having her come back if she didn't love him? And how could he even pretend to love her? A man didn't treat a woman he cared about the way Sly treated her. That had been the problem from the beginning.

So what did he have in store for her?

She went over to peer through the slats of the blinds that covered the front window. She didn't see Sly's car, didn't notice headlights down the drive or movement about the yard. But that didn't mean anything. Tucked away as her house was, she *wouldn't* see anything. He could still be out there.

Would they have another argument, one in which she'd have to cajole and appease Sly for Jayden's sake?

She wouldn't sleep with him again, no matter what. She couldn't. She lost a piece of herself every time she succumbed. But it wasn't fair that Jayden should be awakened and frightened by such angry voices as he'd heard in the past. Sadie didn't want that

kind of emotional, upsetting life for him —
or herself. Why was she the only parent he
had who cared about that sort of thing? Sly
did exactly as he wanted, fought dirty if that
was what it required to win, while she was
handicapped by trying to protect their son.

"When will it all be over?" she grumbled.

For a brief moment, she allowed herself to
fantasize about packing up and slipping
away in the middle of the night — going
someplace where Sly would never be able
to find them. She could start over, build a
new life and try to forget.

But how far would her rattletrap El
Camino take them? What if it broke down
in the very next town? And how would she
find a place to live, when she had no money,
no resources? Besides, they couldn't have a
good quality of life if she was always looking over her shoulder. If Sly ever did find
her, he'd have a compelling reason to sue
her for custody — and would likely win.

Although she cherished the dream of
escape, that was all it was — a dream. She
was stuck in Silver Springs, had no choice
except to try to cope with the man she'd
grown to dislike so immensely.

With a sigh, she checked her phone again.
Should she text him? She wanted to know
how worried she should be. She could be

driving herself mad for no reason. What if he'd cooled off — or had something pressing at work? An emergency of some sort? If she knew there was no danger, she could relax and get some sleep so that she'd be able to handle whatever happened tomorrow. But . . . hearing from her could also start something new.

With a sigh, she tossed her phone aside. She wished Maude were awake and out in her yard, so they could chat. It was times like these that she missed her parents, especially her mother. She needed to hear someone else's voice. As the night stretched on, she felt so alone, so inadequate.

But wishing for Maude was silly. Her landlady couldn't help her. It wasn't even fair to ask.

Although Dawson told himself not to worry about Sadie, a sense of foreboding hung over him for the rest of the evening. She'd sounded so upset; he doubted she would've gotten that way unless she felt there was good reason.

He showered and called Angela as he did most every night. Then he tried to sleep — Lord knew he was tired — but every creak or thump had him up, checking the windows, the doors, the driveway or his phone in case Sadie tried to reach out for help. He'd seen the face of tragedy, knew the worst *could* and sometimes *did* happen, which made it almost impossible to sleep. The blood from his parents' murders was still down the hall, the scene he'd encountered when he found them forever etched in his mind.

Finally, at two in the morning, he texted Sadie: You okay?

He wasn't sure what he'd do if he didn't hear back. Silence could mean she was sleeping; it could also mean that she *wasn't* okay . . .

As the minutes dragged on without a reply, he decided to go into town, since he couldn't sleep, anyway. He had her address; it was on the résumé she'd submitted. He'd drive by her place to see if everything appeared normal. Maybe that would give him some peace of mind. He understood that Sly could also target *him.* She obviously thought the chances of that were good. But Dawson had a feeling he'd direct his displeasure at her first. He was used to tormenting Sadie, felt entitled because she "belonged" to him in some way. Sly would also see her as a much easier, more predictable target.

Almost every muscle in his body complained as Dawson dressed, scooped his keys off the dresser and descended the stairs. He'd been sore in one place or another since he got home from jail and put in his first hard day of work. Just when one muscle group stopped complaining, he'd do something a little different and antagonize another, which was okay during the day. He could compensate for it, overcome it, when he was moving around. At night those muscles stiffened up, so his back ached and his thighs burned.

A full moon hung low in the sky. After he climbed into his truck, he sat behind the wheel for a few minutes, staring out at the moon before starting the engine. The night he'd picked up that hitchhiker had been so much like this. He remembered a big, portentous moon and the same cool breeze blowing the trees, carrying the fecund scent of moist earth and growing things . . .

But the similarity didn't mean anything. He was merely letting his fears get the best of him.

He shifted his gaze to the left, in the direction of his parents' graves. He'd buried them on the farm, in the far corner. He'd felt they'd want that. He needed to take Angela out there, to show her their headstones and let her say goodbye. Maybe then she'd quit asking when their parents were coming back, as she had again tonight.

Shifting into Reverse, he backed out of the drive.

The highway was empty, as he'd expected. Even the two bars in town would be closed this time of night. He figured there might be a few cops out — was afraid he'd be unlucky enough to run into Sly or someone else on the force.

Fortunately, that didn't happen. He breathed a sigh of relief as he turned down the street where Sadie lived, a few blocks off the main drag, and rolled slowly past the expensive home that fronted her one-bedroom.

Everything looked quiet in the neighborhood, but he couldn't see Sadie's place from the street, so "quiet" didn't tell him anything. After parking at the corner, he walked back to be sure.

A light glimmered around the edges of the blinds in her front window, but that wasn't necessarily reason for concern. Maybe she couldn't sleep, either. Maybe she wanted to be prepared in case something happened, or she'd fallen asleep reading and hadn't gotten up to turn it off. She might even leave that light on at night for the sake of her child, so he could find the bathroom or whatever.

Dawson didn't see a patrol car or any other vehicle parked behind her El Camino. If Sly was there, arguing with her — or doing anything else — he would've had to block her in, because the drive was so narrow, or park out on the street, as Dawson had, and Dawson hadn't seen him.

He checked his phone, as he'd been doing every few minutes. Nothing. She hadn't responded to his text.

Briefly, he considered knocking on the door. He'd come this far, hated to go home without achieving any reassurance. But chances were he'd only wake her child or scare her to death by appearing so unexpectedly in the middle of the night.

Convinced he'd done all he could do, he turned to leave. But then he heard his phone chime and glanced down at it.

There she was.

I'm okay. You?

He scratched his head. He was fairly certain his hair was standing up on one side. He hadn't put much thought into his appearance when he left the house.

I'm fine.

Why aren't you sleeping? You were exhausted when I left.

He was always exhausted these days. He
was working too hard not to be. Because
I'm not in bed.

Don't tell me you're working!

No, I'm standing outside your door.

What? Why?

You sounded so upset earlier. I was concerned there might be trouble — wasn't
sure how bad things might get. But now
that I know you're okay, I'm leaving. See
you tomorrow.

The door opened before he could get too
far and she called out to him in a loud
whisper. "Dawson!"

She was wearing an overlarge T-shirt, her
legs and feet bare, her face devoid of
makeup and her hair mussed. Obviously,
she'd taken no thought for her appearance,
either. But he liked it — more than if she'd
been all made up. There was something
sexy, intimate about seeing her this way.

He walked closer so they could talk without waking her landlady or anyone else.

"Sorry to disturb you. After what happened to my folks, I guess I was . . . assuming the worst. I let my imagination get the best of me."

"I can't believe you came to check on me, especially so late. That's *really* nice."

"It's no big deal. I'll see you tomorrow —"

"Wait! Where's your car?"

"Down the street."

That seemed to bring her some relief. "That's good. With Sly dropping by all the time . . . Well, never mind. Anyway, would you like to come in for a drink before you go? I mean, you're already here."

He was about to say no. He had to work in the morning; nothing mattered more to him than saving the farm. But she was right. He *was* here, and he was more than a little curious about how she lived — not to mention intrigued by her apparel, or lack of apparel.

"I don't know about you, but I'm too on edge to sleep, anyway." She gave a nervous laugh. "The slightest noise disturbs me."

He understood. It'd been the same for him. Expecting some sort of reprisal from a man like Sly had a way of putting a person on pins and needles. After what he'd been through, both with the death of his parents and what he'd experienced at the hands of police since, Dawson felt like he was particularly sensitive to the possibilities.

"It'd be nice to . . . to have someone to talk to for a few minutes," she added when he hesitated. "A little adult conversation might give me the chance to get my feet underneath me again."

She needed company, someone close at hand to provide a sense of security, at least until she could calm down.

He decided to stay. Why not? He'd been up this long. "Sure. What do you have to drink?"

She held the door so he could come in. "I have a bottle of Pinot Grigio, which should be much better than the wine I brought to your place," she added with a self-deprecating smile.

He tried not to let his gaze fall to her bare legs — or her shirt, since it was obvious she wasn't wearing a bra — but that was exactly where his eyes tended to go. He hadn't been with a woman in *so* long. Although he'd initially thought Sadie wasn't his type, that he wasn't attracted to her, the more he got to know her, the prettier she became. She had the most gorgeous legs, and her breasts, though small, looked like the perfect size to fit the palm of his hand.

In an effort to keep his mind — and his attention — where it should be, he circled the room, inspecting his surroundings. Her place was clean and neat but sparsely furnished with what looked like thrift-store purchases or hand-me-downs. "That's what you typically drink?"

"I don't typically drink anything. I can't afford alcohol," she said with a wry laugh. "I've been saving this."

Stopping in front of a side table, he picked up a photograph of her and her son. They were on a beach, the same towel wrapped around them both as Sadie kissed Jayden's cheek. "For what?"

"A celebration."

He put the photograph down and looked over his shoulder. "Of . . ."

She shrugged. "My neighbor gave it to me for my birthday last month."

"Why didn't you open it?"

"I decided to wait for something better to come along."

"What's better than a birthday?" he asked, but he hadn't celebrated his birthday this year, either. He'd spent it in jail, wondering if he'd be convicted of murder.

"My divorce. The day I receive my final papers. The day it will all be over."

"What's holding that up?"

She rolled her eyes. "Sly, of course. He's doing everything he can to sabotage the process."

"Don't tell me opening this wine signifies that you're giving up."

"No. I'd just really like to have a glass, especially now that I have someone to drink it with. You interested?"

For however long he stayed, she wouldn't be alone. "Sure."

She went into the kitchen and returned with a regular water glass filled almost to the halfway mark.

"That's a lot of wine," he said as he accepted it.

"Sorry. I don't have any wineglasses."

He took a sip, found it to be as good as she had promised — much better than what she'd bought the other day. "What happened to your belongings? I mean, I can't imagine you've always lived in such a . . . spartan fashion."

"I had to leave most of my stuff behind," she explained. "It was hard enough just to get myself and Jayden out of that house."

"Where'd you live?"

"In one of the new homes on the other side of town. We had some nice furniture, too. Nothing like this. Sly can be stingy with his money, but he likes quality — things that make him look good to his friends."

"So . . . he lives there alone now, with the good furniture?"

She nodded. "I didn't take anything, knew that would only make it harder for me to leave. I did try to get my clothes. But even that didn't work. He threw away what I couldn't carry in that first load."

"And he thinks *I'm* bad," Dawson grumbled.

She studied the liquid in her own glass. "He has a way of justifying — or excusing — the most terrible things." She gestured toward her threadbare couch. "Would you like to sit down?"

To avoid hovering over her, he took her up on that offer and made himself comfortable. The room was so small it was the only way to put a little distance between them. "What made you marry a guy like that?"

"I wish I knew," she replied. "In the beginning he seemed . . . different than he turned out to be. But I was barely eighteen when we married. What did I know?"

Dawson took another sip of his wine. "When did things start to go bad?"

She leaned against the wall opposite him. "I can't really pinpoint a date. He grew more demanding and irritable as the years passed, especially after he had to share my attention with Jayden. He'd withdraw or sulk if he didn't get his way — or rail at me until I gave in just to appease him. He became so controlling there were times, lots of them, when I felt I couldn't breathe. If not for my son, I would've left him long ago — and I wouldn't still be living here in Silver Springs, where he can continue to harass me. That's for darn sure."

"Why can't you move away?"

"And take Jayden from him? The court would never allow it."

He found his gaze drifting back to her legs. For all he knew, she was wearing a pair of shorts under that old, soft-looking T-shirt. But he wasn't picturing shorts. He kept picturing a pair of lacy white panties — and imagining what her thighs would feel like if he ran his fingers up under the hem of that shirt . . .

An awkward silence fell. He realized that she'd spoken last and he should've said something to keep the conversation going. Once he dragged his eyes up to meet hers, the flush to her cheeks indicated she'd noticed his preoccupation with her bare legs.

Knowing that his interest couldn't be comforting to her, not after all she'd been through and the doubts she probably still harbored where he was concerned, he cleared his throat, set his glass aside and stood. "Sorry for . . . staring. I'd better get going."

Her eyebrows came together in a look of despair. "Already?"

Her response surprised him. She'd just caught him ogling her; didn't she want him gone? "You'd like me to stay even though . . ."

"It's okay." Her blush deepened. "I know it's probably been a long time for you, and . . . and there's nothing wrong with looking, right?"

"There is if it makes you uncomfortable. I didn't mean to do that. I . . . got distracted. It *has* been a long time for me since . . . since I've been with someone in that way. But I would never come on to you, never put you in a compromising situation. All you have to do for me is cook and clean and look after my sister." He lifted his hands. "I promise you that."

"Thank you. The reassurance is . . . appreciated. And, knowing how tired you must be, I wouldn't ask you to stay any longer except . . . having someone here is nice, you know? It gives me a little break from having to be quite so diligent. Sometimes, late at

167

night, it feels like I'm going out of my mind."

"You're just tired."

"Yeah. But not only physically. I'm tired of keeping watch. Of being worried. Of never knowing when he might appear to challenge me in some way." She made a negating gesture with one hand. "That isn't your problem, of course. I don't mean to drag you into anything. I just thought we could spend a few more minutes chatting about our lives, or something else, if you prefer. You know . . . have the chance to calm down before facing the rest of this nerve-racking night."

She didn't need to chat with anyone; she needed a chance to recover, to feel safe. And she needed more sleep than she was getting. "Bring me a blanket and a pillow," he said. "I'll stay here for a few hours, on the couch, so you can rest without worry."

Her eyes widened. "You don't have to go that far —"

"It's fine."

"But you must be as weary of your battles as I am mine."

He *was* weary, but as harrowing as his ordeal had been, it'd lasted only a year. He got the impression she'd endured her "hell" for much longer. "Whether I crash here or at home doesn't matter. After sleeping on such a thin mattress while I was in jail, I can nod off just about anywhere."

A look of relief came over her face. "That'd be great. *Really* great. If you're sure you wouldn't mind. I'm normally not like this — just sort of at loose ends tonight."

"Like I said, it's no trouble."

"Good." The tension seemed to leave her body. "Then I wouldn't have to worry that Sly might be . . . bothering you out at the farm, and that it would be my fault."

"You don't have to worry about me. Go sleep. I'll let myself out in a few hours."

"Okay." She put down her wine, left the room and returned with an old quilt and pillow. "I'd let you take the bed, since you're doing me a favor, but my son's in there and moving him would risk waking him."

"You share a bed with Jayden?"

"A mattress, actually. That's all we've got."

No doubt Sly preferred Jayden to be sleeping with his mother. Then she'd be unlikely to invite another man into her bed.

She downed the rest of her wine, gave him a grateful smile and told him good-night.

After she went into her room, he sat on the couch sipping his own wine for another ten or fifteen minutes. He couldn't get the image of her bare legs out of his mind. Even after he'd drained his glass and lain down, he couldn't seem to rein in the desire that kept him rock-hard. Now that he'd thought about sex, he couldn't *quit* thinking about it.

That she'd given him *her* pillow didn't help. He could smell her perfume on the case.

9

What'd just happened?

Sadie's heart thumped against her chest as she crawled into bed with Jayden. Dawson had never given her the impression he found her attractive; she'd assumed he didn't. She'd noticed certain things about *him,* of course — like his perfect backside, since the fit of his jeans made that obvious, how the corded muscles of his arms and shoulders rippled as he worked, or the way his lips moved when he talked or smiled. Like Sly had said, *most* women noticed Dawson. They'd have to be blind not to. But he'd seemed completely indifferent to *her.*

Until a few moments ago.

Remembering the hunger in his eyes took Sadie's breath away. He wanted a woman — so badly she wasn't sure he was feeling very particular about which one. Acknowledging that helped her cool off a little. It wasn't *her* he wanted; anyone would probably do.

Still, she hadn't felt young or attractive for some time. She'd become a cliché, had fallen to the unappealing status of "beleaguered mom anxious to get out of a bad marriage" and was happy if she could just get an extra hour of sleep in a night or a generous tip at the diner. Romance hadn't even entered her consciousness, so achieving the interest of a man who was *that* good-looking, even though there was still a great deal of suspicion surrounding him, reminded her that she wasn't too old or too far gone to feel the kind of titillating desire depicted in movies. For the first time in ages, she *wanted* to make love. And she was so unaccustomed to the arousal flooding her body that she didn't know how to combat it.

Having Dawson stay probably wasn't the best way. She had to admit that. Knowing he was in the other room made her want to go back out there, but . . . God, it felt good to feel attractive again.

Closing her eyes, she allowed herself to imagine what it might be like if he were to kiss her with those full, soft-looking lips, imagined his large hands sliding up under her shirt to touch her breasts — and jumped out of bed again.

Stop, stop, stop! She couldn't let her mind go there. Allowing herself to fantasize about Dawson Reed wouldn't improve her situation. What if she acted on those fantasies? If she did, and Sly found out they'd been together — well, she didn't even want to contemplate what would happen if Sly found out. And that wasn't the only thing. Dawson was her boss! She needed the job he was providing.

Kneeling by the mattress, she forced herself to focus on the small body curled up under the covers. Jayden. Her son. She had to be smart, for his sake. Working for Dawson gave her an opportunity, made it possible for her to one day get out from under Sly's thumb so she could build a better life for them both.

She couldn't do anything to blow that.

Dawson woke to find a small face staring intently into his. Startled and unsure of where he was, he sat up rather abruptly, and the boy jumped back.

"Mo-om!" the kid cried. "There's a man in our house!"

Dawson's ears rang with the unexpected noise as he glanced around, trying to regain his bearings. He'd fallen asleep at Sadie's

— so deeply he hadn't gotten up and gone home as he'd intended. And now it was . . . morning? Tough to tell with the blinds down . . .

"Shh. It's okay," he said to Jayden. "Don't wake your mom. I'm leaving." Shoving the quilt he'd been using out of the way, he got to his feet but staggered there for a moment. Still groggy, he hadn't given his sore muscles any warning that they would suddenly be bearing his weight.

"Mom! Hurry!"

Dawson shoved a hand through his hair, trying to get it to stay down. If he had his guess, he looked pretty scary, especially to a small person. But he wasn't sure there was anything he could do to change that. They were in such a tiny house he couldn't even back away. "It's okay. I'm not going to hurt anyone," he said and started searching for his keys. They weren't in his pocket. He remembered taking them out because they were cutting into his leg while he was sleeping, but . . .

"Dawson?"

At the surprise in Sadie's voice, he whirled around to see her standing in the doorway of her bedroom, looking as rumpled as he was. "I'm sorry to still be here," he said. "I didn't wake up as planned. I guess I was more exhausted than I thought. But I'm going now — if only I can find my keys."

"Who *is* it, Mommy?" the boy whispered loudly.

"Jayden, it's okay. This is Dawson Reed, Mommy's boss."

Her son gave him a skeptical once-over. "Why's he sleeping at *our* house?"

Dawson racked his brain, searching for a safe answer that would also appease the boy. He'd stayed to be nice, to offer Sadie some reassurance so she could sleep, but he knew it wouldn't look like a favor if Jayden mentioned his "overnighter" to Sly, the landlady or someone else.

Fortunately, Sadie spoke up. "He came over to see Mommy last night and was too tired to drive home. We can share our couch with him, can't we?"

Jayden didn't seem too sure about that, but he was calming down now that he could tell his mother wasn't alarmed. "I guess," he said with a measure of reluctance.

"What time is it?" Dawson asked.

Sadie rubbed her face. "Almost seven."

"When do you have to be at the restaurant?"

"Not until eight today. My alarm will be going off in five minutes."

"So you'll be out to the farm at one."

She covered a yawn. "Unless I get done early."

"One is fine. I'll see you then." Spotting his keys on the floor, he stooped to grab them, but Sadie hurried after him, still wearing that darn T-shirt he'd dreamed of pulling off her for half the night, and intercepted him at the door.

"Actually, I was thinking maybe you could stay for breakfast and then . . . you know —" she lowered her voice "— leave after we do."

He froze with his hand on the knob. Now that he was on his way, he didn't want to be held up. He had the feeling he should never have come here. He hadn't been ogling Sadie at the farm. He'd been able to keep his mind where it should be, for the sake of his sister. "Because . . ."

"My landlady gets up early, and she . . . she looks for me in the mornings, for a bit of chitchat before I head to work. After that, no one will be paying any attention to my place, and I wouldn't want her to, you know, think the worst."

By seeing a strange man come out of her house . . . That was the part she didn't add. "Right. Okay." He had a lot to do and was suddenly damn uncomfortable hanging out here. But he figured he could tolerate another few minutes.

Letting his breath go in a long sigh, he returned to the couch.

Jayden was still staring at him. "You live on a *farm*?"

He'd said that as if Dawson lived on a spaceship or the moon or something *really* exciting. "I do."

"What kind of animals do you have? Do you have any pigs?"

"I don't have animals right now. I grow artichokes."

Jayden looked disappointed. "What's an arti— What did you call it?"

"Artichokes are vegetables. I'll have to send one home with your mom so you can try it."

"I don't like vegetables," he said.

Dawson couldn't help chuckling. "Then I'm glad I'm not depending on you."

He wrinkled his nose. "What'd you say?"

"Nothing. I didn't like vegetables when I was your age, either."

"Jayden, why don't you go potty and get dressed?" Sadie said. "And please don't put so much toilet paper in the toilet this morning. If you stop it up again, Mrs. Clevenger is going to want to kick us out."

"I don't do that," he said, but he shot Dawson a glance that was just devilish

177

enough to indicate otherwise.

"Hurry," Sadie prodded. "We can't be late."

"I'm going," her son said, but he was barely inching along. Clearly, he was more interested in keeping an eye on Dawson.

"Hurry," she said again. "Breakfast will be ready soon."

"What're we having?" he asked.

"How about French toast? You like French toast."

He clapped his hands. "Yay! My favorite! Do *you* like French toast?" he asked Dawson.

"Sure, French toast sounds delicious to me," Dawson replied and hoped Sadie would put on something a little less revealing while she cooked — almost as much as he hoped she wouldn't.

Sadie peeled off the T-shirt and the shorts she'd worn to bed and tossed them in the pile to be washed. She was going to take a quick shower, but removing her clothes while Dawson was in the house felt rather . . . erotic, especially after what she'd imagined last night. She could hear his voice as he talked to Jayden, which made him sound very close . . .

Something had changed between them,

she decided. The attraction that'd flared last night wasn't gone. He'd grown aware of her in a sexual way — and she liked the attention.

"You gotta be smart," she reminded herself with a stern glance in the mirror. Then she pushed those feelings of excitement to the side, doing her best to ignore them, so she could get ready and wouldn't be late. She hated to make Dawson stay until she and Jayden could get out the door, but what had seemed so innocent last night — having him stay for a few hours because she needed the company — felt entirely different now that she'd spent hours dreaming about feeling his naked body against hers.

"Ready, Mom?" Jayden hung on the doorknob with one hand while fighting to keep the bag they took to and from Petra's each day on his shoulder with the other.

She straightened the apron that was part of her uniform for Lolita's. "Yeah. Let's go."

Dawson was watching the news when they came through the living room. He hadn't been able to shave, so he had a dark shadow of beard growth on his chin. That together with his wrinkled clothes made him look a little unkempt, but Sadie liked him that way. He looked good sitting there on her couch in those faded jeans and that Tennessee Williams T-shirt. She'd found him attractive from the start, but his sex appeal seemed to be growing fast, which worried her. They'd be spending a lot of time out at the farm alone — and she'd only be spending more time with him once she was finished working at the diner.

"Have a great shift," he said.

"Will you be here when we come home?" Jayden asked.

He chuckled as he shook his head. "No. You'll have your couch back."

"You can use it. We can share," he said, repeating what Sadie had told him earlier. To her ear, Jayden sounded a little disappointed, which surprised her.

"Thanks, but I should be okay at my place. I'll be careful not to drop by when I'm so tired."

Jayden hitched the bag higher on his little shoulder. "Maybe I can come see those things you grow sometime."

"I've already told your mother she can bring you whenever she wants."

Jayden immediately turned to her. "Can I go today?"

He had been at Petra's so much recently. Sadie knew he missed being with her. And some of her previous fears seemed unfounded — given that Dawson could've murdered them both in their sleep last night and hadn't so much as given them a threatening look. But she was still worried about Sly's reaction. Ironically, she was far more frightened of her ex than her new employer.

"Can I, Mommy? Please?" Jayden begged.

If Jayden came only for this afternoon, would Sly have to know?

He could too easily find out, she decided. He'd been keeping such a close eye on her — had *always* kept a close eye on her, but more so now that she was working for Dawson.

"I'll think about it while I'm at the diner." She was so tired of letting Sly dictate what she could and couldn't do, but she had to be careful or he'd sue her for custody.

She took the bag from him and they walked out to find Maude Clevenger spraying off the stepping-stones in the yard.

"Mornin'!" Maude called and turned off her sprayer in anticipation of their usual chat.

Sadie breathed a sigh of relief that she'd asked Dawson to stay inside until after she left. Maude would go in for breakfast in a few minutes. Then no one should be paying any attention to what went on at her place.

"Morning," she responded and smiled as Maude approached.

"I've got something to show you," her landlady told Jayden, eyes sparkling with excitement.

He hurried over. "What is it?"

"Only the biggest snail I've ever seen," she replied.

"A *snail*? Where?"

Sadie put the bag in the back of the El Camino and followed her son to a table where Maude had put the snail in a large plastic bowl. While they oohed and aahed, Sadie pulled her phone from her purse and texted Dawson. My landlady is outside, all right. But she should go in after we leave. Can you keep an eye out for her and make sure she's gone before you come out?

You got it, came his response.

When she had Jayden in his safety seat and was backing out of the drive, Sadie sighed in relief. She thought she'd pulled off keeping Dawson's presence a secret. Jayden had been so excited by the snail he hadn't mentioned the fact that they'd had a visitor, and with as quickly as his mind moved on to whatever was happening at the moment, she couldn't imagine he'd pipe up with that later — not unless something jogged his memory. With any luck, that wouldn't happen. She should be in the clear.

But then she caught a glimpse of a black-

and-white sedan turning at the corner and realized that Sly had probably been behind the wheel. He'd just driven past her house. Again.

She searched for where Dawson had parked his truck and nearly gasped when she spotted it not far from where the patrol car had turned. There it was, plain as day!

Had Sly recognized it?

He had to have. Like her car, that truck was distinctive . . .

"Why aren't we going, Mommy?"

Jayden was so used to her backing out of their drive as fast as was safely possible, rushing to get him to Petra's so she wouldn't be late for work, that he'd noticed the hesitation. They were sitting in the street, her foot on the brake as she gaped at Dawson's truck. She was trying to convince herself that what she'd seen a moment earlier was merely her imagination — fear getting the best of her — and not her ex-husband's cruiser.

"We're going." She gave the El Camino some gas, but instead of heading straight to Petra's, she rounded the corner and headed toward the center of town. She wanted to know if that was Sly . . .

"Can I go to the farm?" her son asked.

Her heart was still pumping erratically,

knocking against her chest and making it difficult to concentrate. "What'd you say, honey?"

"Can I go to the farm today?"

"I told you I'd think about it at the diner. I'm not at the diner yet."

"Why can't I know *now*?"

She reached California Street — the main thoroughfare in Silver Springs — and looked both ways, searching for any sign of a patrol car, but saw nothing. "I'll call you on my break and let you know."

"I can't wait that long. I want to go to the farm!" he pleaded. "You'll be there, won't you?"

She decided to stop by the store while she was heading in the wrong direction. "Yes, I'll be there."

"Then why can't I come? Dawson said I could!"

She wanted to say, "Because your father would use it against me." But she refused to undermine Jayden's relationship with Sly. They struggled to get along as it was. "Today might not be the best day, that's all. There will be plenty of other opportunities."

Because he wasn't happy with her answer, he continued to beg her both before and after she stopped to get him and Petra's kids some fruit snacks for later, but Sadie held fast. If Sly had recognized Dawson's truck, there'd be a confrontation, and she didn't want Jayden to have any part of that.

She was still feeling nervous after she'd dropped him off and was pulling into the diner — but a text she received from Dawson brought her a bit of relief.

All is well. Your landlady turned her back to put away the hose, and I slipped right past her. Houdini couldn't have escaped more cleanly.

She smiled at the image he'd created of himself sneaking away. He made her feel good — from when he stood up to Sly at the door to when he helped her down from the roof to when he tried to fire her, for her own good, and couldn't quite succeed because he had too soft of a heart. He wasn't what other people thought he was. He was the best-kept secret in town.

But she couldn't get too excited. Sly would somehow wreck what she had going, if he could.

10

Since Dawson had been released from jail, he'd thought only of getting the farm up and running and bringing Angela home, where she belonged. He owed it to his parents. They'd essentially saved his life when they adopted him, gave him a good home and provided a solid education. More than anything, they'd given him love, which was what had finally made him whole — or as whole as he was going to get. He didn't even like to think about what'd come before. But ever since last night, whenever he let his mind wander, he didn't dwell on how many more plants he could put in if he cultivated another five acres, or how he might respond if he received a difficult question from the state representative who was coming in five days to see if he'd be able to provide a stable environment for Angela.

He thought about Sadie.

186

"Damn it, stop!" he growled at himself. There was no one around to hear him; he could do and say what he wanted. But no amount of censure seemed to change the pattern of his thoughts, not since last night. He'd had to put his sexuality on a shelf, had to focus on other things to survive. Now that the danger was past, and he was left to pick up the pieces, however, that all-too-human part of him was reasserting itself with a vengeance. Those gorgeous legs and what he might've found had he lifted that T-shirt she'd been wearing remained center stage in his mind, which affected other parts of his body, as well.

He should've hired someone else. A man.

Except he couldn't hire a man to help bathe his sister . . .

As the sun moved higher in the sky, he found himself glancing toward the drive more and more frequently. He kept asking himself why it mattered to him what time Sadie arrived. She was going in to clean. It wasn't as if they'd have much interaction. But he was looking forward to seeing her in spite of all that.

Shortly after noon, a car arrived, but it wasn't Sadie. Although he couldn't be sure, since he was standing at such a distance, Dawson was fairly certain it was Aiyana's oldest two sons parking in his drive. He'd met them when he attended school at New Horizons Boys Ranch and had been friends with them ever since. Like Aiyana, they'd stood by him despite the doubt and suspicion he'd faced almost everywhere else, but he hadn't spent any time with them since he'd been home. He'd been too focused on what he had to accomplish, too busy to even return their calls.

"I guess we have to drop by unannounced to get to speak to you," Elijah said as they met halfway between the field where Dawson had been working and the drive where the Turners had parked.

"Sorry," Dawson said. "It's nothing personal."

Elijah exchanged a knowing glance with Gavin. "We don't doubt that. You've been through hell. I'm not sure I'd be particularly friendly after a year in jail, either."

"Exactly," Gavin chimed in.

"I figured you'd come around when you were ready — didn't want to push," Elijah continued. "But you know my mother."

She'd tried to call him. He'd been meaning to get in touch . . . "Aiyana sent you?"

Elijah lifted a bucket. "With cleaning supplies."

Dawson removed his cap and wiped the

sweat from his brow. "She expects you to *clean*?"

"Just the . . . you know, the bedroom."

Realization dawned. "The murder scene."

"She asked us if we'd mind," Gavin chimed in. "And we don't."

"Better us than you," Elijah added. "She told us you were preserving it for some forensics expert, so we purposely held off to give you time. But if that's happened already, we'd like to take care of the washing up for you."

Gavin, who had a darker complexion and a smaller build, with tattoos covering both arms, propped his hands on his lean hips. "Has the forensics dude been here?"

Dawson nodded. "Guy by the name of Ed Shuler came out the day after I was released."

Elijah spat in the dirt. "Good. He find anything that might be helpful?"

"Don't know yet. He took all kinds of samples — fiber samples, wall swabs, drain swabs, blood samples, fabric samples and who knows what else. But he told me it could take months to process everything."

Elijah frowned. "That's disheartening."

"Like everything else that's happened this year," he said.

"So now all you can do is wait?" Gavin

189

chimed in.

Dawson shoved his hands into his pockets. "That's about the sum of it."

"But you're done with the room, right?" Elijah asked. "Have you cleaned it yet?"

"Not yet." Dawson knew it needed to be done — and before he brought Angela home. No one in his or her right mind would let him take custody of his sister with their parents' blood still spattered all over the walls. But every time he decided to get scrubbing, he couldn't quite bring himself to follow through. He hadn't even been able to make himself go inside the room yet. The day he got home, he'd been physically ill, nauseous, as he climbed the stairs. That was why he'd locked their door — and tried to put what was behind it out of his mind. Even when he let Ed Shuler inside, he hadn't gone in with him. He'd used some flimsy excuse that he had to take care of something else to get as far away as possible.

"So we can do that for you now?" Gavin pressed.

He almost said yes. He sure as hell didn't want to do it himself. But washing up smacked too much of moving on, and moving on made him feel disloyal. "No. I'm not ready."

"Not ready," Elijah repeated.

"It's complicated," he said.

Elijah arched one eyebrow. "My mother's afraid you'll let what happened consume your life. On the chance you refused to let us clean, she told me to tell you that your parents loved you and would want what was best for *you,* and that might be letting go. She says she'd feel that way about us, if she were in your parents' situation."

"The killer took a year from you," Gavin concurred. "Don't let him take any more."

"I'm going to catch the bastard," Dawson said. "I have to. I won't be able to live with myself if I don't."

Gavin let his breath go in a long, audible exhale. "What does that mean?"

"It means I have to do this my own way. I'll clean the room when I'm ready."

"I wish you'd let us take care of it for you," Elijah said. "But . . . I don't want to make things worse for you. I'll tell my mother that she'll have to come out here and talk to you herself if she feels that strongly about it."

"Tell her I appreciate the support she's given me. The same goes for you. A person in my situation . . . having someone in your corner makes a big difference."

"We know you better than everyone else,"

Elijah said.

Gavin kicked a pebble in the dirt. "I feel terrible. If only I'd been home when you came by after shoving that hitchhiker out of your truck, I could've corroborated some of your story."

"I could've gone back to the bar to see you, but I didn't want to drink anything else, didn't want to get sucked back into that scene for any length of time. I was just wasting fifteen or twenty minutes until I could go home and get some rest. I had to work the next morning."

"And you didn't want to let your parents down by being unable to do that."

He chuckled without mirth. "That's the irony."

The sound of a motor caused them to turn. Sadie had arrived. She parked to one side so the Turners could still get around her and climbed out carrying a small, white sack.

"Hey." Elijah obviously recognized her and seemed startled to see her.

She glanced from one brother to the other. "Hi."

"Sadie works for me now," Dawson explained to avoid any misunderstanding. "She'll be taking care of Angela, once we get the house cleaned up and I can bring my sister home."

"You quit the diner?" Gavin asked her.

"I'm still there, but only for another week or so. This job will give me more hours. I needed to get something that paid a bit more."

Elijah nodded. "I see."

Dawson dug the house key out of his pocket. His parents had never locked the house during the day. They'd rarely bothered to lock it even at night. When they were murdered, the house had been left wide-open, and Dawson knew it was because they figured he'd lock up after he got home. They'd felt safe. But after what he'd been through, he wasn't about to allow anyone, including the vandals who'd come after, the chance to get inside his home ever again. "Here you are. You can go inside and get started," he told her.

"Okay. See you in a minute." She offered them all a self-conscious smile before leaving.

"*Sadie,* Dawson?" Elijah whispered once she was out of earshot. "What about Sly?"

"What about him?" Dawson asked.

"He's super possessive, for one. I can't imagine he'll be okay with having her out here — with you — even if you weren't —" he paused, grappling for words until he ended with "— public enemy number one right now."

"I've been tried. I was found *not* guilty."

"That won't matter," Gavin muttered, showing his complete agreement with his brother. "Not to him."

Dawson scratched his neck. "She applied. She was qualified and close by and needed the money. I didn't see why her ex should have any say in the matter."

Elijah looked less than comfortable. "Don't mess with Sly, man. He can be a real ass."

Dawson was finding that out. "He's not going to tell me who I can and can't hire. That's not fair to me or her."

Gavin cleared his throat. "I applaud your fighting spirit. And I can see why you'd feel that way. So would I. But I've seen that dude in action. Like Eli said, he's a real prick — a prick on a power trip."

"Most cops are," Dawson joked. "At least the ones I've met."

Eli dipped his head as if to say he could understand. "I'm sure you haven't seen the best side of law enforcement. Everyone on the Silver Springs force is convinced you're guilty. But you've been through enough. I'd hate to see you wind up in trouble again."

"So what are you suggesting?" Dawson

asked. "That I fire her and let him starve her out? Allow him to force her to come back to him because she has no other way of feeding her child?"

"Jayden is *his* child, too," Gavin said. "Sly won't let him go hungry."

"I'm not so sure," Dawson argued. "He seems to care more about himself than his son — or his desperate-to-be-rid-of-him wife." He thought of how frightened Sadie had been this morning that someone would see him coming out of her house. Sure, she was concerned about what her landlady would think, but she was more afraid that Sly would find out. "She hasn't said much, but everything she has told me suggests he's not playing fair."

Eli leaned around his brother, checking to be sure Sadie had gone into the house and wasn't standing off in the shade somewhere, listening. "I don't know him that well, to tell you the truth. You might be right. But Sly's a snake, a *jealous* snake. A few weeks ago, Sadie must've found someone to watch her kid, because I saw her at the bar. Sly was there, too, and stared daggers at anyone who dared approach her. He made it *very* clear he still considered her to be his property and wouldn't put up with interlopers. So . . . watch your back."

"I'm not interested in her romantically." What Dawson had been feeling since last night called him a liar, but he hadn't intended their relationship to be anything other than employer/employee and wasn't going to let it move in that direction.

"The reality doesn't matter," Eli said. "He'll perceive you as a threat and give you grief over anything he can."

"I asked her to dance when we saw her the night Eli's talking about," Gavin said. "I felt sorry for her sitting off by herself, you know? And, just for that, he almost started a fight with me right there in the bar."

Dawson slapped his jeans to get the dust off. "Yeah. I've seen a bit of that kind of behavior."

Eli's eyes widened. "*Already?* When did she start working for you?"

"Just a few days ago. But the beginning of anything is always the hardest."

"You think he'll settle down and let it go," Gavin said.

Dawson settled his cap back on his head as he looked up at them again. "Once he gets used to the idea. What else can he do?"

Eli made a clicking sound with his mouth. "I don't like what comes to mind."

"Legally," Dawson stressed. "He's a cop, right?"

"The fact that he's a cop makes it worse, not better," Gavin said.

"Who's going to hold him in check?" Eli agreed.

Dawson turned to stare at the fields he'd been working so hard to cultivate. He'd hate to see all his effort wasted. He had to stay focused. And yet . . . he couldn't abandon a woman who was being bullied. "I guess *I* will, if necessary," he said as he turned back.

"Don't do *anything.*" Elijah's voice grew firm. "If he comes over, call one of us. He'll be less likely to act out with a witness around. You can't let it come down to his word against yours."

"Sure thing," Dawson said. But he knew if Sly came out, there'd be no time to invite the Turners.

He waved as they left. Then he pivoted and saw Sadie's face at the window, looking out at him. He wanted to go in and talk to her, to see how she was doing.

And that was specifically why he averted his gaze and went right back to the field where he'd been working.

Because the diner had been slow, they'd cut her an hour early, giving Sadie time to swing by a small clothing boutique, where she'd purchased a new blouse. Perhaps it wasn't wise to waste money in her current financial crisis. She could continue to get by without another top. But she couldn't remember the last time she'd had something new. She was working two jobs right now, so she had more money coming in than since she'd left Sly, and it'd been fun to feel as though she had someone she wanted to impress. She hadn't bothered with that type of thing in ages, had barely let herself *look* at the eligible men in the area.

The sheer, sparkly fabric that covered a solid nude-colored tank underneath made her feel pretty, maybe even sexy in a subtle way, but Dawson had barely glanced at her when she arrived — and then he hadn't come in. She stood at the window mired in disappointment as she watched him move away from her until he disappeared from view.

"What did you expect?" she said aloud. She'd been a fool to buy a new blouse. Last night had been an anomaly. Dawson wasn't interested in her. She'd be crazy to get involved with him even if he was. She had nothing but his word and her instincts to rely on when it came to the issue of his parents' murder. And Sly would become even more insufferable if he thought he had competition. It was better to keep her

relationship with Dawson professional —
which she'd known all along, of course.

Trying to shake off a sudden melancholy,
she went up to his room to borrow an old
T-shirt. She hadn't worn her new blouse for
more than an hour. If she took it off now,
before she could spill or splash on it, she
could possibly return it. And since she did
Dawson's laundry, and he never showed up
at the house unless it was time to eat, she'd
just change back before dinner and then
wash and return his shirt to his closet with
the next batch.

His T-shirt nearly drowned her. She'd
never weighed much, but the longer she'd
lived with Sly, the harder it had been to keep
any meat on her bones. He made her so
anxious she didn't care to eat. Sometimes
she'd throw up if she did, and that problem
was continuing now that they were separated and financial worries added to the
other concerns that weighed so heavily. She
never knew what to expect from him; he
kept her constantly on edge, constantly
wary.

After folding her new blouse, she set it on
the dresser and went about cleaning the
room. She hadn't made it upstairs before,
so she figured it was time to dig in on the
second story. Although she'd taken the dirty

laundry from Dawson's room, there was more, and the clean clothes she'd left on his bed before were now piled on the floor in a haphazard fashion because he hadn't taken the time to put them away.

"Good thing you got me," she mumbled and changed his bedding, dusted, vacuumed and cleaned and straightened the closet and drawers. She also wiped down the lighting fixture and ceiling fan and scrubbed the window, which looked out onto the front yard and the highway beyond.

While pausing there to rest for a moment, she saw a police cruiser go by. Whoever was behind the wheel didn't slow down or turn in, but the sight of any cop car was enough to remind her of the panic she'd endured earlier when she thought Sly had noticed Dawson's truck parked on her street. She hadn't heard from her ex today — not while she was working at the diner and not after — so she'd begun to relax. But as the minutes ticked by with no word, she realized that could be foreboding. He *always* checked in, did whatever he could to remain in her thoughts and to encourage her to see him. She had no doubt that once he got her to come back to him, and was secure in the relationship, he'd treat her the same as before, but he swore that would never happen.

Her hair was falling from the ponytail she'd pulled it into after changing into Dawson's T-shirt, so she took a moment to put it up again. Then she went downstairs to retrieve her phone from the counter, where she'd left it.

She'd received a text from Petra.

Jayden took the news that he couldn't come out to the farm pretty hard.

I'm sorry, she wrote back. I didn't mean to get his hopes up. She wasn't the one who'd gotten his hopes up. Dawson had done that by agreeing to let him come to the farm, thereby putting the decision squarely on her shoulders. But she couldn't tell Petra how the possibility had cropped up, didn't want to draw Dawson into the conversation. She hoped Jayden hadn't mentioned him, either.

He's fine now, came her response. I was just surprised by how badly he wanted to go. Usually he gets over disappointment much quicker.

I'll bring him here when I can, she wrote but had no idea when that might be. It depended on Sly and how he behaved in the next few days — whether he calmed down or continued to cause trouble.

She checked her missed calls and her voice mails. Nothing from him so far. Where was he today?

Relieved that she hadn't heard from him — and nervous at the same time — she turned on her music and poured herself a cup of coffee. She was about to carry her phone upstairs so she could listen while she cleaned Angela's room when the sack she'd brought, which was on the counter with the coffeemaker, reminded her that she'd purchased a piece of Lolita's homemade apple pie for Dawson.

She decided she'd change back into her blouse and take it out to him in an hour or so, but before she could go back upstairs, she heard a noise directly behind her and nearly jumped out of her skin.

"Whoa! Take it easy! It's me," Dawson said when she screamed and whirled around like she was about to be attacked.

She pressed a hand to her chest in an effort to slow her galloping heartbeat. "Sorry. I . . . I didn't hear you come in."

"Probably because of the music. I wasn't being quiet and certainly didn't mean to startle you. I just ran out of water." He lifted his thermos, but then his eyes lowered to her chest and she watched as the fact that she was wearing his shirt registered.

"I apologize for . . . for appropriating your clothes for my own use. I —" She didn't know what to say. She didn't feel comfortable telling him she'd worn a blouse to work she couldn't actually work in.

"It's fine," he said before she could even come up with an excuse.

"Thanks. I'll wash it, of course. I planned to put it through the laundry. It's not as if . . . well —"

"How much do you weigh?" he asked, cutting her off.

She blinked in surprise. "A hundred and twenty pounds."

He tilted his head, giving her a look that indicated he didn't believe her.

"Okay, I only weigh about a hundred and eight, maybe a hundred and five. But . . . I'm trying to eat enough to build back up."

"Why isn't it working?"

She cleared her throat. "I guess I'm a high-strung person. Turns out nervous energy can really amp up metabolism," she added with a humorless chuckle.

"You look like a teenage girl."

She felt her smile slip from her face. She'd bought a new blouse, hoping to please him. She'd thought he'd liked what he saw — last night, anyway. This let her know that he didn't find her attractive after all. She could tell by the censure in his tone.

"Yeah, I . . . I've struggled with my weight for a few years now." She turned away to hide the fact that his comment had stung — because that was an unreasonable reaction. She *was* too thin. She had no business fantasizing about him, anyway.

Fortunately, she spotted the sack she'd brought with her, which gave her a way to divert his attention. "I brought you a piece of pie," she mumbled and handed it to him. Then she escaped from the kitchen before he could react.

11

Dawson dropped the sack to his side without even looking in it and closed his eyes as he heard Sadie's feet on the stairs behind him. What had possessed him to say such a thing? He hadn't intended to hurt her. He'd simply been trying to remind himself that he wasn't attracted to her, to shove that between them in hopes it would help him keep his thoughts where they should be. Lord knew he had to do *something* to gain control over his libido. He'd just dumped out the rest of his water under the flimsy excuse that it was getting too warm to drink so that he could come inside and see her!

He pictured the expression on her face as she'd whirled around to grab the sack with the pie. She'd looked crestfallen, as if he'd struck her for no reason.

Shit . . . It was coming upon her in his T-shirt, he decided. After last night, he'd liked the sight of that a little too much.

He considered following her upstairs to apologize. With Sly in her life, she'd probably had about all she could take of unkind men. But he could hardly explain what had caused him to act as he had — that he wanted her and was simply trying to find, or even build up, some flaw he could focus on that'd make him want her a little less.

No apology, he told himself. He needed to stay put. Better to let that little snippet of conversation go and simply be more polite in the future. But it didn't make him feel any better that the pie was so delicious, some of the best he'd ever tasted. What'd made her think to bring him a piece?

He liked her. She seemed nice, and he hadn't had enough nice people in his life.

"I don't remember Lolita serving pie like this when I lived here before," he called up the stairs. He was hoping to hear a few words from Sadie, achieve some assurance that they could just move on, but she didn't answer.

When he finished, he put the empty plate in the sink and went up to make sure she wasn't crying. His bedroom was already spotless. He poked his head in there before he found her wearing her own blouse again while cleaning Angela's room. "I'm not sure if you heard me, but I said the pie was really good." He stopped short of entering the room, preferred to stand in the doorway. "Thanks for bringing it."

"You're welcome." She kept her face averted and continued working so he couldn't get a bead on what she was feeling.

He leaned against the doorjamb. "Tasted homemade."

"It was." She still had her back to him, was busy putting clean linens on the bed.

He didn't have anything else to say, and he needed to get back to work, but he was reluctant to go. "What's for dinner tonight?"

"I was planning to make beef Stroganoff. Do you like that?"

This achieved a glance, but he couldn't hold her gaze. "Don't know that I've ever had it."

"It's good. Noodles, ground beef and mushrooms in a delicious gravy."

"*Sounds* good. Anyway, I trust you. I've enjoyed everything you've served so far."

Once the bed was made, she straightened — and finally faced him. "Are you hungry now?"

She hadn't been crying, but something had changed. She was no longer open to him, had the same guarded look in her eyes she'd had when they first met and she'd been so frightened of who and what he might be.

"Not yet," he said. "That pie was delicious, though."

"Do you want me to go get you some more?"

She obviously couldn't figure out why he was inside talking to her and not out working, like usual — had no idea that he felt terrible for insulting her. "Not today. Maybe another time."

"Okay."

"How much do I owe you for this piece?" She'd had to spend some money to get it for him, hadn't she?

She bent to plug in the vacuum. "Nothing. Wasn't much."

When he didn't leave, she hesitated. "Is there something else?"

"No." Resigned, he shoved off the lintel so he could go but stopped immediately. "Just so you know, I didn't mind that you were wearing my shirt. I have a lot of old T-shirts. You can borrow one whenever."

"That's okay. I have this. I just . . . didn't want to get it dirty."

"I can see why. It's pretty."

"Thanks," she said, but curtly and in such an offhanded tone that he could tell she'd deemed the compliment insincere. She believed what he'd told her earlier — that she looked like a teenager and was therefore unattractive to him — and had slammed the door on future signals that might contradict that statement.

"What I said about your weight a few minutes ago was . . . rude," he said. "I'm sorry."

She lifted a hand. "I'm not offended. I know I'm too skinny."

He offered her an apologetic smile. "I wouldn't go that far. You're on the thin side, but you have *gorgeous* legs."

"Thanks."

He'd meant what he said, but this compliment met with the same disbelief that'd caused the demise of the first.

"Have you heard from Sly?" he asked.

She gathered a handful of the electrical cord in anticipation of starting to vacuum. "Not yet. But I'm sure he'll call or text me soon. He never stays away for long. Why?"

"I don't want him to cause you any trouble."

"He's my problem. I'll take care of . . . whatever happens."

He was afraid she wouldn't be able to take care of it. How could a 105-pound woman ever fend off a man Sly's size? Dawson hadn't weighed 105 pounds since elementary school . . . "Hopefully, he's not as bad as he seems."

"Like most people, he's got his good points." She would've been hard-pressed to come up with what those were, given how she'd been feeling about him lately. Fortunately, Dawson didn't ask.

"I suppose so," he said. "Well, I'd better get back to work."

"Don't forget to take out some more water," she said, and he heard the vacuum go on as he descended the stairs.

Once he reached the main floor, Dawson stood there for several minutes. He still felt bad about being so rude earlier, wished he could go back up and fix what he'd broken. Sadie had thrown up a wall to shield the soft, vulnerable part of her she'd started to show him before.

But maybe that was for the best. They both had enough going on in their lives. They didn't need to complicate anything by getting too close to one another.

Sadie said very little when she served dinner, and this time she didn't eat.

"Aren't you going to join me?" Dawson asked as he watched her pack up for the day.

"No, that's okay. I need to get over to my

babysitter's so I can pick up my son."

"You should take some dinner with you — enough for you and Jayden."

"Why? They're *your* groceries."

"Doesn't matter. There's plenty."

"You don't have to eat it all tonight. It'll make good leftovers, help you get through the weekend, since I won't be back until Monday."

Dawson had lost track of the days. Since all he did was work, one tended to blend into the next. "It's already Friday?"

"You didn't realize?"

"No." Not until he thought about it. He knew Robin Strauss from the state was coming on Wednesday, which meant there had to be a weekend between now and then. He just didn't want his first few days as Sadie's employer to end on such a negative note.

She slung her purse over her shoulder. "Don't forget you have meatballs and other food in the fridge, too. The meatballs would make a good sandwich."

"Gotcha."

"Call me if you need anything. Maybe I can come over for a few hours here or there. I'm scheduled at the diner on Sunday morning, but I'm off tomorrow. I won't have a babysitter, but if it's just for a short time, I might be able to bring Jayden if . . .

well, it depends."

"I'll bear that in mind," Dawson said, but he planned to leave her alone. Maybe if he didn't see her for a couple of days, his hormones would settle down, and she'd forget what he said to her earlier.

"What do you do for fun?" he asked impulsively, before she could get out the door.

"I'm a single mother."

"And that means?"

"I take a nap," she said with a laugh.

He chuckled. "Right. I'll see you on Monday."

She gave him a beleaguered smile. "Have a good weekend."

As soon as he finished dinner, Dawson went out and worked until the sun went down and he could no longer determine a dirt clod from a rock. He was exhausted when he came in, figured he'd take a shower and fall into bed. But he made the mistake of letting his mind drift while he was standing under the hot spray, and it went exactly where he didn't want it to go — to Sadie. After that, he *couldn't* sleep. He kept wondering what she was doing, if she was already in bed and whether Sly had contacted her. He almost texted her to check — that was his natural inclination — but he refused to succumb to the temptation.

After prowling around the house for two hours, until it was almost eleven, he gave up. He'd been reluctant to go into town, hated being the subject of such doubt and suspicion. He'd never been much of a "people" person to begin with. But if he was ever going to blend into the community, he had to circulate, had to get his official "return" over with so that seeing him wouldn't be such a remarkable thing.

What better place was there to start than the bar?

The Blue Suede Shoe hadn't changed over the past year, but Dawson had. Before the murders, he'd managed to let go of most of the anger that'd driven him to misbehave in his youth. But the dark emotions that'd skulked beneath his skin in the old days were back.

After a year spent sitting in a jail cell, he supposed that was normal. Even if it wasn't, he couldn't change anything, not until he found the man who'd murdered his parents. He'd never been much of an innocent, anyway. His reputation was partly what'd made it so easy for folks around here to blame him for the murders. As the son of a crack whore, he'd seen more by the time he turned eight than most teenagers had seen by eighteen. Had his grandmother not found him and his mother living in a bug-infested apartment with several people they barely knew, drug paraphernalia strewn about and little food, who could say where he'd be? Not long after Grandma Pat took him in, his mother died of an accidental overdose, so he would've been stranded in that situation without a single caring adult — at least one he knew about or could figure out how to reach at such a young age. He had no idea who his father was. His mother had never been able to tell him. She'd made up stories at first, but those stories always changed — in one his father would be a policeman, in another he'd be a rich businessman. That was what finally convinced Dawson that she didn't know; she was just trying to tell him what he wanted to hear.

As nice as it sounded for his grandmother to swoop in and save the day, however, she was no picnic, either, or his mother wouldn't have run away in the first place. Dawson didn't get along with Grandma Pat much better than his mother had, which was why, after five years of struggling, she sent him to the boys ranch and allowed him to be adopted by the Reeds. Aiyana, the teachers and his new parents were supposed to train him to be a decent man. He'd expected to hate Silver Springs, had considered New Horizons a punishment one step short of juvenile hall, which was where he would've ended up — mostly for fighting — had he not been accepted into the school. But he wouldn't have met the Reeds if he hadn't come to New Horizons, and it was then that his life had finally changed for the better.

For years, he'd credited the Reeds and what he'd learned at the school with saving him from falling into the kind of life his mother had lived. But, eventually, he learned to appreciate the fact that Grandma Pat had done what she could, given her own emotional and financial limitations. At the end of her life, during the years she was suffering from cancer, they actually became quite close. He lost her right after college. That was partly what had motivated him to move back to Silver Springs when he lost his job instead of staying in Santa Barbara. Her death had served as a stark reminder that life didn't last forever. He'd wanted to look after the Reeds while he could. Other than Angela, they were all the family he had left.

Now he wished he hadn't made that decision. If he hadn't been living in Silver Springs, he wouldn't have picked up that hitchhiker. And if he hadn't picked up that hitchhiker, he believed his parents would still be alive.

But he'd been with them in their final years. He tried to console himself with that. He felt like he'd done his part to return the love they'd given him.

Now he just had to find their killer.

Ignoring the curious stares he received as he walked in, he found a seat at the far end of the bar.

"Look, it's the dude who killed his parents! He's out of jail."

Dawson heard a man at a nearby table whisper that loudly to his companion. The pair gaped at him, as did everyone else, but no one got up to confront him. Dawson considered that a good thing. He was afraid of what he might do to anyone who tried to throw him out.

Half expecting the bartender to be the one to walk over and ask him to leave, he felt like a tightly coiled spring until the man wiping down the bar merely looked up and nodded. "Be with you in a minute," he said and, true to his word, came down as soon as he'd tossed his rag into the sink. "What can I get for you?"

Dawson felt the tension in his body ease. "I'll take a Guinness."

"You got it."

The bartender looked to be in his mid-twenties. Dawson decided he hadn't paid much attention to the murders, or he didn't care about a crime that didn't directly affect him. But when he returned with the beer, he said, "You been out to see Aiyana yet?"

Dawson lifted his eyebrows in surprise. The guy spoke like they knew each other, like they were friends. "No, but Eli and Gavin stopped by the farm. Why? How do *you* know the Turners?"

"I went to school at New Horizons, too."

"When?"

"Graduated seven years ago. That's a bit after your time, but I heard about you, of course. Everyone's heard about you. My father's a criminal defense attorney in LA. A good one," he added. "Aiyana had me set up a meeting with him."

"She did?" She'd never mentioned that to Dawson. "Why?"

"She was hoping he could help."

"And? Did that meeting ever take place?"

"It did, although nothing really came of it. He took a look at the evidence to see if there might be something more he could suggest to your attorneys. But my dad told Aiyana that your team was doing a good job, that you should get off, and you did."

Dawson sipped the foam off his beer. "Nice of her to go to the trouble. Nice of your father, too."

"He has his moments," he responded. "I wouldn't have been sent away to a boys school if we'd been able to get along. But . . . things are better between us now."

"What was the problem?"

"I wish I could say it was him, but I was a spoiled brat, needed to grow up."

Dawson liked this guy already. "And now?"

"I'm damn near perfect. Can't you tell?" He grinned as he walked off to refill someone else's glass.

As Dawson drank his beer, he eyed some of the women in the bar. He'd come here for a much-needed diversion. Considering the amount of flesh on display, he felt he'd come to the right place. If anything could distract him, it should be this. It'd been so long since he'd had a woman, and he was beginning to feel every one of those days.

And yet . . . he wasn't as interested as he'd thought he would be.

He told himself it was because ogling the cleavage he saw felt a little desperate and shallow and he'd outgrown that type of thing. But he was afraid it was more than that. He was afraid someone else had already captured his imagination, someone he'd at first thought was too skinny to be attractive to him. It wasn't her breasts so much as her big eyes and that full mouth that turned him on — not to mention her legs —

"Would you like another?"

The bartender was back.

"No, thanks. I've got to work in the morning."

"I hear you're getting the farm up and going."

This guy was pretty friendly. "What's your name?"

"Gage. Gage Pond."

"Who told you I'm getting the farm up and going, Gage?"

"You're kidding, right? You're all anyone can talk about these days."

"I'm all anyone has been able to talk about for a long time."

"True, but with the verdict and your release . . . well, that has them all stirred up again."

Them. This guy didn't consider himself one of "them." That was apparent. "People will always talk. Nothing I can do about that."

"True enough." He hesitated as if he had more to say. Then he smiled and walked off as if that was it, only to come right back. "Look, I realize you might want to put the whole thing behind you . . ."

"But . . ." With that kind of a lead-in, Dawson expected several uncomfortable questions, including *Did you do it?* He didn't want to deal with that, but he liked this Gage enough to indulge him, to a point.

"But that hitchhiker you told the police about?"

Dawson sat up straighter. He hadn't expected Gage to bring up the hitchhiker. No one wanted to talk about the hitchhiker because most people didn't believe he existed, and if he did exist, they couldn't be so sure of *his* guilt. "Yes?"

"Guy came in here a few weeks after the murder. I'd just served him a drink when some news piece about the crime came on TV, a clip where you described the man you thought killed your parents. He looked a little startled. Then he said he'd seen a homeless-looking dude who matched that description at the same service station the night before your parents were murdered."

Dawson's heart began to pound against his chest. "Did he have any interaction with the guy? Could he provide a name or . . . or where the guy was from?"

"Doubt they even talked. Didn't sound like it."

But he could corroborate that the hitch-hiker existed. So far, no one had even been able to do that much, not that the police had tried very hard to find the person Dawson felt certain was responsible for killing his folks. Detective Garbo had been too determined to get a conviction, to be able to say he solved this gruesome case, and he had a much greater chance of doing that with Dawson than some stranger who might not have had any believable motive. "Do you know the guy's name who came in here?"

"Don't think he ever mentioned it. But I know he lives in Santa Barbara. I remember talking about it because I'd like to move there myself one day."

"What was he doing here?"

"Said he had a job building a bunker out on Alex Hardy's property."

"A bunker."

"Yeah. Alex is a bit of a survivalist."

"Maybe Alex has his name."

"He could've kept it, or he should have some paperwork on that bunker somewhere. I told the guy he should go to the police and tell them what he told me. When he left here, he acted as if he was on his way."

But Dawson had already been arrested at that point. With the police convinced they had the right man, why would they pay some stranger from Santa Barbara any attention? If Dawson had his guess, they hadn't even bothered to take a report.

Dawson wanted to head out to Alex's place right now. He finally had something — small thread though it was — to pursue on the strange man he'd fought with on the night that changed everything. But it was after eleven. He, of all people, had no business approaching someone's house that late. The police had already made him out to be some sort of psychopath. Tomorrow would have to be soon enough.

But it wasn't going to be easy to wait.

Sadie hadn't heard from Sly all day. After she got Jayden to bed, she poured herself a glass of the wine she'd opened for Dawson and turned on the TV. But she wasn't paying much attention to the program she was watching. She didn't have cable or satellite, so her choices were limited to begin with. She kept glancing at her phone, wondering why Sly hadn't asked what she was doing tonight. On a Friday. He always seemed particularly interested in what she might be up to on a weekend, was so afraid she might start seeing another man.

She replayed their argument in her head again. He didn't like to lose. He found it embarrassing, demeaning — a statement that he wasn't everything he pretended to be. So . . . he'd never let her have the last word.

If you think I'll ever let you divorce me, you have another think coming. That statement — the way he'd said it — gave her chills because she believed that far more than this uncharacteristic silence.

If it weren't so late, she would've called her mother-in-law to ask if Marliss would like to see Jayden this weekend. Sadie tried to take him by once a week, just to show good faith — that she wasn't trying to deny Sly or his family contact with their own flesh and blood. Marliss always treated her coolly, which made their encounters awkward, but Sly's mother had heard only his side of what had gone wrong in their marriage — and he blamed her. Sadie didn't think she could expect any more, so she tried not to get upset by how their relationship had suffered. Most mothers were blind to their children's faults. Sadie knew she'd never convince Marliss that Sly was so controlling and abusive; she just thought if she could talk to Marliss, Marliss might mention that

Sly was sick or *something* to explain his sudden and complete silence.

Would you like to see Jayden this weekend? I could drop him off for a few hours if you're not working.

Sadie typed that message to Sly instead of his mother but couldn't bring herself to send it. Jayden wouldn't welcome that idea, and she couldn't throw him under the bus just because she was going out of her mind trying to figure out what Sly was up to. Besides, as worried as she was on the one hand, the silence was kind of nice on the other. She hated to break it.

She watched a couple of programs, which helped occupy her mind. Hoping that she'd finally be able to sleep, she got up to shut off the TV and set her glass in the sink. That was when her mind returned to Dawson, but she immediately steered her thoughts away. What she'd been dreaming about last night had been crazy. She wasn't interested in her boss. She was just lonely — so lonely that she wasn't making good decisions.

She'd left the light on in the bedroom so she wouldn't have to get ready for bed in the dark. Light didn't seem to bother Jayden. He could sleep with it on, and sometimes did until she joined him.

After she changed into a tank top and

sweatpants, she read for twenty minutes or so before turning out the light. She was just drifting off, was almost asleep, when she heard three distinct thumps on the side of the house. She was so tired, she tried to ignore the noise, but then she heard it again — louder and more insistent.

Someone or something was outside, trying to rouse her. A raccoon or a squirrel didn't make that deliberate *bang, bang, bang . . .*

Alarmed, she crept out of bed and crossed to the window, where she parted the blinds to peer out. There was only one window in the room, and it looked out on a very small yard and a gate leading to the narrow alley behind the house, not the side yard. She didn't expect to see anything, was merely doing what she could — which was why she covered her mouth to stop herself from screaming and stumbled back when she spotted a man. She couldn't tell who it was. His face was hidden beneath the hood of a black sweatshirt, but she could see his basic shape, even his shadow in the moonlight. He looked up at her, then jumped the fence and ran down the alley.

Who was that? Sly? She'd barely caught a glimpse, couldn't even say with any certainty that the person she saw had his build. He was dressed in a way she'd never seen him dressed, and it'd happened too fast. But who else would come by in the middle of the night?

He'd probably been watching and waiting to see if Dawson would join her again — and, even though that hadn't happened, he was angry enough about before to give her a little scare.

After unplugging her phone from its charger, she carried it with her into the living room so she could peek out the other windows, but none looked out on the side yard. She couldn't determine what her visitor had been doing, and she wasn't about to venture beyond the safety of her locked doors — not when that man could so easily come back. For all she knew, she'd just seen the hitchhiker who'd hacked the Reeds to death.

She considered calling Sly. He was, after all, a police officer. He'd know how to handle something like this — if it wasn't him. But it *could* be him, which meant she couldn't call 9-1-1 or anyone else on the police force, either. Whoever came to see what was wrong would contact Sly immediately, or tell him what happened afterward, and he'd want to know why she didn't reach out to him like he'd probably been setting her up to do.

Without letting herself think any more about it, she texted Dawson. She still felt a little awkward about assuming he was interested in her when he wasn't, but, for the most part, he had been nice so far, and she needed a friend, especially one who wouldn't take Sly's side in any given situation or share anything she said.

You awake? she wrote.

She hesitated to disturb him, which was why she didn't call. She figured, if he was sleeping, he probably wouldn't notice that he'd received a message. A ring was more intrusive. So she was surprised when he texted her right back.

Yeah. What are you doing up so late?

To be honest, I'm a little nervous. There was someone at my house a minute ago. A man.

What do you mean — at your house?

Outside, doing something. Someone knocked on the side of the house, then came around back where I could see him from the window. I think it was Sly, but I can't be sure.

227

And you have no idea what he was doing?

None. Do you think he was just trying to scare me? The less secure I feel, the more likely I'd be to move back — or at least go there tonight.

Whatever you do, don't go there.

So do you think it was nothing? Should I just go back to bed? Whoever it was had been on the side, not where he could've been watching her.

But there was nothing to say he'd been on the side for long. Had he been outside her window before that, staring through the gap between the blinds and the wall while she undressed? *Peeping?*

Do you have your blinds down? Dawson texted.

I do. I know he comes here a lot to check up on me, so I always keep them down. But they don't fit the window very well. There's a two-inch gap that someone could easily peer through if . . . if they wanted to be that intrusive. She felt violated just imagining that, even if it was Sly. So what if he'd seen her before? They weren't together any longer. She deserved some privacy.

228

I'm coming over.

This time she was surprised *by* his response, not that she'd received one. No! You don't have to come all the way to town. I just . . . I needed to tell someone, I guess. Needed to hear someone say I'm being silly and there's nothing to be afraid of.

She knew where his mind would go, because hers had already gone there. His response confirmed it. You're not going to hear that from me, not after what happened to my parents.

I admit — I keep thinking of that hitchhiker. That's why I texted you, I guess. You don't think he's back . . .

I can't say it isn't possible.

The idea that it might be him gives me the creeps . . .

It's okay. I'm almost there.

How? It took longer than two or three minutes to get to her house, but that was the length of time they'd been communicating with each other.

I'm not at the farm. I'm coming from the bar only a few blocks away. I'll swing by and take a look around, make sure everything's okay.

That he was so close made her feel much better. Everyone was wrong about him. He didn't frighten her; he made her feel safe. After all, he could've done anything he wanted last night, but he hadn't even gotten off the couch.

She breathed a sigh of relief as they disconnected — but that was when she began to smell smoke.

12

Dawson was turning down Sadie's street
when his phone rang. "Stay away! Oh my
God, whatever you do, stay away!" Sadie
screamed and then she was gone.

The panic in her voice caused Dawson to
stomp on the brake. There had to be a
reason she'd called him off. But what could
that reason be? What was happening?

He tried to reach her again. She didn't
answer, so he didn't turn around. He knew
how slight she was. What if she was trying
to protect her little boy? What if Sly was
there, giving her trouble, and that was why
she'd called to tell him to stay away — to
avoid a fight between them?

Dawson didn't bother to park down the
street. He was in too much of a hurry. He
pulled in front of her landlady's house, got
out and jogged around to the back. He
could smell something burning before he
heard a disoriented "What is it, Sadie?" And

then, even before Sadie could answer, the speaker — a woman — seemed to realize what "it" was, because her voice suddenly grew strident. "Fire! Vern! The bungalow's burning. Call 9-1-1!"

The door to the house that fronted Sadie's slammed shut as whoever had said that — which had to be her landlady — went back in to, presumably, make sure her orders were carried out right away.

Fortunately, Sadie appeared to be safe. Dawson could see her standing on the lawn dressed in the same T-shirt she'd worn last night and a pair of sweatpants. She was holding her little boy, although he was half as big as she was, who kept trying to get down. She wouldn't let him go, however. She clung to him for dear life — until she saw Dawson. As soon as Dawson called out to her, she started toward him and, for a brief moment, he thought he saw a flash of relief in her eyes, which disappeared as soon as she reached him. "You have to go," she said. "Hurry! I shouldn't have called you."

"What's happening?" he asked.

"Someone set my house on fire!"

"On *purpose*?" He could hear the loud crackle, see orange flames leaping and dancing through the front window.

"Yes!"

He remembered hearing the old woman mention calling 9-1-1. "You haven't called for help yet?"

"I didn't have a chance. Once I hung up with you and smelled the smoke, I grabbed Jayden and got out. Maude's calling the fire department now."

"Maude" had to be the name of the landlady who'd just hurried into the front house. "Who could have done this?" he asked.

Sadie shook her head as if she didn't know, but he wondered if there was more that she wouldn't say. She probably didn't want Jayden to hear her accuse his father, but Dawson guessed that was what she believed. She'd said she thought it might be Sly who'd knocked on the house, so it followed that he might also have set the blaze . . .

Dawson reached for Jayden. "Here, let me take him. He's too heavy for you."

She pulled away so that he couldn't lift the boy from her arms. "No, you have to go."

"Why? What does any of this have to do with me?"

Her eyebrows slammed together. "Don't you see? Whoever did this has to have someone to blame — and who would make a better candidate than you? If you're here, if everyone sees you, that'll only make it easier for —" she was starting to shiver "— for whoever did this to connect you to it. Please, go home."

"Who's *this*?" The old lady had re-appeared, this time with a silver-haired man who looked about the same age she did.

"My b-boss," Sadie stuttered, likely from shock as much as the cold. "I . . . I called him when I heard someone outside, and he . . . he came to make sure everything was okay."

Her husband hurried to the garden hose and unwound it as fast as he could, but the woman hesitated for a second. "You're Dawson Reed," she said.

He could tell she wasn't exactly pleased to make his acquaintance. Fortunately, given the situation, there wasn't time to have any further interaction. He nodded once to acknowledge his identity and turned back to Sadie while Maude went to help with the hose. "Let me take Jayden," he insisted.

Sadie looked as though her knees were about to buckle. Maybe they were, because she allowed him to pull her son away, which Dawson hadn't fully expected, despite his efforts.

"Tell me he didn't do this," she whispered as they transferred the boy.

Dawson scowled at the sight of her burning house. The flames were starting to take hold, creating a terrible stench as they consumed paint and plastic and other materials. The smell surprised him; it was far worse than any wood fire. He knew the fumes from a burning house could also be toxic, so he pulled Sadie out of the path of the breeze. "You would know what he's capable of more than me," he murmured.

"Who, Mommy?" Jayden asked. "Daddy? Did Daddy start the fire?"

What kid asked if his father was the one who'd tried to burn down their safe haven — *while they were in it*?

"No, not Daddy. A . . . a hitchhiker," she said vaguely.

"What's a hitchhiker?" Jayden asked.

"In this case, it's a bad man," she replied.

Dawson thought the boy might struggle to reach his mother, or get down, since he'd been trying to get down when she was holding him, but he seemed surprisingly content where he was. He even put his arms around Dawson's neck as if he was quite comfortable.

"I can take Jayden. You've got to leave," Sadie said, her face drawn and pinched as she looked up at him.

He could only imagine how difficult it would feel to be victimized like this, to know that someone had purposely tried to harm her — in her own home, where she should feel safe — and that the person responsible might be the father of her child. Knowing she could lose all of her belongings, when she had so little to begin with, had to be almost as difficult. "I'm not leaving, not unless you and Jayden come with me. It won't do either of you any good to stand out here in the cold, breathing in this toxic air and watching —" *what little you have go up in smoke "— this."*

"We can't leave," she said. "There will be . . . questions I'll have to answer."

"Then I'll wait, too, make sure everything goes okay," he responded.

She shook her head. "That's not a good decision."

They could hear the wail of sirens growing louder as the emergency vehicles drew close.

"Sly will come," she said. "Someone . . . someone will call him. And regardless of . . . of how this got started, he won't be happy to see you here. He'll assume . . . the wrong things."

The mere mention of Sly made Dawson

clench his jaw. "Maybe he'll assume the *right* things."

She gave him a look that indicated she couldn't possibly understand what he meant by that.

"That he'll no longer be able to push you around," he explained. "I've had it. I won't allow it anymore."

Her mouth formed a worried O. "I don't want to draw you into this — not to that degree. I just . . . needed to talk to someone who . . . who wasn't connected to the life I lived before, someone I felt was strictly *my* friend and not his."

Dawson watched the flames leap higher. "Then you chose the right person, because I'm definitely *not* his friend."

The temperature wasn't much less than fifty degrees, so not exactly freezing. But the shock and upset of what was happening, in addition to the cool breeze, made Sadie shiver uncontrollably. As the fire trucks arrived and cut their sirens, which had become almost deafening, Dawson took off his coat and insisted she put it on.

Sadie could smell the scent of Dawson's cologne before that far more pleasant scent was overwhelmed by the stench of the fire. She could've gotten a jacket or blanket from

Maude, but Maude was busy trying to direct her husband on where to aim the garden hose, and Sadie didn't want to interrupt. Although the two had started to spray the house where Sadie lived, hoping to save what they could, the hose provided such a pitiful trickle compared to what was needed that their efforts seemed to do little or no good. Dawson soon persuaded them to spray the surrounding shrubbery and their own house in an effort to stop the fire from spreading instead of trying to put it out altogether.

The first firefighters on the scene yelled for them all to stay back, but the yard was so small there wasn't anywhere to go. Dawson, still carrying her son, guided her around to the front and insisted she and Jayden get in his truck. He climbed in, too, and started the engine so that he could back down the street to allow more room for the emergency vehicles now gathering en masse, and turn on the heater.

"You warm enough?" he asked Jayden.

"Yeah." Her son, who was now sitting between them, climbed up on his knees to be able to see out the window. "Can I go watch the firefighters?"

"No!" Sadie replied. "You could get hurt.

We need to stay here. You heard what they said."

Several of the neighbors streamed out of their houses to see what was going on. Sadie watched them gather in a frightened and questioning cluster on the opposite side of the street.

"Is that Daddy?" Jayden pointed when the first police car appeared.

Sadie's heart jumped into her throat as she squinted against the glare of headlights. But the man who climbed out from behind the wheel once those lights were turned off wasn't Sly; it was Leland Pinter. "No, that's not him." She breathed a sigh of relief, but it wasn't more than ten or fifteen minutes later that Sly did pull up. She curled her fingernails into her palms as she watched him get out. She had a feeling he'd cause trouble. He didn't hurry to the back like everyone who'd arrived before him. He didn't seem to care about the fire, not as much as he cared about the fact that Dawson's truck was parked so close to her place and she was sitting in it.

How had he even noticed them? If he'd just heard her house was burning, wouldn't he automatically run to the back to see if she and Jayden were okay?

Apparently not. Nothing got past him. He

239

didn't even look worried as he approached her side of the vehicle. Expression hard, eyes flinty, he looked angry instead.

She glanced at Dawson in a silent appeal to let her handle Sly and rolled down the window.

Sly's eyes narrowed even further as he looked over at Dawson. He didn't even acknowledge Jayden when Jayden said a soft "Hi, Daddy."

"What's going on?" he demanded without preamble.

Thankfully, Dawson refrained from responding. Given Sly's volatile temper, Sadie was grateful for Dawson's forbearance.

"*Someone* set my house on fire." She was so upset she had a hard time keeping the accusation out of her voice.

"*Someone,*" he repeated, obviously grasping that she believed he was to blame.

"Yes. You wouldn't know who, would you?" Since he'd already guessed what she believed, she couldn't help lifting her eyebrows in challenge.

A muscle moved in his cheek. "How would *I* know?"

"Whoever it was knocked on the side of the house, then came around back. I saw him, for a second, before he ran away."

"What'd he look like?" Sly angled his head

toward Dawson. "This guy right here?"

Sadie felt the tension between the two men edge up a notch, but, to Dawson's credit, he didn't take the bait. "Like a man dressed in black. He was wearing a hoodie that covered his face, so I couldn't see it."

Once again, Sly indicated Dawson. "And then this guy shows up right away? You don't find that suspicious?"

Sadie was no longer cold. She was beginning to sweat. But she was still shaking. She knew how her response would sound to Sly, how he'd interpret it. "No, because he didn't 'show up.' I called him."

"*You* called *him,*" Sly repeated.

"I was scared," she explained.

He pulled out his phone. "I don't see where you tried to reach me."

"Because I didn't. Why would I? We're divorced, Sly."

"Not yet. And I'm still Jayden's father, and a police officer. A police officer would make sense to most people. But not you, I guess. You're so stupid you call a suspected murderer."

Dawson seemed to have reached his breaking point. "Your son's sitting here," he growled, his voice a warning.

Hoping to save Dawson from Sly's reaction, Sadie jumped out of the truck.

"Look, why don't we go somewhere we can talk privately?" She took his arm and tried to lead him away, but he shook her off, his gaze riveted on Dawson's coat.

"Where the hell did you get that?" he growled.

"Does it matter?" she asked. "Please! I've been through enough tonight. Let's not fight. Dawson doesn't want to fight with you, either. We're merely trying to cope with what's happened."

"By cozying up together."

"*Cozying up?* Don't you care that someone set fire to my house, Sly? That we could've burned to death in our sleep? You'd think you'd be more concerned about the fact that there's an arsonist running around than whether or not I'm wearing another man's coat!"

He shoved her back toward the truck. "Get Jayden."

Sadie wasn't about to do that, not with an argument brewing. "No. We're both exhausted and upset. We might've lost the only belongings we have left, and we were barely scraping by to begin with."

"We'll talk about that later. *Get Jayden.* I'm taking you home."

"*Home?*"

"To the house we bought together. That's

still home, Sadie. Where else are you going to go?"

Holy shit! This was exactly what he wanted. He thought she'd come back to him; he thought, without her rental house, she'd have no choice. "Oh my God," she whispered.

"What?" he snapped.

"You did it! You burned my house down so I'd have nowhere to live, so that I'd have no resources and would have to come back to you."

"Now you're talking crazy," he growled. "I'm a police officer. Be careful who you accuse of arson!"

"Who else would do such a thing to me?"

"It could be anyone! I told you not to hang around a murderer. For all we know, it was him — the very man you called!"

"It wasn't him," she insisted. "If he wanted to hurt me, he's had plenty of chances. You're the only one who's ever made my life miserable."

"What have I done to you?" he cried. "You're such a baby. But we'll talk about all of this later. Get Jayden."

He had no conscience. He'd do anything to retain control of her. He'd said as much — and tonight he'd proved it. "What about the collateral damage, Sly? Do you realize what you've done to Maude and Vern? They didn't deserve this."

"If you won't get Jayden, I will."

He started to go around her, but she grabbed his arm. "Don't you dare! I won't drag him out of that truck just because you can't stand to see me in the company of another man. Dawson's my boss, Sly. And . . . and a friend. He doesn't like me in the way you think. He's made that clear."

The sudden fury she'd expected when she accused him appeared now. "He has, has he? You've talked about it? The two of you?"

"Don't twist what I say!"

"I'm not going to let this no-good bastard come between us, Sadie."

"He's not *trying* to come between us!" Their voices were so loud she guessed Dawson could hear bits and pieces, if not everything. "He's being a nice guy, helping me out."

He shoved her again, hard enough to make her stumble back. "He's a murderer!"

The driver's-side door opened, and Dawson got out. "Get back in the truck, Sadie." He spoke in a cordial tone as he came toward them, but Sadie could tell he'd had all he could take. She wanted to do as he said, to escape Sly as soon as possible, but she couldn't. She had to remain between them. She was afraid of what might happen if she didn't.

"Please, let me go with him," she said to Sly. "I wouldn't come back to you even without Dawson in my life. I was unhappy. Don't you understand that? So unhappy that I could barely get up in the mornings. I don't love you anymore. The only thing I want is for you to let me go!"

His hand whipped out and grabbed her arm, fingers digging deep into her flesh, like they had so many times before — deep enough that she'd have bruises. But the pain wasn't what alarmed her. Almost as fast, Dawson gripped Sly's arm in the same "I'm in charge" manner.

"Let her go. *Now,*" he gritted out.

Sadie watched Sly's eyes flare in surprise. He was so used to doing what he wanted — and getting away with it almost uncontested in this town — that he hadn't expected Dawson to go so far in her defense. His top lip curled under and his other hand went for his gun with such determination that Sadie felt sure he'd shoot Dawson. She opened her mouth to scream, but, in that moment, someone besides the three of them called out to Sly.

"What's going on, Harris?"

The chief of police had pulled up while

they were arguing and was getting out of his car. He obviously thought Sly was about to apprehend Dawson, but the sound of his boss's voice caused Sly to let go of Sadie, back away — and leave his gun holstered. "Nothing," he muttered.

"Then what're you doing out here when everyone else is in back?" Thomas demanded.

Sly's chest was rising and falling fast, but he managed to modulate his voice so that he sounded somewhat normal. "I was — I was checking on my wife and son to . . . to make sure they're okay."

Chief Thomas strode toward them. "And?"

"I'm fine," Sadie said, but her heart was pounding so fast she thought she might faint.

The police chief turned his attention to Dawson — and grimaced when he recognized him. "What're *you* doing here?"

"He's my boss," Sadie cut in. "I called him when I heard someone outside my house, and he was kind enough to come."

Shouting from around back drew the chief's attention. Sadie supposed the noise had been going on all along. The firefighters were still battling the blaze back there. She'd seen the frenetic activity before Sly had shown up, but, somehow, she'd been so caught up in what was happening right here over the past several minutes, she hadn't noticed the noise since.

"Are they getting the blaze under control?" Thomas asked.

"I haven't been around back to see," Sly grudgingly admitted.

"I'm in good hands," Sadie told Sly. "You can . . . You can go ahead and do your job now."

She was sort of surprised that the chief didn't raise a fuss about Dawson, given what he believed Dawson to be. Obviously, he was more concerned about the fire than trying to control the company she was keeping, as Sly should've been. That her ex had focused so quickly on her, despite the fact that her house was burning, served as yet more proof that he'd known about the fire all along — and didn't care. He was only concerned about the fact that she was fleeing in the wrong direction.

As Sly stalked off with his chief, Sadie covered her mouth and breathed slowly through her fingers, trying to calm down. She thought he might turn and glare at them both, but he didn't. Maybe he was as shocked as she was that he'd almost done something even more reckless than setting fire to her house.

"I can't believe that happened," she murmured as she dropped her hand. "And what could've happened if Chief Thomas hadn't arrived when he did."

Dawson was the one glaring — at Sly's back. "He almost drew his weapon," he said, his voice filled with the same shock and anger she felt.

She checked to make sure Jayden was still in the truck and saw him standing up in the seat, hands on the dashboard, nose almost pressed to the glass. "Sly's not right in the head," she whispered. "He's obsessed with . . . with making sure I don't get away."

Dawson shook out his hand, which had been curled into a fist. "He's the one who set the fire."

"Yes," she agreed. "He wasn't the least bit surprised that there was a major blaze going on. Did you notice?"

"He thought you'd have to move in with him."

Where would she go? The full extent of where she'd be without her small cottage hit her in that moment. Although she'd been worried all along, she'd been holding out hope that her house and most of the things inside it could be saved. She was *still* hopeful. But even if they could save her belongings, the fire had to have done enough damage by now that she'd probably have to live elsewhere while the cottage was being repaired or rebuilt. Where would she go? She didn't have any family she could stay with. And Petra didn't have room for her. She couldn't see herself moving in with Petra and her family, anyway. She couldn't see herself trying to stay with Maude and Vern, either. They were nice, but she doubted they'd even make the offer.

She'd have to hit up one of the waitresses she worked with to see if she could move in and pay half the rent, but she hated how awkward that would be, especially because she wouldn't be able to afford a great deal. She'd have to spend what money she was making on replacing clothes and other basic necessities.

"I'm so tired," she mumbled as she gazed at the little person who was depending on her to take care of him.

"Everything'll be okay," Dawson said. "Let's go to the farm."

"You won't mind letting me stay the night?"

"Of course not. You can stay until you have somewhere better to go."

He'd made it easy. His kindness brought a lump to her throat. He'd been through a lot himself, and yet he'd stepped up to help her, even though he was already helping her by providing a job with pay on which she could actually survive. Everyone expected her to be skeptical of his help, but she could tell Dawson had no ulterior motive. He was what she thought he was — a nice guy.

"Are you sure?" She blinked rapidly, trying to suppress the tears that threatened in the wake of so much drama, fear, anger and upset. She'd cried in front of him once before. She didn't want to cry again, didn't want to give him any more reason to regret befriending her.

"You work there, anyway. Consider it part of your pay, if that helps."

"But you're already paying me well."

"I have the mortgage whether you stay or not. It's not like it'll cost me any more to have you."

Would she have been this generous to him, had their roles been reversed? Like the rest of Silver Springs, she'd been so prejudiced against him, so conditioned to believe that a monster lurked behind that handsome face. "I just . . . I feel bad for leaning on you. You're already carrying a heavy load."

"There's plenty of room at the farm." He shrugged off his kindness as if it wasn't a big deal. But it was a huge deal to her.

Before she even knew what she was about to do, she grabbed him and hugged him — partly so that he wouldn't be able to see the tears gathering in her eyes.

"Thank you," she said. "I can't tell you how grateful I am for your help."

He'd stiffened when she grabbed him. The contact had obviously been unexpected. But then she felt his hands slide up her back and became instantly aware of his large, firm body. At that point, the hug turned into something a little more intimate than she'd intended, but the contact felt so good she couldn't let go. She clung to him, even went so far as to close her eyes and let her fingers briefly slip through the hair at the nape of his neck.

He was the one who pulled away. "We'd better get some sleep." After setting her gently to one side, he walked back to the truck as if that hug had never happened.

Sadie could hardly breathe for the acrid smoke billowing into the sky. Sly was in back, probably trying to keep the neighbors who'd wandered over, and the fire truck chasers, at a safe distance. She knew, if she got into the vehicle with Dawson, she'd be driving a wedge between her and her ex-husband, his friends on the force, almost everyone in town. She could easily become

251

a pariah like Dawson. He'd warned her as much. So . . . was she making a mistake?

She feared she might be. She'd known Dawson for only four days. But in that time, he'd been a better friend to her than anyone else in Silver Springs.

Squaring her shoulders, she turned her back on everything that'd come before and got in the truck.

"Would you rather I take you to a motel?" he asked as she put on her seat belt. He'd already buckled Jayden in. Jayden's safety seat was in her car around back; there was no way she could reach it.

She tried to imagine herself at one of the three local motels. The Mission Inn was the cheapest, but even that would cost over $100/night. She wouldn't be able to stay there long even if she went there tonight. "No."

"Are you *sure*?" he asked.

"I'm sure," she replied.

13

Sadie was glad she'd already cleaned Angela's room. That made it possible for her and Jayden to fall into a clean bed. But as exhausted as she was — physically and emotionally — she couldn't drift off. She kept wondering if all of her belongings had been destroyed and worrying about what it would cost to replace their basic clothes and toiletries, not to mention Jayden's toys. She couldn't bring herself to even think about trying to replace the furniture she'd managed to cobble together secondhand. And what about the sentimental items she might never see again? Like the professional photographs she'd had taken of Jayden when he was a baby? Her only pictures of her parents were in that house!

Could Sly really have done something so terrible to her? He claimed to love her, to have changed. He swore up and down that he'd treat her like a queen if she came back to him. But the memory of their encounter on the road just after she'd pulled out of the farm the other day had haunted her since it happened. The determination and hatred she'd seen in his eyes contradicted his proclamations of love, made her believe he *did* start the fire — to take his revenge on her for embarrassing him by defecting as much as to force her back to him. He didn't really care about her, but he refused to lose her, couldn't stand being the one left behind.

As she stewed over how the fire might or might not be progressing at her place, she heard Dawson moving around downstairs. He had to be tired, too. Why wasn't he in bed, asleep?

Once she could slip out without disturbing Jayden, she got up. The clothes she'd been wearing at the fire had reeked so much of smoke she'd thrown them in the washer as soon as she arrived and Dawson had loaned her a clean T-shirt and some sweatpants. Although his sweats drowned her — she could only keep them on because of the drawstring at the waist — she wasn't about to leave the room in nothing but his T-shirt, despite the fact that it hit her at midthigh.

"What's going on?" she asked when she found him standing in the living room, gazing out the large picture window.

All the lights were off in the house. Obviously, he wanted to be able to see what might be happening in the front yard and, possibly, the highway beyond.

"Nothing," he replied.

"Then why are you still up? You've got to be even more tired than I am."

"The night's not over yet."

"What do you mean?"

"The police will be coming. They'll need to get a statement from you."

"I already told Sly what I saw and heard."

Dawson grimaced. "You don't think he'll be the investigating officer, do you?"

"Who can say? If he's the one who set the fire, he'll certainly lobby for the job. He'd be stupid not to."

"If that happens, you'll have to complain, try to get someone else. You can't let him investigate."

Raising any sort of question about his integrity would piss Sly off so badly she doubted they'd ever be able to have a civil word with each other again. But what did he expect? He'd gone *way* too far, had forced her into a corner. She had to fight back. It wasn't as if he'd been allowing their divorce to proceed, anyway.

"I will." Even though it would make her

life more difficult. For sure he'd seek custody of Jayden at that point. "I'm just hoping whoever will be investigating will wait until morning to question me. I'm not sure I'm up for it right now."

"Even if that happens, Sly will come by tonight — if only to see whether you're here instead of at a motel or somewhere else."

Of course he would. Had she not been so frantic, so shocked and upset, she would've been expecting him, too. "That's what you're waiting for," she said.

"Aren't you?" he asked in surprise.

She sighed. "I've been too distraught to even think about it. But now that you mention it . . . I can see him coming over. He wouldn't miss an opportunity to make my life difficult — and I'm sure you're now on the same short list I am."

He shoved a hand through his hair, which was sticking up as if he'd done the same thing many times already tonight. "You haven't heard from him?"

She hadn't checked her phone. She'd been so grateful to get away from the melee and have some quiet time in which to recover that she'd shoved her phone in her purse and left it there. She was dying to know if any of her stuff could be saved, but, at the same time, she was afraid she'd hear the opposite — that the firefighters hadn't been able to salvage anything.

She wasn't sure she could take that kind of news right now. "One sec."

She went into the kitchen, where she'd set her purse on the counter. "Nothing," she called back when she'd pulled out her phone. No missed calls. No texts. Did that mean the blaze had grown out of control? Was Sly and everyone still there, caught up in the emergency? Was Maude's house in danger?

"This is a bad sign," she said as she returned to the living room with her phone in hand.

Dawson turned to face her. "What's a bad sign?"

"That he hasn't tried to reach me. That makes me wonder if my entire house is burning to the ground — with everything I own inside it."

"It's natural to be worried, but try not to jump to any conclusions."

How could she not? "I feel bad for . . . for interrupting your life," she said. "I know you're under a lot of pressure to move Angela out of that facility, and to get the farm up and running —"

"This won't stop me," he interrupted.

"I don't even want it to *delay* you. I'll help

in the fields tomorrow."

"Don't you work at the diner?"

"No. Saturday's my day off, remember?"

"How can they spare you? Isn't that a busy day for the restaurant?"

"The busiest, but Petra can't watch Jayden. She volunteers at her church on Saturdays, so they always give me Saturday off."

"Why can't his father watch him? I mean, not tomorrow. Sly's working late tonight. But he should be available *some* Saturdays."

She nibbled at her bottom lip while trying to decide how much to say about her ex's parenting. "You'd think so."

"Have you ever tried to arrange it with him?"

"No."

"Because you don't want to deal with him?"

"Not only that. He's not very good with Jayden," she admitted.

A car passed on the highway. Dawson fell silent as he watched it but returned to the conversation the moment it went by without turning in. "Jayden's Sly's son, right? He's not from another relationship."

"I've never been with anyone else."

"How old is Sly? Your age?"

"No, he's your age. Two years older than me."

He leaned one shoulder against the wall, still keeping a vigilant watch on the drive while he spoke. "Why didn't you go off to college? Give yourself some time before settling down?"

"Part of me wanted to. But Sly didn't want me to leave, and we were so in love. I didn't see any reason to put off getting married. He'd already joined the police force, so he had a good job and . . . and I thought we'd have the perfect life together. We did have a perfect life together — at first," she added.

"Was the way he treated Jayden part of what came between you?"

She moved so that she could gaze out at the highway herself. "Definitely."

"The boy's only five, and he seems like a good kid. What could possibly be the problem?"

She was now close enough to Dawson that she could smell his cologne. That scent stood out because he didn't normally wear cologne. At least, she'd never noticed it before, and it made sense. Why would he put on cologne to go out and work in the fields?

But tonight, he'd gone to the bar.

Had he been hoping to find a woman?

With his looks, she couldn't imagine he'd have any trouble, despite his reputation.

"Sadie?"

She blinked at him. "Hmm?"

"What was the problem between Sly and Jayden?"

She'd been staring at him, imagining him at the bar dancing with . . . who knows who, and it made her feel . . . what? A trickle of *envy*? "Sorry, I'm tired," she said as she dragged her gaze back to what lay beyond the window. "Maybe you haven't noticed, but Jayden's sort of . . . sensitive. He likes art and dance, but he's not too big on sports."

"He's young yet," he responded.

She liked that he didn't put Jayden down for his interests, didn't seem to think it was the end of the world that a boy might not like what were traditionally considered "boy" things. Being different didn't make Jayden any less than other little kids, and she got the impression Dawson agreed with that kind of thinking. "Yes, but . . . I doubt he'll ever change. Sly keeps blaming me for making Jayden 'soft.' "

"Making him soft?" Dawson repeated.

"Yeah. He's always telling me to stop babying him. But I don't think *I'm* the reason Jayden doesn't like what Sly wants him to like. He just came to us that way."

Although she wasn't looking back at him, Sadie could feel the weight of Dawson's stare.

"He's going to have to accept his son for what he is at some point," he said. "It'd be smart not to screw the kid up too badly before that happens."

"I agree. But Sly doesn't get that. He thinks he can 'toughen him up.' "

"And how does he do that?"

She scrubbed a hand over her face. "By saying hurtful things that make Jayden feel inadequate. 'Come on, you don't want to be a dancer! Dancers are pussies.' That sort of thing. I hate the constant put-downs. If not for that, I'd probably still be with Sly. I was so beaten down, so convinced I could never unravel the mistake of marrying him — especially given that I had a child to care for and no education — that I wouldn't have left for only myself. To me, 'for better or for worse' meant exactly that. But the need to protect Jayden forced the issue. I hate knowing Sly's embarrassed of his own son, that he wants him to be anything other than what he is. It's so . . . damaging and hurtful — to both of us."

"If Sly's that hard on Jayden, how is it

that he has partial custody?"

"Sly hasn't been *physically* abusive." At least to Jayden. What he'd done to her — pressing her to have sex with him when she didn't even want him to touch her — definitely crossed that line. But she was too embarrassed to tell anyone about that. She felt as if most people wouldn't think it was a big deal, considering she'd slept with him for so many years before.

"Did you tell the judge about the put-downs?"

"I tried to, but he cut me off. The nuances I've shared with you . . . they weren't enough to get him to take action against Sly. This judge thinks of Sly as a fine officer of the law."

"Wow." Dawson rubbed his jaw. "As if I didn't hate your ex *before* we had this conversation."

"He's emotionally toxic," she said. "There isn't a better way to describe him."

Dawson didn't get the chance to respond. A pair of headlights swung into the yard, drawing his attention back to the window.

"He's here," he said.

14

Sly wasn't alone. Dawson watched as the police chief got out of the patrol car, too. Dawson hadn't had a lot of direct contact with Chief Thomas, but he was leery of the entire Silver Springs police force. When his parents were murdered, they'd focused on him right away, wouldn't believe a single thing he said. He'd never been treated worse, especially at such a terrible time.

Why did you kill them? What kind of a man takes a hatchet to his own parents? They didn't have to take in your worthless ass, you know. They did it out of the kindness of their hearts, and this is how you repay them? The detective who'd been given the case had kept him shut up in a cold, uncomfortable interrogation room, drilling him with those questions, as well as many others, for twelve hours — until he'd grown so weary of trying to fend off each new attempt to trick him into incriminating himself that he'd asked for an attorney. He'd made that choice not long before dinnertime the day after his parents were killed. He'd been at the station the whole day, had had *no* sleep, but it didn't matter that he'd tried to work with them for so long. In their eyes, asking for representation only confirmed his guilt. And all of this had been going on while the real culprit got away.

"Thank goodness," Sadie murmured.

"Thank goodness?" he repeated as the two men came toward the house. What did she have to thank goodness about right now?

"Chief Thomas is with him," she explained.

Apparently, she was even more afraid of Sly, and what he might do, than Dawson had realized. But he couldn't blame her. They both believed her ex was the one who set the blaze that'd very likely destroyed everything she owned. What regular arsonist would make so much noise, wait for confirmation that she was up — so she could get herself and Jayden out of the house — and then run away?

How he could do such a thing was another issue entirely. What if she hadn't smelled the smoke? What if she'd gone back to bed or tried to get their things out first? Or the fire caused an explosion he hadn't anticipated? How could Sly take the risk of killing the woman he supposedly loved *and* his own child?

He could do it because he'd rather her die, rather Sadie and Jayden *both* die, than let her follow through with the divorce, which revealed just how proud, arrogant and determined he was. His police uniform meant nothing. He was *not* one of the "good" guys. But after what Dawson had been through, it was tough for him to look at any law enforcement in a positive light. He'd seen the system up close, had learned that justice didn't always prevail and even trained officers stretched the law to accomplish what they hoped to accomplish. They could be as small-minded and prejudiced as the general public, maybe more so.

The knock that sounded came off brisk and purposeful. Sadie moved to answer the door; she knew it was for her. But Dawson caught her arm and held her in place for a second to indicate that he would handle this. This was *his* home. He needed to establish the fact that nothing would happen here of which he didn't approve. He had rights as a property owner. Remaining in charge, letting Sly and his fellow officers know that he would not tolerate another abuse of power, could be the only way to maintain some vestige of control over what was happening.

He took his time turning on the lights so they'd think they were dragging him out of bed — and that he hadn't anticipated this all along.

When he swung open the door, he didn't greet them or invite them in. He saw no point in the usual courtesies. He was beyond that sort of thing with Sly and the Silver Springs Police Department. They would never be friends.

"We're looking for Sadie Harris," Chief Thomas announced as a chill wind whipped at his hair and clothes and flooded into the house. "Don't suppose you know where she is."

Sly glared at him, so Dawson glared right back. He wanted to be sure Sly knew he wasn't going to forget what'd happened in the street in front of Sadie's house.

"I do." Dawson spoke to the police chief but only after he felt he'd made it clear to Sly that he would not be intimidated. "She and Jayden are here."

Sly opened his mouth to speak, but Chief Thomas lifted a hand to indicate he not get involved at this point. "Will you please let her know we're here? We'd like to speak to her."

"No problem." Leaving them standing on the stoop in the cold, Dawson shut the door. "You ready for this?" he whispered.

"Do I have any choice?" she replied.

"I can send them away, tell them to come back tomorrow."

"No, as frightened as I am of the truth, I'd like to hear about the fire — if it's out, if anything was saved. And if I have to talk to Sly, I might as well get it over with while Chief Thomas is around to keep him in line."

"Just be aware that Chief Thomas isn't necessarily your friend," he said.

"What do you mean?"

"His first inclination will be to protect his officer. Any bad behavior on Sly's part will reflect on him and the department as a whole. So take some time to recall what happened and tell it *exactly* as it occurred. Keep it simple and don't deviate from your story no matter what they ask or this could go down as unsolved. I don't want them to be able to establish any doubt or trip you up."

Her stomach churned with anxiety as she rubbed her hands on the sweatpants he'd loaned her. "How can they do that when I'm telling the truth?"

He frowned. "All too easily. I was telling

the truth, too."

With a quick nod, she signaled that she understood, and he opened the door, stepping to one side so that she could be seen in the opening, as well.

"Sadie, I'm so glad you're safe," Chief Thomas said.

"Thank you." She hugged herself as she glanced at her ex-husband. The expression on his face seemed to make her even more nervous.

"I hope you're here with good news," she told them. "Have they . . . Have they put out the flames?"

"They have."

"And?"

"I'm afraid there's significant damage to the living room and bedroom. What the fire didn't destroy, the water from the fire hoses might have damaged, so I'm not sure what you'll be able to salvage from those rooms. But the kitchen, bathroom and laundry areas are all intact."

"When will I be able to go back?"

"Not for a few days. It's a toxic mess right now, but if you'll give me a list, I can have someone grab whatever necessities you need, if they're still serviceable. Once we've finished looking things over, someone will let you know and then you can return and sift through what's left."

Dawson could only imagine how hard it had to be for her to hear those words. He'd never forget the night he was released from jail and came home to find the damage that'd confronted him. As if returning to the place where his parents had been murdered wasn't difficult enough, he'd been greeted by that graffiti: *Murderer.* The sight of it had felt like a kick in the gut. And then he'd had to walk through the house, through all the trash people had thrown in it, to find the damage to his folks' pictures and furniture and such.

"How's Maude's house?" Sadie asked.

"It's fine," Thomas replied. "The fire didn't reach that far."

"I'm so glad. And no one was hurt?"

"Not physically, no. Maude will have to file a claim with her homeowner's insurance, and it'll take some time to rebuild the place. That can't be good news to either of you. But things could've been worse. I'm proud of our firefighters for putting that fire out as fast as they did. They did a great job."

What a shame that they'd had to risk their lives in the first place.

"I'm grateful they arrived so quickly," Sadie said. "Maybe it means I'll still have some of my belongings."

The wind howled outside, tossing tree branches against the windows with an eerie scraping sound.

Thomas adjusted his belt. "I hope that's the case."

Sadie blew out a sigh. "Thanks. I appreciate the news."

"No problem," he said. "And now, if you wouldn't mind, I'd like to hear a bit more about how the fire got started. I know it's late, and you've got to be tired and upset, but I'd rather we have this talk sooner rather than later — while all the details are fresh in your mind."

"I understand," she said.

"It's too windy out here, though," Thomas told her. "Why don't you come sit in the car with us?"

Dawson expected her to agree, but she made no move to leave the house. "Since I called Dawson when it happened, and told him all about it, he might have something to contribute," she replied. "Let's talk in here." She looked to Dawson. "Is that okay?"

Dawson thought it was the smartest move she could make. Then they couldn't isolate and pressure her the way they'd isolated and pressured him a year ago. She wasn't suspected of a crime like he'd been, but if Sly started the fire, he'd have a vested interest in getting her to say some things and not others, or trying to discredit her story in various places.

Silently applauding her, Dawson moved out of the way so they could come in out of the cold. "Of course."

Sly wasn't pleased by his ex-wife's response. He lagged behind on the stoop for so long Dawson almost wondered if he'd refuse to come in. But he didn't want to be left out, or he wouldn't be here. He seemed to realize that if he *didn't* go with the flow, the conversation would proceed without him. Chief Thomas seemed somewhat indifferent to his displeasure — or at least undeterred by it. He'd already stepped inside, so Sly followed suit just before Dawson closed the door.

"Have a seat." Sadie took charge. Dawson refused to offer them anything, but the fact that she seemed so comfortable in his house — or maybe it was that she was wearing his clothes — further agitated her soon-to-be ex. As Sly brushed past, he hit Dawson's shoulder with his own, hard enough to knock Dawson back a step, so Dawson immediately shoved him against the wall. The exchange would've erupted in a fight, except the police chief whipped around and grabbed Sly, yanking him out of reach and standing between them.

"We'll have none of that!" he snapped.

"This is ridiculous," Sly grumbled. "Why are we doing this here? Let's grab Sadie and figure out what happened at my place, without this bastard."

"That's up to Sadie." Chief Thomas looked to her. "Given Dawson's history with this town, and how my officers feel about him, maybe we'd be better off —"

"No," she broke in. "I'm not leaving here. Jayden's asleep, and after what we've both been through, I don't see any reason to wake him."

Chief Thomas smoothed down his hair, which was still ruffled from the wind outside. "That's understandable." He arched an eyebrow at Sly as he gestured toward the couch. "Sit down."

Although Sly obeyed, he did so grudgingly. And he kept glowering at Sadie as if she'd betrayed him personally. Dawson considered that hugely ironic, given what they believed *he'd* done.

"What happened tonight?" Thomas asked, withdrawing a small notebook from his shirt pocket. "I'll take a few notes, if that's okay."

"Of course it's okay," she said. "There's just not a lot to tell. Someone set fire to my house. It's that simple."

"Do you have any idea who?"

When she hesitated, Dawson thought she might accuse Sly, as she'd done earlier, but she didn't. "No."

"You didn't see anything that might help identify the perpetrator?" Thomas asked. "Hear anything?"

The dark circles under Sadie's eyes seemed more pronounced than before. Besides the shock of having so recently escaped a burning house, it was nearly four in the morning and she hadn't gotten any sleep. "I heard some rustling outside. I tried to convince myself it was nothing. Houses have . . . settling noises and such."

"How do you know it *wasn't* a settling noise?"

"Because it turned out to be more than a little rustling."

Dawson couldn't help studying Sly while Sadie spoke. Her ex wasn't expressing any concern. Was he too angry to feel concern? Or did he already know what happened — as they suspected?

"What was the sound like?"

"Someone banging on the side of the house. My bedroom window looks out on the back, not the side, but when I got up, I spotted a man standing in the yard looking at me."

"How close was he?"

"About twenty feet from my window."

"Did you recognize him?"

She clasped her hands in front of her. "I can't say for sure. He was tall and slender, I know that."

"What was he wearing?"

"Jeans and a black sweatshirt."

"Did you see his face?"

"No, it was too deeply shadowed. He had the hood of his sweatshirt pulled up."

"What was he doing?"

She lifted Dawson's sweats so they wouldn't drag as she walked over to the chair across from the couch. "Just standing there, staring at me," she said as she perched on the edge of it.

"Did he come any closer? Yell anything? Make any gestures?"

"No. Once he saw me looking at him, he just turned, hopped the fence and ran down the alley."

"What kind of shoes was he wearing?"

"I didn't notice," she replied. "I was so freaked out to have a man in my yard in the middle of the night, especially a man in a black hoodie, that I panicked and nearly screamed. I was just trying to get a grip and calm down when I smelled smoke and realized the house was on fire."

"You're convinced it was the man you saw who started the fire?"

"Who else could it be? The fire started on that side — the side where I'd also heard the rustling and banging."

"I see." He took a moment to jot that down. Then he said, "Do you have any known enemies? Anyone who might have a grudge against you or wish you harm?"

Again, Dawson could see her deliberating on whether or not to voice her suspicions, but habit — and fear — got in the way.

"She has no enemies," Sly said, speaking for her. "Like I told you on the way over, I'd know if there was someone she didn't get along with. Whoever set that fire has to be this guy right here." He pointed at Dawson. "He's the only thing that's changed in this town over the past couple of weeks. And we already know what he's capable of."

Dawson wasn't surprised by the accusation; he'd been anticipating it. Now that he was out of jail, he was the town bogeyman. Even Sadie had tried to keep him away from the fire, knowing he'd likely get blamed if someone saw him at the scene. "And what would be my motivation for that?" he asked calmly.

"Maybe you like her. Maybe letting her move out here under the guise of trying to help her is your way of getting her into your bed."

Sadie started to say something, but Dawson overrode her. "Sadie's my employee," he said. "There's nothing more between us."

"Let's face it," Sly said. "You didn't like the way I reacted to her working here, so you did it to get the best of me."

Dawson chuckled at that. "Nice try. I admit I have no affinity for you. But this time I do have an airtight alibi. I was at the bar when the fire broke out and didn't drive to Sadie's until she called me. Several people saw me, one of whom was the bartender. I paid my bill *after* she called. The fire was already going by then."

"No one's accusing you," Chief Thomas said. "Officer Harris is going through an emotional time right now, but he will behave more professionally in the future, *right, Officer Harris*?"

Sly's nostrils flared, but his boss glared at him until he recited the desired answer. "Yes."

"Because we don't jump to conclusions," Thomas explained, speaking mostly to Sly as if he were talking to a recalcitrant child. "We're police officers, which means we investigate and go where the leads take us."

"What if those leads take you to one of your own?" Dawson asked.

Sadie stiffened at his words. Dawson could sense her tension. But he kept his gaze riveted on Sly. If Sly could throw accusations around, so could he. Maybe it would get Sly to state what he'd been doing when the fire broke out — if he had a solid alibi.

"What's that supposed to mean?" Sly jumped to his feet.

"*I* had nothing to gain by burning Sadie out," Dawson replied. "You, on the other hand, have been trying desperately to get her to come back to you."

"How dare you!" Sly charged toward him, but once again Chief Thomas intercepted by jumping up and grabbing the back of his shirt.

"If you value your job, you'll sit down and shut up!" he snapped. "I only brought you here out of respect for your connection to Sadie. So if you can't control your temper, I'll send you to the car, and you can wait there until I come fire your ass. *Do you understand?*"

Sly's face flushed red. It galled him to take a dressing-down in their presence. He knew how powerless it made him look, and being

277

perceived as powerful and important, being admired, was what he loved most. Dawson didn't know him well, but he was willing to bet on that.

"I won't stand for you, of all people, to ruin my life," he growled to Dawson and stomped out and slammed the door.

"Forgive Officer Harris," Chief Thomas said. "He's an . . . impassioned person, but he means well."

"Does he?" Dawson challenged.

Chief Thomas looked him up and down. "He's never been tried for murder."

"Well, if you do your job, he'll soon be tried for arson," Dawson said. "Or, since two people were in that house when he set the blaze, I'm thinking the charge could be *attempted* murder, which isn't too far off."

Thomas dropped the feigned politeness he'd exhibited so far. "You'd better watch yourself, son," he said. "I don't take accusations against my officers lightly."

"He's not the one making the accusation," Sadie said. "I am."

Thomas studied her more carefully. "You need to be careful, too, Sadie. You're talking about your husband."

Her chest lifted as she drew a deep breath. "I'm talking about my *ex*-husband, the person who's been stalking me for months."

There was a moment of silence. Then Chief Thomas said, "If he's been stalking you *for months,* why is this the first time I've heard about it?"

"I was afraid of what he might do if I reported him. The divorce isn't final. We're still fighting over money and custody issues. I knew lodging a complaint against him would only make matters worse. So I tried to convince myself that if I could keep the peace long enough, we'd eventually wade through the divorce and he'd move on, find someone else. I never dreamed the opposite would occur. That he'd only get *more* fixated on me. That the behavior would escalate. That he'd go so far as to burn me out of my house!"

"These are serious allegations," Thomas said. "Are you *sure* you want to make them?"

"I have a little boy to protect, and I may have lost everything I own tonight. I don't need any more trouble, so I don't do this lightly. I'm afraid of Sly, Chief Thomas. I need you to know that. I'm not saying I *know* he's guilty of setting my house on fire. But I am saying my gut tells me he did it, so please don't let him be the one to investigate."

Chief Thomas rubbed his chin for several

seconds before responding. "This puts me in a very difficult situation."

"Because you're his boss?"

"That and I can't believe he'd ever go so far as to commit arson. Sure, he acted up a bit tonight. But it's killing him to lose you. And he's worried. He feels as if his wife and son are out here alone with a man who hacked his own parents to death. How do you expect him to react?"

Sadie seemed so weary when she answered. "As I keep saying, I'm his *ex*-wife. That means I can stay where I want. And if he really cared about his son, he'd —" she caught herself and finished with what Dawson figured was a broader statement than she'd originally intended "— treat us both differently."

The police chief studied her. "It's been a hell of a night."

"That's why I'm hoping you'll honor this one request," she said.

"Dawson has an ax to grind when it comes to the department," Thomas said. "You realize that."

"I do. But from what I've seen, he's got good reason."

The police chief stiffened. "That won't help, teaming up with a suspected murderer against all the rest of us law-abiding citizens.

Now you're giving *Sly* some credibility."

"I have a right to my opinion. Dawson was found innocent. That means, in the eyes of the law, he has the same rights as the rest of us. I think it's time we consider him innocent until proven guilty."

"Fine. I'll put someone else on it," Thomas snapped and stalked out.

Dawson shoved his hands into his pockets as Sadie closed the door. "Do you think whoever he asks to investigate the fire will be impartial enough to do a decent job?"

"I doubt it. Sly is friends with everyone on the force. He'll be doing everything he can to poison the minds of those working the case. And let's face it — even if that weren't true, the police would rather villainize you than him."

She seemed so wiped out Dawson couldn't help feeling sorry for her. He understood that kind of weariness; he'd experienced it. "You shouldn't have sided with me."

When she said nothing, simply moved to the window and looked out, presumably at the taillights of the squad car Chief Thomas and Sly were in, Dawson added, "So why'd you do it?"

"I believe you're innocent," she said without turning. "That means I *had* to say it. What kind of person would I be if I didn't?"

"That's not a popular position here in Silver Springs."

Closing her eyes, she pressed her forehead to the glass. "Oh well." She straightened again. "Sometimes, the truth is just the truth."

He wished he could touch her. He'd had plenty of sexual thoughts where she was concerned, but this was more about comfort. "If Sly set that fire, he could be capable of almost anything. So if it makes any difference, I think you did the right thing telling Thomas about him."

"Except it might push him further."

"Or it might be the only thing that keeps him in check."

She sighed. "I hope it goes that way, but I don't think it will. I'm pretty sure I just started World War III."

And she had a child to protect. The odds were stacked against her. But Dawson wasn't going to let Sly get the best of her, not if he could help it. "Like I said, you can stay here until you get on your feet."

"Thanks," she murmured, but he could tell her thoughts were a million miles away. Was she psyching herself up for the battle ahead? Or was she remembering past times when taking a stand had only made her situation worse?

Putting his arm around her, he gave her shoulder a quick squeeze. He didn't want her to think he was hitting on her; he just didn't want her to feel so alone. But he wasn't even sure she noticed. She didn't react to his touch. She just stood there staring out at the darkness.

15

When Sadie woke up, Jayden wasn't in bed with her. Her chest tightened in panic as she sat up and looked around. How was it that she hadn't felt him get up? Where had he gone? They were no longer in their little house with the small, fenced yard and Maude puttering about outside. They were on a large piece of land — especially from his perspective — and that piece of land had lots of places to get hurt or lost. It even had a pond.

The instant terror tempted her to call his name, but she held off in case Dawson was still sleeping. As late as they'd both gone to bed, he *should* be sleeping. The clock on the nightstand indicated it was only nine-thirty. That wasn't *too* late, considering it had been almost five when Sly and Chief Thomas left. No wonder she hadn't felt her son slip away. She'd been passed out from exhaustion.

Without so much as a thought for her tangled hair, she scrambled out of bed and hurried past Dawson's room, pausing only long enough, once she saw his door standing open, to see that he wasn't in there. She was halfway down the stairs when she heard Dawson talking in a low whisper. "You want more cereal?"

"More chocolate milk!" Jayden's eager enthusiasm made his voice much louder.

"Shh!" Dawson said. "We're trying to let Mom sleep, remember?"

Sadie reached the ground floor as Dawson poured her son more chocolate milk. "It's okay. I'm up."

"Look, Mommy! We have cold cereal!" Jayden cried.

"Where did we get that?" She was the one who'd bought the groceries so far, and she hadn't purchased any processed cereal. Dawson had never mentioned that he wanted some, and she rarely let Jayden eat that kind of thing. The carton of chocolate milk Dawson put back on the table was new, too.

"We went to the store!" Jayden held up a sucker. "And I got *this*!"

"For later," Dawson quickly inserted. "After lunch or dinner. We talked about that, remember?"

Jayden didn't seem pleased about waiting, but he set the sucker reverently by his plate. "Yeah."

A grin tugged at Dawson's lips. "I wish everyone was so easy to please that a sucker would make all the difference," he said in an aside to her. "My sister's like that."

"Children are so innocent. She sounds the same. I'm looking forward to meeting her."

"She's definitely innocent." He gestured at the chair next to Jayden. "Want to sit down and have some cereal?"

Sadie almost said no. She doubted she could eat even if she tried. Her stomach hurt every time she thought about last night — the fire, whether or not she'd have anything left once the police allowed her to go back in, Sly's behavior when he came out to the farm with Chief Thomas. Everything she'd tried to avoid with him seemed to be happening, despite her efforts. But Dawson had turned what could've been a confusing and sad morning into a happy one for Jayden, and she didn't want to spoil her son's fun. "Sure. I'll have a bowl."

Dawson slid the box and the milk over to her. "You okay?" he murmured while Jayden was busy pretending his spoon was a rocket ship blasting off from his bowl.

"Yeah. I think so."

"You didn't get much sleep."

She covered a yawn. "Neither did you. And then you got up with my kid. I'm sorry. I didn't even realize he'd climbed out of bed."

"I had those guys coming to clear away all the junk and take it to the dump this morning, so I had to get up early. I couldn't miss them."

"So that pile of stuff that was in the yard is gone?"

"It is."

She crossed to the window to check. Sure enough, all the broken furniture and other things Dawson had thrown out were no longer cluttering up the place. Somehow that helped, was yet another thing from the past that'd been squared away. "Looks great. It'll be nice to have it gone, but I'm sorry you didn't get to sleep in, like I did."

"They were so loud I'm surprised they didn't wake you. Jayden certainly enjoyed watching the process."

"I feel bad you got stuck babysitting for me."

"I didn't mind, so don't worry about it. I hope it's okay that I took him to the store. I would've asked, but I hated to wake you, and I didn't dare leave him here alone while you were sleeping. I haven't been around him much — haven't been around kids in general — so I have no idea how far he might wander."

"I appreciate you being cautious, especially with the pond out back. But wake me if something like this ever happens again. I don't expect you to take care of my child."

"I wouldn't mind helping now and then."

She took a bite of cereal but couldn't even taste it. "I wonder what the police will find out about the fire," she said when she'd swallowed.

"I wouldn't get your hopes up too much."

She gripped her spoon that much tighter. "Why not?"

He glanced at Jayden, who was still making motor sounds with his mouth and pretending to send his spoon to "outer space."

"If it was who we think it was, I'm sure he was careful not to leave a trail."

She stirred her cereal around in the milk, trying to gain enough enthusiasm to take another bite. "He's smart," she agreed. "I doubt he would've done something like that unless he was sure he could get away with it."

"Exactly. Then there're the other factors — that he could possibly sway whoever investigates or tamper with the evidence. I wouldn't set my sights on getting some resolution for fear you'll only be disappointed. But we *can* hope that the fire was put out before you lost too much. What I heard last night made that sound like a real possibility."

"Yeah. I don't know how I'll replace what has been lost, so I'm praying it wasn't a lot."

He seemed to notice that she wasn't particularly interested in her food. "Try not to worry, okay? It won't help."

"Then we should stay busy. Are we going to work in the fields today?"

"With Jayden?"

"He'll just play close by. I'll keep an eye on him."

"No, you stay inside. Maybe you can both have a nap later. I'll take care of the fields. But I'm not going to work until afternoon. Last night Gage Pond, the bartender at The Blue Suede Shoe, told me a vagrant matching the description of the hitchhiker I picked up a year ago was spotted the same night by a man building a bunker for Alex Hardy."

"What man?"

"He didn't get a name — or can't remember it if he did. Do you know Alex?"

"I do. He comes into the restaurant all the time."

"What's he like?"

"He's about thirty-five. Shaves his head. Wears camouflage. Collects guns. Talks about buying junk silver and stocking up on ammo and food. Brags that he could survive on his property for a year even if the rest of civilization went to hell in a handbasket."

"He married?"

"Divorced. His wife moved away last year, after they split, with both kids. He didn't have a problem with it." She'd been jealous that Hannah Hardy had so easily managed to leave Alex behind. She wished she had the same option.

"Do you think he'll talk to me?"

"Might. He's anti-government, which makes the police nervous. Sly talked about him every once in a while, said he was building up an arsenal and the department was watching him with a skeptical eye. The fact that there's no love lost between them should be a good thing for you. At least you know he wouldn't be likely to take their side over yours."

"That's good. I'd rather not get shot trying to approach his place," he said with a humorless laugh.

"Why don't I go with you? That should make the approach easier. I could introduce you, explain what's going on. He'll recognize me."

"You think it would be safe to go along? And take Jayden?"

"I want to go!" Jayden said, even though he'd obviously just tuned in and didn't know what they were talking about.

Sadie ruffled his hair while she answered. "Of course. Alex has never hurt anyone, not that I know of. And I'd like to feel as if I'm doing some good somewhere. Might take my mind off my own troubles."

Dawson closed the cereal box before putting it in the cupboard. "Okay, then. We'll leave as soon as you're ready."

Getting ready wouldn't take her long. She had only one change of clothes — the T-shirt and sweats she'd washed last night — and no makeup or anything. Dawson had stopped and bought her a toothbrush at the 24-hour mini-mart, at least.

She helped her son down from the table and wiped his mouth and hands before dumping the rest of her cereal down the sink. As she put the bowl in the dishwasher, she noticed Dawson frowning at her.

"I hesitate to say this because I don't want you to think I'm criticizing your appearance again. I feel bad that I ever did that. But you need to eat more — for the sake of your health."

"My health is fine," she said. "As for taking it the wrong way, it doesn't matter how skinny I get. No one's going to want me as long as I've got Sly dogging my every footstep."

"I wouldn't say *no one,*" he said. At least that was what Sadie thought she heard, but he spoke in a mutter, as if he wasn't even really talking to her, and left the kitchen before she could ask him to repeat it.

The barbed wire fence surrounding Alex Hardy's place had half a dozen Keep Out and No Trespassing signs posted along the road. Once he saw that, Dawson was glad he'd brought someone who knew the property owner. Given the anger that simmered just under his skin these days, it wouldn't take much to get him in a fight. Sometimes he wished for a target, some way to vent his despair and frustration. And the person who owned this land looked like he'd be happy to interpret anything as a threat.

"Alex Hardy is coming off as seriously antisocial," he grumbled as he eyed the cabin-like home beyond the safety of the fence.

"He's not as unfriendly as you might think," Sadie said. "He just likes to look tough."

Dawson could feel her leg against his

whenever she moved. They'd swung by her place to get Jayden's safety seat out of her car, which had been necessary, but seeing the charred side of the house had been difficult for her. She'd barely spoken since. He'd pointed out that the other half of the house looked just fine, that there had to be some things left she could recover, but she hadn't really responded. She'd just turned her back on the whole sad affair, put Jayden's safety seat on the passenger side, because it required a shoulder strap, and climbed in next to him.

Fortunately, and sort of surprisingly, given all the signs, the gate to the driveway of Alex Hardy's place stood open. Dawson pulled in behind a red truck that sported several NRA bumper stickers and one that depicted a woman with bare breasts. "Should we leave Jayden in the truck, just in case?" he asked. "After all the press about me, once this guy recognizes who I am, there'll be no telling how he might react."

"He's not going to do anything." She unstrapped her son, and they all walked to the front stoop together.

They didn't have a chance to ring the bell. The door swung wide before they could even reach it.

"Wow. Alex. That was fast," Sadie said.

"Don't tell me you have motion sensors on the property these days."

A burly man with a long *Duck Dynasty* beard and a rifle tattooed on his arm looked out at them. "Not yet. Might get some, though. That'd be cool. I saw you from the window. Who's this?" He gestured at Dawson.

Sadie started to reply, but Alex cut her off before she could.

"Wait! I recognize you! Saw you on TV. You're that dude who killed his parents a year or so ago."

Dawson felt his muscles bunch. No matter how many times he suffered that accusation, it never got any easier. "They were killed, but I didn't do it," he said. "That's why I'm here."

Alex ignored his response and focused on Sadie. "Since when did you become friends with *him*?"

"We're not friends, exactly. Well, we *are* friends. But we're more employer/employee."

"You work for him? What about the restaurant? I just saw you there a few days ago."

"I've still got another week at Lolita's, but it wasn't paying me enough, so I had to look elsewhere," she said. "Dawson has hired me as a caregiver for his sister."

"Whoa! You're quitting Lolita's and working for the Reeds' son even though we don't really know . . . I mean, what does Sly have to say about that?"

"It's none of Sly's business."

"Since when did that ever stop him from getting involved?" he said with a laugh.

"You have a point," she replied. "He thinks he can weigh in on everything. That he owns this town, owns *me*. But I'll deal with it." She stopped Jayden from trying to slip inside the house to pet the cat that sat watching them with its black tail twitching from side to side. "Listen, Alex. Gage, down at The Blue Suede Shoe, mentioned that someone who put in a bunker for you saw a homeless man fitting the description of the hitchhiker Dawson picked up the night his parents were murdered. Do you remember anything about that?"

"He was from Santa Barbara," Dawson added, hoping to jog his memory.

"We need to reach him," Sadie continued, "to see if he can tell us any more about that vagrant — if he talked to him, what his name was, where he was from, where he was heading, if he had any tattoos or other distinguishing characteristics. You know, anything that might help us find him."

"*Really?*" Alex said.

Dawson was taken aback by his response. "Really. Why? What do you mean?"

He tugged on his beard as he talked. "You're looking for a needle in a haystack, man. I don't even remember the name of the guy who built my bunker. And even if you end up tracking him down, what're the chances *he's* going to remember anything about a bum he saw a year ago?"

"I admit the chances aren't good," Dawson said. "But I have to start somewhere, and it's all I have. I'll worry about the rest once I get that far. So do you have a receipt or work order or anything else he might've signed?" Dawson asked.

"Sorry. Don't keep crap like that. But the company was called Safety First. I remember because there aren't a hell of a lot of companies in this area that build bunkers, you hear what I'm saying? Maybe they can tell you the name of the dude they sent out. If you're *real* lucky, it might even be that he still works there."

"We'll see what we can find." Dawson lifted Jayden into his arms so that Sadie wouldn't have to keep him from trying to approach the cat and started back toward the truck.

"Thanks, Alex," he heard her say.

Although Alex lowered his voice, Dawson

could still make out his words. "I know Sly was no picnic, Sadie. I've had a couple of run-ins with him myself. But are you sure you haven't jumped from the frying pan into the fire by moving on to *this* guy?"

"We're not together, Alex. I just work for him," she reiterated.

"Seems to me like you're pretty set on helping him."

Even Dawson could hear the skepticism in Alex's voice.

"Because Dawson hasn't killed anyone," she said, her tone turning defensive. "He's a nice guy."

"Then I hope Sly doesn't kill him."

As angry as Dawson was, at the police, at Sly, at the vagrant who murdered his parents — at the whole world right now — he almost wished Sly *would* come after him. He craved the opportunity to put Sly Harris down in any kind of meaningful way. Sly deserved it.

Except he knew Sadie's ex wasn't the type who would ever fight fair.

16

Sadie took her son from Dawson as soon as they got back to the truck and strapped Jayden in his safety seat while Dawson used his phone to research the contact information for Safety First in Santa Barbara. He found a listing and shot her a "wish me luck" look before dialing. There was always a possibility that the company wasn't even in business anymore.

She fended off her son's pleas to eat his sucker two or three times with a "not now" or "after lunch" while trying to listen to Dawson's side of the conversation. Finally, she gave in, just to keep Jayden quiet. She figured one treat at an irregular time shouldn't cause any lasting damage.

Dawson had already identified himself and asked for the owner. She could hear him saying, "When will he be in?" and "Can you tell me if you have access to job orders for the company going back thirteen months or so?" over the crackle of the wrapper.

When he hung up, she raised her eyebrows in expectation. "So?"

"That was a woman by the name of Amber."

"And?"

"The good news is that they have every single job order since they opened their doors eight years ago."

"What's the bad news?"

"She wouldn't give me any more information. Said I'd have to speak to the owner, who won't be in until Monday."

"Did you get his name?" She'd heard him ask for it.

"Big Red."

"That's it?"

"That's all she gave me."

"I'm sorry you have to wait even longer."

"That isn't all bad. At least I still have hope," he said and waited for Sadie to get in before climbing behind the wheel.

"You let him have his treat?" Dawson asked, hitching a thumb at the pleased-as-punch Jayden.

"He couldn't wait any longer."

"You mean you got tired of saying no," he said with a chuckle.

"Essentially," she agreed.

Dawson leaned forward to see her son.

"You got lucky today, huh, bud?"

Jayden offered him a sticky but toothy smile.

Sadie was surprised when Dawson parked in front of The Mint Julep instead of continuing on to the farm. Silver Springs didn't have a lot of clothing stores. There was no mall, Target or Walmart, just a few small, expensive shops that catered to the wealthy tourists who came through. Sadie had purchased her blouse the other day from this place; it was her favorite boutique. But she'd found the blouse on the clearance rack. Typically, she couldn't afford to shop here, even though she stopped in once in a while to browse.

"What are we doing?" she asked as Dawson cut the engine.

"You need clothes," he said simply.

"I can wait. Chief Thomas told me I could give him a list of the things I need. I was planning to do that today."

"He also said that the bedroom was one of the most damaged parts of the house. I doubt there'll be much to salvage, and in the meantime I'm sure you'd like a few things — beyond that T-shirt and those baggy sweats."

She was so glad she'd grabbed her shoes before running out of the house, or she'd need those, too. She just wished she'd managed to save more of her and Jayden's belongings. She'd been afraid the electrical box or something else would explode, or she'd get blocked in if she lingered. "But . . . I don't really have the money right now. And what little I do have I need to reserve for Jayden."

"We'll get him some things, too. There's a 'nice twice' place for kids a few blocks off the main drag."

"I'm familiar with it." That was where she'd purchased most of his things since leaving Sly.

"We'll go there next." He lifted a hand. "No need to worry about the money. I'll front what you need as an advance against your wages."

Problem was, she'd need every bit of those wages for other things — like car insurance, day care, rent and utilities, so she could move out of the farmhouse and get back on her own two feet. She hated having to lean on someone she hadn't known all that long, someone who had enough of his own problems.

But what could she say? She and Jayden were wearing what they'd slept in. At a minimum, they'd need underwear and socks for when they bathed or showered later.

Which meant she had to buy them.

"Okay. Thanks." She scooted out the driver side right after he did and would've walked around to get Jayden, but Dawson beat her to it, and Jayden didn't seem to mind. He didn't reach for her once, didn't even look over at her as he would have if his father were carrying him. She found it so ironic that they both trusted Dawson more than they did Sly — intuitively — in spite of how everyone else felt about him.

Jessica Spitz, the owner, was inside the shop, creating a new display. She glanced up as the buzzer sounded over the door and stopped what she was doing. "Sadie! I read about the fire in the paper this morning. I'm *so* glad you're okay."

Sadie managed a smile, even though she felt extremely uncomfortable in what she was wearing, given how fancy the shop was, and how Jessica was always dressed like she was ready to walk down a red carpet in LA. It didn't help that she didn't have much money with which to rectify her situation and would have to check price tags so carefully. "Thanks. It's a bummer — that's for sure."

"But you have renter's insurance, right?"

Sadie didn't. She'd been so broke she hadn't even considered an additional bill.

But Jessica made it sound as if every renter would have insurance, so she avoided answering more honestly by saying, "I'll be okay," as if she *did* have coverage.

"How do you think the fire got started?" Jessica asked.

"What'd it say in the paper?" Sadie hadn't even thought to look. She'd been too distracted with the simple act of recovering and helping Dawson find the vagrant he believed murdered his parents.

"Not much — just that a fire broke out in your home after midnight last night and destroyed half of it before the fire department could put out the blaze. I hope you didn't lose too many of your things."

Sadie drew a deep breath. "So do I. The police won't let me go back yet, so it'll be a day or two before I find out what's left."

"I read that they're still investigating the origins of the fire."

"Yeah. That's what they told me, too." She wasn't about to mention that she thought it was arson. She supposed there was a chance that seeing a man in her yard right before she smelled smoke was a coincidence, but it had to be a very small one.

"I'm guessing it was faulty wiring," Jessica mused. "My aunt once had an electrical fire break out while she was on vacation. Burned her place to the ground."

"Wow. I'm sorry to hear that," Sadie said.

"Don't worry about it. Happened years ago." Her gaze shifted to Dawson. "And you are . . ." Once again, Sadie witnessed recognition dawn before she could introduce her new employer. "Dawson Reed," Jessica finished before they could answer.

Sadie knew he couldn't enjoy the notoriety he'd gained, but he dipped his head politely in spite of that. "Nice to meet you."

To Jessica's credit, she offered him a smile. "It's nice to meet you, too. So . . . what can I do for the both of you?" Her gaze swept over Sadie's comfortable but shapeless apparel. "I take it you need a few things to wear."

"A blouse and a pair of jeans should get me through, for now." Sadie didn't want Jessica to suggest too much, didn't want Dawson to feel as if he'd have to buy her a lot. Not only was she sensitive to the fact that she couldn't really afford to shop here, she didn't want him to feel she was taking advantage of his willingness to loan her what she needed until payday.

"I have a new brand of jeans that'll look great on your slender figure," Jessica said.

Slender sounded better than skinny, but mention of her size made Sadie self-conscious in front of Dawson. She knew what he thought of her weight. "Great. I'll try on a pair," she said. If Jessica liked the jeans, she knew she would, too, but she had no real hope that she'd be able to buy the latest and greatest, so she slowly gravitated over to the clearance rack, where she found a lightweight sweater that might work and a long-sleeved blouse.

Dawson was playing with Jayden. Sadie could see her son darting between the racks, trying to hide from him, could hear the squeals of delight when Dawson "found" him. Dawson seemed preoccupied until Jessica returned with the jeans she'd suggested and asked if Sadie was ready to "start a room." Then he looked up as if he was interested to see what she'd chosen.

"Sure." Sadie followed her into the two-stall changing room in the corner of the boutique.

"Make sure you come out so we can take a look," Jessica told her as she left.

Sadie checked the price on the jeans first thing — $125. She wasn't even going to bother putting them on, she told herself.

She tried the sweater first. She liked it, but it was on sale for $44 and the blouse was only $35.

"Are you coming out?" Jessica called.

Afraid she'd sound rude if she refused, Sadie reluctantly pulled on the jeans and walked out to model them. "I like the blouse, but . . . I'm going to pass on the jeans."

Jessica's face fell. "Why? They're stunning on you. Look at that ass!" She glanced over at Dawson for support, but he immediately went back to playing with Jayden. "And don't worry about the price," she added. "I'm going to give you whatever you need half off. It'll be my way of helping you bounce back from the fire."

"That's *very* kind of you," Sadie said. "But . . . are you sure?"

"Positive."

"Thank you." Although Sadie was grateful, she hated having to accept charity.

Jessica waved her off. "It's the least I can do after what you've been through."

Sadie allowed her gaze to stray to Dawson. Jayden had hid again and was waiting quietly to be found, but Dawson wasn't going after him. She'd thought, when everything grew quiet, that he must be on his phone, but he was looking at her, and the expression on his face surprised her.

"I think someone else likes the way they look, too," Jessica teased, but that only made everything grow awkward very fast. Dawson instantly shuttered the appreciation that'd been so apparent a moment before and pretended, like Sadie did, that he hadn't even heard what Jessica said and started patting the clothes rack Jayden was in as if he didn't already know Jayden was there.

"You should get them," he said once he'd flushed Jayden out.

She was still deliberating in front of the mirror. Together with the blouse, she'd be spending close to $100, even with the discount. That sounded like a fortune to her. She'd had to watch every penny for so long. But she couldn't complain about the expense, not when Jessica was giving her such a good deal, and she needed clothes right away. She'd been trying to figure out how to say no so that she could visit a thrift shop instead — she'd gotten really good at finding gems other people had given away — but with Dawson supporting Jessica, she felt cornered. Suppressing the nagging worry that she'd need the money she was spending, she smiled. "Okay. I guess I will."

When she came back out of the dressing room, she found Jayden sitting on Dawson's shoulders. "Look, Mommy! See how tall I am?"

At least *he* seemed to be having a wonderful time . . . Briefly, she wondered why his own father couldn't make him this happy.

"You'd better get some underclothes," Dawson said before she could approach the register. "You need that most of all, right?"

She didn't even get the chance to answer before Jessica jumped in. "Oh, I've got the perfect thing!"

The shop owner went to the lingerie section, where she picked up a pair of champagne-colored lace panties with a matching bra that'd been on display.

Sadie had never seen anything so beautiful and delicate, but that was what told her it would be out of her price range.

"Isn't this *gorgeous*?" Jessica said. "We have it in a small, too, which would be your size."

Sadie opened her mouth to try to direct Jessica to something more affordable. She didn't even need to see the price tag to know that set wasn't for her. But Dawson spoke before she could formulate the words. "We'll take those, too," he said and pulled out his wallet.

One carefully manicured eyebrow slid up on Jessica's lovely face. "*You're* taking care of the bill?"

He didn't answer that question, either. He just handed her his credit card, as if that should speak for itself, and she shot Sadie a knowing smile. Dawson had been watching Sadie's son while she tried on clothes, and now he was paying for what she'd selected — was even buying her underwear. Sadie knew how it appeared.

While Jessica took her time wrapping everything in perfumed tissue paper and putting it all in a pretty sack with a pink ribbon, Dawson started out ahead of her. Not wanting to be far behind his new hero, Jayden hurried after him, which gave Sadie a moment alone with the shop owner. "We're just friends," she said, hoping to set Jessica straight.

But Jessica wasn't buying it. "A man doesn't look at a friend like that," she said with a laugh.

As they picked up a few things for Jayden at the secondhand shop and then drove home, Dawson kept picturing Sadie as she'd probably look in the lacy underwear and bra set he'd just purchased. He tried to distract himself by turning on the radio. When that didn't work, he started going over everything he had yet to do today. And when that didn't work, he tried to think about whether or not he'd find the man who might've seen the hitchhiker he'd picked up the night his parents were killed. Usually, the murders triggered enough anger to drown out any other emotion, even sexual desire, but the vision of Sadie in those snug-fitting jeans had elicited such a deluge of testosterone it was hijacking his brain. The bra and panty set only made matters worse.

He was so consumed with fighting a constant erection it took him a while to realize Sadie hadn't said anything since they left the nice-twice shop.

"You okay?" he asked, glancing over at her.

She stared straight ahead. "Yeah. Fine. Thanks for fronting the money back there — for both of us. I'm grateful."

"And yet . . . you don't sound grateful. You sound upset."

She checked to see what Jayden was taking in — Dawson saw her do it. But the boy was so absorbed in playing with the measuring tape he'd found in the truck he wasn't tracking the conversation. "I'm not upset, exactly. It's just . . . that boutique we went to for me was expensive," she said. "And I have a lot of bills to cover."

He'd known her situation when he stopped at The Mint Julep, which was probably what was bothering her. "You need clothes," he pointed out.

"I know, but there are other places to buy them. I could've gotten mine secondhand,

310

just like what we did for Jayden."

"There's nothing like that here for adults."

"There's one in Santa Barbara."

"You were planning to drive to Santa Barbara today?"

"I could have. I might have. But it was so nice of Jessica to give me a discount, and you to loan me the money, that I felt as if it would be rude to refuse, and now I'm worried about what I've done."

Thanks to the space Jayden's safety seat took up, he could feel the warmth of her next to him. He liked having her so close, but it certainly didn't help him rein in his libido. "Sadie, you don't have to pay me back. As a matter of fact, I don't even want you to. I only said it was coming from your wages so you'd relax and, hopefully, enjoy yourself. Otherwise, I knew you'd refuse."

"Because I *want* to pay you back. Don't you get it? I appreciate your kindness and understanding, but I don't want your *pity*. I'm in a bad situation, which puts me at a disadvantage at the moment, but I'll get back on my feet eventually."

"So I bought you a couple of things," he said with a shrug. "What does it matter?"

"It matters because . . ." Her words fell off and she blew out a sigh.

"I'm listening," he said.

"It matters because I like you." She answered grudgingly while continuing to stare straight ahead. "I want you to be able to respect me."

He swerved around a pothole. "I *do* respect you!" Otherwise, he wouldn't be working so hard to keep his mental and physical distance. Not only was he trying to give her a little help, he was trying to give her the time and space to recover from ten years of emotional abuse — without asserting his own needs and desires.

"Then you can't treat me like a charity case," she said. "It makes me feel like you'll never view me as . . . as a responsible, likable, respectable adult. Someone who could . . . you know, be your equal."

He slowed to turn in at the farm. "Sadie, buying you those clothes had less to do with you than it did me, okay? Sure, you need them, but that only gave me the excuse."

She seemed surprised by his statement. "What do you mean?"

"It felt good to forget about my situation by buying you something pretty. Something you didn't have to reject because of price. Something that would be beautiful on you. And, okay, maybe even something that was a little extravagant. That was the appeal of it. I wanted to feel like a man again and not a suspect for murder or someone who, like you, has a lot to rebuild. I only said you could pay me back when we went in so you wouldn't refuse. I never planned on taking the money out of your wages. I know I chose things you wouldn't."

"But you spent so much on . . . on *underwear*!"

He couldn't help grinning. "I know. That was the best part."

Dawson's words stuck in Sadie's head for the rest of the day. She insisted on going out and helping him in the fields, but Jayden wouldn't stay close enough for her to be as effective as she wanted. She had to keep stopping to catch him before he wandered off. Not only that, she wasn't accustomed to such physical labor. And she was already battling such fatigue from being up so much last night.

"Go in and relax," Dawson told her. "You look like you're about to faint."

She dusted the dirt off her sweatpants. "I'm doing okay," she said, but his assessment had been far more accurate than she cared to admit. "If you can keep going, I can."

"I could keep going a lot longer if you'd go in and make us something to eat," he told her.

But they'd had lunch when they got home — meatball sandwiches — and it was only four-thirty. "You're hungry *again*?"

"I'm always hungry," he joked.

Breathing a silent sigh of relief, she pulled off the gloves she'd been using to protect her hands while she fought with some particularly deep-rooted weeds. "What would you like?"

"Why don't you warm up some of that Stroganoff? That's my favorite of what you've made so far."

"I can do that." She had the sneaking suspicion he was only trying to provide her with a good excuse to give up, but she was just weary enough to let him. "I can help more tomorrow, once I get back from the restaurant," she said. "I'm just so darn tired."

His muscles flexed as he kept fighting with the stubborn plant he was determined to remove. "You should take a nap after we eat."

"If I do, I won't sleep tonight. Nights are hard enough, you know? I can make it. Aren't you tired?"

She grew self-conscious when he looked up at her. She was covered in dirt and sweat. "I am, but I promised Angela I'd come see her tomorrow, which means I won't be able to work for a big part of the day. I need to make some progress this weekend."

"I feel bad," she admitted. "I'm the one who's getting in the way — me and all my baggage. I've just sort of . . . crashed into your life."

"It's fine. What happened last night was Sly's fault and not yours, anyway."

"Or whoever set the fire," she added.

Dawson leaned on his shovel. "You no longer think it was him?"

She shaded her eyes to be able to see Jayden. Her son had finally settled down and was digging in a muddy hole at the edge of their row. "I talked to Chief Thomas before I came out here. I had to tell him what to get, if he can, from the house."

"What has he found that would lead him to believe it wasn't Sly?"

"Nothing, yet. But he had a few things to say that made sense to me."

"Let me guess. He said that Sly would never do anything to hurt his own son."

"He did, but you already know I'm skeptical of that."

He stretched his back. "So what's causing you to second-guess yourself?"

She lowered her voice, in case any part of what she said carried over to Jayden. "He wouldn't want to do something that could possibly ruin his image or get him kicked off the force, let alone sent to prison. He loves his badge. It makes him a big shot, gives him power in this town. And power is what he loves most."

Dawson shook his head as he went back to work.

"You don't agree?"

"It's none of my business," he said.

"I'm asking your opinion."

He stopped again. "Honestly? I think he did it. Maybe what Chief Thomas mentioned — his badge and his ego — would stop him if he believed there was any chance he could get caught. But he thinks he's too smart for that."

"People blamed you for something terrible because you seemed like the logical choice, and they were wrong. I'm tempted to believe he did it, too — you know that. But I'd hate to make the same mistake with Jayden's father."

"I wouldn't wish what's happened to me on anyone, even Sly," he said. "But I was blamed for being in the wrong place at the wrong time, essentially. I didn't mistreat them beforehand, wasn't bullying, threatening or abusing them, the way Sly has bullied and threatened you. There was no pattern of aggression, not that anyone cared to cut me any slack for that. I was adopted, had a rough past and found them. That was all it took." He jammed his shovel even deeper into the ground. "If I have my guess, Sly didn't like that you suddenly had an ally, some other way to make money and survive. He felt he was losing his grip on you and needed to do something to shore it up, something that would force you back under his control once and for all."

He was echoing her own thoughts — the thoughts she'd had before Chief Thomas got in her head, anyway. "Yeah. You're right," she agreed. "It's just hard to believe that . . . that he would do such a thing. Because if he would go *that* far — what might he do next?"

"Good question," he said. "Regardless of what Chief Thomas had to say, you have to stay on your guard. We both do."

17

Someone was skulking around her house, a dark shadow that Sadie could see from her window but couldn't completely make out. He was wearing a dark hoodie, pulled over his face. *He's back,* she thought. Only, suddenly, she wasn't at *her* house peering through the window at all — she was at the farm, gazing out at the fields, and she could smell smoke again. She was trying to scream, to warn Dawson to get out of the house, when she opened her eyes and, heart pumping, blinked at the semidarkness.

There was no smoke. Everything smelled like it usually did — a little musty, since the house was so old. Those sights, sounds and images were all a dream.

It felt late, yet the light was still on in the hallway, the TV blaring downstairs. She'd left it that way when she came up to lie down with Jayden because she'd been planning to go back and wait for Dawson to finish up outside. She'd wanted to feel secure in the fact that they were both in for the night before retiring but had fallen asleep as fast as Jayden had.

So where was Dawson? After she'd served him the leftover Stroganoff, he'd said he'd work for only another hour or two. Had he ever come in? Was he in his bed? If so, why'd he leave the TV and lights on?

Maybe he'd been too tired to bother with that sort of thing, she thought, but she knew, instinctively, that would be odd for him. He was a man who took care of things. He took care of people, too; she was an obvious example. He would've locked up and turned everything off before going to bed.

Still struggling to overcome the last vestiges of sleep — and the effects of that nightmare — she leaned up on one elbow and squinted to see the clock. It wasn't as late as she'd thought — only eleven. Dawson could easily be watching the TV she heard.

Jayden was snuggled close to her. After kissing his forehead, she slid him over so she could get out of bed. She was wearing Dawson's clothes again; she'd put her own sweats in the washer after working outside.

Although she was plenty warm, the hardwood floor proved cold enough that she wished for her slippers. It was so easy to take the little things for granted — until they were gone.

Thoughts of how she was going to recover from the fire threatened to commandeer her mind yet again. Before she'd gone to sleep, she'd decided that, with the way things were going, she had only one option: she had to save every dime she could and leave Silver Springs as soon as possible. Dawson was right. That Sly would set her house on fire was a warning sign, and she'd be stupid not to heed it. He'd finally gone too far, so far she felt justified in escaping any way she could, and in taking their son with her.

But she knew it would be some time before she had the money to leave, and she didn't have many options in the meantime except to watch her back, so she pushed away those worries. Chief Thomas had called just before she put Jayden to bed to say that he had someone going through the house at that very moment, and he'd bring the items on her list — what they could salvage — tomorrow. The officer he'd sent said he couldn't find the pictures of Jayden or her parents, which concerned her, but that didn't mean they weren't safe. The officer didn't say they'd been destroyed, only that the plastic storage container she kept them in wasn't in the bedroom closet where she'd told him to look, which was potentially good news. If the container wasn't there, the pictures weren't, either, so she must've moved them.

Hopefully, she'd put them in a safe spot. Which might've been the case. No spot could've been worse than the closet.

So, overall, she should be feeling grateful, not panicked, she told herself. Her situation might not be as bad as she'd first thought, on the recovery end of things, anyway. She was just overwhelmed by how hard it was going to be to escape and start over — and it didn't help that she was disoriented and uneasy right now, especially when she passed Dawson's room and found the door standing open and the bed made.

She checked the bathroom. He would've showered before bed. He was particular about his hygiene. But she couldn't detect any recent moisture or anything else that might suggest a shower had recently taken place.

He had to be downstairs, she decided, must've fallen asleep on the couch. But when she reached the living room, it was empty. So were the kitchen and laundry room.

"Dawson?" Despite trying not to let herself be spooked so easily, she could hear a tremor in her voice.

After searching the ground floor again and peering out the windows, she returned to the foot of the stairs and gazed up at his parents' room. Surely he wasn't in *there*. But where else could he be? He had to be home. His truck was in the drive.

Her stomach cramped as she crept slowly back up the stairs and tried the knob.

Locked. Thank the Lord. Except that did nothing to explain where he might be. It was pitch-black outside. He couldn't be working . . .

You have to stay on your guard. We both do. Those words came back to her as she tried his cell phone. He'd been talking about Sly.

She listened to see if she could hear his phone buzzing or ringing in the house but heard nothing.

"Answer, damn it," she muttered, but he didn't pick up. And when she tried again, his voice mail came on for the second time.

This is Dawson Reed. Leave a message.

Had he caught a ride into town? Was he sitting in The Blue Suede Shoe? He'd gone there last night, hadn't he? And it was a weekend. Maybe he came in from work, realized she was sleeping and left.

But she felt certain, because of Sly, he'd leave a note or something in case she woke up.

She was afraid her ex-husband had driven out, waited for it to get dark and ambushed Dawson while he was coming in from the fields . . .

She covered her mouth as a vision of what that might look like flashed before her mind's eye. That told her what she *really* thought when it came to what Sly was capable of, didn't it?

"Shit. Shit, shit, shit." She hurried back downstairs and began rummaging through the "junk" drawer she'd reorganized in the kitchen. She'd seen a flashlight in there . . .

Fortunately, it wasn't hard to find — and it worked. The beam wasn't as strong as she would've liked, but she also had her phone. Although hesitant to leave Jayden after what'd happened last night, she was only going out on the farm. Everything seemed fine at the house, except that Dawson wasn't in it. She'd lock up and keep an eye out while she checked the fields. She couldn't leave Dawson out in the dark alone; he could need help.

"You better not have done anything," she told Sly, even though he wasn't around.

Had he come out here and caused trouble just as they'd anticipated? What else could've happened?

She remembered how quickly Sly had reached for his gun while her house was burning, and that was right in the street! If Chief Thomas hadn't shown up when he did, her ex might've drawn his weapon — and used it.

The weather was cold enough that she pulled on the coat she found hanging on one of the hooks in the mudroom — the one Dawson had loaned her before.

Please be okay . . . After the fire and how belligerent Sly had behaved at the house, not to mention her nightmare and what had happened at this farm a year ago, she was having a difficult time *not* imagining the worst. What if she found Dawson lying in a pool of his own blood?

Or worse . . . What if she couldn't find him at all? What if Sly had killed him and dragged him off to some remote burial site where his body would never even be recovered?

Sly wouldn't do that, she told herself. But she'd seen crazier things happen in the true crime shows she watched.

The door, when she closed and locked it behind her, sounded overly loud. She feared

Sly would jump out of the darkness at any moment and choke her, or kill her in some other way. If he got away with it, he'd have full custody of Jayden without even having to fight for it. Then he could make sure Jayden was no longer "babied," that he was brought up to be a "man" according to Sly's definition. Sly wouldn't even have to worry about how he'd raise Jayden on his own, since his mother would do most of the work for him.

The hair on the back of Sadie's neck stood on end as she swung the beam of the flashlight across the yard. What she saw in that white circle seemed innocuous, but it was what she didn't see that scared her. What was moving around outside it?

She dearly hoped it wasn't her ex-husband.

Drawing a deep breath for courage, she left the back porch and headed to where she'd been with Dawson earlier. He might've stopped working there to fix the watering system or repair the barn, which meant he could be almost anywhere. But he hadn't planned to stay out very much longer. Given that, she guessed he wouldn't have taken on a new project, that he'd try to finish what he'd been working on and then quit.

Once she got out there, however, she saw no sign of him — just his shovel cast off to one side as if he'd tossed it away or dropped it.

Her heart began to race; she could feel it bumping against her chest. "Oh God," she whispered. "No, please."

Directing her flashlight at the freshly turned earth, she began searching for blood or any other sign of foul play. If Sly had harmed Dawson, he wasn't going to get away with it. She'd see to it that he was punished, no matter what she had to do. But the thought that Dawson might be hurt was almost more than she could take in the first place. She'd feel bad if *anyone* were hurt, but especially him. Maybe she hadn't known him long, but she'd begun to care about him.

Her eyes filled with tears, making it that much harder to see. As she moved her light in an ever-widening circle, she hoped to find *something.* But she didn't. She was about to go in and call the police. Sly was part of the force, and most of the other cops were poisoned against Dawson, but what else could she do? Time could be of the essence, which meant she needed to act quickly. She could only hope that there was someone who would respond with a measure of integrity in the performance of his job.

Then she spotted something. There, under the tree.

Her breath caught in her throat as she lifted the flashlight higher to get a better look.

A second later, she realized what it was: Dawson's boots.

Sadie's hands were on his body, up under his shirt, feeling his chest. Dawson wished those hands would move lower. He hadn't been touched intimately in eighteen months or more — other than the one cell mate who'd tried to grab his junk in the middle of the night and lost a tooth for the effort.

He felt his body react, felt himself grow hard before he realized they weren't even in the house, let alone his bed.

What the hell? What were they doing outside? Was this another of his many fantasies?

"Dawson? Can you hear me?" she said.

He managed to lift his heavy eyelids so that he could take in the sight of her. She was bent over him, wearing a big coat — *his* coat, he realized — crying. A flashlight lay on the ground beside her, its beam shooting off across the field. "What's wrong?" he mumbled.

"That's what I'm trying to figure out. What'd he do to you?"

He caught and held her hands before she could get him any more worked up. "What are you talking about?"

"Sly!"

"He was here?"

"That's my guess. Did he hurt you?"

Dawson couldn't remember seeing Sly tonight. He didn't feel any pain, either. But he was so groggy — the result of all the sleep deprivation he'd suffered since being released from jail. And it was awfully strange to find himself outside. How did he get here?

Suddenly, the answer came to him. He'd been too exhausted to keep working but was too stubborn to quit. He'd promised himself he'd take fifteen minutes and rest under the closest tree before finishing the row he was on. At that point, he must've sacked out, fallen so deeply asleep that he would've spent the whole night out here if Sadie hadn't awakened him. "Wait. Sadie, it's okay. *I'm* okay. I fell asleep, that's all."

He expected her to pull away, but she didn't. He could see the shine of the moon in her eyes as she stared down at him, her chest rising and falling rapidly from her fear and upset.

"You scared me," she whispered.

"I'm sorry." She was so upset he couldn't help letting his own hands slip inside that heavy coat. He was seeking the soft feel of her skin, which he found at her waist, but he was also hoping to calm her, to let her know he was right there, all in one piece, and she had no reason to fear. "Nothing happened."

"So . . . Sly hasn't been out here?"

"No. Everything's okay," he replied, except that they were both touching each other and neither one seemed eager to let go.

"God, you feel good," he said with a hoarse laugh, but he felt too guilty making a move on her to continue. She worked for him. And she hadn't even escaped her last relationship yet. He didn't want to give her the impression that she had to put out for him in order to retain his friendship or his support — or to have a place to stay or keep her job or whatever. "Sorry, I . . . I didn't mean to get out of line." He forced himself to let go of her, but she didn't seem offended. On the contrary, she caught his hands — and moved them higher, to her breasts!

The testosterone that shot through him in that moment drew every muscle taut. "Sadie . . ."

She must've heard the desperation in his voice; he heard it himself. He was trying to warn her that it wouldn't be difficult to push him past his own restraint. He hadn't been living a normal life for the past year; that put him at a distinct disadvantage. But she still didn't withdraw. She covered his hands with hers, holding them in place. "Don't talk. I won't listen. I *can't* listen, not right now. I just . . . I want to touch and be touched. I want to experience something besides anger and remorse and fear." She lowered her voice. "I want to make love to a man I actually desire. I can't even imagine what that would feel like."

"But you don't realize how much this could complicate things," he said, struggling to keep his head clear. "We don't even know each other all that well, and we're both in a mess. It's too big of a risk."

"I don't care about the risk," she said. "I'm tired of fighting *everything* in my life. I need a time-out, the chance to experience something breathtaking. As long as we both want this, what will it hurt? I mean . . . I may not be all that attractive to you, but sometimes the way you look at me makes me think —"

"Don't say that," he interrupted before she could even finish. "You're wrong. I think you're beautiful."

"Then what's one night? Why can't we let ourselves have a few hours of mind-numbing pleasure before we go back to the battle that has become our regular lives? In the morning, we'll pretend it never happened. We'll be responsible and cautious again. Just . . . not right now."

Dawson wasn't sure they could ignore having crossed such a line. But he couldn't bring himself to argue anymore, not when she came off so earnest. And once she straddled his hips, he knew he'd lost the ability to refuse. The pressure of her bottom against his erection set off an atom bomb of sexual energy that made him want to rip off her clothes.

"Okay. Sure. One night. We can forget about it tomorrow. Now let me taste you," he said, and a moment later they were kissing deeply, frantically, and fumbling to reach bare skin.

It didn't take long for Dawson to find the latch on the lacy bra he'd bought her earlier and snap it open. Sadie felt the tension give right before he peeled off the coat she was wearing as well as her shirt. She'd never had another man's hands on her breasts. As Dawson's fingers slid lightly over her nipples

331

— seeking, exploring, enjoying — she gasped and heard a guttural sound come out of him in return.

"We'd better take it slow, or I'm afraid I'll disappoint you," he muttered. The pounding of his heart, which she could feel beneath his solid chest, indicated he wanted to take it anything *except* slow. But she wasn't worried either way. She didn't care how he "performed." She just needed to feel close to someone — a man she could admire — for a few minutes. And, in that regard and many others, this was exactly what she craved, even if she never reached climax. In this moment, she was no longer isolated, no longer alone.

"All I need is to feel your body and let you feel mine," she told him as she pulled off his shirt. "To get drunk on desire. To pretend as if I'm someone else, someone who hasn't screwed up and missed all the good things in life." She didn't want him to feel any pressure. She preferred he let go and enjoy himself as she was doing — allowed himself to get carried away. He deserved a time-out as much as she did . . .

The earth felt cool and moist as he rolled her onto her back. She guessed they'd be filthy when they were through, but, as he stared down at what he'd revealed when he removed her coat, shirt and bra, she didn't care. Although she couldn't make out his expression, not with it being so dark and the moon creating a halo around his head, she didn't need to. She could tell he liked what he saw and that he wanted to see more, because he stripped off the sweats he'd loaned her next and ran a finger over her new panties — where the thin fabric covered the most sensitive part of her.

She shivered at his touch.

"I knew you'd look beautiful in these," he said. "I almost hate to take them off."

"I hope you're not going to let that stop you," she said with a breathy laugh.

"Hell no," he responded and slid them down over her hips so she could kick them off.

Sadie was literally throbbing with the desire to feel him inside her. Had she ever been this eager for Sly? If so, it'd been years ago. For the first time in ages, *she* was choosing who she wanted to touch her. That felt as liberating as it was intoxicating.

After he spread out his coat for her to lie on, she reached for the zipper of his pants, but he stopped her. "Not yet," he murmured and bent his head to kiss her neck, her collarbone and then her breasts.

Sadie could hardly catch her breath for

the excitement pouring through her. The smell of the earth around them, the cool night air wafting over her bare skin and the moon shimmering high above made the experience almost surreal.

Maybe she was dreaming, she told herself — except a dream had never felt *this* good.

"That's out of this world," she said as he took her nipple in his mouth. The warm wetness of his tongue sliding over her nearly melted her bones . . .

He moved to the other breast, but he didn't only focus there. While one hand continued to stimulate the nipple he'd just left, the other traveled lower.

Sadie jerked when he touched her. She wasn't sure she'd ever been so aroused. And he'd hardly done anything yet.

"You like that?" he murmured.

"I've never wanted anything more," she said.

His teeth glinted in a smile as he lifted his head to watch her while he slipped a finger inside her.

Sadie gripped his wrist. She wasn't sure why. What he was doing was just so . . . intimate. She felt the need to hang on to him, especially as the tension began to build in her body. She was going to climax quickly and easily, which hadn't been the case in several years. Sly hadn't been a *terrible* lover. He'd insisted she come every now and then. But those encounters had almost been worse than the ones where he simply took his pleasure and went on his way. She'd had to work so hard with him, and he got so angry if she couldn't achieve what he wanted. The effort and energy required on both their parts often made him cross before they were through. Rarely did she feel any closer to him after.

But this . . . this was an entirely different experience, something fresh and new and beyond titillating. She liked the way Dawson handled her body. He was confident yet respectful. And although he seemed to be as caught up in her as she was him — as eager for his own release as any man would be — he made her believe that the more she enjoyed their lovemaking, the more he enjoyed it, as well.

Maybe that had been the problem with Sly. Even when they were having sex, she'd felt alone, or merely a means to an end. Occasionally, he'd gone so far as to show her a porn flick in order to teach her how to "really" turn him on, which made her feel as if she didn't have the power to turn him on as she was, and that only made matters between them worse.

"I wish we were in the house so I could see you clearly," Dawson breathed as her legs began to quiver. "I love watching this, love watching you."

She didn't need any encouragement. She'd had too many fantasies that involved him. But what he said certainly didn't hurt. A moment later, the most spectacular climax rushed through her. With a groan, she let herself soar with it, let herself embrace the pleasure he was providing.

The release felt so welcome, so cathartic . . .

She closed her eyes, savoring the moment, and didn't open them again until he pulled her earlobe into his mouth. "That was nice," he murmured.

"That was the best thing I've felt in a long, long time," she admitted.

"Good." She could hear the satisfaction in his voice. "I'd like you to come again, when I'm inside you, but I shouldn't make any promises. You've got me so excited I'm not sure I can hold out for long."

He'd taken the safe route to guarantee she wouldn't be disappointed. She recognized that — and found it endearing.

"Remember, you're dealing with a guy who's been in jail for a year," he added.

"You don't have anything to worry about,"

she told him. "You've already surpassed all my expectations. I just wanted to be with someone and have it be free and easy and enjoyable for a change." Although she made it sound as if almost any man would do, that wasn't true. She'd felt an attraction to him from the first moment they'd met, and that attraction had only grown stronger as she'd come to know him. She just didn't want him to think she was taking this too seriously when she'd promised otherwise. And, since she'd be leaving as soon as she could save enough money, she didn't want to misconstrue what he could expect in the future.

"Should we go inside — to my room?" he asked. "You can't be too comfortable out here."

She considered the suggestion but shook her head. This was a moment out of time, and it needed to stay that way, needed to be separate from the lives they were living, or it could change everything, and she couldn't afford to have it do that. She needed her job. She also needed a safe place to stay, until she could get out on her own.

"No. That's where reality resides," she said. "This is . . . something else, a dream, and I'm not ready to go back to reality quite yet."

He seemed to understand, because he didn't press her. "Okay." He kissed her — slowly and gently at first but with more need and urgency as their tongues met and intertwined. After that there was no time for talking. Sadie didn't want to talk, anyway. She was too busy removing his pants.

"What about birth control?" he asked.

She could tell he'd been putting off the question, that he hadn't wanted to ruin what they were experiencing by forcing her to face the possibility of pregnancy.

"I don't have anything," he admitted.

She was still on the pill, because of what Sly had done, insisting she provide sex even though they were split up. She wasn't about to allow her ex to get her pregnant. One child with him was enough. "I've got that covered."

She was afraid Dawson would question her. If she and her husband had been split up for a year, and she hadn't been with anyone else, why would she still be on birth control? Any guy would wonder. But Dawson was too caught up to think about the ramifications. In this moment, he wanted only one thing, and that one thing precluded critical thinking.

"Thank God," he responded and pressed inside her.

18

He was having sex with his sister's caregiver on the ground outside, and she'd worked for him less than a week. On some level, Dawson knew it was pathetic that he'd caved in to his libido so soon. From the beginning, he'd pretended he hadn't hired Sadie because he was attracted to her. He'd told himself she was too skinny, that he was only trying to help her, that he had too much going on at the moment to worry about satisfying his sexual urges.

Now he knew that was at least partially a lie. He'd *tried* to keep his thoughts where they needed to be, but he liked so many things about her. And those legs! Every time he'd seen her since that night at her house, he'd felt a tug down deep in his gut. He'd gone to the bar, hoping to find someone with whom he could safely vent his sexual frustration, but no one had been remotely appealing to him. Sadie had been all he could think about even then.

In any case, he couldn't regret succumb-ing — not when feeling her beneath him brought such sweet pleasure. Since he'd already gotten her off, he thought she might become sort of impassive. He'd had a partner or two like that before, who reacted mechanically. But what happened earlier didn't seem to make any difference with Sadie. She remained engaged and respon-sive, which excited him even more. He enjoyed every second with her, loved the way she cast all reservations aside and threw everything she had into making love with him. Despite the fact that he was the only person she'd ever been with besides her ex-husband, she wasn't timid.

He'd been right that it wouldn't take him more than a few minutes to reach climax, however. The pleasure was too intense to be able to hold off. As the tension built, he wished he could prolong the moment even as he couldn't wait to reach that pinnacle. For a change, he was facing a good problem, the best kind of problem there was . . .

As he let himself go, he felt her hands in his hair, her mouth on his neck, and knew one time with her would never be enough. He'd barely finished, yet he wished he could do it all again. But he didn't know how this would affect her, what she might be like tomorrow. He worried that she'd feel some remorse. As he'd said, they didn't know each other all that well.

"We need a shower." He was slumped over her, trying to catch his breath. He hadn't had to put in a lot of work or effort; it was the level of excitement that had his heart racing. "I've done a lot of things in these fields, but I've never made love in the dirt," he said as he eased his weight to the side.

"You should do it more often," she said. "You're good at it."

That she could be so cavalier with that suggestion bothered him a little. She didn't seem to care one way or another if she was his partner when that occurred. But after what she'd been through, he couldn't blame her. He wouldn't want to get into another relationship, either, not if someone like Sly was all he'd ever known.

After pecking her lips, he got up and gathered their clothes as well as the flashlight.

"Hey, some of those are mine," she said when she understood that he wasn't going to hand them back.

"But you can't put them on or you'll just have to take them off and wash them in the house," he said. "We've been naked for the past fifteen minutes or more. We can last a bit longer. Come on!" Grabbing her hand, he helped her to her feet and together they ran for the house.

"You locked it?" he said when they reached the back door and couldn't get in.

"I was afraid something had happened to you! I couldn't leave Jayden vulnerable while I checked."

"True. Where's the key?"

"In the pockets of the sweats I was wearing."

He had her hold the flashlight while he fumbled around with what he was carrying until he came up with it. "Whew! Good thing. Or we'd be banging on the door, hoping to wake a five-year-old so he could let us in."

"If that were the case, we'd *have* to put on our clothes whether we were dirty or not," she said.

They were both laughing at how funny it would be to get locked out while they were naked as they spilled into the house. Then Dawson dropped their clothes on the floor and pulled her into the bathroom.

"What are we doing?" Sadie asked.

"I told you. We're going to take a shower," he replied.

"Together?"

He turned on the water. "Why not? It's no more intimate than what we just shared. And it's still tonight, isn't it?"

Her eyes twinkled with a mischievousness he hadn't seen in them before. She was having a good time. So was he. "It is."

As he tested the temperature, she stood back and looked him over.

"I don't think I've ever been examined so closely," he said.

"It was too dark outside to see you very well."

"So you're making up for it?"

"What can I say?" A playful smile curved her lips. "I've never seen a man who isn't circumcised."

"I'm glad I get to be the one to broaden your education."

"You have a beautiful body."

They'd given themselves until tomorrow to resume their usual roles. That meant he could kiss her. And he did. He lifted her chin and covered her mouth with his as he'd been dying to do since that night at her guesthouse when he'd forced himself to remain on the couch. He'd kissed her outside, too, but this was different, more meaningful because there was no sexual intention behind it — no *immediate* sexual intention, anyway.

When her arms went around his neck, and her naked body came up against his, he clasped her to him. *That* was a nice feeling, almost as good as sex itself, he thought.

"And did I tell you I like the way you touch me?" she asked, gazing up at him as he lifted his head.

He slid his hands down her back and over the rounded cheeks of her ass. "You're going to have to give me another chance — whether it's tonight or some other time."

"Another chance to —"

"Make love to you," he finished. "In a bed, when I don't have to fear you're uncomfortable, and when I'm not coming off eighteen months of celibacy, so I have the stamina to last."

"You're more frank than I expected," she said with a laugh.

"We're just being honest here, right?"

"We're just being honest," she agreed and kissed him as if she was testing out how it might feel to take the initiative.

"I've got an idea," he said against her soft lips.

She seemed reluctant to pull away. "And that is . . ."

"After this, let's go upstairs."

"I think that was always the plan. We have to go to bed at some point."

He could hear the teasing note in her voice. "I'm not planning to sleep. I want you in *my* bed, not yours."

"I'm not sure that would be wise," she said, but she didn't seem entirely committed to her refusal, which told him more than mere words.

"It's still tonight," he reminded her, making what she'd said before a commitment.

"But we're supposed to be keeping what happened outside separate from what happens in here," she reminded him. "We're not doing a very good job of that."

He, for one, was glad. "We'll worry about tomorrow when tomorrow comes. Tonight, I want *you* to take the lead."

She pulled back. "What?"

"That's right." He tugged her into the shower with him. "You make all the moves. Do whatever you'd like to do, and I'll go along with it."

"You're putting *me* in charge."

Nudging her beneath the spray, he grabbed the soap and began to run it over her breasts. "Why not?"

She watched his hands as they moved. "I probably won't be any good at it. I've never had the opportunity."

Because she'd been dominated by a control freak ever since she was in high school.

"I guessed as much. That's why I want it. I'd like to see what you'd do if you could do anything," he said, but only an hour later, when they were in his bed as he'd wanted, he wasn't sure they should've acted on that idea. The way she'd made love to him was so sweet he knew he'd never be able to forget it.

Sly was waiting for her when she arrived at Lolita's the following morning. Sadie noticed him sitting at the counter with Pete, both of them in uniform, and nearly turned around and walked out. She was only finishing up at the restaurant because she'd said she would. She could use the money, of course, but what little she could make today would hardly compensate her for having to deal with Sly. Neither would it make a big difference as to when she'd be able to leave this town. The fire had already set her back months.

After what she'd experienced last night with Dawson, she didn't want to see her ex. She was still basking in the afterglow of what it had felt like to be in someone else's arms — someone whose touch excited her.

She'd barely turned on her heel when Lolita, a determined if not fiery redhead with a curvy figure, came up behind her.

"Boy, am I glad to see you. Missy called in sick this morning, so we're shorthanded. Any chance you could handle a table in addition to the breakfast bar? I understand it'll be stressful to manage that much, but it's stressful for all of us this morning. We're so busy, and we don't have any other options."

Sadie opened her mouth to say she wasn't feeling well herself. She wanted to leave so badly. But she couldn't lie. Lolita had been good to her. She wouldn't leave her in the lurch. "Sure. No problem. I'll take two tables, if you need it."

Lolita squeezed her arm. "I appreciate that. You always come through. I'm so sad to be losing you."

"Thanks."

When her boss rushed off to take a few orders, or to see to the smooth running of the kitchen, Sadie drew a deep breath, squared her shoulders and told herself to get to work. She'd simply treat Sly like any other patron.

He didn't speak to her when he saw her, and she didn't speak to him. She pulled her pad from her pocket and took a couple of orders down the bar, which she turned in to the cooks, before approaching him and Pete.

"What can I get for you this morning?"

she asked, forcing a polite but distant smile.

Pete ordered; Sly didn't. He sat there glaring at her as though she'd done him dirty.

Sadie recognized that look. She associated it with the anger and reprisal that so often went with it but was determined to be professional. "Well, if that's it, I'll get this order in."

"Don't you *dare* walk away from me," Sly growled.

Pete glanced from Sly to her and back again. "Whoa, take it easy, buddy," he murmured to his friend. "You heard what Chief said this morning."

Sly ignored him. "You're sleeping with him, aren't you!" he said to her.

"Sly, no." Pete grabbed his arm, but he shook off his friend.

"You are, right? Tell me you aren't. Just *try* to make that believable. I heard he bought you some panties yesterday. Spent a pretty penny for them, too. Whole town's talking about it. You must be giving him *something,* the way he's taking care of you."

A denial rose to Sadie's lips. She didn't want to be embarrassed in the middle of the crowded diner. She knew almost everyone there, which made airing their dirty laundry in public that much worse. Besides, she wasn't with Dawson in the way he

349

thought. They weren't an *item*. They were just two desperate souls seeking shelter from the storm, and they'd taken a little pleasure in each other last night. Was that really such a terrible sin? She wasn't in a committed relationship and hadn't been for some time. Who knew how many women Sly had slept with in the past year? She felt as if she should have the same right. "Yes," she replied. "Last night. Several times. And I've never enjoyed anything more."

His jaw dropped. Sadie was surprised, too. She hadn't expected anything like that to come out of her mouth, wasn't sure what had possessed her.

"And you're proud of that?" A crash reverberated as Sly swiped his water glass and utensils to the floor. "You whore! No wonder I couldn't get along with you! You don't want a decent man. You want some dirty murderer in your bed."

Sadie clenched her jaw. "Dawson's no murderer. He's a far better man than *you*. You're the one who set the fire. I saw you outside my window! You knew I wasn't coming back to you, so you tried to burn me out. To make sure I had nowhere else to go!"

He went silent. He wasn't used to having her come back at him, let alone casting any aspersions on his character. In the past, she'd always tried to placate him, to keep the level of emotion down — for the sake of Jayden, for the sake of those around them, for her own safety. Especially if they were in public. But she was tired of his emotional vomit. If standing up to Sly meant war, there was no way to avoid it, because she couldn't tolerate what he was doing to her any longer.

"You'd better kiss that little boy of yours goodbye," he said, "because I'm going back to court, and I'm going to take him away from you."

"Boy of *mine*?" she said. "He's your son, too, and you're an even bigger monster than I thought if you'd deprive Jayden of his mother just because I was so miserably unhappy with you!"

He grabbed for her. In that instance, she thought he was going to take hold of her and punch her. She dropped her pad and pencil as her arms came up to protect her face, but Pete grabbed him in a bear hug and hauled him back before he could reach her. "Come on. We're getting out of here. Now!" Pete said and half dragged Sly from the restaurant.

Sadie was shaking when she bent to collect what she'd dropped. Everyone in the room was staring at her, and for good reason. She'd just had a knock-down-drag-out with her ex, who happened to be on the police force, after admitting to sleeping with the guy everyone believed killed his parents — with a hatchet, no less. A scene didn't get more salacious than that. She'd be the talk of the town for weeks.

"Oh my gosh! Are you okay?" Lolita came rushing toward her.

Sadie wasn't sure she had the strength to stand. She'd experienced such extremes this weekend — fear and anger on one side, ecstasy on the other. She wasn't sure her emotions could swing in a wider arc.

Fortunately, Lolita helped her to her feet. "Here, hang on to me."

"I'm sorry." Sadie could feel the shock and amazement in the room and chafed beneath the unwanted attention. "I didn't mean to cause a scene. That isn't right, not in a place of business."

"You've never caused a problem before. It was that ex-husband of yours who was spoiling for a fight. Jealousy can turn people into the ugliest possible version of them-selves."

Lolita assumed this was an anomaly, that Sly was a normal person and extreme circumstances had led to extreme behavior.

She had no idea what Sadie had lived with on a daily basis for over a decade. "I'm afraid he'll try to take Jayden from Petra's, to scare me if for no other reason. I've got to go. I know it's not a good time, so I hope you'll forgive me, but . . . I have no choice," she said. "And this is it, my last day. I won't leave Jayden again."

Dawson was surprised to see Sadie pull into the drive. When he'd dropped her off at her car this morning, so she could drive herself home after work and would have transportation thereafter, he'd expected it to be noon or one before he saw her again, but it was barely ten o'clock.

He left the field he'd been weeding to meet her. He'd been thinking of her all morning, hadn't been able to get the touch and taste of her out of his head. He'd been with plenty of women over the years, especially in college, but sex with Sadie had been different somehow, more fulfilling. Although he'd been trying to convince himself that he was overreacting, that a year in jail and becoming the most hated man in town would make a person more grateful for every kindness, every soft touch, he feared he felt more than mere gratitude for her "friendship." Somehow, Sadie had really gotten to him. And he was pretty sure she felt the same. When he'd awakened this morning, she'd been gone from his bed, but every time he caught her eye, she'd smile and blush as if she was thinking about the same thing he was. She'd even sat a little closer to him in the truck when he took her to get her car.

Jayden came running toward him. "Hey! I get to be with you!" he yelled as if that was the greatest thing in the world.

Dawson couldn't help smiling. At least he had one admirer.

Jayden squealed in excitement when Dawson swung him up on his shoulders. He loved riding there, loved any kind of affection. He was such an easy, good child — it made Dawson wonder how Sly could be disappointed in him. "Why are you back so early?"

"My mom came and got me," the boy replied.

That didn't answer the question, but it was probably all Jayden knew. Dawson held the boy's ankles so he wouldn't fall off as he finished closing the distance between him and Sadie. "What's going on?" he asked as he reached her.

She lifted a box that reeked of smoke out of the back of her El Camino. "I got a call from Chief Thomas. He had my things, so I swung by the station to pick them up."

Dawson saw a stack of folded clothing piled on top of who knew what else. "Did you get everything you asked for?"

"Not everything, but I've got my toiletries and some clothes — the ones from the dresser opposite the closet. I lost what was *in* the closet, since it was on the side of the house that burned."

"That sucks. I'm sorry."

"I'm grateful there's *something* left."

"Here, let me take that." He reached up to put Jayden on the ground so he could help, but she circumvented him with the box.

"It's okay," she said. "It's not heavy."

Something was wrong. Sadie wasn't treating him as she had this morning. And she sure as hell wasn't treating him as she had last night.

Letting Jayden remain on his shoulders, Dawson followed her to the house. "How'd you get off work so early?"

After a slight hesitation, she said, "My boss didn't need me today."

That should've been believable, but it wasn't. She seemed upset. "Aren't Sundays busy?"

"They are."

"So what happened?"

She put the box on the kitchen table and began pulling all the clothes out, presumably so she could wash the stench out of them before taking them upstairs. "Nothing," she said. But that couldn't be true. She was acting too remote. Had she lost the pictures she was worried about recovering? Heard bad news from Sly? Gotten in a fight with the restaurant owner? Been taunted for associating with him?

Dawson would've pushed her for a more convincing answer, but he figured she might not be willing to talk in front of Jayden.

"Anyway, Jayden and I are available to help in the fields today." She managed a smile, but it looked too brittle to be convincing.

"I won't be outside much longer," he said. "I'm going to see Angela, remember?"

"You're leaving?" Her eyes, which had looked everywhere since she'd been home except directly at him, latched onto his face.

"I was hoping to take you with me," he said. "So you could meet Angela."

"How far away is she?"

"She's in LA, so we'll have a bit of a drive — two hours there and two hours back, providing traffic isn't bad, but traffic shouldn't be bad on a Sunday."

Sadie's gaze lifted to her son, who was still sitting happily on Dawson's shoulders, his head nearly touching the ten-foot ceiling. "What about Jayden?"

He put the boy down. "We'll take him with us."

Some of the tension in Sadie's face and body seemed to ease. "Great. The sooner, the better. When can we go?"

"The sooner, the better?" he asked, hoping for some clarification.

"It'll be nice to have a change of scenery," she explained, "a break from Silver Springs."

He lowered his voice as Jayden caught a glimpse of one of his toys and hopped up on a chair to get it out of the box. "Did Chief Thomas tell you something about the fire? Something that makes it all worse?"

"No. He said they're still investigating. That it'll be a few days before they know anything."

"So . . . are you going to tell me what's wrong?"

She put a hand on her son's head as he drove his toy car along the edge of the table. "No, it's not your problem. You're my employer. You shouldn't have to worry about anything more than paying me for what I do."

Last night he'd been more than just her

employer. This morning she'd acted as if she couldn't get enough of him, too. What was going on? "Your employer. Okay. Sure. But . . . I thought we were friends, at least."

Their eyes met. For a second, he thought she'd break down, but she didn't. Throwing her shoulders back, she lifted her chin. "I'm sorry. There's only one way out for me."

"Can we talk about it?"

"That won't help," she said and pulled her gaze away.

With a sigh, he shoved a hand through his hair. "Let me finish up outside and we'll leave in an hour or so."

"I'll help you," she said. "Jayden can play nearby."

That hadn't worked out so well before. She'd spent more time trying to keep her son close — not that Dawson had minded. He liked having her out there with him. It just wasn't necessary today. "No need," he said. "That's not part of your job. But if you'd make some lunch so we can eat before we go, that'd be great."

"Okay."

He hesitated a moment longer, hoping he'd be able to figure out what had changed, but she'd already turned to start lunch. Something from this morning had caused her to back away from him. Was it the regret he'd feared she'd feel? A degree of doubt someone had placed in her mind about whether he'd murdered his parents? *What?*

19

Sadie hung on to her son's hand as Dawson signed in to see his sister. They'd barely spoken on the long drive. She'd read to Jayden and tried to keep him occupied until he'd fallen asleep, and then the movement of the vehicle had put her to sleep, as well. But she felt it was better to keep some emotional distance between them. She'd let herself get too close to Dawson last night. As much as she'd enjoyed his touch — as much as she'd needed those few precious hours — she had to maintain some emotional distance. She couldn't allow herself to get too involved with him, to care a great deal, or it would be that much harder to leave Silver Springs. And she *had* to leave. For her own sanity and safety. For the sake of her son. Sly held too much power here, and he wasn't to be trusted. If not for Pete, he would've struck her this morning, and maybe he would've continued to strike until she was seriously injured. He'd been *that* angry, *that* scary.

Even worse, he claimed he was going to take Jayden away from her.

She wouldn't allow that to happen. Jayden wasn't happy with his father, and because his father had no idea how damaging he was to those around him — or didn't care if he did — it wasn't as if she could expect him to change. After the incident at the restaurant, she was no longer willing to give Sly the benefit of the doubt where the fire was concerned, either. Chief Thomas had made some sense to her. But he didn't understand that logic only worked with stable people, and Sly was not stable. Her ex's behavior had grown progressively worse since the day she married him, and most especially after Jayden was born. He'd felt replaced by their son, jealous of the love she felt for their child, and the more she retreated from him, the more tyrannical he became.

Once Dawson had signed in, he led her and Jayden into a sterile-looking waiting room, the kind one might find in any hospital.

"You've been here before?" Sadie murmured.

"Yeah. A couple times," he said.

"That's nice of you."

He didn't respond. When he picked up a magazine, effectively ending the conversation, she wondered if he was mad at her. She hated the thought of that. But there wasn't a lot she could do to fix the situation. She could only keep her eye on the one path that would lead her out of the mess her life had become.

One step at a time. The first step was to save the money she would need to start over somewhere else. That was why she needed the job Dawson provided and couldn't do anything to put it in jeopardy.

They'd waited only a few minutes before a young woman with long brown hair pulled into a ponytail came out to get them. "She's been waiting for you," she told Dawson with a smile that suggested his sister was somewhat of a handful. "She's packed her bags again, thinks you're taking her home with you tonight."

He shook his head. "Don't let her fool you. She knows better. She's being stubborn, trying to force the issue."

The woman looked a little surprised when Sadie and Jayden came forward, too, making it apparent they were with Dawson. "You've brought some friends, I see."

All business now, Dawson introduced Sadie as Angela's new caregiver. He'd seemed surprised — maybe even slightly hurt — by her withdrawal earlier. The eagerness of the smile he'd been wearing when she first greeted him at the farm had been replaced with a certain wariness, as if he wasn't so sure she could be trusted anymore. But since she'd reestablished their roles as employer/employee, he'd respected those boundaries. Although she'd sat right next to him in the truck — thanks to where they had to put Jayden's safety seat — he hadn't tried to touch her.

"This is Megan, the woman who takes care of Angela in the evenings," he said, finishing up the introductions.

"Looks like you're getting ready to bring her home, all right," Megan said, referring to the fact that he'd already hired a caregiver.

"I have a meeting with the state on Wednesday. Everything hinges on that," he told her.

"I responded to the letter they sent here, put in a good word for you."

"Thanks."

"No problem. I've seen how you are with her," she said in a tone that left no question as to how much *she* believed in Dawson. "She adores you."

Megan punched in a code that allowed

them access to a special wing. Sadie heard the door swing closed behind them, the echo of their own footsteps and the TVs playing in several of the rooms they passed. Angela lived at the end and had decorated her door like that of a kindergarten class. Sadie took a moment to examine the toilet-paper flowers and hand-drawn pictures taped up there. The picture in the middle nearly broke her heart. It showed what could only be Angela with her parents and Dawson — her "baby" brother. The four of them were holding hands.

Dawson saw it, too. Sadie noticed how, when he paused to look, a muscle moved in his cheek, and she couldn't help touching him. As much as she told herself it wasn't wise, he'd done so much for her, and she could tell the sight evoked a poignant emotion.

When he felt her hand on his arm, he looked over in surprise. A confused expression drew his eyebrows together before the moment was lost and Angela realized he'd arrived.

"My brother! That's my brother. He told me he'd come. Here he is." She spoke overly loud and nearly knocked into Megan in her attempt to reach Dawson. Then she clung to him as if he were a lifeline, and, wearing an affectionate smile, he let her squeeze him tight.

She might've hung on to him for the duration of the visit if she hadn't spotted Sadie. At that point, she let go, but before he could even introduce them, she saw Jayden. Then everything changed. With a gasp of absolute joy, she burst into tears. "Dawson!" she cried. "You brought me a little boy? You know I always wanted one! You were too big. I never got to carry you around. I couldn't lift you even once. But I loved you anyway," she was quick to add. "You're a good brother. I'm just so happy to have a *little* one."

With that she scooped a surprised Jayden into her arms and swung him around, laughing and crying at the same time. "I can't believe it," she said. "You brought me a little boy. I knew you'd bring me something good, but . . . *this,*" she said, as if a child was the fulfillment of all her dreams.

Fortunately, Jayden didn't object. He tried to push away so he could see into her face, but she was hugging him too fiercely. "I'm going to play with you and sing to you and push you on the tire swing," she told him. "And I won't let you get near the pond. The pond's not safe." For a moment, her voice took on the qualities of an adult voice, an echo of what she'd probably been told so many times herself. "I just love you," she added.

When she squeezed him even harder, Jayden looked to Sadie as if to say, "Get me out of here." But Dawson tossed aside the present he had bought her — a child's camera — and moved first.

"He's going to be staying with us for a while, but you don't get to keep him," he told his sister. "And you have to stop hugging him so tight, or he won't want you to touch him. Remember the puppy? How I taught you to hold the puppy?"

"Oh, yeah. I'll be careful, Dawson. I just forgot. That's all." Although she ducked away from her brother so that he couldn't take Jayden away from her, she did loosen her grip. "I won't never hurt you," she told Jayden. "I'll be so careful, just like the puppy. I never hurt the puppy. My mom was allergic, that's all. So the puppy had to live with someone else."

"Angela."

She was so engrossed in Jayden that Dawson had to say her name twice before he could get her to look up.

"Don't you want to know who *this* is?" Dawson indicated Sadie.

"The lady who's going to let me come

home?" Angela guessed.

"You mean from the state? No. Robin Strauss is coming to check the house on Wednesday. This is Jayden's mother, Sadie. She's going to be staying with us and helping to take care of you — the way Megan does here."

"Oh. No." She shook her head. "I don't need her, Dawson. Megan's coming home with me. She'll take care of me, and I'll take care of Jayden."

"Angela, I have to stay here," Megan said, trying to keep the humor from her voice. "I have other people to care for, remember? What about Scotty, down the hall? And Mary? What would they do without me? You now have Sadie. She'll love you just as much as I do."

"And if *she* can't stay, neither can Jayden," Dawson pointed out.

That seemed to get through. "Oh, I didn't mean she *couldn't* stay," Angela said, quickly retrenching. "You can stay, Sadie, and I'll help you take care of your little boy."

"I appreciate that," Sadie said. "We can all help each other."

"So you're not mad at me?" Angela peered closely at her.

Sadie smiled to reassure her. "No. Of course not."

They gave Angela her camera, which she liked, but she was too preoccupied with Jayden to visit with them for long. Even her beloved brother couldn't distract her. She took picture after picture of Jayden. Then she "read" him a book she'd obviously memorized and helped him make a bracelet with her bead set.

After about ten minutes, Megan had to leave to see to other responsibilities, which left Sadie alone with Dawson while Angela and Jayden played.

"What do you think?" he asked when the door closed softly behind Megan.

"About . . ." Sadie responded.

"Angela. Will you be able to cope with her?"

"We should be fine. She seems sweet."

"She can be a little . . . determined."

"She must not be *too* difficult. Megan seems fond of her."

"Fortunately, to know her is to love her, but, like anyone, she has her moments."

"So does Jayden. Everything will be okay." Sadie averted her gaze, hoping there'd be something to distract them, but Angela and Jayden were still happily engaged in the jewelry-making endeavor — and when she glanced back, Dawson was still watching her.

"I'm sorry if you regret last night," he said.

The memories she'd been trying to forget, or at least force into the back of her mind, flooded over her with just that simple statement. "Let's not talk about it. I was the one who started everything, and I'm embarrassed I came on so strong."

"Believe me, I didn't mind."

She felt her cheeks grow warm at the inflection of his voice. The way he'd said that meant more than the words conveyed.

"Still, you have no reason to apologize for anything."

He lowered his voice even though Angela and Jayden weren't paying any attention. "But you *do* regret it. Is that it? Is that what's wrong? I hope not, because the fact that we chose to be together won't change the way I treat you, whether or not you can live at the farm or whether or not you have a job. Sex isn't a requirement. And I'm not like Sly. You can back away from me at any time, because I'm only interested in what you *want* to give. Nothing else holds any meaning for me. In case that's the problem," he added.

Now he was beginning to guess at what was going on in her head, and he was imagining all the wrong things. She knew he wasn't like Sly. And she didn't regret last night — not in the way he assumed. "It's not that," she said.

"Then what is it?"

Fear. She was beginning to feel something for him, and she couldn't allow it. "I can't afford to build a new relationship here, Dawson, can't afford to let myself care about anyone or anything. Sly will never leave this place. He was born here. His mother lives here. He loves his job because it makes him feel like a big shot. That alone would be enough to keep him in Silver Springs. Which means *I* have to go."

He rocked back. "Whoa! What are you talking about? You're *leaving*?"

"I have no choice. I realized it when Sly almost pulled his gun on you. Something terrible is going to happen if I stay."

Angela couldn't get one of the beads on her thread and brought it to Dawson. He paused to help her before returning to their conversation. "But . . . where will you go?"

"Out of state," she replied. "Maybe the east coast. As far away as I can. I can't take him breathing down my neck anymore. He could've killed me and Jayden when he set that fire."

"I agree he's out of control, but . . . when are you planning to leave?"

She felt bad telling him this, since he'd

370

been kind enough to help her, but she'd never dreamed Sly would set fire to her house when she accepted the job Dawson offered. "As soon as I can save enough to make it feasible."

Dawson watched his sister play with Jayden, but Sadie could tell his mind wasn't on what he was seeing. "So this is all about the fire? Nothing's happened since then?" he asked at length. "Maybe when you went in to pick up your stuff at the station?"

She didn't want to tell Dawson about the scene at the restaurant. She was afraid to draw him into her problems any further for fear he'd get hurt. "Not really."

He gave her an "I'm not buying it" expression. "What happened?"

She began digging at her cuticles, something she often did when she was anxious or upset.

"Sadie . . ."

"Fine," she responded with an exasperated sigh. "I'm sure you'll hear about it anyway, since I filed a police report."

He stiffened. "You filed a police report? Today?"

She nodded.

"Why?"

"I had no choice." She'd tried so hard to get away from Sly peaceably, had turned herself inside out trying to respect his needs and wishes — had even given him sex long after she wanted to allow him that kind of intimacy. But none of that had done any good. He wouldn't let her go. And since their relationship had deteriorated so far, she had nothing left to save, no reason *not* to go to the police. Maybe it wouldn't help, but she had to try. "Sly came to the restaurant this morning. He was angry, knew that you'd bought me —" she checked to make sure neither Angela nor Jayden were cluing in to their conversation "— some underwear."

"Because you didn't have any — thanks to him!"

"That's not the direction his mind went, of course. He accused me of —" unable to maintain eye contact, she looked down at the damage she was causing her fingers "— of doing what we did last night."

"And what did you say?"

"I told him he was right — and that I enjoyed it."

Dawson laughed at her unexpected response. "Are you joking?"

"No."

He sobered. "What did *he* do?"

"He went crazy, caused a scene. If Pete — his friend on the force — hadn't been with him and interceded . . ." She let her voice trail off.

Dawson leaned closer. "What? Don't tell me he would've hit you."

"He wanted to. When he raised his fist, I could see the hatred in his eyes, knew he wasn't in his right mind."

Dawson's muscles bunched. "That son of a bitch doesn't know when to quit."

"There's something seriously wrong with him," she agreed. "But the situation is what it is. I need to accept reality and do what I can to protect myself and my child."

Dawson got up and began to pace the short distance between Angela's bed and her walk-in closet.

"You can't let it upset you," she told him. "Like I said, it is what it is."

He pivoted to face her. "Can I ask you something?"

The gravity in his voice made her uneasy. "That depends . . ."

"Last night, when you told me you were on the pill . . ."

Apparently, the oddness of her response in that moment hadn't slipped past him, after all.

She put up a hand. "No. Don't ask."

He stopped in front of her. "It's because you've still been sleeping with him, right?"

Damn it. He'd asked anyway. And she couldn't blame him. If she were him, she would've guessed the same, would also have wondered why. "No! I mean . . . not recently and not like you probably assume. It's just . . . since I left him, he's come by the house a lot, insisting we have some family time with Jayden — for Jayden's sake so that we keep things as normal as possible."

"And then he'd turn it into something more."

"Yes. After I put Jayden to bed. Whenever I'd refuse, it would start a fight. So there were a few times — three, to be exact — when . . . when I gave in to avoid the upset and abuse I'd get otherwise. I was looking for a way to get rid of him without having my son wake up to another blistering argument." She rubbed her face. "Sometimes I think I'd do *anything* to avoid another fight. At least I thought that until the last time. He came over just before Thanksgiving, drunk and belligerent, and he wouldn't leave until . . . well, *until,* and that was such an awful experience I knew I could never do it again, not even to stave off a fight." She closed her eyes as she remembered how rough and demanding he'd been.

"And yet you stayed on the pill."

She forced herself to look at him again..

"In case . . ."

"In case he were to force you," Dawson guessed, spelling it out.

She hesitated to go that far. Sly hadn't ever *raped* her, exactly. It was more that he made her feel cornered, as if giving him what he wanted was the only way out — or the best way out. "Maybe, in the back of my mind, I fear it's a possibility. Because I've been absolutely religious about taking that pill. It's an act of defiance, in a way. He'd love it if I were to get pregnant again. Then I'd *have* to come back to him. It was during my last pregnancy that he became so controlling, because he knew he had me at even more of a disadvantage."

Dawson shook his head. "You have no idea what I'd like to do to that man."

She got off the bed, too. "See? That's why I didn't want to tell you. There's nothing you can do about Sly, nothing that won't get you hurt or in trouble. Our hands are tied. The only answer is for me to leave town — and to make sure he can never find me."

"That's *not* the only option," he argued. "You should be able to live where you want. He's a police officer, for God's sake. I'm going to pay him a visit and let him know that he'd better not ever touch you again."

She grabbed hold of his arm. "No! You

have to promise me you'll stay clear of him. I couldn't live with myself if something happened to you or anyone else."

"Are you mad, Sadie?" The emergency in Sadie's voice had finally drawn Angela's attention. "Dawson, did you make Sadie mad?"

He cleared his throat. "No, I'm mad at someone else."

"Who?" she asked.

"A bad guy," he responded.

"What bad guy?" she asked.

"You don't know him, honey. And you don't have to worry about it. I've got everything under control."

Too interested in what she was doing to bother asking any more about some generic "bad guy," she returned to making jewelry with Jayden.

"Dawson, please," Sadie whispered. "I've got enough to worry about. You can't get involved."

"*Someone* has to stop him," he said.

"The police will do that. Like I told you, I filed a complaint against him today, and I applied for a restraining order."

He shoved his hands into his pockets. "And how was that received?"

She could hear the skepticism in his tone. "Chief Thomas was a little patronizing," she admitted. "He suggested I might be exaggerating, especially after he called Pete, and Pete said he'd seen what happened and it wasn't that big of a deal. But Chief Thomas promised me he'd talk to Lolita, too. She could tell the threat was real. She'll back me up."

"Even if she does, he didn't actually strike you, so they'll minimize it and sweep it under the rug. You realize that, don't you? In their minds, he hasn't done anything to be suspended over, and they can't have an officer on active duty walking around with a restraining order against him."

Again, it came back to the fact that she had nowhere to turn. But she couldn't expect Dawson to do any more than he already had. "Even if Thomas only threatens him to stay away from me, it should help. I only need to buy a few months."

"Maybe it's time to go on the offensive."

"Offensive how?"

"Sly believes he's got his boot on your neck. That's why he had the nerve to set the fire in the first place."

"He *does* have his boot on my neck," she pointed out with a humorless chuckle.

"It's time for the power paradigm to shift," he mumbled as if he wasn't really talking to her.

"What'd you say?" she asked.

"Nothing," he replied. Angela had decided she wanted more of Dawson's attention and asked him to come over and make her a necklace. "We'll talk about it later."

20

After they left Stanley DeWitt, Dawson was too tired to drive home, as originally planned, and it wasn't comfortable for him to sit in the middle so Sadie could drive. He was too big for that spot. So he suggested they get some dinner, stay over at a motel and head back early the next morning.

He thought Sadie might balk. A motel room was close quarters, and neither one of them had money to waste on renting two when they could get by with one, but, when he mentioned it, she readily agreed. He got the impression she was eager to be gone from Silver Springs for as long as possible. She wanted to be gone *for good.*

He didn't feel too great about seeing her go, however. He had no idea if their relationship would progress, but he was enjoying her friendship and support, even if she never gave him anything more. He hated to think of her on the run, always looking over her shoulder for fear Sly would catch up. He also hated that Sly had had her at such a disadvantage — and capitalized on it — for so long. In Dawson's mind, there had to be a better way for her to escape her current situation than to start over somewhere else, with nothing and no one except her child.

Fortunately, Sly might've unwittingly provided her with a better chance to escape. If they could only prove he set the fire, he'd go to prison.

"We need to hire an outside investigator to take a look at the fire evidence," he said when they were talking about the problem over dinner. "Like I did with the forensic specialist who examined my parents' bedroom."

Sadie looked startled by the suggestion. "How? Hiring someone like that costs money, which is something I don't have."

"They don't cost that much."

"I'm sure they do by my standards!"

"But consider the possibilities." Pushing his chimichanga platter aside the moment he finished with it, he spent some time on his phone, looking up crime scene investigators that included fire inspectors on the internet and showing those who looked to have extensive experience to Sadie. One of the most promising lived right in LA.

"There's nothing to indicate rates," she said as she passed his phone back to him and finished her margarita.

"Ed charged me two grand plus travel. Shouldn't be more than that. It's definitely cheaper than moving," he pointed out. "And if we hire the guy from LA, there shouldn't be much travel. Just a tank or two of gas."

Now that Jayden was full and only playing with his bean-and-cheese burrito, she stacked the plates so that he'd have more room to finish coloring his paper place mat. "Still. Moving is later. When I've had a chance to save up. Hiring an arson investigator would require immediate money, and even $500 is a fortune to me."

The waitress came by, so Dawson waited until their plates had been removed. "I'll loan you what you need," he said. "I feel that strongly about it."

She dipped a tortilla chip in the salsa. "Like you loaned me the money for the clothes?"

Dawson had had two margaritas, enough tequila to feel loose and relaxed in a way he hadn't been relaxed in a long time. The motel they'd rented was right next door, so they could walk over when they were finished, wouldn't need to worry about driving, which was why he'd allowed himself to drink a little more than he would otherwise.

He gave her a lazy smile as he remembered the panty purchase — and the fact that he'd had the pleasure of removing those panties from her body later.

What he wouldn't give to do that again . . .

"What?" she said when he didn't speak.

He tried to steer his mind back to safer territory. "Doesn't hurt to call and ask."

"But how will we know the guy we choose to hire is any good? And even if he is good, what if he doesn't find anything to prove Sly's complicity? It's a risk, you know?"

He straightened in the booth. "I believe we know who did it," he said, in deference to Jayden.

"So do I," she said without hesitation.

"Then let's prove it. We can check with Ed Shuler, the specialist I hired. See if he has any recommendations. He's an ex-cop, might've worked with someone he could suggest. If not, we'll have to use one of the guys I've found here." He gestured at his phone. "The one from LA."

She turned her glass around and around on the table, making a solid ring out of the condensation.

"Unless you *want* to leave town." He studied her. He was essentially asking if there wasn't *something* in Silver Springs she liked and, when she glanced up, he knew she understood that.

"I *did* want to go," she said. "I've dreamed about it for a long time."

"And now?"

Her lips curved into a self-conscious smile. "I wouldn't be in any hurry if . . . if not for Sly."

Dawson scooted lower in the booth. "Good. Let's do it, then. We'll split the cost."

She grimaced. "No. I can't let you bear any of the expense, not when you have so much at risk yourself, what with the farm and your sister and everything. It'll be a loan, nothing more — and only if you're positive you can afford to lend it to me without ruining what you're trying to accomplish."

"I've got a little padding."

"Okay. But it'll definitely be a loan. I won't accept anything else."

He lifted his glass. "Fine, a loan, then."

The check came, and she tried to insist on paying for half of it.

"We're here on business," he said, handing her credit card back before the waiter could collect the tray.

"Eating Mexican food and drinking margaritas is business?" she scoffed.

"I brought you to LA to meet Angela, didn't I? I'm covering meals and expenses."

"Okay. But this feels more like a vacation. I can't remember a meal I enjoyed more."

"You're easy to please." He liked that about her, liked that she was real and down-to-earth and sensitive to other people's situations and not just her own.

Something passed between them. Dawson almost reached across the table to take her hand. He thought she might let him, but he resisted. He needed to move slowly, to give her time to acclimate to having a different man in her life. He also needed to be careful. He'd never really fallen in love, didn't have a lot of experience with it, and he definitely didn't want to start something if it wasn't going to work out.

She helped Jayden finish his picture while Dawson paid. Then they walked over to the motel. There were two double beds. Sadie and Jayden would be in one; he'd be in the other. But, as tired as Dawson was, he wasn't sure he'd be getting any sleep. Long after the lights were out and they were settled in for the night, he found himself staring across the space that separated him from Sadie.

■ ■ ■ ■

They were in the truck, driving home the next morning, when Dawson tried to reach Big Red at Safety First. He tried once at eight and once at nine, but it wasn't until they were nearly to Silver Springs that he finally got through.

Knowing what hung in the balance, Sadie wanted to listen to the conversation. She was praying he'd get good news — in her opinion, he deserved a little — but they'd just pulled over to get gas and Jayden needed to use the restroom.

By the time she took her son into the mini-mart, bought him an apple after they were finished in the restroom and returned, Dawson was off the phone.

"What happened?" she asked.

He removed the gas nozzle from his tank and screwed on the cap. "It was a guy by the name of Oscar Hunt."

"Who built the shelter for Alex? That's who saw the vagrant you picked up and mentioned it to Gage Pond at The Blue Suede Shoe?"

Dawson opened the passenger door to lift Jayden into his safety seat. "Yep."

"Did you talk to him?"

385

"No, he's out on a job."

"He doesn't have a cell phone?"

"He's somewhere in the Nevada desert, doesn't have service. They won't give me his personal information, anyway. But Big Red said he'd give Hunt my number as soon as they have contact with him."

"Did you ask if Oscar has ever mentioned the incident?"

"I did. Big Red had no idea what I was talking about, though. Said he doesn't recall."

"That doesn't mean anything."

"No," Dawson agreed, but she could tell he was nervous that the lead wouldn't go anywhere. He had only this Oscar's sighting of a vagrant fitting the right description and the hope that the forensics specialist he hired would be able to find something of evidentiary value, when all he'd had to start with was a crime scene that'd already been scoured by police. The odds were not in his favor.

"We have only a couple of days to get ready for Robin Strauss," he said, obviously trying to distract himself.

"From the state?"

He nodded.

"We'll be ready," she promised. At least she could help him with that.

Sly was at the gym on Tuesday morning when his phone started to buzz. Pete was trying to reach him. They both had the day off, were going to the range later. They often went target shooting — if not at the range, where they had to put in a certain number of hours to remain on the force, then out in the mountains, where they shot things up for fun. Although they probably spent equal time developing their skills, Sly took great pride in the fact that he was the better marksman.

Because he was lifting, he let the call transfer to voice mail so he could finish his curls. He would've waited to call Pete back until he was on his way home, so he wouldn't be interrupted and could finish quicker, but Pete seemed determined to reach him. When the phone rang again, Sly slouched onto the weight bench where he'd left his phone and answered.

"What's up?"

"Where are you?" Pete replied.

Sly straightened his right leg to admire the definition in his quads. He looked good. The Stanozolol he'd been taking was making a big difference. "Charlie's Fitness, why?"

"I just stopped by your place."

"But we weren't supposed to get together until after lunch . . ."

"I know. I have something to tell you. I hope you're sitting down."

This sounded ominous. Sly dropped his foot back to the mats that covered the floor. "Is there a problem?"

"There might be. When I went in to the station this morning to finish a report I was supposed to turn in yesterday, I overheard a snatch of conversation I don't think you're gonna like."

Sly wasn't too worried. He grabbed his towel, which he always left on the bench with his phone while he lifted, and wiped the sweat from his face. "I'm sure you were getting an earful. Chief Thomas is still pissed at me for what happened at Lolita's on Sunday, but don't worry about it. I'm having dinner at his place tonight so that we can discuss my 'recent behavior,' as he put it. I'll just tell him about all the shit Sadie's been putting me through, how she's been playing me hot and then cold, sleeping around when I think we're getting back together and trying to turn my own kid against me, and he'll understand. What man wouldn't? Thomas might curse and yell, but he's always got our backs. That's what's important on the force, right? Solidarity. He says it himself all the time — we're stronger if we stand together."

"Thomas will come around," Pete agreed. "He always does. But . . . this is something else."

Sly tossed the towel aside. "The complaint Sadie filed against me? I already know about that. Thomas called me first thing." He laughed without humor. "She's got her nerve, man, thinking anyone at that station would take her side over mine."

"No, it's not that, either, buddy. If you'll just listen . . ."

Sly felt his first trickle of unease. What else could there be? "Fine. I'm all ears," he said. "Shoot."

"There's a guy, a Damian Steele, coming from LA. Sounded like he was some kind of forensics specialist, so —"

"Are we still trying to gather evidence on the Reed murders?" Sly broke in, hoping he'd figured it out at last. If so, that was a *good* thing. He'd love nothing more than to see Dawson Reed go to prison for the rest of his life, or worse. Without him standing in the way, providing food and shelter and work for Sadie, she wouldn't be acting the way she was. She'd have nowhere to turn, would be down on her knees, *begging* him to take her back.

"I thought maybe that was the case, too. It's killing me that he's running around town as if he's as innocent as everyone else. But when I looked up this Damian dude on the internet, I found out that he's an *arson* investigator. A good one."

Sly's stomach plummeted to his feet. "What'd you say?"

"You heard me." There was a moment of silence, then he said, "That's not a problem, is it?"

"What do you mean?"

"Sadie's telling everyone you had something to do with the fire. After what I saw at the diner, I thought . . . I don't know. I thought maybe you did do something stupid."

"Hell, no. Of course not. I'm not an idiot."

"Whew! I'm relieved."

"You thought I might have . . . ."

"Not really. You just . . . haven't been yourself lately, that's all. Sadie . . . she's gotten inside your head."

Sly was reeling so badly he was having a difficult time sounding convincing. He'd been so careful that night. But . . . had he left anything behind? "That's bullshit. I can't believe you'd even consider it."

"Yeah. You're right. Sorry, bro. Doesn't matter who comes to town. Just wanted you to know — in case."

"I appreciate that. So . . . the department is hiring someone else? An outsider?"

"Not the department. Thomas was surprised by the call. He tried to say we had it covered, but the guy must've convinced him he had some right to see the property, because Chief Thomas set up a time to meet him there."

"When?"

"Noon on Thursday."

"You've *got* to be kidding me," he said, kicking over his water bottle. "We don't need no outsider meddling in our business."

"Yeah. No one likes it much, but it is what it is."

Sly took a moment to process everything he'd just heard. "The weird thing is . . . if we didn't hire him, who did? The fire department?"

"Doubt it. They don't have the money for that kind of thing, not for a fire where no one was actually hurt."

"Is it Maude, then? She's got money. Is she not satisfied with the investigation?"

"The landlady? Come on. She wouldn't think to call in a specialist. Anyway, her homeowner's policy will pay to rebuild whether it was arson or not."

"Whoever invited this guy *has* to be paying a lot. Someone like Damian Steele is an important man. He's not going to drop everything and drive out here on his own dime," he started, then stopped. Son of a bitch! It was Dawson Reed. It had to be.

That prick was coming after him.

21

Dawson spent a long two days trying to make up for the time he'd lost over the weekend, but thanks to the desire he felt for Sadie, which he was trying so hard not to act upon, the nights were longer still. He'd managed to get through them, however, managed to make it all the way to Tuesday night — which felt like a real accomplishment — but now he was facing another hurdle. The time had come to clean his parents' bedroom. He couldn't put it off any longer.

As he stood in the hallway, staring at that locked door with the cleaning supplies in a bucket at his feet, he would've procrastinated yet again if he could have. But he had no excuse to do so. Just yesterday he'd spoken to the forensics specialist he'd hired. Ed hadn't learned anything from the samples he'd collected quite yet, said it would be several weeks before the results came in, but he'd reiterated that he was done with the bedroom.

The only thing stopping Dawson from cleaning it was his own reluctance. Why didn't he allow Eli and Gavin to handle the gruesome task for him? Then he wouldn't have to face his feelings, could continue to compartmentalize his grief.

He looked down at his hands. They felt awkward and clumsy, and he hadn't even inserted the key. He'd stood in the same spot many times and managed his emotions just fine, but this was different. He had to actually *open* the door, couldn't shove the memory of what was inside into the back of his mind and walk away, like before.

Downstairs, he heard Sadie and Jayden come into the house. They were back from the store. Already. He'd thought he'd have more time, didn't want to be doing this with them in the house. But the woman from the state would be here first thing in the morning. He could easily imagine what *she'd* think if she found the murder scene pretty much as the police left it. She wouldn't understand the conflicting emotions that made him so reluctant, wouldn't understand that washing away the last of his parents' blood somehow erased them, too — or what was left of them — when he hadn't quite let go, *couldn't* let go until he'd found the person who murdered them. She'd merely assume he wasn't coping as well as he should be, and she'd decide that Angela would be better off remaining at Stanley DeWitt.

He closed his eyes as he listened to Jayden downstairs.

"Want me to carry it, Mommy?"

"No, honey. It's too heavy for you. Here, let me."

"I can do it!"

"No, you get the other one. There's nothing that can get broken in there."

Planning to go in and lock the door behind him, before Jayden and Sadie could even realize he was in the house, Dawson picked up the cleaning supplies, removed the key from his pocket and, with a sigh, inserted it into the lock. He had to do this, and he had to do it now. He couldn't let Angela down. He'd already let his parents down by picking up that hitchhiker. If he hadn't done that, they'd probably still be around and Angela wouldn't be in an institution —

He froze in the open doorway. There was no blood spatter on the walls or bed, no overturned or broken furniture, no mangled lamp. Even the smell was different — not musty stale but tinged with disinfectant.

His gaze shifted from the bed frame, which no longer had its mattress (the police had taken that when the crime occurred and never brought it back), to the drapes flapping near the *open* window, to the dresser where what hadn't been broken and removed had been carefully arranged.

"Sadie?" he called.

He heard her tell Jayden he could have only one of something before footfalls indicated she was climbing the stairs.

He turned as she stepped into the room behind him.

"I didn't realize you'd come in from the fields." Her eyes dropped to the cleaning supplies before returning to his face.

He gestured around him. "Did you do this?" It *had* to be her, didn't it? Unless, while the three of them were in LA, she'd let the Turner boys come in, there was no one else.

She seemed a little nervous when she nodded, as if she feared she might've overstepped.

"When?"

She cleared her throat. "After you were asleep last night I got the key off your dresser, where you put . . . well, where you put all the stuff from your pockets when you undress."

He couldn't believe she'd found a time when he was unconscious enough not to hear her. He felt as if he'd spent most of the past two nights hoping she'd visit his room, but for very different reasons than to pick up a key. *"Why?"*

She averted her gaze. "Because I knew it had to be done, and I couldn't bear the thought of you having to do it. I hope . . . I hope it doesn't upset you that I was so . . . presumptuous. I was afraid if I offered, you'd only turn me down — like you did Eli and Gavin."

"I would've turned you down. It couldn't have been easy to . . . to do what you did."

"It wasn't." She wiped her palms on her jeans as if she was still trying to get the blood off. "It was one of the hardest things I've ever done."

"I didn't mean for you to get stuck with the job. I told you in the beginning that I didn't expect you to take on something like . . . like this. That it wasn't part of your duties." He shook his head in disbelief. "I was planning to do it myself."

"I'm just glad you don't have to." She touched his arm. "Thanks for everything you've done for me," she said softly, and taking the bucket away from him, she carried it back downstairs.

Dawson closed the door before walking over to the window. He hadn't cried since the murders occurred. He'd been too damn angry. He didn't want to break down now; he just couldn't help it. A tear rolled down each cheek as he stared at the box spring that no longer had a mattress. His parents were *really* gone, completely out of the house. He'd known that acknowledgment would be hard. But it was Sadie's kindness that had been his undoing.

While Jayden watched cartoons, Sadie put away the cleaning supplies and unpacked the items she'd purchased — the hamper she'd been meaning to get for Dawson, a few groceries for the meals she had planned in the next few days and some more under-wear and clothes for Jayden. She hadn't heard Dawson come out of his parents' bedroom even though there wasn't anything left to be done in there. As difficult as it had been to see the blood, the missing mat-tress, the broken lamp and the hatchet marks on the headboard and wall, all of which had made the details of the killing so much more vivid, she'd ignored the reality of what she was doing and scoured that place from top to bottom.

So what was he doing now? Was it just that she couldn't hear his footsteps above the TV?

After she put the butter, cream and chicken breasts in the fridge, she walked to the base of the stairs and gazed up. The door was closed, but she was pretty sure he hadn't come out. Was he okay? She didn't want to intrude, but she was beginning to wonder if she should check on him, see if he needed a little consolation.

Her phone went off before she could decide whether to go up. She thought it might be Lolita from the restaurant. She'd been waiting to hear all about her boss's meeting with Chief Thomas, but it was her landlady, Maude.

"Maude, how are you?" she said.

"Fine. More important, how are you and Jayden?"

Because she and Maude had checked on each other before, Sadie knew this was merely an intro to something more important than the usual small talk. She figured Maude had some information from the insurance company or an estimate from the police on how much longer it would be before they could start the cleanup and reconstruction phase. "We're okay, thanks to Dawson."

At the mention of Dawson's name, Maude hesitated. Sadie knew her former landlady wasn't quite comfortable with Sadie's new situation. But Maude couldn't complain too loudly. Sadie was a grown woman and could make her own decisions. "Sly's very unhappy that you're staying out there with the Reeds' son," she said at length, shifting the concern to Sadie's ex so she didn't have to claim it herself.

After checking to make sure Jayden was still glued to the TV, Sadie walked toward the back of the house and slipped inside the bathroom off the porch so that her voice wouldn't carry upstairs. "How do you know?"

"He came by here a few minutes ago."

"Why'd he do that? Please don't tell me he's part of the investigation." She immediately assumed he was there to destroy any evidence he might've left behind. "Or did he just want to see what was left of the house?"

"He didn't even go in back. He came to talk to me."

Sadie sat on the edge of the tub/shower combo. "What'd he have to say?"

"He told me that Dawson has hired a special arson investigator to determine the origin and cause of the fire."

Sadie curled her fingernails into her palm. So her ex knew. She'd wondered if and when he'd find out about Damian Steele — and how he'd react once he did.

"Is that true?" Maude asked when Sadie didn't volunteer a response.

"Yes." She'd tried to tell Dawson not to spend the money. But once they'd returned from LA, and he'd gone onto the computer to show her more of the website belonging to the investigator he'd found who wasn't even that far away, she hadn't been able to refuse. If they could prove Sly was responsible for the fire, he'd never be able to get custody of Jayden. "I feel it's important," she explained.

"Who's paying for it?"

"Dawson. For now. You know I don't have the money. But I'm going to pay him back. It's just a loan."

"Are you sure it's necessary to spend the money in the first place, Sadie? You can't seriously believe that Sly might be responsible for what happened."

Sadie gripped the phone tighter. "Sly told you we think *he* set the fire?"

"Yes. He was insulted, upset. Swore he would never do such a thing, that he loves the two of you and, as a police officer, he'd never willfully destroy property, etc., etc.

He was quite impassioned."

And convincing, obviously. "He's a pretender, Maude. He's pretended our whole marriage to be far more law-abiding than he is. Trust me, he'll do what he thinks he can get away with. And he thinks he can get away with this."

"Has he ever hurt you?" she asked, sounding unsure.

"Not yet. But he's done plenty to lead me to believe that he's capable of it. One was starting that fire."

"Why would he risk the lives of people he loves?"

"Because he didn't think he was risking us. He made sure I was awake, remember?"

"But what about his career?"

"Like I said, he did it because he believed he could get away with it. He never expected me to have the resources to hire my own investigator. He thought destroying the home I was living in would leave me with no choice except to come back to him."

"You wouldn't have had the resources without Dawson. But are you sure you can trust *him*? I mean . . . it seems to me that you have things backward here, Sadie. We've known Sly for years. Whatever his faults might be, I'm convinced he loves you. He's also on the police force. That should give him *some* credibility. At least he's never been accused of murder!"

"Well, I'm accusing him of arson."

"You're *that* certain."

Sadie wished she had seen more of the man who'd been in the yard Friday night. That dark figure was almost like an apparition — just an amorphous shape with little or no detail that she could tie to her ex. "I have no other explanation for what happened."

"That doesn't mean it was him!"

"Who else could it be?"

Maude didn't answer that question. "He asked me not to permit a secondary investigation," she said.

"He what?" Sadie cried.

"He says it's a waste of money, that the work has already been done. So what's the point? It'll just drag his reputation through the mud for nothing. And he's owed more than that after all the service he's given this town. I've always liked him."

"You barely knew him before I moved in, Maude. And since then, you've liked him because he wants you to like him. He wanted you to welcome his visits, think nothing of how often he stopped by, speak to him freely and give him whatever information about me that you would. He can't be trusted. *Please* let the inspector come onto the property and do what we've hired him to do. I wouldn't spend money I don't have if I wasn't completely convinced it was necessary."

"But Sly's a police officer!"

"That's the problem! Because he's a police officer, he knows how to get away with things other people might not. And he knows that no one on the Silver Springs force would want to find anything that leads to him, so there's a little bit of safety there, too."

"*Safety?* You're saying the Silver Springs police force would protect him even if he were guilty? You're accusing our entire department of corruption?"

"I'm not accusing the department. Given my suspicions, I believe I should have an unbiased party take a look — that's all. The expert who's coming will have no vested interest in pointing a finger at an innocent party. I'm not fabricating a case, Maude. If I were trying to do that, I'd lie and say I saw the man's face when I looked out the window. Instead, I've been honest. I'm merely in search of the facts. If the facts drag someone's reputation through the mud — Sly's or anyone else's — maybe that's the way it needs to be." What about Dawson's reputation and what had been done to that? Sadie thought, but she didn't bring it up, since she knew Maude would only defend his detractors. "Please? Let the inspector come," she pressed. "Let's see what he finds. That's the only way I'll be able to put my mind at ease. If I'm wrong about Sly, I'll be the first to apologize — to both of you."

Maude sighed into the phone. "Okay. He won't be happy about it. I feel bad that he'll perceive me as siding against him. But if this specialist you've hired can bring us some resolution, I'm all for it. At least then, like you say, you'll be able to breathe easier."

Sadie closed her eyes in relief. "I hope so."

"Just tell me this isn't because you've grown infatuated with Dawson Reed," Maude said. "I don't know anything that can cloud someone's judgment quite like a new romance."

"No," she said. "How I feel about Dawson has nothing to do with it."

"Really? Because Sly claims you're sleeping with him. That you announced it at the diner."

"I didn't *announce* it, exactly. Sly accused me — as he always accuses me whenever I'm around another man — and I told him what he deserved to hear."

"So it's true . . ."

Sadie wasn't willing to lie. "What happens between Dawson and I has no bearing on anything else."

"Love makes people do crazy things, Sadie. I'd hate for you to be taken in if . . . if Dawson isn't the man you think he is."

"I understand. You have nothing to worry about. I'm not acting the way I am because I'm infatuated with him," she said. And that was true. Dawson wasn't the reason she believed Sly set the fire. Dawson wasn't the reason she felt she should have the origins of the fire examined by an independent third party. Sly alone was to blame for that.

It was true, however, that she was developing feelings for Dawson. Although she'd cleaned his parents' room because she wanted to be kind to someone who had suffered enough, someone who'd been there for her when she'd most needed a friend, kindness wasn't what had her lingering outside his door every time she got up to go to the bathroom late at night.

22

"You're quiet tonight."

When he spoke, Sadie shifted her gaze to Dawson, who was sitting on the couch not far from the chair she'd taken. Since she'd put Jayden to bed an hour ago, she and Dawson had been flipping through channels, catching part of the news and then a little Sports Center. They had the house ready for Robin Strauss's visit first thing in the morning. Every room was spotless, the vandalism had been fixed, the fields were in the process of being tamed — which showed that Dawson could likely support Angela — and all the broken junk and trash had been removed from the yard. But there were still things that needed to be fixed, things that weren't as high on Dawson's priority list, so Sadie guessed Dawson was nervous. He'd been quiet, too.

"Just tired, I guess."

"Would you rather watch something else?"

he asked.

"No." Although she wasn't a big sports fan, she didn't see any reason to make him change the channel. She wasn't paying much attention to what she saw on the screen. She had so many worries, and yet all she could think about was the night she'd made love with Dawson in the field — how raw and visceral and incredibly satisfying it had been, and how badly she wanted a repeat of that experience or the one that'd come after, in Dawson's bed. The strength of her desire, the way she craved the opportunity to touch him whenever she saw him, surprised her. Maybe she didn't have a low libido as Sly said — he was always telling her stuff that made her feel as if she didn't measure up to his expectations in some way — because it was all she could do not to get up and straddle Dawson right now, while he was sitting on the couch.

"What are you thinking about?" he asked.

The feel of his skin. The taste of his kiss. The weight of his body as he pressed her into the mattress. That seemed to make the terrible stuff go away, at least for the moment. But she couldn't say so. They'd managed to redraw the lines they'd crossed, needed to wait and see what the fire investigator found before making any decisions on whether or not to pursue a relationship. She was too dependent on him right now, couldn't afford to get any more intimately involved in case it ended up ruining her job situation. Even if things between them worked out, chances were she'd have to move. Sly was in a more volatile state than he'd ever been. Why start something she might not be able to finish?

"What Maude said on the phone," she replied, just to have an answer. "I'm shocked Sly would have the nerve to come right out and ask her not to allow Damian Steele access to her property. I mean . . . I lived behind her for a year. That he believed *he* could hold sway with her over me shows how delusional he can be."

"I'm not shocked by that at all," Dawson responded. "I'm shocked that she was even tempted. From what you told me of your conversation, it wasn't all that easy to convince her to oppose his wishes."

"I don't hold that against her. She's a fair person. Doesn't like conflict. And he can be very persuasive."

Dawson turned off the TV and set the remote on the coffee table. "Regardless of her excuse, I'm encouraged he made that move."

"Encouraged?" she echoed.

"It shows that he's worried."

"I agree." Turning off the TV seemed to create a vacuum of sound. The sudden silence made her even more self-conscious. She tucked her feet beneath her. Because the box of items she'd picked up at the police station had included only a few things, she was still limited on clothing, so she was once again wearing his sweats with one of his T-shirts. "I wonder what he'll do when he finds out that Maude's going to allow it despite his request."

"What *can* he do?"

"Treat her crappy from here on out. That's how he operates. He's nice as long as you give him what he wants. If you refuse, he tries to punish you." She pulled the tie from her ponytail and raked her hair back so she could redo it. "I'll feel terrible if he targets her for petty driving or parking citations he would've overlooked before. Now he'll be searching for any excuse."

"Did he do those types of things to people when you were married?"

"All the time. He used to laugh when he got the better of someone. It makes him feel powerful."

Dawson's lip curled in contempt. "It's time people quit putting up with his bullshit."

She drew a deep breath. "Yeah, well, I think he understands that I'm not coming back to him now, don't you?"

"Would he take you back? After you told him you slept with me?" A faint smile curved his lips. "And that you liked it?"

She wasn't sure they should be talking about this. Just the mention of their night together made her tingle. "I don't know. He accused me of cheating on him a lot while we were married. But I never did. I never even dared to have a male friend, let alone a *boy*friend."

"About the other night . . ."

Her heart started to pound. "Yes?"

He opened his mouth to say something. Then he shook his head. "Never mind. We have a big day tomorrow. We'd better get some sleep."

"Right. Time to turn in," she agreed, but when he went upstairs, she didn't move. She sat there for several minutes, hoping to stifle the desire that had made it almost impossible to stop her gaze from following him wherever he went.

Although she went down the list of reasons she'd be foolish to act on that desire, it didn't make any difference in the end. All resistance fell by the wayside the moment she passed his room. He was just coming out. She wasn't sure where he was going, and she didn't ask. She simply walked into his arms, caught his face between her hands and kissed him as if he was all that mattered in the world.

Sly turned off his headlights as he pulled off the highway and crept through the countryside along the canal in his cruiser. He knew the way, had been here three times before.

The route he'd chosen was filled with large potholes, but it would eventually lead him to the rear of Dawson's property, and getting there without being seen was all that mattered. Chief Thomas had chewed his ass out for what he'd done in the restaurant — and threatened his job if he went anywhere near Sadie again. Thomas wasn't going to let Silver Springs PD become the subject of the next documentary on the abuse of power — that was what he'd said.

Sly cared about the force, too. The force was his *life*. But he refused to let Dawson Reed get the better of him. The same held true for Sadie. He'd do whatever he had to. He just wasn't sure what that should be. Everything that came to mind, everything he imagined, was vicious. And if Dawson and Sadie suddenly went missing, he'd instantly become the prime suspect.

He had to be smarter than that, had to figure out a way to retaliate without putting his own ass on the line.

"You're going to be sorry," he muttered. He'd been saying that since he learned about the arson specialist, and his anger had only grown hotter since Maude Clevenger had called to let him know she was going to allow the investigator to come, after all. Sadie had talked her into it; Maude had said she owed it to Sadie to grant the request. Maude had also indicated that if he wasn't responsible for setting the fire, he had nothing to worry about.

Except he *did* have something to worry about. He had a lot to worry about. Dawson and Sadie could cost him more than he could afford to lose — his job, the respect of his friends and family, even his freedom.

How dare Sadie work against him. Embarrass him by announcing to everyone in the diner that she was glad to be in someone else's bed. File a complaint with the police force *he* worked for. Try to put him behind bars by proving he set the fire.

That fire had definitely turned into a lot more than he'd expected. It had spread so fast. But even then, it wasn't such a big deal that it should destroy his whole life. Before he left her place that night, he'd made sure no one was going to get hurt. And Maude's homeowner's insurance would cover the damage. If it went down as unsolved, everyone could be okay. That was how it *should* go.

But Sadie and Dawson refused to let it. And if the truth came out, no one would believe he hadn't intended to harm anyone. He'd be charged with attempted murder — and Sadie would be the first to testify against him.

The unfairness of that rankled so badly he couldn't help grinding his teeth. *Damn* them. He wasn't going to let them get away with it, wasn't going to let them ruin *his* life.

He slowed as he came to a particularly narrow spot in the road and edged over to one side so he wouldn't hit an irrigation pump. He was getting close, he could see the outline of the farmhouse in the moonlight only 200 feet or so away.

His tires crunched on the rocks that filled a low spot in the dirt road as he slowed even more. From there, he inched along until he reached the same vantage point he'd used before and cut the engine. He could see the yellow glow of a light through a second-story window. Was that Sadie's room? Or

Dawson's? And it was late. Why was the light still on?

After what Sadie had said in the restaurant, he thought he could guess, but imagining her having sex with Dawson — moaning in pleasure as he pumped into her — created such a thirst for violence. He kept imagining sliding his hands around her neck and squeezing until her face turned blue, which made it impossible for him to focus on anything else. She'd had him so worked up the past few days he couldn't eat or sleep!

You're sleeping with him, aren't you . . .

Yes, and I've never enjoyed anything more . . .

That was essentially what she'd said to him. The mere memory of her defiant expression made him long to smash her face. How dare she taunt him, when she knew his biggest complaint had always been how complacent she was in the bedroom. That was why he'd gone elsewhere occasionally: for some excitement! A man needed a good thrill every once in a while. It wasn't as if he'd *cared* about those other women. He would never have touched them if she hadn't been so resistant to trying some of the things he'd shown her in various porn flicks.

She was boring. Too straitlaced for him.

He was glad to be rid of her, he told himself. Now he could do whatever he wanted, and he had no one to answer to. She couldn't even give him a decent son. While other men's boys were out playing baseball, his child was in the bedroom playing *Barbies*. Jayden was an embarrassment. Yet she stood up for him all the time, refused to let his own father teach him how to be a man.

He didn't want her back. Not anymore. He just couldn't take her running around town, acting as if she was so much happier with someone else, especially *Dawson Reed*. And he couldn't let her bring that damn investigator to town.

His door creaked as he opened it, but there wasn't anyone in the fields to hear. He waited and listened, to be sure. But it was every bit as quiet as it had been when he'd come here before.

After he climbed out, he closed the door softly and walked toward the house. Although he didn't have any specific plans, he couldn't make himself stay as far back as he always had before. That light, imagining Sadie inside, drew him closer — and closer.

Once he reached the yard, he crept across it and tried to peer through the windows. But everything was dark downstairs. Whatever was happening was happening above him, and he wanted to know what, if anything, that was. Otherwise, he could achieve no satisfaction.

He needed to get inside, he decided. Just to listen. Knowing they were so close, so *vulnerable,* would make him feel as if he was still in control of the situation — for a few minutes, anyway. He wouldn't stay long.

After checking, once again, to make sure he was going unobserved, he approached the back door — and tried the knob. *Son of a bitch!* It was locked.

But that wouldn't stop him. He'd just have to find another way in.

Dawson could hardly catch his breath for the intensity of Sadie's kiss. Even though he'd been dying to touch her again, he'd promised himself he wouldn't press her. She needed time.

But his body had acted almost of its own volition. When he'd heard her footsteps on the stairs, he'd intercepted her, intent on saying something, anything, to stall her for a few moments. He told himself he just wanted to talk, but, truth was, he couldn't stand the thought of spending another night in his bed alone.

Fortunately, it hadn't come to that. She acted as if she'd only been waiting for the right opportunity, because she certainly wasn't holding back.

"Trying to leave you alone has been torture," he said as his hands found their way up the back of her shirt where he could splay his fingers against her soft, smooth skin. "I've been miserable. Constantly imagining you naked against me. Imagining myself inside you. Hoping but not wanting to ask."

"With everything that's going on, it's crazy I can even think of sex," she said with a husky laugh. "But I haven't been able to get you off my mind, either."

"Then I'm glad you broke down."

She kissed him again and again — hungrily, as though she might never get enough. "Tell me we're not making a mistake," she said as they gasped for breath. "Because I've never wanted a man like I want you. I can't quash the desire, can't even curb it."

"You don't have to," he said, and she put her legs around his hips to make it easier when he lifted her and carried her to the bed.

"Wait. There's so much that could go wrong for us . . ." she said.

He didn't wait. She wasn't committed to refusing. He could tell by the fact that she didn't stop him when he pulled off the sweatpants he'd loaned her. "There's also a lot about this that feels right." He could understand her hesitancy, the fear she had to be feeling that she might be making another mistake. But practical concerns were difficult to remember, and even harder to heed, while deluged with so many hormones.

"Okay, one more time," she said. "Then that's it."

"No." He was done fighting. As far as he was concerned, they were in a relationship. Whether that would turn out to be good or bad, for either one of them, remained to be seen. But there was no going back. The fact that they were once again straining to come together, when it had been only a few days since the first time, proved that.

"No?" she echoed, sounding a little panicked.

"It's too late. All we can do now is go for it — and hope for the best."

Putting her hands on his chest, she pushed him far enough away to be able to look into his face. "That terrifies me as much or more than anything related to Sly."

"I understand. But think of this. Maybe it's meant to be. Maybe finding each other will be the one good thing to come out of all the shit we've been through."

"It's just so fast, *too* fast . . ."

"We've been trying to make it go slower. We just . . . can't. So I say we let go — grab hands and jump off the cliff, enjoy the fall."

She laughed again. "Is that supposed to convince me? That sounds as ominous as it does exhilarating!"

"To me, it just sounds exhilarating. I don't want to miss out on what might be the best thing to ever happen to me. Do you?"

She ran her hand over his cheek in a gentle caress. "No," she said, and with that the tempo of their lovemaking changed. They were no longer in such a hurry. Giving themselves permission to feel something deeper than the physical created a completely different kind of experience — one even more fulfilling.

Sly sat in Dawson's living room, listening to the rhythmic creak of the bed overhead. Dawson and Sadie were so busy he probably could've used his shoulder to bust open the back door — splintered the whole damn thing — without drawing their attention. Instead, he'd been careful, oh so quiet as he used a screwdriver from Dawson's own toolshed to dig away at the dry rot in one of the window frames until he'd made a hole large enough to reach his hand through and release the latch.

Dawson might notice the damage in the morning. Or maybe he wouldn't. There'd been so much vandalism that he hadn't been able to repair it all. Either way, Sly didn't care. Dawson and Sadie wouldn't be able to prove a damn thing. He'd been wearing gloves when he used the screwdriver — was wearing gloves now. And if it ever came down to an extensive evidence search where a strand of his hair or some of his DNA was found in the living room, so what? He'd been here before — with the chief of police, no less. He could've left hair or DNA then as easily as now. He wasn't frightened. He was too livid to be frightened — *so* livid he could hardly see straight.

Squeak, squeak, squeak. As he listened to what was going on upstairs, he tapped the tire iron he'd used as a lever to help open the window against the palm of his left hand. The blood was rushing through his body so fast he could hear the roar of it in his ears. Even a month ago, he would never have dreamed he'd find himself in this position, had never considered the possibility that another man could come between him and Sadie. She'd always been *his* — since she was old enough to date.

Then Dawson had been let out of jail and,

421

just when Sly felt as if he was making some progress toward putting his marriage back together, everything had fallen apart. Now, here he was, listening to another man take his place between her legs.

He stared at the tool in his hand. He wanted to use it on them. Get rid of them both so he didn't have to think about them ever again. Put an end to his own torment that quickly, that easily. Even if he became the prime suspect, no one would be able to prove anything. Then there'd be no one to pay the fire inspector who was coming to town, and there would be no worry that some hotshot might be able to find what their own far less experienced department could not.

Look what you've reduced me to, he silently berated Sadie. *An arsonist. A man who wants to commit* murder.

And she thought he'd ruined *her* life. She had no idea what she'd done to him. He'd never be the same.

Unable to take the sound of that bed squeaking any longer, he decided to put an end to it. Imagining the humiliation he'd face if the arson investigator somehow proved he was responsible gave him the perfect excuse to do what he wanted to do anyway.

He stood up, but before he could reach the stairs, a pair of headlights flashed through the front windows of the house.

Someone was here.

Panic surged through him, clearing his head. He had to get out. *Now.*

Taking the screwdriver and the tire iron with him, he hurried to the back door, let himself out and slipped into the darkness.

Once he reached his car, he was relieved to be out of the house. He didn't think he'd been seen. But he didn't know for sure. And, just in case someone was watching and listening, he waited, didn't dare start the engine because of the noise.

As he sat there with his heart beating in his throat, he saw headlights again, only this time the car was moving back toward the highway. He didn't think there could be two cars, so whoever had come to the farm was leaving. Already.

Had whoever it was even gone to the door?

No. There wouldn't have been time. At least, Sly didn't think so.

He held off another five minutes before starting his cruiser, turning around and rolling slowly and cautiously back toward the highway. From there, he took side streets — as much as possible — to his house so that he wouldn't run into anyone he knew.

Not until he got home, where he'd left his phone so that his whereabouts couldn't be tracked after the fact, did he understand what'd happened. It was Pete who'd visited the farm. Sly had missed half a dozen calls from him, texts, too.

Where the hell are you, man?

Don't tell me you're out at Dawson Reed's place. That would be crazy. You realize that, right?

You gotta leave Sadie and Dawson alone. They aren't worth your future.

Why won't you pick up? I know you're not home. I've been by your place twice already.

You're not at your mother's either. What the hell, dude? Are you trying to get yourself kicked off the force?

Pick up. You need to listen to me.

Pete had driven to Dawson's in order to keep him out of trouble. But he would never know just how close Sly had come — because Sly could never tell him.

Dawson woke up when Sadie pulled away from him. "You're leaving already?" he mumbled sleepily.

"Yeah. I've got to get back to Jayden."

"But it isn't morning yet."

"I'm afraid I'll oversleep if I don't go now, and it's best if he wakes up to find me where I usually am."

Dawson had an alarm set for fairly early, but he didn't mention that. Jayden could always wake up before the alarm went off. Besides, things were going fast enough as it was. Sadie would probably feel more comfortable sleeping with her son, like she usually did. "Just tell me one thing before you go."

She was putting on her clothes. "What's that?"

"You're okay, right? You're not too freaked out?"

"Right now I'm not freaked out at all. Right now I'm pretty happy."

He knew she was referring to the climax he'd given her and smiled even though she couldn't see him. "Then try to remember, in the morning, that everything's going to be fine. Even if things go . . . bad between us at some point, we'll figure out a way to be kind to each other, to end as friends. You won't go through anything like what you've been through with Sly. I promise."

"You're a good man," she said. "I'm glad I met you."

You're a good man. That wasn't something he'd heard very often in his life. He'd been a troubled kid and barely out of that difficult stage of life when he'd been accused of murder. The whole town still believed he'd taken two lives with a hatchet — and not just any lives but the lives of his *parents.*

Maybe that was why he rolled her words around and around in his head for so long after she left the room. Her belief in him felt even better than the pleasure she'd provided.

23

Robin Strauss wasn't a minute late. With her gray hair combed into a bun at her nape and a multitude of lines around her mouth, she appeared to be about fifty-five and rather . . . harsh.

Sadie could tell that Dawson grew even more nervous once he saw her. The media hadn't been kind to him, and the media reports had to be at least part of what Robin Strauss would use to judge him by. With her sober demeanor, button-down suit and thick glasses, she looked like a no-nonsense nun, or maybe a spinster librarian — someone who would view him as skeptically as possible.

Once they let her in, she didn't say anything overtly negative, but she wasn't friendly, either. She walked through the house, peering into each room before pausing at the master.

"This is where it happened?" She turned

to Sadie, since Dawson had stopped at the doorway rather than follow them inside.

"Yes." Sadie had asked Petra to watch Jayden for a couple of hours. She hated to leave him, in case Sly tried to cause trouble, but she'd known it wouldn't be wise to have him here during the visit in case the discussion turned to the murders, and Petra had assured her she wouldn't let Sly take Jayden no matter what.

"Is anyone using this room?" She focused on the box springs that didn't have a mattress.

"Not yet."

Ms. Strauss turned around to address Dawson. "What do you plan to do with it? Anything?"

"Sadie and Jayden will move in here once Angela is allowed to come home," he said.

Her eyebrows, carefully drawn in with pencil, rose slightly. "Sadie doesn't mind the fact that there was a double homicide here?"

Sadie spoke up before Dawson could attempt an answer. "I'm not pleased by the idea, of course. No one would be. But, as we've already explained, I'm living here because Dawson felt it would be better for Angela to have round-the-clock care. Or are you saying the bedroom should be closed off and never used again?"

Ms. Strauss seemed to realize how impractical the alternative would be. Despite the Reeds' deaths, there were still living and breathing people who needed shelter. A house couldn't be boarded up or burned down every time someone committed an act of violence inside its walls. "Some people are funny about those types of things — superstitious — is all," she said.

"I'm not superstitious," Sadie told her, but she had to admit, at least to herself, that the thought of sleeping in this room was a little discomfiting. She didn't feel it was fair to put Angela here, however. And she knew how hard it would be for Dawson. So she'd insisted on being the one. Given that she wasn't paying rent, it only seemed fair. "And just so you know, Dawson isn't to blame for what happened, despite what you might've read about his case. He's currently looking for the man he believes to be responsible."

Ms. Strauss pushed her glasses higher on her nose. "That's what he told you?"

Sadie couldn't help bristling at the skepticism in her voice. "Yes. And I believe it's true."

She made no comment, merely clasped her clipboard to her chest. "So where is

Angela's room?"

"That's where Jayden and I are staying at the moment. Right this way."

Dawson stepped aside as Sadie led her back into the hall.

Ms. Strauss peered into Dawson's room before taking a long look at Angela's. "I've spoken to Angela," she announced, rather abruptly.

"Did she tell you how badly she wants to come home?" Sadie shot a hopeful glance at Dawson. He'd rejoined them once they came out of his parents' room, but he wasn't doing a lot of talking. Sadie was trying to fill the long awkward silences, to make Ms. Strauss more sympathetic, if possible.

"She did."

"She loves her brother. He's always been good to her."

"How long have *you* known Dawson?" she asked.

There was that skepticism again. Sadie barely managed to keep her smile in place. "Not long, which is why it's so great that you don't have to take my word for what a nice guy he is. The one person in town who's known him the longest, since he was a freshman in high school, has said all along that he could never have perpetrated such a

430

terrible crime. Feel free to talk to her, if you need a character reference."

"I'll do that," she said, but Sadie got the impression she only agreed in order to be thorough. "Who should I contact?"

"Aiyana Turner. She's the owner of New Horizons Boys Ranch."

"Where he went to school."

She'd done her homework. "Yes. Her sons also know Dawson and believe the same thing she does. His detractors, on the other hand, are virtual strangers. They're judging him by what was presented in the media — which is, of course, what we both hope you *won't* do. For Angela's sake."

When the older woman's eyes narrowed beneath those thick glasses, Sadie feared she might've been a little *too* zealous in his defense. She didn't want to reveal her romantic interest. That would only make Ms. Strauss question her credibility. "You told me that you started working here a week ago, correct?"

What Ms. Strauss really meant was, "How would you know?" Sadie could tell. "Yes."

"Were you familiar with Dawson before that?"

"Not really, no."

"Well, you certainly seem to be getting along so far."

That would be a good thing for Angela, wouldn't it? But Sadie wasn't sure Ms. Strauss meant her statement in a positive way.

After that, she tried to keep her mouth shut. Dawson finished the tour, answered several more questions — about where Angela was when the murders occurred, how much she saw, what she understood.

Before Ms. Strauss left, however, she asked if Sadie would walk her out to her car — and made it clear that Dawson wasn't to join them.

A rush of nervous energy flooded through Sadie as she agreed. "Sure."

Sadie guessed Dawson was watching from the window while they crossed the porch and descended the stairs. Ms. Strauss didn't speak immediately — didn't say anything until they were well out of earshot of Dawson. Then she used her key fob to unlock the doors to a black sedan and turned. "You seem very supportive of Mr. Reed."

"I am," Sadie admitted. "I've spent a lot of hours with him over the past eight days and have seen nothing that would lead me to believe he would be anything other than a devoted brother. We've even been to visit Angela at Stanley DeWitt together. He wanted to take me along, so she could meet me."

"Eight days isn't a long time," she said, refusing to be persuaded.

"Like I said, you can speak to Aiyana, Elijah or Gavin, if you're looking for someone who has known him longer."

"I'm not sure they could convince me."

Ms. Strauss spoke with such resolution, Sadie felt her jaw drop. She was going to deny Dawson's request for Angela to come home! "Because . . ."

"If we turn Angela over to him, and something happens to her, the blowback could be severe. The press will make a lot of the state releasing a mentally handicapped woman to a man we had reason to believe might be dangerous, and —"

"Whoa, wait a minute," Sadie broke in. "He was tried and found innocent. I think the state has done all it can do."

"Not in this regard, I'm afraid."

"But refusing to let Angela come home makes no sense," Sadie argued. "Dawson wants her here, and she wants to be here. Why would the state insist on continuing to pay for her care when she has a family member who's willing to step up?"

Unperturbed, as if she dealt with emotional situations all the time — and, of course, she probably did — Ms. Strauss climbed behind the wheel. "Because we're responsible for her well-being. I don't feel it's wise to take the risk, not when Angela is receiving the care she needs at Stanley De-Witt."

Dawson was going to be heartbroken. He would believe he'd let Angela down — and his dead parents by extension.

Sadie caught the door before Ms. Strauss could close it. "But you can't believe the media reports," she said. "Please. They don't always get it right."

She put her key in the ignition. "I'm *not* basing my decision on the media reports."

"You have to be! What else could be influencing your decision?"

She sighed audibly. "I received a call from someone yesterday that definitely made an impact."

Sadie's mind raced as she tried to imagine who might've contacted the state in regards to Dawson getting his sister back, but no one came to mind. Who else would care? Distant relatives? The prosecutor? The detective? "From *who*?"

"From someone who's very concerned about this situation, concerned enough to let me know where things *really* stand."

"*Who?*" Sadie repeated with more insistence. "It couldn't be anyone who knows what he or she is talking about."

"It was an officer on the Silver Springs police force," Ms. Strauss announced, as if that cinched it. "He let me know in no uncertain terms that Dawson Reed has gotten away with murder."

Sadie felt the blood rush to her head. *"Excuse me?"*

Ms. Strauss looked a little shocked by the power behind her outburst. "I was saying that I have it on good authority —"

"No. That isn't good authority. The officer who called you was Sly Harris, wasn't it."

A hint of color crept into her cheeks. "Yes. How did you know?"

Closing her eyes, Sadie shook her head. "Because he's my ex-husband. He hates that I now have a job that enables me to move on without him, so he's been doing everything possible to make life for me miserable — Dawson, too, since Dawson's been kind enough to help me. Officer Harris wasn't acting in Angela's best interest when he contacted you, Ms. Strauss. He was acting in his *own* best interest, was trying to cause trouble for Dawson."

"I'd rather not get involved in any domestic disputes." She lifted a hand as if to indicate that what Sadie had said was none

435

of her business.

"Then don't," Sadie responded. "I'm telling you Dawson Reed *didn't* kill his parents. Why would he be so intent on catching the real culprit if he was the guilty party? Why would he spend over $2,000 on a forensic specialist to come out and collect specimens from the bedroom? Why would he move back here, where he's been treated like a pariah, and try to take care of his mentally handicapped sister, when he could take the money he received from his parents' estate and start over, footloose and fancy-free, somewhere else?"

"To make himself look innocent, of course."

Sadie shook her head in disgust. "Don't you see how weak of an argument that is? He wouldn't waste the time *or* the money. Especially because nothing he's done so far has changed anyone's mind! He'll have to find the culprit and *prove* his innocence in order to make the people of Silver Springs believe him, and he knows he has little chance of that. He's only fighting because he feels he owes it to his parents."

A scowl suggested she would continue to resist Sadie's logic. But what she said next indicated *some* softening. "I'll think about it."

There was nothing left to do but let her close the door. Sadie's heart sank as she watched Dawson's only hope of getting his sister back put her car in Reverse and start backing down the drive. She didn't want to go in and tell him that his sister would have to remain institutionalized.

"Damn it. Can't *anything* go right?" she mumbled.

Knowing that he was waiting to hear what Ms. Strauss had wanted to talk to her about, and feeling the weight of the inevitable, she turned, heartsick but resolute, toward the house. She needed to leave town sooner rather than later, she decided. Sly would not leave Dawson alone as long as she was here with him.

Before she could go more than two steps, however, Ms. Strauss stopped, rolled down her window and poked her head out.

"Fine," she called out. "I'll check into it. If what you say is true, that Officer Harris has a personal interest in this situation and there are others who will vouch for Mr. Reed's character, I'll recommend that the state allow Angela to come home."

Sadie couldn't believe her ears. "Call the chief of police. I'm not asking you to take my word alone. You could visit Lolita, who owns the diner in town, too. She saw Officer Harris nearly strike me in the restaurant on Sunday. It was right after that I applied to get a restraining order against him — although I haven't yet had my hearing on that." She thought about telling Ms. Strauss about the fire. In her book, Sly had done a lot more than *almost* strike her. But she had no proof he was the arsonist and didn't want to come off as unbalanced or *too* acrimonious.

"It is what Angela wants, so . . . I'll reevaluate and get back to you." Her lips curved into a smile — the first Sadie had seen from her. "Tell Dawson he's lucky to have you in his corner."

Sadie let her breath go in relief. "I'm equally lucky to have him in mine," she said and waved as Ms. Strauss left.

The following morning, nervous sweat ran down Sadie's back, causing her blouse to stick to her as she stood, with Chief Thomas, at Sly's door. After telling Dawson the good news about Ms. Strauss, she'd spent the rest of the day and night thinking about how she could neutralize the threat Sly posed, if not to herself — that had proved impossible, thanks to his obsession — at least to Dawson. And this was the best she could come up with: something she couldn't tell Dawson about because she knew he'd try to dissuade her.

Although she'd stopped by the police station and asked for an escort, she'd nearly come away without one. None of the other police officers would even speak to her — not like they used to, anyway. A few cast her dark or disgruntled glances. Others muttered under their breath. All gave her a wide berth.

Sly had done a solid job of making her look like the bad guy. No doubt he'd painted her as a woman he couldn't rely on when he needed her, a wife who wouldn't support him in his difficult job, an ex who was launching slanderous and unfair accusations and had now taken up with a "known" murderer, as if that was the last piece of proof anyone would ever need in order to be convinced that she was "the problem."

But she got lucky when Chief Thomas happened to hear her talking to the sergeant at the front desk. Although Dixie Gilbert should've been more sympathetic — she and Sadie got their hair done at the same place and were casual acquaintances — Dixie wasn't about to break rank with her brothers in blue. As the only woman on the force, it was probably hard to fit in, so Sadie could understand. She just couldn't admire her lack of courage. Dixie was giving Sadie the brush-off by telling her that someone would "be in touch" — while Sadie knew that call would probably never come — when Thomas saw her, came out of his office and asked what was going on. As soon as Sadie told him, he said he'd be happy to drive her over to Sly's place so that she could speak to him.

Sadie was fairly certain he was hoping to play mediator. He wanted to bring them together so they could arrive at an understanding, one in which she wouldn't embarrass the department by pursuing the restraining order (she did, after all, have witnesses to Sly's explosive temper at the restaurant, which gave her legitimate grounds). She, on the other hand, merely wanted the opportunity to deliver a message to him without creating a record on her phone of calling or texting him after telling the police she was afraid of him. She knew how quickly Sly would capitalize on that to try to prove she wasn't remotely intimidated by him.

As soon as Sly opened the door, squinting out at them and stinking of alcohol, she was glad she hadn't come alone. Not that she ever would have. She knew better than to give him an opportunity like that. But she was frightened even with Chief Thomas at her side. She'd never seen Sly looking so rough. He'd always been a big drinker. He prided himself on his ability to "hold his liquor." But that was just it — he'd never been a "sloppy" drunk, never let himself go.

Chief Thomas didn't like what he saw, either. "What the hell's the matter with you? You smell like you just crawled out of a bottle."

Sly managed to stand up straighter. "Couldn't sleep last night. Insomnia's a bitch."

So he'd tried to drink himself into a stupor? Judging by the way the light hurt his eyes, he'd managed that quite nicely — and now he had a raging hangover.

"What are *you* doing here?" he growled, glaring at her.

Chief Thomas gestured to draw his attention. "Whoa! Let's not start off like that. We're here to make peace. Can we come in?"

Sly shook his head. "I don't want her in this house. She's the one who walked out of it. But . . . we can talk in back. Let me comb my hair and brush my teeth. Let yourselves through the side gate and meet me on the patio." He glared at her. "*She* knows the way."

Sadie felt Chief Thomas's frown, rather than saw it, as she led him through the side yard to the patio. The large barbecue that had been Sly's pride and joy when they were married stood open without its cover and his barbecuing utensils lay scattered about, along with several plates, some with wasted food, and a slew of empty beer cans.

"Looks like you had a party last night," Chief Thomas said when the sliding door opened and Sly came out.

"It's been a few days," he said with a shrug. "Some of the guys came by. That's all." He knocked a plate with a half-eaten hamburger, covered with ants, off the closest chair, swung it around to face them and slouched into it. "What's going on now? Why are you here?"

"I'm trying to help you save your job. That's why *I'm* here," Chief Thomas said. "And, judging by what Sadie's told me already, she might be able to help you, too."

Sly hooked his arm over the back of the chair. "How? She certainly hasn't helped me so far."

"Things don't have to be like this between us, Sly," Sadie said. He had to get a grip on his life, on the divorce. Soon it would be his weekend to have Jayden, and although he typically didn't exercise his custodial rights, and he hadn't mentioned this weekend specifically, he could always surprise her. She wouldn't put it past him. She didn't want to let Jayden go with a man who might've set fire to their house and who looked so uncharacteristically out of sorts now, even if Sly was his father. "I never wanted any trouble to begin with," she added. "I'm hoping we can back up, take a deep breath and find some way to avoid the bitter divorce so many others experience."

"You think you're going to accomplish that by shacking up with Dawson Reed?"

"Sadie has a right to work — and even sleep — with anyone she wants, Sly," Thomas interrupted. "You two have been split up for some time. That's no longer any of your business."

"I'm not supposed to care?" he argued.

"Caring is one thing. Creating a problem is another."

"So *I'm* the problem? What about the restraining order? She knows how that looks — accusing me of stalking her, of being *dangerous*." He wiggled his fingers like he was impersonating a bogeyman.

But he *was* dangerous. Maybe Sadie was the only one who truly believed it, but she was absolutely convinced. That was another reason it scared her to think he could take

Jayden this coming weekend.

She cleared her throat. "I'll forget about the restraining order, so long as you fulfill a few of *my* requests."

He looked around as if he was wishing for a beer, despite the fact that it was only ten-thirty in the morning. "I'm all ears," he said when he couldn't find an unopened can.

"I want you to stay away from Dawson, quit trying to make his life miserable."

"I haven't done shit to that asshole," he growled.

Maybe he hadn't done what he wanted to do, but he'd done what he could. "You called the state and tried to convince them not to let him bring his sister home."

A smile slashed his face as if the mere mention of that was some sort of victory. "I was acting as a concerned citizen."

"You're *not* a concerned citizen. You identified yourself as a police officer and implied you had insider knowledge to suggest that Dawson was guilty. You understood you'd be taken seriously and that you could severely damage his chances to get his sister released, and that's not fair. You don't know anything about him, nothing more than what's in his police file, anyway. And he's had enough trouble. I don't want to make his situation any worse, just because he was

444

nice enough to try to help me."

"*Help* you?" His gaze swept down over her breasts. "Believe me, he's getting what he wants out of *that* deal."

Sadie squared her shoulders. This wasn't a topic she cared to discuss in front of Chief Thomas, but she doubted Sly would let her out of it, so she dived in. "If you're talking about sex, he could get that from plenty of other women, Sly. You've said it yourself. Women have a thing for him. It's not as if he's hard to look at."

A glint of surprise and possibly jealousy flashed in his eyes as he rubbed the beard growth on his cheeks. "Got a soft spot for the guy you're riding these days, do you?" he said when he finally dropped his hand.

"How Sadie feels about Dawson also has nothing to do with this conversation," Thomas broke in. "She can fall in love with him, sleep with him, marry him, whatever. None of that's illegal, which means none of it's your concern — or the concern of the department."

Afraid that Sly would reject her offer out of hand, Sadie hurried to get back to the conversation. "Not only will I drop the restraining order, I'll accept your last offer of child support and no alimony." She wanted to bring up the issue of Sly exercising his parental rights this weekend, but she knew the moment she let him know she didn't want him to take Jayden, he'd make sure to insist. Her best chance of keeping her son out of his company was to pretend she would welcome the break — so she could spend the weekend alone with Dawson. That was how she planned to handle it if he asked when he could come get Jayden tomorrow.

His bloodshot eyes latched onto her face. "So now you're in a hurry to get it over with."

"Yes. That way we can wrap up the divorce and be done with each other."

Sly spat at the cement as if it were her words that'd left a bad taste in his mouth and not the alcohol he'd drunk before bed. "He doesn't need you to come over here and beg for him. I'm sure he can take care of himself."

"He doesn't even know I'm here, Sly. I doubt he'd agree with it if he did. This is me talking. I want to . . . to stop what's happening before it goes any further. I don't like that you're out to get him. He's never done anything to you."

Sly sprang to his feet. "Except hire a specialist to try to prove me guilty of arson!"

"*I'm* behind that! It has nothing to do with him."

"Bullshit! He's coaching you and helping you and loaning you money and shit."

Chief Thomas, a dark scowl on his face, rose to his feet. "If you didn't set that fire, you have nothing to worry about. So what if Sadie and Dawson have hired an independent investigator?"

Sly's mouth opened and closed twice before he managed to say, "Silver Springs can handle the investigation! We have competent personnel. You've said so yourself."

"That's true. But if Sadie and Dawson want to pay for someone else to redo the same work, I'm fine with it, because being 'fine with it' proves that the department isn't trying to hide anything, that we're not merely trying to cover your ass. That aspect should appeal to you, too. If their arson inspector can't prove you're guilty, you'll never have to worry about this popping up again."

"What if he pretends to find something that isn't there?" Sly asked.

"What are you talking about?" Thomas snapped. "*Why* would he do that?"

"Who knows? Maybe they're paying him a little extra." Sly focused on Sadie. "Get rid of the investigator, too, or I'm not making any deals with you."

Sadie couldn't go that far. If he set the fire, it wasn't safe to leave him out on the streets. Even if *she* could get free of him, what would happen to the next woman who became part of his life? "I'm sorry. It's too late for that. He'll be here today — in just another hour."

"You could meet him at the property and send him away."

"That's true." She adjusted her purse in her lap. "But I won't. I have to do this for my own peace of mind. You say you didn't do it. I'd like to believe you. But I can't take your word for it. I need to see what he has to say."

He kicked over a can near his feet. "You're so full of bullshit! You come here with *my boss,* pretending to offer me an olive branch, but you're still going after me."

Thomas lifted one eyebrow. "She's not going after *you.* She's going after the criminal who set fire to her house, right?"

Sly flung out a hand. "You're taking *her* side?"

Thomas stared him down. "You know what? You're really starting to piss me off. She's offering you a fair deal. I suggest you take it."

"You couldn't possibly understand all the

nuances between us," Sly argued.

"I don't need to," Thomas said. "You're essentially divorced. She has the right to move on. And you're going to let her do it. Furthermore, if you set that fire, you're going to prison. It's that simple."

Although Sadie had always suspected Sly was the culprit, she was never more positive of it than in that moment. Something about his expression gave him away. But when he quickly recovered and shouted, "I had nothing to do with it!" he was *so* convincing.

Was she wrong?

She wanted to believe she was. She just couldn't.

"Good. Then you have nothing to worry about," Thomas said. "So we can leave, knowing that you're going to leave both Sadie and Dawson alone in the future. Is that true?"

"Of course," Sly grumbled, now sullen, but Sadie knew then that she'd wasted her time coming here. Regardless of what he told Chief Thomas, Sly wouldn't back off. Maybe he would've appreciated her concessions on the restraining order and the divorce if he didn't have something much bigger to worry about. But he did. He had the fire. And if the truth came out, he'd lose everything that mattered to him, including his freedom.

As Sadie walked out, she realized there was no telling what he might do. She'd never had more reason to be frightened of him.

24

Dawson heard his name and turned to find a petite woman with a long black braid and skin like burnished copper standing at the edge of the field, trying to get his attention. Aiyana. He'd called her this morning, to thank her for sending Eli and Gavin over to clean, even though he wouldn't let them, and to tell her how things had gone with the state yesterday — that Ms. Strauss was tentatively in favor of letting Angela come home. But his onetime school administrator had been busy and hadn't been able to talk more than a few minutes. She'd said she'd call back, that she really needed to have a longer conversation with him.

Evidently, she'd decided to swing by the farm instead.

He didn't mind. He'd missed her — just didn't realize how much until he saw her beaming at him. He should've reached out to her as soon as he was released from jail.

He wasn't sure why he hadn't.

Stopping his tractor, he wiped the sweat from his face, climbed down and walked over so that she wouldn't have to come through the loose dirt in order to speak with him. "Hey, look who's here! Silver Springs royalty," he said.

"Oh, listen to you," she responded with a laugh.

He was too dirty, wouldn't have made physical contact, but she didn't give him a choice. She grabbed him as soon as she could reach him, dirt, sweat and all.

Clasping her to him, he swung her around. She was the closest thing he had to a mother these days, so he wasn't in any hurry to break the embrace. He closed his eyes and smiled to himself as she gave him a convincing squeeze, one that felt a lot like "I love you."

"It's good to see you, especially looking so fit and handsome," she said when he put her down.

"*Fit?* Is that how I look?" he said with a laugh. "I was thinking dirty might be more appropriate."

"Okay, dirty but strong as an ox."

He bent to knock some of the dust off the bottom of the long, colorful skirt she wore. "Maybe that hug wasn't such a good idea."

She made a sound that signified she wasn't concerned. "Who cares about a little dirt here and there? I've washed these clothes before, I can wash them again."

"You've always been able to focus on what's important." Without her perspective, and the fact that she'd entered his life at such a critical juncture, he wasn't sure what he'd be like today. She was the one who'd helped him make sense of the world, who'd taught him to live a more disciplined life. She'd also facilitated his adoption by the Reeds — had approached them with the idea of taking in one of her "boys" with the promise that she had the "perfect" one in mind.

"Because I'm older than I look. Perspective comes with age," she said with a wink. "So how are you *really* — on the inside? Coping okay?"

He sobered. "Managing. How are things out at the ranch?"

She tossed her braid, which had come around front, over her shoulder. "Busy as ever. That's why it took me so long to pay you a visit — that and I didn't want to descend on you before you were ready for company. Sometimes it's easier to deal with pain when we have a little space. At least I'm that way. But I hope you know I've been thinking about you, pulling for you — and I'm always available if you need me."

"I do know that. It means a lot. Thank you." He gestured toward the porch. "Should we sit for a minute? Can I get you something to drink?"

"I'll take a chair, but I don't need a drink. I won't interrupt you for long. I just had to see you with my own eyes — needed the reassurance."

"I'm glad you're here."

She chose the old rocker where his mother used to read on long summer evenings while waiting for his father to come in from the fields. Dawson felt a tinge of nostalgia at the sight of her sitting there. His mother should still be alive to enjoy those quiet hours before dusk. Why would anyone harm such a fine person?

It didn't make sense, especially the way it happened, so randomly. But after getting to know the men he'd served time with, Dawson understood that senseless crimes were perpetrated far too often. Some of the things the men he'd met liked to talk about turned his stomach. He wouldn't let someone just like them get away with murdering his folks. He'd made himself that promise. But it would help if he could hear from Oscar Hunt at Safety First. There'd been no word since Dawson had spoken to Big Red on Monday.

Was the man who installed Alex's bunker still at a remote location with no cell service? Or had Big Red either forgotten or not bothered to pass along the message?

Dawson decided he'd let one more day go by and then call again. "Are you sure I can't get you something to drink?" he asked Aiyana.

"I might not be here long enough." A wry grin claimed her lips. "I'm afraid you'll send me away the moment you hear what I'd like to talk about."

Dawson tensed for the first time since realizing he had a visitor. "Something wrong?"

"Not wrong, exactly. It's just that . . . I don't want to see you get into any more trouble."

He sank into the seat not far from her. "You think I'm headed for trouble?"

She glanced around. "Sadie isn't here, is she? I didn't see her car in the drive . . ."

"No. She left a couple of hours ago. She had to drop Jayden off at the babysitter's so she could meet the arson investigator at the house she was renting. You heard about the fire . . ."

"I did. How upsetting."

"No kidding."

455

She peered closer at him. "Sounds like you and Sadie are close."

"I've hired her to be Angela's caregiver."

"Eli mentioned that. I also heard she's been staying here since the fire."

"She is."

"How's that working out?"

"Great. She's doing a fine job helping me get this place ready."

"I like Sadie, Dawson. She seems like a nice girl." She shifted uncomfortably. "But that ex-husband of hers. I felt a niggle of concern when Eli first mentioned that she was here, but that niggle turned into something much more akin to panic when I ran into Lolita, who happens to be a friend of mine, at the grocery store yesterday."

"Lolita from the diner."

"Yes. She told me that Sly had to be dragged from the restaurant on Sunday, that he nearly attacked Sadie."

Dawson grimaced. "He's an asshole. There's no way he should be on the force."

"I agree. He's too volatile to be a police officer. But that isn't up to either of us. We have to deal with what is."

"Meaning . . ."

"You should keep your distance from Sly Harris, even if you have to keep your distance from Sadie to accomplish it. I know it's none of my business, but when I imagine all the heartache you've already endured, I can't bear the thought of you finding more trouble. That's why I'm here." She gave him a sheepish look. "Now . . . do you still want to offer me a drink?"

"Of course. But I should warn you that it's too late to stop anything where Sadie's involved. I've already bought in."

"You can always let her go. There's got to be someone else who can help you out here, and with Angela."

"The point is . . . I don't want anyone else."

She reared back in apparent surprise. "You're saying you care about her."

He stared out across the fields, at his tractor sitting in the middle of the section he'd been getting ready for planting, and the tree, in the distance, by which he'd buried his folks. He loved this farm. Loved the land, the area. He had a lot of good memories here. This was where he'd finally found home. He felt that same sense of having found something important, something he both needed and wanted, in Sadie. And he, of all people, knew better than to think that was an easy thing to come by. "I do."

"Already?"

He stretched his neck. "Neither one of us

are in a good situation. We recognize that. But she's brought some happiness and companionship back into my life. I'm not going to let Sly take that away from me. We deserve the chance to see if it goes anywhere."

Aiyana crossed her legs and smoothed her skirt. "Well. That changes things, I suppose."

He arched his eyebrows. "It does? In what way?"

"Makes it worth the risk."

She spoke so matter-of-factly he had to laugh. "You're going to change your mind that easily?"

"What can I say?" She sighed in an exaggerated fashion. "I'm a romantic. To me, love is always worth the risk."

"I don't know that it's love," he said, trying to back her off a little. "Not yet. Who can say where it will go? But there's a chance. I definitely feel . . . a spark."

"Even the hope of love is worth the risk," she clarified.

"Good. Then how about a cup of coffee?"

"Why not?"

He jerked his head toward the house. "Come on in. I'll make a fresh pot."

"What do you think of Sadie's son?" she asked as she followed him inside.

"Jayden's a great kid. Why?"

"I'm just curious how you'd feel about becoming a father."

"Whoa!" Stopping, he turned to face her. "That's really jumping ahead. Let me get used to having a girlfriend — with a cute boy — first."

Some of her enthusiasm dimmed. "You realize that Sly will be part of your life for as long as you're with Sadie . . ."

"Hopefully, he won't be part of her life *or* mine, no matter what happens."

"That's unrealistic. Jayden's his son."

He led her into the kitchen and motioned her into a seat as he started the coffee. "We believe he set the fire that nearly burned down her rental, Aiyana. And if we can prove it, he'll go to prison."

She looked aghast. "You can't be serious! I've heard rumors rumbling around town that she's accused him, but I never dreamed it was a real possibility."

"It's real, all right." He explained the logic behind their suspicion while the coffee percolated. By the time he carried two cups over to the table, they'd already moved on to how much she liked Eli's fiancée, Cora, how she wished Gavin and some of her other boys could find a good woman and settle down and how much attendance at the school she'd founded so long ago had grown over the years. She said they had more students than ever.

Dawson enjoyed the conversation. He especially liked hearing that she was dating someone herself, after being alone for so long. Cal Buchanan, a local cattle rancher, had always had a thing for her. He used to hang around the school as much as possible, even when Dawson was going there. Apparently, they were openly seeing each other now. Aiyana even admitted that he'd asked her to marry him — and that she was considering it.

Their conversation made Dawson feel more normal than anything since he'd been released from jail. He had work to do, but he was still sorry to see her go when she left an hour later. He waved as she backed down the drive. Then he whistled some silly tune as he walked toward the place where he'd been working. But before he could reach his tractor, he saw a section of plants off in the distance that looked as if they'd been mowed down — something he probably wouldn't have noticed if he hadn't been taking his time and looking around, taking stock of everything. He was usually too focused on what lay directly in front of him to pay much attention to what lay off to one side.

Curious to see what'd caused the damage, he followed the canal to where it looked as if a car had driven into his crops while making a three-point turn in order to go back the way it had come.

"What the hell," he muttered as he squatted to finger the tire tracks. He hadn't driven his truck back here, not in ages. Which meant someone else had to have come recently — and, judging by the number of times a vehicle had turned around in this very spot, more than once. But why would anyone come here the first time, let alone again and again? There was nothing but dirt and artichoke plants.

Unless . . .

Dawson stood and turned. He had an unobstructed view of the house from this vantage point, and it wasn't that far away.

A creeping sensation came over him as he realized that this would be the perfect place to park at night if someone wanted to do a little snooping — on him and Sadie. And Dawson had a good idea who that person might be.

Dawson was trying to call her, but Sadie couldn't talk right now. The arson investigator had just pulled into the drive and was walking up to greet her. He was late, thanks to traffic he'd encountered leaving Los Angeles. When he'd let her know it'd be an extra hour or so, Chief Thomas, who'd been planning to meet him with her, had gone to the station and left her to handle the appointment on her own. He'd also given her permission to go in and get what was left of her belongings. He told her the firefighters had salvaged what they could and staged it in the kitchen, where she'd be able to get to it from the back door. They didn't want her to go anywhere near the side that had been burned for fear she might get hurt. She probably could've searched through what they'd saved while she waited for Mr. Steele, but she'd been putting that off. She didn't want to be too emotional when the arson investigator arrived.

Normally, Maude and Vern — or at the least Maude — would've kept her busy chatting, but they were gone today, visiting their daughter in Palm Springs. So Sadie had been sitting alone on their patio, using the internet on her phone to entertain herself while she waited.

Planning to call Dawson back later, she silenced his ring before sticking out her hand to shake with the stern-looking, military type who was, apparently, her arson investigator. "Sadie Harris. Thank you for coming."

"Damian Steele."

His name sounded like a movie star's. She supposed it was fitting that he lived in LA.

"So," she said, "is there anything you need from me?"

He had a notebook in his left hand, seemed ready to get down to business. "Nope. Just access." He gestured at the scarred building in front of them. "Looks like I've got that, since this must be the place."

"Yes." Surprisingly, when the wind kicked up, she could still smell the acrid scent of smoke. "I've got the key if you'd like to get inside."

"I do. I'll take a look at everything."

At least he seemed thorough.

She handed him the key and returned to Maude's patio while he brought some paint cans and other things from his vehicle and walked the perimeter of the property before kneeling on the left side, where the fire had started. He spent some time there, collecting samples he put in those cans before going inside.

Sadie would've trailed after him — she was dying to see the house. But she wasn't supposed to go anywhere except the kitchen, and something about the efficiency of his actions and his complete absorption made her feel like she might mess up his mojo or something if she tried.

While he was in the house, she returned Dawson's call. "What's up?"

"Has the arson investigator arrived yet?" he asked.

"Just got here." She'd texted him about the delay, but he hadn't responded. She'd assumed he was too engrossed in his work.

"What's he saying? Anything?"

"Not yet. He's looking it all over carefully, taking samples."

"Have you been inside?"

"No. Call me superstitious, but there's so much riding on this. I don't want to have touched or disturbed one little thing, for fear that will be the one thing that might have given the culprit away if I hadn't."

"I doubt you have to worry about that *inside.*"

"Still. I'm staying away from everything until he's done. I've waited this long, you know? I can wait another hour or so. Then I'll go in and . . . and comb through what's left."

He must've heard the anxiety in her voice, because he said, "Do you want me to come over and help with that?"

It was a nice offer. The people of Silver Springs would be surprised to learn how sensitive he could be. But she preferred to do it alone. The fire had not only forced her out of her rental, it had acted like an ax, severing the last of the bond between her and Sly. She was looking forward to having a few minutes in her old space, even if it was just the kitchen, to savor the fact that she no longer had to smile when she opened the door to him. No longer had to pretend she wasn't dying a little inside when he insisted on spending time with her and Jayden. No longer had to worry that he'd hit her up for sex and put her in the position of trying to say no without starting a major argument. She had other things to worry about, of course — everything she'd been trying to avoid by making nice for so long — but there was a strange sort of relief in escaping her old problems even if it meant taking on new ones.

She also wasn't sure how she'd hold up if the photos of her parents and Jayden's baby pictures had been ruined, didn't want Dawson to see her go to pieces if they were gone any more than she wanted the arson investigator to witness such a scene. "No, I've got it."

"Okay."

She expected him to say goodbye and hang up, but he didn't.

"I found something a few minutes ago, something that has me concerned," he said.

"What's that?" she asked.

"Tire tracks, out near the canal at the back of the property. Someone's been sitting out there, watching the house."

Her stomach tightened. "And you think it was Sly."

"Who else could it be?"

Her ex had kept close tabs on her ever since she left him — even before that. But she didn't want to believe he was sneaking around the farm after he'd been warned by Chief Thomas to stay away. If he wasn't careful, he'd get himself kicked off the force. Then where would he be? "Maybe some teenagers were out there partying — smoking pot or having sex."

"I'd be more tempted to pass it off as harmless if whoever it was had come only once. But I can see where a vehicle — the same vehicle judging by the similarity of the tracks — has been in and out of here at least three times since the last rain, and that was the day I hired you, remember?"

A chill rolled down her spine. She wished she could continue to argue that those tracks might be innocuous, but she couldn't. It would be like Sly to press his luck in that way.

So what, exactly, had he been up to? Had he been peeking through the windows? Stolen or booby-trapped something? Was he running some kind of surveillance so that he'd know exactly what was going on?

As extreme as that sounded, it was plausible. After what she'd seen this morning — the state of the house and the way Sly had been living — she thought he was coming completely undone. "I remember the rain."

"Not only that, but I found a back window that looks like it's been tampered with. I'm afraid he's been inside the house. That's what really concerns me."

"No!"

"Yes."

She'd thought she was relatively safe, living with Dawson. But instead of causing Sly to back off, it'd provoked him further. He had a weapon — issued by the city, no less — and he knew how to use it. He could hurt, even kill, both of them. Maybe Jayden, too.

"You've been confident that the pride he takes in being a police officer would hold him in check —"

"Chief Thomas has an eye on him and he

knows it," she said, hoping to justify that confidence.

"But he doesn't seem to be respecting his boundaries even still."

"He isn't doing well," she confided.

There was a slight pause. "What do you mean? You've talked to him?"

"Chief Thomas and I went over there this morning."

"What for?"

She'd done it for a lot of reasons. Dawson was one of those reasons. But so was Jayden. "He still has partial custody of my son. Legally, I have to let Jayden spend the weekend at his place. But with the way things stand between us, it's going to be terrifying for me to see that happen."

"You told me Sly hasn't taken much interest in Jayden since you left him."

"That's true — so far. He rarely exercised his visitation rights. Even when he did, he kept Jayden for only a few hours or, once in a great while, overnight. He didn't want to make my life any easier, didn't want to allow me the chance to have some fun or date. Making sure I always had Jayden was another way he could control me. But now that he knows I'm sleeping with you, that having Jayden isn't standing in the way, I'm afraid he'll take him just to show he can. In other words, he'll do whatever I'd rather he didn't. That's all I can rely on where he's concerned. So, in an effort to get ahead of that, I tried to calm him down, to call a truce."

"How'd that go?"

"Not so good," she admitted. "Sly has always been fastidious when it comes to his personal hygiene and belongings. But the house must've been a wreck, because he wouldn't let us in. He had us meet him around back. Even the patio was nothing like I've ever seen it before. He's partying a lot, and not cleaning up. And he's not limiting that kind of behavior to the weekend. He reeked of alcohol when he opened the door, gave me the impression he was up drinking until very late."

"Probably because he didn't start until he got back from spying on us," Dawson said with a dose of sarcasm. "Anyway, how'd he treat you?"

"Very coolly. He's blaming me for everything that's going wrong in his life, can't see how he's contributing to his own downfall. I told him I'll accept his latest offer on child support and forgo any alimony, and that I'd stop pushing for a restraining order, which would take some of the pressure off him at work, if he'll just stop trying to cause trouble and leave us alone. But I don't think it'll do any good. He demanded that I also call off the arson investigator."

"I hope you refused. You must have, since the investigator is there."

"Yes."

"What'd Sly say then?"

"He got belligerent again."

Dawson made no reply.

"Hello?" Sadie said into the silence. "You still there?"

"Yeah."

She brushed a few fallen leaves off the patio table. "What are you thinking?"

"That I hope he comes back to the farm tonight."

"Why?"

"Because the next time he sets foot on my property, I'll be waiting for him."

Sadie gripped the phone tighter. This was not going the way she wanted. "Don't even talk like that. Don't you see how dangerous a private, late-night encounter with him could be?" Dawson was beginning to feel some of the frustration and desperation *she'd* felt for a long time, which was only making the situation *more* volatile.

"I can't allow him to skulk around the house," he said. "If he's trespassing, I'm going to do something about it."

Sadie pulled her sleeve down over her free hand. It was colder out than she'd expected. "And what happens if it comes to an altercation?"

"I guess he'll learn that I'm not going to tolerate his bullshit."

"No. Don't you see? He's willing to go further than you are. He proved that when he almost drew his gun the night of the fire — which means you could get hurt instead. And even if you don't, you could be arrested if *you* hurt *him.*"

"Chief Thomas knows Sly's been out of line."

"So? He also thinks you killed your parents! He won't protect you. If, in making sure Sly gets what's coming to him, you go back behind bars, Thomas will think justice has been served all the way around. Two problems solved at once."

"I have to do *something*! I can't wait for him to murder us in our sleep. After what happened to my parents, I have to be able to protect those I care about."

Sadie caught her breath. Had he really just said that? She'd promised herself, if she could only get away from Sly, she'd never give any man the right to lay claim on her again. She couldn't afford to make another mistake. But she couldn't pretend she didn't

471

have feelings for Dawson. It didn't matter that they hadn't known each other all that long.

She needed to get out on her own. To figure out who she was these days and what she wanted.

"I understand," she said. "We just have to be careful. Let's get Chief Thomas involved, have him waiting for Sly if he comes back tonight."

"What will that do?"

"It'll prove that he's disobeying orders. Did you get pictures of those tire tracks?"

"I did."

"Email them to him."

"Even if I do, and Thomas agrees to come out here, he'll just confront Sly and send him home. He won't arrest him, Sadie. He may suspend him, but then Sly will have even more reason to hate us — and more time to act on that hate."

"But we only have to avoid trouble until the investigation here is complete. Hopefully, that won't take too long."

"And if Damian Steele doesn't find anything?"

"I'm hoping it won't go that way," she said, because if there was no evidence linking Sly to the fire, she'd have only one escape. She'd *have* to leave, find someplace

Sly could never find her, as she'd been thinking of doing before.

Then whether or not she was falling in love with Dawson would be a moot point. She'd have to sever ties regardless.

Dawson felt uneasy as he hung up. He didn't have any good options when it came to stopping Sly Harris. That meant he had to at least *try* to go about it the "right" way. But he'd be giving up the element of surprise, and for what? He had no trust for the local authorities, wasn't sure sacrificing that advantage would do any good in the end, especially because asking for their help included the expectation that they would act against one of their own.

He'd already lost so much. He didn't want to lose any more. But he couldn't figure out a better way to go.

He was just about to give in and call Chief Thomas when his phone rang. The number wasn't one he recognized — there was no name attached to it — but he was glad he answered.

"This is Oscar Hunt." The caller spoke in a loud, gruff voice. "Big Red told me to give you a jingle."

Oscar. At last. The possibility this man represented set off a riot of butterflies in Dawson's stomach. "Yes, thank you. I appreciate you getting back to me."

"No problem. Red said you're calling about that vagrant I met in Silver Springs a year ago, when your folks were killed. But I'm not sure I'm going to be able to help you. I mean . . . what more can I do? I went to the police, gave them a full report."

Somehow Dawson's defense attorneys had never been made aware of that report. Otherwise, they would've tracked this guy down and asked him to testify. "Do you remember who you talked to?"

"No. It's been too long. But I'm pretty sure it was the detective investigating the case. I remember, because they had me wait at the station until he could come in even though he'd left for the day."

"John Garbo."

"That sounds right."

"Would you recognize him if you saw him?"

"Certainly. I've never given a statement before, so it was memorable. The detective was a strange-looking fella. Built like a cannonball. Bald. Funny little triangle of hair below his bottom lip."

That was John Garbo, all right. He had to be the only man in Silver Springs who was over forty sporting a soul patch on his chin. So what'd happened to that report? Had he deep-sixed it? Stuck it in with a pile of papers no one would ever go through? Maybe he'd put it in the file and just hadn't mentioned it to anyone. From the beginning he'd been so sure that Dawson was his man he hadn't been willing to take a close look at anything that didn't fit the case he was building — just like Dawson's attorneys had said. "What'd you tell him?"

"Just what I saw, man. That there was a tall, skinny dude trying to bum a ride to Santa Barbara at the station right there as you come out of town."

The memory of that night, the fight that had ensued when the dude wouldn't get out of his truck and the creepy sense that he wasn't right in the head made Dawson slightly queasy to this day. By the time he'd gotten rid of his belligerent passenger, he'd had such a terrible feeling about him — as if he'd been lucky to get away. And then he'd found his parents dead. "When did you see this 'tall, skinny' dude?"

"Night before Valentine's Day, around ten-thirty."

That was the night his parents were killed,

all right. "How can you be so specific? It's been over a year." Dawson didn't want to get suckered in by one of those strange people who fed off the excitement surrounding a high-profile case and tried to insert himself in it. Hard as it was to believe, he knew there were such people.

"Easy. I worked fifteen hours that day so that I could finish the bunker I was building in time to head home to my family. Still didn't get done, had to go back two times after because I'd screwed up and needed to fix what I'd done wrong, but I wanted to be there for Valentine's Day. My wife had just received a call from her doctor, saying she was cancer-free. We were going to celebrate."

"Congratulations," Dawson said. "I hope your wife is still in remission . . ."

"Sure is. Just had her annual checkup."

"That's wonderful. So . . . you were returning to Santa Barbara?"

"Yeah. I would've given the guy a ride, but I had so much equipment in the back of my truck that I'd had to put my luggage in front. Wasn't room."

Too bad Dawson hadn't also refused. But he'd felt confident he could handle himself, if necessary, and he'd never dreamed he'd need to fear for his family. "He spoke to you? Asked you for a ride?"

"He did. I was sort of tempted to figure out a way to make it work, like I said. But I was too loaded."

"When did you go to the police to let them know you'd seen this person?"

"Not until a few weeks later. I learned of the murders when everyone else did. It was all over the news. But I didn't think I had any information — not until after they arrested you and I saw a clip where the anchor gave your version of the night's events. Then I realized that I'd seen the same guy."

"You don't happen to know where that hitchhiker is now . . ." Dawson held his breath, but the crushing response came anyway.

"No clue. Could be anywhere."

Dawson let his breath go as he struggled to cope with the bitter disappointment. But then Oscar spoke again.

"I can tell you what he was doing in town, though."

"You can?" Dawson's hope skyrocketed again, almost giving him an emotional whiplash.

"Yep. Told me he came to see his little brother at the boys ranch you folks got out there."

"New Horizons."

"That's it. I remember because he was royally pissed that they made him leave at lights-out, wouldn't let him stay on campus even though he had no way to get back to Santa Barbara, where he had friends."

Dawson clenched his fist. *There* was the connection he'd been looking for, and what a hopeful connection it was! His heart began to race as he considered the implications. Because of privacy laws, Aiyana wouldn't be able to give him a list of all the students she had a year ago, but she had to have access to such a list, and he felt certain she'd be willing to call them all herself, if need be.

Dropping his head in his free hand, he had to blink several times to overcome a sudden upwelling of emotion. At last, he had a small break that could lead to the one thing he craved more than anything else: justice. "Thank God."

"You don't think what I've told you will do any good, though, do you?" Oscar asked. "I mean it didn't do any good when I reported it last year."

Filled with a new sense of resolve, Dawson lifted his head. "I didn't know about it last year."

Chief Thomas had asked Sadie to call him

when the arson investigator was done. He wanted to meet him, to speak with him. She'd just texted Dawson that he was leaving soon and was about to let Chief Thomas know as well when Damian Steele said he was going to swing by the police station on his way out of town, anyway. Figuring that would take care of it, she asked if he'd found anything.

He explained that he needed to do some more research and run a few tests before answering that question, but he left her with the promise that he'd be in touch as soon as he had any news.

"Something has to go my way eventually," she muttered as she walked around to the back.

A flood of nervous energy made her feel slightly shaky as she opened the door and saw all of her belongings from the living room, bedroom and bathroom piled up and crammed into the small kitchen. She wouldn't be able to get through to the living room from here even if she wanted to go in there. The firefighters had blocked it off. But, after taking a cursory glance at the towels, one nightstand, a side table, two lamps and a couple of boxes of storage items from the coat closet, she realized that there were no surprises here. The couch must've been destroyed. The mattress she'd used as a bed and a second rickety nightstand were gone, too. So were a lot of Jayden's clothes and toys and her own clothes. Everything that had been against or near the wall that went up in flames would need to be replaced.

Thankfully, none of those items held any sentimental value. But neither did any of the stuff in here. She went through the boxes carefully, just in case someone had put her photographs inside without making a note of the fact that they'd found the one thing she'd been asking for. But there were no pictures.

Her hands felt clammy and she had a tension headache by the time she finished. She'd been told to stay out of the other side of the house, but she'd watched Damian Steele go in there and come out unscathed, and she wasn't about to wait another day before launching a full-fledged search for her photos. She needed some resolution, some peace of mind there, at least.

She went outside and around to the front, where she made sure no one was watching before letting herself into the living room.

The sun poured through large holes between the burned studs of the left wall. Almost everything below that was scorched black and looked ready to disintegrate. She didn't want that to happen while she was there. With her luck, the roof would collapse. But she needed only a few minutes, just enough time to look in places the firefighters and police might not have thought to check.

Problem was, her house was so small that there weren't a lot of places her pictures could be. She might've taken them out and left them on the couch. She'd been doing a little scrapbooking to pass the time. But she didn't think that was the case. Dawson had been on the couch one of the nights before the fire, and she was pretty sure she'd remember if she'd had to move the plastic container she kept them in.

The side table had a sliding door. Maybe she'd stuck them in there and the firefighters hadn't noticed that it opened . . .

She found some pictures Jayden had colored or drawn at Petra's that she'd saved. Surprisingly enough, they were okay. The table had protected them. She was happy to find *something* that held sentimental value, but those hand-drawn pictures couldn't replace the photographs she'd had a professional take of him as a baby, or the photographs of her parents.

Where could she have put that plastic

case? It had to have been in the closet, under the couch or in this side table.

Unless she'd shoved it in the bottom of the painted armoire in her bedroom. She'd had more clothes before the fire, but still not a great deal. There'd always been plenty of room in that armoire. She'd put various odds and ends in there . . .

The bedroom had suffered more damage than the living room. A lot of the floor was gone, showing the crawl space underneath. She tested each step to make sure it wasn't going to give beneath her weight as she moved gingerly to the charred armoire near the devoured mattress where she and Jayden had slept for the year she'd been separated from Sly. The sight of it frightened her. Had she not been sufficiently awakened and capable of getting them out . . .

If Sly set that fire, he really had lost his mind, she decided.

She couldn't get the armoire open. It was too damaged. Filled with renewed hope — because a jammed armoire door could easily explain why the firefighters hadn't found the plastic container she'd requested — she used a crowbar from the Clevengers' garage to break open the door.

That was where her hope died. Although she had some books, various notes, bills and checking account information in there, stacked on the small shelves to one side, the pictures she most wanted weren't to be found.

This was the last place they could be. She wouldn't have put them in the attic or crawl space. She was afraid of spiders, avoided those places entirely — and had no need to use them. She hadn't had enough belongings to worry about the extra storage space.

Standing back, she stared glumly at the odds and ends she'd discovered. There were a few loose pictures of Jayden, but they weren't the ones she loved the most. The ones taken when he was nine months, that had best captured his sweet little smile and spirit at the time, were gone. So were the only pictures she had of her parents.

Sadie had never felt more alone in the world than at this very moment. She was standing in a house she believed her ex-husband had torched, most of her stuff was damaged or destroyed and everything that really mattered to her was gone. Not only that, if she couldn't figure out some way to tie Sly to what he'd done, she'd be facing the daunting prospect of moving to a completely new place, where she wouldn't know a soul, in order to be rid of him for good. How would she start over without so much as a babysitter she felt she could trust to watch Jayden while she worked? Where would she go? What would she do?

She wished she could talk to her mother, wished she hadn't lost her so soon. Her father had done a good job in her mother's absence, but then she'd lost him, too. She'd had only Sly in her life from that point forward, dominating and controlling everything and making her doubt her own abilities — sometimes even her sanity.

She didn't try to stop the tears that rolled down her cheeks. Crying was self-indulgent. She was feeling sorry for herself and she shouldn't, but she didn't care. The sense of loss was too overwhelming. Pictures were only pictures, but the people those pictures represented were gone, and the pictures were all she'd had left.

She didn't hear the door. She'd sunk to the floor, buried her face in her arms, which rested on her knees, and was sobbing like a child when she heard her name.

Startled, she looked up to see Dawson crouched beside her.

"Everything's going to be okay," he said as he drew her to her feet and pulled her into his arms.

"They're gone," she said, her voice muffled by his shirt. "All of my pictures. I feel like I can't even remember what my mother looked like without them."

He didn't say anything, just held her close.

"I hate him," she said after gulping for breath. "I hate him and I hate love. Love is what got me into this. I don't ever want to love anyone again."

She was essentially telling him she didn't want to love *him,* either, but that didn't seem to upset him. Maybe he knew it was too late, that love had already made a joke of her words, because his hands were gentle as they moved in a comforting fashion over her back. "Love isn't the problem, Sadie," he said, his voice soothing. "Love is the answer. That's what makes life worth living."

"It's made my life a living hell." And she knew it wasn't going to get easier if she had to leave town, leave him. She lifted her head to peer into his face. "Why'd you take me in? Have you lost your mind? Look at me! I'm in *such* a mess. I have a little boy to take care of and literally nothing to take care of him with."

"You have all you need," he said. "You'll see."

She scowled in defiance. "You didn't answer my question. You should've turned me away, especially once you realized my ex is a freaking psychopath. I gave you the chance. Now you're having to deal with his actions, too."

A contemplative expression claimed his face as he smoothed the hair out of her eyes. "I don't know why. I guess if you search hard enough, there's always a glimmer of sunshine in life. I used to watch for it through the slats of my cell. That was literal sunshine, of course. It's what kept me hanging on — that little patch of light. Not a lot to cling to, but enough. I see something similar, something hopeful and warm, when I look at you."

She studied his handsome features. "I make you feel better?"

"You do. I told you before, you make me feel like a man again."

"Because we have mad, wild sex. We can't keep our hands off each other," she said sulkily.

He tucked her hair behind her ears. "It's more than that. At least it is for me."

It was a lot more than that for her, too, but she didn't care to acknowledge the fact.

"I like that I'm needed, wanted and able to help," he added.

Her heart was beating hard, knocking against her ribs. "That scares me to death."

He smiled. "What does?"

"What if I fall in love with you? I can't do that. I can't trust my own heart. Not after what I've been through."

"Don't worry about 'what ifs'. We're just going to take things one day at a time."

"But I doubt the investigator will come up with anything. I mean, look at this mess." She gestured around her. "What can he or anyone else tell from *this*?" She kicked a burned shoe to one side. "It seems as if Sly always gets away with whatever he does. There's no justice in the world, Dawson. What happened to you is a perfect example."

He wiped her tears with his thumbs. "It's not over yet. For either one of us. But maybe I'm feeling optimistic because I heard from Oscar today."

She sniffed to stop her nose from running. "You did? What did he say? Does he remember the drifter?"

"He does. He could also tell me why that drifter was in town. He's the brother of one of the boys who went to New Horizons last year."

This was encouraging. "Which boy? And is he still at the school?"

"That's what I need to find out."

"Aiyana will jump all over that."

"I've already called her. She's working on

it. Could take a couple of days. Shouldn't be much longer."

Sadie drew a deep breath. Hearing this news made a difference. So did having Dawson's support. As much as she didn't want to lean on him, didn't want to admit that having him come, even though she told him he didn't need to, made her feel capable of going on in spite of the despair. "That's wonderful," she said.

He frowned as he gazed around at the burned bedroom. "Are you sure your pictures are gone?"

"I've looked everywhere. They're not here. No plastic container. No pictures."

"I'm sorry."

"I guess we just have to take the blows life deals us and, when we get knocked down, get back up again, right?" What other choice did she have? She couldn't give up.

"That's right. And you can do it. Getting up is hard, but it's all that counts in the end."

With a nod, she slipped her hand in his. "Okay. Let's go. I don't want to be here anymore."

"Why don't you ride with me? We'll pick up Jayden and take him out for ice cream before coming back to get your car. Ice cream won't fix everything, but —"

She wiped the last of the wetness from her face. "It's better than sobbing on the floor," she finished with a broken laugh. "Thank you. I don't know what I would've done without you the past couple of weeks."

He squeezed her hand. "Don't even mention it. You've saved me, too."

That made her smile. She'd grieve over her pictures later, she told herself. When she had the fortitude. Right now she had to soldier on — for Dawson, who could have a chance at proving that the transient he encountered at the gas station was not only real but possibly culpable of his parents' murder, and Jayden, who was depending on her to be strong.

26

There was no one at the ice cream parlor. That came as a relief to Sadie. She didn't want to encounter anyone with her red, swollen eyes. Having to face the girl behind the counter was bad enough.

They each picked their favorite flavor. Dawson got a double scoop of mocha almond fudge; she and Jayden each got a single cone of chocolate.

Assuring her they'd come back to town to recover her car later, Dawson drove them home so they could prolong the peace they'd found together. That simple gesture, keeping her with him even though it wasn't the most practical thing to do, made her appreciate him even more. She was falling in love again, all right. She didn't want to be — especially with her future in Silver Springs being so uncertain — but she couldn't deny what she was feeling, couldn't pretend otherwise. That fact became all too clear when Jayden fell asleep on the way and, once Dawson carried him into the house for a nap, she caught hold of his hand before he could go out to work.

"What is it?" he murmured, sounding surprised.

She didn't explain. She simply led him to his bedroom, where she closed and locked the door before peeling off his clothes. Because she didn't know how long she'd get to be with him, she felt a certain urgency to make the most of every minute.

Fortunately, he didn't seem to mind another delay. "I'm glad that you're getting comfortable with me," he said.

"I've never been like this," she admitted. "I can't get enough of you. I want to make love all the time."

"That makes two of us," he said before his mouth came down on hers.

The taste and feel of him ignited the same raw hunger she'd experienced when he made love to her before. From that moment on, Sadie was lost — sailing away on a rapid current of desire. After he took off her clothes, he picked her up and tossed her onto the bed, making her laugh. But once he climbed into bed with her, all levity disappeared. She closed her eyes, savoring the rush of eagerness and expectation that charged through her as his hands moved over her body. This was what desire felt like, she told herself.

He seemed to be in no hurry, but when he eventually rolled her beneath him, the pressure of him pushing inside her, filling her, made her feel complete. She clung to him as he began to thrust, enjoying the slightly salty taste of his skin, the solidness of his chest as it slid against her bare breasts and the ropey muscles of his back she could feel bulging beneath her fingertips.

"You're so talented at this," she gasped as the pleasure began to build.

His laugh sounded ragged, proof that he was experiencing the same escalation of breathing and heart rate. "I don't think this requires any talent."

"It requires a little intuition, at least. I've never felt anything like being with you."

He paused, resting part of his weight on his elbows as he stared down at her.

"What?" she said, taken aback by the intensity of his gaze.

"You're not going to leave me, are you?" he asked softly.

She didn't know what to say. If they couldn't tie Sly to that fire, couldn't get him out of their lives, she'd be doing Dawson a favor by leaving. "I hope I won't have to."

He frowned at her words, obviously not satisfied by her answer. But before he could press the issue, she dragged his mouth to hers, compelling him to move again. He did, and he spent the rest of Jayden's nap convincing her with every kiss, every touch, that she'd be sorry if she didn't stay.

They could hear Jayden playing with what few toys he had left in the next room. He was awake, but he seemed perfectly happy, so Sadie didn't jump up to dress. She seemed reluctant to get out of bed, and Dawson felt the same way. Languid and satisfied, he closed his eyes as he rested his head on her shoulder and she raked her fingernails gently over his back. "It's hard to make myself work when you're around," he teased.

She smoothed his hair back. "Sorry I kept you from the fields. I know you're feeling pressure to get things done."

His hand covered her breast. "Don't be sorry. I wouldn't have traded this for anything."

"It could've waited until later, I suppose."

"I don't think it would've been the same." He lifted his head to give her a lazy grin. "Sometimes you have to seize the moment, you know?" He put his head back down so she wouldn't stop scratching. "Tonight wouldn't have been a good option, anyway. We have a date with the chief of police."

She'd been so caught up in the fact that she'd lost her pictures, he could tell she hadn't been thinking about what he'd discovered out by the canal. "You got a hold of him?"

"Just before I saw you at the rental earlier. He's coming tonight."

"You told him about the tire tracks?"

"Yeah."

"And he believed you?"

"I think so. He sat on the other end of the line in silence for a few seconds. Then he said Sly 'better not' be trespassing when he'd been told to stay away."

"Did you email him the pictures?"

"I did, but I haven't heard from him since then."

"So what's the plan?"

"He said he'd call a meeting to bring Sly to the station at the end of Sly's shift. But instead of being there to conduct the meeting, Thomas is going to have someone else stand in for him while his wife drops him off out here. That way, we'll know Sly is occupied while Thomas gets into position, and no one else on the force will know what's going on."

"So they can't alert him."

"Exactly."

"Then what?"

He slid his hand down the curve of her waist. She'd been eating better lately. He could tell because she'd put on a few pounds, didn't seem so anxious all the time. She deserved to have more peace of mind than Sly had given her. "Then we just wait and see what happens."

"What if Sly *doesn't* come?"

"We'll have to try again tomorrow."

"How many times do you think Thomas will be willing to come out here?"

"Not more than two or three. So . . . we have to hope, if Sly *is* stalking us, that he proves it soon."

Her phone started vibrating on the nightstand. She was getting a call. With a sigh that showed her reluctance to move, she leaned over to get it. "Speak of the devil," she grumbled.

"Seriously?" Dawson sat up. "He's calling you right now?"

"Should I answer?"

"Might as well. See if you can get some idea what's going through his mind."

"I can guess that."

"What would you guess?"

The phone transferred to voice mail, but

she didn't put her phone down. "He has visitation rights this weekend, remember?"

"You think he's calling about that?"

"What else? It's the only thing that gives him a legitimate reason to get in touch in spite of what Chief Thomas said — to stay away."

"He can't expect to take Jayden after setting that fire."

"He's claiming he didn't set the fire, remember?"

"We know he did." But how to handle this? "What happens if you refuse?"

"The law would be on his side — unless I go through with the restraining order. That would probably stop him."

"You told him you wouldn't do that."

"*If* he leaves us alone. You and I both know he won't. Those tracks out back sort of prove it, right?"

Her phone started to ring again. This time she answered it. "Hello?"

Dawson felt the peace and tranquility they'd been enjoying disappear from the room, watched the old haunted look come over Sadie again.

"But he doesn't like baseball," he heard her say. "I'm not trying to start a fight . . . I know it's your weekend. It's just . . . Never mind. Of course you can take him. That'll

497

be perfect. Dawson and I were thinking of going away for a couple of days, anyway."

This was news to Dawson, but he waited until she'd hung up to ask for the details. "What's going on?"

"He wants to take Jayden for the weekend. I knew he would. He's looking for any way to get the best of me, and he knows he can always do that through my son."

"What was that bit about us going away for the weekend?"

She shoved a hand through her hair. "My way of trying to fight back. If he thinks I want him to take Jayden, he'll back out."

"Did he?"

"Sadly, he didn't fall for it."

"Damn. So now what? We can't let Jayden go to his place. We can't trust him."

The way she nibbled on her bottom lip suggested she was contemplating something.

"Sadie?" Dawson prompted.

"We need to rile him up, provoke him. If we make him mad enough, he'll show up here tonight for sure."

"Where he'll be caught by Chief Thomas."

"Yes. Then I'll be able to go through with getting the restraining order, after all — with Chief Thomas's blessing."

Dawson punched his pillow and propped

it behind his head. "That wouldn't take much. Just seeing us together would be enough to make him apoplectic."

She pecked his lips. "So how can we bump into him? We can't exactly show up at his house."

"No, but he's working this evening, right? Chief Thomas indicated as much. So let's take Jayden to Petra's — if anything happens, we won't want him involved in it. Then we'll drive around town, make sure we're seen at the gas station, eating at the drive-in, shopping at the grocery store, having a drink at The Blue Suede Shoe. Who knows? Maybe we'll get lucky and run across him. He'll be patrolling, so he should be keeping watch on what's happening in town."

A rueful smile curved her lips. "I usually consider myself lucky if I *don't* run across him."

"How often does that happen?"

"Not often. He seems to find me no matter what — is always watching."

"Great. For once, his obsession will play in our favor."

"And driving around town together is harmless enough," she said in a voice that suggested she was mulling it over. "We should be able to go where we want."

"Mommy?" The door handle jiggled as Jayden tried to come in.

Sadie jumped out of bed and started pulling on her clothes. "What, honey?"

"What are you doing?"

She shot Dawson a guilty look. "Just . . . cleaning."

"Is Dawson cleaning with you?"

Obviously, he'd heard their voices. Dawson couldn't help grinning as she said, "Yes, we're . . . ah . . . folding clothes."

There was a slight pause. Then Jayden said, "Can I come in?"

"Of course. Just a sec."

Once they were both dressed and had made the bed, she took a stack of folded T-shirts out of the drawer before letting her son into the room.

Dawson thought Jayden would go straight to Sadie. He was still a little groggy from his nap. But he slipped past her and lifted his arms for Dawson to pick him up. "Can we get more ice cream?" he asked as Dawson pulled the boy into his arms.

"Not tonight, buddy. Maybe tomorrow, though."

Sadie lifted her eyebrows as if to say, "What's up? My son goes to you instead of me?"

Dawson winked at her, but he didn't get a

chance to say anything. This time *his* phone was ringing.

He pulled it out of his pocket and tensed as he saw the caller ID: Stanley DeWitt. He was out of time on his promise to bring Angela home. She'd been calling him crying the past few days, telling him seven was seven and asking him to come pick her up. He had a difficult time getting through those calls because he didn't know what to tell her. The state was taking its sweet time, even though he'd called Robin Strauss to let her know how hard the wait was on his sister and that the delay was forcing him to break a promise.

"Is it Angela?" Sadie asked.

He nodded.

"Here, let me take Jayden so you can talk to her."

Dawson let Jayden go to his mother as he sat on the edge of the bed and pushed the Talk button. "Hello?"

"You did it!" She spoke so loud he had to pull the phone away from his ear by a few centimeters. "You did it, Dawson, just like I knew you would. Megan says I can come home." Someone spoke in the background, trying to calm her. "But only if I wait till Tuesday," she added. "Not seven days. And not till Christmas. Just till Tuesday."

That was still five days, but she seemed pleased, so he didn't point that out. He wasn't quite sure whether to believe her in the first place. "Are you certain of that?" he asked.

"Talk to Megan!"

The phone transferred and Megan came on the line.

"Is what Angela just told me true?" he asked.

"It is." He could hear the warmth in her voice. "The paperwork came through this morning. I'm sure they'll be calling to let you know once we get it back to them, but from what I saw, she's set to be released into your custody early next week."

"Wow." He felt such relief he didn't know what to say. He'd just come through another hard-fought battle — and won. First his freedom, then his sister's. "That's great."

"You'll be able to come get her, right?"

"Of course. I'll be there as soon as she can leave."

"Great. We'll let you know when, exactly, we can release her on Tuesday."

Sadie was standing in the doorway with Jayden, watching as he hit the End button.

"What is it?" she asked.

"I guess Ms. Strauss has finished her investigation."

"And?"

"Angela's coming home."

She put Jayden down and crossed over to him. "That's wonderful, Dawson. I'm so happy for you," she said and, resting her hands on his shoulders, kissed his forehead.

He looked up at her in surprise. This was the first time she'd shown him any affection in front of her son. To him, that was significant. It also reminded him that he wasn't done fighting. Maybe he'd secured his freedom and Angela's, and was making strides toward finding the man who'd murdered his folks, but he still had to force Sly to let go of Sadie and Jayden. Then, even though he wouldn't have his parents, he would have taken care of all the family he had left.

27

Sly couldn't believe that Sadie had had the nerve to bring his boss — the chief of police, no less — to his house as some sort of enforcer this morning. He'd been fuming about it all day, could hardly think about anything else. It was amazing how, now that she had a little help, she believed she'd gained the upper hand. But she didn't know him very well if she thought he'd ever let her get away with how she was behaving. He'd set her straight, couldn't wait for the right opportunity to do exactly that. He'd been racking his brain all day, trying to figure out how best to accomplish it, but he hadn't figured it out quite yet. He'd tried to put her at a disadvantage by telling her he planned to take Jayden for the weekend, but she'd actually seemed *relieved.* He hated the idea that having him sit home and babysit would only enable her to devote every minute of her time to Dawson . . .

The thought of that conversation made him even angrier, especially when he paired that with what she'd said to him in Lolita's. She claimed she was finally enjoying sex — only, with someone else.

As Sly drove slowly down the main drag of Silver Springs, he eyed the citizens and drivers he saw on the road with an especially critical eye. The mood he was in, no one was getting away with *anything.*

He spotted a sleek red sports car pulling out of the gas station and recognized it as belonging to Monty Tremaine, a student this year at New Horizons, and flipped on his lights. Monty hadn't done anything wrong that he could see, but Sly had never liked him. He'd run into him a time or two at the bowling alley, didn't feel as if Monty had the proper respect for authority. The boy was too full of himself, too proud of his own status. Most of the students at the boys ranch didn't even have a car while they were in Silver Springs, but Monty's father was a movie exec in LA and had lots of dough. Monty's convertible BMW cost far more than any car a kid should own. What had he ever done to earn anything, except give his parents enough trouble that they'd finally resorted to sending him to a school devoted to behavior control?

Once Monty spotted Sly's cruiser and the lights flashing behind him, he pulled over at the edge of town. He was on his way back to the school, Sly decided, was headed in that direction. "That's it, you little bastard. You'd *better* pull over."

He felt a familiar rush of adrenaline as he parked behind the BMW, got out and approached the driver side. It bothered him that Monty hadn't automatically rolled down his window, however. Sly had to wait while he found the button.

"Something wrong, Officer?" The boy looked bewildered — and none too pleased.

That he could be irritated by getting pulled over, instead of frightened, made Sly eager to put the fear of God in him. Who did he think he was, anyway? His father? Someone who mattered in the world?

"Driver's license, registration and proof of insurance, please."

Monty gaped at him. "What for?"

Sly didn't answer, simply held out his hand to show that he could demand whatever he wanted without an explanation.

Monty sighed and reached over to the glove box. He handed Sly his registration and insurance card while he dug his wallet out of his back pocket so he could produce his driver's license.

"Are you going to tell me what this is about?" he asked.

Sly fixed the documents to his clipboard and used his flashlight to study them. "I'll be right back," he said and returned to his cruiser to run the boy's information through the computer. He was hoping to find something he could legitimately cite Monty for — expired registration, lack of current insurance, even an unpaid parking ticket, if not something bigger — but everything seemed to be in order. No doubt his rich daddy had seen to that.

Still, this little jerk wasn't going to drive off without *some* sort of citation, not with *his* disrespectful attitude.

After taking a few moments to jot down the boy's name, address and other information, Sly walked back to Monty and handed him his registration, insurance card and license. "Here you are."

The boy seemed confused. "So . . . can I go?"

Sly took his time filling out the rest of the ticket. "Not quite yet."

Monty removed his hand from the gearshift, where he'd put it when he briefly thought he was free to leave. "Why not?"

"Why do you think?"

"I have no clue, man. I haven't done

anything wrong."

Sly eyed him with a measure of disdain. "You ran a stoplight back there."

His eyes flared wide. "What are you talking about? I didn't run any stoplight!"

"You sure did. Just after you came out of the gas station."

"That's not true. I saw you. I wouldn't have been stupid enough to run a stoplight. I wasn't speeding, either."

Hearing such umbrage in the young man's voice made Sly feel a bit better. "I saw you."

"You couldn't have seen me, because I didn't run anything," he argued. "I'm not going to take a ticket. I'll fight it."

"Feel free. But it'll be a waste of time." Sly smiled. "What judge is going to take your word over mine?"

Monty's mouth dropped open. "Especially out here in the boondocks. Is that it?"

"Are you saying our judges are corrupt? I'll make a note of your opinion, in case I see you in court." Sly handed him the clipboard with the ticket attached. "Sign here."

"I'm not going to sign that!"

"Would you rather I take you down to the station?"

"I can't believe this," he muttered. "What'd I do? Nothing!"

"You're not admitting guilt by signing. You can always take it up with the judge, if you want."

"Sure I can," he grumbled and scribbled an "X" on the signature line.

"Have a nice evening," Sly said and gave him the ticket before returning to his cruiser, where he slid behind the wheel. God, he loved his job. He was about to swing around and head back into town, to see if he couldn't find someone else who deserved a little reminder of the power of the local police, when his cell phone rang. He hoped it would be Sadie. He always hoped it would be Sadie, but he wanted to hear from her now more than ever. He was still holding out hope that she'd plead with him not to take Jayden this weekend, or show some other sign that she'd rather he didn't. Having Jayden for so long would only be fun if it bothered her.

It wasn't Sadie, however. It was Dixie Gilbert, the only woman on the police force. She'd been calling him recently, wanting to hang out. He'd gone over there once and let her give him a blow job. She had a thing for him, had made that clear in the past few months, but he wasn't interested in her. Although he didn't mind letting her get him off when he didn't have a better option, he couldn't be seen with someone so over-weight and unattractive. He could do better — much better.

"Hello?"

"Hey," she said, her voice artificially husky. She was striving for sexy, but he found the affectation annoying.

"I'm on duty tonight," he told her. "What's up?"

Taken aback by the brusqueness of his response, she hesitated. "Sorry, I didn't re-alize you were busy. It's not like there's a lot going on in this town even when you *are* on duty. What, did I interrupt your dough-nut break?"

"Is there a reason you called?" he asked.

He expected her to invite him over. She'd offered to make him dinner on three differ-ent occasions. So far, he'd only accepted her invitation to watch a movie late at night, and he'd parked down the street so no one would see his car. If the guys on the force thought he was sleeping with her, they'd tease him mercilessly. It wasn't as if he'd stayed long, anyway. He'd had her blow him as soon as he possibly could, said he was too tired to stay longer and left. "No. I don't want to upset you. Never mind."

"What is it?" he pressed. "With what's been going on in my personal life, I haven't had the best day."

"Well . . . I'm fairly certain that what I have to tell you will only make it worse, so . . ."

This piqued his interest. Apparently, she wasn't about to issue another invitation to dinner, after all. "What is it?"

"It's about your ex-wife."

He almost corrected her. He and Sadie weren't divorced yet and wouldn't be until he decided to let her go. But he bit his tongue. He was getting tired of saying that, would have to prove it instead. "What about her?"

"She's here, at The Blue Suede Shoe."

"What's she doing *at the bar*?"

"Dancing. With Dawson Reed. They're here together — and are having a darn good time from the looks of it."

He gripped the phone so hard the plastic dug into his fingers. "What do you mean by that?"

"They're dancing about as close as two people can. Looks like she's madly in love with him. A murderer. Who would've thought? Who goes from a cop to a criminal — and then flaunts it around town? She should be ashamed."

"She isn't in love with him. He's messing with her mind, that's all, making her think

511

he can fix everything that's wrong in her life. She'll come around, get straightened out once it dawns on her that isn't the case."

"No, she won't," Dixie argued. "She's gone, Sly, and she isn't coming back. I think it's time you let her go — and realize that there are other women out there who can make you happy. Haven't you been through enough with her? I mean, let it end."

Dixie was glad to see Sadie out with someone else, especially Dawson, Sly realized. She thought it would make him forget about his wife and start seeing her. "I gotta go," he said.

She hesitated. Then, with a bit more determination, she said, "I'm heading home now and will be there all night, if you'd like to come by. Sometimes it's easier to get over someone when you have someone else to hang on to, you know?"

He hit the gas pedal, peeled out and swerved into the road, narrowly missing a car coming from the opposite direction. He saw the panic on the driver's face, but he didn't care that he'd nearly caused an accident. "I'm not in the mood, Dixie. Not tonight."

"So what are you going to do? Go home and pout? Drink some more? Word around the station is that you're drinking too much as it is. People are starting to worry about you."

"I don't care what the 'word' is. What I do when I'm off duty is my own business. But I'm not going to drink tonight. I'm going over to the bar to knock some sense into Sadie. That's what I'm going to do."

"Don't, Sly. You need to let her go!"

"I'll decide when it's time for that," he said and disconnected.

"I haven't seen him," Dawson said. "You ready to move on to another location?"

Sadie hugged him a little closer. "Stairway to Heaven" was playing — an old song, but a good one. She could've danced with him like this all night. They weren't out just to have a good time, but she was having fun in spite of that. She enjoyed being with him regardless of what they were doing. "Not yet."

"I'd like to stay, too," he said. "But we've been here for over an hour. If we want to gain Sly's attention, we need to spread ourselves around."

She noticed Dixie Gilbert coming back into the bar and frowned. "Maybe not."

"What do you mean?"

"See that woman over there? The one with the short, dark hair?"

Dawson turned her as they danced so that he could take a look without seeming too obvious. "Yeah."

"She's on the force with Sly." Sadie hadn't thought much of seeing Dixie when they first came in. If Sly spoke of her, it was usually with contempt. He claimed the city had only hired her so that it wouldn't come under fire for being sexist, that she was a terrible officer. But the loyalty Dixie had shown to Sly when Sadie went in to the station, and the way she was behaving tonight, as if she relished the idea of seeing Sadie out with another guy, made Sadie wonder if there wasn't something between them in spite of what he'd said about her in the past.

"Unless Sly's coming to meet her, I don't see where that's going to help us," Dawson mused.

Neither did Sadie. But Dixie had left her seat at the bar, gone outside and returned a few minutes later, as if she'd gone out for a smoke. Except Dixie didn't smoke. Sadie was thinking she might've made a call, might've told Sly what she'd been seeing at the bar.

Or was that assuming too much? Most of the patrons in The Blue Suede Shoe were keeping a wary eye on them. That trip outside could simply have meant that Dixie needed a breath of fresh air.

When Dixie paid her bill and gathered her coat, Sadie decided she must've been mistaken. "You're right. It's probably nothing," she told Dawson. Just more of the usual bias against him. "Let's go."

As soon as Dixie saw them making their way over to the bar, she stopped and waited. "I'd get out of here, if I were you," she said without preamble.

Sadie blinked at her in surprise. "Excuse me?"

"Sly will be here any minute, and he's pretty pissed. Who knows what he'll do?" She started to walk out, but Sadie caught her arm.

"You called him?"

Although Dixie didn't respond, her silence confirmed what Sadie had already guessed.

"Dixie, I know you'll probably attribute this to jealousy, but I promise you it isn't. This is one woman trying to look out for another. You don't know Sly, not the way I do. Unless you want to screw up your life, stay away from him. He's no good."

Jerking away, Dixie made as if to leave but turned back at the last moment. "Why would you want to help *me*?" she asked, suddenly uncertain.

She'd obviously marked the sincerity in

Sadie's voice. "Because I wouldn't wish a man like Sly on anyone," Sadie said.

With a brisk nod that suggested she accepted the truth in that statement, Dixie hitched her purse higher on her shoulder. "Like I said, get out of here. That's me returning the favor."

Except they'd been *hoping* to run into Sly. That he'd been alerted that they were at the bar, and was coming to see for himself, was perfect — providing they could avoid an altercation.

"Sounds like Sly's upset. Do you think we've done enough?" Sadie asked Dawson as they watched the door swing shut behind Dixie.

"Just by having a drink and doing a little dancing? No."

The old uneasiness crept up on her. "Did you say *no*?"

"We need to put an end to what's happening, Sadie — the sooner, the better. And the best way to do that is to piss him off so badly he'll come out to the farm tonight for sure."

She pictured the expression on Sly's face when he'd nearly pulled his gun the night of the fire. "That's a little terrifying, don't you think? He might not settle for peeping, and I don't want this to get you killed. Me, either, as far as that goes."

"We'll only be safe once he's behind bars. Let's deliver him into Chief Thomas's hands and hope that Thomas will see what's been going on all along — and put a stop to it."

Taking a deep breath, she nodded and let him lead her back onto the dance floor.

Dawson wasn't looking at the door, but he knew the second Sly walked into the bar. He could sense the change in the room. Sadie seemed to feel the same disturbance. The way she tightened her grip on him as they danced indicated she was uneasy.

"Don't worry," he murmured. "We're in public. He can't do anything here."

"He could always follow us home," she said.

"He has that meeting at the station, remember? We'll stay until he leaves. Then we'll go to the farm and wait for him there." He pulled her slowly toward the far side of the room, where Sly would have to go to some effort to watch them. Dawson didn't want to make it too obvious that they were tweaking his nose.

Sadie craned her head to get a peek at her ex. "I can see him searching the crowd."

"Maybe you should stay at Petra's tonight," Dawson said. "Let me handle this."

"What are you talking about? You know Petra and her family took Jayden with them to her parents' place in Ojai."

Thank goodness Petra had been willing to do that, or Sadie would've been even more nervous. "Doesn't mean you can't sleep at her place, out of the fray."

"No. I'm not staying there, or anywhere else, alone."

She made a good point. What if Sly didn't come out to the farm but went to Petra's instead, hoping to get hold of Jayden? That would be the worst possible outcome — for Sadie to have an encounter with him on her own. Dawson fully believed he'd harm her if he could. "What about a motel? He won't be able to find you if we put you in a motel."

"I'm not leaving you, so don't even suggest it."

Dawson was tempted to insist. He probably would have if the chief of police wasn't coming to the farm. How out of control could things get as long as Thomas was there? "Okay."

The crowd parted as Sly cut through. "Where's our son?" he demanded, confronting them while they danced.

"He's with Petra," Sadie said.

"Don't you think he spends enough time there?"

"What are you talking about? He's hardly there at all anymore. I'm able to keep him with me now that I work for Dawson."

"I'm going to get him." He turned as if he'd act on those words, but she spoke before he could get more than a step away.

"They're out of town, Sly. Won't be back until tomorrow. She took Jayden with her."

"What kind of mother are you?" he snarled.

Dawson wanted to punch him in the face. No one had ever deserved it more. But if he started a fight, he'd only enable Sly to claim *he* was the aggressor, would be playing right into Sly's hands.

Sadie ignored him, too. They continued to dance until Sly had no choice but to move out of the way. But he didn't leave. He leaned up against the closest wall and glared daggers at them.

"Hey," Dawson murmured to Sadie. "Look at *me.*" He could tell she was worried when she lifted her face. "You okay?"

"Yeah," she said and surprised him by kissing him — deeply and with far more passion than he would've expected in public.

"He deserves that," he whispered, trying not to laugh.

"I didn't do it for him," she said.

He framed her face with his hands. "Good. Just stay focused on me."

Sly trailed them around The Blue Suede Shoe from that moment on. If they went to sit down, he followed as far as the bar and stood with his hand resting on the butt of his firearm as if to suggest he had the ability to enforce whatever he wanted. If they danced, he leaned against the wall as close as he could get, wearing a menacing frown.

Whenever Dawson caught his eye, Dawson grinned as if he wasn't bothered at all. He knew that was probably going too far, but he couldn't help it. What gave Sly the idea that even a police officer could act the way he was acting?

When it came close to eight — time for the meeting at the station, according to what Chief Thomas had told Dawson — Sly left, as expected, and, shortly after, Dawson guided Sadie out to his truck. "Let's get home while we've got the chance," he said. He was eager for Chief Thomas to show up so they could explain what Sly had been doing and, hopefully, put an end to it. But just as they pulled into their drive, he received a text message from Thomas.

Something has come up. I'm not going to

be able to make it tonight. Will call you tomorrow.

Sly couldn't believe it. He sat in the police chief's office, stunned, as Thomas railed at him. Only the chief wasn't yelling loudly. He was speaking in a harsh but low voice so that the other officers milling about the station couldn't hear. His wish for secrecy, more than anything else, told Sly that he was really in trouble this time. Usually, Thomas didn't hesitate to scream regardless of who was around. "I told you not to go anywhere near that farmhouse!"

"I haven't!"

"Stop saying that. Do you think I'm an idiot? You're lying, and I know it!"

"I'm not lying!"

He opened a folder and slapped some pictures on the desk. "Then what the hell are these?"

Sly pulled them closer so that he could take a look. There were no landmarks in the photos, just an up-close shot of some tire impressions in brown dirt. He didn't recognize their significance until he noticed the water pump in one corner. "Oh shit," he mumbled, covering his face before Chief Thomas could say any more.

"Those tire tracks match the brand of tires

on our cruisers," he said. "I checked."

That meant any cruiser could've made those tracks. These pictures weren't good enough to show the small imperfections that set his tires apart from all the rest. But Sly knew better than to make that argument. He'd lose all credibility if he tried.

"You're a police officer, for God's sake," his chief went on. "What are you doing *stalking* your ex-wife?"

Sly shot to his feet. "She's not my ex!"

"Only because you won't let her go. What's the matter with you?"

"Nothing's the matter with me! I'm trying to protect her, that's all. I'm terrified that he's going to hurt her. He's a murderer!"

"We've been over this. She has the right to stay with anyone she wants."

"The cop in me agrees. But the man behind the badge? How do you think I'd feel if she were to wind up like the Reeds? And what about my child? Jayden lives out on that farm, too. You can't tell me you wouldn't be hanging around in case of trouble if it were your wife and child."

Thomas rubbed a hand over his face. "I'll be honest, Sly. That's the only reason we're sitting here. Dawson and Sadie set up a little trap for you tonight. They asked me to come out there, to be waiting for you when you showed up at this particular spot." He tapped the pictures. "But I couldn't do it. You know why? Because if I caught you out there, I'd have to suspend you for disobeying my direct orders. Instead, being the nice guy that I am, I've decided to give you *one* more chance to remain on the force. Do you hear me? I understand that you care about Sadie and Jayden, so much that losing them is making you a little crazy. But you can't break the law and expect to keep your job. Stay away from the Reed farm. This is your final warning."

Sly bowed his head as if he was taking every word to heart. "I will. I swear. Thank you."

"I mean it," Thomas reiterated as Sly headed for the door. "This is your last chance."

Hunching his shoulders as if he'd been sufficiently berated and felt terrible for the trouble he'd caused, Sly nodded again. But as soon as he was free of the station, he straightened. He'd never been more livid in his life, never more determined. Sadie and Dawson would not make a fool of *him.* He wouldn't take his cruiser back to where he'd parked it before. But he would go to the farm, and he'd do what he should've done already: prove — at least to everyone else

— that he'd been right about Dawson Reed all along.

The fact that Jayden was with Petra tonight gave him the perfect opportunity.

28

Sadie couldn't believe that Chief Thomas had canceled on them, especially at the last minute. Obviously, he didn't believe Sly was a real threat. No one did. They saw his uniform and his badge and judged only by that; with Dawson, they saw the media reports and did the same. But how could *Chief Thomas* not see the reality? He'd witnessed Sly's behavior around her. She'd gotten the impression he was on her side during their visit to Sly's house.

It was because Sly was such a good liar, she decided. He could lie his way out of anything . . .

The moment they received the chief's message, Dawson had her go inside and lock the doors. He also told her to keep her cell phone handy so they could contact each other at any given moment. Then he went out back to dig a small pit where Sly had been backing into the artichokes. Dawson said, because the moon was full, he should have barely enough light, and once Dawson covered the hole with plants and straw, Sly would never expect it to be there. If Sly returned to the same spot, he'd back into it when he tried to leave and wouldn't be able to get out. And if his car was there in the morning, or he had to call for a tow, they'd have proof that he was still harassing them — proof that didn't depend on Chief Thomas seeing Sly on the farm with his own eyes.

Dawson said it wasn't much, but it was better than letting Sly peep into their windows at night without any repercussions.

After seeing the look on Sly's face while they were at the bar, however, Sadie was afraid he'd do far more than peep. She'd never made him so angry, mostly because she'd spent their entire married life trying to appease him. And if Thomas had given away the fact that she and Dawson knew about his late-night visits, Sly wouldn't fall into Dawson's trap. He wouldn't go anywhere near it. All of Dawson's work would come to nothing.

Hoping to talk Chief Thomas into fulfilling his commitment, she called the police station. She was told he'd left for the night, so she tried his home. That didn't help, either. His wife simply said he was "unavailable."

What the heck did that mean? Sadie wondered. Where could he be? What could he be doing that was so important? She and Dawson were in trouble. She felt as if Sly had finally snapped. The way he'd behaved at the bar — so openly hostile despite the presence of many witnesses — proved he was dangerous. To make matters worse, he had no fear of punishment, believed he lived above the law, because he could live above the law so long as Chief Thomas supported him. Something terrible would have to happen to change that, and Sadie didn't like to consider what that "something" might be.

She paced in the kitchen while waiting for the police chief to return her call, but that call didn't come. His lack of response was beginning to smell like a purposeful dodge. He was acting to protect his officer, just as Dawson had always thought he would. And it was only getting later and darker. By now, Sly would be off work and out of the meeting — if there really had been a meeting.

She sat down to compose a couple of letters — one to Chief Thomas and one to Jayden. After she sealed them each in a separate envelope, she called Petra and asked to be able to say good-night to her son.

"Where's Dawson?" Jayden asked once Petra put him on the phone.

Sadie couldn't help smiling at that. He was so enamored with the new man in their lives. "He's still working."

"In the dark?"

"In the dark." That concerned her, too. She'd been trying to suppress the worry that plagued her by telling herself that it was early yet. But Sly could still show up, could just as easily shoot Dawson while he was out on the tractor as any other time.

She hurried to the back door so she could check on him, just in case, and was mildly reassured by the rumble of the tractor. He was okay for now.

After closing and locking the door again, she returned to the kitchen.

"He needs to come in now," Jayden was saying. "It's bedtime."

Sadie chuckled at her son's bossy tone. "You're right. I'll make sure he does."

After she told Jayden she loved him and that she'd see him tomorrow, Petra took the phone back. "He's having a good time, is about to go to bed," she said. "Don't worry about him, okay?"

"I won't. Thank you. I hope . . . I hope

it's not too much of an imposition that I asked you to take him with you."

"Not at all. I know you wouldn't ask unless you really needed it. And my parents love him. How are things in Silver Springs?"

She drew a shaky breath. "Tense."

Petra's voice took on a more serious tone. "What's going on?"

Sadie had shared a little of her concerns about Sly. That was why Petra had agreed to take Jayden. Otherwise, she would've said she couldn't babysit, that she wasn't going to be home. "Sly is acting a bit . . . threatening."

"He is."

"Yes."

"You're frightened."

"I am," she admitted. "If anything happens to me, would you —"

"Whoa," Petra broke in. "You don't think this thing could go *that* far."

"No, of course not." She didn't want to scare Petra, but, in Sadie's heart, she believed it *could* get that bad. She'd always believed it could get that bad, or she wouldn't have let Sly control her for so long. "I'm just saying if the worst happens — not that it ever would — Sly's mother will take Jayden. But will you make sure he gets the letter I'm putting under the front porch of the Reed farmhouse? He won't understand what it means at this age, of course. So wait until he's older, if you can. There should come a time when . . . when it will be important to him."

There was a long pause before Petra said, "This is sounding pretty ominous, Sadie."

"It's a worst-case scenario, that's all," she said, trying to play it off. "Since most of our things are gone —" also thanks to Sly, she was fairly certain "— I'd like Jayden to at least have my words, my love. That's all I've got to give him."

"If you're writing a letter like *that,* I think it's time to call the police. I mean . . . someone else on the force, besides Sly."

"Yeah. I'll do that," she said, even though she'd already tried — to no avail. "It'll all work out. Just wanted you to know about the letter." She didn't tell Petra about the second letter. She figured Petra would find it when she collected the one for Jayden — and then Chief Thomas would understand how badly he'd misjudged both Sly and Dawson.

"I'll keep it in mind. I hope it never comes down to that, though."

"So do I." She heard Dawson come in.

"Sadie?" he called.

"I've got to go," she told Petra.

Her former neighbor seemed reluctant to end the conversation. "My parents have a guesthouse. Maybe you should come stay here in Ojai with them for a month or two. Sly wouldn't know where to find you and . . . and maybe some time will be all that's necessary to get things to settle down."

"That's a nice offer, but I'm the one who got Dawson into this. I can't abandon him with the problem."

"What about Jayden? Your leaving town would be better for him, don't you agree?"

She shoved a hand through her hair. "I do. Definitely. But . . . maybe I'm just tired and blowing this out of proportion. I hope that's the case."

"Either way, I guess we can talk about it tomorrow," Petra said.

"Right. Thanks." Sadie hung up as Dawson came into the kitchen.

"It's done," he said, looking exhausted. "We have a nice trap."

"Will Sly be able to see the pit?"

"Not unless he suspects it's there, not unless he's specifically looking for it. And on a darker night he wouldn't be able to see it at all, so if he comes tomorrow or —"

"He'll come tonight," she said.

He studied her, obviously surprised by the

confidence in her voice. "How do you know?"

"He won't be able to stop himself." She slipped her arms around his waist and rested her cheek against his chest. "He's too angry. And he's never been capable of delaying gratification — not when it comes to satisfying his anger."

"I'll stay up," Dawson said. "You try to get some sleep."

Sadie refused to go to bed without him. He was just as tired. Besides, she didn't want to be caught at a disadvantage if Sly did show up.

"Let's watch some TV," she suggested. She put the letters out, but after two or three hours spent lying on the couch with Dawson, during which nothing happened, his breathing steadied out and her own eyelids grew too heavy to lift.

Getting the hatchet had taken much longer than Sly had anticipated. It wasn't as if he could go out and buy one. He'd had to steal Pete's from Pete's garage, which meant he'd also have to return it before morning. He knew how the coming investigation would go, had to be prepared for it. That was why he'd gone to his mother's house almost as soon as he left the station. He'd told her he was in trouble, had broken down in tears saying he needed help with his drinking or he was going to lose his job — and she'd been so concerned she'd bought every word and blamed Sadie just as he had.

"That girl isn't who we thought she was," she'd said, her lips pursed in disapproval. "She's not worth it, Sly. You need to let her go."

"But she's not safe," he'd replied, playing the good guy. His mother wanted to see him as the knight in shining armor he portrayed, so it wasn't a hard sell. "She's living with a murderer."

His mother had wrung her hands at that. "We've got to get Jayden away from her somehow. He's not safe out there."

He'd agreed that he had to sue for custody of his son, even though he knew he'd never have to pay his attorney another dime. Then he'd "reluctantly" acquiesced when she'd insisted he stay the night rather than go home and "face that empty house."

"That's probably for the best," he'd told her. "I'll only try to drown my sorrows if I have the chance, and I can't turn to the bottle anymore."

After she went to bed, he'd gone into his room and stuffed the pillows under the blankets so it'd look as though he was sleeping if she came to check on him.

Once he was satisfied that she was down for the night, and all the neighbors would be, too, he'd dressed in the jeans and black hoodie he'd worn when he started the fire, taken his late father's 8mm pistol from the closet and pushed her car out of the garage so he wouldn't have to start the engine. It was important that his cruiser remain conspicuously parked in front of her house, so the neighbors could report that it had never moved and, with the garage door down, no one would know he'd simply used her vehicle.

Just to be safe, he'd pushed her Pontiac Grand Prix clear to the end of the street before getting behind the wheel. But that was when the hunt for the hatchet had started. Before he remembered seeing one at Pete's place, he'd almost decided he'd have to shoot Sadie *and* Dawson. Two bullets accomplished the same goal. Except . . . he liked the idea of hacking Sadie to pieces and letting Dawson take the blame for it. Dawson would be dead, too, of course — his body hidden so well that it would never be found — which meant he'd never stand trial for her murder, but that didn't matter. His disappearance would be enough to convict him in the minds of everyone who

mattered. Sly would then be totally vindi-
cated for his actions the past few weeks and,
so long as they couldn't prove he had any
part in Sadie's murder and Dawson's disappearance, life would go on pretty much as it
had before Sadie decided she had the nerve
to stand up to him.

In other words, he'd win the battle they'd
started.

"Poetic justice," he muttered as he went
over his plan, again and again, while parking his mother's car on a deserted side road
not far from the farm and walking the rest
of the way. He would've preferred to get
closer. He'd have to bring the car to the
house after he killed Dawson so that he
could dispose of the body before morning,
which would eat up valuable time. But —
he felt the solid weight of the hatchet he
carried as he walked — if he was going to
pull this off, certain things had to be handled in a certain way.

Fortunately, he was a cop: he knew exactly
how to get away with murder.

Dawson came awake. He wasn't sure why,
since dawn was obviously a long way off
and he couldn't hear or see anything he'd
consider alarming. Although most of the
lights were off, they'd turned them off and

left the TV on. Some '80s sitcom blared in the room.

Sadie, still asleep in his arms, started to rouse when he moved. "Something wrong?" she murmured, and then she came awake, too, as if she suddenly realized that they'd fallen asleep and shouldn't have.

"Everything's fine," he told her. "I'm just going to check."

"No." She grabbed him before he could slide out from under her weight. "Let's stay together."

"At least let me look out the window." He wanted to do more than that — wanted to go out and see if he'd caught anything in his trap — but he hesitated to leave her alone. He knew she was frightened, and he felt she had good reason to be.

He couldn't see anything to be concerned about in the front. He checked a few of the other windows, but clouds had rolled in front of the moon, dimming its light. He couldn't make out anything except an abundance of shadows, some of which *could* indicate the presence of a human being, but probably didn't. "Where's your phone?" he asked. "Why don't you see if Chief Thomas has returned your calls?"

Sadie sat up, rubbed her face and reached for her cell, which was on the coffee table.

"Nope."

They'd had the ringer on, wouldn't have missed it, but he thought maybe a text had come in. "Nothing at all?"

"No call, no text, nothing."

The police had really left them on their own. But Dawson wasn't surprised. Since when had they ever done *him* any favors? "What time is it?"

"One-fifteen."

There was a lot of night left.

"I hate that we're letting Sly disrupt our lives like this," he grumbled. "He wins as long as we are always watching our backs, can't live a normal life."

"That's nothing new for me," Sadie said. "But I feel bad I've dragged you into his sights."

"You didn't drag me. I put myself there."

She cast him a discouraged look. "I'm still sorry."

He pulled her to her feet. "Don't be. You're worth it. The fire investigator will find something. Then we'll be out of this. But for now, let's go to bed. We can't wait up, expecting the worst, every night."

She seemed reluctant, but after making sure all the doors were locked — again — he convinced her to accompany him to his bedroom. "If he does something tonight,

Chief Thomas will know we were right about him."

"That'll be small consolation if we're dead."

He didn't respond. What could he say? She was right.

They used the bathroom and brushed their teeth before falling into bed. Dawson was still tired, but he didn't go to sleep right away. He curled around Sadie, hoping to offer her some comfort and security.

"I've been trying so hard not to love you," she whispered.

He kissed her neck. "How's that going for you?"

"I'm failing. Miserably."

He couldn't help smiling. "Like I said, maybe we were meant to be together."

"Or maybe, just when I'm finding some happiness, Sly will put an end to that, too." Her hand pulled his up to her mouth so she could kiss it.

"That's not going to happen."

"The same type of thing has happened to other people."

He held her tighter. "I'm not going to let it happen to you," he promised, but it was only a few moments later when he heard a subtle noise, a rattle, that told him someone might be trying to get inside the house.

29

This wasn't going to be hard, Sly told himself. All he had to do was draw Dawson to the door. As soon as he opened it — *boom!* The sound of the gun would cause Sadie to scream. She might even come running. And the hatchet would do the rest. In a few minutes, the whole thing would be over. She would've gotten what she'd been asking for, what she deserved. Sly would then drag Dawson's body outside while he went back for the car. He preferred Dawson didn't bleed too much in the house, but even if he did, and the police found it, those who wielded weapons like hatchets often injured themselves in the process of trying to hurt someone else. The presence of his blood wouldn't prove anything — especially if Sly did a good job cleaning up.

He turned the handle of the back door again and brushed against the side of the house. He had to be careful, couldn't be *too* obvious, or Dawson would simply call 9-1-1. Sly needed him to come take a look to see what was going on first. It wasn't as if a man recently charged with murder would be overly hasty to call the police anyway, though. Dawson knew there wasn't anyone on the force who'd be eager to help him.

When the ambient light he could see filtering down from the hallway upstairs went off, Sly knew someone was coming. He pressed himself to the back of the house and began to count. He had no specific number in mind. He just needed to remain calm until the door opened. Only then could he fire. Dawson might expect a confrontation, a fight, but he'd assume Sly was laboring under some hesitancy to take things too far, wouldn't expect to open the door and be shot immediately.

That was why Sly felt his plan would work.

Sadie crept down the stairs behind Dawson. She had her phone in her hand, planned to call 9-1-1 at the first hint of trouble. She had to make sure they had a legitimate reason first, though. She couldn't be perceived as someone who was trying to make Sly look bad, not when most of the officers on the force believed that Dawson was a murderer and she was an unfaithful wife.

"Be careful," she whispered.

"Stay back," Dawson warned.

There was still a small part of her that wondered if they were overreacting to be so defensive and frightened. When she'd married Sly, she'd certainly never expected to find herself in such a situation. He'd seemed normal then. But he hadn't been normal for a long time. She didn't care if her reaction was extreme. She wasn't going to lower her guard.

Dawson lifted a hand, indicating that she should remain on the stairs as he hit ground level and turned toward the back door. Unfortunately, there were no windows that looked out on the porch, but there were several small triangular-shaped windows in the door itself. Sadie held her breath as she leaned over the banister to watch Dawson peer out of those. They'd left the lights off downstairs so that whoever it was wouldn't be able to see in, except via the dim light filtering down from above. But that meant Dawson seemed to get swallowed up in the darkness.

He must not have seen anything, because he didn't open the door, didn't go on the porch. She heard him move into the kitchen instead, and then the living room, checking to see if he could learn anything from what he could see outside the other windows in the house.

"Anything?" she whispered.

"Not yet."

"Is there any chance we could've imagined those noises?"

"We didn't imagine anything. But there's always a chance it was a raccoon or possum."

"Should I call the police?"

"Not yet. What would you tell them? That we heard someone on the porch? I doubt that would bring them running."

He made a good point. They didn't have anything to report yet . . .

She heard a creak, again coming from the porch, and felt her heart rate spike. Someone or something was out there; she was certain of it. She was about to ask if Dawson had heard the same thing, but he'd already switched directions, indicating he had.

"Stay back," he murmured again.

She didn't get the chance to respond before she heard breaking glass. She lifted her phone to call the police, but before she could even punch in the digits, a single gunshot rent the air.

Sly hadn't wanted to break the door. He hadn't had any choice. Dawson was too leery to come out, too smart to put himself at such a disadvantage, and Sly didn't have a lot of time to mess around. He wasn't too worried about it, though. He'd just stage the scene to make it look as if Sadie had tried to lock Dawson out — which was reasonable if they'd started to fight or she was afraid of him — and he'd forced his way in.

Sly heard her scream as he kicked the door open to find her frozen on the stairs, a look of horror on her face as she gazed down at Dawson. Sly hadn't been able to see what he was shooting at, but he'd hit his target. Dawson had crumpled to the floor. Sly could sense Sadie's uncertainty and desire to run toward her new boyfriend, which surprised him. She cared so much about him . . .

But then she saw the hatchet and realized what was in store for her.

A burst of adrenaline made Sadie's legs so rubbery they would hardly carry her up the stairs. She wanted to call 9-1-1, but there was no time. Sly would be on her before she could complete the call.

All she could do was try to reach the bathroom. Once she got in there and locked the door, he could break it down with the hatchet, of course, but at least that might afford her the precious seconds she needed to reach emergency services.

She thought she might make it, but the terror of hearing his footsteps pounding up the stairs so close behind her nearly caused her legs to give out on her entirely. *Go, go, go!* her mind yelled. *For Jayden.* She didn't want to leave her son motherless — with only a murderer for a father.

But panic had robbed her of her usual strength.

Somehow she managed to grip the door frame and launch herself through it. But she couldn't close the door in time. She felt the pressure of Sly's hand forcing the panel open despite her efforts to push it shut as he raised the hatchet.

She screamed — just as Dawson yelled Sly's name.

Sly's face registered shock as he turned to find Dawson staggering up the stairs, leaning heavily on the banister. Blood soaked his shirt, and he could barely lift the arm he used for most everything, but he was trying to stop Sly anyway.

"What the hell? You want *more*?" Sly screamed and turned on him, giving Sadie the chance to slam and lock the bathroom door.

Her hands shook as she dialed 9-1-1. She was terrified Sly would shoot Dawson again. Sly no longer had his gun in his hand, which gave her some hope, but he still had that hatchet, which could do just as much damage. Jayden's father had completely lost his mind.

Before she could get the call to go through, however, she heard more footsteps, pounding up the stairs. Then she heard someone yell, "Freeze, or I'll shoot!"

Chief Thomas! Sadie scowled at her phone in confusion. She hadn't spoken to anyone yet. How was it that Chief Thomas had shown up?

"Chief?" she yelled.

He didn't answer. He was too busy giving commands. "Get down on the ground! Now!"

Heart pounding, Sadie cracked open the door to find Thomas standing, gun drawn, over Sly, who was now lying facedown on the floor, his arms and legs spread out. Somehow the police chief had gotten past Dawson on the stairs, but Dawson was still trying to drag himself up to reach her.

"Are you okay?" he asked the moment their eyes met, his face pale and anxious.

"I'm fine, but . . . what about you? I thought . . ." She fought the lump that rose in her throat. "I thought he'd killed you."

He pressed his left hand to the bullet wound in his shoulder. "No. I'm okay. Hurts like a mother, but . . . I'll get some meds."

"Call for help. He needs an ambulance," Thomas said, but she didn't need anyone to tell her that. She was already dialing.

Sadie sat in the waiting room of the Ojai Valley Community Hospital, the closest hospital to Silver Springs, while Dawson had surgery. She'd been in such a rush to climb into the ambulance with him when it came that she'd forgotten to grab a coat. Fortunately, Chief Thomas had arrived not long after she did and insisted she take his. The waiting room wasn't that cold, but she was so jittery, so worried. Dawson had seemed okay in the ambulance, had kept re-assuring her. But he hadn't been seen by a doctor at that point, so she had no way of knowing how bad off he really was. What if he'd lost too much blood? Or the bullet had struck a nerve or damaged muscle tissue that would mean he'd lose the use of his right arm? He depended on his ability to use his hands in order to make a living.

"You okay?" Chief Thomas asked.

He'd been on his phone since he arrived, so they hadn't yet had a chance to talk. "I am. I'm just afraid for Dawson."

"I'm sorry about what happened."

She'd been hunching over, clasping her hands between her knees while staring at the floor, but now that he seemed to be available for a conversation, she sat back. "How did you know?" she asked. "How did you get to the farm in time?"

"I was already there waiting and watching for him."

"Where?"

"At the back, by the canal, but when it started getting late and nothing happened, I decided to go home. I was exhausted, couldn't stay awake anymore. But when I tried to turn around, I got stuck. I was just coming to the house to get Dawson to pull me out with his tractor when I heard the gunshot."

"Wait. You're saying you got stuck in Dawson's trap? That you would've been gone if not for that?"

"It was a trap?"

"For Sly, not you."

"Well, it caught one of us. And it's a damn

good thing."

"Why didn't you let us know you were coming? Why did you cancel in the first place?"

"I was trying to have some faith in my officer, was trying to do everything I could to save him. I even warned him. But after I canceled with you and spoke with him, I received word on something that changed my mind."

She lifted her eyebrows in question. "What? It didn't come from Damian Steele, did it?"

"No. Although it might appear to you that we haven't done much, we have been conducting our own investigation of the fire. That investigation included checking the various stores outside Silver Springs for video footage of a man purchasing a black hoodie and dark jeans."

"That had to be like looking for a needle in a haystack!" she exclaimed.

"It was, except I remembered Sly mentioning something about going to Santa Barbara not long before the fire. I figured, if it *was* him, he would've picked up that stuff there — since it wasn't so close to home."

"You found the footage to prove it?"

"I did. He's on video — clear as day — purchasing those items from Walmart. I believe it's the same clothing he had on tonight."

Sadie gaped at him. "That connects him to the fire."

"Let's just say it's a piece of the puzzle, some fairly strong circumstantial evidence. We'd need more than that to get a conviction. But he's going to prison regardless — for attempted murder."

So whether her arson investigator came through with more evidence didn't matter. She had what she needed.

She covered her mouth as she drew a deep breath. Her ex would no longer be around to intimidate, threaten or frighten her. It was almost too good to be true. "I'm free."

"Yes."

"Thank God," she whispered, mostly to herself, but she sent the police chief a sideways glance. "Aren't you going to warn me about making another mistake by getting involved with Dawson?"

He straightened his uniform. "No."

"Because . . ."

"I've learned something about Dawson, too — something that makes me believe Dawson isn't the man we thought he was, either."

She tried to read his expression. "That's good, right?"

"Yeah, that's good. Aiyana Turner called me a few hours ago."

At the mention of Aiyana's name, Sadie came to her feet. "She was able to discover the name of the brother of that drifter Dawson believed killed his parents!"

"Yes. She worked on it all afternoon and evening. And that discovery led to the drifter's name — Ronny Booker, a onetime welder and drug addict with a rap sheet a mile long."

She curled her fingernails into her palms. "Will you be able to locate him, though?"

"Already have."

"Where is he?"

"Jail, awaiting trial on a separate case."

She wished Dawson could hear this. "For what?"

"Robbed a house about nine months ago — and killed three of the occupants with a butcher knife. They have his DNA as well as a witness who survived — a fourth member of the family. Booker will go to prison for sure, and he'll never get out."

"Oh my gosh!" she cried. "Dawson *knew* the man he met that night was the one, could tell he was unstable, not right."

Chief Thomas's voice filled with caution, but she could tell that he believed Ronny Booker was their assailant, too. "We don't have a lot of hard evidence to pin the Reed murders on him yet, but —" he gave her a sheepish smile "— he does wear a size nine shoe."

For a moment, Sadie wasn't sure why that was so significant. Then she remembered the footprint found outside Dawson's parents' house — the one that was too small to have been left by Dawson. "Wow," she said. "That wasn't left by a random stranger as I heard reported in the news."

"We don't think so now."

"That's wonderful. Incredible, really. But . . . why didn't Aiyana call *us*?"

"She planned to. She was just giving me a head start, didn't want Dawson to get involved too soon and accidentally screw anything up — or do something he might regret."

In other words, she'd still trusted Chief Thomas after Dawson had lost faith in him. "Thank you for following up on that lead. Ronny Booker killed the Reeds. I know he did, because it wasn't Dawson — and no one else had any reason to hurt them. Booker was the only stranger around that night."

"If it was Ronny, we'll prove it."

"Dawson hired a forensics specialist —"

"I know. If he finds anything, it will help,

but I don't think it'll even be necessary."

"I'm stunned," she said as she sat back down. Dawson had tracked down his parents' killer. He'd no longer have to live under the terrible suspicion that had plagued him since their murder. And Sly would go to prison even if they couldn't prove he set the fire.

"Where is Sly now?" She'd paid little attention to what was happening with Sly once Chief Thomas stepped in. She'd been too worried about Dawson.

"They're booking him at the county jail. He'll be there until his trial. Then he'll go to prison, like I said."

She tried to imagine what the future might be like without him — and felt such hope and excitement. She'd be able to do whatever she wanted with her life with no thought as to how he'd react or whether he'd approve or let her. "I never want to see him again."

"I don't blame you. You won't have to. He's a cop. Any judge he gets is going to give him the longest sentence possible."

The memory of Sly coming after her with that hatchet chilled Sadie to the bone. He'd shot Dawson and would've killed her if Chief Thomas hadn't come charging in when he did. She and Dawson would both be dead. "He's a monster," she said.

"That's another thing. Just before I left for the farm, as if what I'd already heard wasn't enough, the bartender from The Blue Suede Shoe called to tell me how intimidating he'd behaved at the bar. I'm afraid he's not the man I hired over a decade ago."

Sadie didn't get the chance to respond. The doctor had walked in. "Is there a Sadie Harris here?"

She stood up again. "Yes. I'm Sadie Harris."

"Dawson is asking for you," he said.

She swallowed against a suddenly dry throat. "Is he going to be okay?"

"I had quite a time removing that bullet from his shoulder, but I managed, and because I managed, he should make a full recovery. He just needs to rest up."

Sadie smiled in relief as she turned to Chief Thomas. "He's going to be fine."

Thomas returned her smile as he got to his feet. "I think he's going to be even better than fine once you tell him the good news."

"*You're* not going to tell him?" she asked in surprise.

"No. I'll leave that to you. I'm going home."

She tried to return his coat, but he refused

to take it.

"Bring it by the station tomorrow or the next day. There's no rush."

"Thank you," she said. "I can't tell you how grateful I am that . . . that you were there tonight. We thought you . . ."

"I know what you thought." His voice carried a trace of disappointment as he continued, "I didn't want to show any doubt in my men, in case I was wrong. Something like this is . . . well, it's so unfortunate, especially now, with the way people are feeling toward law enforcement."

"You're not all like Sly," she said.

"I'm glad you realize that — and I'm happy it worked out as well as it did for you and Dawson."

She put out her hand to shake with him. "It only worked out because you did your job. Thanks again."

EPILOGUE

Angela was standing in front of Stanley De-Witt with her luggage and Megan by her side when Sadie and Dawson pulled into the parking lot. Dawson's sister recognized his truck the second it came into view and started to wave wildly.

"Look how excited she is." Sadie chuckled as she slowed to avoid another car that was coming down the row from the opposite direction. She was driving, since Dawson was barely out of the hospital. He should've been resting in bed, but he said he wouldn't disappoint Angela by not showing up to get her.

"She won't be happy when she realizes we don't have Jayden with us," he said as he used his left hand, since he couldn't use his right, to wave back at her.

They'd had to leave Jayden with Petra. Four people couldn't fit in Dawson's truck or Sadie's El Camino. Dawson was already talking about buying a sedan capable of fitting the entire "family," though, so Sadie knew that wouldn't continue to be a problem.

She came to a stop at the curb and put the gearshift in Park. "I'll go grab him as soon as we get back, so she'll get to see him soon."

"Dawson!" Angela cried and would've thrown herself at him as soon as he got out if Sadie hadn't intervened.

"Whoa! Be gentle, okay? Dawson's hurt right now," she explained.

His sister frowned at the evidence — she couldn't see the big bandage under his shirt, but she could see that his arm was in a sling. "You told me you were okay, Dawson. You were in the hospital, but you said it wasn't a *big* owie." Her tone came off accusatory, as if his getting hurt had been intentional.

"It's nothing, honey. I'll heal, with time. I just have to be careful not to pull out my stitches, or I'll start to bleed again."

"I don't like blood," she said.

"Neither do I," he responded.

She eyed him speculatively, as if she was deciding how much to believe. "What are stitches?"

He pulled the neck of his T-shirt over to show her the bandage. "I've got some threads holding my skin together under here."

"Can you take off your shirt so I can see it all?"

"Not right now. It's covered by bandages, anyway." He gave her the best one-armed hug he could, but she seemed upset in spite of the excitement she'd exhibited only moments before.

"What is it?" he asked.

"You're not going to die like Mom and Dad, are you? You're not going away again . . ."

"No, I'm not going away again. Ever. I'm just fine."

"Are *they* coming back?"

He shot Sadie a sad look before answering his sister. "No. But I'll show you where you can visit them whenever you miss them."

"I miss them *now,*" she said.

He nodded. "So do I."

Sadie and Megan had to insist that Dawson not try to load the luggage himself. They took care of that while he went in to handle the paperwork.

"It's all done," he said when he came out. "We're free to go."

"I bet there were moments when you thought this day would never happen," Megan said to him.

"There were a lot of them," he admitted.

They thanked her before loading up and starting off for Silver Springs.

"Can I have an ice cream cone?" Angela asked almost as soon as they pulled out of the parking lot.

She knew her brother was a soft touch, and she was taking immediate advantage of that, but Sadie would've indulged her, too, so she couldn't point any fingers at Dawson. They stopped at a shop and enjoyed the Los Angeles sunshine a little before starting the drive home. After that, Angela tolerated the drive for about an hour before she started asking, "How much longer?" and "When are we going to be there?"

Sadie smiled to herself as Dawson told Angela they had another hour, forty-five minutes, half hour, etc. He possessed a gentle strength. Sadie had never been more proud of him. He always treated Angela with such kindness and patience.

"When will I get to see Jayden?" Angela asked.

This was another frequent question. "I'll pick him up as soon as I drop you and Dawson off at the farm," Sadie told her, but going to get Jayden proved unnecessary. When they pulled into the farm, it looked as though half the town was there to meet them. Petra and Jayden stood right out front, holding a Welcome Back sign. There were other signs as well, even a big one that read, We're sorry, Dawson, mixed in with all the balloons and other greetings.

Once she got out, Sadie learned the church the Reeds had attended had organized the party. Not only did they have tables filled with food, they'd brought workers who were there to help Dawson finish weeding and planting before the weather could turn too warm to be good for his crops. A few were even fixing various things Dawson hadn't been able to get around to on the house. Besides the church members, Aiyana and her sons were there. So were Maude and Vern and Lolita, as well as several of the waitresses from the restaurant. Chief Thomas had come, too, with Pete and George, Sly's friends. They looked the most sheepish.

Dawson was clearly astounded by the crowd, especially when everyone began to greet him and Angela. A line quickly formed as folks came up to offer him an apology. *I was wrong about you . . . I'm so sorry . . . We should've listened to Aiyana. She's always right . . . I'm here to help . . .*

Dawson would've been justified in rejecting their apologies. They'd been so judgmental. But he didn't. He shook hands with anyone who approached him, even allowed some to give him half a hug on his uninjured side.

Sadie stood nearby, enjoying the spectacle while talking to Maude, who'd winked at her and said, "You followed your heart, and it was *your* heart and no one else's that was right."

When Maude drifted off to talk to other friends and Angela called out, trying to get Dawson to come over and help her with something, Sadie let them both go. Chief Thomas was approaching her. "Thanks for coming today," she told him.

"No problem. Glad to be here." He jerked his head to where Dawson was tying a balloon for his sister. "He deserves a party — and a lot more after what he's been through. But you've had a rough time, too."

"I'm just glad it's over." She'd noticed that Sly's mother wasn't in the crowd. She doubted his mother would ever have a kind word for her again, despite what he'd done.

"So am I. I'm also happy to give you a bit of good news."

She expected him to tell her about some evidence they'd acquired that would help put Sly or Ronny Booker away. "You've heard from the fire investigator?"

"Yes. He's confirmed our findings that an accelerant was used — probably gasoline. But that's it so far. This is something else."

"What?"

"We've found your pictures."

"My *pictures*?" she echoed.

"Of your parents — and Jayden when he was a baby."

She felt her jaw drop. "Where?"

"Under Sly's bed. They were there when we went through his place yesterday — in the plastic container you told us they'd be in, which is a little melted on one side, from what I hear, but otherwise unharmed. One of my officers will bring them over tonight. I didn't want to miss the moment you arrived here to see the surprise, or I would've picked them up for you myself."

"Tomorrow's fine, thank you. But . . . how did *Sly* get them?"

"He was there the night of the fire. Once it was out, I'm guessing he went in and poked around — or in the days immediately after. I still believed in him then, wasn't watching him as closely as I should have."

"I don't understand why he'd ever take them in the first place. I mean, I can see him wanting Jayden's baby pictures, but I'd already offered him the opportunity to make copies, and he never acted on it. I would've done it myself if I'd had the money."

Thomas scratched his neck. "Maybe this was another attempt to hurt you."

"I'm sure of it," she muttered. No doubt Sly loved knowing he had what she wanted and could decide if or when he'd ever give it to her.

She chatted with the police chief for a few more minutes about what the fire inspector might find or the forensics specialist Dawson had hired to search for further evidence on his parents' murder, and marveled that whatever they found would help but wouldn't change the ultimate outcome for Sly or Ronny Booker.

Dawson returned to her side only a moment after Thomas walked over to get a cupcake. "What is it?"

Because she didn't want to turn the focus away from him and what he was experiencing, she figured she'd tell him about the pictures later. "This." She smiled up at him. "It's wonderful, isn't it?"

"It *is* wonderful." He leaned in for a kiss. "But having you and Jayden in my life, and Angela back home, is by far the best part."

ABOUT THE AUTHOR

New York Times and *USA Today* bestselling author **Brenda Novak** has penned over 45 novels. A two-time Rita nominee, she's won The National Readers' Choice, The Booksellers' Best, The Bookbuyers' Best and many other awards. She runs an annual online auction for diabetes research every May at www.brendanovak.com. To date, she's raised over $2 million. Brenda considers herself lucky to be a mother of five and married to the love of her life.

THREE BROTHERS

Three Brothers

Peter Ackroyd

Chatto & Windus

LONDON

Published by Chatto & Windus 2013

2 4 6 8 10 9 7 5 3 1

First published in Great Britain in 2013 by
Chatto & Windus
Random House, 20 Vauxhall Bridge Road,
London SW1V 2SA
www.randomhouse.co.uk

Addresses for companies within The Random House Group Limited can be
found at: www.randomhouse.co.uk/offices.htm

The Random House Group Limited Reg. No. 954009

A CIP catalogue record for this book
is available from the British Library

ISBN 9780701186937

Typeset by Palimpsest Book Production Limited,
Falkirk, Stirlingshire

Printed in the UK by
CPI Group (UK) Ltd, Croydon CR0 4YY

Contents

I

Cheese and pickle

I N THE London borough of Camden, in the middle of the
last century, there lived three brothers; they were three
young boys, with a year's difference of age between each of
them. They were united, however, in one extraordinary
way. They had been born at the same time on the same
day of the same month – to be precise, midday on 8 May.
The chance was remote and even implausible. Yet it was
so. The local newspaper recorded the coincidence, after the
birth of the third son, and the Hanway boys became
the object of speculation. Were they in some sense marked
out? Was there some invisible communion between them,
apart from their natural affinity?

The interest soon subsided, of course, in a neighbourhood
where the daily struggles of existence were still evident four
or five years after the War. In any case, there were other differences between the boys – differences of temperament,
differences of affection – that soon became manifest. These
diversities, however, were still mild and pliable. They had
not yet become the source of great disagreement or hostile
division.

The three boys were young enough, and near enough
in age, to enjoy the same pastimes. On the pavement

outside their small house in Crystal Street they chalked the squares of hop-scotch. They played marbles in the gutter with fierce concentration. They hardened the seeds of the horse chestnut with pickle juice and brine, so that they could compete with conkers. They raced each other on the common, at the edge of the council estate in which they lived. They explored the deserted tracts of land beside an old railway line, and trod cautiously among the debris of an abandoned bomb shelter.

On the common, too, they played the old game 'Run Run Away'. One of them, with a scarf wound about his eyes as a blindfold, repeated a few well-known words as the others ran as far as they could; when he stopped speaking, they had to remain quite still. He then had to find them, and the first one he touched became 'it' when the whole game began again.

On one particular afternoon the youngest of them, Sam, was standing, his eyes blindfolded, and he began to shout out the words.

'When I was standing on the stair
I met a man who wasn't there.
He wasn't there again today.
I wish, I wish he'd go away.
Here I come, ready or not!'

After a minute or two of threshing around he caught hold of his oldest brother, Harry. But there was no real excitement in the game. They had played it too often.

'Listen,' Sam said, 'what do you both want to be when you grow up?'

'I want to be a pilot.'

'I want to be a detective.'

'Do you know what?' Sam told them. 'I don't want to be anything.'

The sky was growing darker, and a cold breeze had started

up across the common with the promise of light rain. 'Come on,' Harry said, pointing to the abandoned bomb shelter, 'let's all go under the ground. I've got some matches. We can start a fire. Mum won't miss us till teatime. Let's start a fire that will go on *for ever!*'

'I dare you.'

'I double dare you.'

So one by one, in single file, following each other, they descended into the earth.

They had a small back garden, in which they investigated the lives of earwigs and other insects. At the bottom of this garden there was an old stone basin often filled with rainwater, and in this they raised tadpoles caught from the pond on the edge of the common. They put their heads together and peered down into the murky water, their sweet liquorice breath mingling with the dank odour of moss and slime. They tried to grow beans and peas in the garden, but the shoots withered and rotted away. It was, in short, a London childhood. They had never seen mountains or waterfalls, of course, but they lived securely in their world of brick and stone.

They recognised by instinct the frontiers to their territory; a street further north, or further south, was not visited. It was not welcoming. But within their own bounds they were entirely at home. They knew every dip in the pavement, every front door, every cat that prowled along the gutter or slumbered on the window sill. They knew, or at least recognised, most of the people they saw. There were few strangers in the neighbourhood. They lived among familiar faces.

Any stranger who happened to walk through the neighbourhood would not have come away with any distinct impression. It was a council estate, built in the 1920s, of two-storey red-brick terraces. That was all. One row of houses was interrupted by some small shops – a newsagent, a hairdresser, a butcher among them – and on the corners of the narrow streets were general stores or public houses. There was a fish-and-chip shop, and a bakery, in the street where the Hanways lived. The district smelled at various times of dust and of rain, of bonfire smoke and of petrol. Its sounds were not of cars but of trams and milk-floats, with the distinct but distant roar of London somewhere around the corner. It had the forlorn calm of a poor neighbourhood, yet for the three brothers it repaid the closest possible attention. It was the source of curiosity, of surprise, and, sometimes, of delight. The centre of their lives was very small, but it was brightly lit. And all around stretched the endless streets, of which they were largely unaware.

Their first memories of childhood differed. Harry recalled how he had managed to walk unaided across the carpet of the small living room, praised and encouraged by his parents sitting on a yellow sofa. Daniel, between his brothers in age, remembered being taken out of a pram and held up to the sunlight, in which he seemed to soar. Sam's first memory was of falling and cutting his leg on a shard of broken glass; he had cried when he saw the blood. Had their respective memories ever come together, they might have had some understanding of their shared past. But they were content with these fragments.

They attended the same primary school, a red-brick building set beside a grey-brick church, where the signs for 'Boys' and 'Girls' were carved in Gothic script above two portals. The school smelled of soap and carbolic disinfectant, but the classrooms were always cluttered and dirty with a faint patina of dust upon the shelves and windows.

The Hanway boys were in separate classes, according to their age, and in the playground they did not care to fraternise. Harry was the most gregarious and thus the most popular of the brothers; he laughed readily, and had a circle of acquaintances whom he easily amused. Daniel had two chosen friends, with whom he was always deep in consultation; they collected bus numbers and cigarette cards, which they would compare and contrast. Sam, the youngest, seemed content to remain on his own. He did not seek the company of the other children. And they in turn left him alone. But Sam had a temper. One morning, at the gate of the school, a boy remarked on the fact that Sam had torn his school jacket. Sam struck out at him with his fist and knocked him to the pavement. His two brothers witnessed the event, and adjusted to him accordingly.

Harry Hanway was ten, Daniel Hanway was nine, and Sam Hanway was eight, when their mother disappeared. They returned late one afternoon from school, and found an empty house. Harry made sandwiches of cheese and pickle. They sat around the kitchen table, and waited. No one came.

Their father, Philip, was employed as a nightwatchman in the City. He always left the house in the afternoon, stopped at a pub on Camden High Street, and then took the bus to the financial headquarters where he worked. He would put on his dark blue uniform, kept in a small locker off the main hall, and then sit behind an imposing central desk. He always had with him pencils and paper. After a few minutes of concentration he would begin writing, slowly and hesitantly; then he would stop altogether. For the rest of the night he would smoke and stare into space.

He had been called up for the army, in the third year of the War, but in fact travelled no farther than Middlesbrough where he was assigned to the barracks as a clerk of munitions. He remained in that post until the end of the War when, with army pay in his pocket, he returned to London. He had been brought up in Ruislip, but he had no intention of returning. Ruislip was the place where he had waited impatiently for his real life to begin. Instead he set off for Soho. He believed that he was destined to be a writer. When he was a schoolboy, he had read an English translation of *The Count of Monte Cristo* over several weeks; he had devoured it, page by page, elated and terrified by the turns of the plot. The day after he finished the novel, he began his own story. He never completed it. He put the pages in a biscuit tin, where at the time of this narrative they still lay. Yet he was not discouraged. He began writing other stories, to which he could never find a satisfactory conclusion. The more disappointment he suffered, the more intense his ambition became. He recalled the last words of *The Count of Monte Cristo*, 'wait and hope'.

So he migrated to Soho in search of publishers, of magazines, of fellow writers, of critics, of any stimulus – he was not sure of his way forward. He rented a small room in Poland Street, and indulged in what seemed to him to be the bliss of bohemian life. He woke late; he drank coffee in dirty cafés; he lounged and sipped Guinness in shadowy pubs. Yet he could not write. He sat down at the folding table in his room, pencil in hand. He could find no subject.

When his army funds were low, he sought work in the neighbourhood. He became a barman in the Horn of Plenty, a pub in Greek Street that was the chosen spot for a group of hard-drinking and sometimes bellicose Soho residents. Philip Hanway was happy here. He called himself a writer, and enjoyed the anecdotes of the journalists and advertising copy-writers who frequented the bar. And then he met Sally Palliser. She worked in a cake shop, or 'pâtisserie', in Meard Street. He had passed its window, with a display of almond tarts and buns and pastries, and had seen her delicately picking out an angel cake for a customer. His first impression was of the graceful way she moved behind the counter, her skirt slightly creasing as she bent forward. On the following morning he paused, opened the gaily painted door, and ordered a macaroon. He purchased a macaroon every morning for the next few weeks.

Sally had been impressed when he told her that he was a writer. He was young, and looked very smart in a grey suit, grey overcoat and grey trilby.

'I like grey,' he told her. 'I can disappear.'

'Now that's interesting.'

'I promise you, I will *always* say interesting things to you. I can't help myself.'

'But what will *I* say?'

'You just have to smile.'

When he first took her out she ordered a pink gin and smoked Woodbines. This delighted him. They went dancing at the Rainbow Room in Holborn to the music of Harry Chapman and his orchestra. After three months, much to her parents' disapproval, she moved into Philip's small room.

'Living in sin is not right,' her mother said. 'It will come to no good. Mark my words.' She was always enjoining her daughter to mark her words. 'And what are you going to live on? Spam and baked beans?'

In fact there was a fish-and-chip shop in Dean Street. And the pastries were free. She brought back the stale ones at the end of the day.

After a violent argument with the staff of the Horn of Plenty, Philip Hanway lost his job.

'Where are you going?' the landlord asked him.

'I'm going *outside*. For good.' He wanted to slam the door but it swung limply to and fro.

'Well,' he said to Sally when he returned home, 'at least I can concentrate on my writing.' She surmised that he would be happy to survive on her small income.

When she first realised that she was pregnant, she panicked. She enquired about abortionists, of whom there were several in Soho, but the stories of injury and even fatality dissuaded her. 'Sometimes,' a friend told her, 'they stick a knitting needle up your you-know-what.'

'Ouch.'

'Have you ever seen a dead baby? Looks like a mole.'

So Harry was saved.

She informed her parents of the pregnancy before she told Philip. She wanted to present him with a family ultimatum. And so, five weeks later, Sally and Philip were married in the registry office on St Martin's Lane. Philip then exerted himself to find work, and applied for the job of night-watchman. The two of them formally requested a council house, as a newly married couple, and to their relief they succeeded. So they moved to Camden, where Harry was born four months later.

The three brothers had been sitting in silence around the kitchen table. Sam was fiddling with two elastic bands he had tied together. 'I'm going to have a drink of fizz,' Harry said. 'Anyone else want some?'

'Where is she?' Daniel asked him.

'I think,' he replied, 'she's been delayed.' An old alarm clock was ticking by the sink. 'Dad will know what to do.'

Philip Hanway did not seem particularly surprised by his wife's disappearance. 'She has gone away for a while,' he told his sons. That was all he said. He offered no other explanation. In fact he never afterwards spoke of her. He continued his work as a nightwatchman, and the boys saw little of him. They grew accustomed to looking after them-selves. Philip provided them with pocket money that they pooled. After a few months they forgot that their life had ever been different.

In the days immediately following her disappearance, however, Sam was very quiet. On going to school in those mornings the boys encountered a thick smog, and under its cover Sam wept softly without the others knowing. They explained nothing to their school companions or to their teachers. On the matter of their mother, they were wholly silent. Something – something vast, something overwhelming – had happened. But they could not speak of it. The neighbours, curiously, did not seem to notice Sally's absence. The three brothers were left to themselves.

A year after the disappearance Harry progressed, as he had expected, to the secondary modern school on the other side of the borough. He had sat the 11-plus examination, but he had not excelled in any of the papers. He changed from one school uniform to another, and caught a bus in the morning. Then, a year later, Daniel passed the same examination with much higher marks.

Daniel seemed to have a natural propensity for study, and a love of reading. Often, when Harry and Sam would busy themselves with sports or games on the common, he would stay behind with a book. In this he could be said to take after his father. But Philip knew very little of his son's secluded life. Daniel visited the public library on the boundary of the estate, and brought home each week a selection of adventure novels and popular histories. He took out on an extended loan each volume of *Arthur Mee's Children's Encyclopaedia*, and vowed to memorise the contents.

His work was rewarded when it was announced, after passing the 11-plus, that he had won a place at Camden Grammar School. If his mother had been there, she would have danced with him around the kitchen; she would have lifted him up, and pressed her nose against his. Philip simply shook his hand, and gave him half-a-crown. Harry joked with him about a school for swots. Sam never mentioned the subject.

But there was now a change in the Hanway family. Daniel had to strive with his contemporaries. He had to compete. He was given homework every night, and would sit at the kitchen table while Harry and Sam were free to roam. He became more deliberate and circumspect; he saw his life as a series of hurdles over which he was obliged to jump.

Then Harry started playing football for his school team. He enjoyed the exhilaration of the dribble with the ball, the clever pass, and the sudden shot at the goal. He enjoyed the exercise of his own body – the exercise of his power in the world. He called out to his teammates, he shouted at the linesmen, he whooped with triumph at every goal his team scored. It was a world of expressive noise. The physical sensation of movement delighted him. He revelled in the wind and rain and sunlight as he ran across the pitch.

In this, he was different from his brothers. Gradually the intimacy between them began to fade. Sam was left to himself. He spent many hours making elaborate contraptions out of wood and cardboard. Even though he did not know the word melancholy, he began to experience it. He would turn, head over heels, on his narrow bed in order to make himself dizzy and disoriented. He did not prosper at school. As a matter of course he was sent to the same secondary modern school as his older brother. He made no friends there, and Harry seemed to avoid him.

II

The path is clear

HARRY HANWAY left school at the age of sixteen, and was already eager to join the world. He was active, determined, and energetic. At school he had won popularity for his cheerfulness and bravado. He had become captain of the football team. He had retaliated against one notorious school bully by knocking him to the floor. He had his own recognisable phrases, which were instantly imitated. 'How the heck are you?' was his standard greeting. He also said, in mock irritation, 'What the heck?' So he became known as Harry Heck.

'I don't want to go to college,' he told his father as his leaving day approached. 'I want to get a job.'

'Say that again.'

'I want to get a job.'

'Just so you're certain.' He looked away for a moment. 'There's nothing worse than a dead-end job.'

It was a Sunday afternoon. Philip Hanway was about to leave for the City. He now worked seven nights a week in order to support his family. 'I'll come back with money, Dad.'

'It's not about the money. It's about you.'

'But what do you think, Dad, of the newspapers? That's a good life, isn't it?' Harry loved newspapers. He enjoyed the appearance, and even the texture, of them. He liked their smell. He relished the size of the headlines and the neat rows of type. He was excited by the thought of thousands of copies despatched from the printing plant into waiting vans. In the evenings, after school, he flattened the *Daily Sketch* on the kitchen table and slowly turned its pages. Sometimes he read out paragraphs aloud, just like the news broadcasters on the wireless.

'Newspaper boy?' Daniel was writing in an exercise book, but now looked up at him.

'Dry up.'

'I was only asking.'

'Sod off.'

'There's no need for a fight,' Philip said. 'We have to think about this seriously.'

'I have thought about it seriously.'

So Harry arrived at the offices of the local newspaper, the *Camden Bugle*, and asked if they needed a messenger boy.

He was astonished to discover that the offices of the *Bugle* comprised two small rooms, one marked 'Editorial' and the other marked 'Advertising', above a row of shops along the high street. Its premises were on the second floor above a barber, and the candy-striped pole could be seen from the desks of 'Editorial'. The floor was covered with scuffed lino-leum, and the interior needed repainting.

The *Bugle*, quite by chance, did need a messenger boy, the previous occupant of that post having just handed in his notice in order to become a gentleman's outfitter in Bond Street. The editor, George Bradwell, prided himself on making his decisions in an instant. And he reckoned Harry to be a lively young man. 'Do you run or do you walk fast?' he asked him. He had a gruff voice that seemed to come from his chest rather than his throat.

'I run, sir, when I see the path clear.'

'That's good. That's what you must do.' He had an emphatic manner of speaking, reminding Harry of the fairground barkers who came to Camden once a year. George Bradwell was not used to being interrupted or contradicted. He explained that Harry was supposed to take the 'copy' from the office to the printer, and then bring the 'proof' back to the *Bugle*. Copy of what? Proof of what? It was very mysterious. Bradwell then showed Harry some pages of typing, with various scrawls and symbols in the margins. 'These,' he said, 'have been marked up.' Harry nodded, as if he understood perfectly what he was being told. The air was heavy with the stale odour of tobacco. 'Cadogan Street.' Pinned to the wall was a large map of the borough. Bradwell pointed with tobacco-stained finger to the street in question. 'On the right is Lubin the printer. Just tell him you're from the *Bugle*. This is Tony, by the way.'

Tony was a middle-aged man of florid complexion, with the indefinable air of having been disappointed in life. He boasted a thin pencil-like moustache, and a clump of hair perched precariously on his head. 'You can't miss Lubin,' he said. 'He is the Jew boy.' Harry knew at once that Tony wore a wig, and he suspected that the moustache was dyed. Tony looked like a man perpetually in disguise.

Tony, in turn, took an instinctive dislike to the new recruit; any young person threatened him.

Harry soon became accustomed to his duties. He was so exhilarated by his new job that he mastered its details easily enough. He dashed from the *Bugle* to the printers. He ran between 'Editorial' and 'Advertising', picking up the copy from both departments. In 'Editorial' Tony was news. George was interviews and reviews. An elderly man, Aldous, was sports. Aldous hardly ever spoke, and seemed to Harry to exist in a state of self-pitying gloom. Stress and tension were

13

always in the air. Bradwell would answer the telephone and announce himself as 'editor in chief'. Tony would then give a sarcastic smile. Bradwell would often snatch his hat and coat, and stride purposefully out of the office. Sometimes he would not come back for an hour or more. Then he returned with an air of mystery, and with the odour of alcohol.

In the background there was always the stutter of a type-writer, as Tony or Aldous put together a paragraph. Aldous described the triumphs, or the miseries, of the Camden Rovers. He praised the exploits of a Camden schoolgirl who had won a North London javelin competition. He denounced the closing of the bar of the Camden Cricketers' Association. He typed down all this with the same air of gloom. Tony celebrated a lucky win on the football pools by a Camden pensioner. He described the closure of a cottage hospital in East Camden. He reported the theft of a jukebox from a Camden public house. He sat over his typewriter like a bird of prey.

On the whole, Harry preferred 'Advertising'. It was run by a small woman with a strong Scots accent. To Harry, Maureen seemed marvellously exotic. She wore a skein of artificial pearls over her hair and, according to Tony, dressed like something out of a shop window. He referred to her as Queen of Scots or Bloody Maureen. She supervised the work of two young men who were, again according to Tony, 'slaves at her feet'. Maureen had overheard the remark; she had arched her eyebrows and sniffed. She considered Tony to be, as she put it, 'a drastic little creature'. 'Excuse me,' she said, 'but I think he's a very common type of person. And that wig looks like a dead cat.' Harry could not disagree.

Harry enjoyed his time in Lubin's printworks. He savoured the pervasive smell of ink, and the steady metallic beat of the electrotyping machines. He saw the curved plates of metal type being inserted into the presses, and watched as the paper flowed between them. It was a cheerful and good-humoured place, filled with shouts and the noise of the machinery. This was the newspaper world that Harry had envisaged — a strident, exciting, declamatory world.

Harry was walking back from the printer one evening, after delivering the last of that day's copy, when he noticed a man in a dark raincoat walking ahead of him. He was in his thirties, or so it seemed, but he was much smaller and slighter than Harry. He was carrying a shopping bag in each hand, containing something bulky or heavy. He had difficulty in maintaining an even pace, but he looked calmly from side to side. On a whim, or instinct, Harry decided to follow him. The man crossed the road, and then began walking down a street of semi-detached dark red-brick houses. The area was gloomy enough in the day, but on a winter evening it was a place in mourning. It was one of those parts of London that sunlight never seems to enter, an almost subterranean world of domestic privacy and seclusion. Net curtains were hanging at every window, and the gates of the small front gardens were all closed.

Harry knew that the brick church of Our Lady of Sorrows stood at the end of this dark red avenue, opposite a small park. He suspected that the man was about to enter the park, but then he saw him vanish into the deep shadow of the church itself. He followed him through the porch, and then sat quietly in a pew at the back. The church was deserted. The man had walked slowly up the aisle and had halted at the wooden rail before the altar. It seemed to Harry that he had knelt down and, with his head bowed forward, begun to pray. But that was not what he was doing. Harry heard rustling, and noticed that he was taking something out of the bags. He walked towards him silently and cautiously; then, to his alarm, he saw two large cans of petrol. He did not hesitate. He shouted out 'Heck!' and rushed at the man, knocking him to the floor before pinning him against the rail. The man looked at him, mildly, and did not try to resist.

The cry had roused the curate of the church, who had been dozing in the sacristy amidst the mild perfume of lilies and beeswax polish. He came running out, and was astonished at the spectacle of Harry straddling the man and pressing him against the floor of the church. Harry suggested to him that he might go in search of a policeman. A glance at the cans of petrol convinced the curate. 'I'm in no possible hurry,' the man said as Harry continued to sit upon him. 'Don't you think this church is rather wonderful?' It was ornate and comfortable, with candles and flowers and images; statues of the saints stood between the Stations of the Cross, and a wooden confessional box was against the south aisle. 'My mother used to frequent this place a great deal. She used to sit here with me. I was only a boy, naturally. That was in '44. When the bombing got a trifle on the heavy side.' He had a plaintive or earnest expression, as if he were trying to solve a curiously subtle problem. 'I can remember the bombs very well. I was never scared, you see. It was the excitement. Glorious feeling.' His voice, echoing in the empty church, was very gentle. 'I was one of the Blitz boys. Have you heard of us by any chance?' Harry shook his head. The War was, for him, very distant. 'We were the ones who put out the fires. We had buckets of sand and a hand-truck. We had iron bars to force our way in. We were absolutely fierce. We were ready to *eat* fires, even if I say so myself.'

The curate came back with three policemen. Harry rose to his feet and two officers took the man away. The third remained to take down Harry's statement.

Harry told George Bradwell the following morning. He became so excited by his own narrative that he knelt on the floor to demonstrate the manner in which he had pinned down the arsonist.

'I think,' Bradwell said, 'that we can make a story out of this.'

'But it's true.'

'A news story. *Bugle* reporter foils arson attack upon church. Commended by the police for his heroism.'

'But I'm not a reporter.'

'You are now.' He glanced at the unoccupied desks of Aldous and of Tony. Harry sensed, then, that he did not altogether relish their company. 'You know how to hold a pen, don't you?' Harry nodded. 'That's a good start.'

Within a very short time Bradwell taught him how to construct a news story; he explained to him that he should begin with the simple fact, in a short sentence, and then gradually elaborate. He pointed out the places where Harry might acquire news – the magistrates' court, the town hall, the police stations, the office of the coroner. He gave him lessons in typewriting, and even sent him on a course of shorthand. Bradwell seemed to be reliving the earliest stages of his own career; he saw in Harry a version of his younger self. He wished him to succeed. And Harry did. He had a natural gift for vivid description, and a keen eye for a likely story. Another messenger boy was hired.

Tony was furious at Harry's appointment. He believed himself to have been supplanted and, in effect, humiliated. But he did not show his fury to those who had instigated it. He concealed it from Bradwell and Harry, but he vented it to Aldous. 'He can't write,' he said as they sat in a local public house. 'He can't spell. He is an ignorant little bleeder. I think he may be a pansy. What do you think?' Aldous was deeply uncomfortable about any such allusion. He merely shook his head. Tony's anger emerged as genial malice in Harry's presence. He was careful not to criticise him directly, but tried to unsettle him with jokes and insinuations. Harry feigned not to notice his resentment and bitterness.

He spent most of his time, in any case, out of 'Editorial'. He rushed after stories of burglaries and assaults. He attended weddings and funerals. He waited outside the local police station for the arrival of the Black Maria van. He spent hours talking to the elderly clerk of the magistrates' court, Mr Peabody, who was a source of local information. Mr Peabody was a grave and dignified gentleman, with a taste for whisky. He would speak eloquently of the foibles of a certain magistrate, or the surprising conclusion of a certain case; but as he drank he grew more thoughtful, until his conversation came to a lingering end. Harry knew that, at this stage, it was time to withdraw. He would leave Mr Peabody at the bar, glass in hand, staring solemnly at the row of bottles above the cash register.

'Hanway? Hanway?' he asked Harry one evening.

'Yes, Mr Peabody?'

'The name is known to me. I can recall it. It is an unusual name. Most unusual.' He reflected. 'There was a young woman, by the name of Hanway, connected with the court in some way. Some years ago. I seem to remember her crying.'

Who was the young woman, crying? Could Mr Peabody have some vague recollection of his mother? But, then, what had she to do with the magistrates' court? Harry sensed, at that moment, that all this had something to do with her disappearance.

He decided to consult the court's files. He knew the approximate date of his mother's disappearance. It had been in the early winter. He recalled the smog. He had been ten years old. So he turned back to the records of October 1957. It was weary work, going through the reports of cases and incidents long forgotten. But he read on through evidences and judgements – until one name arrested his wandering

18

attention. Mrs Sally Hanway was brought before the court on 22 October 1957. He started to sweat, and looked away at a printed notice fixed to the wall. With an effort of concentration he turned back to the page, from which he had been momentarily distracted by a pang of anxiety so great that he caught his breath. At that instant, too, Daniel Hanway and Sam Hanway were seized with a sensation close to panic. Harry carried on reading and learned that Mrs Sally Hanway had been found guilty of soliciting and of offending public morals. The magistrate had sentenced her to a term of three months' imprisonment.

Harry got up from his chair and walked down the long corridor of the building. He came out of the entrance, descended the stone steps, and was then sick on the pavement. He steadied himself against a pillar, and breathed in deeply. He had a sudden image of her, standing on the steps of the magistrates' court, with her finger to her lips. He went back to the library, and replaced the heavy volume on the shelves.

It was only when he had walked out again into the street that he realised something else. His father had known of this. That is why he had evinced no surprise. That is why he had never spoken of her disappearance. And the neighbours must also have known of his mother's arrest. Out of pity or embarrassment, they had not remarked upon her absence to the three young brothers. He realised, too, that with this knowledge he could no longer remain in the house with his brothers.

The life of the Hanway household was not, in any case, as it once had been. The brothers had steadily grown apart. Daniel spent his evenings in study, while Harry pursued his new work. Without the company of his older brothers, Sam had become aimless. He had no friends and spent his time, outside of school, roaming through the streets – in search of what? Their father had changed his job. He gave up his post

19

as nightwatchman, and had become a long-distance lorry driver with a regular run from London to Carlisle; as a result he spent less time than ever at home.

Harry took advantage of his father's absence to leave quietly and quickly. He found a small room in a street close to the offices of the *Bugle*. He had few possessions; what he owned could be carried in a suitcase.

Daniel saw him packing. He asked him where he was going.

'Now that's an excellent question. I'm going away. I'm taking off.'

'For good?'

'Nothing is for good, clever boy.'

'Dad won't like it.'

'Dad will like it. You will have more space. Sam can have my room.' He closed the lid of the suitcase. 'Dad doesn't even know I'm here. When is he ever at home?'

'Where are you going then?'

'Carver Street.'

It was a street of small houses and of small shops. They were some of the first buildings ever erected in the fields of Camden, in the early nineteenth century, but they did not wear their age gracefully. Their yellow brick had faded with grime and decay; the doors were peeling, and the windows were dusty. A sudden gap in the row of houses marked the spot where a stray doodlebug had flattened two houses; they had not yet been rebuilt, and the open site was covered in weeds and refuse. The windows of Harry's room overlooked this waste-ground. He rented the room from an elderly Irish couple, the Stantons, whose son had recently died of polio-myelitis. It was the son's room that Harry now occupied. A crucifix hung on the wall above the bed.

Harry had never been alone before. He had never thought of himself as solitary. He had lost contact with his erstwhile school friends, but he would have denied ever being lonely. He never once used the word. But now he sat by himself in any number of cheap cafés, where the principal resource was egg and chips and brown sauce. It was the sauce, in fact, that effected his introduction to Hilda. She was sitting at the table next to his in the Zodiac Café for Working Men. He was shaking the bottle of sauce so vigorously that it splattered over her plate of spotted dick and custard.

He offered to buy her an untainted pudding, an offer that she gracefully accepted. It was the least he could do. Then they began to talk.

'I expect,' she said, 'that you will be laughing at me soon.'

'Why would I do that?'

'Everything I do seems to be funny. Not funny peculiar. Funny ha ha. People laugh at me for no apparent reason. I'm *serious*.' She had a direct manner, but it was accompanied by a shy smile that Harry found charming; she had a round face, but it was a pretty one. 'My name is Hilda. That makes you laugh, doesn't it?'

'No.'

'It should do. Hilda is a stupid name. *Everyone* in Southend is called Hilda.'

'But they can't all be as pretty as you.'

'Now that *does* make me laugh. I don't suppose you've ever been there.'

'Where?'

'Southend.'

'I have, actually. I felt the need for fresh air.'

'Did you find any?'

'No. It just smelled of seafood and candy-floss.'

'That's it. That's *it*.'

'Yet I enjoyed it. I liked the gloom.'

'That's where I *come* from.' Then she did laugh. Harry

thought that it was a delightful laugh, an innocent laugh. 'What's your name and rank?'

'Harry Hanway. First-class.'

'Where are you from, Harry Hanway?'

'If you seek my monument, look around you.'

'A local yokel?'

'That's me.'

So Harry and Hilda became friends long before they were ever lovers. Hilda worked in the 'typing pool' of a City bank, from which she emerged every evening with stories about her colleagues. She seemed to be in a continual state of amusement at the absurdities of the world, and often began her sentences with 'You'll never guess' or 'Don't laugh, but . . . ' Harry did laugh. He began to write a short weekly column in the *Bugle*, entitled 'Don't Laugh, But . . . ', in which he retold some of Hilda's anecdotes.

'I'm a bit of an orphan, actually,' she had told him. 'I was found. On a doctor's doorstep in Tilbury. Where the docks are.'

'Was your father a sailor?'

'I don't know. That's the *point*. Anyway I was called after a nurse in the hospital. That was before I was taken on.'

'Who by?'

'Mum and Dad. Well, *honorary* Mum and Dad. That's why I ended up in Southend, you see. They had an ice-cream van on the front by the pier.'

'One of those ones with a chime? A tinkle?'

'"Singing in the Rain." Mum used to serve ices like Chocolate Melody and Vanilla Creamsicle.' She laughed. 'The van was the colour of strawberries.' She suddenly had a memory of the strawberry van against the blue sea, its melody sometimes drowned by the sound of the waves. 'My favourite was Raspberry Wriggle.'

She lived now in a hostel for single young women, with a strict rule against male visitors. Harry could hardly have brought her to his little room in the Stanton household, with the crucifix above the bed. So they existed on the fringes of lovemaking. They met in the park. They retreated to the back rows of the local cinemas. They were passionate but furtive. What others might have found embarrassing, they considered to be amusing. It was part of the comedy of life.

Whenever she saw love stories on the screen, Hilda wept. 'I can't *help* myself,' she said. 'It's daft, I grant you that, but there it is. But let's face it. I'm a *girl*. And Robert Mitchum is so handsome. He looks like you.' Harry remained dry-eyed, and slightly bored, through the films that Hilda enjoyed.

One late afternoon he had spread the pages of the *Morning Chronicle* over the grass in the neighbourhood park, so that they might be protected from the damp ground. At the beginning of spring they both enjoyed this part of Camden. Harry was just about to roll on his back when he glimpsed an item in the newspaper. It announced a competition, sponsored by the *Morning Chronicle* itself, for young writers. The challenge was to complete a profile of a neighbourhood personality. 'Now this is interesting,' he remarked to Hilda. 'This is just the ticket.'

And then he thought of the Blitz boy, the arsonist whom he had forestalled in the church of Our Lady of Sorrows. He was a fine subject for a pen portrait, connecting the carnage and mayhem of 1944 with his own obsession. The arsonist wanted to live in flame. And, in London, there would always be a time when fire broke out.

Mr Peabody recalled the case very well. Harry himself had wanted to attend the trial, but the man had pleaded guilty to all charges and had thus dispensed with jury and witnesses. He had also confessed to two other offences of arson, connected with a garage and a gentlemen's lavatory. He had been sentenced to three years and despatched to Wormwood Scrubs, where he would be subject to regular medical reports.

Mr Peabody consulted the registers and uncovered the name of Simon Sim.

Harry applied for permission to interview Sim, and the prison authorities obliged. He then wrote to Sim, introducing himself once again, and to his surprise received a friendly response. So, on an early summer morning, he arrived at Wormwood Scrubs. The name itself was sinister. What could be worse than a wood full of worms? It had been designed to resemble a fortress, with a wooden gateway between two great towers. Harry's pace slowed, and he approached the entrance with some hesitation. He had the curious sensation that, once he entered, he would never get out again. He went up to the prison officer on duty, and explained his presence. Doors were opened, and gates were unlocked. He was led into 'C' wing, and taken to a small room containing nothing more than a table and three chairs. One chair was at each end of the table, and the third was by the door. The air of the prison smelled of wet paint and stale potatoes mingled.

Simon Sim was accompanied by a warder, who sat by the door. 'Wonderful to see you again,' Sim said. 'I haven't been well. But I wanted to talk to you. I know that I know you. Isn't that peculiar?' Harry did not understand what he meant. 'This is a fine place to have a fever, actually.' He looked appreciatively at the grey walls and the barred window. 'It calms you down. Helps you to think.'

'Are you feeling better?'

'Over the worst. Just the occasional shake or two.' He fixed his stare upon Harry with the same plaintive force as before, when they had struggled in the church. 'May I enquire, I mean, why do you want to see me?'

'I wanted to ask you about the Blitz.'

'Oh that's an enormous subject. Vast.'

'What was it like?'

'What was it *like*? Golly, that's a hard question.' His laughter turned into a cough. 'This is what it was like. The glass was raining down. It was raining glass. If you looked up, you would have been blinded. But that was not the worst thing.' His voice was curiously melodious. 'I'm glad that you caught me. It would just have gone on.'

'How old were you when you began?'

'Eleven. Twelve. A ripe old age. Terrific noise sometimes. We were out one night, after the sirens had sounded, when the bombs came down on the high street. I saw one girl. Her face was smashed where pebbles had lodged in her cheeks. One man was running down the slope of Hannaford Street, making for the shelter, when a falling bomb got him. I saw his head rolling along like a football.' He paused for a moment. 'We were as keen as mustard.' Sim then told him of the bombing of a jam factory, where the dead were found covered in marmalade. He told him of a girl whose back was blown off, so that her kidneys were exposed; she had continued talking as she was taken away. There were other stories that he related with a peaceful and sometimes even blissful expression. Harry wrote down all of them. 'I told you,' Sim said, 'that I knew you. As soon as you wrote to me, I remembered. Your name is Hanway.' Harry nodded. 'I knew your parents. I knew your mother. Lovely lady.' Harry looked at him in alarm. 'After the War I worked in the grocer's on Sutcliffe Street. Do you remember it?'

'It's still there,' Harry said.

'She used to buy bacon for you. Sometimes one of you boys came with her. She was always cheerful. And now you're here. Isn't it curious how things come about? But then, dear me, you found me. I never found you. Isn't it astonishing?'

'I wanted to ask you,' Harry said, hesitantly, 'about the fires.' He glanced at the warder who was clenching and unclenching his hands.

'About my fires? Goodness me, I don't know. I don't enquire into my reasons. I don't like to pry, you see.'

'Do you think there is some connection with the Blitz?'

'I wouldn't speculate on that. It might just be an amazing coincidence. Coincidences do happen. Your mother bought bacon from me. There's one. And a fine one. Where is she now, by the way? Your mother?'

'She's dead,' Harry replied.

'Is she? We used to talk about the terrible shortage of matches. And of flypaper, actually. There wasn't much of it around. And, goodness me, there were plenty of flies.'

So Harry wrote his profile of Simon Sim. He described his fever; he described his calm and melodious voice. He read it out to Hilda on one Sunday afternoon. They had decided to walk along the river at Chelsea. They liked to look into the windows of the houses there, and imagine occupying those large and opulent rooms. 'Do you think we ever shall?' she asked him.

'Oh yes. I should hope so.' And then he added, after a pause, 'I intend it. And I will do it.'

They sat down on a bench overlooking the Thames, and Harry took the article out of the pocket of his jacket. Hilda listened intently. When he had finished she put her arms around his neck and kissed his cheek. Someone was walking past them. When they had finished their embrace, Harry looked up. He seemed to recognise the figure. He was taking long strides, and his head was bowed. It was Sam. Harry was sure of it. He called out to him. But Sam – if indeed it was Sam – quickened his pace. Then he began to run. He did not look back.

Harry was unsettled by the unexpected sighting of his younger brother. He had not visited his father. He had not heard from his father. Now he believed that Sam had avoided

26

him out of anger, or disappointment, at his sudden departure. Still, Harry was of sanguine temperament. He rarely thought of his family. He put the matter out of his mind.

After he had sent the profile of Simon Sim to the *Morning Chronicle*, he endured some weeks of suspense. He had told no one, at the *Bugle*, of his intentions. Tony, however, sensed something in the air. 'You're nervous, Harry,' he said, barely restraining a smile. 'Anything up?'

'Nothing at all.'

'Just thought I'd ask.' Then Tony noticed that he read the *Morning Chronicle* every morning with unusual attention. 'Are you thinking of leaving us, Harry?' he asked as soon as he saw that George had entered the room.

'Of course not.'

'As long as you're sure.'

'Well. I am sure. Thank you for asking, Tony.'

Then on a Saturday morning, three weeks later, the *Morning Chronicle* printed his profile of Simon Sim. Harry had won the competition. He looked at his name in ten-point type. He could not bear to stand in the street, but walked into a café and ordered a cup of tea. He was nervous, and his hand shook as he held the cup. He thought that he had seen his future. He had tasted ambition. He received a letter the following week, asking him to collect the £25 cheque in person at the offices of the *Chronicle*. This was his opportunity.

He decided that he would not take Hilda with him. She would laugh, or out of nervousness say something absurd. Harry knew that, to attain his goal of acquiring a job as a reporter on the *Chronicle*, he would need to remain calm and attentive. He would need to convey an air of seriousness and professionalism. Of course they all knew at the *Bugle*. George Bradwell had shaken his hand, and expressed the wish that he would remain with them. Aldous had looked grave, and nodded. Tony had never mentioned the subject, and avoided Harry's eye. Maureen had embraced him, and congratulated him, while her two young men stood up and clapped. The new messenger boy, Percy, had pretended to blow a trumpet. 'That's the bugle,' he said, 'of the *Bugle*.' Percy was a cheerful boy.

In the following week Harry took the 48 bus to Fleet Street. He had passed through it before, but he had never stopped here. He had never been here in earnest. Now he was struck by the pace, and the intensity, of this narrow valley between tall buildings. He found the offices of the *Morning Chronicle* easily enough; they were based in what seemed to be a new building of plate glass and Portland stone. In the lobby there was a constant stream of people coming in or going out. Harry announced himself to a woman standing behind a large desk and was directed to the office of the deputy editor on the fifth floor. Harry could sense the beating of his heart as he entered the lift. He felt faint. He made his way along a corridor. He glimpsed a large room where several middle-aged men were sitting hunched over their typewriters. Telephones were ringing. A small man in a brown suit was standing by the open door, his hands on his hips. 'Where,' Harry asked him, 'can I find the deputy editor?'

'You have found him.' His glance was very sharp. 'And who are you?'

'Hanway, sir. Harry Hanway. I won the competition.'

'Oh did you?' He was very carefully dressed, with a white handkerchief discreetly visible in the upper pocket of his jacket. His tie was tightly knotted, his cuffs crisp. He was short but he seemed to Harry to be plumped up and perky; he looked like a pigeon about to mate. 'Well, young man, I have a cheque somewhere about me.' He was scrutinising him very carefully. 'Where do you work?'

'At the *Camden Bugle*.'

'No! And how's George?'

'Sir?'

'I started on the *Bugle*! With George.'

So the connection was made. The deputy editor, John Askew, was immediately impressed by this coincidence. What a tight little world, and a tight little city, this was! He asked Harry if he carried a union card. Harry did. George Bradwell had arranged the matter as soon as Harry had joined the staff of the *Bugle*. 'What a chance this is,' Askew said, almost to himself. 'It is too good.' He went into his office and telephoned Bradwell. Bradwell was of course reluctant to part with Harry, but he gladly acknowledged his skills as a reporter. He wanted Harry to succeed where he had failed.

'Arranged, arranged,' Askew said as he joined Harry in the corridor. 'Just a word with the editor.' He came back, twenty minutes later, singing 'Oh I do like to be beside the seaside'. 'You are in,' he said, almost casually. 'Now where's that cheque?'

So in the spring of 1965, at the age of eighteen, Harry Hanway became a reporter for the *Morning Chronicle*.

III

My life begins

'AT REGINA *gravi iamdudum saucia cura.*' In his small
bedroom, Daniel Hanway was reading the opening of
the fourth book of the *Aeneid* to himself. He repeated the
words out loud, savouring the rhythm of the Virgilian dactylic
hexameter. Dactylic hexameter. He was pleased that he knew
the phrase. No one else in the street would know it. He
assimilated his school books easily and readily. He was a
natural scholar, and translated Latin with such rapidity that
his companions looked at him with suspicion.

Daniel preferred to stay in his room, despite the emptiness
of the house. He did not enjoy the emptiness, and preferred
the clutter of his books and papers. He kept the curtains
closed. He did not like the view of the shabby street, in rain
or in sunshine. In sunshine it seemed angular and obdurate,
unyielding; it smelled of hot dust and dirt. In rain it seemed
mournful and desolate, absorbent, encompassing. When he
walked down this street, and the other streets of the council
estate, he felt contempt and betrayal.

He kept a diary in which he disclosed the feelings he could
not otherwise have expressed. 'Today I walked five miles. The
further away I got from this place the happier I became. I
could actually *smile*. I don't belong here. Which is a pretty

obvious thing to say. But sometimes I feel like screaming it out loud. I don't want to be a part of Crystal Street or Camden Town. I *hate* it when someone comes up to me in the street. I am a prisoner of war, planning for my escape. The people here are so *common*. None of them have any manners. God, they *sicken* me with their boring opinions. What's the point of them? Well, I hope I can rise above it all.'

He had been given by his father, last Christmas, a gramophone. He had bought a long-playing recording of Beethoven's Ninth Symphony. He played it loudly and, with both arms outstretched, he would conduct the Berlin Philharmonic Orchestra. He twirled around; he jumped up and down; he leapt onto the bed, and conducted from there. He had an image of himself surrounded by triumphant sound, yet somehow the sound seemed to issue from him. He was always at the centre. In his fantasies and ambitions he was always striving ever higher. He sensed something within himself that would not let him rest.

So at school he was quick, nervous, eager. He never stayed still. One teacher compared him to a sparrow that darts its glance in every direction. Sparrow became his nickname. He was now spare and lean. At a younger age he had been slightly plump. He used to slap his cheeks to see if he could diminish them. As soon as he entered the grammar school, however, he grew thin with tension and concentration.

He had two especial friends by the time he had reached the sixth form. Richardson was a boy of quiet and humorous cynicism. He could impersonate everyone, and took great delight in doing so. Palmer was strict, methodical and reticent. They were both attracted by Daniel's wild energy. They never discussed girls. They discussed ideas. 'It's all so Kafka-esque,' Daniel might say. Or 'hell is other people, according to Jean-Paul Sartre'. He described the school itself as 'Orwellian'.

He had an hysterical laugh. A word would set him off.

31

One day, in a history lesson, the teacher spoke of 'some old cobblers' reading Tom Paine's *Rights of Man*. Daniel looked at Richardson, and Richardson looked at Daniel. Richardson snorted, and Daniel was obliged to stuff a dirty handkerchief in his mouth.

Palmer looked at them severely. 'You behave,' he said afterwards, 'like a couple of schoolgirls.' This set them off again choking with laughter.

When they rode home on the bus Daniel had the habit of getting off three stops before his neighbourhood. He did not want the others to know where he lived. In his early days at the school he had lied about everything. 'My dad,' he said, 'has a Buick.' He pronounced the name of the car as 'Brick'. Or he might say, 'My dad was one of the Dambusters'. One of his first assignments in the geography class had been to draw a scale-plan of his house. He exaggerated the size and the number of rooms, so that the small council house in Camden was transformed into a large suburban villa.

He had other secrets. He never mentioned to his friends the fact that he was attracted to boys rather than to girls. They would not have welcomed the information. They would not have known how to respond to it.

He saw Harry, one Saturday afternoon, walking slowly along Camden High Street. He was arm in arm with a young woman, who was laughing at something he had said.

'Oh there you are,' Harry said airily, as if they had parted company an hour or so before. 'Have you finished school yet?'

'Another year.' He detected a slight note of sarcasm in his brother's voice. 'Are you still at the *Bugle*?'

'No fear. I'm going up in the world. I'm on the *Chronicle* now.' Daniel tried not to show that he was impressed by this news. 'In Fleet Street.'

It was only now that Harry introduced Hilda to his younger

brother. She put her head to one side and remarked, 'You *look* like each other. Oh Hilda. What a very silly thing to say. Anyway, you do.' She had noticed something else. She had noticed some communion between them. It was not of character, or of temperament. It was something harder and deeper, something almost impersonal.

'And what about you?' Harry asked him.

'What about me?'

'What are you going to do?'

'I sit my exams. And then I intend to go to Cambridge.'

Hilda recalled how Harry had used the same phrase, 'I intend to', with the same directness. 'That will be nice,' she said.

'Rewarding,' Daniel replied.

'How's Dad?' Harry asked him.

Two evenings before, when Daniel was lying on his bed reading, he had heard his father opening the front door. He must have returned from another long journey. He always entered the house quietly, not letting the door slam. Daniel resumed his reading. Then he heard a crash, and a yell. He got up from his bed, and walked slowly down the stairs to find his father standing in the living room with an old cloth armchair upturned on the floral-patterned carpet. There was a smell of dust in the air. 'It just fell over,' Philip said. 'I never touched it.'

At that moment Sam came into the house; without greeting them he went straight to his room.

'A leg must have been loose.' Daniel settled the armchair upright.

Philip promptly sat down in it, and asked his son to pour him a whisky. 'How does Sam seem to you, Danny?'

He hated being called Danny. Danny was the young child on the council estate. His name was Daniel. 'I don't know how Sam seems, Father. I know not "seems".'

'What?'

'Hamlet. Shakespeare.'

Philip was immediately impatient with his son. He had come to the conclusion that Daniel was prim and affected. He did not understand how this had happened. Once he had been so likeable and cheerful. Perhaps he also realised that his son now disliked him. Or, rather, that Daniel felt disdain for him.

In truth Daniel blamed his father for life in a shabby house in a shabby street. He resented the lack of ambition that had consigned the family to this council estate. He disliked Philip's weary look, and detested his air of defeat and resignation.

'I suppose,' Philip said, after a pause, 'that you are doing well at school.'

'I think so.'

'Whatever you do, Danny, you must . . . ' He trailed off.

'What did you want to tell me, Father?' There was some malice in his voice, which he did not believe he had intended.

'You have brains. You are quick. Don't let it go to your head.'

'My head is fine. So are my brains.'

'Don't be clever.'

'That's exactly what I intend to be.'

They were not looking at one another; they were staring into infinite space.

Philip began again. 'So you want to go to university?'

'To Cambridge.'

'That's a big step.'

Daniel seemed to consider this truism for a moment. He disliked his father's faint cockney accent, especially since he had gone to some trouble in removing all traces of his own. He had managed to hypnotise himself. He had drawn a large black dot on the ceiling of his narrow bedroom, and stared at it with concentration until he felt his ordinary awareness slip away. Then he repeated certain words out loud – corn-flake, lunar, rain – without any London intonation. Much to his surprise, the method worked. 'It *is* a big step,' he said. 'That's why I'm making it.'

'Are you ready for it?'

'Ready?'

'There will be people there with a lot of money. There will be a few snobs, too.'

'So?' How dare his father assume that he would be the victim of snobbery?

'There won't be many of you.'

'Many what?'

'Working-class boys.'

Daniel was too angry to speak for a moment. 'I don't think these divisions mean anything.'

'Wait and see.' It occurred to Daniel that his father was jealous of his success. He had no knowledge of Philip Hanway's early ambitions, but he sensed his father's envy. 'I'm only a lorry driver, Danny. I never expected to be a lorry driver. I don't want to be a lorry driver. So I don't amount to much.' Daniel did not reply. 'When I was your age I had ambitions. I know. The same old story. But you get beaten down. You get distracted. You get betrayed. That's when some people become sick. That's when some people die.'

'The horror of life.' Daniel had recently come across the phrase.

'Is it? That says it. The horror of life.'

Daniel knew that he ought to feel pity for his father, but instead he was still filled with anger and resentment. 'Why did Mother disappear?'

'She ran away with another man. That's all I know.'

'Did you try and find her?'

'What was the point? She didn't want us.'

'You could have tried.'

'When you drive long distances, you can dream. Dream of the past. Dream of what might have been. I spend my time dreaming.' Daniel noticed that his father had changed the subject, but he did not interrupt him. 'My life is over. I know that. That's why I worry about Sam. I wouldn't want to see him —' Philip put his hand up to his face, and started to weep. Daniel was horrified by this display of feeling. He should, perhaps, have gone over to his father and tried to comfort him. Instead he sat solemnly in his chair, staring at him but not daring to speak. 'That wasn't meant to happen,' Philip said after a few seconds.

'No,' Daniel replied. 'I don't suppose it was. I still have some homework to finish.' He rose and left the room.

'How's Dad?' Harry repeated the question.

'He is — he is — fine. As far as I know.'

Daniel replied to his brother's question in as easy and nonchalant a manner as he could muster. He wondered whether he should mention their father's explanation for their mother's disappearance. He looked up at Harry, and Harry's eyes told him to stay quiet. He thought that he had seen, within them, the image of a woman with her finger to her lips.

'Got a girl yet, Dan?'

'He's only a child,' Hilda replied for him. 'Fancy asking that.'

Daniel resented being called a child. 'I do have a friend,' he said. 'She works in a flower shop near my school.'

Harry knew, from the way that Daniel put his hand up to his neck, that he was lying.

'Let's have a walk in the park,' Hilda suggested. 'It's ever such a nice day.' Daniel winced.

He joined them reluctantly. He did not care to be seen in their company. He started walking a few paces behind Harry when Hilda noticed another similarity between the two brothers. Their pace was equal. Their posture was alike. The direction they were taking, without appearing to notice one another, was identical. They were advancing towards the same destination without being aware of the fact. They stopped beside a fountain and small pool. A short distance away was a stone folly, wooden benches set up inside, its roof ornamented with stone doves and weeping angels. It was a secluded spot from which to sit and stare at the rising and falling water.

'I used to come here,' Harry said, 'when I had finished at the *Bugle*. It was quiet, in the evening. I used to watch the ducks getting ready to sleep.'

'I used to come here,' Daniel said, 'on a Sunday afternoon. It was so cheerful and peaceful then. I used to watch the children feeding the ducks.'

'I used to lose track of time.'

'I used to fall asleep.'

The sparkling of the sun on the water of the fountain cast a strange light over them, and they seemed to Hilda to have grown taller. Harry put his arm around her shoulder. 'Cup of tea?'

There was a café in the park, the haunt of solitary people, pensioners and pigeons. The mild light of early spring shone upon the paper cups and plates. 'It all comes down to this, Dan,' Harry was saying. 'You've got to take your chances where you find them. No one gives you help in this world.' He seemed to have forgotten George Bradwell. 'Every man for himself.'

Hilda burst out laughing. 'Oh look. Isn't it funny?' She was watching as a terrier chased a squirrel across the grass. The squirrel then scampered up a tree, leaving the dog staring upwards and barking furiously. 'They never catch them, do they?' she said. The little dog was trembling with purpose and desire, his body shaking with fierce energy. The squirrel, clasping the bark, remained quite still. He gazed down at his pursuer, while the dog directed his bright and eager glance upwards. Their eyes met, and darkness called to darkness.

'As I was saying, Dan, life is a struggle. A battle.'

'I don't want to fight.'

'Then you'll do nothing. You'll go down.' He jerked his thumb towards the ground.

'I won't go down. But I don't have to fight.'

'You two.' Hilda was laughing again. 'You would think there was a war on.'

Harry felt contempt for Daniel's passivity, but he took care not to show it. Nevertheless Daniel felt it. The little dog was still barking. 'I saw Sam recently,' Harry said.

'Where?'

'He was walking along the Embankment. Chelsea. He didn't seem to notice me.'

'He doesn't see anything. Not really. He sees what he wants to see. What he intends to see. Sometimes he stares and stares into space. But he's happy enough, I think. He sees something I don't see.'

'Nutter?'

At that moment Sam cried out in his sleep. He was still in his bed, having walked through London for most of the night.

'I don't know,' Daniel replied. 'I hope not.'

'Does he have a job?'

'Dad – Father – gives him money. I don't think he wants to work.'

Daniel walked home sensing that he had made a bad impression on his brother. Harry had looked at him strangely when he had said that he had no wish to fight. But it was the truth. He disliked confrontation of any kind, and could not bear disagreements or disputes.

38

'I hate sports,' he wrote in his diary. 'I hate team games. Wednesday afternoon is my black afternoon. Everything about it repels me. Packing up the kit. Walking to the playing fields. Undressing in the changing room. It is all so *undignified*. And unnecessary. What is the point of running around in the mud with a ball on a winter's day? Everything is cold and wet and dismal. Cricket is worse. I went to the public library to find out the rules, and I still don't know them. I hate that hard little ball coming anywhere near me. I always duck it. That's why no one ever chooses me. I'm always the last one standing. It's embarrassing. Anyway I can't stand the team spirit. Savages in a pack. I don't know how they can get so worked up over *nothing*. And the communal bathing is misery. It is all so grotesque.'

He had a horror of being late for the first class of the morning, and was often the first to arrive in the schoolyard. This schoolyard sloped down towards a wooden fence that separated it from the road. That road had once been a river, and the sloping yard a grassy bank. There had been a river here for hundreds of thousands of years, a remnant of the vast ocean that had once covered the site. Where Daniel stood and dreamed, there had swum the plesiosaur and the coelacanth. But the ocean had gone, leaving behind the river. This river created fertile ground. To its banks came hippopotami and elephants the size of small dogs. Some early settlers had encamped just where Daniel was standing. There had been a fight here. A man had been struck in the face with a rock, and had died. He had fallen at Daniel's feet.

Battles had also been fought in this favoured region of the river. And Daniel watched as slowly the yard was filled with the noise and dispute of schoolchildren. Something glinted at his feet. He stooped down to pick it up, when suddenly he felt an overwhelming desire to throw himself upon the ground; he steadied himself, by putting his hands on the tarmac, and remained crouched for several seconds. The sound of winds and waters was in his head. Then it passed. 'Ready, steady, go,' someone shouted at him. He had looked as if he were about to start a race.

He worked hard, throughout the last autumn and winter of his school years, preparing for his final examinations. 'Exams are three days away,' he wrote. 'I must not panic. I must revise everything one more time. I hope it's Cicero or someone else easy. I hope it's not Tacitus or Ovid. Now I feel sick. I don't suppose I'll get an hour's sleep between now and exam day. I must concentrate. I have to be steady. Otherwise I will become like that tramp.'

He had seen the tramp a week before. 'I saw a beggar by the road today. I didn't feel pity. I felt fear. Fear that I could become like him. One little slip and I could go down. It's all so hopeless. I don't think anyone understands me. Hell is other people.'

Yet his fears were unwarranted. He received high grades in his examinations and at once, through the agency of his school, he applied to both Oxford and Cambridge.

He had visited Cambridge in a day of gentle sunlight and shadow, iridescent in the watery atmosphere of the neighbourhood. He had gone up in the train with his schoolfriend, Palmer, who had also applied. His memory, ever afterwards, was of undergraduates sitting and laughing by the side of water, of empty courtyards, of great establishments of enduring stone, all unimaginable and unattainable. 'It is very civilised,' Palmer said as they travelled back. 'I can see us there.' Daniel, who thought nothing of Palmer's chances, merely nodded. As he returned to London he felt mournful, as if he were leaving all his hopes behind.

'What college did you like most?' Palmer asked him.

'I don't know – I don't want to think about it. Not yet.'

'I liked Clare. I liked the little bridge and the gardens.'
'There's more to life than gardens.'

Philip Hanway insisted on driving him to Cambridge, on the day before the beginning of the university term. This horrified Daniel, who had a vision of arriving at his new college in his father's lorry. He tried to persuade him that he was perfectly happy to travel by train, alone; but, no, his father insisted that he would hire a car for the day. He wanted to make sure that Daniel was 'settled in'.

'Do you think,' he asked Daniel as they drove together along the A11, 'do you think that you will ever write?'

'Write?'

'Novels. Plays.'

'I don't know. I don't think so.'

'Oh.'

'Why do you ask?'

'No reason. Curious.'

There was something happening on the right-hand side of the road. Daniel thought he could see people running – running at the speed of the Morris Minor in which he and his father were driving – running figures even then overtaking them. And then they vanished into the distance. It had been a trick of the light reflected in the window.

'And now,' he said to himself, 'my life begins.'

IV

Are you hungry?

S AM HANWAY had not prospered at school. He had made no friends. He did not antagonise anyone; he simply preferred his own company. He was absorbed in some private world, of rage and affection, which did not encircle other people. He did not excel in his studies; he was wayward and inconsistent. He would approach a subject with interest and great excitement for a week or two, and then would lose concentration.

Outside school he wandered around the estate, picking up a stone or examining a brick; he would study them with wonder and concentration, absorbing them within his being, before discarding them. He was a large boy, with a round face and powerful limbs; he had grey eyes and wore spectacles. When he took off his spectacles, his face seemed to flinch; he had the slightly blank look of someone running through mist.

'When I leave here,' he told one of his teachers, 'I want to go to a circus school. I want to learn how to do tricks with animals. Zebras, most likely.' This was not considered to be very practical and, as soon as he reached school-leaving age, he enrolled at the labour exchange.

Sam found work in the local supermarket. Here he was

employed to stack goods upon the shelves, and to pack the shopping bags of customers. He had to look tidy, and to act smartly. With uncharacteristic energy, on the first day, he rose early and washed himself in the bathroom sink; he put on a shirt and tie, and took from his wardrobe the cheap grey suit that his father had purchased for him. It did not fit him well, and under a leaden sky he hastened to the supermarket on this first morning.

He took off the jacket and put on a striped apron and white hat. The changing room was beside the ventilation system for the dairy counter. It smelled faintly of cheese or curdled milk, a disquieting and even depressing smell. 'Sam? Is that your name?' He nodded. He was being addressed by a young woman with pale prominent eyes; her flaxen hair was tied back, and Sam tried not to notice the pimples on her face. She looked vulnerable, as if a layer of skin had been stripped from her. 'I've got to get you started,' she said. He felt uncomfortable in the presence of females, and had not mastered the art of talking to them. 'There's nothing to it, really.' She put out her hand, as if it belonged to someone else, and placed it limply in his. 'This is cheese. This is milk. This is butter.' He could see what they were. 'You don't have much to say for yourself, do you? Well. Keep smiling. It won't be as bad as all that.'

He learned how to unpack the goods, and arrange them on the shelves. He sized and sorted the various bottles, tins, packets and boxes; he carried in the fruit and vegetables; he replaced the cheese, the milk and the butter. The girl with the flaxen hair sometimes watched him. 'Worse things happen at sea,' she said.

His ordeal started when he was asked to stand by the till and pack the bags of the customers. Each face became a terror. He was being judged. When he was slow, or clumsy, he blushed. He realised that people were cruel because they were unhappy. He thought he saw lines of suffering humanity, shuffling towards him with their wire baskets or trolleys. He detested the children looking up at him with blank incurious eyes. If somebody complained, he insisted on explaining himself. He would look at them quietly and attentively before answering them in a low voice. He outlined in detail the proper way of filling a shopping bag, with bulky dry goods at the bottom and perishable goods at the top. So the days passed, one like another. It was as if he were living in a cave. If nothing mattered, then he could exist like this.

He did not eat in the canteen. He disliked the smell of beef and custard and tomato sauce. He bought a chocolate bar, instead, and sat in a bus shelter on the high street. So he remained apart from the rest of the staff. They were not malicious, but they were not particularly friendly. They would grow impatient with his long explanations. They greeted him hurriedly, and walked on. He knew all these things; but he never took offence.

One Saturday morning he was standing by the till, as usual, packing the bags. He glanced down the waiting line of customers. There was a middle-aged woman standing at the end of the queue. He looked at her a second time. She was wearing a blue cardigan and white blouse. He knew that face. It was her. It was his mother. She became aware of him in the instant that he recognised her. They gazed at each other. In his consternation he bowed over the counter and, when he looked up again, she was gone.

'What's the matter with you?' A man, harsh and impatient, was standing in front of him. 'You don't know how to do this, do you?' Without any thought, Sam lashed out at him. The woman on the till moaned, with a sort of pleasure, when the man fell to the floor. There was general uproar and Sam was hauled away by the manager before being dismissed from the staff. It happened within an hour. And in that hour Sam's life changed.

He vowed that he would never work again. He had no plan of action, no goal, but the very act of working seemed to him to be a form of death. He could live off the food in the house, purchased by his father; his father had a habit of leaving his wallet on the mantelpiece, when he returned from his long hours of driving, and Sam took small sums. He did not tell anyone that he had been fired. He left the house at the same time each morning, and returned at the same time each evening. He wore the same grey suit. He wandered.

One late afternoon he was walking along one of the paths in the local park, not far from the café where Harry and Hilda and Daniel had drunk tea beneath the trees. There was a young man sitting, slumped, upon a wooden bench. His clothes were old and soiled; he looked weary, his face hollowed by exhaustion or want. He was sighing, or groaning, it was hard to say which; he was trembling, slightly, as if he were trying to ward off pain. His eyes were closed, and there was spittle at the corners of his mouth. Sam sat down quietly beside him. He stared straight ahead, frowning slightly, and from time to time he would glance at this fellow on the bench. The young man opened his eyes and stared at him. Sam said nothing, and looked ahead once more. He could have sat there indefinitely. He had no reason to move on. One place was as good as another. But a sudden thought struck him. 'Are you hungry?' he asked him. The young man did not reply. 'Hang on,' he said. 'I'll be back in a minute.' After a few minutes he returned with two packets of crisps and a bottle of Tizer. The young man took them without a word. From that day forward, at the same time, Sam always brought two packets of crisps and a bottle of Tizer to the bench where the young man was waiting for him.

Now that he had lost his job, Sam also seemed to become part of a floating world. There was, for example, the matter of the stone post. It stood at the corner of Lowin Street and the high street. Its function was obscure, and Sam had no idea of its age. It was a weather-beaten piece of old stone that may have been on that spot since the building of Camden Town; it may even have stood there in an earlier period. Who could tell? Now, from across the street, Sam had the time to observe it. A young boy came up to it, placed his hands upon it, and began to beat it like a drum; he seemed to derive enormous pleasure from this. Someone called him, and he ran off. Sam continued to stand and watch. He noticed a curious fact or coincidence — most of those who passed the post put out a hand and touched it. It was an unwitting, and perhaps even an unconscious, gesture. Yet the stone post was being endlessly patted and felt.

As he continued watching the stone, it seemed to become aware of his presence. Sam was astonished when the stone rose several feet into the air; as it hovered there several ribs and pillars of stone, several arches and mouldings, began to exfoliate from it, creating an intricate shrine or shelter of stone. He thought he could hear the sound of hammering, of banging, of the labour of construction. Then it began to fade into the air. The stone post, once more a solitary presence, hovered above the ground before descending and resuming its original position. All this may have been the work of a moment. Or it may have taken many centuries.

If he had shouted aloud, he would have drawn attention to himself. He wanted to find somewhere in seclusion, somewhere he might sit and think. There was such a place. The church of Our Lady of Sorrows, the church where Harry had thwarted the arsonist, was only a few hundred yards away from this corner of the high street. Sam had passed it many times.

He bowed his head as he went into the porch, struck suddenly by the coolness of the air. The church itself was empty. He walked down the aisle, and then hesitated. Above the altar was a cross on which hung the figure of the suffering Jesus – this was not what he had come for. But then he saw the lady, smiling, with her right hand raised in greeting or in blessing. She was dressed in blue and white. Sam crossed the aisle and walked over to the Lady Chapel.

He sat down on the narrow wooden pew and bowed his head. Then, after a long silence, he began to speak to her. 'Do you mind if I talk to you? I have no friends, you see. I have no one to tell. I could have gone home, and forgotten all about it, but that would have been wrong. That would mean nothing had happened. But everything has happened.' He spoke in a slow, soft voice. 'But now I have been chosen. I have been chosen to experience – well, you can call it a miracle if you like. I think it was a miracle. What do you think?' He looked up at her, wondering, enquiring, reflecting. She regarded him with pity, and put her finger to her lips.

He sat in silence once more. He felt secure here, as safe as if he were in his own room at home – no, safer, because he was under the protection of the lady. He was suffused with warmth, although he could not tell whether it came from within or without. Who was that standing a short distance away? An old nun had come up to the altar with lilies in her hands; she crossed herself before the statue, and then changed the flowers in the silver vases to either side of it. She had noticed Sam but she seemed to pay him no attention. She crossed herself again, and left the chapel as quietly as she had entered it.

After she had gone Sam looked up again at the lady. 'She has offered you something,' he said. 'I have nothing to give you. Do you need anything from me?' She did not reply. 'Probably not. But I promise you this. When I see a person

47

in trouble, I will try to help.' He thought of the young vagrant on the park bench. 'That will be helping you, I hope.' He stayed there a little longer, until with a sigh he got up from the pew and left the church.

He came back to the chapel on the following morning. He sat in the same place, and gazed impassively at the statue of the lady. He noticed now that she had blue eyes, and that three tears ran down her right cheek. Perhaps she had wept last night. He wondered what had caused this. Did she know already of the young man? 'Don't worry,' he said. 'Everything will be all right.'

He came each day, and soon realised that three or four different nuns in turn changed the flowers and the altar cloth. He knew them all by sight, but they had not broken their silence. Then one of them surprised him. It was the oldest of them, the one he had seen on his first visit to the chapel. She was about to withdraw, having completed her ministrations, when she turned and walked over to him. It seemed to be a sudden decision.

'Are you troubled, son?'

'No. I'm happy. I think I'm happy.'

'You pray to Our Lady?'

'I speak to her.'

'Do you?'

'On the first day she put her finger to her lips.'

She made the sign of the cross, and walked away.

The nuns began to pay more attention to Sam. They smiled at him as they dusted the altar and polished the rails; they would walk down the aisle and nod as they passed him. One of them left a missal in his accustomed seat and then, a week later, he found a rosary there. He did not know what to do with it. He put it in the pocket of his trousers, and would sometimes slide his fingers through the hard wooden beads.

He washed his clothes in the kitchen sink at home, and dried them in the garden, but of course he became more shabby. There came a morning when one of the nuns approached him. 'Do you know anything about gardening?' she asked him. He shook his head. 'Well, you can learn. You're strong, aren't you?'

'Yes.'

'We need a handyman. Mother Placentia thought of you.'

Of Mother Placentia, he knew nothing. He had vowed never to work again, but he was drawn to the company of these women. 'I can do that,' he said.

'Good. Come into the sacristy.'

He had not known that there was a convent attached to the church of Our Lady of Sorrows. This small establishment lay behind the church, surrounded by a high red-brick wall. If you had asked any of the local residents about the nuns, they would not have known how to answer. No one knew when, or from where, they had come. They had always seemed to be part of the neighbourhood. But they were rarely seen. They stayed behind the high walls.

Sam entered through the gate of the convent in the company of Sister Eugenia, the nun who had come up to him in the church. They crossed a courtyard, with the basin of a dried fountain in the middle where fallen leaves rustled in the dust. There was a sundial in the corner of the lawn, its gnomon broken. A bird was perched on the stone rim of the basin of the fountain, singing its eternal song; yet it seemed to Sam that it sang more slowly than any bird he had ever heard.

Sister Eugenia led him down a corridor, on the walls of which were hanging woodcuts and engravings of sacred scenes. The sister approached a door at the end of the corridor, and knocked upon it gently. 'Who is knocking?' asked someone within.

'Eugenia, Mother.'

'Enter in God's name, Eugenia.'

She opened the door, and asked Sam to go in before her. 'It is the young man,' she said.

'Is it you? You are younger than I expected.' Mother Placentia was a small, plump woman with an expression of brutal amiability; her head was shaken by a slight but continual tremor. On the wall above her was a portrait of the Virgin, hands clasped in prayer or pity, her outline traced in blue and gold. 'How old are you?'

'Seventeen.'

'So you are the young man who sees visions in the heart of London.' He said nothing but continued to look steadily at her. 'You are as still as a lamb. That is good. Do you know the saying, "rise up west wind and refresh my garden"?' He shook his head. 'You must be our wind. You must refresh our garden. Can you do that?'

'I hope so.'

'What is your name, young man?'

'Sam. Sam Hanway.'

'Hanway?' She seemed momentarily distracted. 'A good name. An old name.'

'We may be old without being good,' he said.

She burst into laughter which ended with a fit of coughing. 'The Lord has given you wit,' she said.

The garden smelled sweetly of several herbs, but there was little for Sam to do. One of the nuns, Sister Idonea, tended the sage and the thyme and the rue. He was there to remove the weeds, water the lawns and beds, and burn the dead leaves of autumn. He also performed the tasks that the nuns could not; he built shelves, he painted doors and fences, he restored the stone paths that crossed the courtyard. Yet it seemed that the nuns simply wanted him to be part of their community; he had been given a sign by the Virgin, and they wanted to see what might happen to him.

He came to know the sisters very well. Mother Placentia ruled over them with the same forceful amiability she had displayed to him. She was massively calm, she was dispassionate, she was obdurate. Sister Delecta and Sister Prudentia, for example, had been involved in an argument over the number of wax candles needed for the vigil of the Assumption of Our Lady. Their quarrel had been loud, and had reached the ears of Sister Idonea. She had stopped shelling peas and listened to them with great eagerness, registering the use of such words as 'pitiful' and 'ridiculous'. She repeated the conversation, with some exaggeration, to Sister Clarice who was known to be a particular favourite of Mother. The abbess called in the two offending sisters. As soon as they had entered her office she rose up from her chair and slapped them both on the right cheek.

Sister Idonea was listening at the door, and later gave an exultant report to anyone who cared to listen. '*Ave genetrix*,' Mother Placentia had said. 'You give birth to quarrels and dissensions, do you? You fight like sows in a sty?'

'No, *madame*,' Sister Delecta replied. She was the youngest, and supposedly the demurest, of the nuns. 'We had a difference of opinion.'

'There will be no differences in this place. All are one. On your knees.'

They fell to their knees as Mother Placentia, standing before the portrait of the Virgin, began to pray in a loud voice. 'Hail Mary, full of grace, the Lord is with thee. Blessed art thou among women.' The two nuns joined in the prayer, murmuring in low voices. When it was complete she turned to them. 'Leave this place on your knees and creep to the cross in the chapel. There you will prostrate yourselves for an hour, before rising and resuming your duties in a cheerful spirit.' So the nuns painfully and slowly made their way towards the chapel in another part of the building. Sam had seen them. He had entered the chapel in order to mend a broken transom light, when he glimpsed them lying on the chilly tiled floor. He backed out of the door. He gathered later that there had been much recrimination between Sister Idonea and Sister Prudentia, conducted in frowns and grimaces rather than words. The whole convent had taken sides. Salt and pepper were not being passed down the table; bread was in short supply for one or two nuns; there was much coughing and clearing of throats whenever certain nuns sang the divine office.

Yet the days passed tranquilly for Sam. He would arrive at the convent early in the morning, and would begin work at once; he hardly spoke to anyone in the course of the day, and would eat whatever food Sister Idonea had left him for lunch. In the evening he visited the young man in the park; he rarely spoke to him but gave him the crisps and sweet drink, which he could afford from the small wage the convent paid him.

It came to the attention of Mother Placentia that there were what she called 'poor men and women' in the vicinity of the convent; she said that they were drawn to the place as to a shelter. If she could not accommodate them, she could at least nourish them. So she instituted an afternoon meal to be distributed at the gate of the convent. Sam volunteered to hand out the bread and soup or stew. He felt at ease in the company of tramps and wanderers. He was even comforted by their presence. He was not shy, or awkward, with them. They had looked with mild curiosity at this young man among the nuns, but soon he was expected. That is what he had always wanted – acceptance. He did not want to be singled out, to be looked on with pity or condescension.

He soon learned that no one vagrant was like another. They were all in one sense touched by misery, but it manifested itself in different ways. In some of them it was not manifest at all. These were the cheerful ones who, in the extremity of failure or distress, still laughed at the absurdity of the world. One of them wore an old and heavy coat, in the pockets of which he kept a surprising variety of objects. He would pull out a trowel, or a chipped cup, with all the delight of a conjuror successfully performing a trick. One old woman, the creases of her hands and face lined with dirt, would sometimes dance in the middle of the road. She called Sam 'sweetheart'. Yet others remained gloomy and silent. These were the ones who most interested Sam. He tried to speak to one middle-aged man, whose head was always covered by a hood, but the man had merely sighed and walked off.

Some kept themselves apart. Where the others would form groups, or pairs, they would sit by themselves on the pavement – their backs against the convent wall – or stand alone a little way off. The reason for this solitariness was clear to Sam. He had experienced it himself. It was the fruit of pride and introspection. Pride is possible even in misery. In his own misery, Sam had not wanted anyone to come too close. So he respected those who stayed aloof. He glanced at them quickly, when he handed them the food, and then looked away.

There were those who engaged him in conversation. Some of them spoke quickly and eagerly, like children, while others spoke softly and slowly. Yet it seemed to Sam, strangely enough, that they spoke with one voice; or, rather, that one voice spoke through all of them – the way that a hundred birds seem to sing the same song. That, at least, was how he put it to himself.

'Do you think you'll be joining us?' one middle-aged man asked him. He had a bald spot on the top of his head, with long black hair cascading from its rim.

'Joining?'

'Coming along with us. When this place goes.'

'It won't go.'

'Oh yes it will. I see it all the time. I'm used to it.'

'I don't know whether I'll go with you or not.'

'I think you will.'

Nothing disturbed the even tenor of the days. Sam still lived at home, but he rarely saw his father. He had not told him that he worked in the convent; it was a secret thing, belonging to a secluded part of himself. He kept the rosary on a little wooden table in his bedroom; it reminded him of his life with the nuns; it reassured him, in its plainness and simplicity. He knew now that each bead was a prayer, a prayer perfectly formed, a sphere of grace. So he would hold the rosary, grip it tightly, and close his eyes – then he saw images, images of flame and ruined walls, of sunlit fields and hills, of innumerable faces gazing upwards. He did not know what these images meant, but he was touched by them. He still sometimes visited the Lady Chapel, too, where he sat in front of the statue of the lady. 'Thank you,' he said one day, 'for letting me stay. I feel safe here.'

Yet, on a day after one of these visits, everything changed. He set off from his house early that morning, making his familiar way to the convent. But he could not find it. The gate and the walls were not there. The convent had disappeared. He ran through the streets, returning by different routes to the same place. The convent was gone. He looked for signs of the tramps and beggars who had wandered through the neighbourhood; they, too, had vanished. He asked several people if they had seen the nuns, but they looked at him curiously and shook their heads. Nuns? What nuns? He was distraught. He cried out – to what, or to whom, he did not know. Weeping, he beat his fists against a stone wall.

Eventually he went back to the church. There was no chapel. There was no lady. The nave was dark. He sat down in a pew and began to beat his head against the wooden rail in front of him. That was the day when the young tramp in the park also disappeared.

V

A marmoset

HARRY HANWAY was bent over his typewriter, smoking as he read the page still in the machine. He was writing a story – he used the word casually and naturally now – concerning the resignation of a middle-ranking minister from the Wilson government. It was not the stuff of headlines, but with careful nurturing it could grow. Harry knew that the minister had been hastened from office as a result of his affair with his secretary, already a married woman. So Harry chose his words carefully, hinting rather than stating impropriety, lending an air of ambiguity to all his phrases, making it clear that the minister was a married man with three small children. He enjoyed this process. It gave him power.

His career at the *Morning Chronicle* had so far been a success. He had begun work as one of the reporters filing copy for the gossip column, purportedly written by 'Peregrine Porcupine'. Harry found himself at parties and at first nights, at society weddings and at political conferences, on the chance that he would see and talk to a 'famous name' or would pick up some gossip that could be repeated to the newspaper's readership. His ready charm, his affability, and his London accent distinguished him from the mass of ex-public-school boys who staffed other gossip columns.

He looked, and sounded, as if he could be trusted. He soon impressed his superiors with his ability to deliver 'scoops' over his rivals.

It was Harry, for example, who broke the news that Joey Hanover had been lured by ATV from BBC Television with the offer of five thousand pounds for each half-hour programme. He had seen Hanover sitting alone at a table in a pub close to Portland Place, and had sat beside him. He did not look, or behave, like a journalist. He was an ordinary Londoner. So Hanover, slightly the worse for drink, had confided in him. 'You and I, chum,' he said, 'are idiots. Sitting here and drinking in the middle of the afternoon.' He stared balefully at Harry for a moment. 'What do you do?'

'I work in a shop. A shoe shop. It's my day off.'

'Is it now? What kind of shoes?'

'All types.'

Hanover was silent for a moment. 'Do you know who I am?'

'You're Joey Hanover. Everyone knows you.'

'Oh do they?' Once more he lapsed into a morose silence. 'What if I were to tell you that Joey Hanover is a chump? A right disaster?' Harry sensed, with growing excitement, the approach of a good story. But he took care to remain calm, and even unimpressed. 'I am about to walk away from my closest mates. And for what? Lucre. Filthy lucre.'

'There's nothing wrong with money.'

'You're right. There is nothing wrong with money. Where would we be without it? But bang goes the old team. Whoosh.' He threw up his hands. 'Excuse me.' He came back from the bar with what looked like a large gin and tonic. The other customers were still pretending to ignore him. 'And what's it all for? Five thousand per show.'

'That's a lot of money.'

'Anyway, it's too late now. It's done. Hello ATV.'

Eventually Harry rose from his seat, on the grounds that he had to meet his girlfriend, and made his escape. He hailed a taxi and within half an hour he was at his desk. He opened *Spotlight*, and found the telephone numbers of Hanover's manager and press agent. The story was on the front page of the first edition.

On the following morning the editor asked to see him. This was an unexpected summons, since Andrew Havers-Williams did not generally mingle with the junior staff. Harry considered him to be something of a 'toff', a man of impeccable and even dandified dress; he wore silk waistcoats and silk ties; he swept his luxuriant white hair back in bouffant fashion; his enunciation was clipped and precise; his voice had the timbre of an expensive education. 'Well, Hanway,' he said as Harry entered his office. 'Well done. Very well done. The proprietor likes this sort of thing.' His tone suggested that the proprietor, Sir Martin Flaxman, was a man of comparatively simple tastes. 'Personally I know nothing about this Hanover chap. Comedian, is he? Where did you find him?'

'In a pub, sir.'

'A pub? I see. Well done.' He had an air of forced cheerfulness, as if he were aware of a disparity between them that could only be negotiated by a show of bonhomie. 'How long have you been with the paper?'

'Two years.'

'Two years on Porcupine is long enough, don't you think?' Harry nodded. 'I'm going to hand you over to the news desk.'

That had been Harry's aim from the beginning. 'I would welcome that,' he said.

'Talk to James White.'

James White was the news editor. He was middle-aged, tall, balding. He had been an officer during the War, and had retained the manner ever since. He owed his post solely to

58

the fact that he had attended the same school as the editor, and he was widely disliked by the staff of the news desk. He was something of a martinet, something of a bully. 'Don't just stand there,' he said on the first day. 'Do something. Make yourself useful. Wait. I want you to go to the Old Bailey. See if anything's happening.' That was how he always addressed Harry – 'I want you to . . .' He was generally stiff and condescending; he was always irritable, as if he was chafed by some inward discontent.

Yet Harry soon learned how to deal with him, as he learned how to deal with his other colleagues. They were immensely susceptible to flattery. 'Good piece,' he would say. 'Good piece.' Or he would pat someone on the back. 'Terrific story. Terrific.' He realised that many of them lacked self-confidence. They had wanted to be barristers, or politicians, or writers; but they had ended up as journalists. They gathered at the end of the day in the Duke of Granby, a long and narrow pub near the corner of Chancery Lane and Fleet Street. Here in an atmosphere of forced joviality they discussed the day's stories and events at the newspaper itself; they gossiped mercilessly about their contemporaries; they mocked the journalists on rival newspapers; they were sarcastic about the politicians of the day; they drank great quantities of beer or lager to keep themselves in good humour. They prided themselves on knowing the ways of the world, as a little tap on the side of the nose would signify. They were generally red-faced, with wary eyes.

Three political journalists were employed on the *Chronicle*, the most senior of them being an excessively neat and fastidious man. George Hunter was always rearranging the objects in front of him. It was said that he could not enter a room without emptying the ashtrays. He had a gentle and unemphatic voice, sometimes trailing off into silence. It was said by his colleagues that this was a ruse – that his silences were a way of extracting confidences from otherwise reticent politicians. No one likes silence in a conversation.

'Well, George,' Harry might say in the Duke of Granby, 'have you had a good day?'

'Yes. A good day.'

'It's warm in here.'

'It *is* warm in here. Yes. What are you drinking?'

'A pint of Courage. The very best.'

'A pint of the very best, Suzanne.'

He was a perpetual echo. This was another secret of his success. He never seemed to have any opinions of his own. He was cautious and circumspect. He spoke respectfully of Mr Harold Wilson and Mr Edward Heath. He alluded to various political events and arguments in a low voice, as if they were still decidedly confidential. Yet he was observant. He missed nothing.

His two younger colleagues did not share his inhibitions. They talked of politicians in terms of personal intimacy, called them 'Willie' or 'Jim'. They professed cynicism but, as Harry noticed, they were thrilled to be addressed or recognised by these apparent worthless ministers. Yet Harry enjoyed their company. They were high-spirited and facetious, causing each other to laugh helplessly at some absurd or improbable fiasco. Nick Salmond was a good mimic; he could impersonate Wilson's flickering eyes and snake-like tongue, and Heath's convulsive shuddering laugh. They knew all the gossip, too, about the sex lives of prominent politicians. They luxuriated in speculation and innuendo. James Thorn was plump and pale; he always wore a flower in his buttonhole, and always dressed in a pinstriped suit. He had a voice, as Harry once said to Hilda, like an organ pipe. Both Salmond and Thorn were longing for George Hunter to retire, although uneasily aware of the rivalry that would then rise between them. They sat on opposite sides of the same desk in the newsroom, beating out stories on their typewriters as the deadline drew ever closer. Harry had come to realise that words were cheap, and that they could be manufactured by the yard. The journalists would write something, and then write it again. Then they repeated it as if it were a new thought, and then recapitulated it in a slightly different way. They would conclude the paragraph with the same sentiment. And so it went on.

There was no subtlety or profundity in what they wrote. Neither of them pretended that there was. They repeated the conventional wisdom – the wisdom, if that is the word, shared by the majority of other political journalists at any one time. They both wrote editorials on political matters, in which they attempted to be authoritative. They relied upon portentous cliché masquerading as strong opinion. They were stern and, in the guise of anonymity, they were self-righteous.

Harry began to understand the way in which the political world worked. It was driven by ambition, and anger, and jealousy, concealed beneath the pretence of honesty and good intention. Nick and James realised the subterfuge well enough, and their conversation was filled with gossip about the weaknesses and vices of the politicians; but they wrote only about policies and issues, helping to sustain the deceit. George Hunter seemed genuinely to believe in the virtues of public office. He was considered to be old-fashioned. Nick and James merely gave credence to the lies they saw through. Over a drink, Harry felt at ease with them. He felt that they understood the world in which he, too, wanted to play a part.

He and Hilda Nugent had, on the strength of his new income, moved to a basement flat in Notting Hill. It was a part of London that neither of them knew, and at first they had been alarmed by its air of decay and general dilapidation. The large terraced houses and stucco mansions had been divided into small flats and rooms for a population of beatniks, immigrants from the West Indies and transient workers. It was called 'bed-sit land'. It suited them. They were still unmarried. Harry did not want to marry. He had told Hilda that he feared the expense and responsibility of a child. She might have suspected that there were other reasons but, if she did, she hid that thought from herself. She supposed that she was content with her present life. In turn Harry did not choose to enquire about his future with her. He did not reflect upon it. He did not believe that reflection was necessary.

So, as an unmarried couple, they found a place among the transient or louche population of Notting Hill. They felt at home with the peeling stucco and the untidy balconies, the unswept basement areas and the faded paintwork. They had not chosen the area deliberately. Perhaps the area had chosen them.

Hilda had found work as the manager of a coffee shop in Bayswater, called 'The Wait And See'. When she had first told Harry the name she had become helpless with laughter. 'Wait and see?' he asked her. 'What is the hidden meaning in it?'

'There isn't one.' And then she added, 'Wait and see.' She rearranged three small china bowls on the mantelpiece. 'Haven't you got anything else to ask me?'

'Anything else? As in?'

'Well, how do I *like* it?'

'Like it?'

'Yes. Enjoy. Take pleasure in. Derive comfort from.'

'How do you like it?'

'The job is just fine. Thanks for asking. There are times, Harry, when I feel that you don't care for me at all.'

'That isn't true.'

'Well, now I've said it.'

Sometimes she described to him the events of the day. 'An old man came into the café today. He was perfectly dressed, bowler hat and all. He was tall and stout and wore a three-piece suit. "Hello," he says. "I am Arthur Effles." That's a *funny* name, isn't it? "May I just order a cup of tea?" Then he sits down, very deferentially I thought, and lights a fag. "You see, young lady, I am here with a purpose. I have rented a room in the neighbourhood. Just a plain, simple room. I have rented rooms in other parts of London. Then I fan out, so to speak, from street to street. At present I am on your street, which is Coppice Street. I visit every establishment – just like this one – and make myself thoroughly familiar with it." He kept on making little bows and blowing little kisses. He had a beautiful smile, like a *patriarch*. Do you know what I mean?'

'I suppose so.'

'Do you *suppose* or do you know? Oh forget it. It doesn't matter. So anyway he smiles this lovely smile. "I talk to a person such as yourself, and I find out all about the neighbourhood. When I have walked down all the streets, and discovered all its secrets, I leave my lodging and rent somewhere else." Then he gets up and sits by the window. For the rest of the morning he just looks into the street. I could tell from the way he sat that he loved windows.'

'He sounds like a daft old bastard.'

'I wouldn't describe him as *daft*. Perhaps a little bit *cracked*.' She sensed that she had bored him with this story. So she said no more.

Late one afternoon, as she stood behind the counter, a young man entered the coffee shop. He lingered over the menu, asking her carefully and specifically about every item. Even as he did so it seemed to Hilda that he was troubled by some inward thought or inward distress. Without knowing anything about him, she pitied him. Eventually he ordered a ham sandwich and a cup of tea. She watched him surreptitiously as he chewed the food, and drank the tea; he was staring far away.

She presented him with the bill.

'I'm afraid I can't pay this,' he told her. 'I have no job. No money.' He looked at her without expression.

She was so surprised that she did not know how to reply. 'No money?' He shook his head. She stood there for a moment, and then impulsively went back to the counter and put three pastries into a paper bag. He took them and, without a word, left the coffee shop. She sat down at one of the tables, and burst into tears. Hilda told Harry the story that evening, omitting the detail of her tears.

He sighed, and looked away for a moment. Somehow he knew that she had encountered Sam.

She followed Harry's career with more interest than her own, questioning him about his work and colleagues. 'How is the balding bully?' she asked him. She was referring to James White, the news editor.

'Getting more beastly every day. Whenever I think of him, I feel an inexpressible sensation of weariness. Or boredom. One or the other. What is the point of these people? He's so damned superior. But he has nothing to be superior about. He has a companion. A comrade in arms who has a pudgy face and smokes all the time. That's all I know about him. All I want to know.'

One evening, she said to him, 'I saw that man you interviewed. Cormac something.'

'Cormac Webb?'

'That's it. Webb.' Cormac Webb was a junior minister in the Department of Housing. He had been interviewed by Harry because he was the youngest member of the Labour government. Webb had struck him as being brash, exuberant and opportunistic – all the qualities that Harry admired. He had told Harry, off the record, that he preferred champagne to beer and that his favourite restaurant was Simpson's in the Strand. He exuded a sort of charmless bonhomie. 'Where did you see him?' he asked her.

'He was going into that Ruppta's building.' These offices were immediately across the street from The Wait And See. Asher Ruppta was a businessman, of ambiguous nationality, who had become the subject of hostile controversy and bitter complaint in Notting Hill Gate. He was known as a brutal and rapacious landlord, buying up old houses and subdividing them into smaller and smaller flats that were then rented to immigrants from the West Indies. It was reported that he terrorised the older residents until they were forced to move out or to sell their properties to him. Then he would bring in new tenants and charge them exorbitant rents. His 'agents' always had bull terriers with them. 'Then I saw them walking towards the park. Later, that is.'

What would Webb have to do with Ruppta? The fact that Webb was in the housing department occurred to Harry as soon as he asked himself the question. But why would he visit Ruppta's offices? Why did not Ruppta go to Whitehall? 'Did you tell me once,' he asked her, 'that Ruppta's staff use the coffee shop?'

'That's right. Lunchtime. She eats *so* much. She orders *three* sandwiches.'

'Who does?'

'The secretary. And then there's a typist, who looks a little bit like a mongoose. No. A marmoset.'

'What does a marmoset look like?'

'Like *her*. Anyway she's leaving. I don't think she likes it there.'

'You remember how to type, don't you?'

'Of course I do. Have you forgotten how to breathe?'

'Are you any good?'

'Any *good*?'

In his excitement it did not occur to him that Hilda might want to stay at the coffee shop.

It did not take him very long to devise a scheme whereby Hilda would enter the office of Asher Ruppta. She took the secretary and typist into her confidence. 'You know,' she told them, 'I am *sick* of making sandwiches.' Later she added, 'I used to be a typist, like you. I *loved* it.'

'Well, you can go back to it,' the typist said on the following day. 'I'm off. I've had enough.'

So Hilda entered the employment of Asher Ruppta. He was a short thickset man, in middle age, of olive complexion. He had gold rings on the second and third fingers of his right hand; he wore an expensive silk suit, and a pair of horn-rimmed spectacles hung from a silver chain around his neck. He could have been a banker, or a heart surgeon. Hilda later described him as 'very *sleek*'.

'So you know my ladies,' he said to Hilda on the morning she had come for an interview. 'My ladies are very special. They are very good ladies.' He could not have been more polite, more gallant. Could this have been the man who threatened old women with bull terriers? He looked at her with a certain amount of merriment, as if he had divined her question. 'Julie says that you are an excellent typist.'

'I hope so. I think so.'

'How many fingers?'

'Excuse me?'

'How many fingers do you use?'

She held up her hands. 'All of them.'

'Excellent. You have a pianist's hands.'

'I can't play a note.' She was laughing.

'You can make music on the typewriter. Please to sit there.' She sat down in front of a large Remington. 'Now, Miss Hilda, you can begin.' He started to dictate to her a letter concerning the freehold of a property in Lancaster Gate. He seemed to Hilda to be making up the figures as he went along.

She and Julie Armitage, the secretary, now shared an office. Julie was thin, but she rarely stopped eating. She kept a pocket knife and a jar of Colman's mustard in the drawer of her desk. She cut up a Scotch egg, or a pork pie, into several very small pieces; then she spread mustard on each one of them evenly before placing them in her mouth in a rapid but somehow absent-minded fashion.

Julie was not happy with the world as she found it. Her face looked as if it were incapable of smiling, and the sides of her mouth were sure proof of the theory of gravity. She complained about the weather, about the bus service, about the previous night's television programmes – and of course about her own job. 'I've got too much on my plate,' she said one afternoon. That was true, Hilda thought, in another sense. 'Mr Ruppta doesn't understand.' She pronounced his name in a deliberately formal way. 'I am that busy. I hardly have time to take a wee. And my back is giving me gyp.' Hilda could not help laughing. Julie looked at her in a pained fashion. 'It's all right for some.'

'Let me help.' Hilda tried to sound apologetic. 'Give me some of your paperwork.'

'Would you?'

So Hilda became better acquainted with all aspects of Ruppta's business. 'He's claiming for payments he never made,' she reported to Harry. 'That's thieving, isn't it? He makes up lists of works that were never done. He lies about the number of tenants in a property. I know that for a fact. I have the real numbers in my desk. Sometimes I hear him talking on the 'phone. He is ever so smooth and polite. A real *charmer*. He talks very carefully and precisely. Like a walking dictionary. He never loses his temper. Not *him*. I should think he would stay calm in an avalanche. Yes, he *would*. He is never even *annoyed*. Which is annoying. But I don't think he's a gentleman at all. I think he is a bit of a villain. I have to pass on messages to him. "Flat 38 is done." Or "number ten is vacant". That kind of thing. Very suspicious. But he just smiles and puts a finger up to one of his eyebrows. He likes to smooth them down. "Thank you, Miss Hilda," he says.' Harry had been taking notes.

There had as yet been no further sign of Cormac Webb. Then, one evening, he walked into the office. Asher Ruppta had been to the bank earlier in the day, and had drawn out a large sum in cash. Hilda knew this because he had taken with him a black attaché case equipped with a safety lock. He always used this to carry money.

Webb did not identify himself to Julie or to Hilda but went over to Ruppta's door and gave it a sharp double rap. 'Ah,' Ruppta said as he opened the door, 'my very good friend!' The two men shook hands, and entered Ruppta's private office. Hilda pretended to be checking her pages of typing, but in fact she was listening as carefully as she could without arousing Julie's suspicion. She heard stray phrases, such as 'the provision' and 'the regulator', but the rest was murmured conversation. After a few minutes Webb left the office, carrying the attaché case. He still did not seem to notice the presence of the two women. But he was smiling.

Harry was delighted with the news. 'This is it,' he said. 'We've bagged him.'

He cleared the story with James White. 'That little cripple,' White said with some satisfaction. Cormac Webb had a slight limp.

The news editor then took the story to Andrew Havers-Williams who remarked that 'Webb is not one of nature's gentlemen'. It only remained, he said, for 'that chap, Hanway, to catch him at it'.

Julie volunteered the next piece of information. 'That person,' she said to Hilda on the following morning, 'comes here every month. On the dot. I don't know who he is and I don't want to know. He has ever such a cruel mouth. What does he do with all them attaché cases?'

Hilda observed that, on the day after Webb's visit, Asher

Ruppta purchased a property in Queensway that had previously been subject to a 'building order'. It seemed that this order had been lifted only a week before. A 'building order' gave tenants certain rights of appeal and of rehousing.

Looking back over the files, Hilda noticed that other 'building orders' had been allowed to expire or had been lifted. In one file she noticed a letter, dated 31 October 1968, with the heading of the Department of Housing. It was signed by Webb himself. It was couched in formal style, but the gist was clear enough. Asher Ruppta's property holdings were due to be investigated by an official from the department, but the government had decided that such action was neither necessary nor desirable. It seemed that Webb had intervened and stopped an investigation into Ruppta's business.

'I'll tell you what he's doing,' Harry said to Hilda that evening. 'He is giving Ruppta inside information. That's what he's doing. I wonder how much he's being paid.'

'*Hundreds.*' She opened her eyes wide.

'Heck.' He had a habit of scratching his face that Hilda still found endearing. 'When is he coming next?'

'The first of next month. Around five.'

On that day, Harry and a photographer from the *Chronicle* were sitting in The Wait And See. They were drinking coffee and watching the street from the window. There was a new girl behind the counter, Millicent, who had been handed a pound note for allowing them to stay there. 'Here he is,' Harry said. He had become very excited. The photographer swiftly picked up his camera from the Formica table, and took several photographs of Cormac Webb walking down the street and entering the building. Thirty minutes later, he photographed him coming out of the premises with an attaché case.

Webb had seen them. He seemed to Harry to have some

difficulty in mastering his expression as he walked across the road towards them. The photographer kept on snapping him.

'You can put that fucking thing down,' Webb said as he came into the coffee shop. 'Can we speak outside?'

'Sure,' Harry replied. 'We can speak anywhere.'

'I know you. You're from the *Chronicle*. You interviewed me.'

'That's right. Can I ask you about your relationship with Asher Ruppta?'

'I don't have one. And that's that.'

'What's in the case?'

'That's none of your business. I warn you. I don't remember your name.'

'Harry Hanway.'

'I warn you, Hanway, that if you publish any of this you will be out of business.'

'Out of business? That's a curious phrase.'

'You will be finished. Do you understand that?'

'That really depends on whether you have done anything wrong or not.'

Webb glared at him, and limped away.

Harry spent the next two days preparing the story. He consulted the Land Register. He found out the leases attached to various properties. He found the title deeds and records of 'building orders'. There was a significant pattern of Ruppta buying up properties within a few days of the 'building order' being lifted. Harry was not able to prove directly that Webb had sold Ruppta information, but he knew how to surmise and suggest within the bounds of libel.

He was about to give the story to James White when he was called to the office of the editor. To his surprise he was greeted there by the proprietor of the *Chronicle*, Sir Martin Flaxman. He was a small man and seemed frail; but he had

70

a full head of sleek black hair which was, perhaps, a little too long at the back. He had a forceful manner, with a bluffness that might have been mistaken for geniality. Harry wondered how such a small man could make so much money. In fact Flaxman had made his fortune from selling medical supplies in Asia and Africa.

'Well, Harry,' he said, 'I've been hearing all about you. You know when to go for the balls, don't you?' He squeezed Harry's arm. 'Fuck it. I'm frightened of you already. Look at me. I'm shaking.' Andrew Havers-Williams, strangely divorced from the conversation, was looking out of the window towards the steeple of St Bride's Church. 'Do you know what I tell Andy here? Spread enough shit around and something will grow.' He was still holding onto Harry's arm. 'There's good shit and there's bad shit. I'm looking out for you, Harry. You're my boy.' And with that he abruptly left the room.

'Very colourful.' The editor cleared his throat. 'That story about Webb and Ruppta.'

'Yes?'

'How far has it got?'

'As far as it can. I was about to pass it over to White.'

'That won't be necessary.'

'I don't –'

'We won't be going on with it.' Harry remained silent. 'Sir Martin doesn't want to publish it.'

'Why ever not?'

'I'll tell you something in confidence. I shouldn't, but I will. I owe you an explanation. In the past Sir Martin has been in business with Ruppta. As a good reporter, you will be angry. I understand that. But as an employee of the *Chronicle*, you have to accept it. For the sake of your career.'

Harry did indeed think of himself as a 'good' reporter, whatever that meant, but he did not want to jeopardise his future at the *Chronicle*. That was more important. Sir Martin

Flaxman had, after all, expressed an interest in him. The abandonment of the Webb story was exasperating, but he might be able to use it to his advantage in the weeks and months to come.

VI

Squeeze in

'ACTUALLY, I don't much care for the place. It isn't exactly what I expected.' Daniel Hanway was confiding in his former schoolfriend, Peter Palmer, who had come to see him in the middle of the second term. Palmer had been given a place at the University of Liverpool.

'Have you made many friends?'

'Friends? No. Not really.' He did not want to admit loneliness or the fact that he looked warily upon his contemporaries.

'I bet,' Palmer said, 'that you don't feel as clever as you used to.'

'What do you expect? My director of studies isn't interested in anything I have to say. He just sits there smoking his pipe. He has the most boring opinions I have ever heard. He's in love with Ben Jonson, for Christ's sake. You're right. I don't feel so clever any more. I think there are people here who are cleverer than me. I hate that. I might as well be invisible.'

They were sitting in two black leather armchairs before a small gas fire. It was the biggest room Daniel had ever possessed, and a small bedroom lay off it. He had refused to put posters on the walls, so that his surroundings had a quality of bleakness that secretly he enjoyed. It suited his mood.

'I feel,' he said, 'that I'm on the sidelines of everything. There's something really great going on somewhere, but I have nothing to do with it.' They could hear from the room upstairs the sound of music and laughter. 'Come on,' he said, 'let's walk to Grantchester.' It was a walk he had already done many times, along the path and the fields beside the river Cam, where he could brood on his unhappiness. 'I can't stand the lectures,' he was saying to Palmer as they crossed the first bridge on the outskirts of Cambridge. 'Total waste of time. I have come up with a plan to avoid those wankers. Do you want to know what it is?' He savoured a few seconds of silence. 'This is what you do. Say that you are studying the poetry of Browning. If you've got a strong enough stomach, you don't have to *read* him. Not as such. You read nine or ten books about him. They will be so boring that you can sort of skim them. Then you take their main arguments, mix them up, blend them together and press them into shape. Hey, you've got yourself a great piece of cookery. A great essay. Then you memorise it for the exam.'

'Isn't that, well, a bit mechanical?'

'The syllabus is mechanical. Exams are mechanical.'

They walked on a little way until they came to a small stone chapel standing five or six feet back from the bank of the river. 'This is the place,' Daniel said, 'where the Virgin Mary was supposed to have appeared before a female hermit. Thirteenth century. So they built this little shrine.'

'You don't believe that stuff?'

'I wouldn't rule it out. Do you smell that lovely scent?'

'Water lilies.'

They were silent for a while. 'What's with the moustache and long hair?' Palmer asked him. He had been waiting to ask the question all day.

'I just woke up one morning and decided to grow them.'

'You and a thousand other hippies.'

'What's that supposed to mean?'

'The spirit of the age. The new youth.'

'That's all romantic shit. I just wanted to grow a moustache. Isn't that a good enough explanation?'

'A band of brothers.'

'Listen to yourself. You're as bad as those cunts who go on *sit-ins* and organise poetry *workshops*.'

'You can't just dismiss them.'

'Yes I can. They're pathetic. What does it matter to me that I'm living in the 1960s? Does that make anything so different?'

They had come to the fields outside Grantchester. 'Sunday is the worst day,' Daniel said. 'Don't you feel it? It is so empty. So melancholy.'

'Now who's the romantic?'

When the bell rang for dinner in Hall that evening, Daniel put on his black gown and walked down his staircase. The bell might have signalled a funeral.

'Squeeze in, dear.' Ernest Hughes was a plump young man who believed that he bore a resemblance to Oscar Wilde, whom he called 'Oscar'. 'There's always room for one more. If there is semolina again, I shall scream.'

This prompted a snigger from Stanley Askisson, a young man from the north who had a great affection for the novels of D. H. Lawrence. Ernest looked at his soup with a placid expression. 'Don't you think, Stanley –'

'I do think.' He sniggered again. 'Don't I think I should be more polite?'

'Don't you think that we should bring back the sedan chair?'

'Don't talk shite.'

'I happen to believe it is the perfect form of transport.'

'You're an idiot.'

'Oh dear.'

'There's a difference between me and you, Ernest. Not in money. Not in class. Not in brains. I have my gods. You have your gods.'

'Oscar said that gods are vulgar.'

'Oscar Wilde was a great fat insect. A spider.'

Ernest blinked and breathed hard. 'You don't know what you're talking about.'

'I know a fake when I see one. He was false. False to himself, and false to others. Each man kills the thing he loves. I don't think so.' He was very fierce. 'Not unless that love is unnatural and obscene.'

Ernest now seemed close to tears. He put his spoon in the soup and said nothing. Daniel enjoyed sitting beside Stanley. He savoured his presence, and would from time to time lean over so that their bodies briefly touched.

The conversation, formal and hesitant, turned to a new album by a rock group of whom Daniel had never heard. 'I hate that capitalist shit,' Stanley said.

'Capitalist? What's so capitalist about entertaining the people?'

'The people? The people are fuckers.'

Daniel and Stanley went together to the college bar. 'Hughes is a slug,' Stanley said. 'He leaves a trail of slime. He uses words without knowing their meaning. He is all pretence.'

'I don't mind him,' Daniel replied.

'Oh you don't mind anything. You don't mind the world. You want to get on in it.'

'What's wrong with that?' Daniel experienced a sudden sharp surge of anger. No one had ever made him angry before.

'What's wrong with it? Wherever you look, there's hypocrisy. There's sham. No one ever dares speak the truth. Say what they really think.'

Daniel felt that Stanley was accusing him of some crime that he was not aware he had committed. 'Why do you think I want to get on?'

'Because you're weak.'

'Like Hughes?'

'No. Not like that. He is weak in the soul, in the life force. You are weak in the mind.'

'I don't think so.'

'You don't know yourself. So you don't trust yourself.'

Again Daniel felt the anger rising within him. He felt threatened. He felt that he was being goaded. 'I don't know how you can say that.'

'I am not attacking you. I am attacking the false you. The false Daniel Hanway who works too hard and is nervous all the time.'

'That's very kind of you.'

'Cruel to be kind. That's the phrase, isn't it?' Stanley went over to the bar, and brought back two more pints of lager. 'Sup up,' he said. 'Where I come from, we can drink that down in two minutes.' He had a cheerful grin that Daniel had not noticed before. 'You mustn't take me too seriously.'

Another student came up to them. 'Have either of you got a copy of *Troilus and Criseyde*?' They shook their heads. 'Oh well. Thought I'd ask.' When he walked away, they sat in silence for a few moments.

'Why is it,' Stanley asked him, 'that we are all so uneasy with each other?'

'Lack of confidence?'

'Something like that.'

'I've been looking for some ideal friend. Some companion.' Daniel had been hoping to say this for some time. 'But I've found no one.'

'I don't think,' Stanley said, 'that I'll make it to thirty. I won't survive that long. I'll burn the years away. I'm always going to be poor. I know it. But I don't mind that. Poverty sings.' His eyes were very bright; he was looking away, over Daniel's shoulder, with an expression of eagerness upon his face. 'I don't think I could stand to live for very long. It just gets harder all the time.'

'I know what you mean,' Daniel said. 'Everything is difficult. I can't look forward at all without shuddering.'

'Shudder. That's a good word. Like slither.'

'Or mother.'

Stanley looked perplexed. 'Now that's a strange association. What have you got against your mother?'

'Nothing. I haven't seen her for ten years.' Then he told him the story of his mother's disappearance. He had never discussed it with anyone before. But in the company of Stanley he wanted to make an emotional impression; he wanted to convince him that in some way he had been deprived of love. In the telling of the story he feigned more hurt and surprise than he believed he felt. But his words were more truthful than he realised.

They were sitting in a corner of the bar, within an alcove on the walls of which were various *film noir* posters. Daniel had fallen silent after explaining how his father had never mentioned his mother again. Stanley then bent forward and kissed him on the lips. There was no one else near them. Daniel's eyes widened, and he looked at Stanley in astonishment. Then he returned the kiss with such passion that he bit Stan's lip. 'Be careful,' Stanley said curtly. And then he added, 'I don't want this thing to happen. But it will happen.'

Daniel was still breathless. He was shaking with nervous excitement. 'Do you want us to?' Stanley nodded. 'I never thought − I never knew −'

'That I was queer? Well, I am. Sort of. And I am not. I knew you were. As soon as I saw you.' Daniel blushed.

They determined to keep their liaison a secret. It was not difficult. Their contemporaries would never have recognised or understood a relationship of this kind – it was beyond any possible range of their experience. Ernest Hughes may have sensed something – in a look, or in a gesture – but he said nothing. Sometimes he pursed his lips and looked superciliously at Daniel; but Daniel looked back at him with as innocent an expression as he could muster.

Daniel had hoped that in Stanley Askisson he had found his ideal companion, but he was soon disenchanted. There were many times when Stanley was curt and angry with him; Daniel came to dread his harangues. Their lovemaking was often awkward and unsatisfactory. Stanley would lie on his back, looking up at the ceiling, while Daniel would try to arouse him; when he did not succeed, he felt humiliated. Stanley would pick arguments with him, and even insult him.

'This is your life,' he said one day. He picked up a sheet of paper, and drew a series of squares with a pencil. 'You are in a box every hour of every day. Work. Work.' He stabbed each square with the pencil. 'I feel sorry for you. I pity you.'

'You want me to be more like you, I suppose.'

'You arrange your hours as if you were in some sort of military campaign. But who precisely is the enemy?' Daniel was silent. 'Come on. Get out of your box. Let's go for a walk.'

They competed with each other in their studies. One afternoon Daniel entered Stan's room in order to see what books he was reading and what essay he was preparing. He wanted to look at his notes. 'What are you doing here?' Stanley had come in unexpectedly.

'I was waiting for you.'

'So why are you going through my papers?' Daniel had disordered them on the desk.

'I was curious.'

'You were spying on me.'

'Why?' The word stuck somewhere in his throat.

'So that's it. *I* am your enemy.'

'No. Of course not.' He did not sound convincing.

Their supervisor, Eric Hamilton, was an academic who had spent his career in the college. Despite all the appurtenances of middle age, including a brown tweed jacket and a pipe, he looked oddly boyish. His clothes were always crumpled. The bottoms of his fawn trousers were spattered with mud, after his bicycle ride to the college from his small terraced house in Trumpington Street. He had a habit of tilting his head to one side, listening with a slight smile to his students' remarks.

'It seems to me,' he said in one morning supervision, 'that *Volpone* comes from a city vernacular tradition.' It seemed to Daniel that half of his sentences began with 'it seems to me that'. 'What is the phrase Jonson employs? "Language that men do use." That is the vibrant thing. I would like to say that this has the sheer edge of actuality. Felt life. Do you see?'

Daniel had no idea what he was trying to say, and simply continued reading his essay in which Hamilton took no particular interest. Hamilton seemed more ready to listen to Stanley Askisson, however, who could talk about felt life and the vibrant thing for as long as was necessary. Daniel sensed the favouritism, and resented it.

So he retreated to the safety and the silence of the university library. He became known to the staff, and was told that there would be summer work in the understaffed accessions department. 'You are very familiar with books,' the sub-librarian said. 'Not to mention keen on them. We can do with you.'

Daniel put his name forward, for work in the vacation, and was accepted. He was also allowed to keep his room in college during the summer months. He wrote a short letter to his father, announcing the good news, and prepared himself joyfully for a summer of toil. Stanley Askisson was going back to his mother's house in Hartlepool.

And so the summer passed. He hardly noticed it. After finishing work in the library he drank alone, most evenings, in a small pub close to the college which was used by a local population of shopkeepers, workmen and retired couples. No one from the college or the wider university frequented it. He sat in the back parlour, drinking pints of bitter.

One evening, late that summer, a stranger walked into the pub and ordered a pint of cider. 'Is anyone sitting here?' he asked Daniel, pointing to the bench beside him. Daniel shook his head. 'Ta.' He had thick dark hair, swept back and rendered glossy with brilliantine; he seemed to Daniel to have a coarse but pleasing face, with a day or two's growth of stubble. 'Your very good 'ealth,' he said, raising his glass.

'Thanks.'

'Don't mention it. I won't.' He drank down some cider, and sighed. 'That's sweet. That's the ticket. What do you do then?'

'I'm an undergraduate.'

'Ah. An under*graduate*.'

'What do you do?'

'This and that. Sometimes this, and sometimes that. Sometimes both together.' He tapped the side of his nose. 'You're queer, aren't you?'

Daniel was alarmed and embarrassed. 'What makes you think that?'

'The way you looked at me. Don't get me wrong. I don't mind queers. I like them. What do you study?'

'English literature.'

'*Lit*erature? Is that a fact? What's your name?'

'Daniel.'

'Pleased to meet you, Dan.' He held out his hand. 'I'm Sparkler.'

'That's a strange name.'

'You can call me Spark or Sparkie or Sparkle. I'm quick, you see.' The young man now held up Daniel's watch. 'Never shake hands with a stranger, Dan.'

'How did you do that?'

'It's a gift, isn't it. Can you keep a secret?' Daniel nodded. 'Let's go to another pub.' When they got outside Sparkler turned the corner and led him into the back yard. 'Look,' he said. He plunged his hands into his pockets, and brought out watches and wallets.

Daniel was astonished. 'Are you a thief?'

'That's right. A tea-leaf. I came down here because the coppers don't know me.' He stuffed the objects back into his pockets. 'Let's move.'

Daniel walked with him in a state of some bewilderment. He found himself enjoying the company of this good-looking young man, and was in fact exhilarated at the thought of his being a petty criminal. 'How long,' he asked him, 'have you been doing –'

'The thieving? Ever since I was that high. I'm a natural, aren't I? It's my calling. I get to travel. I'm my own boss. I don't pay no tax.'

'Have you ever been caught?'

'Caught? *Caught?* Can you catch a firefly? You can catch fleas, I know, but not with your hands you can't. No more can they catch me. You ask too many questions, under*graduate*.' He laughed, and put his arm around Daniel's shoulders, causing him a shock of pleasure. 'You've got to be hard. Hard and smart. And *quick*. These mods aren't hard. They're all flannel. You're a Londoner, aren't you?'

'Camden.'

'Why is a London boy doing literature, then?'

'I just like it.'

'Can you write good English?'

'I hope so.'

'Let's go in here.' Sparkler took his arm from Daniel's shoulders, and led him into another pub. 'Two of your very finest pints, landlord,' he said as he went up to the bar. 'I feel a terrible thirst coming on me. Makes me see red.'

'Pints of what exactly?'

'Two pints of Bulmer's best. My young friend here insists on the best. Now then, gentlemen. I have a pack of cards about me somewhere.'

'No betting allowed,' the landlord said.

'No bets. No bets. Just a bit of harmless fun.' Then he performed a card trick, to the delight of the locals, before retiring with the two glasses to a corner of the pub where Daniel was sitting. 'Keep them happy,' he said. 'And then they don't ask questions. They accept you. So you can write good English, can you?'

'Yes. I can.'

'I have a load of stories to tell, don't I? You can write them down for me. How many pockets can a pickpocket pick before he pips Sparkler? I'll give you something in return.' He winked at him, and then stretched his legs beneath the table. Daniel's mouth went dry, and with trembling hand he raised his glass and drank from it. 'This is what we'll call it. The Sparkler Papers.'

'It has a ring to it.' Daniel was still thoroughly bewildered by the events of the evening. Why had this good-looking stranger taken such an interest in him? Had they really met by accident or coincidence?

'I'll tell you about the time when I met a very kind lady. She took care of me when I was broke. She looked after me.

One day you may meet her. When you come up to London. Have you got a pen on you?'Then he wrote down a telephone number. 'Ring me the week before. Then I can give you my address.' He leaned forward and whispered in his ear. 'You can suck my cock.' So began Daniel's 'transcription' of The Sparkler Papers.

Whenever Daniel went up to London, he told Stanley Askisson that he was visiting his father. In truth he had forgotten all about his family. It was something from which he had escaped. So in the vacations, instead of returning to Camden, he resumed his job at the university library. He was allowed to stay in his college rooms, too. Except for his one day a month in London with Sparkler, he devoted his time to work among books.

Daniel and Stanley stood outside the examination schools, where their finals were to be held. Daniel had not been able to sleep the previous night. He was filled with such alarm that he was sick that morning, retching violently into the hand basin in his bedroom. The world spun about him. Only when he had washed and dressed did he regain some semblance of ordinary life. Outside the building he dug his hands deep into his pockets to keep them from shaking. Stanley was smoking a Players cigarette, and was making nervous jokes about running out of ink.

Three months later the results were published. Daniel had obtained a first-class, and Stanley a second-class, degree.

'Now I see things from the point of view of failure,' Stanley said. Then he burst into tears.

Daniel put his arm around him. 'It will be all right,' he said.

'No. It won't be all right. It will never be right again.'

'You're taking it too seriously.'

'And you're not?'

There was an immediate change in their relationship. They were no longer intimate. In fact they tried to avoid one another as much as possible. Daniel had performed so well that he was offered a research fellowship by the college, a post that he accepted with enthusiasm. This was the place in which he now wished to settle and to prosper. Stanley Askisson drifted to London where, after taking a civil-service examination, he found himself a junior clerk in the Ministry of Housing. Soon enough he was working directly for Cormac Webb. Daniel Hanway, meanwhile, had begun work on his dissertation on 'The Criminal Element in Eighteenth Century Literature'. He continued to see Sparkler in London.

VII

Red red robin

I T WAS raining, a mild and gentle rain that shrouded the
city in a pearl-grey light. Sam was walking through what
was for him still an unfamiliar part of London, south of
the river. He sensed a difference of atmosphere; there was
no urgency, no energy, in the air. The rain billowed around
the houses like a bland mist. He pushed open a gate and
walked up a small front path between patches of grass; he
rang the bell, and the door opened a fraction before he
was admitted.

Fifteen minutes later he came out across the threshold. It
was still raining. He was accompanied by a middle-aged
woman, who stopped and put her hand up to a pocket in
her jacket. 'I almost forgot,' she said. 'Take it.'

'I don't want this, you know.'

'Still, I like to give it to you.'

He took the envelope and, without looking back, went
into the street. He did not look up until he passed St George's
Church in Borough High Street. An old woman was sitting
on its worn steps, her hair tied together with rags. Sam
reached into the pocket of his jacket, and gave the envelope
to her. He knew that it contained a five-pound note. He was
given the same amount every week, and always handed the

money to the first vagrant he saw. And who was the woman in the house from whom he had received the money? Sam had found his mother at last.

Three months earlier he had entered the church of Our Lady of Sorrows in Camden, where he had first seen the statue of the Virgin. He had been hoping, ever since, that the chapel and the statue would somehow reappear and that the nuns would also return. What had come and gone might come again.

He sat at the back of the church, his hands clasped in front of him; he repeated some words that the nuns had recited to him. '*Ave maris stella, virgo et puella.*' The door leading from the porch was suddenly opened, and there stepped a woman into the nave wearing a white raincoat and a blue scarf. She entered one of the pews, and Sam saw her for a moment in profile. Hurriedly he left the church and stood on the gravel path outside the porch. What should he do? Should he talk to her? Would she recognise him? He feared another rejection — that was how he put it to himself — and so he decided to wait in the street where she would not notice him. A few minutes later she left the church and came out, taking off her scarf as she swung open the wooden gate in front of her. She turned left and walked quickly away. Sam decided to follow her, at a careful distance.

She entered the underground station at the top of Camden High Street, and stood in line for a ticket. Sam hated this station. It had an acrid smell of old machinery, and the booming sound of trains echoed from the depths; the dank atmosphere was filled with foreboding. He did not appreciate the world under the ground. Yet he waited in the queue, unwilling to let his mother out of his sight, and then followed her down the escalator to the southward-bound platform of the Northern Line.

He sat at the other end of the carriage, from where he kept on glancing at his mother. He had known her at once, in the supermarket and in the church, but he had not recognised her by sight; he had recognised her by feeling. He had been drawn to her by some bond of sympathy or perception that was instinctive and unassailable. She was staring straight ahead, immersed in her own thoughts. She seemed to Sam to be troubled; he wanted to approach her, and to comfort her, but he could not do anything so bold.

She left the train at Borough and Sam followed her through the wind-haunted passages, past the peeling advertisements and the grubby white tiles, past the piss-stained corners and the rusted metal grilles, until she came out into the hall of the escalators. He watched her rise slowly, and then himself stepped on the moving stairs so that he would not lose her. She came out onto Borough High Street and began walking south, taking the old pilgrim trail from Southwark. Sam felt curiously light-hearted as he followed her. Eventually she turned up the path of a small terraced house.

There was a low wall on the other side of the road, bordering a wild waste of garden in front of an untenanted house. Sam sat there, and waited. At regular intervals cars drew up to the parking spaces in the road outside. Individual men would then enter the house, leaving after an hour or so. Two young women came up, arm in arm, and were admitted. They did not leave.

Sam came again the next day, and then the next. He did not know what he was waiting for. He knew only that this was what he was supposed to do. He noticed that all the curtains of the house were drawn, and that he could hear no noise. Then on the third day he walked up the narrow path and rang the bell. A young woman, holding a plastic cup in her hand, came to the door. 'Can I help you?'

'I've come to see Mrs Hanway.'

'Who? There's no one of that name here.'

'I know her.'

'Let him in.' It was his mother's voice.

The young woman moved aside, and Sam crossed the threshold into a hall decorated with crimson flock wallpaper and a number of watercolours of pastoral scenes in heavy gilt frames. He went towards his mother standing at the end, at the foot of a staircase.

'Well, Sam, you have found me.'

'I saw you in the church. In Allington Street.'

'I go back there sometimes. I like it.'

'So do I.'

He looked away from her for a moment, but she did not look away from him. 'I would know you anywhere, Sam. Your hair is not as light as it used to be. Come in here. Mary, will you make us a pot of tea?' She led him into a small room with a window overlooking an empty yard and a brick wall. A blue vase of tulips had been placed on the table at which they sat. 'I haven't seen you for a long time,' she said.

'I was seven.'

'You're nineteen now, aren't you?'

'Eighteen.'

They were silent for a moment as Mary brought in the tea.

'So you've left school.'

'Yes.'

'What are you doing now?'

'Nothing.' She stared at him for a moment, with a fixed attention. 'What do *you* do?'

She threw her hands up in the air. 'This.' Then she questioned him about Harry, and about Daniel, listening eagerly as he tried to remember all the details of the immediate past. She never once mentioned Philip Hanway.

'Why did you go away?'

89

'Why does anyone do anything? No. That's unfair on you. I was in trouble. That's all I want to say.'

'Where did you go?'

'I went away. It doesn't matter where.' He remembered now the paleness of her pale blue eyes. 'I didn't want to leave you. I didn't mean to leave you. Your father wanted it. He didn't want to see me again. It wasn't easy.' She paused for a moment. 'It was the hardest thing in my life.'

'You thought it was for our own good.'

'Yes. That's it. Your own good.'

'We knew that something was wrong.'

'What did your father tell you?'

'He didn't. He never said a word.'

'Didn't you ask?'

'We talked about it to each other. But we never wanted to mention it to anyone. I think we felt guilty for something, but I don't know . . .'

'*You* felt guilty? How do you think I felt? I have never felt anything else.' She reached over and touched the vase of tulips. 'You never spoke to your father?' Sam shook his head. 'You boys were always very private. You never gave anything away. You were the strangest boys in the world. Nothing will stop Harry. Nothing will trouble Harry. Danny is more fragile. And you were always the dreamer. I was always most concerned for you. Do you remember the time when – No. Let's not talk about the past. You're grown-up now. You're an adult.'

'So what should we talk about, as *adults*?'

'How do you get by?'

'Get by?'

'If you have no job, what do you do for money?'

'Dad helps me. I live at home. I don't cost much.' He laughed. 'I've nothing to spend it on.'

'Don't you have a girlfriend?' He looked at her, and said nothing. 'Don't you have *any* friends?'

'Who would want to be friends with me?'

'Don't say that.'

'I just did.' He looked at the vase of flowers. 'There are lots of people in the world who have no friends. Sometimes I see something interesting. Or I feel something. But I know that I have no one to tell.'

'And the red red robin comes bob bob bobbing along.'

'What?'

'Nothing. It was a song I knew as a kid.' They stared at one another. 'Now that I've found you,' she said, 'I'll never let you go.'

'Is that another song?'

'No. It's the truth.' She stood up and left the room, returning a few moments later with a five-pound note in her hand. 'Here. Take it.'

'I don't want it.'

'Take it. I need to give it to you.'

'To buy myself a friend?'

'Buy whatever you want, Sam.'

So began the series of their strange meetings. On the same day each week, at the same time, he would ring the doorbell and would be admitted. He looked forward to the pot of tea brought in by Mary; he looked forward to the fresh flowers in the blue vase. He looked forward to hearing his mother's voice. It was nothing she said in particular, but the soothing syllables of her conversation induced in him a feeling of repose.

'I see faces before I go to sleep,' she said to him one afternoon. 'I don't know them, but I think somehow I recognise them.'

'Ancestors?'

'Do you think so? That *is* a nice idea. One of them did look a bit like you. He had your smile.'

'Sometimes,' she said on another occasion, 'I smell the strangest things. The smell of burning rags, where there is nothing burning. Sometimes I smell the perfume of roses on a busy street.'

A fortnight later Sam said to her, 'I've got a job.'

'Oh yes?'

'As a nightwatchman. I'll still be able to come around in the afternoon.'

'That's what your father used to do.'

'He was the one who found it for me.'

In fact Philip Hanway had become more and more concerned about his youngest son. When he eventually discovered that Sam had no work, it occurred to him to contact his old employer: there was no qualification needed to be a nightwatchman. So, on Philip's recommendation, Sam was hired.

'You may get lonely,' his mother said to him.

'Me?'

'Your father used to complain.'

'I'll get used to it, I expect. I get used to everything else.'

'Have you mentioned me to your father?' she asked him a week later.

'Do you want me to?'

'No. Some things are better left unsaid, don't you think? What about your brothers?'

'What *about* them?'

'Have you seen them?'

'I don't think so.'

'And what does that mean?'

'Sometimes I think I see their reflections. Sometimes I think I see them across the street. I see them in my dreams all the time.'

'You know, Sam, you baffle me.'

'Just begin at the beginning. You'll find your way.' He

looked at the blue vase. 'How do you pronounce it? Vase as in stars? Or vase as in maze?'

On another visit he spoke to his mother about his work as a nightwatchman. 'I like it. I like to sit and think. Why do I prefer blue to red? If colours were words, what would they say? Why do eyes get tired?'

'Some questions, Sam, have no answers.'

'Do you know who you remind me of? The unknown soldier. You don't have much expression, do you?' It was Julie Armitage. Sam had been given work at a newly built office block along Kingsway; just before his arrival, the property business of Asher Ruppta had taken premises in the same building. Julie immediately felt sympathy for one whom she considered to be a fellow sufferer in the world. 'Here. I've made you a nice sandwich. Do you like Spam? I *love* it.'

He picked up a neatly quartered piece. 'You have some, too.'

'Oh no. It's for you. Oh well, all right then. If you insist.' She bit into it while all the time keeping her eyes upon Sam. 'What do you think of corned beef?'

'Take it or leave it.'

'I like it with pickle. Not that piccalilli muck. I can't abide it. Just regular Branston. Next time I'll bring you a pickled egg.'

'I've never seen a pickled egg.'

'It's just an egg, really. They sell them in pubs.'

So began the friendship between Julie and Sam. He came on duty at five in the evening, and she finished work at six. She would come down with a 'snack', as she called it, and sit down beside him as he ate it. She began to confide in him. 'He's planning something.' 'He' was Asher Ruppta. 'He sits very still and smells his fingers. I know the signs. Sometimes he whispers a word or two. As if he was praying.'

'What does he do?' Sam asked her on another evening, between mouthfuls of cold sausage sandwich.

'Now there's a question. What doesn't he do? He does this and he does that. Am I making myself clear? As clear as mud?'

'Perhaps it is mud.'

'You are a sharp one, aren't you?' She was silent for a moment. 'I think you're right, actually. It is mud. Deep and dark. But you would never know it. It all looks good on paper.'

'I think there's something going on,' she announced two weeks later. 'He has been meeting people out of the office. He never does that. I've had to book him tables in restaurants.' She seemed excited by these events.

Sam now visited his mother two or three times a week, before setting off for his work. He mentioned Julie Armitage, and Sally laughed. '*That's* a coincidence. I knew −' But when he spoke of Asher Ruppta, her eyes widened and she looked away. From that time forward she sometimes asked about Julie and her employer, in an indirect and only slightly curious way.

Sam saw Ruppta often enough. He would walk out of the lift at approximately the same time every evening, and pass the young nightwatchman on his way to the street. He was courteous, politely nodding to Sam before putting on the black Homburg hat that he always wore. Yet he rarely looked directly at him; whenever he did so, his hooded eyes seemed to flash with some inward fire. Sam then saw the spirit of Ruppta as a hawk or some other bird of prey. He thought that he had seen such a bird, perched on the roof of the building, its wings unfurled, but in a moment it was gone.

One evening a young man rang to enter the lobby. 'I'm here to see Mr Ruppta's secretary,' he said. He looked at Sam curiously, as if trying to recall where he had met him.

'I'll call her,' he said. 'Can I give her your name?'

'Stanley Askisson.'

Julie came down with a small package wrapped in brown

paper. She gave it to Stanley Askisson, who thanked her and walked out. Before he left the building, he stared once more at Sam.

'There's something going on,' she said. It was her favourite phrase. 'Do you fancy some pork scratchings? I'll bring them down. There was money in that packet. Banknotes.'

'Who is he?'

'I don't know. Ruppy just told me —'

'Who?'

'That's my secret name for you know who. Ruppy told me to give the money to someone called Askisson.'

'He seemed to know me. But then he didn't know me.'

Stanley Askisson came back two weeks later, and waited in the lobby until he was given a package by Julie. 'Do you know what?' she said to Sam as soon as Askisson had gone out into the street. 'There's no reference to him in any of the letters or papers. This is the problem. There is no mention of the money anywhere. It might as well be fairy gold.'

'Fairy gold?'

'It fades away.'

'But he won't fade away, will he?'

'He could be a blackmailer. Is that what you're thinking, Sam?' Julie put a great deal of faith in Sam's sagacity; she interpreted his periods of silence and withdrawal as wisdom.

'Wait and see,' he replied.

'Next time I'm going to follow him. There's something going on.'

'Won't he mind?'

'Who?'

'Ruppta.'

'He won't know anything about it.'

Stanley Askisson returned a fortnight later, by which time Sam and Julie had formulated a plan.

She left the package with Sam before slipping out into the street wearing a scarf and a nondescript beige coat. On Askisson's arrival Sam gave him the package, with the excuse that Julie had left early for a dentist's appointment. Askisson seemed surprised, but made no comment. Once more he looked at Sam curiously, as though he had known him in some other circumstance. He left the building and, as usual, turned right. Julie followed a short distance behind. She did not want to be seen, of course, but she need not have taken any great precaution. Askisson would not have known her. He never recognised the faces of young women.

Everyone became anonymous on Kingsway, a barren valley carved through the teeming alleys and lanes of nineteenth-century London. All the life of the neighbourhood had been laid waste by the clearance for this site, and none of it had returned. Stanley Askisson walked south towards Bush House before walking around the curve of Aldwych towards a bus stop on the south side of the Strand. The sky was blood-red with a fiery setting sun. Julie kept him in sight. When he boarded the 173 bus she followed him, sitting on the long seat close to the conductor's platform.

Askisson left the bus at the stop halfway down Whitehall, where Julie also alighted. She followed him down Whitehall until he turned into the portal of one of the government departments. When Julie passed it, she saw that it was the Ministry of Housing. The next morning, before Ruppta arrived in the office, she telephoned the ministry and asked to speak to Stanley Askisson. He answered the 'phone in his customary manner. 'Office of Cormac Webb.'

'Sorry. Wrong number.' Now she knew. Webb was a name familiar to her. Ever since she had shared an office with Hilda Nugent, she had been aware of his connection with Ruppta. It seemed that the payments were still being made, indirectly through Askisson, and of course she suspected the nature of the bargain. What had happened to Hilda, by the way? She had telephoned one morning to say that she was ill, and had never returned to work. Ruppta had seemed preoccupied at the time, and so Julie never raised the matter with him.

She told Sam about her pursuit of Askisson. 'Ruppy is giving money to Cormac Webb,' she said. 'He wants something. Information.'

'Planning permission,' Sam replied. 'He's a property developer, isn't he?'

'Don't you think it's *exciting*? I do.'

He had not considered it in that light. He had not really considered it in any light at all. But now he took more interest in Asher Ruppta. And Ruppta began to take more interest in him. He would stop at Sam's desk, before leaving the building, and engage him in brief conversation. 'How are you, Mr Sam?' he would say. 'Has Julie brought you anything nice today?' He was always watchful, somehow looking all around Sam as if searching for his shadow. Ruppta believed in the spirit world. He had been brought up by his mother on a small island of an archipelago in the Celebes Sea. And now he sensed something about Sam. He was not sure what it was, as yet, but there was a quality associated with the mystery that Ruppta had experienced as a child.

'He's been asking after you,' Julie said to Sam one evening. She had just presented him with a sausage sandwich. 'Tuck in. He thinks you've got promise. Potential.'

'Potential for what?'

'Fire bombing. No. I'm joking.'

On the following day Ruppta came up to Sam in the lobby. 'You are a young man,' he said. 'Do you want to sit behind a desk like this for ever? Is it right?' Sam shook his head. 'I need a smart young man. On my island, Sam, there were conjurors. *Aslohi*. They had assistants. *Mekini*. These assistants would help them with their tricks. They would climb up poles and disappear. They would rise into the air. They would fall into a trance. You can be one of my *mekini*.'

'How do I fall into a trance?'

'This will not be necessary. You can deliver little items from me. You can receive letters for me. Perhaps you will follow people. Who knows?' He was about to walk away, when he turned back to Sam. 'On my island there were creatures you could not see and you could not hear. They hid in the green tapestry of the forest, in the humid air, in the great old rocks. Do you have such creatures in London, Sam?'

'Not to my knowledge.'

'It is not a question of knowledge.'

So Sam became a courier, and messenger, for Asher Ruppta.

VIII

What is it?

ARRY HANWAY began to rise among the journalists of the *Chronicle*. He had become chief news reporter, and his byline now appeared on the front page almost daily. He had not forgotten about Cormac Webb; indeed he had kept all the material for possible use at a later date, but he had been willing to suppress the story at the request of Sir Martin Flaxman. This prompt and willing acquiescence recommended Harry to the proprietor of the *Chronicle*, who started to invite him to parties at his house in Cheyne Walk.

For the first time in his life Harry was being introduced to the powerful and to the merely famous. Most of them were cordial and self-deprecating, although Harry realised that success had made them so. It was extraordinary that they all knew, or professed to know, each other; a television presenter was on first-name terms with a businessman or a bishop. It seemed to Harry that, for them, the rest of the world did not really exist.

He began to understand, too, how alliances and affinities might be formed. Here was an admiral talking to a leading businessman; there was a politician talking to a pop star. Despite the air of bonhomie, what brought them all together was self-interest.

'They call me a muck-raker.' Sir Martin was talking to a small group of people. 'What's wrong with raking muck? If you spread enough shit, something may begin to grow.' He laughed very loudly. 'But you have to get the best journalists. Like Harry here. Most of them are arse-lickers. Tame poodles pretending to be guard dogs. But not Harry. He knows what he is. And he likes it.' The little group broke apart, aimlessly colliding with other little groups.

Harry stepped back, and found himself standing beside Cormac Webb. Webb looked at him without betraying any feeling. There had been a flash of recognition, and resentment, but this had been followed by an impassive expression; he was pretending not to remember him. 'How are you, sir?' Harry asked him.

'Tremendous.' He smiled. 'Nose to the grindstone.' He was oddly chastened. Harry noticed that there were white specks of dandruff on his dark pinstriped suit. He seemed shorter, and slighter, than Harry had remembered; he was more vulnerable, as if he had suffered some loss of power.

Sir Martin took Harry aside, put his arm around his shoulders, and whispered to him. 'I've been told that Webb is about to retire. For personal reasons. No more use to me now. He won't be coming here again.' Then he added, under his breath, 'And here's another cunt.' Harry looked up and saw a Conservative front-bench spokesman holding an animated conversation with an actress. 'He wants to get into her knickers.' Sir Martin took Harry over to him. 'Robin,' he said, 'let me introduce you to Harry Hanway.' The actress walked away.

Robin Green concealed his annoyance very well. He had a smooth and well-oiled manner, with a delicate persuasive voice. 'Delighted,' he said. When he smiled he showed his teeth.

'Harry's my boy. He can sniff out secrets like a pig can scent truffles. Secrets smell. Do you have any secrets, Robin?'

'Alas no.' He did not look at Harry, but glanced in his direction. 'Sorry to disappoint you.'

'I don't believe you, Robin.' Sir Martin was as always very emphatic. 'Every man has a secret.'

'And every woman, too,' Harry added.

'Is that so?' Sir Martin looked at him with amusement. 'You must tell me about her some time.'

'Her?'

'I'm sure you had someone in mind.' Harry had been thinking of his mother. 'You must meet my daughter, Harry. Guinevere! Guinevere! Come over here.'

A girl of nineteen or twenty reluctantly crossed the room. 'I sent her to finishing school,' he told the two men. 'I wanted her to become a toffee-nosed bitch and marry a millionaire.'

'Dad!'

'Now she wants to be a social worker. I told her to get a proper job.'

Harry was drawn to Guinevere. She had long dark hair, and large brown eyes; her lips were slightly parted, as if she were about to speak. For some reason Harry saw her swimming in the ocean. She was suspended in the bright blue water.

'Are you one of Dad's attack dogs?' She was smiling.

'I'm probably a poodle.'

'But poodles can bite.'

'I am tame.' They looked at one other for a moment, held by the mutual gaze. 'So you want to be a social worker?'

'Don't laugh.'

'I am not laughing. It's a very good thing.'

'Now you're making fun of me.'

'I'm not. I promise you. I would hate to make fun of you.'

'Would you?' She looked at him with genuine gratitude. 'That's all Dad ever does. I don't think he likes women.'

'I don't think he likes anybody.'

'I don't know why I'm telling you this. What was your name again?'

'Harry.'

'The trouble with Harry.'

'What?'

'It's a novel.'

'I never read novels.'

'Good for you.'

'I don't see much point in them.'

'But you journalists write novels, don't you? You call them stories. Dad is always going on about "good stories".'

'It's just a term,' he said.

'God, I hate these parties.' She looked quickly around the room. 'Mum always stays in the country. She can't stand his friends. She says that it's a dance of death.'

'I can see why.'

'Do you know why I want to be a social worker? I want to get away from all this. Do you know how people are forced to live? One family in a room. No hot water.'

'I know.'

'But do you know? *Really* know? Come with me one day. I'll take you to Limehouse, where I'm being trained.'

'Of course.' He did not want to disappoint her.

They met three days later, on a Saturday morning, outside Limehouse Underground Station. He did not know how to greet her, but she put out her hand. 'It's quiet around here,' she said. They were at the end of a long narrow street dominated on both sides by warehouses of dark brown brick, derelict and empty. 'The local people want them torn down. They need council flats. Come on. I'll show you.'

They walked away from the immediate environs of the river and turned down a side street of dilapidated terrace houses. These were all multiple dwellings – the front doors were open and there were sounds of babies crying, of voices being raised in small rooms. A group of children was playing in the street, while two or three disconsolate men in tattered suits sat on the front steps and watched them. 'Irish,' Guinevere said. 'Or Jamaican. Whoever has the least money.'

A settlement of round huts, created out of mud and straw, had once been raised here by the river. Their roofs had been made of thatch, and they had been built in two parallel lines just like these nineteenth-century tenements. The same sounds, and the same voices, had come from these frail huts; children had played in the space between them, and men had watched them as they sat upon the ground by the threshold of their dwellings. Now someone called out, 'Peter! Peter!'

Guinevere led him into one of the houses. A powerful smell of damp in the hallway mingled with the stale air. 'I visit the family on the first floor,' she said. She walked up the stairs that were covered in chipped and broken linoleum, and knocked on the door at the next level. 'Mrs Byrne,' she called out. 'It's Guinevere.'

A middle-aged woman came to the door. 'I've just finished feeding them,' she said. 'You'd better come in.' Three children were sitting around a Formica table; they were all holding slices of bread, their white faces slightly smeared with jam. They looked up at Guinevere and Harry without expression.

'This gentleman is a journalist,' Guinevere said. 'I wanted him to meet you. To see how you were getting on.'

'Oh we get on. We're not complaining.' Harry observed another room, to which the door was closed. 'My husband's still sleeping. He has the fits.'

'Tell the gentleman how much you live on.'

'Twelve pounds a week. He draws it from the social security.' She looked at the closed door. 'Twelve pounds doesn't go far these days. Not with five of us.' Harry went over to a window that overlooked the grimy street. As his eyes grew accustomed to the dirty brick and the dust upon the windows, he was astonished to see his brother leaving one of the tenements. There was no doubt about it. It was Sam. He walked down some steps into the street, paused for a moment, and then turned left. Harry took a pace backward when he thought that Sam had stared up at him. Then Sam walked off and was gone.

'That Ruppta,' the woman was saying. 'He is a tartar.'

'What was that?'

'We're talking about her landlord,' Guinevere told him. 'Asher Ruppta. Have you heard of him?'

'Yes.'

'He comes down terrible hard on people such as us,' the woman said.

'If they can't pay one week's rent, he threatens them with eviction.'

'Out in the street, sir. With three little ones and him with the fits.'

'He owns most of the houses in this street,' Guinevere said. 'They were going to be torn down, but then the decision was reversed.'

'Is that so?'

'There are a lot of blacks,' Mrs Byrne said. 'I've nothing against them personally.'

Harry experienced a strong desire to leave this small room, and get out into the air. He went over to the window, and looked impatiently down into the street. Guinevere sensed his mood, and reacted accordingly. 'We should go now, Mrs Byrne,' she said. 'I just wanted to say hello.'

Harry put out his hand, and then surreptitiously left a ten-pound note on the Formica table. Mrs Byrne saw it, but she said nothing. Like her children, she stared at him without noticeable expression.

'Thank you for coming,' Guinevere told him as they walked back into the street.

'Thank you for inviting me.'

'I hope you weren't too bored.'

'Bored? Never.'

'How can it happen?'

'What?'

'This.' She gestured at the mean houses. From one of them came the sound of 'Old Man River'.

'That is something to ask Asher Ruppta.'

'How much do you know about that man?'

'Enough.'

'Why don't you write about him? Expose him?'

'You know,' he said, 'you have the loveliest hair.' He felt as if he were poised on a bank beside clear water, about to jump in.

Hilda Nugent's instinct and secret wish was to marry. On her occasional visits to Southend, her foster-mother constantly brought up the subject. 'It's not right,' she said. 'Living in sin.'

'Don't be so old-fashioned, Mum. Everyone does it nowadays.'

'That doesn't make it right.'

'We are as good as married.'

'I wouldn't say that without a ring on your finger. Mark my words.'

And, secretly, Hilda agreed with her. She would allude to the subject, with Harry, from time to time. 'Are we putting down roots in Notting Hill?' she might ask him.

'Roots?'

'Are we going to stay for a long time?'

'I really don't know. What do you think?' He was irritated by her constant use of 'we'.

'We have a good routine, don't we?'

'I suppose so.'

'We are comfortable.'

Yes. You are as comfortable as an old armchair. He did not say it but he considered saying it.

The result of such conversations was always inconclusive. 'Sometimes,' she said, 'I think I'm living with a stranger. I don't really understand you.'

'There isn't very much to understand.'

'There you go again. You're keeping me away. You don't want to be touched. *Disturbed*. Sometimes I think I should just get up and walk away.' She had in fact never thought that.

He looked at her and said nothing.

'You just like to use people. You don't give a damn for any of them. All you really care about is you. Y. O. U.'

'I can spell, Hilda.'

Whenever she considered the possibility of Harry leaving her, she panicked. She expressed her doubt and fear in oblique ways. 'It really is terrifying,' she said to him one evening.

'What is?'

'One single little day might change everything. I could be run over. Extinguished.'

He laughed. 'I don't think it's a question of extinction.'

'How do you know?'

Harry stayed on the track of Asher Ruppta, not knowing where it might lead. He decided to approach him directly, and to seek an interview with him. He telephoned Julie Armitage; he knew all about her from Hilda's descriptions but, fortunately, he had never met her. That would have been a complication. He told her that he was writing a profile of her employer; she seemed strangely excited, and promised to phone him. He believed that he could hear the rustle of a crisps packet as she spoke to him.

On the following day he received a telephone call from Ruppta himself. 'I do not give interviews,' he told Harry. 'I keep silent. If I am silent, then I am not disturbed. Good day to you, sir.'

'I just had a few questions.'

'Alas, I do not know any answers.'

'There were some planning permissions – '

'It would be better if you did not come too close, Mr Hanway. You have an interesting name, by the way.'

He found out that Ruppta owned a large mansion on the corner of a quiet avenue in Highgate, and he drove there one evening, curious to see if he entertained any visitors. The property was protected by iron railings above a brick wall, and there was a large security gate in front of a gravel drive. He parked close by, and waited. It was a quiet late-summer evening in the leafy street, and Harry wound down the window to enjoy the perfume of the luxuriant trees and hedges. On an evening such as this, all London seemed to be still. Then he heard the unmistakable clicking of high heels. A woman was walking quickly along the street. She stopped by the security gate, and looked up nervously at the house. Then she pressed a bell. Harry realised, after a moment's incomprehension, that it was his mother.

'Hello?' Harry recognised Ruppta's voice.

'It's Sally.'

A buzzer sounded, and the gate swung open.

Harry sat in the car, staring straight ahead but seeing nothing. He could not move, or think. He knew that he should drive away, but he had not the strength to turn the key. What was she doing there? Was she still in her own old business? What had Ruppta said to him? You have an interesting name. Ruppta had not threatened him, but he had laid down a warning. Harry now realised that there would be an unspoken pact between them. He would no longer pursue his investigation of Asher Ruppta.

Harry and Guinevere met for the third time in Fountain Court, part of the gardens of the Inner Temple where a small fountain played into a pond fringed with trees.

'I don't know anything about you,' she said.

'What is there to know? I'm twenty-one and I'm single.'

'What? Harry Hanway? No girlfriend?'

'I do know a girl, but we're not really close.' The light of the water gleamed in his eyes. 'Actually I don't see her that often.'

'You never mention your parents.'

'I don't have any.'

'Oh.'

'They were killed. In a car crash.'

'That's a terrible thing.'

'I don't really like to talk about it.'

'Do you have any brothers or sisters?'

'No. Just me. Only me.' Then he leaned over and kissed her.

They continued to meet at Fountain Court. 'I think you're very ambitious,' she said to him one afternoon.

'How can you tell?'

'The way you carry yourself. The way you dress. When you took me to that restaurant last night, you looked at the menu for a moment and then made up your mind. You're impatient, too.'

'I'm sorry.'

'No. I like it. You know what you want.'

'I know what I like.' He kissed her on the cheek.

'You talk quickly, too.'

'Perhaps I have a lot to say. How is Mrs Byrne, by the way?'

'She says she is very poorly. My boss is thinking of taking the children into care.'

'Care? Is that the right word? Oh look. There's a squirrel.'

'There's a change in the air about you,' Hilda told him.

'What on earth does that mean?'

'I don't know. But I feel it. I see it.'

'Why are you trembling?'

'I just am.'

'Are you not hungry?'

'I wouldn't mind if I never ate another thing.'

'What is the matter with you, Hilda?'

'You are the matter, Harry. I think that everything is going to be different.' He looked away from her briefly, as if something had caught his eye in the corner of the room.

'What if I were to get sick?' she asked him on another occasion. 'Would you look after me?'

'Of course.'

'No, you wouldn't. You would tell me, ever so nicely, that it was *my* problem and that you had other things on your mind. Then you would creep away, but not before blowing me a great big kiss from the door.'

'Honestly, Hilda, I just can't *win* with you.'

'Oh but you have won. And you know it.'

As she hugged him one evening she smelled some other perfume on the lapel of his jacket. She held onto him, clinging for life. 'Now what is it?' he asked her. She broke down in tears. 'What *is* it?'

'You know what it is.'

Gently he disengaged himself from her, and left the flat.

Hilda sat down, trying to steady herself with the arm of the chair. Some music started playing in the flat next door, and the refrain of the song rang through her head after the music had stopped. 'It's all about your eyes. They hypnotise.' Slowly she got to her feet, put on her coat, and opened the door of the flat. As she left she heard a child crying in another room, and she realised that she was still crying too. It had been raining, and the pavement shone with the reflected light of the street lamps. The autumn had arrived two or three days before, with a sudden chill in the air. 'The Americans,' she said to herself, 'call it fall.' As she walked towards Portobello it began to rain again, a slow and fitful shower, but she went on bare-headed without noticing it. Two days later she knocked on the door of the ice-cream van by the beach at Southend. 'I missed the Raspberry Wriggle,' she said.

IX

A cat may look

'SEVENTEEN HOURS of supervision?'

'*Mea culpa*. But I *do* have to admit that I am a trifle *squashed* by the end of term.'

Daniel Hanway, in the middle of dinner, was listening to a conversation between History and Biology at the high table. After completing his doctorate, he had been elected a junior fellow and deputy supervisor in English at his college.

Classics now joined the conversation. 'I trust that you acknowledge that it is your job.'

'I would like to say that it is part of my *job*, as you put it.'

'But I put it so well.'

History was short, with a slightly hooked nose, and a mass of fuzzy hair. He looked as if he had experienced an electric shock. Biology was bushy-haired, bushy-bearded and bushy-eyebrowed; he chortled rather than laughed. Classics was more saturnine; he wore a brown corduroy jacket, brown corduroy trousers, a green tie and white shirt. He had several other ties, jackets and trousers of the same colours so that he could remain in costume for his students.

Mathematics and Philosophy were arguing about the depth of nuclear bunkers. Philosophy 'hazarded a guess' at seventy feet, at which Mathematics smiled politely, if mockingly. 'Fifty feet?'

'Oh no.'

'Thirty feet?'

'No, no. The figures are quite wrong. Absurdly so, if I may say so.'

'But wouldn't I be *dead* otherwise?'

'No, not dead at all. Far from it. Very much alive. You need only dig thirty-six inches. The radiation is blown away.'

History and Biology had moved on. 'Oh these skinheads are absolutely ancient. They resemble the Mohocks of the eighteenth century. As Professor Leavis said —'

'*Dr* Leavis.'

'The *mobile vulgus* are always with us. What does our colleague from wildest London think of the *vulgus*?' History addressed the question to Daniel, whose origins in Camden Town were already well known.

'*Odi profanum vulgus*,' he replied, '*et arceo*.'

'Oh really? Where did you pick up your Horace?'

'He has been a good friend of mine for years.'

'Is that so? But do you really despise the crowd?'

'I despise anyone who cannot think for himself.'

'So you admire Oswald Mosley?'

'I know,' Classics said, 'let's look up Mosley in *Who's Who*.'

On returning to his rooms after dinner, Daniel continued his letter to his old schoolfriend Peter Palmer. Palmer had been appointed a junior lecturer in history at Durham University, and they corresponded now on their respective roles. Long-distance telephone calls were so expensive.

'Yesterday,' Daniel wrote, 'the English faculty met for the first time this term. When I say met I mean *collided*. Someone is teaching structuralism. Someone else is teaching Marxism. And then someone else is teaching old-fashioned lit crit. Did you ever hear of Lionel Manning? He wrote a book years ago on George Eliot. Rubbish, actually. But he's supposed to be an authority. Whatever *that* means. He considers himself to be a wit, but he just says absurd things in a high-pitched voice. "The French don't think," he said to me, apropos of some existentialist nonsense he had been discussing. "The English *can't* think. That is why they produce very good novelists." You get the general idea. He also has bad breath.

'You must have heard of Reginald Pearsall. He of the polo-necked sweater and black leather jacket. He has a face like a skull and when he smiles it is positively revolting. Very rigorous. Very low church. He goes on about moral belief and moral certitude. His favourite phrase is "what, precisely, do you mean by . . . ?" He adores George Orwell. A great bore, in other words.

'I have some younger colleagues. Dominic Tennyson likes to be called Dave. His surname is suspect, too. Could he have changed it by deed poll? He has just published, in *The Journal of English Literary Studies*, an article entitled "The State of Jacobean Coinage with Relation to the Plays of Philip Massinger". I'm not making it up. He has a deadly rival in Jeremy Jones. Now Jones has published an essay in some other journal. "The Use of the Term 'Almighty' in Eighteenth-Century Sermons." What is the *matter* with these people?

'And then there's the poet. Paul Wilkin. Remember him?'

Paul Wilkin had enjoyed a modest success several years before. He had published his first book while in his twenties, where it had been acclaimed by the usual poetry reviewers as 'a startlingly original voice' and 'an impressive debut'. On the publication of the second volume, Wilkin was described as 'one of the leaders of his generation'. But then of course there came along other young poets, who were reviewed in equally trite and effusive terms. There was never any shortage of praise for first or even second books of poetry. Now in his forties, Wilkin was an envious and distrustful man.

He had been published once by the famous firm of Connaught & Douglas, before, as he put it, 'moving on' to a smaller publisher; yet he had remained a guest at their annual parties for the last fifteen years. So he spoke fondly of 'Jack' Priestley, of 'Willie' Maugham and of 'Wystan'. Of his contemporaries, however, he was scathing and dismissive. He scanned the literary pages of the newspapers and magazines for any mention of his name, and realised soon enough that these references were becoming more and more infrequent. He had a long thin face, and long untidy hair; his mouth was thin and small; his chin was weak, and was emphasised by a narrow moustache.

At their first meeting Daniel Hanway had professed admiration for Wilkin's poetry. In truth he regarded it as no more than adequate, and on occasions old-fashioned and mediocre. But Wilkin had been delighted by Daniel's enthusiasm. Immediately he saw in him a young academic of great promise; in the future, perhaps, he might become influential. He might even be persuaded to write a book about the poetry of Paul Wilkin.

So Wilkin became very friendly with Daniel. He invited the young man to tea in his rooms, and then eventually to dinner at his house. Wilkin lived with his wife Phyllis, a middle-aged philologist, in a semi-detached house close to the railway station. They had two Persian cats, and the house smelled of damp and pet food. Mrs Wilkin was a timid and bedraggled woman who hardly spoke at all, but who seemed to look reproachfully at Daniel as she served him small portions of unappetising food.

Wilkin himself hardly stopped talking. He had a flat expressionless voice, but it had a rasping note when he became angry. He was in turn boastful and querulous, complaining about a certain 'bastard' of a reviewer or 'prick' of a poet. His conversation settled on his own triumphs and tribulations, with reference to the prizes he had won or the magazines in which he had been published. The literary world, in his conversation, seemed to Daniel to be a vast boxing ring in which 'contenders' and 'young pretenders' vied for mastery. There were 'heavyweights' and 'lightweights'; it was a world in which intense rivalries, and enmities, could develop. Somebody had been given a 'thrashing' in the *Observer*, while someone else had been 'put down' by *The Listener*.

'I settled my account with Hunt,' Wilkin had said to him. He almost spat out the name. 'He went for me in the Staggers –' This was the name, among the literati, for the *New Statesman*. 'He tried to demolish me. But I was still standing. Then lo and behold, a book of his essays was published last month. Can you imagine the conceit of it? Collecting your own articles? Anyway as a critic he is complete crap. Complete. So I just pointed out his mistakes. Just left it at that. Did you see the piece in the *Journal*?' Daniel nodded, although in fact he never read that newspaper. 'I made short work of him, I must say. He can't write. He simply can't write. I saw him off.'

'When did he review your book?' Daniel asked him.

'Oh, three or four years ago.'

'Graham Maland?' he said to Daniel on another evening. 'I wouldn't trust him as far as I can spit.' Graham Maland was a young novelist who had published three novels within the space of five years, all of them widely praised and admired. Wilkin did not reserve his animosity only for his fellow poets. 'Have you ever seen him?' Daniel shook his head. 'He's a fat little pudding. Full of suet. And what a shit. I happen to know that he got a ten-thousand-pound advance for his next novel. Ten thousand pounds! It's ridiculous. Anyway, there's a rumour going around that he's a plagiarist. Someone sent the manuscript of a novel to him, and he just copied the plot. That's what people are saying. And I tell you what. I'm sure he's queer.'

Daniel still went to see Sparkler in London, where he lived in a small flat on the same terraced street that Harry and

Guinevere Flaxman had once visited. 'Would you like to go to a queer pub, Dan?' he asked him one evening.

'In Limehouse?'

'No. Across the water. We'll swim.'

It was crowded and noisy. They went up to the bar where two middle-aged men were standing, identically dressed in dark slacks and scarlet blouses; both had a small scarf tied around the neck. 'I'm Pooky,' one of them said, 'and she's Spooky.' They were heavily made-up, but no amount of powder or mascara could conceal the years of humiliation and panic.

Daniel looked down the other side of the bar. A young man, wearing a black leather jacket, was talking over his shoulder to someone whom Daniel could not see. 'If you come near me one more time, you bastard,' the young man was saying in an off-hand manner, 'I'm going to break all of your fingers.'

'That one over there?' Spooky was talking to Sparkler. 'Oh she's been around for *years*. Her trousers are so tight you can see her piles.'

'He's got a boner.'

'Everyone gets a boner in here. You should go into the gents.'

'Who's your thin friend?' Pooky asked Sparkler.

'Dan.'

'Danny Boy. Oh Danny Boy, the pipes, the pipes are calling.' Pooky had a pleasant baritone voice. 'Can I hold up your umbrella, Danny?' Daniel looked perplexed. 'It's just a *camp*. What do you do, Danny Boy?'

'I'm a teacher.'

'Ooh, Miss Comprehensive. Do you fancy chicken?'

'Under-age boys,' Sparkler told him.

'No. I don't.'

'No harm in asking. A *cat* may look at a *queen*. And I know what you do, Sparkie. I've heard all about you. From a certain older gentleman.'

'Oh yes? Who?'

116

'He is known to us as the bony queen of nowhere.'

'I know exactly who you mean.'

'Oh my gawd.' Spooky raised a glass to his lips. 'Here she is.' An old man, wearing a tweed suit and red jumper, was approaching them. 'Good evening, cunt face.'

'Hello, pussies.' He had a distinguished, if slightly fruity, voice. 'Good evening, Sparkie boy.'

'Evening, major.'

The major's rheumy eyes travelled in Daniel's direction. 'Who is this one?'

'A friend.'

'A friend? Oh well done, Sparkler. Have a banana.' It was clear that the major believed Daniel to be more a customer than a friend. 'Anyone seen Tony Cointreau?'

'Over there.' Spooky nodded in the general direction of the dance floor. 'Looking for trade.'

Tony Cointreau was wearing a square pork-pie hat made out of leather, a loose-fitting shirt and torn jeans embroidered with stars. He never stopped moving, swivelling his hips, tapping his feet, half-turning. 'That young man,' the major said, 'gave me crabs.'

'You shouldn't be sleeping with rent, you old cunt. Apologies, Sparkler.'

'No offence. No offence.'

'But at my age −'

'At your age you should be dead.'

Tony Cointreau came over to them. 'More old queens than in Westminster Abbey.' The remark was ignored. It had been made before. 'Whose round is it?'

'Yours, you silly slut.'

'Do you know what I fancy?' Pooky asked no one in particular. 'A nice bit of black cock.'

The major turned round from the bar. 'Yum yum. Sloppy seconds for me, please.'

Two men were kissing in a corner, inviting looks of disapproval or envy. The whole darkly lit space was filled with looks, glimpses, sneaks, peeps, glances, winks, nudges, touches, strokes, nods interspersed with grins and smiles. The air was filled with the smell of beer and leather and cigarettes. Daniel enjoyed his time with Sparkler.

'Why not come to a party in London?' Wilkin was sitting with Daniel in the cafeteria of the English Faculty. 'I can't promise you'll enjoy it. But you may meet some interesting people. It's the annual bash of Connaught & Douglas.' Daniel accepted the invitation readily enough. He was intrigued by the prospect of seeing what Wilkin called 'the literary mob'. 'I'll tell you what,' Wilkin told him the following morning. 'We'll have lunch with some chums first. They always meet on Fridays.' Daniel then learned that there was a lunch club of young writers and journalists known as the Ancient Druids after the public house in which they met.

They travelled together on the train to London. 'Did you know,' Wilkin said, slapping his leg with his hand, 'that Jemimah Slater is in trouble for plagiarism? She wrote an article for *Eighteenth Century Studies* on a possible source for *The Rape of the Lock*. It turns out that she got it all from a post-graduate thesis she was supervising. It couldn't happen to a nicer girl, could it?'

'Will she be suspended?'

'Oh no. She'll get away with it. It will be hushed up. It always is. That's the way they operate.'

'*They*?'

'Did you see that piece on Tom Eliot by Gardiner? Gardiner gave me a good review once. Fine critic.'

By the time they arrived at Liverpool Street Daniel was exhausted.

They took the underground to Tottenham Court Road;

from there it was a short walk to the Ancient Druids in Poland Street. They entered the pub and walked up a steep staircase to a small dining room on the first floor. Already sitting at the table was a burly young man introduced to Daniel as Denis Davis. He was an American or Canadian (Daniel did not know which) who had come to London to earn his living as a poet and literary journalist. He greeted Wilkin warily, and looked with suspicion on Daniel. 'You Cambridge types scare the shit out of me,' he said cheerfully. 'You are so moral. So analytical. Frank Leavis still rules. Is that right?'

'I am not a Cambridge type,' Wilkin replied. 'I happen to teach there. That's all. And Dr Leavis has retired.'

Then there entered the room a young man with round spectacles, and a diminutive moustache. Wilkin introduced him to Daniel as Clive Rentoul, who specialised in interviews for the arts and books sections of the *Globe*. Both Davis and Rentoul were wearing turtle-necked sweaters. Daniel began to regret his suit, white shirt and tie.

The next arrival was Virginia Crossley, a young novelist who had been at Oxford with Clive Rentoul. She seemed to Daniel to be shy but not at all ill at ease; she observed intently everyone around her. The last to arrive was Damian Etheridge, announced to Daniel as the literary editor of the *Chronicle*. He sat next to Daniel at the table. 'Daniel Hanway,' he said. 'I've heard of you.'

'You have?' Daniel was flattered.

'And I know another Hanway. I wonder if you are related.'

'Who is it?'

'Harry Hanway. Our deputy editor.'

'He's my brother.'

'Oh is he? Your brother is doing very well. He is about to marry the proprietor's daughter.'

It was Daniel's turn to be surprised. 'Is that so?' He had

not forgotten meeting Hilda Nugent with Harry in the Camden park, four or five years before.

'And she's the only child. If you know what I mean.' He rubbed his thumb and forefinger together.

'Graham Maland?' Clive Rentoul was saying in an incredulous tone. 'A marginal figure. A Little Englander. He's not a serious writer.'

'The serious writers,' Denis Davis said, 'are Jo Heller and Saul Bellow. Maybe Mailer. They're the heavyweights. Saul is superb. And Jerry of course.'

'Jerry Lewis?' Crossley asked him in what she thought was an ironic manner.

'Jerry Salinger. Raise high the roofbeam, carpenters. Great steal from Sappho.' Daniel had no idea what he was talking about; he suspected that Denis Davis had none, either. 'The Americans are the future. I want to say —'

'Oh,' Rentoul said, 'What do you *want* to say?'

'Have you ever thought of reviewing?' Damian Etheridge asked Daniel. 'I'm always looking for new talent for the book pages.'

'I would be happy to try. I don't know if I would be any good at it —'

'Nothing to it. I'll send you some new novels. Have a go at them.'

'You're very pleased with yourself, aren't you?' Virginia Crossley was leaning towards Damian Etheridge.

'I don't think so, Virginia.'

'Why are you giving novels to someone you have just met? Excuse me, I think you should show a little more respect for fiction.'

'Respect?'

The others sensed the beginning of an argument, and looked uneasily towards Virginia and Damian. 'And you review five or six at a time. As if they were tins of baked beans.'

'There are just so many of them.'

'I waved a flag,' Denis Davis said to her, 'when I read your piece in the *Standard*.'

This seemed to mollify her. 'The one about new fiction?'

'When you said that in history you can make things up, but in fiction you have to tell the truth.'

She laughed at her own remark, as if she were hearing it for the first time. 'Well, that is the case.' It occurred to Daniel that her apparent shyness was actually slyness – and that she had a high opinion of herself. Her voice had a slight rasp, a metallic quality that was oddly intimidating. 'At least,' she added, 'I take fiction seriously.' She looked at Damian Etheridge.

'I bet you take everything seriously,' he said.

'And what is wrong with that?'

'Nothing. Nothing at all.' A few minutes later he whispered to Daniel, 'That's what's wrong with her books.'

'Wrong?'

'They're very heavy. Teenage suicides. Back-street abortions.' She heard the word 'abortions' and glared at him. 'As I was saying,' he added in a louder voice. 'The French *nouveau roman* is doing very well here. In critical circles.'

Daniel could hear Rentoul's voice in conversation with someone else. 'You *must* have come across totalism. It comes out of situationism. Have you read Derrida, by the way? You simply *must*.'

'I've tried. I don't understand a word of it. I prefer Heidegger.'

'Oh that's very old hat. All that *Dasein* business. A real German bore.'

'I've just turned in,' Davis was saying, 'a piece on Jimmy Baldwin.' Daniel had never heard the phrase 'turned in' before, but he assumed it was of common currency.

They carried on drinking into the late afternoon, their

voices getting louder and their conversation more animated. They were arguing about the books pages of the various newspapers and periodicals – which had the best contributors, which chose the most interesting books. Clive Rentoul was complaining about the favourable treatment given by the *Observer* to the poetry of Sylvia Plath, Thom Gunn and Ted Hughes whom he denounced as the 'Cambridge versifiers'. Wilkin had nothing to say in their defence, of course, but he objected to Rentoul's description.

It was time to attend the party at Connaught & Douglas. The offices of the publishing house were in New Bond Street. So they crammed into a taxi, excited by their sudden physical proximity, and made their way through central London. In this company it seemed to Daniel to become an unfamiliar city, brighter and more colourful than the one he had known as a youth. It had become a place of promise as well as of pleasure. When they arrived at their destination they all clambered out of the cab, leaving Daniel to pay the fare.

The party was held in the board room and chairman's office of the company, taking up the first floor of a late-eighteenth-century house. Wilkin immediately went up to a tall, doleful man who did not seem particularly friendly towards him. Wilkin beckoned Daniel over. 'This is Max Sitwell,' he said. 'Max works on the *Sunday Times.*'

'Daniel Hanway.'

'Are you a poet, too?'

'Far from it. I teach.'

'At Cambridge?' Daniel nodded. 'I was at Cambridge. Caius. A million years ago. I hated it.'

'I don't think,' Daniel replied, 'that it has changed much.'

'Oh look,' Wilkin said, 'there's Graham.' He went over to a portly young man, wearing large horn-rimmed spectacles, whom Daniel recognised to be Graham Maland. With a nod to the doleful man Daniel joined the two of them. Clive Rentoul came over, too. 'I loved the last novel,' Wilkin was saying to Maland. 'Superb.'

'My favourite character,' Rentoul said, apparently laughing at the memory, 'was the taxidermist. Hilarious.'

Daniel noticed that their appreciation of Maland's work had risen very quickly. Maland seemed embarrassed by their compliments, as if he suspected them of not being quite real. 'That's very kind of you,' he said. 'How about you, Paul? Are you publishing another volume?'

'Not yet. Not yet. I'm waiting for the right time.'

Maland quickly turned away and introduced himself to Daniel Hanway. Daniel was now quite drunk, and he was amused at the self-composure with which he greeted the famous young novelist. In other circumstances he might have searched for something to talk about. 'I wouldn't necessarily believe,' he confided in Maland, 'everything that they say.' Later he would not remember using those words.

'I don't.' Maland smiled. 'I don't believe any of it.'

Daniel felt relieved and reassured by this answer, as if a whole complex of problems had been resolved. He joined another group that included Damian Etheridge. 'I do think that Benny Hill is the true successor to Puck,' someone was saying.

'Do you? What an interesting point. But surely he is Falstaff? And Hancock is Hamlet.'

'Perfect.'

He then found himself in a group around a television journalist who had just published his memoirs. He was a man in late middle age but he was glossy, perfectly preserved, with a shine on his skin and a shine on his suit. Daniel noticed that the others gazed towards him, as if some source of enchantment was to be found in the glowing cheeks and forehead. He did not appear on television. Television appeared on him. Despite his modest stature he was larger and more capacious than those around him. But then it seemed to Daniel that some kind of bright liquid was flowing down his face and falling onto the ground. He was beginning to dissolve.

Daniel overheard conversations. 'Oh the *Spectator*. Terrible circulation. Shadow of its former self under Lawson. Gale has just appointed some teenage literary editor. Ridiculous. Think of all the perfectly good literary journalists there are.'

'The opera was so − so Shakespearean.'

'Tremendous fun.'

'There was a dog in it.'

'I thought the dog was *marvellous*.'

Then Daniel dropped his glass.

He found himself leaning against a wall on the pavement outside; he was smoking a cigarette which (had he known it) he had begged from a passer-by. He was swaying, with half-opened eyes, and was in danger of toppling forward into the street. Then someone put an arm around his shoulder. 'Are you all right, Danny boy?' It was Sparkler.

X

That's the way to do it

SAM HANWAY had become Asher Ruppta's 'odd-job boy', as Ruppta called him, expected to perform various tasks from visiting the bank to sorting out the diverse files created by the business. He spent much of the time with Julie Armitage in a small back office, where every morning he would find an offering of food on his desk – a ginger biscuit, a packet of nuts, a sausage roll, a pork pie, a bar of Bounty. He felt like a pet rabbit. Soon Julie would be stroking him.

He was often asked to collect the rent from Asher Ruppta's various properties. Julie Armitage used to commiserate with him, for what she considered to be an unenviable task, but in fact Sam felt no awkwardness or embarrassment as he went from door to door with his rent book. He looked forward to the opportunity of talking to people, of learning about their problems, of hearing their complaints. He took an almost aesthetic interest in speculating about the truthfulness of those whom he interviewed. He would speak to them in a slow and steady voice; he was infinitely patient with them, but he was determined. He could wear down the most spirited or most volatile of the tenants with his politeness. He had an air of remoteness about him, also, as if he were not quite sure what he was doing in any particular place. He looked as if he might ascend into the sky at any moment. His eyes were pale, lending his face an air of placidity and calmness.

He also liked talking to Asher Ruppta: Ruppta would sometimes break off from business and, stretched out in his chair with his hands behind his head, he would tell Sam about his childhood on the island of the Celebes Sea. He would tell him stories of creatures of shifting shape that lived in swamps or marshes, of ghost birds that could be heard but never seen, of spirits that waited for the living in the shadow of barns or old buildings. His face then seemed to Sam to be set in a more cruel and ferocious look than the pliancy and passivity of his customary expression. On Ruppta's island each dwelling had its own familiar soul, to whom offerings were made at dawn.

One evening Ruppta told Sam the story of the boy who became a tree. It began when his palms started to itch; he scratched and scratched, but the itching would not stop. Then the tips of his fingers began to tingle, and he began to tap them relentlessly on the crude wooden table in his small house. He woke one morning to find two fingers of his right hand covered in warts or growths, so strong and tough that they looked as if they were made of horn. He could not cut them with a knife, and when he tried to tear them away from his flesh the pain stopped him. After two or three weeks, the fingers of both hands were covered with these strange growths. The local doctor was baffled by the symptoms; he gave the boy some ointment, made from hyena fat, but it had no effect. Then the boy's mother took him to the wise woman of the district. She took one look at his warts, and then turned away. Already the woody warts had covered the skin up to his wrists; they were of mottled texture, and dark brown in hue. They resembled the bark of a tree. The wise woman told the boy's mother

126

that there was nothing to be done, but that he would not die. It was a disease, she said, that came from the forest. There had been stories of it over many generations. It had no name.

It was at this time that the boy began to sense a heaviness in his legs. There were small bulbous lumps swelling on the soles of his feet, and his toes were beginning to sprout the same dark wart-like growths. The layers of wood had also become thicker and harder upon his hands, and soon began to move upwards along his arms. One morning he saw some ants crawling among the layers; it seems that they had found something sweet to eat.

The growths had soon covered his feet, and were moving up his legs; he noticed that twigs and small branches were growing where his toes had once been. When he tried to walk, there was a soft scraping across the floor. Patches of green mould formed on the bark along his arms and, if he scraped them, pieces of the wood would become detached and fall away. He called out, day and night, '*Pahintuin! Pahintuin!*' Make it stop! Make it stop!

By now the bark had come up to his chest, and wooden growths had reached the back of his neck. He felt them moving onto his scalp and into his hair. Then he felt flecks of wood within his eyelashes. He sensed that there were little pieces of wood underneath the skin of his face. He was now helpless. He lay upon the ground outside his little house, where his mother fed him. He could no longer move, since the tendrils coming from his body had fastened themselves into the earth.

Eventually the people of the village could bear it no longer. He was an abomination. Against the protestations of his mother, and of his younger brother, they dragged the boy into the forest and left him there among the trees. He did not die. He seemed to find some nourishment within himself, and the frequent rains quenched his thirst. Eventually the bark covered his eyes, and his limbs were entirely engulfed in its mantle. It is also possible that certain roots slowly penetrated his skull and somehow changed the nature of his brain. His mouth was the last human trace of him, but that turned into what looked like a knot of wood. The boy now resembled a fallen tree of gnarled or rotting bark, a haven for small insects. The birds alighted upon it, and pecked at grubs or larvae.

The boy's mother visited the forest every day, and sat beside what was now no more than a fallen log. She stroked the green moss that had grown across its bark, and passed her hands slowly over the rotting wood. It smelled now of vegetable decay. She was sure, sometimes, that she felt a sensation of warmth. How did Asher Ruppta know this? He was the boy's younger brother.

'The Byrnes are very troubling to me,' Ruppta said to Sam one morning. 'They are never paying their rents. They must be taught a lesson.'

Sam visited Mrs Byrne on the following day. 'I need the housing benefit for *him*.' She nodded towards the closed door of the bedroom. She offered two or three pound notes. 'For the sake of the children, sir. Look at them. Can't you see their poor pale faces?'

Reluctantly Sam accepted the money, and noted down the amount still owed.

'God bless you, sir. I'll pay it all back to you. I'm expecting a parcel from Belfast.' She stared at the closed door. 'He had one of his fits last night. I had to sit on him. My own health is terrible poor.' The three children were eating bread with Marmite, their lips and cheeks smeared with the brown paste.

After the unsatisfactory interview with Mrs Byrne, Sam walked up the next flight of stairs and knocked on the door of the flat immediately above. The tenant knew Sam's touch, and the door was flung open. 'Come on in, Sammy boy. Time for daylight robbery, is it? Smash and grab? You should wear a hood and mask.' It was Sparkler.

Sparkler had been a tenant in Britannia Street for four years. He had always lived in this part of London, and he relished the anonymity associated with it. But he enjoyed the weekly visits of Sam with his rent book. 'Now then, Sammy boy,' he said, 'cup of char? Soak your powerful mind in tea.'

As they sat together Sam told Sparkler stories about the other tenants whom he visited. He called him Spark. 'Well, Spark,' he said on this afternoon, 'the Robertsons have vanished. Everything has gone. Bed. All the furniture.'

'As clean as a whistle, is it?'

'A bone picked clean,' Sam replied. 'Nothing left at all.'

'That is a very remarkable thing, Sammy. How did they manage to get away without making any noise at all?'

'The area is strange like that. Nothing ever seems to stick. Everything just fades away.'

'I know exactly what you mean, Sammy boy. The streets will swallow you up. They're misty. Like the Thames next door. It was tough in 1944.'

'What made you say that, Spark?'

'I was thinking of mist. And smoke. I was six at the time. There was this shelter. I hated it. Mum hated it, too. So we stopped going.'

'Wasn't that dangerous?'

'Oh yes. Of course. It was a big oblong room, with a wooden bench along each wall. There was a tin tacked to one corner, with a candle stuck in it. It smelled terrible of piss and vomit. It's gone now. At least I think it's gone. What if it were still there? Still smelling? It don't bear thinking about, do it?

'Boys like to explore, don't they?' Sam was silent for a moment. 'I used to go down into the ground.'

'Yes. Boys go where they are told not to go. I'm still that way. I *won't* do what I'm told. There was an underground bomb shelter on the common. A big one. Still there, I think. Its entrance was boarded up after the War, but I knew a way of wriggling through. There is always a way, you know. You just have to know how to look for it. There was rooms on either side. Do you believe in ghosts?' Sam nodded. 'Do you? Do you *really*?'

'I do.'

'This was the curious thing. I was lagging behind a friend of mine. His name will come to me in a minute. Keith Watson. I was creeping past one of them rooms, when I saw something out the corner of my eye. It was like a flickering light coming from inside. I went back and there — you'll never believe it, I know you won't — there was a garden. A lovely garden full of flowers. And in the middle was an old gentleman tending to it. It was only there for a moment. And then it faded away. I wasn't scared or anything. I was happy. But I never told Keith Watson.' Sam now smiled at the memory.

Sparkler and Daniel Hanway were sleeping in the same bed when they were woken by shrieks coming from the flat below. 'Smoke!' Sparkler shouted in alarm. He threw on a robe and rushed out into the hall. 'Call 999!' He rushed downstairs, where a fire was eating Mrs Byrne's front door. He kicked out at it, and one of the panels fell apart. 'Open it,' he shouted, 'open it!' Mrs Byrne had the presence of mind to unlatch it, and Sparkler rushed in. 'Get me some water,' he said. 'Let me get to the sink.' The flat was full of smoke, and he could not see the children. He soaked his robe and then draped it across the door. Some of the flames were extinguished. He performed the same manoeuvre three or four times until the door was merely smouldering. Sparkler flung open the windows to disperse the smoke hanging in the air. The children, in their pyjamas, were huddled in the kitchen; they did not cry, or speak, but stared solemnly at Sparkler. He went into the adjacent bedroom to check on Mr Byrne but, to his surprise, found no one. It looked as if Mrs Byrne was accusomed to sleep alone in the bed.

By the time the firemen had arrived, there was little to do except to secure the damaged door. They were intent, however, on finding out the cause of the sudden blaze. 'Do you have any idea what happened?' one of them asked Mrs Byrne. She shook her head, but then looked towards Sparkler. She knew better than to speak, and he understood her. Another fireman then discovered some burnt rags, smelling of paraffin. 'Do you have any enemies?'

'The poor Irish always have enemies.'

'Anyone in particular?'

'I don't think so. No.'

'Hooligans,' the fireman said. 'Yobs. There are some nasty gangs in this part of the world.'

Mrs Byrne went into the kitchen. 'All of you get dressed now. We're going to your Aunty Theresa.' Sparkler had followed her, and now she whispered to him. 'Lend me five pounds for a taxi?'

He went back upstairs, and borrowed the money from Daniel. He came back into bed a few minutes later, and embraced him. 'At least you're still nice and warm,' he said. 'Why didn't you come downstairs?'

'I was scared.'

'You're always scared.' Sparkler kissed him again. But he could not sleep. He lay in bed with his head propped up on a pillow. 'I wonder,' he said.

'Wonder what?'

'I wonder if Ruppta was trying to frighten them away.'

'Your landlord? That would be a dangerous thing to do.'

'He may be a dangerous man. I will have a word with Sam.'

'Sam?'

'He is Ruppta's collector. I don't know his last name. Everyone just calls him Sam.' Daniel stared up at the ceiling, glimmering in the dark room from the light of the street lamps outside. 'There was no Mr Byrne.' He told Daniel the story of Mrs Byrne's husband and his fits. 'But he wasn't there.'

'I suspect,' Daniel replied, 'that he hasn't been there for some time.'

'But she still picks up his social security.'

'She tells them that he is too ill to collect it himself.'

The next morning Mrs Byrne returned by herself, with two large shopping bags and a suitcase. Slowly, and with great care, she packed all the food stored in the kitchen cupboard; she folded the sheets and towels, putting the plates and cups between them. There was nothing else that belonged to her.

Sparkler came down to help her. 'I'll be all right,' she said. She seemed to him to be meek and uncomplaining, as if she had been expecting misfortune all along. 'I'll just be on my way,' she said. 'I won't keep you.'

'Is there anything I can do for you, Mrs Byrne?'

'Keep an eye out for Ruppta.'

Sam was surprised and shocked when he arrived to collect the rent on the following morning. He stared at the charred front door of Mrs Byrne's flat, knocked, rattled the handle, and, realising that there was no one inside, hurried up the stairs to Sparkler. Daniel was still staying with Sparkler in the little flat. Alarmed by Sam's knocking, he rushed into the bathroom and closed the door. He did not at first recognise Sam's voice.

'What's going on?' Sam asked Sparkler. 'What's happened?'

'Someone set fire to Mrs Byrne's door.'

'Whoever could have done such a thing?'

'I don't know, Sam.' He turned and looked out of the window. 'I have no idea. What do you think?'

'She never paid all of her rent.'

'You told me.'

'I explained this to Mr Ruppta. I explained that her husband was unemployed, and that she had three small children.'

'There is no husband.'

'What?'

'He didn't live there. But she's still collecting his social security.'

'Oh.' There was no expression in his voice.

'Tell me this. It may be important. What did Ruppta say?'

'He never said anything.'

'Is it possible, Sam —'

'That he wanted to scare them away? It is possible. Yes. And I will find out. I promise you.'

Sam was now feeling uncomfortable in the small room; he was perspiring, clutching the notebook in which he kept account of the rents. 'I can't believe that he would do such a thing.'

To Sparkler's surprise he then crouched down on the floor, bent forward, and seemed to be attempting a handstand. 'What are you doing, Sam?'

'I am going to stand on my head. It clears my brain. It helps me to think.' This is what he proceeded to do. He managed to balance gracefully upon his head, his arms outstretched upon the carpet. After a minute he relaxed his stance and brought himself gently to the floor before standing up. 'I know what to do now,' he said.

Daniel was astonished. He recognised his younger brother's

voice when he said 'I know what to do now'. He shrank
away from the door.

Julie Armitage had prepared a plate of small sandwiches for
Sam's return. 'Spam or fish paste?' she asked him as soon as
he came into the room.

'A bit of both.'

'Ooh.' She squealed in delight. '*Cheeky*.'

He knocked quietly on the door and entered Asher
Ruppta's inner office. Ruppta was sitting in his chair, looking
carefully at his hands. 'Mrs Byrne's front door has been set
on fire,' Sam said.

'Is that so? That is very unfortunate. Was anyone hurt?'

'No. But she left with the children straight after.' He stared
at Ruppta. 'I don't know how it could have happened.'

'Shall we call the police, Sam?'

Sam remembered the absent husband. 'I don't think so. We
need to find a new tenant.'

'We should really call the police.'

'They never do anything.'

'But the police protect us, Sam.'

'Too much trouble.'

'Well, if you say so.'

It seemed to Sam that his employer could not have instigated the arson. Why was he so eager to summon the police,
if he had been the guilty party? No, there was another cause
for the attack. He was reflecting on these things on his way
to his mother's house.

She greeted him with a kiss, and then folded back the
side of her hair with her hand. It was a gesture that he
remembered from childhood. 'And what have you been
doing?' she asked him.

'There was a fire in Britannia Street.'

'When?'

134

'A few nights ago.'

'Bad?'

'Not really. But one of the families left. They didn't feel safe, I suppose.' Then he told her about Mrs Byrne and the three children.

'Poor cow,' she said. 'I know what it's like. What number?'

'Twelve.'

'But that's where Sparkler —' She stopped, confused, and her face reddened.

'How do you know Sparkler?'

'Friend of a friend.'

'Friend of whose friend?'

'I know a man who knows him. Would you like a pot of tea?' She went out of the room for a moment. 'Mary will bring you one. Do you think Mr Ruppta is responsible for the fire?'

'I hope not.'

'He is a most unusual man. From what I have heard.'

'What have you heard, Mum?'

'Nothing in particular.' She seemed perplexed, almost worried. 'Where *is* that tea?' She went out and came back with a full pot.

When he returned to Camden that evening he found his father lying on his side upon the worn carpet. 'Thank God you're back,' he said, 'I can hardly breathe.' His voice was high and quavering. 'Someone crept up behind me and gave me a great thump. I can still see his shadow.'

Sam telephoned for an ambulance. 'Is it your heart, Dad?'

'I don't know. I don't think so. Your mother —'

They carried him on a stretcher into the ambulance, where they placed an oxygen mask over his mouth and nose; his forehead seemed to Sam to be suffused with a pale glow, or was it the brightness of the sweat against the skin? Philip

Hanway looked up at the roof of the vehicle, his eyes flickering and darting as if he were deep in prayer. When they arrived at the hospital he was content to be lifted and handled, willingly giving up the burden of his body to others. He was no longer responsible for it.

He was taken to intensive care, and then wheeled on a trolley to the operating theatre. Sam remained behind in the small ward, where a male nurse was smoothing the bed in which his father had been placed. 'The ambulance came within ten minutes,' Sam said. 'It was quick, considering the traffic.'

'Oh they can drive, those boys. I'm surprised they never kill anybody. Still, it's all in a good cause.'

'What are they doing to Dad?'

'I imagine that they are giving him an angiogram.'

'Angelogram?'

'They insert a small cardiac catheter in the vein of the leg. Just by the groin. They proceed along the vein, right up into the chambers of the heart, through the pericardium and the atrium, into the pulmonary veins and semi-lunar valve.' He recited this without much thought.

Sam grimaced. 'Will he be in pain?'

'I am told that veins have no feeling.'

Their conversation was interrupted by the arrival of another patient, a very large man perched on what in comparison seemed to be a very small trolley. He was followed by a young man and woman who seemed more distraught than he was. 'What is his name?' the male nurse asked them.

'We call him Uncle,' the young lady replied.

'We can't do that in a hospital, can we?'

'Benjamin. Rabbi Benjamin.'

'Benjamin.' The nurse leaned over him. 'Can you hear me, Benjamin.'

'He was so full of life. So full of words. Then he fell over, and was silent. He is a great man. A holy man.'

'Can you hear me, Benjamin?'

'Let me be.' His voice was low and powerful.

'I have to take some blood.'

'Don't touch me.'

'You need to be tested.'

'I need nothing. I need no one.'

'That's not strictly true, I'm afraid.' The nurse placed the syringe in his arm. 'That's good. That's lovely. Nice and smooth.' He turned to the two young relatives, who were looking on anxiously. 'Don't worry. I'm not going to drink it.'

When he had removed the syringe, and sealed it, he walked over to Sam. He whispered to him confidentially, in the high voice of Punch, 'That's the way to do it!' He went over to the relatives. 'Does he have to pass water, do you think?' He approached the bed. 'Do you need to spend a penny, Benjamin? Don't fret. We're used to it here. We would like you to use a bottle, Benjamin, if you can.' Once more he addressed the relatives. 'A lot of patients can't bring themselves to mention it. Not until it's too late. So I always raise the subject myself.' There came a groan from the bed. 'He's probably not urgent, though, is he?'

He left the ward with the syringe but returned a few minutes later and sat down beside Sam.

'How did you end up here?' Sam asked him.

'End up? That's a way of putting it, I suppose. Better than a prison or asylum, where a man of my talents might *end up*. But I'll tell you something. It's a horrible place at night. They say that suffering brings you wisdom. Understanding. Patience. Pain is supposed to purify the soul. It's all crap. Bollocks. I'm sick of hearing it. Suffering makes you weak. It makes you helpless. It leaves you at everyone's mercy. People you could spit on come to pity you. I've seen it. You are sick. They are healthy. They don't want to care for you. They want to triumph over you. Or they want something out of you. Gratitude. Love. A mention in the will.'

'That's not a very nice thing to say.'

'It's not a very nice world.'

A doctor came in, looked at Sam with a mild expression, and shook his head.

The three brothers sat side by side in the chapel of the crematorium, looking straight ahead. 'It's been a long time,' Harry said. 'You've put on weight, Sam. The way I see it is this. We can look back and weep, or we can look forward. When did you last see Dad, Daniel?'

'Six years ago, I think.'

'Precisely. The same with me. You only saw him, Sam, because you still live in the house. We weren't a family any more.'

They looked at the coffin as it slid slowly behind the curtain.

Their father looked back at them. He had no regrets now.

XI

Easily led

Now that Hilda Nugent had gone, leaving a scrawled note about Southend, Harry Hanway began to see Guinevere more frequently. He moved out of Notting Hill Gate, considering it now to be a seedy area, and rented a small flat in Walpole Street, off the King's Road and conveniently close to the Flaxman mansion in Cheyne Walk.

He met Sir Martin, quite by chance, at the corner of Tite Street. 'Hanway!' Flaxman yelled. He was wearing a dark overcoat and a black trilby, with a pair of brightly polished black shoes.

Harry was startled. He had been thinking of an appropriate present for Guinevere's twenty-fifth birthday, and had not come to a satisfactory conclusion. And there was her father waving and shouting at him from the other side of the street. Harry walked over to him. 'I'm delighted to see you, sir.'

'So you want to fuck my daughter, do you?'

'I wouldn't put it quite like that.'

'How *would* you put it? Shag? Penetrate? Deflower? Or none of the above?'

Harry tried to laugh. 'I'm very fond of Guinevere.'

'Ditto.'

'I respect her.'

'Well, don't go near her cunt then.' Sir Martin put his arm around Harry's shoulders. 'You know she's a virgin, don't you?' Harry made no response. 'And I insist that she remains that way until the day of her wedding. She isn't one of these London slags. Do you have a J. Arthur when you think about her?'

'Sorry?' He knew what Flaxman meant, but he wanted him to spell it out.

'J. Arthur Rank. Wank.'

'No. I don't.'

'I bet you don't think about her at all.' Harry really did not know how to respond to this. 'Come and walk with me back to the house. I like you well enough, Harry. You're a decent boy. And a good hack.' He clasped his arm with a very strong grip. 'I want you to do a favour for me. I want you to stick it to Pincher Solomon.' Solomon was the owner of a string of betting shops in South London; he was known as 'Pincher' because of his unorthodox ways of doing business. 'I happen to know that he is defrauding the Revenue. I just can't prove it.'

'So what —'

'Investigate him. Make him nervous. Get one of your financial people to drop a few hints.'

Harry knew that Sir Martin was bidding for a franchise in racecourse gambling. Pincher Solomon was obviously a competitor, and Sir Martin was willing to employ the resources of the *Chronicle* to blackmail or intimidate him. It would not have occurred to Harry to refuse his proprietor's request. It was his newspaper, after all. So now as deputy editor, without consulting the editor, he began a dossier on Pincher Solomon and asked one of the financial journalists to consult the records of Solomon at Companies House.

He met Guinevere now two or three evenings each week; they walked by the Thames in the direction of Lambeth, and ate in an Italian or Indian restaurant at the upper end of the King's Road. 'Your father has told me to be careful with you.'

'That's very good advice. For once.'

'Am I allowed to kiss you?'

'On the cheek. When we meet or part.'

'Can I hold your hand?'

'That is going too far.'

So they talked of other things. 'Why is English life so unbearable?' she asked him.

'What do you mean?'

'One of my clients is dying in agony because she can't get the right cancer treatment. And there's my mother going on about pearl *necklaces*. It's all so wrong. So –'

'Unfair?' In his childhood Harry had been surrounded by poor people, just a step away from destitution, and he had felt no pity for them.

'Worse than unfair. It's evil.'

'Have you told your father that?'

'He just smiles at me.'

'He's good at that.'

'You know,' she said to him on another evening as they sat in the Italian restaurant, 'there are a lot of prostitutes in Limehouse.'

'Oh really?'

'All they drink is tea.'

Harry shifted in his seat. 'Extraordinary.'

'Some of them go round to one of the flats in Britannia Street.'

'To a customer?'

'No. A friend. They call him Sparkler. I think he's queer. Sorry. Homosexual. Sparkler has lots of stories.'

'I bet.'

'That reminds me. Do you remember Mrs Byrne?'

'The one with the three children.'

'Sparkler told me that she had been scared out of her flat. Someone set fire to the front door.'

'Who?'

'That's what he wants to find out. He knows the neighbourhood very well. He suspects the landlord —'

'Asher Ruppta. I remember him.'

'But it could just be a street gang.' She had been picking at a seafood pizza. 'Who can tell? Who can know?' He leaned forward and kissed her on the cheek. 'That's not allowed. We are not meeting or parting.'

'I'm a very lucky person. Having you.'

'What do you mean — having me?'

'I mean, well —'

She really did not want her question to be answered. 'There's no such thing as luck. I don't believe there is, anyway.'

'You make your own?'

'Well, put it this way. You are charming.'

'Thank you.'

'You are confident. Yes. I think you have made your own luck. I don't know what drives you forward. Ambition, I suppose. I accept that.'

'I am ambitious for both of us, Guinevere. I love you.'

'I don't think you actually love me. I think you love the *idea* of me. I am the heiress. I am the only child.'

'Of course. Everyone knows *that*. But I'm the best person to guide you. You said that I was ambitious. But I am also realistic, Guinevere. Maybe that's why your father introduced us.'

Guinevere took him to a concert at the Albert Hall in the

following week. 'They say,' she told him, 'that music soothes the savage breast.'

'I don't think so.'

'Wait and see.'

'I feel sorry,' Harry said as they left the building after the performance, 'for those musicians.'

'What do you mean?'

'Once they wanted to stand out. I bet every single one of them wanted to be a famous violinist. Or whistler.'

'Flautist.'

'They all expected to be the best. What is the word?'

'Virtuoso.'

'Exactly. They wanted to excel. But they ended up as part of a crowd. They must feel depressed when they wake up in the morning.'

'I'm sure they enjoy making music together.'

'You don't understand the world.'

'I want a bit that's rare,' Sir Martin Flaxman said to his butler, staring at a haunch of cold roast beef. 'As if it's just been carved from the cow. Speaking of which, where is your mother?'

'She has a headache.' Guinevere was sitting opposite him at the dining-room table.

'Headache? That's a woman's way of saying fuck you. Isn't that right, Harry?'

Harry was sitting beside Guinevere. 'I wouldn't really know.'

'Is that so? Hark the vestal virgin sing. Are you keeping your promise to me?'

'Of course.'

'What promise?' Guinevere asked her father.

'None of your business.'

'I promised,' Harry told her, 'to get him some details on a rival company.'

'That's right. And I heard some good news yesterday. The old Jew has pulled out of the racing business.' He was referring to Pincher Solomon. 'That will teach him.' He took a thick slice of roast beef, and covered it with a mound of horseradish sauce. 'I like it hot, Harry,' he said, drooling slightly at the mouth. 'As hot as hell.' Then he put a boiled potato in his mouth, and swallowed it. Suddenly he burped. There was a scent of horseradish in the air. 'I'm going to get rid of Havers-Williams.' He was talking about the editor of the *Morning Chronicle*. 'He's a useless bastard. He mumbles.' He took another bite out of the beef and horseradish. 'I come from nothing, Harry. I'm a bastard. Did you know that?'

'I have heard.'

Flaxman laughed very loudly. 'No. A real bastard. Wrong side of the sheets. Do you know how that makes you feel? It makes you feel different. It makes you feel special. I made my first deal in the army. I sold military supplies to civilians. Does that shock you?' Harry shook his head. 'Well, it should do.' Flaxman swallowed another potato. 'I am telling you this because you are almost part of the family. Almost. But not quite.'

Guinevere suddenly spoke up. 'Let's put an end to this nonsense. Do you want to marry me, Harry?'

'Yes.'

'Daddy, will you sign on the dotted line?'

'You see what a romantic she is, Harry?'

Lady Flaxman entered the dining room. 'I warn you in advance, Martin,' she said to her husband, 'that my nerves are bad today. Good afternoon, Mr Hanway. What's all this about marriage?'

'I was telling Harry, Maud, that he is almost part of the family.'

'Why he should ever want to be part of this family is

beyond me. We are a frightful shower aren't we, Mr Hanway? Simply frightful.'

'He's after my money.'

'Do you see what I mean, Mr Hanway? There is no refinement here. No elegance.' Lady Flaxman was a tall, thin woman with a voice of the purest diction and a black dress of the most elegant cut. She wore her jewels as if she had inherited them. In fact she came from a family of small traders in Enfield. 'Are you sure you aren't making a most terrible mistake?'

'Oh no. I love Guinevere.'

'Love is a very small word.' Flaxman was sucking on a piece of fat. 'For a very small thing.'

'You see, Mr Hanway, my husband has no finesse. He is nature, red in tooth and claw.'

'I'm not the only one.'

With a pained smile she sat beside her husband. 'Is there any beef left?' Then she looked, slowly and sorrowfully, at Harry. 'Like a lamb to the slaughter,' she said.

'He is not being slaughtered, Mummy, he is getting married to me.'

'The married state is like a butcher's shop, dear. Blood on the floor. Everything. The works.' She toyed with a piece of potato. 'If there is to be a marriage,' she said, staring disapprovingly at her daughter, 'it must be somewhere rural and delightful. A medieval churchyard. Graveyard. Yew trees. Bells. That sort of thing.'

'As long as there is no confetti,' Guinevere replied.

'Aren't you supposed to tie an old boot to the car?' her father asked her. He was looking at his wife.

'We don't want anything sexual,' she said. 'My mother will be there.'

'The graveyard may come in handy.'

'Oh I really can't bear it. I haven't got the strength to fight you any more, Martin. Where is the horseradish?' Harry

145

handed her a cut-glass jar and its acccompanying silver spoon. She spread the contents delicately, and then began cutting up the meat in small squares. 'I presume, Guinevere, that you will be wearing white?'

'If you say so, Mother.'

'It is not what I say. It is what you may or may not have done.' Sir Martin laughed. 'It is not a laughing matter. A virgin bride is a wonderful thing. I should know. I was a virgin once. I was the cynosure of all eyes.' She popped a morsel into her mouth. 'I am very feminine, you see, Mr Hanway. I am my own worst enemy. I am easily led.' She glared at her husband. 'Not that anyone considers my feelings any more. I might as well be deaf and dumb. I might as well be blind. Like those poor mice.' Guinevere looked towards her father and raised her eyebrows. 'Of course,' Lady Flaxman announced to Harry, 'there's no question of children.'

'Mummy!'

'Guinevere is too frail. Too weak. It would kill her.'

Harry looked at his intended wife without any expression.

The wedding took place on a grey and overcast day. The ceremony in the Guards Chapel was, at Guinevere's request, very simple. But she wore a white bridal dress, and Harry had bought a dark morning suit. They smiled pleasantly at one another when the union was pronounced by the priest. It was in fact Sir Martin who cried, sobbing quietly as he stood beside his daughter. As the newly wed couple walked down the aisle one of Harry's colleagues remarked that he seemed very pleased with himself – 'As well he might,' he added in a whisper. Guinevere, on the other hand, had an expression of faint bewilderment.

By the time of the reception, in the Ritz Hotel just across the park, Sir Martin had recovered his composure. He had already decided that he wished to make a speech, and so a microphone had been set up in a corner of the large room in which the party was being held. The walls glittered with long mirrors, and the thick scarlet carpet glowed in the light. The sun shone through the high windows so that the chandeliers, with thousands of pieces of intricate glass, seemed to swim in the general brightness. It had been noticed by some of Harry's colleagues that this was entirely a Flaxman affair; none of Harry's family had appeared, and it was presumed that none had been invited. Did he in fact have a family at all? One suggested that he was a Barnardo's boy, while another speculated that the Hanway relatives were too poor or too uncouth to be shown.

'I stand here a happy man,' Sir Martin Flaxman was saying into the microphone. 'Almost as happy as Harry. He is the cat who gets the cream, isn't he? I never thought Guinevere would marry. I thought she would become a nun. Seriously. I hope for Harry's sake that she doesn't behave like one.' There were loud guffaws from some of the male guests. 'I wish you luck, Harry. You'll need it.'

'Really this is too much.' Lady Flaxman had turned to her elderly mother. 'He has no finesse. No style. No bearing.' Her mother suffered from severe tremors in the lower part of her face, and could scarcely get the glass of champagne to her lips. When she felt the rim on her teeth, however, she gulped it down greedily. She was about to reply. 'Shush!' her daughter told her. 'I need to listen to this.'

'I have an announcement to make,' her husband was saying. 'When I die – if I die – I intend to leave the business entirely in Guinevere's hands. I have watched her. I know her. She will make a good chairman of the board.'

'Jesus H. Christ. This is an absolute insult.' Lady Flaxman turned to her trembling mother. 'I have a much better business brain. Guinevere is a mere girl. Do say something, mother. Please.'

In the middle of the night, one month later, Harry was lying awake beside Guinevere; she was sleeping, although she was as always restlessly dreaming. He could not sleep; he was making intricate plans for the future, visualising every scene and scheming every move. So he remained alert. But then he saw something. He saw what seemed to be a structure of light rising from Guinevere's body and taking her shape. This silver outline then seemed to sit upright. It was taller than Guinevere, by a few inches, but it bore the impress of her features. Then it bowed down, apparently in sorrow, before disappearing.

XII

The goddess of wind

'I DON'T blame Harry for not inviting me to the wedding. I understand. I sympathise.' Daniel Hanway was writing to Peter Palmer. 'He wants to escape from his past. Including his family. I don't want to see him any more than he wants to see me. Other news. I have started writing fiction reviews for the *Chronicle*! The literary editor there is called Damian Etheridge. Very much a *journalist*. A bit stupid, actually, but friendly enough. He sends me notes with the books saying "Don't hold back" and "Lay down the law".

'I know you are going to say that I have always despised novels. This is true. I stopped reading them when they reached the twentieth century. The funny thing is that this is the best possible preparation for reviewing contemporary fiction. Most of it is just embarrassing. *Excruciating*. You have never seen such garbage. Yet of course the regular reviewers treat these so-called writers as if they were Tolstoy or Proust. If I see the phrase "an accomplished debut" or "a return to form" or "a magisterial performance" or "voice of his generation", I shall scream and scream until I'm sick.

'It actually makes me angry, although I admit that anger is an unworthy emotion. As you know I am the most

149

mild-mannered person imaginable. But put me behind a typewriter and I become a *fiend*. I like to go for the established names. Braine. Golding. Greene. What a lot of charlatans they are! And I get paid thirty pounds a review!'

Still, he was getting noticed. At literary parties, for which he often travelled to London, his name was becoming recognised. 'So you,' one writer said to him, 'are the *enfant terrible.*' He pronounced the French phrase exquisitely.

'I wouldn't say that.' As usual, Daniel was very modest.

'Oh I would.' There was a touch of contempt in his voice. 'You like to pick a fight, don't you?'

'I don't think so.'

'Why don't you do some serious reviewing?'

Daniel did not understand why he was so angry with him. Daniel discovered later that he had criticised a novel by one of his friends.

'You are making waves,' another writer said. 'Make sure that you don't go under.'

At Cambridge of course he was ready to dismiss his journalism as a matter of no consequence – if anyone had asked him about it. But his colleagues did not mention it. He knew very well that it was considered vulgar and even indecent to appear in the 'public prints'. Yet he had an advantage over his contemporaries in the English Faculty. He had been commissioned to write a book.

One of the editors at Connaught & Douglas, Aubrey Rackham, had invited him to lunch at The Tramp in Air Street. 'I have been keeping an eye on you,' Rackham said as they sat down at their table. He had a low rasping voice, at once affable and conspiratorial. 'You are terribly naughty in your reviews.' He always wore a bright red handkerchief in the breast pocket of his suits, and was known to his acquaintances as 'Hanky Panky'. 'Pure poison, dear. You are a wicked *witch*. I'll have a gin and It, please.' He nodded to the waiter, and then winked at Daniel. 'In this restaurant, they know what "It" is.' Daniel had no idea what he was talking about, but he laughed all the same. 'Bottoms up,' Rackham called out as the drink was placed in front of him. Daniel was then greeted with another expansive wink.

'Is there a book in you?' Rackham asked him after the first course was over.

'I beg your pardon?'

'Not literally, dear.' Rackham squealed with delight. 'You should be so lucky. I mean, do you think you could write a book?'

The idea had in fact often occurred to Daniel. There was, however, one obstacle to his ambition. He could never hit upon an appropriate subject.

'I admire your style, you see,' Rackham was saying. 'It just needs direction. Thrust.' He settled comfortably into his seat. 'A little bird told me that you are a cockney boy.'

'I was born in Camden Town.'

'Out of earshot of those silly bells. But you are a Londoner.'

'Oh yes.'

'I come from Devon originally. Home of old cows. Just up to lipstick level, darling.' A waiter was refilling his wine-glass. 'There is a book I would like you to think about. Can you guess what it is?' Daniel shook his head. 'The Writers of London.'

He was perplexed and a little disappointed. He had been expecting Rackham to mention an academic topic, perhaps a book of literary criticism, or a new edition of a celebrated classic. The writers of London had never been part of the university curriculum. 'London writers, or writers about London?'

'You can have it both ways, my dear. If you know what I mean.' Another wink. 'Look at that waiter. Straight out of Caravaggio.'

So a few weeks later, after Daniel had prepared a synopsis, he was commissioned to write the book. He tried casually to mention the fact to Paul Wilkin.

'What?' He looked incredulous. 'Who has commissioned you?'

'Rackham at Connaught & Douglas.'

'Hanky Panky? That old queen?'

'Is he?'

'*Is* he? Is the pope Catholic?' It was quite like him, Daniel thought, to use a vulgar phrase.

'How much advance are they giving you?'

'A thousand pounds.'

'A thousand pounds!' Wilkin tried unsuccessfully to conceal his envy and resentment. 'So what's it about?'

'The writers of London.'

'So it won't be a long book then.' Now he was sneering at him.

Daniel decided that he had seen quite enough of Wilkin for the time being. He invented an urgent meeting and walked away.

He visited Sparkler on the following Sunday. They kissed amicably when he arrived at the little flat in Britannia Street. 'I do believe,' Sparkler said, 'that you are looking well.'

Daniel laughed. 'How was I looking before?'

'You were looking like a piece of warm dripping. But now you look better. A few months ago —'

'Oh now you're going back to that drunken night at the party —'

'You was so drunk I could hardly see you.'

'In —'

'New Bond Street. Next to the hatters. Opposite the jewellers.'

'How do you know that?'

'Know? There is nothing about London I *don't* know. I'm

on first-name terms with the sparrows and very chummy with the pigeons. I'm like a black cab. I get about.'

They went that evening to the Spit and Sawdust, a public house close beside the river. It was a few yards down from the local police station, and so was patronised by many officers. But it had also become a haunt for Sparkler, who enjoyed their company; they knew him to be a petty thief and a part-time prostitute, but this was no reflection on his character. Two of them were sitting in the saloon bar when Sparkler and Daniel entered.

'There you are,' one of them said with a laugh.

'You are absolutely right,' Sparkler replied. 'Here I am. This is a friend of mine. He doesn't say much. What can I get you, Bill? And you, Ben?' He never did call them by their right names. He brought the drinks over, with the help of Daniel. 'Bungho!' he said as he raised his pint of Guinness.

'Here's looking at you!'

'One in the eye!'

'That hit the spot.'

Daniel said nothing. He did not feel at ease with these two policemen.

'What have you been up to, Sparkler?'

'Well, gentlemen, that is a leading question which I may not be at liberty to answer.'

'Let me guess.'

'Now don't embarrass me. I have feelings, don't I?'

'I'm weeping.'

'Enlighten me on one thing, Bill. I came into your station about a month ago. To tell you about the arson attack on my block.'

'Oh did you?'

'Yes I did. No one never gave me a ring about it.'

'Did they not?' They looked at each other and smiled.

'You know that Asher Ruppta is the landlord.'

'The wog? Of course we do. He is the big cheese around here.' Ben was rubbing together his thumb and first finger. 'He's got the lolly.'

'If it was him what did it, and I only say if – if it *was* him, then he should be stopped.'

'Where does your friend come from? Not around here.'

'University.'

The two policemen looked with suspicion at Daniel. 'He ain't a student.'

'I am a lecturer.'

'Is that so?' He looked back at Sparkler. 'You don't want to be worrying about Ruppta.'

'I want to find him out.'

'He has a lot of friends.'

'I'm not scared of him. I'm not scared of anyone or nothing.'

The other policeman had been watching Daniel. 'What's a nice boy doing with a villain like this?'

It was not an easy question to answer. 'Dry up,' Sparkler answered for him. 'None of your business.'

'But it's yours, is it?' Both officers burst into laughter.

Daniel blushed, and looked away.

Sparkler changed the subject. 'I might need a little bit of help.'

'For what?'

'Finding them.' It suddenly occurred to Daniel that this was the reason Sparkler frequented the Spit and Sawdust – 'help' was offered and taken in both directions. Information was passed on.

'And what do you mean by them?'

'Them bastards that started the fire.'

The policeman stared at Sparkler, his level gaze suggesting perhaps that this was not the best idea. But he said nothing. Then his colleague offered a diversion. Someone was sitting at a nearby table. He was a tall and emaciated figure, with long yellow hair. He must have been in his early twenties, but he was wearing the clothes of a middle-aged man – a black overcoat, black trousers, and a black cap. 'Do you know who that is? That's the jackdaw.'

'The jackdaw?' Sparkler looked up with surprise and interest. 'What's he doing around here?'

'Sizing up the neighbourhood, I should think. You've got competition.'

The young man with the black cap looked over towards them with what seemed to Daniel to be a contemptuous expression. The 'jackdaw', as Daniel soon learned from Sparkler, was a notorious thief and receiver of stolen goods who operated south of the river in Southwark and Bermondsey. He had a reputation for viciousness. Although Sparkler had never met him, he was acquainted with several people who had been slashed or beaten by this emaciated young man.

Daniel noticed the thin creases upon his face, and the lines about his mouth; he noticed his slightly curled lip, and his insolent stare. The black coat and the black cap were old-fashioned. And there was something else. He was wearing brown shoes. Black trousers and brown shoes. The jackdaw was not someone who paid attention to his appearance or, rather, he was someone who advertised that fact.

'How long has he been here?' Sparkler asked them.

'A couple of days. No more. He's got nerve. He knows this is our pub.'

'I wonder what he wants.'

'What do you boys always want?'

'We don't normally cross the water.'

'True.'

'I'll be watching out for him.'

'So will we.'

★　★　★

Sparkler and Daniel walked back slowly to the flat, Sparkler looking behind from time to time. 'What's the matter?' Daniel asked him.

'I want to see the man who isn't there.'

They trod the dark streets in silence. There was fog in the street, spreading from the river; there was an acrid smell in the air, too, as if the fog were smoke from a bonfire. This was a damp and unwholesome place. The lights were burning in the downstairs rooms that they passed; where the curtains were not drawn Daniel could see plates on tables, cheap prints hanging from the walls, plain furniture, and people sitting or standing in silhouette.

Suddenly Daniel heard a most terrible scream: it crescendoed for some seconds and then abruptly stopped. It reminded him of an incident from his childhood. On Camden Common he had watched as a cat was seized by a fox. Daniel stood still, and stared about him.

'Why are you stopping?' Sparkler asked him.

'Somebody,' Daniel replied, 'has been killed.'

'Well, blow me down.'

'Seriously. You must have heard it.'

'I didn't hear nothing.'

'Are you deaf? It was so fierce.'

'I never have heard that scream. Some people have. Some people haven't. My grandfather heard it once.'

Daniel stayed for the rest of the weekend, eating with Sparkler in the now familiar cafés and cheap restaurants of Limehouse. He explored the territory for other reasons also. He had decided to write one chapter of his proposed book on the various novelists who had described the opium dens of the neighbourhood in the nineteenth century. There was one street in particular where the dens had been situated – Bluegate Fields – but it was now part of a park where blocks of council apartments rose. Yet still, in the lie of the territory, Daniel could see the image of the old street and its cobbled stones. He could glimpse it twisting its way among the small red gates and granite paths of the new estate; it would always be here, with its own burden of mystery. It was of the same order as the scream he had heard.

He and Sparkler came back on Sunday night from a meal in a local Indian restaurant, where Sparkler had insisted on ordering the hottest vindaloo on the menu. 'That was a facer,' he said, the sweat running down his forehead. 'That will get the wind up me. Did you ever hear that song. "I'm Doris, the goddess of wind. Tra-la."'

'I am not familiar with it. No.'

'Sung by Mrs Shufflewick.'

They had come up to the front door of the house in Britannia Street. When he put the key in the lock, Sparkler's expression changed. He took out the key and then placed it back in the lock. He opened the door very abruptly and ran up the stairs to the third floor on which he lived. Daniel followed him quickly, alarmed at Sparkler's reaction. The door of the flat was open, and he could hear Sparkler's voice raised in anger. 'What the bloody hell is this?' he was saying. 'For the love of Mike!'

'What is it?'

'I've been burgled. The burglar has been burgled. The thief has been out-thiefed. He's taken the watches. Can you believe it?' Daniel shook his head. 'When one tea-leaf goes after another tea-leaf, what do you get? You don't get a cup of tea. Oh fuck.' Sparkler went over to a small chest of drawers and opened one of its compartments. 'Oh fuck.' He intoned the word more solemnly. 'He's taken my little red book.'

The little red book was Sparkler's record of the visits of his male clients, Aubrey Rackham and Sir Martin Flaxman among them.

Sparkler pretended to strangle himself, writhing in such strange contortions that he alarmed Daniel. Then he lay down on the floor, and began banging his feet on the carpet. 'I'm dead,' he said. 'I'm finished. I'm over.'

'Don't talk like that.' Daniel went over and stood above him. 'Was my name in the book?'

Sparkler gave him a curiously impersonal look. 'Of course not. You're a friend.'

'Who was?'

'I can't tell you. What am I going to do, Danny? What am I going to do?' He rolled on to his front, and lay spread-eagled on the carpet. 'I could go to the police.' He started laughing, quietly at first; but he became louder and more hysterical.

'Calm down, or you'll burst.'

'The jackdaw. That's the one. He must have followed us home the other night.' He was silent for a moment. 'Or those two coppers could have told him where I live.'

'Why would they do that?'

'Did you notice how quiet they got when I mentioned the arson?'

'They were warning you to stay away. I noticed that.'

'So now they have a little bit of insurance against me. The little red book is in their hands, courtesy of the jackdaw. Do you get it?'

Daniel did get it. It seemed likely to him that the two policemen, and some of their colleagues, were somehow collaborating with the arsonists who had driven the Byrne family from their flat.

'I'm going back to the Spit and Sawdust,' Sparkler said. 'I'm not going to be his candyass.' He had an interest in American crime films, and on occasions borrowed his vocabulary from them. 'Am I or am I not a flake?'

'You are not.' Daniel said nothing else for a moment. 'Is this really a good idea?'

'Don't worry. I just want to dance around him. I won't land a punch. I want him to know that I know.'

The jackdaw was standing by the counter in the saloon bar when Sparkler and Daniel came in. 'Well hello, my beauty,' Sparkler said before greeting him with a brief but neatly executed soft-shoe shuffle. 'Having fun?' The jackdaw looked at him warily, and said nothing. 'Not so fragrant here as your side of the water, is it? They tell me that Bermondsey is pure heaven. Do you do a lot of business there?'

The jackdaw's expression was one of amused contempt. 'This and that.'

'More of this? Or more of that?'

The jackdaw sniffed. 'Can it.' He had a hoarse and rasping voice that was very like a growl.

'Now that is not nice. Not nice at all. Anyone would think you had a grudge against me. Next thing I know you will be breaking and entering.' At that moment the landlord came behind the bar and asked them what they wanted to drink. Sparkler was distracted, momentarily, and ordered two pints of Guinness.

The jackdaw and Sparkler were both now standing at the counter of the bar, just a few feet apart.

'Breaking and entering,' Sparkler said to Daniel in a loud voice. 'That's a lovely phrase.'

The jackdaw stared into the space immediately ahead of him. Then he began to whistle a tune that Daniel recognised. But he did not recall the words. The jackdaw whistled a few more notes, and then finished his drink with a flourish before wiping his mouth with a red and white spotted handkerchief. He tipped his hat over his eyes, strolled to the door and, on leaving, looked across at Sparkler. 'Is your friend a nancy, too?' he asked him. Then he was gone.

Sparkler rushed to the door, but the jackdaw had already slipped around a corner. 'Push off,' he shouted in his general direction. He came back into the bar. 'I wonder,' he asked Daniel, 'if I will see him again?'

Daniel knew that he would. 'That tune he was whistling,' he said, 'is called "Sweet Mystery of Life".'

XIII

Cheeky monkey

'Is HIS nibs in?' the odd-looking young man asked Sam Hanway. 'He's expecting me.'

'Who shall I say –'

'The chancer from over the river. Pincher Solomon's friend. He'll know.' He was carrying in his hand a small package that resembled a slim book.

Ruppta must have heard his voice – he was always very acute of hearing – because he opened the door at once. 'Ah,' he said, 'the jackdaw is quick. He likes to chatter.'

'I *am* quick. I told you so.'

Ruppta ushered the young man into his office, from where Sam heard snatches of murmured conversation. He thought he heard the name of Sparkler mentioned, but he dismissed the possibility; there was no reason why his friend should be discussed by this stranger. There was the sound of laughter, and then Sam heard the familiar clicking of the lock to the safe in the corner of Ruppta's office.

They came out of the office, smiling, as if in memory of some shared joke. 'Tell Mr Solomon he has no need to worry now,' Ruppta said. 'I already had one. Now I have the other.'

'Solomon will be very pleased. Hold onto them. Hold on tight.'

'That is my intention. What is that English saying about birds in the hand? But you know all about birds, don't you?'

They shook hands, and Ruppta opened the door for him. 'That young man is known as the jackdaw,' he said after he had gone. 'The jackdaw is considered to be an omen of death. Let us hope it is not the case here.'

Sam left the office early that day, Ruppta permitting his departure on the grounds of what he called 'this inclement weather'.

He had decided to visit his mother at her home, and work-place, in Borough. One of 'the girls', as they were called, came to the door. 'Oh it's you,' she said. 'She's just popped out.' She moved aside and, as Sam entered, she laughed. 'You always bow your head when you come in. You would think this was a church.'

He made his way to the room at the end of the corridor; the flowers were in a blue vase on the table, as usual, and the window had been left open despite the rain. He went over, and leaned against the sill. He liked to gaze at the rain. He did not hear his mother enter the room, and he was startled when she put her hand upon his shoulder.

'Lost in space?' she asked. 'Your father used to like the rain.'

'Yes,' he said, 'I was thinking. I never heard you come in.'

'A penny.'

'What?'

'For your thoughts.'

'Oh nothing much. Nothing special.'

'Your father used to think too much. That's probably what killed him. Is that an awful thing to say?' She leaned over the table and tidied the drooping stems of the flowers in the vase. 'There. That's better.'

162

'I'll tell you what I was thinking. Have you heard of Pincher Solomon?'

'Of course I have.' His mother looked at him intently, almost fearfully. 'He runs this area. Why do you want to know?' Then Sam told her the story of the strange young man with the long yellow hair who had come to Ruppta's office that morning. She stopped him after a moment. 'That's the jackdaw,' she said. 'Watch out for him. Don't cross him. He can be dangerous. Everyone knows about him.'

'Does he live around here?'

'He drinks in the Blue Elephant. Along with Solomon. Don't go near them, Sam. You will only come to harm.'

'What do they want with Mr Ruppta?'

'It doesn't matter. Stay away.' Sally Hanway had dealings with Solomon. He took five per cent of her profits on the understanding that he would protect her from the attentions of the police or the threats of her rivals. 'I wish,' she said, 'that you would find another job.'

'Why? I like the one I have.'

'You shouldn't be seeing these people. You shouldn't be dealing with them. They don't care what they do, Sam. They'll do *anything*.'

He left his mother's house soon after, and began to wander through the streets of Borough. The air was full of noises – a football being kicked against a wall, the faint mosquito crackle of a transistor radio beside an open window, a car accelerating in the road, a child crying, all of them mingling together as the halo of the human world. Then Sam caught sight of the Blue Elephant public house. Instinctively he walked towards it and went in.

The interior resembled a large barn, with a circular bar in the centre of the open space and various chairs and tables scattered across the uneven floor. There were jars of pickled eggs on the counter of the bar, and the air was striated by cigarette smoke and the odour of stale beer. An Irish hound lay sprawled upon the floor, apparently asleep among the loud laughter and conversation of the clientele. A jukebox broadcast the voice of Johnny Mathis. No one paid Sam any attention but, as he went over to the bar, he noticed the jackdaw sitting on a wide deep sofa with three other men.

His companions had a distinctive, and almost shameless, air; each of them was dressed, like the jackdaw himself, in a variety of oddly assorted clothes. One of them wore a mustard-coloured waistcoat with white flared trousers; he had bright red hair that stuck out unevenly. Another had a pork-pie hat with a shiny grey suit; he was wearing white plimsolls. The third of them was older. He wore a blue cloth suit, and a black waistcoat with a watch chain draped across it; his shoes were patched with red and white leather. Sam surmised, rightly, that this was Pincher Solomon. The jackdaw, always quick and observant, recognised Sam at once and whispered to Solomon. 'Over here,' he called out. 'Why don't you come over here?' Sam approached them slowly. 'This is the gent I was telling you of,' the jackdaw said to Solomon. 'He works for old Ruppta.'

'Oh does he?' Solomon had a soft voice with the slightest trace of a lisp. 'Are you a good boy? Are you a slave to your master?'

'No. I am not a slave.'

'You have more of an independent mind, do you?'

'I do my work. That's all.'

'And what is that work?' Solomon seemed to look at him sideways, as if he were examining him secretly as he spoke.

'I collect the rents.'

'That is very sensitive work. Very provoking. Very tiring.'

'I don't find it so.'

'Do you not? Most interesting. Most interesting indeed.

Would you care for a drink? Benedict, will you bring our guest something?'

Benedict leapt to his feet. 'What will it be?'

'Guinness.'

'An excellent choice,' Solomon said. 'What shall we call you, sir?'

'Sam.'

The jackdaw raised his head. 'I knew a Sam once. He ended up in Pentonville.'

'Past history, jackdaw.' Solomon seemed to be concealing the fact that he was annoyed. 'Past history.' Then he turned back to Sam. 'I don't suppose you would object to earning an extra spot of cash? I am not being indelicate, I hope.'

'I don't suppose,' the jackdaw said, imitating Solomon's soft and gentle delivery, 'that you came in here by accident.'

'It may have been a whim.' Solomon replied for him. 'A whim is a good thing. Did you come here on purpose, Sam?'

'I was interested.'

'May I put it this way?' Solomon asked him. 'Your lord and master asked the jackdaw here to help him in a delicate matter. Might Mr Solomon one day ask the same of you?'

'That depends.'

'Oh you are a clever boy.'

'I would do nothing to harm Mr Ruppta.'

'And you are loyal, too. That is a great encouragement to me. That means everything.' Benedict came back with Sam's drink. 'This young man,' he told Sam, 'is as keen as the mustard. Are you not, Benedict?'

'Yes, sir, I am.'

Pincher Solomon exchanged a look with the jackdaw. 'You may be able to solve a little difficulty for me, Mr Sam. We were just discussing it. Before you came in. Isn't that a co-incidence? We need to get a certain letter delivered into the hands of a certain person. It is all very delicate.' He placed the fingertips of both hands together. 'Very sensitive. The jackdaw is too shy, you see. He hates to be recognised. As do all my boys. But you, well, you are anonymous. You look to me like a young man in an old photograph. One of the war dead, as it were.'

'I can mention this to Mr Ruppta?'

'He will be delighted. Overjoyed. Tell him that I am sending a little letter to Sir Martin Flaxman. Have you heard of him?' Sam shook his head. 'Even better. Better and better.'

As instructed, Sam returned to the Blue Elephant two days later. 'Here is the famous letter,' Pincher Solomon told him. 'It is my epistle to the Romans. Fallen brethren, you see. This is what you must do. You must present yourself at the front door of this residence.' He tapped the address on the envelope. 'You must say that you have an important letter to deliver personally to Sir Martin. Personally. There will be the usual bustle and refusal. Then you will say this. "Tell him it is about Tuesday evenings." Repeat the sentence. He will see you then. Take my word for it. Give him the letter. Stay there if you can, while he reads it.'

Asher Ruppta had borrowed the jackdaw from Solomon, so that the practised thief might steal Sparkler's diary; Ruppta knew that Sparkler had been asking questions about the arsonists in Britannia Street, and he wanted to prevent him from doing so. If he had evidence of Sparkler's illegal activities as a prostitute, he could at the very least evict him from his lodgings.

When Ruppta saw the contents of Sparkler's diary, however, he paused and reflected. Here was the name of Sir Martin Flaxman. Ruppta was also interested in another name. It was that of Stanley Askisson, who had carried the bribes from Ruppta to Cormac Webb at the Ministry of Housing.

Of course the jackdaw had first copied out the entries made by Sparkler, and then handed the paper with a flourish to Pincher Solomon. 'The bum boy,' he said, 'has been careless.'

When Solomon saw Flaxman's name, his eyes widened; then he smiled. In the letter conveyed by Sam, he suggested that Sir Martin might like to reconsider his plan to enter the business of racecourse betting.

When Sam knocked on the door at Cheyne Walk, it was opened by an elderly woman wearing an apron.

'I would like to see Sir Martin Flaxman.'

'Well you can't. He's not available.'

'Is he here?'

'It makes no difference whether he is here or isn't here. He is otherwise engaged.'

'Engaged in what?'

'In *what*? How do I know? I'm only the cook.'

'It's urgent.'

'So is my steak pudding. Piss off.'

'Tell him it's about Tuesday evenings.'

'What was that, you cunt?' Flaxman stepped into view.

'Tuesday evenings.'

'Let him in, Mrs A. Come with me.' He took him upstairs to a small office, and Sam took the envelope out of his pocket. 'What is this?'

'It's a letter.'

'I can see that it's a letter. What are these?' He pointed to his eyes. He opened the envelope quickly, and read the letter in an instant. His face flushed, and small beads of sweat formed on his forehead. He glanced briefly at Sam, with such a look of shame or embarrassment that Sam turned away. 'Who do you work for?'

'Mr Asher Ruppta.' It was the truth. He saw no reason to hide it.

'There will be no reply,' he said. And then he walked out of the room, leaving Sam to make his own way out.

As he left the house he heard another woman crying out, 'I forbid steak pudding in this household!'

Sam was working in Ruppta's office on the following morning, when Stanley Askisson came into the room. The door to the inner study opened at once.

'Ah, Mr Askisson, you come at a good time.'

Sam could hear their murmured voices, and put his ear against the door. 'Our friend has gone,' Ruppta was saying.

'You mean Cormac Webb? Yes. He is gone.'

'And who has replaced him?'

'Alford of the bad breath.' There was a pause, an interruption that seemed to Sam to be full of meaning. He imagined Ruppta looking at Askisson, focusing his gaze upon him, imparting his thought without giving verbal expression to it.

'I have come across a diary,' Ruppta said. 'Your name is mentioned. It is all very discreet.'

'My name?'

At that moment Sam heard someone beginning to open the door from the corridor; he took three paces back, and simulated a yawn.

'You should never let a lady see you yawn,' Julie Armitage said. 'It is not polite. Not unless you put your hand over your mouth.' She brought out a large packet of nuts from her bag. 'Do you want a peanut, cheeky monkey? Who's in there with him?'

'That one you followed.'

Her eyes opened widely. 'The one Ruppy gave money to?' Sam nodded. 'Oh my giddy aunt.' They looked at one another with mounting excitement, sharing the same recent inheritance of silence and secrecy. They were whispering. 'What's Ruppy up to?'

'I don't know.'

'Have some more peanuts. They help you think.'

When Stanley Askisson came out of Ruppta's office, he walked to the door without glancing at Sam or Julie – perhaps even without noticing them. They both looked at him carefully, almost greedily, as he opened the door and left the room.

Ruppta came out of his office, whispering or singing softly to himself. 'I am rehearsing a *limbay*,' he said to them. 'It is one of our songs. It brings down a guiding spirit. And then I offer it a sacrifice.' Julie looked at Sam with an expression of irrepressible humour. 'You may laugh, Julie. Laughter is good.'

She swallowed her laughter, and looked around at Sam. 'We were talking about Terry Thomas,' she said.

Another layer of dust had settled in the Camden house since the death of his father. Sam had removed and altered nothing. A coronation mug still sat on the mantelpiece, together with a jewelled miniature of a young woman; they were joined by a small chest, lined in velvet, that held some old coins; there was also a toy music box which, when wound up, played 'Underneath the Arches'. On a side table had been placed a framed photograph of the three brothers at an early age; they were standing, smiling, in front of the stone pillars of some public building. On the wall above the mantelpiece hung a painting of the Embankment that Philip Hanway had purchased before his marriage. A small bookcase beside the mantelpiece contained a score or so of volumes, among them *Cold Comfort Farm* by Stella Gibbons and *Look Homeward Angel* by Thomas Wolfe; Roget's *Thesaurus* stood snugly beside the *Penguin Book of Greek Myths*. On the round dining table against the opposite wall was the copy of *The Listener* that Philip Hanway had been reading before his heart-attack.

Sam sat down in the frayed but comfortable armchair which his father had usually occupied. A slight flurry or ruffle of sound caused him to turn his head towards the mantelpiece, where the coronation mug was sliding slowly to the right. The lid of the small chest then opened, and one of its coins jumped out. The painting of the Thames Embankment came off its hook, and sailed across the room onto the circular table. At this moment the strain of 'Underneath the Arches', as interpreted by tiny metal keys, could be heard. *Cold Comfort Farm* and *Look Homeward Angel* flew from the bookcase and landed on the carpet. Sam watched the proceedings with interest and without any fear. *The Listener* rose from the table and hovered in the air. The coins and chessmen now came out of their boxes and began to fly about the room. Some of them fell noisily to the floor but when they collided with Sam they merely brushed past him like feathers. The photograph of the three brothers sailed above his head, accompanied by the *Penguin Book of Greek Myths*. Sam sat there, entranced, as the familiar objects performed their dance.

XIV

Sausage land

E VER SINCE Harry Hanway had become Sir Martin
Flaxman's son-in-law he was considered to be, in the
words of one of the night-editors, the 'heir apparent'; sure
enough, he was soon appointed as managing editor of the
newspaper, and moved to a large office on the highest floor
of the building from where he could see the steeple of St
Bride's and the dome of St Paul's. He enjoyed his new
eminence in every sense, and discovered to his surprise that
he was capable of malice. He wanted to make sure that the
nominal editor, Andrew Havers-Williams, understood who
was really in charge of the enterprise. To that end he snubbed
or humiliated him in a number of petty ways. He did not
return his calls; he kept him waiting for meetings; he walked
around the newsroom, selecting items and suggesting stories,
without the editor's knowledge or permission.

'Is my daughter a good fuck?' Sir Martin was standing in
Harry's office, looking over the rooftops of Fleet Street.
'Sir?'
'I take it she is no longer a virgin.'
'No. She is not.'
'So you got what you wanted. But I think you are after

much more. Good for you. I like that. You're still hungry. You like to devour, don't you? Money. Power. It's all the same to you, Harry.'

'I wouldn't quite put it like that.'

'Oh but I would. I am like everyone else, you see. I judge people by my own standards. I wonder what I would do if I were in their position.'

'And what is my position, sir?'

'I don't know whether you married my daughter out of ambition or out of greed. Either way, I don't mind. I don't *blame* you for it. I *applaud* you for it. I would have done the same. I am glad that she has married such a dynamic person. I am growing fond of you, Harry.'

Harry was driven home that night in one of the company cars. Flaxman had bought the newly married couple a house in Mount Street, just off Park Lane, in Mayfair. It was a good address, and Harry relished the wealth of the neighbourhood. He had always wanted to live in just such a house and in just such a neighbourhood. He woke up each morning amused by his success.

Guinevere was still a social worker in Limehouse. 'I'm worried about Sparkler,' she told her husband that evening.

'Who?'

'The boy in Limehouse.'

'Oh, the pansy.'

'I don't think that is a good word.'

'All right then. Poof.' Now that they were married Harry did not feel it necessary to defer to her sensibilities in every matter.

'He seems so weak. So *weary*. He coughs all the time. I really don't know what the matter is. It really frightens me. I can get benefit for him, I think, but money is the *least* part of it.' Two days later she had more news about Sparkler. 'The good thing is that a community of nuns lives in the neighbourhood. Poor Magdalens, I think. Poor something, anyway.

I was walking past their convent this morning and I thought to myself, I'll just walk in. Impulse. I told one of the nuns that a sick young man nearby needed care and attention. Do you know what she said to me? "That is *exactly* what we are here for. God has sent you." Isn't that amazing?'

'Amazing.'

There was another matter that concerned Guinevere. 'I don't like "it",' she had said.

'What is "it"?'

'You know. The funny business.'

'What funny business?'

She pointed at his trousers. 'Sausage land. It hurts.'

'Why didn't you mention this before?'

'I didn't want to disappoint you.'

Harry agreed to abstain. He had not married her, after all, for sex.

He was surprised, two weeks later, to find his mother-in-law sitting alone in the dining room of Mount Street with a glass of sherry before her on the table. 'Hello, darling,' she said on Harry's entrance. 'It is all too vile and uncomfortable.'

'Is it?'

'Sir Martin is. He's behaving very oddly.' Guinevere came into the room, and her mother stayed silent for a moment. 'No. I will speak. Am I a pressure cooker? If you conceal your feelings, Guinevere, you can get lung cancer. Or so I have been told.'

'What are you talking about, Mummy?'

'I am talking about your father. And please don't raise your voice to me.'

'What is the matter with him?'

'He has become excitable.' Harry glanced at her; he had noticed the same change in Flaxman's behaviour. 'He jumps whenever the telephone rings. Like a jack-in-the-box.' She laughed at her own description. 'I hate those creatures.'

'They are not real, Mother.'

'That's not the point, is it? And then he snaps at me. I said to him the other day, what's happened to Tuesday evenings? He gives me what I can only describe as a very strange look. What about Tuesday evenings, he asks me. You always used to go to the club to play poker, I tell him. He then utters a profanity about poker that will never pass my lips. Wild horses could not drag it from me.'

'Did he say "fuck poker"?' Guinevere asked her mother.

'That is my daughter for you.' Lady Flaxman was looking at Harry with an expression of mild satisfaction. 'Your wife, I should say. Foul-mouthed. Like her father. I am the first to admit that I am not an angel, but I am not a fishwife either. I do hope that Mrs A. does not intend to boil something in a bag.' Mrs A. was the cook and housekeeper who had moved from Cheyne Walk to Mount Street, where she now lived in a small self-contained flat in the basement – she had been, according to Lady Flaxman, 'practically given away'. 'During the War, you know, corned beef was a great luxury. We live in a very different world. Guinevere dear, pour your mother another drop of sherry. Just the teeniest bit.'

Harry went over to the window that looked out on the back garden, still glowing with the colours of the autumn. He did not know the names of the flowers, or the trees, but he appreciated the spectacle of the golden yellow and the green against the background of the changing leaves. Then he observed a shape emerging from the shade of the trees; it was that of a man standing with his arms apart as if in greeting. Harry saw his father at the bottom of the garden. His father was looking straight at him with that curious piteous glance he had adopted in life. Then he stepped back and was gone.

'Just going outside,' Harry said, 'to get some air.'

He walked down the passage towards the door into the

garden and, as he approached the threshold, he felt a curious sensation in his left arm as if he were being held very tightly by a strong hand. A cloud passed across the sun as he walked into the garden, and the shade deepened. His father was standing where he had stood before, but he had changed; he seemed to have become larger, and more fierce. And then he faded.

'He has made his bed,' Lady Flaxman was saying when Harry re-entered the dining room. 'And now he must eat it.'

'Sleep in it,' Harry said.

'I will sleep where I choose. And that does not include the bed of my husband. If I do, I will have to wear riot gear.'

Guinevere was restless. 'I agree with Mummy. I do think Daddy is unwell,' she said to no one in particular. 'He has a strained look. And he has lost weight. I can tell. Something is worrying him. Is there anything going on at work, Harry?'

'Nothing out of the ordinary.' But then Harry remembered an occasion, the week before, when Flaxman had flinched and stepped back when the editor mentioned Asher Ruppta's name in connection with London criminal gangs. 'No, no,' Flaxman had said. 'We don't want to follow that line. Not at all. Stay clear of it.'

Harry went to work on the following morning with a sore head; he had drunk too much brandy with Lady Flaxman. When he entered his outer office his secretary was waiting for him. 'There is a woman,' she said, 'claiming to be your mother. I put her in the board room.'

'Oh. Good.' He did not know what else to say. 'I'll go and see her.' He felt himself blushing with shame and anger at her sudden appearance. He walked into the board room, where Sally was looking out of the large window over the rooftops of Fleet Street and Ludgate Hill. He stood there without saying anything.

'Good morning, Harry.'

'Why are you here?'

'I wanted to see you. Now that your father's gone –'

'– you wanted to come back?'

'No. Not exactly.' She still had her back turned to him. 'I was hoping that we might talk.'

'Talk? Talk about what?'

'Why are you so hard, Harry?'

'I have had to survive, haven't I?'

'No. You always were hard. When you were a small boy, you were tough. You were determined. Nothing like your father.'

'How can you call *me* hard? You were the one who left. Sam took it worst.'

'Don't.'

'I used to hear him sobbing in his room.'

'I'm sorry –'

'Is that all you can say? We never really had a proper life. A normal life. We just grew older. Dan hid away in his books. That's what he always did. He would go into a book, if he could.'

'And what about you?'

'I'm tough, as you say. You could slam a ten-ton truck into me and I'd survive.'

'And I hear you're married now.'

'I don't want to go into that.'

'Are you happy with her?'

'I don't know. What is it to be happy?' He was silent for a moment. 'Haven't you got a business to run, Mother?'

She turned around to face him. 'You know about that, do you? Did Sam tell you?'

'No. I never see Sam. I found out for myself. I looked up the court records.'

'That was clever of you. I told Sam that your father sent me away after that, but he was too weak to have done that. I left him of my own accord after I came out of prison.'

176

'You left *us*.'

'What else was I supposed to do? All the shame. All the guilt of it. I could cope with that by myself, hidden away somewhere, but not with you boys. Would you like to have seen your mother weeping? And the neighbours whispering behind my back? I thought it was better to clear out altogether. To let you all make a fresh start.'

Harry was not interested in his mother's explanation. 'I saw you in the street.' He scratched the side of his face. 'You have some interesting clients.'

'Have I?'

'Asher Ruppta.'

Suddenly she looked fierce. 'What do you know about him?'

'He interests me.'

'Stay away from him.'

'Oh?'

'He is not safe. He is dangerous.'

'So why did you visit him?'

'He looked after me once. He's a rich man, you know.'

'Yes I do know. What are you trying to say?'

'I have a son by him.'

One night, after the three brothers had gone to bed, there had been a bitter quarrel between Sally and Philip Hanway. She had left the house in a rage, and had walked without knowing where she was going. She found herself outside King's Cross Station, in the dirty and dismal forecourt where people loiter before making their way into the main hall of the station. She had some vague intention of catching a train – to anywhere, to nowhere – and so she pushed open one of the glass doors of the entrance.

She thought better of leaving on a train so late in the evening, and instead she went into a cafeteria and ordered a cup of coffee. She sat over it, her head bowed, inhaling its scent, her hands trembling slightly. She hardly noticed that someone had sat down at the next table.

'Where have you been all your life?' The strange question had been addressed to her. She looked up and saw a foreign gentleman, as she put it to Harry, with large hazel eyes that seemed to be oriental.

'I don't know,' she said. She was, surprisingly, not at all apprehensive. She noticed the refinement of his voice, and the paleness of his skin.

'It is not usual for a lady to drink coffee by herself in the evening. It is not "the done thing".' He put quotation marks around the phrase.

'I was making up my mind what train to catch.' It was the easiest excuse.

'You have a husband and children, do you not?'

'How do you know that?'

'You have a ring. And you look tired. You want to escape for an hour or so. Is that not right?'

She was drawn to this stranger with the precise, careful voice. Then, with an elation she could not explain even to herself, she joined him at his table.

She told Harry that she saw Asher Ruppta from time to time after that first meeting. 'Your father,' she said, 'knew nothing about it. He didn't know about a lot of things.'

'Such as?'

'I had been on the game before I met him. In Soho. Just for the extra cash, you see. So when we needed the money, after you three boys were born —' She grew silent, fearful that in her desire to tell her son everything she had in fact said too much.

'And when you were put in prison?'

'After I got out, I went to Asher Ruppta. I lived with him for a while.'

'That's when you had a son.'

178

'Yes.'

'What happened to him?'

'Nothing happened. He's at a good school. A boarding school.' She paused for a moment. 'Life had been hard, Harry. I always wanted to have money. To be free. But then I met your father.'

'I think you ought to go now.'

So she walked past him and went out into the corridor. The story soon spread around the office that Harry was not a Barnardo's boy after all.

XV

Don't stick it out like that

'HOW ARE you feeling?' Daniel asked Sparkler one morning.

'All right. What's the weather like?'

'Well, it's winter.'

'I know. The sun is low in the sky. Like me.' Daniel looked down at his friend's pale face bathed in sweat, and at his trembling limbs; he heard his rasping persistent cough. 'Is that window open?'

'No.'

'I feel a cold breeze. Could you close the window?' Daniel pretended to close it. 'I won't go to no hospital. The nun is here, isn't she? The doctor says he has given up on me. He can't find nothing wrong, he says. No cause, he says. What is that supposed to mean? The nun says that there's no earthly cause. She has a funny way of talking. Meanwhile I am burning to death.' He seemed to lose consciousness for a moment, and his fingers played listlessly against the sheets. It was as if he were plucking a string. 'Well,' he said, after a while, 'at least I won't grow old.' His face was thinner; his eyes were brighter and more protuberant; his voice was higher. Then there was a flash of his old self. 'I told the nun that I needed strength to steal again,' he said. 'So she went down on her knees to pray for me. "Oh Lord, let him be a thief once more."'

When Daniel had arrived that morning, he had found a small phial of water outside the door to Sparkler's flat. It had a piece of paper taped to it, with the words 'Holy Water' scribbled in biro. One of the inhabitants of the house must have left it there. Daniel put the phial in his pocket, deciding at once that he would not let Sparkler know about it.

When Daniel left the flat that evening, he almost walked into the nun. 'Have you been to see your friend?' she asked him.

'Yes. I have.' He did not know how to address her, and he could not focus upon her face. It floated in front of him like some bright moon.

'You are anxious, I know,' she went on to say. 'But there is no need to worry. He won't die. He is being purged.'

Daniel was so surprised by this that he took a step back. 'Is that so? Are you sure?'

She nodded. 'I have come across this sickness before. It is suffering with a purpose.' She smiled and walked past him towards the door of Sparkler's flat.

Daniel returned by train to Cambridge in a state of relief close to euphoria but, as soon as he got back to his familiar college rooms, his exhilaration vanished. He had had no dealings with nuns before, but he suspected that they were superstitious to a dangerous degree. There was something about her, too, which had seemed to him to be elusive; she had possessed no strong presence.

He looked from the windows of his rooms, and saw Paul Wilkin walking across the quad; from this height he noticed how bald he had become. To his annoyance he then heard footsteps slowly mounting the staircase to his rooms. He closed his eyes briefly at the knock on his door. 'Oh, Daniel, I'm glad I caught you. I thought you might be here.'

'And here I am. Won't you come in, Paul?'

Wilkin entered the room and accepted a glass of sherry. The lines were evident upon his face, and strands of hair had turned greyish-white. 'I wanted to talk to you,' he said. Already Daniel feared the worst, and said nothing. 'My editor has left Aylesford & Bunting. Well, retired, actually. And the bastards there don't want to publish my new book.'

'Of poems?'

'Of course.' For a moment he seemed offended. 'Written over the last ten years. Some of them are bloody marvellous. So I wonder if you could put in a word for me with Aubrey Rackham.'

'Hanky Panky? I thought you despised him.'

'Well, my personal feelings are neither here nor there.' Wilkin was blustering. 'It's important just to get the work published. Connaught & Douglas is a good firm. I have always said so.' No you have not, Daniel thought. 'It would be an honour to be published by them again. They were once my mentors. You can tell them that from me.' No I will not, Daniel thought.

'You had better give me the typescript then,' he said quietly.

'I think it would be better, actually,' Wilkin replied, 'if Rackham wrote to me.'

'You would then avoid the humiliation of seeming to plead.'

Wilkin gave Daniel an angry glance. 'Something like that. Yes.'

'I will certainly mention it to him. I'm having lunch with him on Friday.'

'Oh yes?'

'He wants a progress report on my book.'

'How *is* the book?' He had obviously decided to treat Daniel with more deference than he had done in the past.

'I'm going to concentrate on the city's popular culture. Music hall. Penny dreadfuls. That sort of thing.'

'Barn-storming?'

'Yes indeed.'

'Good for you.' He did not sound particularly enthusiastic, and he took a large gulp from his glass of sherry. 'I might as well tell you, Daniel. I'm having a spot of bother with Phyllis.'

'Oh?'

'She found out somehow that I was having a fling with one of the students. She started shouting. And I walked out of the house. Haven't been back.'

'I see.'

'I suppose it could end in divorce. But how much is that going to cost me?'

Daniel was early for his lunch with Hanky Panky, at the usual restaurant, so he took a walk down Regent Street. He had gone only a few yards when he was suddenly astounded to see Stanley Askisson walking towards him. He had not encountered him since their undergraduate days; they had made no attempt to contact one another. As they met and passed, their eyes swerved away from each other. Daniel quickened his pace.

Aubrey Rackham was already in the restaurant when he arrived; he had his hand on the arm of one of the Italian waiters. 'No more than a drop of vermouth. All the rest is gin.' He caught sight of Daniel at once. 'I always think of Hogarth when I order gin. Gin Lane is in my neighbourhood.' He had a surprisingly deep laugh. 'What have you been up to? I mean, more precisely, how is *it* going?'

'By next month *it* will be finished.'

'You astonish me. You are one of my most remarkable daughters.'

'I have become, you know, by bits and pieces, really interested in the London music hall.'

183

'The Crazy Gang?'

'No. Further back. Dan Leno. Harry Champion. Charles Coborn. They are the real heroes of London.'

'I really don't know –'

'Do you not? That's a good reason to write about them. Their songs are rather wonderful. "Why Can't We Have the Sea in London?"'

'Good question.'

'"Young Men Taken in and Done For."'

'Landladies?'

'Yes.'

'Hussies.'

'"Don't Stick It Out Like That." That was sung by Bessie Bellwood.'

'Lucky Bessie.'

'The sad songs are the greatest. "When These Old Clothes Were New." "My Shadow Is My Only Pal." Far better than the poetry of the period. And then their routines –'

'I suppose their language was *choice*.'

'Beg your pardon?'

'Blue.'

'Oh yes. Very. Indigo.'

Towards the end of the meal Daniel asked, 'Do you remember a poet by the name of Paul Wilkin?'

'Of course. I never thought much of him. Dora Dreary. Rather spermy.'

Daniel did not know what he meant, but he was reassured by his disdain. 'He has a new collection he wants to show you.'

'Oh dear. Isn't he a little bit dated?'

'I would have thought so. But I promised him that I would mention it to you.'

'You have done. He may have been good at the time. But fashions change. Now what about pudding?'

After the meal was over, Rackham sipped his coffee with evident relish. 'I suppose,' he said, 'that Limehouse comes into your book?'

'Of course. Sax Rohmer.'

'I have to go there after this.' He put down his tiny cup with a sigh. 'A dear young friend of mine has become frightfully ill.'

Daniel was surprised by this coincidence with Sparkler's sickness in the same neighbourhood – or perhaps it was not coincidence at all. Could this dear young friend also be Daniel's friend? One of the themes of Daniel's book concerned the patterns of association that linked the people of the city; he had found in the work of the novelists a preoccupation with the image of London as a web so taut and tightly drawn that the slightest movement of any part sent reverberations through the whole. A chance encounter might lead to terrible consequences, and a misheard word bring unintended good fortune. An impromptu answer to a sudden question might cause death.

Flushed by a gin martini and several glasses of white wine, Aubrey Rackham rose majestically to leave. He caught sight of himself, plump and red-faced, in a mirror by the door of the restaurant. 'Just look at me,' he said, 'Not the ruins, but the ruins of those ruins. Silly old *cow.*' He put out his tongue at his own reflection.

Daniel decided, at that instant, to travel to Britannia Street. He would wait there and see if Rackham arrived and entered Sparkler's building. 'Are you going straight there?' he asked him.

'Where?'

'Wherever you said you were going.'

'No. I must pick up one or two things from the office.'

When Daniel reached Britannia Street he meditated on where he might conceal himself so that he could watch Rackham without himself being observed. He found a deserted shop on a corner of the street; from here he had a wide view. The wind on this corner was strong, and scraps of paper were being lifted upwards into the air. Suddenly Daniel saw the nun walking along the street; she looked straight ahead, and seemed uninterested in her surroundings. Daniel knew that she was going to see Sparkler. She went straight up to the door, turned the handle and walked in; he surmised that she must have a key. A few minutes later he saw Aubrey Rackham walking along the street; so he had been right in his assumption, after all.

Daniel walked away from Britannia Street, but he decided to wander through the neighbourhood. After a few minutes he heard music and singing; he walked towards the apparent source of the sound, a building of red brick behind a red-brick wall. A door in the wall was partly open, and he could see a small square yard with a statue at its centre. He could now hear very clearly the words of the song. *Veni Creator Spiritus.* The voices were all female. A nun came into the cloister and walked towards him.

'Have you come about the drains?'

'I haven't come about anything.'

She looked at him with more interest. 'How did you find us?'

'Accident.'

'Oh? That's interesting.'

'I heard the music.'

'I suppose you did. You should be grateful.'

'Grateful? To whom?'

'To your good spirit.'

Daniel walked out of the courtyard and was just turning a corner when he caught sight of Aubrey Rackham.

'Whoops,' Rackham said. 'I hope you're not following me.'

'No.'

'Shame.'

'After you mentioned Limehouse at lunch, I thought I'd come.'

'Opium dens. Sailors with pigtails. What more could you ask?'

'How is your friend?'

'He is very poorly, I'm afraid.' He sighed. 'I don't know what else I can do. He won't go into hospital. A nurse comes round in the morning, but –'

'A nun?'

Rackham looked puzzled. 'Nun? I don't think you'll find many nuns in Limehouse, my darling.'

Daniel visited Sparkler three days later. 'Here! I'm here!' Sparkler answered him from the kitchen; there was excitement, even exhilaration, in his voice. Daniel found him sitting at the kitchen table, a plate of biscuits in front of him. He jumped up when Daniel entered the room, and kissed him on the cheek. His face was flushed, his eyes sparkling. 'I'm all mended,' he told him. 'She said I would come through it. And I have.'

'What do you mean?'

'Can't you see? I'm better. I've been cured. She did it.'

'The nun?'

'Yes.'

'How did she do it?'

'I don't know. I have to tell you something, Danny,' Sparkler was saying. 'When I knew that you fancied me, I thought I could use you. But then I fell in love with you.'

'What?' Daniel was seized by panic. He did not want to be loved by him. He went over to the window and glanced down into Britannia Street; he thought that he could see the nun on the opposite side of the road. She was looking up at him.

He returned a week later, and found Sparkler still shining. 'I saw him,' he said. 'The jackdaw. I thought I *would* see him again. It's not a very big world, is it? I was just idling along the Gray's Inn Road, as you do, getting acquainted with the neighbourhood hounds, when I saw him. As large as life. In an old blue coat. Where he got *that* from, I don't know and don't want to know. Then he clocks me. He smiles in a queer sort of way, sticks two fingers up, and disappears down Baldwin's Gardens where the pump is. I follows him smartish of course. He turns left down Leather Lane at a fair rate of knots, and then sort of loses himself in the crowd. There was a market, I'm sure of it. It weren't a market day but there *were* a market. Otherwise where did all the noise come from? Anyway I just keep my eyes on that old blue coat and stick to him. When he gets to the Clerkenwell Road he stops and looks back at me and makes a sign which is too disgusting to repeat. Then he turns right. This is when these ideas just come to me. He's heading for the river, I say to myself. River? What river? Then I think to myself, maybe he wants to hide in the orchard. But there is no orchard, is there?'

'I don't know the area.'

'Where can you find an orchard in London? There is no such animal.'

'So why did you say it?'

'Most likely my sickness. I am still invalid.'

'An invalid.'

'That's what I said. So then I thought he was going up Saffron Hill, but he turned left down Herbal Hill. More hills in London than in Scotland. He went into Ray Street and then crossed the Farringdon Road. I stopped at the corner there. Where the pub is. Coach and Horses. I could hear the sound of running water coming from the grating. Funny what you remember. Sewer probably. Then I'm on the chase again, and I follow him down to Clerkenwell Green. A lot of people were demonstrating there. Flags and such like. So he slides right through them. He's more like a fish than a jackdaw. Off he goes down Jerusalem Passage with me in pursuit. I hear music. I look up and see an old man smiling and nodding at me. What's that all about?

'He scarpers across the open space there and goes towards the old gate. I forget what it's called. I must have been sweating by now, and I swear that the ground felt hot beneath my feet. It was like walking on fire. And then do you know what happened?'

'What?'

'He *vanished*. Just like that.'

'He probably turned a corner. Or ran down some alley.'

'I know that's what he *ought* to have done. But I swear he just vanished. Well old mate, I said to myself, you are up a gum tree.'

'Oh well.' Daniel looked around the room incuriously, as if he were simply exercising his eyes.

'You are not really interested, are you?'

'Of course I am.'

'No you're not. And I think I know the reason. You're not really interested in me.' Daniel stared at him, not knowing what to say.

XVI

An absolute brick

S AM HAD no reason to think that anything was wrong. Asher Ruppta had telephoned the office the previous day, and asked for certain papers to be brought to his house in Highgate.

'I can't go,' Julie said. 'It's my day off. I've earned it. I'm visiting my sister in Folkestone. Cockles and mussels, alive, alive, oh. I *love* Folkestone.'

'I'll go.'

'There's a good boy. I'll get the address for you.'

'What if he's out?'

'The keys are in the filing cabinet under Q. In case of burglars.'

So it was Sam who had the task of delivering the papers to his employer. He set off with them on the following morning, and made his way by bus to Highgate. The road in which Ruppta lived was quiet, lined with large and solid houses of various styles. It was a reassuring, a comfortable, street. He soon found the house, surrounded by high brick walls and two electric gates. Sam pressed the entry button, but there was no response; so he took out the keys and tried each one in turn before eventually unlocking the gates. He walked up the gravel drive, his attention momentarily distracted by a large crow that hopped along the brick wall nearest to him. It was scrutinising him with evident interest.

The front door was locked but not bolted; Sam hesitated before entering it, nervous of entering the private domain of Asher Ruppta. His first impression of the hallway was one of quiet order; flowers in vases, figurines of marble placed on two cabinets of polished wood, a painting of a bridge over a river. A wide staircase, carpeted in scarlet, led from the hall; Sam looked up at the first landing, and saw it. It was lying there in an unusual position, with the left arm trapped beneath the back.

This was the body of Asher Ruppta. His throat had been cut, and the scarlet carpet was soaked in his blood. The rictus of sudden death was upon his face, but it gave him the appearance of smiling. At the sight of that smile, Sam became suddenly calm. He looked around for a telephone, and walked into the room nearest to him. This room was bare except for a long table on which various artefacts had been placed – a flute, an intricately carved casket, a figurine with a long face, a perforated stone, a knife carved out of amber. He looked at each in turn.

When a telephone rang, he walked towards the sound. It was in another room on the opposite side of the hall. He took up the receiver, and heard the voice of someone talking softly in a foreign language. 'I cannot talk to you now,' he said, and put down the receiver. Then he called the police.

They did not question him for long. His story was consistent and truthful, although he did not tell them about the muttered voice on the telephone. The sergeant had taken one look at the gaping wound in Ruppta's neck. 'A sharp knife,' he said. 'Very neat. Almost perfect, really. You have to take your hat off.'

Sam nodded. 'There is a knife in the next room.' So

they retrieved the amber knife, and placed it carefully in a transparent plastic bag.

When Sam was allowed to leave, he went down the gravel path and found the crow still perched on the high brick wall. He did not know if it was the same crow but he hoped that it was. The bird put its head to one side, and seemed to be listening intently to something that Sam could not hear.

When he had been in the presence of Ruppta's body, he had remained calm and careful; he had not surrendered to panic or alarm. Now that he was outside the house, he felt an overwhelming urge to run and to shout news of the event to anyone he passed. Instead he walked quickly down the road, and then took a bus to London Bridge. He wanted to see his mother as soon as he could. He had to tell *someone*.

When he arrived she was sitting in the back garden, leaning forward, looking speculatively at a patch of soil and considering what to plant there. He bent over to kiss her cheek. 'Ruppta is dead,' he said.

She fell back in her chair. 'What?'

'Murdered.'

'Oh my God.' She put her hand up to her neck.

'His throat was cut.' She put down her hand. 'I found him, Mum. I think he must have been pushed down the stairs first. There was blood all over the place.'

She stared at him. 'Did you say that his throat was cut?'

'Yes. Right across.'

'I can't believe it.'

'It's true.'

'No. I can believe it. When?'

'I've just come from the house.'

'From Ruppta's house?'

'Yes.'

'Who did it? Sorry. Stupid question.' She bowed her head,

and then suddenly she looked up at him with bright eyes. 'What about his will?'

'I don't know about that.'

'But do you know his lawyer?'

'Julie will know. She's worked with him for years.'

'Good. I must speak to her.'

'Why should you be interested?'

'I have known Ruppta for a long time. And I have a special reason.' Sam could see that she was trembling, and that she did not want to look at him.

'I see.'

'You don't see, Sam, but soon you will.'

On the following day Sam went into the office very early. He had not been able to communicate with Julie Armitage; he did not have her telephone number, and she had never given him her address. It was likely that she did not know about the death of her employer; she never read the news-papers, and rarely listened to the radio.

She came in at the usual time; her quick step down the corridor was familiar to him, and he stood up before she entered the room. She glanced at him as she put her raincoat on a wooden peg behind the door. 'What's up with you, *Samuel*? You're not normally so polite. It makes me feel very ladylike. Very feminine.' She was wearing a dress that looked like a dustman's sack. 'Tea for two at Claridge's?'

'Ruppta is dead.'

She looked at him almost without expression. 'I don't believe you just said that.'

'He was murdered.'

She sat down or, rather, she fell into a chair and put her head in her hands. She remained in that posture for a minute or so, completely still. 'Well,' she said eventually. 'I always knew he would have a bad end. Ruppy's finally had it, has he? My word. Gordon Bennett.'

'The police will want to talk to you, Julie.'

'And I will want to talk to them. He had a lot of enemies, Ruppy did. They could have been queuing up to shoot him.'

'He wasn't shot. His throat was cut.'

'That's Ruppy for you. Always goes to extremes.' She listened eagerly as Sam went through the story again and again; she kept on asking him to repeat certain details, or remind her of what he had said before. 'What colour was his blood?' she asked him.

'Well, red of course.'

'You never know.'

He was just about to elaborate upon his description of the amber knife when his mother walked in. He was surprised to see her.

Julie looked up at her, puzzled. 'Can I help you?'

'Good morning, Sam. Yes. I think you can help me, Julie.'

'How do you – ?'

'My son told me. Sam told me . . . '

'I didn't know he had a mother.'

Sally laughed. 'You may know me better as Sally Palliser.'

Julie was astonished. 'What? Are you here?' She rose to her feet, and then abruptly sat down again. 'I never expected to *see* you in all my life.'

'And I never expected to be here with you. And Sam. Life has a way of tricking us, doesn't it?'

Sam looked at both of them with curiosity. 'Do you want me to wait outside?' He was very demure.

'Not at all,' his mother replied. 'You have to know this. Asher Ruppta took me in when I was in trouble. We had a child together. A boy. You never knew about this, Julie.'

'I *thought* there was something,' Julie said. 'He used to be driven down to this school. He said he was on the board of governors.'

'He is. Well, was. I'm going down there today. To pick up Andrew.' She glanced at Sam. 'That is why we must find the will, Julie. I want to make sure that Andrew is protected.'

Sam sensed the presence of something shuddering in the room, coming not from any one of them but from the three of them in combination.

'If there is a will,' Julie was saying, 'then George Flom will have it.'

'His lawyer?'

'His so-called lawyer, yes. His office is in Gresham Street. Above the shirt shop.'

His mother turned to Sam. 'Will you go there? Explain everything to Mr Flom. Tell him to get the papers ready.'

On the following day the police questioned Julie Armitage in the office, and took away a stack of Asher Ruppta's files. Julie seemed agitated after the interview, and was strangely abrupt. 'You should have told me about your mother,' she said to Sam. 'What have you got to hide?'

'Nothing at all, Julie.'

'Shake the other one. Go on. Ring those bells.' She suddenly relented her tone. 'I haven't told them everything I know,' she told him. She looked him in the face, almost greedily. 'What a can of worms.'

When Sally explained to him the details of her relationship with Ruppta and the birth of a son, Sam was delighted. He had sensed that there was some connection between himself and Ruppta, but now that had been proved in the most unexpected manner. When he went to see his mother, three days later, he found the house empty. She opened the front door herself. 'The girls have gone,' she told him. 'They understood.' She led him to the small room with the blue vase of flowers. And there, to his surprise, sat a boy of thirteen or fourteen years. He was wearing a grey school blazer, and grey trousers. He looked up at Sam with a calm and steady gaze.

'This is Andrew,' she said. 'Andrew, say hello to Sam.'

'Hello, Sam.' The boy stood up and gravely shook his hand. 'I'm sorry about your father.'

'It *was* rather awkward. Mother and I are in a bit of a spot, to put it mildly. But my chums rallied round. And my house-master has been an absolute *brick*.' He looked calmly at Sam. 'Half-brother,' he said. He pronounced it very carefully. 'My word. It came as rather a shock. Following my father, if you see what I mean –' He burst into tears, but then quickly recovered. 'Sorry about that.'

'Under the circumstances –'

'I gather that you worked for him.'

'Yes. I did.'

'Did he strike you as being a fair-minded sort of person?'

'I think so.'

'Do you only *think* so?' He did not wait for an answer. 'I believe that my father was not properly understood. He was the soul of charity, you know. Grants to institutions and so forth. But he was a little too diffident for his own good. He was, like me, rather an introvert.' Sam noticed the boy's hair that consisted of tight black curls, as if his personality had somehow boiled over. 'Still, I mustn't gabble on.'

'There is something I want to tell you, Sam.' Sally sat down at the table behind them, and took out a cigarette. 'Asher has left his business to me. To turn it over to Andrew when he is twenty-one. So, you see, you will be working for me. You and Julie will have to teach me all the tricks.'

'I don't think there will be any *tricks*, Mother.'

'It's just a phrase, Andrew.'

'Still, Mother, we must start as we mean to go on. That's another phrase.'

Over the next few days Sam, Julie and Sally sat down together in order to go through Ruppta's investments and properties. Sally was intent upon all of the details – who paid through a bank account and who paid in cash? Who paid weekly or monthly? What was the condition of each flat and house?

'You cannot observe and measure at the same time,' Sam said to her. 'If you measure you cannot observe and, if you observe, you cannot measure. I can measure all the rooms and all the incomes for you. But if I observe instead, I see a picture of human misery.'

His mother looked at him in astonishment. 'Well, Sam, you have set me thinking. You know how these tenants live, don't you?'

'Mainly they live from day to day. They scrape by. They worry about paying me the rent each week. They struggle.'

'I know that Asher made a lot of money out of his flats.'

'But that's the point, isn't it?' Julie's eyes were very bright. 'We're supposed to make money, aren't we? It's all very well for Sam to say that they struggle. We all struggle. I struggle. If Mr Ruppta had not paid me a wage, I would have been in the poorhouse. Where did he get the money to pay me that wage? It stands to reason. From the money you collected, Sam.' She slammed her hand, palm down, onto the table. Sam was surprised by her vehemence, but he chose not to argue with her. He would speak to his mother privately, to see what could be done for the poorer tenants.

On the following day he was asked to go to the police station for a formal interview about the afternoon he found Asher Ruppta's body. He was questioned by the same inspector who had come to the house. 'We have learned a lot more since I last saw you.' Inspector Sutherland had a soft voice and tremulous eyes. 'We know, if I may say so, a lot more about you.' He was polite, almost deferential, to Sam as if he were in some way intimidated by him. Sam sensed this, too, and was bewildered by it. 'You are Sally's son, are you not?' Sam nodded. 'And your mother had – was close to Mr Ruppta? Would that be a fair thing to say?'

'I didn't know about that. Until after.'

'Naturally not. Very understandable.' They were facing each other, across a table, in a small boxlike room without windows. 'You were right about the amber dagger, by the way. You seemed to know about it. I was impressed.'

'It was the only dagger I could see.'

'But how did you guess that he had been killed by that dagger specifically? That was an inspired choice. Hole in one. Was it you who told me that he had fallen down the stairs before his throat had been cut?'

Sam was puzzled. 'No.'

'Funny. I thought it was you. No. Of course not. How could you know such a thing? As it happens, he fell *after* his throat was cut. Some spatters of blood were found on the wall at the top of the stairs. Did he fall or was he pushed? What do you think, Sam?' Sam shrugged his shoulders. 'But if you were a betting man, what would you fancy? Go on. Have a flutter.' Inspector Sutherland looked imploringly at Sam; his expression seemed almost comical. Then he laughed himself, as if appreciating the joke. Sam laughed, too, despite the fact that he was not feeling very comfortable with the tone of Sutherland's questions. 'I suspect that the deceased –' Here he adjusted his tie. 'That the deceased knew his attacker. There is no sign of a forced entry, you see. No sign of a struggle. He might have been having a quiet chat on the landing of the staircase. I can see it, can't you? It's a lovely house, it really is. I've read the will. Your mother gets it.'

'She gets the business, too.'

'Oh yes. Naturally.'

'In trust for her son.'

'Not you of course. The other one.'

'I also have two brothers.'

'Oh?' He seemed interested in this suddenly presented fact. 'Do they know —'

'They don't.'

'Let sleeping dogs lie?'

'Something like that.'

'Well, this has been a most satisfactory conversation.' Sutherland rubbed the palms of his hands together and smiled cheerfully before jumping to his feet. 'I know where to find you. If I should need you again.'

Sam was thoughtful, and a little apprehensive, as he made his way back to Camden Town. A bird fluttered and flew out of a hedge on the road home, startling him. He arrived home at twilight. It was that period, in late October, when the clocks were put backwards by an hour. So the evenings had become darker earlier. He entered the empty house with a sigh, but he did not put on the light. He preferred to sit in the front room until his eyes had become accustomed to the gloom and he could see the familiar objects around him. He did not care for the unnatural light of the electric bulb; it lent a false brightness to the world, and made him uneasy.

Someone knocked very loudly at the door. He hesitated, and then went out. It was his mother. 'I thought you must have been in the kitchen,' she said. 'There was no light.'

'I was just sitting.'

'May I come in?' He made way for her, and followed her into the front room before switching on the light. 'I haven't been here since — since it happened. Nothing much has changed, has it?'

'Dad didn't do much to it. No.'

'Still that old radio. It must be an antique by now. Are you still in your old room?'

'I'm in Harry's.'

'Treating yourself.' She stepped into the kitchen. 'It's smaller than I remembered it.'

'Sometimes,' he said, 'I feel the world closing in.'

'Sam, that's one of the reasons I'm here. I'd like you to move in with us. Andrew is away at school for some of the time, so you would make good company. You would be much more comfortable in Borough. And we can set up the business there. I've given it a lot of thought. There's no need to be in the middle of town. It's a tiring place.'

'What about his house in Highgate?'

'I'm selling it. Andrew wants me to.' She sat down at the kitchen table. 'Make me a cup of tea, will you?' She was silent as he prepared and poured the tea. 'Who do you think killed him, Sam?'

'I think he may have been blackmailing people.'

'That wouldn't surprise me.' She sipped her tea. 'What do you think of Julie?'

'What?'

'There's something odd about her. I can't put my finger on it. Don't you think it funny that, on the day Asher died, she was visiting her sister in Folkestone? She told me that her sister was a bit dotty. Forgetful.'

'What are you getting at, Mum?'

'The dotty sister makes a good alibi, doesn't she?'

'Why on earth would Julie want to murder Mr Ruppta?'

'I don't know. But I'm going to find out.'

XVII

Ants in your pants

WHEN HARRY Hanway broke the news of Asher Ruppta's murder to Sir Martin Flaxman, his father-in-law crowed with delight. 'The crook has been killed, has he? How was it done?'

'I'm trying to find out the details now.'

'Now's the time to go after him. Print everything you've got. Nothing wrong with fucking the dead. You can't catch anything.'

Harry Hanway noted, as he put down the telephone, that Sir Martin seemed to have recovered his good humour.

Lady Flaxman came for dinner that night at Mount Street. 'Pass me the rat poison,' she said almost as soon as she had entered the house. 'The kraken wakes.'

'What do you mean, Mummy?'

'I mean your father. The old fool has come back to life. Jesus wept.' She elaborated on this theme over dinner. 'I knew he was getting better when he swore at me. And he kicked out with his foot. With his foot.' She repeated the phrase very slowly and distinctly.

'What else would he use, Mummy?'

'Nothing is beyond that man. And he has gone red again. Like a cockataw or whatever the horrible creature is called.'

'Cockatoo.'

'More like a lobster. Revolting, actually.' She looked down at a piece of shrivelled meat upon her plate. 'I see we have very slim pickings.' Mrs A. entered the room at this moment. 'Ah, my good woman.' Lady Flaxman greeted her with what seemed to Harry to be artificial warmth.

'I am not your good woman. I will not be called a good woman in this house.'

'Only a turn of phrase.'

'There are turns of phrases and there are turns of phrases.' Mrs A. picked up Lady Flaxman's plate and returned to the kitchen, delighted with her sally.

'Your father,' Lady Flaxman said, 'happened to mention something about retirement.' Harry began to listen more intently. 'Absolute nonsense of course. Is he a shy violet?'

'He is about as shy as King Kong,' Guinevere replied.

'Precisely my point.'

Over the next few days Harry found out more about Asher Ruppta's death; he also learned that 'Miss Sally Palliser' had inherited the business until Ruppta's son reached the age of twenty-one. He was anxious that her married name should not be published, so he decided to steer the story of Ruppta's death in a more sensational direction. He had not forgotten his discovery of the financial relationship between Asher Ruppta and Cormac Webb. Now, with Ruppta gone, Flaxman had more or less invited him to pursue the story with additional vigour. Harry's enthusiasm had been quickened by the fact that Webb had found himself again in government as parliamentary under-secretary at the Home Office. So Harry called in James Thorn, now chief political correspondent of the *Chronicle*.

Thorn was fatter than before, and had acquired a pretentiousness that might have been mistaken for gravity. He still wore pinstriped suits, and had a rose in his buttonhole. 'How can I help you, old boy?'

'What do you think of Cormac Webb?'

'Webb is a coming man. A coming man.'

'He may not be coming for very long.'

'Oh?'

'He may be going. He's put his hand in the till.'

'Is that so?' Thorn was always careful. He knew that Harry liked to disconcert him with a sudden remark or jibe. He retaliated by remaining as bland and as serene as he could manage. That annoyed Harry even more, so that the two men could reach a height of ill temper without either of them betraying the fact.

'I did a story, a few years back, about the connection between Webb and Asher Ruppta.'

'That was when you were a journalist.'

Harry was not sure if this was simply a statement of fact, or a barb. 'It was a good one, too. The story stood up.'

'Why was it never published?'

'Pressure from above.' He raised his eyes to the ceiling.

'From God?'

'As good as.'

'I see.'

'But do you see?'

'Sir Martin, I suppose, had "business dealings" with Ruppta.'

'So we couldn't chase the connection between Webb and Ruppta.'

'Now that he's dead –'

'It doesn't matter. We can go after Webb.'

'You know that Webb is close to Harold Wilson, don't you?'

'Yes. I did know that.'

'I don't imagine that the prime minister will be very thrilled if the *Chronicle* makes a target of him.'

Harry supposed that Thorn wanted to protect himself, and that he would try at all costs to avoid provoking Downing Street. The world of political journalism was run on the lines of a mutual benefit society, where ministers and politicians tried to maintain the most agreeable relations.

'Have you ever heard,' Harry asked Thorn with a smile, 'of the freedom of the press?'

'Of course.'

'It's only a phrase. It doesn't mean anything. But you can use it, can't you?'

'I suppose it is an excuse.'

'That's it. An excuse.'

'People do pretend to take it seriously.'

'Do they really? That *is* good news. So I want you to find out if Webb had any more recent dealings with Ruppta. Or with anyone else. I want to find out how bent he is.'

Thorn found the remark distasteful, but took care not to show it. 'I know his secretary vaguely. Bright young man.'

'He wouldn't want his future career spoiled, would he?'

'I sincerely doubt it. If I were to tell him of your previous suspicions —'

'Proven.'

'Then he might co-operate.'

'What's his name?'

'Askisson.'

'Arrange to meet him for a drink.'

Thorn did not like being told what to do by a man whom, as he told his friends, he considered to be an 'oik'. But he really had no alternative. 'And then pour poison in his ear?'

'Something like that.'

A few hours later, Harry encountered Martin Flaxman in the executive lift; his father-in-law had indeed regained some of his energy. 'Is there a bun in the oven?' Flaxman asked him. Harry must have seemed perplexed. 'Is she up the spout yet?'

'I don't know. I don't think so.' Harry did not want his father-in-law to know that they were no longer lovers.

'You don't *think* so? What has thinking got to do with it? She needs an heir, doesn't she? If you can't do it, I'll get in someone who can.' Harry looked at him in amazement. Flaxman chuckled, and held on to his arm with a strong grip. 'Just joking.' And then he added, 'I *think*.'

Harry returned to his office quickly. He was practically being accused of impotence. He was startled when the subject of his reverie stepped into the room; he quickly rose to his feet and knocked over his chair. 'Ants in your pants?' Flaxman smiled at his discomfiture. 'Not much else.'

Harry had the urge to blot this man out of existence. But he smiled back at him, and said nothing.

'I want you and Guinevere to come to dinner next week.'

'We would be delighted.'

'Oh? Would you?' He did not quite believe his son-in-law.

'Absolutely. Guinevere hasn't seen you in weeks.'

'But she never did want to see me. Before she was married. Silly cow.'

Flaxman went over to the window, and looked down into Fleet Street. It was an overcast day of cold rain. Harry closed his eyes and envisaged his father-in-law hurtling downwards, past the grey and blackened bricks, onto the dark street below. He opened his eyes just as a pigeon fluttered and flew into the obscure sky.

Two days later James Thorn came into Harry Hanway's office or, as he put it, 'just dropped in for a chat'.

'I had a drink with Askisson last night.'

'Oh yes?'

'He is concerned, of course, about your allegations against Webb.'

'Not allegations. Facts. Known as "bribery and corruption".'

Thorn thoroughly disliked the phrase. 'He is worried, quite frankly. He would like to know where he stands.'

'And what does that mean in English?'

Thorn, used to dealing in well-oiled platitudes, was annoyed now by Harry's sardonic manner. 'Let me put it this way. He thinks that he may be able to help you.'

'So he knew about it already.'

'I wouldn't go as far as that.'

'I would go further. He is involved.'

'Now that is going too far, Harry.'

'One of your favourite words, isn't it? Far?' He pronounced it with an Harrovian accent.

Thorn glared at him, but Harry regarded him with calm indifferent eyes. 'Does he want to meet?'

'I think so. He doesn't trust the 'phone.'

'A born conspirator.'

They met beside the Thames, in front of the Royal Festival Hall, with Thorn as a somewhat unwilling third party. It was another leaden overcast day, and the river seemed to Harry to be grey and sluggish in the fading light. He could see at once that Stanley Askisson was nervous, but Askisson's first question surprised him. 'Do you have a brother called Daniel?'

'How did you know that?'

'I was with him at Cambridge. I was a friend of his.'

'Oh.'

'I hear that he's doing well there now.'

'I haven't seen him for years.' He had no intention of mentioning the meeting at their father's funeral. 'We've lost touch.'

'I'm sorry.'

'Don't be. We were never really close. Let's get down to it, shall we?'

'I don't know what you have learned about Cormac. But I had nothing to do with it.'

'What is "it"?'

'You tell me.'

206

Harry looked across the river at the dim northern bank, the water slipping away beneath the level of his vision. 'Bribery. Corruption. Call it what you like.'

'I know nothing of that.' Askisson looked away as he said it, as if his attention had been drawn to something in the water.

'Of course not. But if at some point I were to ask you certain questions —'

'As long as my name is kept out of it.'

'I guarantee it.'

On the following morning he received a telephone call from Cormac Webb. 'We've met before. More than once,' Webb said to him. 'At Flaxman's house — in the house of your father-in-law, I mean — I knew then that you were on the rise. I have a nose for things like that. You have all the right qualities.'

'Oh?'

'Boldness. Ruthlessness. Cruelty. Look at newspaper proprietors, Harry. Bastards.' Harry laughed. 'In a world like that, we can't afford to be meek and mild. Isn't that so, Harry?'

'I wouldn't know, Cormac.'

'Tiger tiger burning bright. That's what you've got to be. In the forests of the night. I don't think you really want to do me any harm, Harry.'

'What makes you so sure?'

'What's in it for you?' That was true enough. 'On the other hand, if I can help you —'

'What do you mean?'

'Calm down. Nothing illegal. As such. I might give you a lead. I might tip you off. Something of that sort. I could help you, for example, with a story about the prime minister.'

'Nothing libellous, I hope?'

'About Harold? Good heavens, no. Whatever gave you that idea?' Webb became more confidential. 'It's going to be the biggest story of the year. If I give it to you, then I need something in return. I need a guarantee that you will drop the absurd interest in my affairs. Then I might be prepared to help in future, you see.'

'I see.'

'If the story I give you turns out to be correct – which it will – then you know you can rely on me. Do you see what I'm offering you?'

Harry Hanway was aware that Webb was desperately anxious to conceal the bribes he took from Asher Ruppta. He could face criminal prosecution, even though Ruppta was dead. 'So what is this news?'

'Do you accept my terms?'

Harry was becoming impatient. 'Yes.'

'The prime minister is going to resign next week, citing pressure of work. But that's not really the problem. His mind is going. There's a word for it. Senility? Is that it? And there may be something else.'

'What?'

'We will have to discuss it privately.'

Harry, curiously enough, believed Webb. He trusted him to the extent of placing a story in the following day's *Chronicle* in which it was insinuated that the prime minister had come to the conclusion that it was time to leave. Harold Wilson's press secretary denied the 'unfounded rumours' the next day. On the day following that, Harold Wilson resigned.

Cormac Webb telephoned Harry that afternoon. 'Congratulations. Everyone is saying that you know more than the Cabinet Secretary.'

'I have good sources.'

'So you do. I have my promise, right?'

'Yes.' He paused for a moment. 'When are we going to have that private meeting?'

'Whenever you wish.'

They met three evenings later, in a small Soho restaurant.

208

'Did you ever read a story by Max Beerbohm called "Enoch Soames"?' Webb asked him.

'Not that I can remember.' In fact Harry had read very little of anything, but he was not about to admit that fact.

'Enoch Soames meets the devil in a Soho restaurant. This is the one.'

'Oh?' Harry looked around without interest.

'Soames was a minor poet who, after talking to the devil, made a pact with him. He would give him his soul in exchange for one favour. He wanted to return to life in a hundred years' time – 1996 – and to find out if he had been remembered by posterity. He would appear in the Reading Room of the British Library and look up his name in the catalogues there. The devil agreed. The deal was done. And this was the point, you see. Enoch Soames had not been remembered at all. His name was absent from the catalogues, except for the titles of two books he had published at his own expense. There and then he is consigned to hell.' Webb looked around with satisfaction at the snug restaurant, with its red plush seats and its artfully shaded lamps. 'You have to be careful whom you meet in restaurants.'

'I've known that for a long time.' They discussed small idle things for a while. 'You said there may have been another reason for Wilson's resignation?' Harry eventually asked him.

'A very interesting one. There may be a plot brewing.'

'What kind of plot?'

'Look around you. Everything is falling to pieces. Strikes everywhere. Unemployment rising through the roof. Inflation going up every month. It can't be sustained.'

'You sound like a Tory.'

'These are just the facts of the matter. Everyone is aware of them.' He leaned forward and lowered his voice. 'There are some people who propose a drastic solution.'

'What would that be? A general election?'

'Oh no. That wouldn't do at all. The government might be returned. A smaller majority, perhaps. No. That would not be drastic at all.'

'What would?'

'A military coup.' Webb sat back in his chair and smiled broadly; his eyes widened, and he looked at Harry with evident interest.

'You aren't serious.'

'Oh yes. Deadly serious. Harold believed that the army was ready to take over the government. So are others.' He leaned forward again, and whispered some names. 'That's why Harold resigned. He wanted to ward off the coup.'

'How many people know about this?'

'A few. The conspirators, naturally. Most of the Cabinet. Some senior civil servants. Two or three newspaper proprietors have been alerted.'

'Among them?'

'Your man? I don't know.'

'So what do we do? What do *you* do?'

'We do nothing. We wait. They have already been unsettled by Harold's departure. We watch and wait.'

After he had left the restaurant Harry walked along Old Compton Street. For the first time it seemed to him to be drab and unprepossessing, with all the signs of weariness and wear. This is what Cormac Webb had meant by 'the facts of the matter'. There could be no doubt that the city was in decline; it looked wan and uncared for, its buildings in a bad state of repair, its inhabitants gloomy and irritable. This was a sullen time.

Three days later Harry and Guinevere Hanway were preparing for dinner with Sir Martin Flaxman. 'Mummy says she won't be coming. When you two get together you behave like fishwives. That's what she says. Nothing but foul language.'

'She is quite good at that herself.'

'That's not the point. According to her. A lady should still be treated like a lady.'

When they arrived at Cheyne Walk, however, they were surprised by the beaming presence of Lady Flaxman dressed in a low-cut red silk dress revealing the beginnings of the darkness between her scrawny breasts. 'I'm so pleased that you could come,' she said to them both, 'I haven't seen you in an age.' She put out her cheek for Guinevere to kiss, but her daughter merely brushed it with her own. 'Darling,' Lady Flaxman said to Harry, 'I do think that you have put on a little weight. It can't be that woman's cooking.'

Sir Martin stood by the fireplace, his hands clenched behind his back; he was rocking slightly, backwards and forwards, as if he were about to take a spring. 'Here she comes,' he said. 'The bartered bride.'

'Good evening, Father.'

'And here is my favourite son-in-law.'

'If you can't say anything nice, Martin, don't say anything at all.'

'I am nice, Maud. Nice as pie.' Sir Martin poured the drinks, and made a point of filling the glasses to the brim. 'May I propose a toast,' he said, 'for the cure of barrenness.' Guinevere blushed.

Harry resisted the urge to hit him. 'A quick word, sir?'

'Well, darling,' Lady Flaxman said to her daughter, 'the fighters are in the ring. There will be blood on the floor. I see it coming. And we have ringside seats. Aren't we lucky?'

'I have had a talk with Cormac Webb,' Harry was saying. 'He told me about a coup. Have you heard anything about it?'

'Coup? As in military coup?'

'That's it.'

'What bloody coup? Nobody tells me anything.'

'The army against the government. Mountjoy. Hatton. Burleigh.'

'Toy soldiers. No lead in their pants. They couldn't arrange a picnic, let alone a coup. Does Webb believe this nonsense?'

'It seems so.'

'He is a cunt. Don't trust anything he says.'

'I have had some confirmation.'

'Oh?'

Harry whispered something to him but, to his evident discomfiture, Flaxman burst out laughing. 'They talk about coups,' he said, 'because they have nothing better to do. They are pathetic. They are just posturing.'

'I don't know if there is a word for it,' Lady Flaxman said, 'but things keep on disappearing in this house.'

'What do you mean, Mother?'

'Little things. Handkerchiefs. Earrings. Only the other day I put down a small pair of scissors and, when I turned round, it was gone.'

'Daft cow,' her husband said.

'Then, yesterday,' Lady Flaxman was saying, 'it turned up in a completely different place. I was mystified.'

'You're going senile.'

'No, Martin, I am not. Don't you agree, Guinevere?'

'When I used to live here,' her daughter replied, 'there were some strange things. Do you remember, Mother, when that little gold pen just went from my desk?'

'Of course. The little gold pen.'

'And then two days later it was back on my desk.'

'Bullshit.' Her father poured himself another drink.

'Where do these things go?' Lady Flaxman asked no one in particular. 'That's all I want to know.'

'I used to get very tense in this house,' Guinevere was saying, 'I would become so anxious that I used to lie down. I would imagine the most terrible things. If I had a headache, I thought that I was suffering from a brain tumour. If my eyes ached, I was sure that I was going blind. Whenever I come back here, I feel a sense of panic.' She turned to her father. 'But things can change for the better. I have a client called Sparkler —'

The face of Martin Flaxman altered colour, and he seemed to choke on his drink. Guinevere watched as her father stumbled and fell against a large sofa covered with red brocade. 'Oh Jesus,' he whispered, 'more trouble.' He looked fiercely at his daughter. 'Where did you hear that name?' Then he slumped onto the floor. 'Why him?' White spittle came from the sides of his mouth.

Lady Flaxman delicately and deliberately put her hand on his pulse. 'Don't celebrate too soon, Mr Hanway,' she said. 'He is still alive.'

XVIII

A comedy sky

DANIEL HANWAY believed the publication party to be
going well. It was being held in the board room
of Connaught & Douglas, which had changed not at all
from the occasion when, three years before, he had
attended the 'bash' as Wilkin had called it. Even the books,
scattered on the small tables, seemed to be the same.
Wilkin was here again, as were most of the people Daniel
had met at lunch above the Ancient Druids in Soho.
Damian Etheridge had lost his job as literary editor of the
Chronicle, and now earned a more precarious living as a
freelance reviewer and literary interviewer. He looked more
haggard than before, and had assumed a peevish or dissatisfied
expression.

Clive Rentoul was as supercilious as ever. The words
seemed to glide from him as if from a great height. 'Well
done, Daniel. You have surprised me.' Daniel concentrated
upon his nose; it was narrow, and slightly curved, with large
nostrils. It implied superiority; it had a look of perpetual
contempt for anything put before it. 'We must have lunch,'
Rentoul said. 'When you're next in London.'

They were joined by Virginia Crossley. 'Now,' she said to
Daniel, 'I expect you to do some serious work.' She had the

same blustering and bullying manner. 'You've got away with it this time. But now we want a masterpiece.'

'Would you excuse me?' Daniel went over to Hanky Panky, who was in excited conversation with Graham Maland concerning the literary feud between two middle-aged novelists. Cressida von Stern had given a bad review to Edgar Cowper, in which she had made a veiled accusation of plagiarism. Cowper had retaliated, three months later, with an attack upon a short book written by von Stern on the modern novel. He had accused her of being 'ignorant' and 'wilful' in her choice of the significant novels of the last decades. None of his had been chosen.

'What he should have done,' Maland was saying, 'is obvious. He should not have responded to her. Silence is the best policy.'

'But I like a good cat-fight,' Hanky Panky replied.

'Cressida is a bitch, not a cat.'

'Oh that is so *naughty*.' Hanky Panky was delighted. 'An interesting crowd, don't you think?'

'Well, all people are interesting if you don't really want to know them.'

'That is the cleverest remark I have heard all day.'

Daniel was about to join the conversation, when someone roughly shook his shoulder. It was Wilkin, who seemed to be swaying slightly. 'He never wrote to me,' he said, pointing his wineglass towards Hanky Panky.

'I did mention it to him.'

'But he never wrote.'

'I'm sorry.'

'Sorry? Who do you think I am? It is not as if I don't have a reputation.'

'You are being orgulous.'

'What? What do you mean?'

'Overbearing.'

'You're a clever little shit, aren't you?'

Denis Davis came over at that moment. 'It's a comedy sky, isn't it?' In the frame of the window pink clouds, inflamed by the setting sun, hovered in a frosty blue sky. 'Have you seen the painted sky in the Palladian theatre at Vicenza? Just like that.'

Hanky Panky turned round to Daniel. 'I spy with my little eye something beginning with "F".'

'Filing cabinet?'

'No.'

'Fireplace?'

'No.'

'Fender?'

'Oh no. That *Fraud* over there.' He was looking at Denis Davis.

'Who is *he*?' Graham Maland suddenly pointed to a portrait from the late nineteenth century just beside the window.

'He? He is our founder. A very distinguished old *Fart*.' It was a picture of a middle-aged man with side-whiskers and a formidable moustache, bearing the stern and almost marmoreal expression of one who is constantly aware of his duties. 'Do you see what is written beneath him? Charles Connaught, Philanthropist and Educationalist. I prefer to read that as Pederast and Hypocrite.'

'You are too cynical.'

'Oh I don't think you can be *too* cynical.'

Virginia Crossley came up to them. 'Do either of you happen to know where the phrase "feasting with panthers" comes from? We were just discussing it.'

'Oscar Wilde,' said Hanky Panky.

'Jacobean tragedy,' said Graham Maland.

At that moment Daniel saw Sparkler entering the room. He became very still as he saw him crossing the room and walking towards Hanky Panky. Why had he come? He must have been invited by Hanky Panky – Daniel had never mentioned the party to him – but for what purpose?

He realised now that Sparkler had seen him, and was raising a glass of wine in his direction. Something had to be done. Daniel stared at him, and walked out of the room. As he hoped, Sparkler followed him.

'What are you doing here?'

'I work here.'

'What?'

'Mr Rackham made sure that I got a job. In the post room. I didn't want to go back to the old game. He asked me to come to a party. I didn't know you would be here, did I?' He put his hand on Daniel's arm. 'Aren't you pleased to see me?' Daniel instinctively recoiled from the touch. 'Oh? Is that the way it is?'

'I don't know.'

Sparkler understood the situation at once. 'You're embarrassed to be seen with me.'

'No.' He sounded hesitant. 'Not at all.'

'Are they your friends in there?'

'Some of them.'

'From Cambridge?'

'And from London.'

'And what am I? The abominable snowball?' Daniel shook his head and said nothing. 'So why don't you come back inside with me?'

'It's complicated.'

'What is?'

'They don't realise.'

'That you're queer?'

'That's one way of putting it. I don't want it to be generally known.'

'So you put your friends before me.'

'It's my career –'

'I was right. You are embarrassed of me.'

'I'm confused. That's all.'

'You know, once I would have done anything for you. I would have died for you.'

'A bit extreme, isn't it?'

Sparkler put down his drink, and walked down the staircase. Daniel felt unwell for a moment, and instinctively put his hand up to his chest. Then he went back to the party, where Virginia Crossley had launched into a violent diatribe against the *Times Literary Supplement*. A young man came up to him. 'You are the author, aren't you?'

'Yes. I am the author.'

'I'm Tristram Ferry. I'm the senior researcher for *Book Ends*.' This was a literary panel show broadcast on BBC 2 every Tuesday evening. 'I think you could rock the boat.'

'Excuse me?'

'You would be good. You have a natural authority.'

Daniel laughed. 'I don't think so.'

'You're an academic, but you're also a reviewer. Best of both worlds. I've read your work.' Daniel presumed that he was referring to his new book. 'In the *Post*. How would you feel about coming on to the show?'

Daniel was delighted. 'I'm not sure,' he said. 'I'm not convinced that I could do it.'

'I know what you mean. There is an art to television –'

'But I am happy to give it a try. Certainly.'

'Do you have an agent?'

'No.' Daniel cleared his throat. 'But I'll give you my telephone number at college. You can contact me there at any time.' Sensing that he may have appeared over-eager, he now frowned slightly. 'But what would I be asked to talk about?'

'We'll know that closer to the time.'

Wilkin lurched toward them. 'I don't give a fuck about

any of this,' he said. 'The fucking publishing scene is corrupt. I despise the lot of you.'

'I'm not a publisher, Paul.'

'That's beside the point. You're all in bed together.' Wilkin leered at Daniel. 'In bed with that old queer.' He was clearly very drunk. 'When a good writer like me is ignored. It's not right, is it?' He stepped closer to Daniel. 'There was a time when I was ten times better known than you will ever be. I won the Poetry Council award for my first book. Do you know that?' Then he seemed to lose interest in what he was saying, and walked up to Graham Maland; much to Maland's discomfort he simply stared at him without any attempt at conversation. Having patted Maland heavily on the back, Wilkin then approached Hanky Panky. 'Well, old dear,' he said, 'I don't suppose you remember me. I'm sorry. Am I interrupting something?' Hanky Panky had been talking to Clive Rentoul.

'I am sure,' Hanky Panky said, 'that you will have something interesting to add.'

'Add this,' Wilkin said and flung the glass of wine he was holding over Hanky Panky. Wilkin then staggered back and fell heavily against the nineteenth-century portrait of the founder of Connaught & Douglas. His right shoulder broke the canvas, and left a hole where the mouth of Charles Connaught had once been.

Daniel was looking down from the double-bowed window when he saw Sparkler; he glimpsed him walking along New Bond Street. His shoulders were hunched, and his head bowed, as he made his way slowly through the crowd.

XIX

Beginning to rain

'I'M JUST popping out,' Julie Armitage said to Sam Hanway. 'To clear my head. I'm a great believer in fresh air.' They were sitting in Sally's house; they had moved Ruppta's business to Borough a few days before. 'May I have permission, Sally?'

'Of course.'

'You are too kind. Ta very much.' In fact she wanted to go outside for a quick snack.

When she had left the house, Sally turned to her son. 'We've got five minutes. She took a bag of doughnuts with her. One minute a doughnut. Where did she leave her handbag?'

It was a capacious handbag, wrought out of leather dyed purple and with an interior lining of green silk. It smelled of mints and of nail varnish, and it contained many half-empty packets of nuts and sweets as well as bus tickets, paper handkerchiefs and assorted items of cosmetics. There was also a small diary, the days neatly divided five to a page. 'What was the day of his death?' Sam asked his mother.

'Four months ago. April the fourth.'

Sam turned to that day. 'She's written down an "F" and

underlined it. She did say that she was going to see her sister in Folkestone.' Then he noticed, at the top of the same page, what seemed to be some blurred letters that had been unsuccessfully erased. He held the page up to the light, and could distinguish numbers rather than letters. There were seven of them. Sam read them out.

'A telephone number,' Sally said.

'I'm going to try it.' He picked up the telephone, and dialled the number.

There was a woman's voice in reply. 'Sir Martin Flaxman's office.'

'Sorry, wrong number.' He told his mother what had been said and then carefully put the diary into the handbag, in the position where he had found it; he replaced the bag beneath Julie's desk.

Julie returned a minute or so later. 'How was the air?' Sally asked her.

'What? Oh yes. Very fresh.' There was suddenly a loud chatter of birds in the garden that distracted Sam's attention, but neither of the women seemed to hear it; they were staring at each other.

The three of them worked on till five, when it was time for Julie to leave. 'You've been quiet this afternoon, Sam,' she said.

'Have I?' He tried to smile at her but the smile froze on his face; he simply gazed at her with a perplexed expression.

'You look,' she said, 'like a frowning soup-plate.'

When she had left, Sam and his mother sat together in silence for a while. 'Let's go outside,' she said. 'It's a lovely evening.'

There had been a brief shower earlier that day, and the air was heavy with moisture and perfume all the more intense for lingering in the dust and shadows of the city;

the generally overheated atmosphere now seemed languorous and restful.

'So now we know,' Sam was saying, 'that Julie has been in touch with Flaxman.'

'Or Flaxman may have contacted her.'

'What did he want? What did she want?'

'What do you think?'

'Money of course.'

'And Flaxman?'

Sam was silent for a moment. 'Information. Either Flaxman offered her money for something, or she approached him. I never told you about the letter, did I?'

'What letter?'

'I was asked to deliver it to Flaxman.'

'Who asked you? Asher?'

'Pincher Solomon.'

'I told you never to get involved with him.'

'That's why I didn't mention it to you. The letter really upset Flaxman.'

'Do you know why?'

Sam shook his head. 'Not really. There was something about Tuesday evenings. Wait a minute. There was a little book. At least I think it was a book.' He rubbed his forehead violently. 'I think,' he said, 'that we should go back to Highgate.'

'Why?'

'I don't know. But we're missing something.'

The house was exactly as he had seen it on the day he discovered the body, except that a 'For Sale' board had been planted neatly in the garden. It now belonged to Sally and to Andrew, but it still retained the personality of Asher Ruppta. Sam wandered into the clean and modern kitchen, where a fly was hurling itself against a window above the sink; with some difficulty he opened the door into the garden and allowed the fly to escape. When he went back into the hall, where he had seen the body lying on the first landing of the stairs, Sally had gone. He called out to her, but there was no reply. He walked into the living room that looked over the gravel drive in front of the house, but then suddenly turned around when he sensed that someone had entered the room behind him and tapped him on the shoulder. There was no one, of course: he had imagined it. Yet he knew now that Ruppta had been murdered by Flaxman.

He left the room and began to climb the staircase, when he heard his mother scream. He ran up the stairs and into a bedroom on the first floor; she was standing at the side of the room, close to the wall. 'I almost trod on it,' she said. It was a dead crow, its black plumage still glistening in the sunlight. 'How did it get in here?'

At that moment the bedroom door closed with a thud, startling them both.

'Open the door for me,' he said. Then very carefully he picked up the dead bird and, carrying it in both hands, took it down the stairs and out through the open door into the garden. He put the bird in the earth, and then covered it with fresh soil. He looked down at the spot for a minute or so.

'I think I know what happened,' he said to his mother as soon as he re-entered the kitchen. 'Julie gave Flaxman a key to the house. She kept three sets in the office. Flaxman was looking for something. I think it might have been the little book I once saw. He was looking for something that had to do with his Tuesday evenings.'

When Julie arrived on the following morning, she seemed distracted and ill at ease. She made herself a cup of tea, and munched disconsolately on a digestive biscuit. 'Are you feeling all right?' Sam asked her.

'Bad dreams. Funny how they affect your mood. They're only ghosts, after all.'

'What are?'

'The people in dreams. They're mostly dead, aren't they?' She spoke with her mouth full of biscuit. 'Do you know that song? "You meet the nicest people in your dreams. It's funny but it's true, that's where I met you." I can't remember the rest.'

'How's your sister?' Sally had come into the room.

'What sister?'

'You know. The one in Folkestone.'

'Oh. She's still very poorly.'

'I am sorry to hear that.'

Julie looked at her suspiciously. 'What is that supposed to mean?'

'Nothing.' Sally looked at Sam, as if asking his permission. 'Except I don't believe you have a sister. I think you made her up.'

'And why would I do a stupid thing like that?'

'To give yourself an alibi. On the day that you met Martin Flaxman. The day Asher was murdered.'

Both women looked pale and strained, their eyes larger than usual, their lips white.

'You don't know what you're talking about.'

'Yes I do.'

'Do you really think that I did him in?'

'No. But I think you gave Flaxman the key to his house.'

Julie's face was suffused with a sudden flush, and she realised at once that she had betrayed herself. 'You can't speak to me like that. That's slander, that is.'

Sam could not bear the tension and animosity between the two women; he got up and, leaving the room, walked up the front path of the small dusty garden where grew roses and geraniums. He could hear their voices rising and falling in counterpoint. There was a silence and, just as their quarrel resumed, Sam went back into the house.

'Flaxman said he wanted a notebook,' Julie was saying. 'A diary. I agreed to help him find it.'

'Why did you do that?'

'Why do you think? Money. Ruppy wasn't exactly a philan-thropist. Anyway, I couldn't find it. I looked everywhere. I was sure that Ruppy had put something in the safe, but it wasn't there.'

'What's in the book?'

'How am I supposed to know? I wasn't Ruppy's keeper.'

'You're shouting again.'

'I have a right to shout. You have been accusing me. Threatening me.'

Again there was a pause, both women becoming quickly exhausted by their argument that seemed as if it might have no end. 'So then what happened? You couldn't find the book. What did you do?'

'Flaxman arranged to meet me at the north end of Battersea Bridge. Funny spot, really. Very windy. A lot of traffic. Maybe that's why he chose it. No one could hear him. He was a strange one. Dressed like a tailor's mannequin, but with the face and manners of a navvy. He had very small hands. I remember that.'

'Why did he want to see you?'

'Why do you think? He wanted my help. Where did I think the book might be? That kind of thing. I told him that it was more likely to be in Ruppy's house than anywhere else. That was my first thought.'

Sally glanced at Sam, as if divining his thought. 'So you decided to give him the key.'

'It seemed like a good idea at the time.'

Sally was indignant. 'How could you betray him like that?'

'Don't use that word to me, Madame Palliser.'

'So you gave Flaxman the key,' Sam said in a voice that he hoped was without blame.

'He knew the address already. They had some some kind of business in the past. Something dodgy, or I'm a Dutchman.'

'And he went there to look for the book.'

'I assume so.'

'This was on the morning that Ruppta was killed.'

'So it seems.'

'Assume? Seems?' Sally went over to Sam, and held on to the back of the chair in which he was sitting. 'You know what happened, Julie.'

'Do I?'

'Ruppta surprised Flaxman, and he was killed. Simple.'

'Is anything ever simple? Do you know the reasons for anything you ever do, Sally? Do you understand the consequences? I don't. I don't think anyone does.' At this moment Julie appeared to Sam to have acquired some kind of power; it was as if he had seen the blue vault of heaven open above her. She moved towards the door. 'Would you like your son to know how his father behaved? Arson. Beatings. He set dogs on some of his tenants. I am sure Andrew would like to read about that. And would he like to learn about his mother? Don't you think I know all about you, Sally? Silence might be the best policy.'

'I don't accept that.' Sally's voice was uncertain, and she looked towards Sam for a response. He sat with his head bowed.

'Well,' Julie said with an expression of triumph. 'There we have it.'

'We can't leave it like that.' Sam raised his head. 'Something has got to happen.'

'Hasn't enough happened already?' Julie got ready to leave.

'You can't work here any longer,' he said.

'Why should I want to? I don't really fancy working for a whore.' Sally walked over to her, and slapped her hard upon her right cheek. Julie put up her hand to her face, and laughed. 'Listen,' she said, 'it's beginning to rain.' Sam also heard the sound of a swift and sudden shower. But when he walked over to the window, there was no rain falling.

XX

A happy shagger

As long as her husband still lived, Lady Flaxman was in charge of the company; only on his death would it pass to her daughter. 'Of course,' she said to Harry, 'I would prefer to be the merry widow. But not everything is possible.' Her care for her husband was exemplary; she had installed a team of three nurses in the house on Cheyne Walk. Whenever she referred to her husband she called him 'Sir Martin' and spoke almost in a whisper. 'I am tiptoeing,' she told Guinevere, 'through the tulips.'

All decisions about the *Chronicle* were now directed to her. Harry was at first dismayed by her ascendancy – thinking that he would only ever have to deal with a more compliant Guinevere – but slowly he began to adapt to the situation.

'You know, Harry,' Lady Flaxman said to him one evening as they sat alone in the office that had once been her husband's, 'he could go on for a long time. Modern medicine is absolutely wonderful. Have you thought about that?'

'Surely you could hand things over to Guinevere?'

'Guinevere hasn't got a clue. She is a social worker. She's practically brain-dead. But you know that, don't you?' She smiled sweetly at him. 'She would need a big man behind her. Are you big, Harry?'

'You must ask Guinevere.'

'Why don't I find out for myself?' She gave a harsh laugh when she saw his expression of horror. 'I won't eat you, you know. Or perhaps I will. Would you mind that, Harry?'

'You're Guinevere's mother.'

'What has Guinevere got to do with it? Have you got something against mothers?' He shook his head. 'I should hope not. Well, we will be very discreet.'

'No. I mean that I can't do this, Maud.'

'Lady Flaxman, please. Think of it as business.' He waited solemnly for her to continue. 'The boss is always right. Isn't that what he used to say?'

'Are you threatening me?'

'Not a threat. An opportunity. I can do things that Guinevere cannot even imagine.'

He closed his eyes for a moment. 'I am not sure what you mean by that.'

'In the sphere of business, Harry. I have plans.' She outlined to him her scheme for an *Evening Chronicle* and a *Sunday Chronicle*, making use of the same building, the same presses and the same staff. 'We won't just be printing newspapers,' she said, 'we will be printing money. Does that excite you, Harry? Will you be a happy shagger?' She came over and grabbed his cock. 'I think something is stirring.'

So began the affair between Lady Flaxman and Harry Hanway. Harry was surprised how quickly he overcame his initial reluctance; she was Guinevere's mother and he began to notice, or to emphasise to himself, the ways in which physically she resembled her daughter. She was not desirable, but she was not altogether repulsive. He was in any case strangely excited by her schemes for the future; he had not believed that he could be aroused by the idea of profit, but had that not been one of the reasons for his attraction to Guinevere?

Lady Flaxman was very eager in her lovemaking, although she often expressed horror at her husband's treatment of her in bed. 'In the past,' she told Harry, 'I have been a common field system for that man. He has ploughed me and fertilised me. It was medieval. I might have been laid out in strips.' 'He would handle me,' she said on another occasion, 'as if I were a church organ. Pushing bits in. Pulling bits out. And all the time paddling with his feet.'

She was not insatiable, but she was demanding. There was a small attic room in the house at Cheyne Walk, where she frequently took Harry; she called it 'the blue lagoon'.

Harry was relieved by the fact that Guinevere was more than ever detached from married life; or perhaps she was simply more distracted by her cares as a social worker. In particular she seemed to be worried about Sparkler; as far as Harry could gather from her comments, the young man had been dismissed by his publishing employers for petty theft, and was now descending into a state of bored and listless drunkenness. 'He used to be so cheerful,' she said to her husband, 'Now he can't be bothered to get up.'

'You can't help someone who will not help himself.'

'If I hear that again, I will scream. It doesn't absolve me.'

Guinevere seemed unaware of the relationship between her mother and her husband. She still invited Lady Flaxman to the house in Mount Street, where she half-listened to her complaints about the business, the state of her husband and of the world in general. 'How's Dad?' was her first question one evening.

'Well, he is not tap dancing. And he's not getting fat on a drip, I can assure you of that.' At this moment Harry entered the room. 'Ah, Mr Hanway. My partner in crime.' She smiled sweetly at her daughter. 'Don't you think your husband is looking well these days, dear? He has such a spring in his step. And I'm sure he's lost weight. How do you do it, Harry?'

'Healthy living, Maud.'

'That's what I like to hear. I don't doubt it for a moment. Do you, Guinevere?'

'What? No. Harry is always good to me.'

'I gather from Mrs A. that you have a healthy appetite. Even for her food. You are very brave.'

'He eats carefully, Mummy.'

In fact the Hanways remained polite and good-natured in each other's company; they had so few mutual interests that they found it unnecessary to quarrel. They shared the house. That was all.

Harry always took a shower after he had returned from an encounter with Lady Flaxman, and then climbed into bed smelling only of almond-scented gel. He felt no guilt about the matter. It was, as Lady Flaxman had said, business. Already he had been promoted to the post of chief executive, with a large rise in salary; the more money he earned, the more fervent became his lovemaking.

One evening Harry, on a visit to Cheyne Walk, heard the sound of high-pitched laughter from behind the closed door of Martin Flaxman's sickroom. He put his ear to the door, and made out the voice of Lady Flaxman. 'Look at you, you old tart,' he heard her say. 'You're all knocked up. Finished. I just wanted to let you know that I am spending your money and fucking your editor. Or whatever he was. Enjoying myself, sweetheart, I really am. That's never happened before. Oh, one other thing. I always hated you touching me. I despised you. But I don't want you dead. Oh no. I want you to be a vegetable. While I'm having fun. Now look. You're dribbling. Does that mean you can hear me? Is that your new way of crying?'

Lady Flaxman was always capable of surprising Harry. 'That day is coming,' she said to him at the beginning of March, 'the holy day.'

'What day is that?'

'Mother's Day. It has always been a sacred day in my book.' She had in fact consigned her ailing mother to an inexpensive care home in Bromley, and had never visited her there. 'Is it for you, Harry? Is your mother that special person in your heart?'

'I have told you that my mother is dead.' He looked back at her impassively.

'Oh yes. Sorry. I forgot.' She put her hands upon her hips and began to sing. '"Sally. Sally. Pride of our alley. You're more than the whole world to me." Lovely old song, isn't it? Wartime. Gracie Fields. Our Gracie.'

He looked away.

Lady Flaxman began to inflict on him little humiliations. She once handed him his tie neatly cut in half. 'I do hate that colour,' she told him. 'It makes you look like a cinema attendant.' On another occasion she ordered him to gargle with an antiseptic. 'The smell of drink on your breath is so vulgar.'

The resentment, and the instinct for revenge, were by now deeply planted in him. At night, while lying beside Guinevere, he would entertain fantasies of following Lady Flaxman and striking her down unseen and unknown.

One morning he went into the drawing room of the house in Cheyne Walk, and found her standing beside a small and highly polished oval table. 'I've had enough,' she said. 'I have decided to tell Guinevere. She ought to know what kind of husband she has. How can I keep a secret like that from my own daughter?'

He looked at her curiously, not clearly taking in what she had said. 'I don't understand what you mean.'

'It's very simple, Harry. I intend to tell Guinevere about us.'

Slowly he comprehended the fact that his life was about to change for the worse. 'Why do you want to do that?'

'What can I tell you? Life's a bitch. And so am I.' She paused to consider. 'Why does anyone want to do anything? I do it because I *can*. I do it because I *like* it. I like you, Harry, hard though it is to believe.' He stepped towards her, but she looked at him defiantly. 'Have you ever wanted to do the one thing you know you should not do? Wouldn't that be a great relief? To press the button that might destroy you? And then it becomes more like a need. The need to fling yourself off the cliff. It would not be right, of course. But what are right and wrong anyway? Just words.' She shook her head. 'I can't explain. I just want something to happen, Harry.'

'You can't do it.'

'I can do anything. Watch.' She picked up the telephone on the oval table, and began to dial a number. So he went towards her, snatched the telephone from her hand, and began to wrap the cord around her neck. She seemed not to resist, or perhaps he did not notice her resistance. He pulled the cord tight and watched her eyes as he throttled her; they soared upwards.

He shook her, enraged by her weak response, and then pushed her violently to the floor; the telephone fell upon her left shoulder, but she was no longer moving. He stood over her for a minute or so, waiting patiently for any sign of life so that he could extinguish it. He realised then that she was staring at him in surprise, almost as if he had made a sudden and unexpected remark.

He left the house and, closing the front door very quietly, he walked across the street towards the Thames. As he approached the river he stopped, and looked around. It was a dry clear day, and the air was very still. A small flock of pigeons, animated with one purpose, landed on the green that lay between the house and the river. He started walking on the embankment road, thinking of nothing. His mind was completely clear and untroubled, doing nothing more than receive the impressions of the world around him.

When he reached Battersea Bridge he was invaded by a sudden fear; he fled in panic. Although he did not know who his pursuer was, he did not dare look over his shoulder. Then it occurred to him that he was trying to run away from himself. At that point his panic subsided; he stopped, his shirt damp with sweat, when he came up to Vauxhall Bridge. He did not think about what had happened. It held no meaning for him.

There were sounds all about him – horns, whistles, bells, shouts and cries surrounded him. He might have drowned in the clamour. Yet he had the strangest sensation that all this noise emanated from himself. He was the source of the commotion. He sat down on a bench beside the river. Wait and hope. Wait for what? Hope? He could see only darkness for him; darkness behind, and darkness ahead.

He was coming up to Westminster Bridge, where the landing stages for the river-boats lined the bank. Ticket sellers were calling out 'Kingston!' and 'Richmond!', 'Greenwich!' and 'Kew'; for a moment he contemplated the choice of one of these destinations. One would be as good as another. But then he changed his mind. He walked onto the bridge. As he approached the rail overlooking the river, he wondered what Sam and Daniel were doing at this particular moment. He tested the rail with his hand, and as Big Ben tolled midday, he eased himself across it and jumped into the water. A dog barked somewhere. It was just an ordinary day.

XXI

Surprisingly good

DANIEL HANWAY approached the television studios of Shepherd's Bush in a state of terror. What if he could not master or remember his words, or sweated uncontrollably, or said quite the wrong thing? He had been asked to participate in a panel discussion on a biography of Mary Shelley, a new novel by Graham Greene, and a history of New York. None of these subjects remotely interested him, but he had forced himself to concoct opinions on all of them. He wrote these opinions on small pieces of paper, and then memorised them.

As he approached the reception desk he felt a curious lightness in his head. He allowed himself to be conducted into a lift, and then into a passage, and then into a small room where he was greeted by a young woman who called herself a researcher. 'I'm Camilla,' she said, 'you're the first. Tea or coffee?'

He was in a kind of trance. 'Yes,' he said, 'that will be fine.'

'Tea or coffee?'

'Neither, thank you.' He did not believe that he had the strength to swallow anything.

The two other guests, on the book panel with him, were a biographer and a journalist who had been the New York correspondent of the *Chronicle*. Daniel knew both of them by reputation, such as it was, but had not met either of them. They seemed to him to be making every effort to appear calm and casual at the prospect of the ordeal.

The biographer was an easy-mannered middle-aged man who seemed to be the very epitome of bland equability. Every word was correct, every expression and gesture measured. He purred his words, and gently chuckled at his own wit. Daniel did not trust him. The journalist was sharp and, even to a stranger like Daniel, a little acerbic; his words came out in a volley, his voice rising and falling in continual exasperation. Daniel was wary of him. He did not pause to contemplate, however, what impression he was making on them.

They were led into a studio, a brightly lit room chill with the air of vacancy; it was unreal, with an abstraction of two sofas and a bookcase. There was a coffee table with a neat pile of books and four glasses of water upon it. A small microphone was being clipped to the lapel of his jacket as the presenter of the programme walked onto the set. Daniel had seen Helen Gurney before, as a participant in various documentaries connected to the arts. She had short dark hair, and wore a large pair of glasses that seemed to magnify the earnestness of her gaze. She spoke forcefully in a low voice, carefully modulated, but seemed to be half-apologetic about introducing anything as vulgar as a book panel. Her favourite phrase was 'it seems to me . . . '. 'Do you not think,' she asked Daniel as the camera turned upon him, 'that feminism has changed the terms of the debate on Mary Shelley herself? It seems to me that her narratives must be deconstructed with much more care.'

How he managed to survive the half-hour of filming he did not know. His voice sounded forced and clumsy in this airless room; he believed that he was talking nonsense, despite the fact that he had carefully memorised most of his lines. It had been an entirely meaningless exercise, in which all of the participants were in some way degraded. 'Yes,' he said at the end, summarising the study of New York, 'surprisingly good.'

'And on that note we must leave it. Goodbye from everyone on *Book Ends*.'

When he came out onto the street on the west side of Shepherd's Bush Green, he welcomed the cold wind as it cleansed him. The Green itself was largely grey, the earth getting the better of the grass, and unlovely. Daniel did not know this western part of London well; it did not have the freedom and the airiness of Camden Town and the rest of North London. It seemed intimate and over-familiar. This was the effect that certain areas of the city had upon him.

He passed a small boy in the street, muttering to himself, shrugging his shoulders, raising his hands into the air and gesticulating wildly. 'What am I supposed to do?' the child was asking with such a look of misery and helplessness upon his face that Daniel turned away. But then he felt the pavement beneath his feet, and the obduracy of London began to enter him. He decided to go underground at Holland Park, and travel to Liverpool Street where he could take the Cambridge train. The lift took him down to the east-bound platform, the sound of its metal gates following him as he walked through the passage. He did not know the Central Line well. He was accustomed from his childhood to the Northern Line, which seemed always to carry with it the sensations of the northern heights of Hampstead and Highgate. The Central Line was closer and more intimate; the platform was warmer, and the sound of the train as it entered the station less harsh.

He settled in the carriage with a sigh of relief. It was

already midday, when the majority of people were at work, and there was a sense of illicit pleasure about the journey. It was almost luxurious. He passed through Notting Hill Gate and Queensway, when the train came to a sudden halt before it reached Lancaster Gate; the brakes shrieked and the train slid a few feet before becoming still. Daniel looked at one or two of the passengers, but there was no sign from them of disquiet or alarm.

He remained still, and looked out of the window at the darkness all around him. This tunnel had been bored through the London Clay, laid down some forty million years before. He was travelling within prehistory, held up by the remains of an unimaginable past. There was a noise as of sudden thunder ahead of the train. He imagined a vast invasion of water or, perhaps, a reawakening of some prehistoric life. But the noise passed; it was that of another train entering a tunnel.

He left the tube at Liverpool Street and made his way along one of the white-tiled passages that conveyed travellers to various parts of the world above-ground. A mild breeze surprised him. It seemed to have come up from the depths and, at the same time, he heard the sound of drums being played somewhere in the distance. It was clear that this was the work of a busker, but that did not lessen his unease; he always felt a slight tremor of anxiety when he passed such people, and he avoided looking at them.

The drums were beating out a recognisable tune in the confined space, where they mixed with the sound of hurrying footsteps. He walked along the curve of the passage, and saw the busker halfway down; he was leaning against the white tiles with the drums strapped around his waist. It was an oddly casual or capricious stance. As Daniel came closer he sensed something familiar about the man. He looked more carefully, and saw that it was Sparkler. His instinct was to turn and run back down the passage, but that would draw attention to himself. He walked on, holding himself rigidly erect; he did not look at Sparkler directly, but he knew well enough that Sparkler's eyes were following him. He expected him to speak, or to call out, but the only sound was that of the beating of the drums. They were beating more loudly as he walked on.

The two young men had been so close, so intimate in the past. Now Daniel had not stopped, had not spoken. He had glanced at Sparkler, and then walked away. Sparkler had seen him – he was sure of that – but had made no attempt to call him back.

The drumming stopped, and Daniel was suddenly convinced that Sparkler had decided to come after him; he fled down the passage and bounded up the stairs, two at a time.

When he stopped at the gateway into the vast expanse of Liverpool Street Station, fighting for breath, he felt an uneasy sensation within his heart. He felt its unnatural beating. He walked more slowly across the concourse to the platform from which he knew the Cambridge train departed. Now he had the luxury of turning round. Sparkler was not to be seen. Yet still Daniel flushed at the thought of their previous intimacy.

A week later, on the same day that Harry flung himself into the Thames, Daniel was feeling more refreshed than he had been for some time. As he prepared a pot of tea, he allowed himself to savour the luxury of his isolation. His first supervision was at ten o'clock, on the symbolism of *Bleak House*, and the second at midday was on the poetry of Tennyson; he took down the appropriate volumes from his shelves, safe once more among his books.

'What we have to explain, in *Bleak House*, is the imagery of the prison.' The first supervision had begun on time. 'It is perfectly obvious that, in most of Dickens's novels, the city itself becomes a form of penitentiary in which all of the characters are effectively manacled to the wall. If it is not a cell, it is a labyrinth in which few people find their way. They are lost souls.'

'But what then,' the young man in spectacles asked him, 'do we make of the continuing use of coincidence?'

'That is the condition of living in the city, is it not? The most heterogeneous elements collide. Because, you see, everything is connected to everything else.'

The undergraduate left the room, and Daniel placed his copy of *Bleak House* on the shelf and took down *The Idylls of the King*.

When he heard the sound of drums, coming from the courtyard beneath his rooms, he was seized with an alarm so great that he almost lost consciousness. He knew what was happening, but he felt the need to witness it. He was in pain as he limped to the window. Sparkler was on the lawn beneath, entirely naked, slapping the small drums with his right hand.

He was looking up at the windows and, now that he could see Daniel, Sparkler let out a wild cry of recognition.

Daniel staggered back, his hand to his mouth, and fell into an old leather armchair. He found it difficult to breathe, and gasped for the air around him. But then the room itself began to tremble. 'This is it,' Daniel said.

The next undergraduate, a few minutes late for his midday supervision, found him dead in the leather chair.

XXII

Anything is possible

As soon as Sam was awake, earlier on that same day, he sensed that Sally had already left the house. He was always aware of the presence of his mother; he felt more settled then, and more assured. Why had she left at such an early hour? When after two hours she had still not returned, he grew more alarmed.

Some days before, Sally had been discussing matters of business with her two sons. 'I will be happy to take up the reins,' Andrew had said. 'When I'm a bit older, naturally.'

'But will you enjoy it, Andrew?'

'I think, Mother, I have a pretty good head on my shoulders.'

'Do you know what I want to do?' She was addressing them both now. 'I want to set up a fair rent scheme. And I want to house some of the homeless. In return they would refurbish the flats.'

'May I put my oar in, Mother?' Andrew seemed perplexed.

'Of course.'

'Aren't you being just a trifle idealistic? I know your intentions are good, but are you sure that these homeless types will *want* to refurbish their flats?'

'What do you think, Sam?'

'I don't really know.' He scratched his face. 'I'll soon be moving on, anyway.'

'Don't say that.'

'I'm a wanderer, Mother. I can't stay still. I don't know what I'm going to do, or where I want to go. Something will happen soon enough.'

By the early afternoon he had become seriously alarmed by her absence. Sally had left him when he was eight years old, and now he returned to that time when he wept for his mother under the cover of London fog and darkness. He sat by the window all that afternoon, looking into the street, caught between fear and indecision. To whom could he turn?

He had to go out. He had to walk through the streets in search of her. So in the waning light he went towards London Bridge. The street lamps shone on the crowd, casting long shadows across the brightly lit hoardings and shopfronts. It was a procession in torchlight, celebrating all the haste and fervour of London. He walked into the middle of the crowd, and slowly his anxieties began to subside. The touch of the stone beneath his feet, and the presence of the people, calmed him. He could feel the forgetfulness of the city rising within him. It was as if individual fear had no place in this concourse, where the great general drama of the human spirit was being displayed in the light of the street lamps.

He walked on across London Bridge and into the City. He soon reached Spitalfields where, in front of the old church beside the market, he saw the man he had once met in the local park at Camden; he was the one to whom he had given Tizer and packets of crisps. He had grown older and greyer, but Sam still recognised him. He looked up at Sam, and then put his forefinger to his forehead in a gesture of salute.

Sam walked further east through the dark streets, surrendering himself to the city. He realised that it had grown cold, and so he made his way towards the first pub he saw. It stood on the corner of Bethnal Green Old Street, as sturdy and as grimy as the street itself with three baskets of plastic flowers hanging above its entrance. He walked inside, enjoying the sensation of sudden warmth and the sour-sweet smell of beer and cigarette smoke.

He had gone over to the bar, and ordered a Guinness, when he became aware that he was being watched. He turned his head, and met the eyes of Sparkler.

'Hello, Samuel, fancy meeting you again.' Sam, in the sudden excitement of seeing him, embraced him. 'Hang on. The locals might get the wrong idea.'

'What have you been doing? Where have you been?'

'I've been wandering. I'm the liberty boy.'

'Where are you living now?'

'Here and there. Everywhere.'

'You lost touch.'

'I suppose I did. But I still see Guinevere. You remember?'

'Of course.'

'She's started a housing charity in Hackney.'

'She'll never change.'

'Oh yes. She has changed. She don't look young any more. I don't think she likes her husband very much. Harry. That's his name. I don't think she trusts him. I think she despises him. I can't be sure. I never met him, did I?' A shadow of a scowl passed across Sparkler's face. 'And her mother's a right old bitch. So she says. I feel sorry for Guinevere, and she feels sorry for me. So we're quits.' He seemed to Sam to be in a strangely excitable mood. 'Guinevere told me a funny story. Not so much funny as weird. She arranged for this couple to move into a council flat on the corner of Britannia Road. Near where I used to live. She said they were a strange couple. But devoted. Then the husband goes and dies. The woman is in a terrible state, breaking down and crying at the funeral. He was *cremated*, by the way. She goes back to the flat and to her job. As an office cleaner. She is too poor to move anywhere else, do you see? And then one day there is a knock at the door. When she answers it, there is her husband. As large as life. He doesn't say anything. He just walks in and makes himself a cup of tea. Just as if nothing had happened. She was glad to see him again. Of course. She doesn't want to ask no questions. She doesn't want to upset him. And they've been living together ever since. What do you think of that, Sammy boy?' Sparkler smiled and put out his hands, as if he had just performed a trick.

'I suppose,' Sam said, 'that anything is possible.'

'You can believe it. Guinevere says that the neighbours have just accepted it.'

Sam pointed to the pair of small drums that Sparkler had placed on the counter. 'What are they for?'

'I'm doing a bit of busking, aren't I? Keeps me occupied. And I earn a few quid. Do you want another one?' In the surprise of meeting one another, they had drunk their beer very quickly. 'I saw your brother this morning. Daniel. Danny boy.'

'You know each other?'

'Oh yes. We go way back. Or we *did*. He looked out of the window. Danny boy. It's a long time since I've been in Cambridge. I was afraid the porter would come after me. But, you know me, I'm *invisible*.' He tapped the drum. 'They seek him here, they seek him there. I was back in London before you could say – whatever people say.'

As soon as Sam returned home, drunk and weary, he knew that his mother was in the house; characteristically she had left her high-heeled shoes at the bottom of the stairs. She did not want to damage the carpets. In his dreams that night, the three brothers were sitting in a darkened space that had no palpable boundaries; then they began to disintegrate, like clouds, and to become part of the darkness.

His mother was already in the kitchen when he went down. 'Sleepy-head,' she said.

'I didn't get in till late.'

'What were you doing?'

'I was looking for *you.*'

'Were you?'

'Where had you gone?'

'It's a long story.' She turned away for a moment towards the sink, and pretended to arrange some dishes. 'I wanted to find Julie.' Sam waited for her to continue. 'I wanted to confront her. I wanted to lay out the charges against her. That sounds very official, doesn't it? I had no real evidence. And what good would it do? I have to protect Andrew, you see. But I wanted her to admit that she had done wrong. Do you want a cup of tea?' Sam shook his head. 'She lives in Camden. In Cooper Crescent. Near where we – Anyway, I waited for her until she came out. She surprised me by going into the church round the corner. The one where you saw me. Ages ago. I was going to walk up to her. I don't know what I would have said, but I would have said *something*. But she knelt down and started to pray. I didn't have the heart to interrupt her. I don't know. She may have been praying for forgiveness or something. A woman came out from the room beside the altar. She was wearing a blue coat. One of the cleaners, probably. She went up to Julie and put her arm around her. Julie looked up at her, and I could see that she was smiling.'

Sam misheard the word. 'Crying?'

'No. I don't think so. But I didn't want to talk to her any more. When I left the church eventually, I just wandered through the streets. I never knew that you were looking for me.' She turned back to the sink. 'Well, that's the end of that. I should get your lunch ready. It's nearly midday.'

'It may not be the end,' he said. 'What was it Dad used to say? Wait and hope.'

'That reminds me. A letter came for you.'

He picked up a slim envelope from the kitchen table, addressed to him. He took out a small piece of white notepaper with the heading 'Our Lady of Sorrows'. The letter was very brief.

'Dear Sam, We appreciate all the work you have done for us. Come back at any time. We have been waiting for you.'